...+ and now lives
...sive reading in the fields
of classical archaeology and medieval and Dark Ages
history and literature has had a clear influence on her
work. Her novels have been published around the world
and she is a bestseller on both sides of the Atlantic.

By Katharine Kerr

The Deverry Series:

DAGGERSPELL
DARKSPELL
DAWNSPELL
DRAGONSPELL

A TIME OF EXILE
A TIME OF OMENS
A TIME OF WAR
A TIME OF JUSTICE

THE RED WYVERN
THE BLACK RAVEN
THE FIRE DRAGON
THE GOLD FALCON
THE SPIRIT STONE

Other Fiction:

POLAR CITY BLUES
FREEZEFRAMES
SNARE

With Mark Kreighbaum:

PALACE

KATHARINE KERR

THE SPIRIT STONE

Book Five of The Dragon Mage

HARPER
Voyager

HarperVoyager
An imprint of HarperCollins*Publishers*
77–85 Fulham Palace Road,
Hammersmith, London W6 8JB

First published in Great Britain by
HarperCollins*Publishers* 2007

www.voyager-books.co.uk

This paperback edition 2008
1

A catalogue record for this book is
available from the British Library

ISBN-13: 978 0 00 712873 0

Set in Fairfield Light by
Palimpsest Book Production Limited,
Grangemouth, Stirlingshire

Printed in Great Britain by
Clays Ltd, St Ives plc

For all my readers
without whom this series would not have existed

PROLOGUE
The Northlands
Summer, 1159

In some sense, every magician is a weaver, merely one who works with invisible strands of the hidden light. With it we weave our various forms, just as a weaver produces cloth, and then stitch them into the images we desire, just as a tailor sews cloth into a tunic or robe. If we be journeymen in our craft, forces will come to inhabit our forms, just as a person will come to buy the tunic and place it over his body. But if we have plumbed the secret recesses of our art, if we are masters of our craft, then we can both weave the forms and place our own bodies within them.

The Pseudo-Iamblichos Scroll

Two men of the Mountain Folk sat on a ledge halfway up a cliff and took the sun. Below them, at the foot of a cascade of stone steps, a grassy park land spread out on either side of a river that emerged from the base of the cliff. Just behind them, a stone landing led to a pair of massive steel-bound doors, open at the moment to let the fresh summer air into the rock-cut city of Lin Serr. Kov, son of Kovolla, was attending upon Chief Envoy Garin, son of Garinna, while this important personage nursed a case of bad bruises and a swollen ankle. A few days previously Garin had been talking to a friend as they hurried down these same steps; a careless engrossment in the conversation had sent him tumbling down two full flights.

'Sunlight's the best thing for the bruises,' Kov told him. 'Or that's what the healers told me, anyway.'

Garin muttered a brief oath, then continued blinking and scowling at the brilliant summer light. *He's getting old*, Kov thought, *ready to stay in the deep city forever, like all the old people do*. At a mere eighty-four years, Kov was young for one of the Mountain Folk and still drawn by life above ground.

'Well,' Kov continued, 'the sun's supposed to help strengthen your blood.'

'Doubtless,' Garin said. 'I'm out here, aren't I?'

Kov let the matter drop. From where they sat, Kov could look across the park land and watch the workmen raising stone blocks into position on the new wall. The city sat in the precise middle of a horseshoe of high cliffs, dug out from the earth and shaped by dwarven labour. Eventually the wall would run from one end of the horseshoe across to the high watchtower at the other, enclosing the park land. Until then, armed guards stood on watch night and day. Everyone in Lin Serr knew that the Horsekin had been raiding farms on the

Deverry border. Although no Horsekin had been sighted up
on the Roof of the World in forty-some years, the Mountain
Folk always prefer safe to sorry.

'What's that noise?' Garin said. 'Sounds like shouting.'

Kov rose to his feet and listened. 'It's the guards.' He
shaded his eyes with his hand and gazed across to the wall.
'Strangers coming.'

A cluster of guards surrounded the strangers and led them
across – four human men, leading riding horses and a pack-
horse. As they drew near, Kov recognized the sun blazons of
Cengarn. One of the humans, a dark-haired fellow, shorter
than his escorts, with the squarish build of someone whose
clan had mountain blood in its veins, also looked familiar.

'It's Lord Blethry, isn't it? The equerry at Cengarn.'

'I think you're right.' Garin held out his hand. Kov handed
him his walking stick. With its help Garin hauled himself
to his feet and looked out towards the wall. 'Yes indeed, that's
Blethry. Those other fellows look like a servant of some sort
and then an armed escort.'

Kov rose, too, and watched as dwarven axemen marched
the human contingent across the park land. At the foot of
the stairs, they paused and allowed Blethry to shout a greeting
in Deverrian. 'Envoy Garin! May I come up?'

'By all means!' Garin called back in the same. 'What brings
you here?'

Blethry waited to answer till he'd panted his way up to
their perch, some hundred and twenty steps high. He wiped
the sweat off his face with one hand and snorted like a
winded horse.

'War, that's what,' Blethry said. 'The Horsekin are building
a fortress out in the Westlands. We figure they want a staging
ground for a strike at our borders.'

'And if they take over your lands,' Garin said, 'they'll be
heading north, no doubt, for ours.'

'No doubt. Gwerbret Ridvar's hoping we can count on
your aid to destroy the place. It's called Zakh Gral.'

'Our High Council will have the final word about that. Now, as for me personally, I hope his grace Gwerbret Cengarn doesn't take this as a slight, but I'll have to send my apprentice here to Cengarn with the news, whatever it may be. I can barely walk.' Garin used his stick to point at his wrapped and swollen ankle.

'I'm sure young Ridvar will understand.' Blethry turned to Kov and bowed. 'My thanks for accompanying us.'

'Most welcome,' Kov glanced at Garin, who was smiling in what appeared to be relief. *It's not the ankle*, Kov thought, *he just doesn't want to leave the safety of the dark.*

'Kov,' Garin said, 'go down and help his lordship's men tether their animals and set up their tents and suchlike. Then join us in the envoy's quarters.'

Lord Blethry had visited Lin Serr several times, but the sheer size of the place always left him awed. The steel doors led into a domed antechamber that could have held Cengarn's great hall twice over. The shaft of sunlight from the open doorway cut across the polished slate floor and pointed like a spear to a roundel, inlaid with various colours of stone to form a maze some twenty yards across. Beyond it, on the curved far wall, tunnels opened into distant gloom and led down to the deep city, forbidden to strangers.

Some ten feet in, well before they reached the floor maze, Garin turned left, hobbling along with his stick, and led Blethry down a short side tunnel that ended in a tall wooden door, carved in a vertical pattern of chained links. Yet for all its massive appearance, when Garin poked it with his stick it swung open without a sound to reveal a small room, bright with sunlight.

'Here we are,' Garin said. 'You've stayed here before, haven't you?'

'I have,' Blethry said. 'It's a comfortable place.'

A big window made the small room seem large and airy, thanks to its view of the green park land far below. Tucked against the inner wall stood a bed, and near it a table and a pair of wooden chairs. On the walls hung steel panels, chiselled and graved into hunting scenes. Garin shoved a chair in to the most shadowed corner of the room, then lowered himself into it with a grunt of pain. Since the last time Blethry had seen him, a thick streak of white had appeared in Garin's close-cropped hair. His short beard had turned entirely grey.

'I'll have Kov bring in another chair,' Garin said. 'Brel will want to join us once he hears the news.'

Indeed, Brel, the avro, to give him his dwarven title of 'warleader', arrived at the same time as Kov and the third chair. He strode in, stood for a moment to glower at Garin, then sat down in a chair near the window and stretched his legs out in front of him.

'The Council's called an emergency meeting,' he said to Blethry. 'They meet down in the deep city, of course, so you're to describe the situation to me, and I'll relay it to them.'

'Very well,' Blethry said. 'In that case, I'd better speak formally.' He cleared his throat. 'I come in the name of Ridvar, Gwerbret Cengarn, to call in the aid owed to us in time of war from the Mountain city of Lin Serr. By treaty and solemn oath we are bound together to render assistance to one another for our mutual benefit.'

'He speaks the truth.' Garin joined this recitation of ancient formulae. 'We did renew our pact on its prior terms after the hostilities known as the Cengarn War, concluded at the date 1116, as is written in the –'

'Worms and slimes!' Brel broke in. 'I know all that. If the Council can't remember it, they have gravel where their intellect ought to be.'

'It's a question of the proper wording,' Garin snapped. 'The Council needs to know that we've heard Lord Blethry speak the proper wording, and that I responded in the same way.'

Brel growled and cross his arms over his chest.

'As is written in the documents pertaining to that war, that time of blood and darkness.' Blethry took over again. 'In that most solemn instance we did celebrate a victory over the army of the peoples known to us as Gel da' Thae or Horsekin, when they made so bold as to besiege our city of Cengarn. In thankfulness for that aid, we did renew our bonds with the Mountain Folk who do inhabit the city of Lin Serr.'

'I too did witness this,' Garin said. 'So be it.'

'Are you two done now?' Brel said.

'We are.' Blethry grinned at him. 'You can tell the Council that we brought a sacrifice to the temples of proper manners.'

'Huh!' Brel snorted profoundly. 'Oh, and welcome! It's good to see you, by the way.'

'My thanks.' Blethry smiled again. 'It's good to see you too.'

Young boys carrying trays of food marched in and began to lay a meal upon the table: a platter of bats, disjointed and fried, a soft mushroom bread, and stewed purple roots of a sort new to Blethry. Kov shut the door after them, then sat on the floor for want of another chair. Garin poured everyone pewter stoups of a thick brown liquor, which Blethry had encountered before. He drank it in small sips and made sure he stopped well before he finished it. He noticed Kov doing the same.

While they ate, Blethry expanded upon his reason for coming to Lin Serr. Some of the savage Horsekin of the far north had turned themselves civilized – they'd become Gel da' Thae, as settled Horsekin called themselves – but living in cities hadn't slaked their thirst for war. They were building a fortress, Zakh Gral, on the edge of the grassy plains that belonged to the Westfolk.

'How did you find it?' Kov said. 'Or was it the Westfolk?'

'Not us nor them,' Blethry said. 'But a gerthddyn name of Salamander. He –'

'Never mind that now,' Brel cut in. 'What matters is that they found it. Details later.'

'We figure that it's only the point of a salient,' Blethry went on. 'Other fortifications will follow, I'll wager. Apparently they want to take over the western grasslands. They need pasturage for those heavy horses of theirs. And of course, they claim that their wretched fake goddess wants them to have it.'

'Alshandra yet again?' Brel said.

'The very one. They refuse to believe she's dead.'

'How convenient for them,' Garin muttered. 'It's amazing how these gods and goddesses always appear when someone wants someone else's land.'

'My thought exactly.' Blethry nodded Garin's way.

'They won't stop at the Westlands,' Brel said. 'But no doubt you realize that, or you wouldn't be here. What's this fortress like?'

In as much detail as Blethry could remember, he repeated Salamander's description of the place.

'It sits on the edge of a cliff over a river gorge,' Blethry finished up. 'Clever scum, the Horsekin.'

'Wooden walls, did you say?' Brel shot a significant glance Garin's way.

'For now,' Blethry said. 'They're working hard at replacing them with stone.'

'Huh,' Brel said. 'We'll see how far they get. I take it that your lords have worked out some sort of plan to bring this fortress down.'

'They have. Gwerbret Ridvar's calling in all his allies, and what's more, Voran, one of the princes of the blood royal, is on hand with fifty of his men.'

'Only fifty?' Garin said.

'At the moment. He's sure his father will send reinforcements. The messages may have reached Dun Deverry by now, for all I know. I left Cengarn weeks ago. As for the Westfolk, Prince Daralanteriel's keen to join the hunt.'

'He should be,' Brel said drily. 'He stands to lose everything if the Horsekin move east.'

'True spoken, of course. He's promised us five hundred archers. Ridvar can muster at least that many riders.'

Brel winced. 'Is that the biggest army you can put together?'

'Until we hear from the high king.'

'And how long will it take to get a full army up here from Dun Deverry?' Brel went on and answered his own question. 'Too long. With what you have, you'll never take the place. You'll have to lay siege and hope you can hold it.'

'I know,' Blethry said. 'Till those reinforcements arrive from Dun Deverry.'

'The Horsekin are likely to see a relieving force before you do. All it'll take is one messenger to slip through your lines when you're investing the fortress. If they've got a town up in the mountains, they doubtless keep a reserve force there. I hate the filthy murderers, but I'd never say they were stupid.' Brel paused to pick a fragment of fried bat out of his grey-streaked beard. 'So I wouldn't plan on a siege. With us along, you won't have to.'

'Sir?' Kov spoke up from his place on the floor. 'What can we –'

'Think, lad!' Brel snapped. 'This fort's perched on the edge of a cliff.'

Kov suddenly grinned. 'Tunnels,' he said. 'We've got sappers.'

'They're our main hope,' Blethry said. 'If the High Council allows you to join us.'

Brel snorted profoundly. 'They will. There's not a family in Lin Serr that didn't lose someone in the last Horsekin war.'

'Kov.' Garin turned to his apprentice. 'What do we owe Cengarn by treaty?'

'Five hundred axemen, sir,' Kov said, 'and a hundred and fifty pikemen, along with provisions for all for forty days.'

'Very good.' Garin nodded at him, then glanced at Blethry. 'Do you think the gwerbret will be offended if we replace those pikemen with sappers and miners?'

'Huh! If he is, and I doubt that with all my heart, then Lord Oth and I will talk some sense into him.'

'Good,' Garin smiled briefly. 'The council meets tomorrow morn. We should know by noon.'

On the morrow, Blethry woke at first light and spent an anxious hour or so pacing back and forth in his quarters. Every now and then he stuck his head out of the window and tried to judge how long he had to wait till noon came around. Well before then he heard a knock on the door. He flung it back to find Garin, stick raised to strike again, with young Kov behind him.

'Ah, you're awake!' Garin said. 'I thought you might be asleep still.'

'Not likely, is it?' Blethry said. 'Well?'

'The Council saw reason quickly, for a change,' Garin said. 'They're organizing the muster now, and the army will march at dawn on the morrow. Five hundred axemen and a full contingent of sappers and miners with all their gear and the like. Oh, and provisions for twice forty days.'

'Splendid!' Blethry said, grinning. 'And my thanks. I'll go down and tell my men the good news.'

Kov slept little the night before the march out of Lin Serr. He packed up his gear, worried about what he might have left out, unpacked the lot, added things, took things away, then packed it all up again. Although he'd visited Cengarn several times, he'd never gone farther west than that city. He'd never seen a war, either. When he finally did fall asleep, he had troubled dreams of shouting and bloodshed.

Just before dawn, Garin woke him when he arrived to give him some final instructions. As well as his walking stick, the elder dwarf carried some long thing wrapped in cloth.

'You're not the apprentice any longer,' Garin said. 'You're the envoy now. Remember your dignity, lad. Speak slowly, listen when you're spoken to, and think before you answer. Follow those simple precepts, and you'll do well.'

'I hope so.' Kov caught his breath with a gulp. 'I'll do my best.'

'I know you will. Now, you've got your father's sword, I see, so here's something to go with it.'

The long bundle turned out to be a staff, blackened and hard with age, carved with runes. Kov took it with both hands and turned it to study the twelve deep-graved symbols. He could recognize Rock and Gold as Mountain runes, and two others as Deverry letters, but he'd never seen the rest.

'Do you know what those mean?' Garin said.

'Well, no.'

'Neither does anyone else. They're very old, but we do know that they once graced the door of Lin Rej.'

'Lin Rej? The old city?'

'The very one. It had carved wooden doors. When the Horsekin arrived, back in the Time of Death, they didn't hold. The besiegers lit a fire in front of them, and when the doors burned through, they finished the job with axes. But one of our loremasters carved these runes here –' Garin pointed at the staff '– on a scrap of wood so they'd be remembered. Over the years, they've been carved on other staffs, but this one came to me from my father's father. It was a hundred years old when he received it as a child.'

'It must be nearly a thousand now, then.'

'Yes. There's a superstitious legend about the runes, too. They're supposed to contain a dweomer spell.' Garin rolled his eyes heavenward. 'Anything that's no longer understood is supposed to contain a dweomer spell, of course. Don't take it seriously.'

'Oh, don't worry! I won't. But now I know why Lin Serr has steel on its doors.'

'We may learn slowly, but in the end, we learn.' Garin paused for a smile. 'Now, spell or no spell, I'm letting you borrow that staff because I can't go to the battle myself. We've never had a formal badge for our envoys, but you're new on the job.'

'Very new.' Kov could hear his voice shake and coughed loudly to cover it.

'Just so.' Garin smiled at him. 'So I decided you might need something to mark your standing and keep your spirits up. This staff's never left the city since the day my father's father brought it inside. Carry it proudly, and never shame it.'

'I'm very grateful for the honour. I'll do my best to live up to it.'

'That's all any man can do, eh? Now get on your way. There's a mule for you to ride, by the by, down at the muster.'

Out in the meadow, five hundred dwarven axemen drew up in marching order, followed by a veritable parade of carts, each drawn by two burly menservants. The sappers and miners were milling around, scrutinizing each cart, repacking some, adding wrapped bundles to others. Kov invited Lord Blethry to come along as he and Brel Avro inspected the muster. Blethry murmured his usual polite remarks until they came to the line of carts. Most carried provisions, ordinary stuff all of it, but those at the head of the line were loaded with mysterious-looking crates, barely visible under greased wraps of coarse cloth that would keep them dry during summer rains. Embroidered runes decorated each cloth. Blethry fell silent, studying the runes, craning his neck to get a better look at the crates.

'Can your read our runes?' Kov said with a small smile.

'I can't, truly,' Blethry said. 'I was just noticing the wheels of your carts here. The design is quite striking.'

Good parry! Kov thought. Aloud, he said, 'A little innovation of ours.'

Blethry nodded, and indeed, to his eyes the wheels must have possessed a fascination of their own. Instead of the solid slab wheels of Deverry carts, dwarven craftsmen had lightened these with spokes radiating from a metal collar that attached them to the axles. Strakes, that is, strips of metal studded to give them a grip on the road, protected the wooden rims.

'Much lighter,' Kov said, 'but just as strong. Easier to fix, too.'

'Stronger, I should think. I trust you'll not be offended if our cartwrights look them over when we reach Cengarn? I shan't be able to keep them away.'

'Of course not. I'm sure our men would take it as an honour if they should copy them.'

'Would you two stop jawing?' Brel turned on them both impartially. 'The sun's up, and it'll be hot soon. Mount up, both of you! Let's march!'

Kov and Blethry followed orders. During the long ride down from the mountains, whenever the contingent camped, Blethry found excuses to walk by the dwarven carts that contained the wrapped bundles and crates, but, Kov could be sure, no one would ever give him one word of information about their contents. The design of a set of wheels they were willing to share, but the formula for the mysterious cargo was going to remain a secret forever, if the Mountain Folk had their way.

They reached the border of Gwerbret Ridvar's rhan when they came to the dun of one of his vassals, a small broch tower inside a high stone wall, perched on a hill wound around by a maze of earthworks. All around it stretched litter from a military camp – firepits, garbage, broken arrows, broken tent pegs, and assorted ditches, hastily filled in. The dwarven contingent drew up to camp some distance away in a cleaner area. Kov remembered this dun as belonging to the clan of the Black Arrow, but men wearing Cengarn's sun blazon on the yokes of their shirts came trotting over to greet them.

'What's happened to Lord Honelg?' Kov asked Blethry.

'I don't know yet.' Blethry gave him a grim smile. 'But I'm assuming he's dead. He turned traitor, you see. When I left Cengarn, the gwerbret was getting ready to march on him. From the look of things, Ridvar took the dun.'

Cengarn's men, left on fort guard, confirmed Blethry's

guess. Lord Honelg was dead, his lands attainted, his young son a hostage, his widow gone back to her father's dun.

'Who's the new lord here?' Blethry said. 'Or has Ridvar reassigned the lands yet?'

'He has, my lord,' the fortguard captain said. 'Lord Gerran of the Gold Falcon. You might remember him as the Red Wolf's common-born captain, but he's a lord now.'

'I do indeed, and he's a grand man with a sword and a good choice all round.'

'We all feel the same, my lord. Are you marching down to Cengarn on the morrow?'

'We are.'

'His grace may have left already. He's mustering his allies at the Red Wolf dun for the march west.' The captain turned to Kov and bowed. 'It gladdens my heart to see your people, envoy, with a war about to start.'

'My thanks,' Kov said. 'But it sounds to me like the war's already started.'

'You could look at it that way, truly,' the captain said, grinning. 'But either way, we're glad you've come in on our side.'

The Mountain Folk weren't the only allies of Gwerbret Ridvar who were readying themselves for the Horsekin war. At the dun of the Red Wolf, a good many miles south-west of the dun that now belonged to the Gold Falcon clan, Tieryn Cadryc and his men were only waiting for the arrival of his overlord to ride out. Preparing the warband for that ride fell to Gerran of the Gold Falcon, its lord and so far one of its only two members, the other being his young page Clae. Despite his sudden elevation to the ranks of the noble-born, Gerran still considered himself the captain of the tieryn's warband, mostly because none of the tieryn's other men could fill the post. Although the tieryn had a son, Lord Mirryn, Cadryc was leaving him behind on fortguard.

Every night at dinner in the great hall, Mirryn would stand behind his father's chair like a page. When Cadryc arrived,

Mirryn would bow to his father, then without a word pull out the chair at the head of the honour table to allow Cadryc to sit down. He would wait to eat, too, until all the others at the honour table had finished their meal. After three days of this treatment, Cadryc had had enough.

'Still sulking, are you?' Cadryc said.

'Well, ye gods!' Mirryn snapped. 'How do you think I should feel, Father, left behind out of the fighting like a woman?'

'And what's this business with my blasted chair?' Cadryc continued without acknowledging the question.

'Since I'm being treated like a servant, I thought I should act like one.'

'Just sit down, and do it right now. You'll drive me daft, hovering like that.'

With a grunt Mirryn sat himself down at his father's left hand, but he crossed his arms over his chest and stared out at nothing. The tieryn swung his head around to glare at his son, who pretended not to notice. Although most of the tieryn's hair was either grey or missing, and Mirryn still sported a thick mop of brown hair to go with his freckles and the family blue eyes, no one would have doubted they were father and son, lean men, both of them, and stubborn.

'If you starve yourself at my table,' Cadryc said, 'you'll be too weak to fight even if I should change my mind, which I won't, so by the black hairy arse of the Lord of Hell, stop sulking and eat your blasted dinner!'

Mirryn went on studying the empty air. Finally Lady Galla, his mother, leaned across the table from her place at the tieryn's right. 'Mirro,' she said, 'please? This has been dreadful for all of us.'

'Oh very well, Mam.' Mirryn drew his table dagger from the sheath at his belt and placed it next to the trencher in front of him. 'Shall I cut you some bread?'

'If you'd be so kind.' Lady Galla smiled at him, then favoured her husband with another smile, which he ignored.

The 'all of us' to whom the lady had referred were the

other occupants of the honour table. Besides the tieryn, his stout, dark-haired lady, and his son, Gerran was now eating with the noble-born, who included Galla's niece, Lady Branna, and her common-born husband Neb. Branna, with her yellow hair and her narrow blue eyes, was a pretty young woman, but Neb was the nondescript sort, brown haired, skinny, neither handsome nor ugly. Most people would have ignored him, but Gerran knew his worth.

Soon, however, Cadryc's allies and vassals would appear to join the muster. Gerran was counting on the table filling up, allowing him to sneak back to his old place at the head of one of the warband's tables over on the other side of the great hall, even though he had to admit that sharing a trencher with Lady Galla's serving woman, Lady Solla, had its compensations. Every now and then her lovely hazel eyes would meet his when he offered her a slice of bread or passed her some portion of the meal. She would blush, and he would find himself at a loss for words.

The times were simply wrong for pleasantries. The coming war filled Gerran's waking thoughts. On the morrow, messengers from their most important ally arrived at the dun. When the gatekeeper came running to tell Gerran that Westfolk were at the gates, Gerran told the man to let them in, then hurried out to greet them. From a distance the Westfolk looked much like ordinary men, but close up their wild blood revealed itself. Their eyes had abnormally large irises, slit with vertical pupils like a cat's. Their long ears curled to a delicate point like sea shells. Rumours claimed they were immortal, too, but that Gerran heartily doubted. At his invitation they dismounted, three archers with their curved short bows slung over their backs and a man carrying the be-ribboned staff of a herald.

'Messages, my lord,' the herald said. 'From Prince Daralanteriel himself.'

'Good,' Gerran said. 'Come into the great hall. The tieryn's there.'

As he followed them inside, Gerran was still wondering over the easy way the herald had called him 'my lord', since his shirt still bore the Red Wolf blazon, not his new gold falcon. Most likely the prince or his cadvridoc had described him at some point. Heralds, after all, remembered everything they were told or they lost their exalted positions.

From the door of the great hall, Lady Branna watched the herald dismount, then hoist down a pair of bulging saddlebags. A dark-haired fellow who looked more human than elven, he seemed somehow familiar, though she couldn't place where she'd seen him before. She followed him to the table of honour, where her uncle was sitting at the head with her aunt at his right. Branna sat down next to her on the bench just as Neb came trotting down the staircase.

'Ah, there you are!' Cadryc called to him. 'Messages from Prince Dar, I'll wager!'

'They are, your grace,' the Westfolk man said. 'My name is Maelaber, by the by, and I'm Calonderiel's son.'

Aha! Branna thought. *That's why he looks familiar.*

'Then twice welcome, lad,' Cadryc said.

'My thanks. We've also come to lead your army to our muster. It's too easy for Deverry men to get lost out in the grasslands.'

'Now that's true spoken.' Cadryc paused for a smile. 'It gladdens my heart to have you with us. Your prince is a far-sighted man.'

'He is that, your grace. I've also got a gift for Lady Branna. Councillor Dallandra sent it.' Maelaber opened one of the saddlebags and brought out a large bundle wrapped in thick grey cloth and stoutly tied with leather thongs. 'Books, I think. She didn't tell us.'

Courtesy demanded that Branna sit quietly until the tieryn gave her the parcel, but curiosity trounced courtesy. Despite her aunt's dark looks, she got up and ran around the table to snatch the parcel out of Maelaber's hands.

'My thanks,' she said with a grin. 'I'll just take these upstairs.'

Branna avoided looking Galla's way as she dashed for the staircase, but she did notice Neb scowling at her – but not for her lack of good manners, she was sure. As the tieryn's scribe, he was going to have to stay at his lord's side until Cadryc gave him leave to go. His curiosity would have to wait.

Up in their chamber, she laid the parcel onto the bed, then flung open the shutters over the window to let in the sunlight. A few slashes with her table dagger disposed of the thongs. She unwound the cloth to find two leather-bound books and a scrap of pale leather bearing a note from Dallandra.

'These belonged to Jill and Nevyn,' the note read. 'They should therefore belong to you. Study them well while the army's gone, especially the larger one. Someday you'll need to carry all this lore in your memory.'

Branna laid the note down and pulled the larger book free of the wrap to lay it right onto the bed, despite the smell of ancient damp from its dark leather binding. It was far too large for her to hold, taller than her forearm was long. When she opened it, the smell of mouldy parchment made her sneeze. She wiped her nose on her sleeve, then saw, written on the first leaf, Nevyn's name. With that sight memory flooded back. She could see the old man opening the book and pointing to a diagram of concentric circles marked by words that, in the memory, she couldn't yet read.

Jill never learned her letters until she was grown, Branna thought. *Nevyn taught her.* Tears blurred her sight, sudden hot tears that shocked her as they spilled. If only Nevyn were alive now, with his vast knowledge, if only he were here – but of course, he was there, opening the door to the chamber, in fact, though he was now as young and ignorant and as nearly powerless as she.

'What's wrong?' Neb said. 'Ye gods, that thing stinks!'

'It does.' Branna pulled a handkerchief from her kirtle. 'It's made me sneeze, and my poor eyes!'

While she wiped her face and blew her nose, he turned a few pages of the book. He frowned a little, mouthed a few words, then suddenly smiled.

'I remember this,' he said. 'Do you?'

'I do. You told me once you'd owned it since you were a very young man.'

Neb looked up, his lips half-parted in shock.

'I mean,' Branna said hastily, 'Nevyn told Jill that.'

'I figured that. It just always surprises me, how much you remember.'

'Me too. What's this second one?'

The smaller book turned out to contain healing lore, first a treatise on the humours, then a vast compendium, page after page of herbs, roots, symptoms, and treatments, and finally some instructions for simple chirurgery. The handwriting wavered, each letter spiky and oddly large.

'Jill's writing,' Neb said abruptly. 'I do remember a few things, here and there. She learned late, you see, and so her hand's somewhat childish.'

'I feel like there's four people in this chamber. Do you feel that, too?'

'In a way.' Neb glanced over his shoulder as if he expected to see Jill and Nevyn standing behind them. 'It creeps my flesh.'

Branna closed the book of medicines and walked over to the window. Outside lay the familiar view of her uncle's dun wall and the green fields beyond. She'd half-expected to see a different prospect, though the details had escaped her memory. *Somewhere I've never been,* she thought, *not as me, anyway. Did I know the silver dragon when I was there?* Ever since she'd seen Rori fly past Cengarn, the silver wyrm had never been far from her mind.

'What were Prince Dar's messages?' she said.

'Um? Jill, what did you say?'

Neb was reading a page in the larger book. He was leaning over to peer at the writing, his shoulders hunched like those of a much older man. Again she remembered seeing Nevyn reading in this same book, sitting at a rough-made table with a dweomer light hovering above him. For a moment she saw their surroundings: a windowless stone room, and at the top of the walls ran a carving of circles and triangles, abruptly broken off as if someone had deliberately defaced it. *Stop!* she told herself. *You're Branna; Branna, not Jill.*

'Neb, stay here!' Branna made her voice as sharp as she could. 'What were Prince Dar's messages?'

With a toss of his head Neb straightened up and turned to face her. 'You're right,' he said softly. 'For a moment I was back there. What did you used to call it? The other When?'

'Just that. But we're here now.'

'So we are. That's going to be our spell of safety, isn't it? Stay here now.'

'It's a good one. We'll need it.'

Neb smiled, nodding a little. 'But the messages,' he went on, 'were all about the army. He's raised over five hundred archers and a good many swordsmen. He's hoping to raise more before we join him.'

'We? You're not riding with the Red Wolf warband, are you?'

'Of course I am. My place is at the tieryn's side.'

For a moment she could barely breathe. Neb caught her hand in both of his.

'What's wrong –' he began.

'I'm terrified you'll get killed, of course,' Branna said. 'Why does he want you to go?'

'To write messages if he needs some sent, of course.'

'Very well, then, but you won't be riding to battle, will you?'

'I won't. Will you look down on me because of that?'

'Oh, don't be stupid!'

Neb grinned. 'I'd be useless in a battle, unless they need someone who can throw stones with a fair degree of accuracy. I used to be good at slinging them at crows and squirrels.'

They shared a laugh, and she felt the fear leave her.

'After all,' Branna said, 'you *are* my husband now. I get to worry. You're supposed to be touched by my devotion.'

'That's true spoken, and my apologies.' Neb made a sweeping bow. 'May I express my complete and total devotion to you?'

'You may. How about the passion that burns within you?'

'That, too. Quite a lot of that, actually. Do you regard me with great esteem?'

'I do, and with affection to match it.'

'Well and good, then. Give me a bit of time, and I'll compose some englynion in your honour.'

'That'd be lovely, but what is this? I'm supposed to sit at my window with the scroll in my lap and long for your return? Huh. I'm going with you.'

'What? You can't do that!'

'Why not? I'll be your assistant. I can gather rushes for pens and all that. It's not like anyone would be asking me to swing a sword, is it?' Branna thought for a moment. 'And I can tear up rags for bandages and help Dalla.'

'Your uncle won't let you come.'

'Then we shan't tell him until it's too late.' She laid a hand on his arm and smiled up at him. 'Don't you want me there?'

'Of course I do. I mean – gods, I never should have admitted that.'

'True spoken. You shouldn't have, but you did, and so let's plan my escape.'

'What about your aunt?'

'She's got Adranna and the children, and Solla now, too. She won't be lonely any longer.'

'There are times when I can see that being married to you is going to be like living in one of Salamander's tales. And I'm thankful to every god there is.' Neb raised her hand and kissed her fingers.

Someone knocked in urgent rhythm on the door. Neb ran to open it and reveal Salamander, who strode in without

waiting to be asked. The gerthddyn frowned and looked
Branna over with stern grey eyes.

'What is this?' Salamander said. 'I've just had an omen
warning about you, my fine lady. You're not planning on doing
anything stupid like following the army, are you?'

'What makes you think I'd do such a thing?'

'Your general temperament, mostly, as well as the way you
blushed scarlet just now.'

'I hate you.'

'Ah, so I'm right.'

'I cannot let Neb go off to war while I stay here, I just can't.'

'What?' Salamander turned to Neb. 'You're riding with the
army?'

'I'm the tieryn's scribe,' Neb said. 'He wants me there.'

'That is profoundly short-sighted, risky, and altogether
foolish of his grace, but since he's a Deverry lord, I'm not
surprised in the least. Isn't Ridvar bringing a scribe?'

'He is,' Neb said, 'but Cadryc can't possibly ask for the
use of him. Have you forgotten his grandson, Matto? Ridvar
did want him killed.'

Salamander said something in Elvish that sounded
immensely foul, though Branna had no idea of what it meant.
'Well, I can read and write.' Salamander switched back to
Deverrian. 'I'm not much for scribing, Neb, but if you packed
me up some inks and pens, I could do a passable job, and
Dar's scribe will be riding with us as well.'

'But it's my duty to –'

'Hang duty! Neb, you and Branna both are far too valuable to risk your lives in a dangerous venture like the one
we have in hand. Don't you understand? Your dweomer is
the hope of the border.'

Branna turned away, saw the books lying on the bed, and
turned back again. Her heart was pounding as badly as if
she'd run a long way.

'I see.' Neb, however, sounded perfectly calm. 'What I
can't see is how to explain that to the tieryn.'

'Imph,' Salamander said. 'No more can I, but it has to be done. I'll consult with Gerran.'

'Does he know?' Branna turned back. 'Gerro, I mean.'

'He does, if you mean about dweomer and Neb having it,' Salamander said. 'And he suspects it about you. He doesn't know the bit about the hope of the border and all that. Think! Even if we wipe Zakh Gral off the face of the earth, this is only the first skirmish in a long war. Do you think the Horsekin are going to go meekly back to their own lands and stay there if they lose?'

'I see your point,' Neb said. 'The more dweomermasters we can muster, the better.'

'It's the best weapon we have against them,' Salamander said. 'We've got some days before Voran and Ridvar arrive. I'm bound to come up with a good tale for the tieryn's ears before then.' He paused for a sunny grin. 'I'm good at tales.'

Whenever the tieryn left the great hall, Gerran went back to his old place at one of the warband's tables. He had the only chair, and he liked to lean it back on its rear legs to allow him to put his feet up on one of the benches. He was just starting on his first tankard of ale for the day when Salamander came trotting down the stone staircase. The gerthddyn hailed him and hurried over.

'I need your advice on somewhat,' Salamander said. 'May I join you?'

'By all means. Fetch yourself some drink.'

Salamander found a tankard and filled it from the barrel over by the servants' hearth, then sat down on the bench not occupied by Gerran's boots.

'It concerns Neb the scribe,' Salamander said. 'He tells me he'll be riding with the army. He shouldn't. He needs to be here in the dun. The fortguard can't keep watch against certain kinds of danger, but he can, if you take my meaning.'

'I do.' Gerran had a long swallow of ale. 'Not that I like thinking about it.'

'I realize that.' Salamander paused for a nervous glance around, but none of the servants were in earshot. 'I can take his place, if our good tieryn will let him stay behind. But I need a tale that will convince Cadryc, some clever ploy, some magnificent obfuscation, a lie, in short, since I can't tell him the truth.'

'There's no need to pile up horseshit.' Gerran set his tankard down. 'You're not inventing a tale for the market-place.'

'Well, what else can I do?'

'Leave it to me. I'll go speak to his grace right now.'

Gerran found Tieryn Cadryc out in the stables, where he and the head groom were making an important decision: which horses the warband would take to Zakh Gral. Gerran waited for a lull in their talk.

'Your grace?' Gerran said. 'A private word with you?'

'Of course.' Cadryc nodded at the groom. 'I'll be back straightaway.'

They walked across the kitchen garden and out to the curve of the dun wall, where no one could overhear.

'What's all this, Gerro?' Cadryc said.

'Your grace, do you trust me?'

'What? Of course I do!'

'And do you trust my judgment? You don't think me daft or suchlike, do you?'

'Of course not! Gerro –'

'Then grant me a daft-sounding boon on my word alone. Neb the scribe should stay here when we ride out.'

For a long moment Cadryc stared at him narrow-eyed. 'On your word alone? No explanation?'

'None, your grace.'

Cadryc shrugged and smiled. 'Done, then,' he said. 'It's an easy enough boon to grant, eh? I can always ask Prince Dar's scribe if I need a message written or suchlike.'

'Better yet, Salamander can read and write. Neb can give him what he needs for the job.'

'Well, there you are, then. Easy and twice easy.'

Cadryc went back to the stables, and Gerran started for the broch. He took a shortcut through the kitchen garden, then realized that someone was lurking behind the cook's little gardening shed. He could guess who it was.

'Come out, gerthddyn,' Gerran said wearily. 'I should have known you'd be eavesdropping.'

'Think of all the effort I've saved you.' Salamander strolled over to join him. 'This way you won't have to tell me what our noble tieryn said. My thanks, by the way. You were quite right. We didn't need the pile of horseshit. I'll just go tell Neb that the matter's settled.'

Salamander trotted off with a cheerful wave. As Gerran followed, he happened to glance up. Far above the dun the black dragon floated on the summer breeze. Although he didn't know where Arzosah was lairing, at various times during the day this strangest of all possible allies would appear, keeping watch over the dun. She'd take a turn or two over it at night, as well, when she was on her way to hunt down a wild meal. Gerran was never sure if her presence was comforting or terrifying. *As long as she doesn't scare the horses,* he thought. With a shrug he went inside to join the warband.

'Well, it gladdens my heart to have that settled,' Branna said. 'I feel horribly selfish, though. I'm just so happy that Neb will be staying here safe in the dun.'

'Why not be happy?' Salamander gave her one of his sunny grins. 'Life is short, so grasp what joy it gives you. As to safe, I hope you both will be, but you'll need to be on your guard.'

'Because of the raven mazrak?'

'Precisely. He may not know who you specifically are, but dweomer can always smell out dweomer. He must know you have it, and that therefore you're a potential thorn in his feathered side.'

'Let's hope I can be a dagger, not a thorn.'

'Someday, mayhap, but not now.' Salamander's voice

dropped to a cold seriousness. 'Never challenge him. Merely watch. He's got a hundred times the power you do.'

'Well and good, then. Will Arzosah be carrying messages back and forth? I can always send you one if I see him.'

'Alas, I doubt it. We'll need the dragons with the army.'

'Rori will be there, too?'

'Oh, of course. He never was the sort of man you could keep out of a good fight.'

Branna felt that she should know exactly what he meant, but the memories eluded her. She was about to ask more, but she heard voices behind her. They were standing just inside the honour door of the great hall, which was beginning to fill up for the evening meal. When she glanced over her shoulder she saw Aunt Galla and her daughter Adranna walking towards them. She stepped aside to let them enter. As they passed, Salamander bowed to both women. Galla favoured him with a smile and a wave of her hand, but Adranna strode on by with her mouth set in a thin line and poison in her eyes.

'Alas,' Salamander said. 'I fear me your cousin will never forgive me. Truly, if I were her I wouldn't forgive me, either. My heart aches for her loss.'

'She's better off without Honelg,' Branna said. 'So are the children.'

'No doubt, but it must be hard on a woman to return a widow to her father's dun.'

'Little do you know how true that is! She and Galla squabble all the time.'

'That must be unpleasant.'

'It is, but at least she's here to help with the spinning.' Branna reflexively rubbed her right wrist with her left hand. 'The more women the better for that. It's so tedious.'

While they waited for the gwerbret's army to ride in, Branna had been spending as much time as she possibly could with her cousin. During their long talks, Adranna occasionally discussed her dead husband and even wept for him, briefly and now and then, but the loss she felt most keenly was nothing so domestic as lord and dun. That evening they left the dinner table early and went up to the women's hall, where they pulled their chairs over to a window and the cooler air.

'You don't know what it's like, Branni,' Adranna said. 'Being part of a clan of believers, I mean. That's how we thought of ourselves, as kin and clan, Alshandra's people all, whether we were farmers or noble-born.'

'I feel that way when we go to the Moon temple on the feast days and suchlike.'

'Oh, that!' Adranna tossed her head. 'That's just tradition. Alshandra is real. You can feel her presence. Our lady's different, truly she is.'

'How can she be? All goddesses are one goddess.'

'That's what the priestesses of the Moon say, but why should we believe them?'

Branna decided to ignore the question. 'Alshandra certainly could be a new aspect of the goddess,' she went on, 'but all that talk of Vandar's spawn and the like – that sounds like the Horsekin men to me, making up a new excuse to start wars and conquer other people's land.'

'I have to admit that it sounded that way to me, too, especially the bit about Vandar's spawn. They do want pasture for their horses, the Horsekin men. The ones that visited us, they practically came right out and said so, but well, I thought maybe Alshandra wants them to live on the grasslands.'

'Grasslands, perchance, somewhere or other. I wouldn't wager high on it. Goddesses don't draw up boundary maps like a village priest, deciding which son gets what when a farmer dies.'

At that Adranna managed to smile.

'Besides,' Branna said, 'why would your goddess want the Westfolk destroyed? She –'

'Hold a moment!' Adranna leaned forward in her chair. 'The Westfolk? I never heard anything against the Westfolk.'

'But that's who Vandar's spawn are, according to the Horsekin leaders. Salamander told me about it. The Westfolk lands are the ones they want for themselves.'

'That can't be true!'

'It is true. Ask Salamander if you don't believe me.'

'And why would I believe one word that lying viper says?'

'Well, why would he make that up? He only lies when he's got a good reason. He told me that he heard it from the priestess Rocca.'

'Still –'

'Besides, Dallandra told me the same thing. Would she lie?'

'She wouldn't.' Adranna whispered, and her hands tightened on the arms of her chair. 'But that's a horrible idea.'

'I rather thought so myself.'

Adranna suddenly noticed, or so it seemed, that she was clutching the wood so tightly that her knuckles had gone white. She let go with a sharp sigh and let her hands rest in her lap. Branna waited for some little while to give her a chance to think things over.

'From everything I've heard,' Branna went on, 'I'd say that the Alshandra cult modelled her on Aranrodda. And Aranrodda's an aspect of the one true goddess, isn't she?'

'She is, truly.'

'Well, then. Wouldn't that mean Alshandra's an aspect herself?'

'Oh. I'd not thought of it that way, but –'

Branna waited. Adranna sighed, leaning back in her chair, her face so uncharacteristically thin and drawn, pale against her dark hair, that Branna nearly wept from looking at her.

'You're exhausted, cousin,' Branna said. 'There's no need to go on talking now.'

'My thanks.' Adranna managed a faint smile. 'We'll have lots of time to talk while the men are gone to war. That's one good thing to come out of this, I suppose.'

'So we will, truly.'

'There's another good thing,' Adranna continued. 'You know, the worst thing about living with Honelg was being terrified. Not of him, so much, though he did have that awful temper, but because of Alshandra. I was always afraid that someone would find us out and tell the priests or the gwerbret. I got so tired of being frightened. Every time someone rode up to the dun, I'd tremble until I found out who it was. I really would, Branni. I couldn't hold a cup of water steady for the trembling. Now the worst has happened and been done with, and the children are safe. I don't much care what happens to me any more, but I prayed and prayed that my children would be safe. So, at least the fear's over now.'

Branna just managed to stop herself from blurting out the truth: the real time of fear had just begun.

Whenever Arzosah wanted to speak with Salamander, she would wait till evening, when the grooms had stabled the horses, safe from the panic her presence would cause. Normally she would fly low over the dun until he noticed, then go land in the meadow just below the motte upon which the dun stood. That particular evening, however, she landed directly on the flat roof of the broch. Salamander, who was up in his top-floor chamber, felt the tower shake as if in a high wind. Out in the ward several maidservants screamed.

'That must be the dragon,' he remarked aloud. 'I'd best go see what she wants.'

He climbed the ladder standing in the corridor outside and shoved open the trap door. In the hot, humid night, the vinegar scent of great wyrm nearly made him choke. He swung himself onto the roof from the ladder's last rung, then stood up to bow to her. He could see her raise her enormous head in silhouette against the stars.

'And a good eve to you, oh perfect paragon of dragon-hood,' Salamander said in Elvish.

'My, you do know how to flatter a lady.' Arzosah made the

rumbling sound that signalled amusement. 'Even minstrels have their uses, I see.'

'And such as my poor skills are, they're at your disposal.'

'Good. I need to know if the dun will be safe if I leave. I have to search for Rori. He was supposed to meet me here, and he's never arrived.'

'That's true. He hasn't. I hope no harm's befallen him.'

'I doubt that very much, since only another dragon could possibly harm him. No, I'm sure he's merely being an utter dolt about facing you and Dallandra.'

'Can't Dalla summon him?'

'No, and all because he's not a true dragon in his soul. When she calls out his true name, he can feel the summons in the dragonish way, but it lacks power over him. He's been ignoring her.' Arzosah clacked her massive jaws. 'He can be infuriating.'

'You have to understand,' Salamander said, 'that it's a hard thing being caught between two peoples. I've spent my whole life that way, and I know.'

'I suppose you're right.' Arzosah considered this for a moment. 'I can see the difficulties Rori goes through. But the worst of them is that it makes so much trouble for me.'

'A terrible thing, truly. Well, once you've found him, why don't you join Dallandra out on the grasslands? I doubt if we're in any danger here, not from armed enemies, at any rate.'

'Good. I'll do that.' She started to spread her wings, then folded them back again. 'You know, you'd best be off the roof before I fly. I'd hate to knock you off it.'

'I'd hate it even more. Good hunting, and I'll see you when we join up with Daralanteriel's army.'

Salamander climbed partway down the ladder, then shut the trap door. Just as he reached the safety of the corridor below, he heard her fly off in a great rush of wings like drumbeats.

Since his chamber was stifling in the summer heat,

Salamander decided to take a turn around the ward in the cooler air before he tried to sleep. When he reached the bottom of the staircase, he discovered that half the dun was doing the same thing, noble-born as well as commoners. Bright points of lantern light danced around the dark ward and glittered here and there up on the catwalks. He could hear men's cajoling voices, speaking softly, and the giggling of serving lasses in return.

Off to one side Gerran stood talking with Lady Solla. In the light of the lantern he carried, his copper-red hair gleamed like the metal itself. Neb and Branna were strolling along arm-in-arm with Adranna's two children trailing after. A crowd of Wildfolk danced around them, led by Branna's skinny grey gnome, and Neb's fat yellow one. A gaggle of crystalline sprites flew above. When Salamander stopped to greet them, Trenni gave him a pleasant 'good evening', but Matto turned his head away and ostentatiously spit on the cobbles. The Wildfolk vanished.

'Let's go inside,' Branna said firmly. 'Trenni, you too. It's time for bed.'

She grabbed a child by the arm with each hand and hurried them into the broch. Neb, however, lingered outside with Salamander. They wandered around the back of the broch and stood in a patch of candlelight falling through a window.

'Do you think that Matto will ever forgive me?' Salamander said. 'I'm afraid I had a great deal to do with his father's death.'

'I'm not so sure it's that,' Neb said. 'More like, he blames you for losing him his home and making his mother so unhappy. Honelg lost every bit of the lad's loyalty when he tried to kill him. Trenni outright hated her father, and I think me our Matto's coming round to her way of thinking.'

'I see. That's truly sad in its own way.'

'It is. It came as a shock to me. And yet, it's odd, but Matto still feels he should hate you and Gerran, too, for the killing of his father.' Neb shook his head. 'I doubt if I'll ever truly understand the noble-born.

'Me either. On the other hand, though my own father and I have our difficulties, if someone killed him, I'd feel the need to bring them to the prince's justice at the very least.'

'My father and I never had any difficulties. I miss him still, but half the people in our town died from that plague. I can't consider myself singled out for grief or suchlike.'

'Truly. A natural affliction knows neither feud nor honour.'

'Of course, the local priests denied that it was any such thing. They told us that Great Bel was angry. They wanted us to find white horses for sacrifice.'

'If it happens again, we know where to find white cows – or won't cattle do?'

'They won't. Bel demands horses, but – here, wait!' Neb held up one hand. 'I just thought of somewhat. I –' He hesitated, visibly thinking.

Salamander held his tongue. Neb's expression of intense concentration had made him seem suddenly older, far stronger. *More Nevyn-like*, Salamander thought. *I wonder if a memory's trying to rise?*

'That plague,' Neb said slowly. 'What if it wasn't Bel's doing nor a natural thing? At the time, I didn't know one cursed thing about the Westfolk and their history. I didn't know about dark dweomer, either. But I do now, and I wonder if someone brought sickness to town, like. It happened so suddenly, and the weather was warm. There'd been a big market fair in town, and there were a goodly number of strangers come for it.'

'I wonder, too. How do the Westfolk come into it?'

'They don't, exactly, but the ancient plague on the Horsekin does. From what you've told me, it gripped their bowels and caused the same kind of bloody flux as –' Neb paused to swallow heavily, summoning courage, 'as I saw. Everything about it sounds the same. If some of it still lurked in that Horsekin city you told me about, and if someone had been there and caught it, and then come to Trev Hael for some reason, well?'

'Indeed! I'm going to tell Dalla about this idea of yours.'

'Good. Now, the town herbwoman decided that since it produced an excess of the watery humour, the fiery humour must be its natural enemy. So she had everyone roasting their food and boiling their well water. When someone died, we burned their blankets and clothing, too. And you know, it did seem to stop the spread of it.'

'That's most interesting. I'll tell Dalla that, too.'

'It was a horrible time.' Neb shuddered and looked away. 'I've not wanted to think about it before this, but truly, it's important, isn't it? I've got this feeling that I need to remember it. Huh, you know, when Clae and I were orphaned, priests of Bel brought us west. They were going to a temple north of Cengarn, but one of them was willing to take us as far as the Great West Road first. There's only one temple north of Cengarn that I know of.'

'Ye gods!' Salamander's voice caught. He coughed and spat onto the ground. 'My apologies, but hearing you say that seems to have clotted my throat right up with omens.'

Salamander hurried up to the privacy of his chamber. He sat on the wide ledge of the unglazed window and looked out at the points of lantern light gleaming in the ward far below. When he thought of Dallandra, her image built up quickly in his mind. She was apparently sitting under a dweomer light of her own making, because a cool silver glow fell across her. With her ash-blonde hair and steel-grey eyes, she seemed made of pure silver like a creature of the moon's sphere.

While Salamander told her Neb's insights about the plague, he could feel her concern.

'I'm glad you told me this right away,' she said. 'If it does come from the Horsekin cities, I hope they don't realize it. They could use it as a weapon against us.'

For a moment Salamander felt as if the solid stone had moved under him. 'Ye gods,' he said. 'Just – oh ye gods!'

'There's a good chance it doesn't, though,' Dallandra went on. 'If the plague were still somehow alive there in the northern cities, why haven't the Gel da' Thae come down with it? Why didn't I get it, come to think of it, when I visited Zatcheka and Grallezar in Braemel, all those years ago?'

'A most soothing and apposite point, oh princess of powers perilous. Deverry towns aren't known for their cleanliness. Maybe it's just something that Neb's birthplace brewed up in its gutters.'

'That seems more probable.' Yet Dallandra sounded doubtful. 'Rinbaladelan's the only one of the ruined cities that's likely to still have pestilence. The plague began there. I've been told that they had underground cisterns for fresh water. Moist, dark places usually do breed one kind of accidental humour or another. It's the slime that accretes, you see.'

'If you say so.' Salamander knew nothing about medicine. The thought of moist, dark slimes made him profoundly glad of it, too. 'What about that priest who brought Neb to his late and lamented uncle's farm?'

'What about him? Don't priests of Bel travel about the kingdom all the time?'

'Yes, they do. Somehow I had the odd feeling that he and the pestilence had some connection. Yet no one in the temple near Honelg's dun was suffering from it.'

'That's true, nor any of their farmers, either. And it's not likely that they'd have been in one of the Horsekin towns, is it?'

'Most extremely unlikely, indeed. I seem to have got obsessed with this wretched illness, probably because of your friends in Braemel. I had a moment of fearing that they'd bring plague with them to the war.'

'Well, it's not likely and doubly so now.' Dallandra's worried mood returned in force. 'Something very odd seems to be happening in Braemel.'

'Haven't you heard from Grallezar?'

'No. I've tried to reach her several times now, but I can't. I can feel her mind, but she seems utterly distracted. I hope things are going well there.'

'Maybe the Gel da' Thae simply don't want to fight against their own kind. They have no love for Deverry men, certainly. What do they call them? Red Reivers?'

'That's right, Lijik Ganda in the Horsekin tongue.'

'Wait – Rocca used a different word for red.'

'The Gel da' Thae have a great many words for all the different colours. Gral means red like rust. Ganda means red like fresh meat.'

'Oh. That says a great deal about the name they chose for Deverry men.'

'True. Now, Braemel allied itself with us and with the Roundears up in Cerr Cawnen out of fear of the Horsekin, those wild tribes of the north. This spring Grallezar hinted at some sort of trouble in her city, something to do with a coterie of Alshandra worshippers, but she never said what it was. I assumed it was none of my affair. The Gel da' Thae can be as clannish as we are.'

'Then we'll know exactly what she chooses to tell us, and naught a thing more.'

'That unfortunately is very true. I could definitely feel her fear, though, when we talked mind to mind.'

In his daily scrying sessions, Salamander had seen changes taking place at Zakh Gral. New troops had arrived, hordes of slaves were building new barracks, and always work on the stone walls went forward. He told Dallandra about these developments in detail. For some while more they talked back and forth, letting their minds reach across the hundreds of miles between them. Salamander could feel himself tiring. Far sooner than usual, he had to fight to maintain his concentration. Dallandra became aware of his difficulty the moment he felt it himself.

'Ebañy, you're exhausted,' she said. 'I know that we need to keep an eye on Zakh Gral, but be very careful that you don't spend too much time scrying. You had to turn yourself into your bird form to escape the fortress. That was a huge strain. Then I got myself into trouble with that astral gate, and you had to come rescue me – another huge strain. I'm worried about you. Your old madness could reassert itself if you keep getting exhausted.'

'Worry not, oh princess of powers perilous! I'm quite aware of that. From now on, I'll scry only twice a day, morning and evening. I promise.'

They broke the link. When Salamander got up from his perch in the window, he felt so dizzy that he lay down on top of his blankets fully dressed. *I'll get up in a moment or two*, he told himself. But when he woke, it was morning.

Technically, Neb and Branna were merely betrothed, not married, but with war looming, there was no time for formal ceremonies and no extra food for feasts. Since Branna's father and uncle had approved their marrying, everyone who knew them assumed quite simply that they were. Upon their return to the dun, Neb had moved the few things he owned into Branna's chamber from his own, and that was an end to it.

With Branna so busy with her cousin and the children, Neb saw little of her during the day. After breakfast he often lingered at table with Salamander, Gerran, and Mirryn, listening to their talk of the coming war. On this particular morning, after Branna and Galla had gone up to their hall, and Tieryn Cadryc had gone out to consult with the grooms, Maelaber, the Westfolk herald, came over to sit with them, though his escort stayed seated with the warband. Maelaber told them in some detail about the preparations the Westfolk were making for the fighting ahead. Gerran listened with the oddly bored expression on his face that meant he was absorbing every scrap of information. Mirryn merely glowered down at the table, so intensely that at last Maelaber fell silent.

'And what's so wrong with you, Mirro?' Gerran said. 'Did the porridge turn your stomach sour or suchlike?'

'You know cursed well what's wrong,' Mirryn said.

'Well, you can't argue with Cadryc's orders,' Gerran said. 'He's the tieryn as well as your father.'

Mirryn answered with a string of epithets so foul that Neb, Salamander, and Maelaber all rose at the same moment and left the table. Neb could hear Gerran and Mirryn squabbling as they walked away.

'Waiting for war's always hard,' Salamander muttered.

'True spoken,' Maelaber said. 'When I left the Westfolk camp, everyone there had thorns up their arses, too.'

Maelaber returned to his escort and the warband, but Neb and Salamander went outside to the dun wall. They climbed up to the catwalks, where they could catch the fresh summer breeze and lean onto the dun wall. Between the crenellations they could see the green meadows and streams of the tieryn's rhan. The sun fell warm on their backs, and Neb yawned.

'Tired already, are you?' Salamander said.

'Being married cuts into a man's sleep.'

'Oh get along with you! Braggart!'

Neb grinned and decided to change the subject. 'Have you heard from Dallandra?'

'I have,' Salamander said. 'She shares our wondering about that pestilence, but she doesn't think it came from one of the Horsekin cities. No more does she think that those priests who took you to her uncle's have anything to do with it.'

'Well and good, then.' Neb turned around to lounge back against a crenel. 'Oh by the gods!'

'What's wrong?'

'Look up!' With a sweep of his arm, Neb pointed at the sky. 'He's back.'

Far above them, a bird with the black silhouette of a raven circled against the pale blue, far too large for any ordinary bird.

'So he is,' Salamander said. 'Our mazrak, home again from wherever his peculiar tunnel led him.'

'He waited to arrive till Arzosah left us, I see. Huh, the coward!'

'I wouldn't call him that. Would you argue with a dragon

thirty times your size? Ah, I see by your expression that you wouldn't.'

Neb slid his hands into his brigga pockets and found the weapons he carried, a leather sling and a round pebble. He brought them out as casually and slowly as he could. 'I wonder if I can get a stone into the air before he notices.'

The raven floated in a lazy circle over the dun, then allowed himself to drift in closer. Neb could see him tilting his head from side to side as if he was examining everything below him. All at once he swung around and flapped off fast, heading north from the dun, a rapidly disappearing black speck against the clear sky.

'He must have seen your sling,' Salamander said.

'He's got good eyes then, blast him!' Neb slapped the leather loop of the sling against a crenel in frustration. 'You know, Salamander, it's a cursed strange thing, but I keep feeling like I know that bird – or the person inside it, I mean. It's as if I can see through his feathers or suchlike. Well, that sounds daft, now that I say it aloud.'

'Not daft but dweomer,' Salamander said. 'Most likely, anyway. You may be mistaken, of course, but somehow I doubt it. I'd say he's someone you knew in a past life.'

'Truly? I certainly don't have any fond feelings for him.'

'Oh, when you recognize a person like this, it doesn't necessarily mean they were a friend. An old enemy will call out to you, like, just as loudly.'

Neb paused, thinking, letting his mind dwell upon the image of the raven and the feelings it aroused. 'An enemy, truly,' he said at last, 'but there's somewhat more as well. It's like a debt linking us, or more than one debt. I owe him somewhat, but he owes me far more.'

'Odd, indeed!' Salamander said. 'Well, meditate upon it. The answer might be important.'

'The chains of wyrd always are, aren't they?'

'True spoken. Very true spoken indeed.'

* * *

Salamander saw the raven mazrak again the very next morning. A little while past sunrise, his regular time to spy on Zakh Gral, he focused through a scatter of high clouds and scried for Rocca. He saw her immediately, standing before the altar in the Outer Shrine. For a moment he gloated over her image. Had she taken care of herself, she would have been beautiful, with her high cheekbones and thick dark hair, but her face looked sunburned and dirt-streaked, framed in messy tendrils of dirty hair. She was wearing a long, sleeveless dress of pale buckskin, painted with Alshandra's holy symbol of the bow and arrow.

Behind her, on the rough stone surface of the altar, sat the relics of her goddess's legendary worshipper, the holy witness Raena. Salamander had seen most of them before – the box with the wyvern dagger, the copper tray with the miniature bow and arrows, the bone whistle, and the obsidian pyramid. A new addition to the hoard startled him. They'd sewn the shirt he'd left behind onto a plain cloth banner and attached it to a long spear. It stood behind the altar and snapped in the wind.

Lakanza, the grey-haired high priestess, stood next to Rocca with a scroll in one hand. In front of them Sidro knelt with her head bowed, while the two Horsekin holy women stood off to one side, their faces grim, their hands clenched into fists. As Salamander watched, Lakanza unrolled a few inches of the scroll and studied it for a moment. Sidro raised her head and looked at Rocca with such venomous hatred in her blue eyes that Rocca took an involuntary step back, but when Lakanza lowered the scroll, Sidro ducked her head to stare at the ground.

Although Salamander could hear nothing, he could see Lakanza's mouth moving in some sort of chant. She raised a hand and beckoned to one of the Horsekin priestesses. The woman stepped forward and took the wyvern dagger out of its box. She grabbed Sidro's long raven-black hair with one hand and raised the dagger with the other. Salamander yelped aloud, thinking he was about to see Sidro's throat slit. Instead, the woman pulled Sidro's hair taut and used the dagger to hack it off, cropping it close to her skull. Sidro endured the ritual with her mouth tight-set and her eyes shut.

Disgraced, Salamander thought. *Serves her right, too, nearly getting me killed like that!* Yet what had she done, after all, but tell the truth and identify an enemy of her people? Salamander's conscience bit him hard. No one would listen to her now, but she had guessed the truth – he *was* one of Vandar's spawn, just as she'd said. His supposedly miraculous escape might well bring disaster upon the fortress and shrine both.

Once she'd cut off Sidro's hair, the Horsekin woman turned and threw it into the wind, which took and scattered the long strands. A few more words from Lakanza, and Sidro rose, picking up the things lying at her feet – a sack and a blanket. Salamander watched as she left the fort and set off on the trail heading north to the forest lands. Had she been thrown out of the holy order? Not likely, since she still wore the painted dress that marked her as a priestess. More likely she'd merely been sent out to preach to the distant believers, much as Rocca had done. She might even be heading to Lord Honelg's dun. If so, she'd walk right into Ridvar's fort-guard and end up a prisoner in Dun Cengarn.

When Salamander widened his Sight to look over the fortress, he saw the raven mazrak drifting on the air currents far above her. *Impossible!* he thought. Less than a full day before, the raven had flown over the Red Wolf dun, a distance of at least three hundred miles. *Ye gods, don't tell me there are two of them!* Salamander broke the vision with a quick stab of fear at the very thought of there being more than one powerful mazrak ranged against them. Then he remembered the astral tunnel.

'Don't you think it's likely,' Salamander asked Dallandra later, 'that he's discovered how to get onto the mother roads?'

'Yes, I certainly do,' Dallandra said. 'Much more likely, in fact, than there being two of these wretched mazrakir. So that's what that tunnel was for! Huh, that's interesting. It's never occurred to me to try to gain the roads from the astral. It's not part of Deverry dweomer, either. I wonder where he learned that?'

'Bardek, I suppose. You thought at one point that he might be from there, didn't you?'

'Yes, and he could be. But however he learned it, that he can work that dweomer means he's a man of great power, so be careful.'

'I shall be, never fear. Let us most devoutly hope that he can't lead armies through those tunnels.'

'It's highly unlikely, since they originate on the astral.'

'An entire army of dweomermasters does strike me as a very distant prospect, now that you mention it. Here's another odd thing. Neb told me that he feels some sort of link to our mazrak from an ill-defined past wyrd they seem to share. He couldn't tell me much more than that. It's not a pleasant link, however. That he does know.'

'Oh by the Star Goddesses!' Dallandra's image looked abruptly weary. 'I don't know why I'm even surprised. Nevyn made a great many enemies during his long life.'

'That's certainly true. I remember a whole ugly clutch of them very clearly indeed, being as I was involved in hunting them down. Off in Bardek, that was, our little war with the dark dweomer —' Salamander abruptly paused, his mind flooded by a surge of memories and omen-warnings both. 'The black stone. The obsidian gem on Alshandra's altar. It has something to do with all of this. I know it in my soul, but I can't say why or what.'

'Then meditate upon it.' Dallandra's thoughts rang with urgency. 'Brood over it like a mare with a weak-legged foal.'

'I shall. I'd wager high that this is a matter of wyrd, something ancient and deep. It involves me, too, though I'm not sure how.'

And indeed, Salamander was right enough about that. During his early childhood, when forming and keeping clear memories lay beyond him, the raven mazrak and the black pyramid had woven a net of wyrd around him. It had snared even a man as powerful as Nevyn, the Master of the Aethyr – which had been Neb's name and dweomer title in the body he wore then, back in those far-off days.

PART I
Dun Deverry and The Westlands
Spring, 983

Every light casts a shadow. The dweomer light
has cast a darkness of darkness. In that vile
night creep those who once were men even as
you, thinking that they craved secrets only to
ease the suffering of the world. Somewhere
along their way, the shadow crept over them
unawares . . .

The Secret Book of Cadwallon the Druid

Built as it was across seven hills, the city of Dun Deverry towered above the surrounding farmlands. Riding up from the south, Nevyn saw it from a long distance away as a cluster of grey and green shapes on the horizon. The road twisted, swinging at times a mile off the straight as it meandered around a lord's dun or rambled along a stream till it finally reached a ford or bridge where a traveller could cross. As the road changed direction, the city seemed to dance on the horizon, now to the east, then to the west, showing him different views as he drew closer. A little while before sunset he finally rode up the last hill, and by then, the city loomed over him like a thunder cloud. The south gates had been repaired since the last time Nevyn had seen them, over a hundred years before, when they'd been only ragged heaps of stone and broken planks. Now they stood twelve feet high and over twenty broad, made of stout oak banded with iron. Each band sported an elaborate engraved design of interlaced wyverns, and on the portion of wall directly above the gates stood a wyvern rampant, carved in pale marble.

Since the stone wall holding them was a good fifteen feet thick, the gates opened into a sort of tunnel, which eventually led onto a cobbled square. Oak saplings, dusted green with their first leaves, stood round the edges. Out in the centre a good many townsfolk were standing around the stone pool of a fountain, gossiping no doubt, but none of them paid any attention to Nevyn, a shabby old herbman leading a laden pack mule and a scruffy riding horse, all three of them covered with dust from the road.

Nevyn, however, studied the townsfolk. As he followed the twisting street uphill past rows of prosperous-looking shops, he kept looking around him, appraising the faces of the people he passed. He'd come to Dun Deverry on two errands. For one, he was searching for a particular young woman who had been his apprentice many a long year before. Everywhere he'd been in the years since her death, he'd searched but never found her. He was hoping that since she'd died in Dun Deverry, she'd been reborn there. She would look very different, of course, but he knew that he'd recognize Lilli when he saw her again. The other errand was far more complicated. To accomplish it, he'd need the help of friends.

Olnadd, priest of Wmm, the god of scribes, lived in a shabby little house not far from the west gate. A brown wooden palisade enclosed the thatch-roofed house, a vegetable garden, and a pair of white geese. When Nevyn arrived at the gate, the geese stopped hunting snails to glare at him. He laid a hand on the latch. Hissing and honking, the pair rushed forward with a great flapping of white wings. His horse and pack mule both threw up their heads and began pulling on reins and halter-rope. As soon as Nevyn let go of the gate, the geese subsided.

'Olnadd,' Nevyn called out. 'Olnadd! Anyone here?'

The front door opened, and the priest hurried out, a slender man with a slick, sparse cap of grey hair. In daily life Wmm's priests dressed much as other Deverry men did, in plain wool brigga with a linen shirt belted over them. Olnadd's shirt sported yokes embroidered with pelicans, the sacred bird of his god.

'Whist, whist,' he called out, 'get back!'

The geese retreated, but not far.

'My apologies,' Olnadd said. 'They're better than watch-dogs, truly.'

'So I see. You don't look surprised to see me, so I take it that my letter reached you.'

'It did.' Olnadd opened the gate and stepped out, shutting it quickly behind him. 'Let's take your horse and mule around to the mews. I've got a shed out there that will do for a stable.'

Once his animals were unloaded and at their hay, Nevyn

followed Olnadd into the house. The priest's wife, a tall, rangy woman who wore her grey hair in braids round her head, greeted him with a smile and ushered them both into her kitchen. They sat at the table near a sunny window. Affyna brought out a plate of cakes and cups of boiled milk sweetened with honey.

'So, then.' Olnadd helped himself to a raisin cake. 'What brings you to us?'

'A rather curious business,' Nevyn said. 'I want to see the king. I've made him a talisman, you see, a little gift for the blood royal.'

'Little gift?' Affyna said. 'If you've made it, it must positively reek of dweomer. Well, I suppose reek isn't quite the word I mean.'

'It will do, truly.' Nevyn grinned at her. 'The question now is, how do I get an audience with our liege to give it to him?'

'That will take a bit of doing,' Olnadd said. 'I don't suppose we should pry, but I can't say I'd mind having a look at the thing.'

'I shouldn't admit this, but I wouldn't mind showing it off. It's taken me a cursed lot of hard work.' Nevyn reached into his shirt, pulled out the slender chain he wore around his neck, and unfastened a small leather pouch. He slid out its contents, wrapped in layers of silk.

'Close those shutters, will you?'

Olnadd got up and did so. One ray of light came through the crack and fell across the table in a line of gold. Nevyn drew a circle deosil around the bundle with his hand, visualized four tiny pentagrams at its cardinal points, and cleared the space around the talisman of all influences – not that evil or impure forces would be lying about the priest's breakfast table, but Nevyn didn't care to have the stone pick up traces of local gossip. He unwrapped the five pieces of silk: the first, mottled with olive, citrine, russet and black; the second, purple; the third, Wmm's own orange; the fourth an emerald green, and the last pale lavender.

In the centre of the silks lay an opal, as big as a walnut, but so perfectly round, so smoothly polished, that it seemed to breathe and glow with a life of its own. Affyna sighed sharply, and Olnadd muttered a few words of prayer under his breath.

'It's commemorated through Bran and the great Gwindyc, you see,' Nevyn said. 'I've linked it up through the Kings of the Wildlands to the golden root of dominion. Not a word of this to anyone, mind.'

'And is there anyone else in Dun Deverry who'd know what I was talking about if I told them?'

'Not half likely, is it?' Nevyn glanced at Affyna.

She smiled again. 'Any woman who marries a priest learns to hold her tongue.'

One piece at a time, smoothing out wrinkles, Nevyn wrapped the opal back up in its silken shrouds. He returned it to the pouch, then wiped the dweomer circle away from the table. Olnadd got up and opened the shutters to let in the spring air.

'And what kind of man is our king?' Nevyn said. 'I knew his grandfather, you see, but I haven't been at court in a cursed long time.'

Olnadd considered, rubbing his chin.

'Hard to say. Now, he used to be the wild sort, Casyl, when he was the Marked Prince, but wedding the sover-eignty changes a man. He's held the kingship only a year now, but he seems to be steadying down.'

'Seems to be?'

'Well, he's a splendid warrior. Very useful just now.' Olnadd considered again, picking up his cup and twisting it between his long fingers. 'But the emotional sort. Given to quick judg-ments and – well – gestures. Things fit for bard songs, a lot of talk about honour – you know the sort.'

'How easy is it for a subject to see his highness? I've brought a good bit of coin to bribe servants.'

'You'll need it, but I can smooth your way and save some of your silver. The scribes all come to the temple, of course, for worship. The head scribe's an interesting sort. Truly, he should have come to us for the priesthood, but he has a taste for power. Coin will be out of place for our Petyc. We'll go down to the bookseller's and see what we can find.'

'A bookseller? Ye gods, Dun Deverry's turning into a grand city indeed.'

'It is, at that. We might find a rare volume, even, but if not, there'll be somewhat there that will make a decent gift. Then I'll introduce you. Petyc will speak to the chamberlain if he likes you. A little gift might be in order for the chamberlain, but a few coins in a pouch should do. There's naught subtle about him, truly.'

'My thanks. I'd like to get this settled before King Casyl goes off to the summer's fighting.'

'Oh, I've no doubt you can. The gossip tells me that he won't ride north for another fortnight or so.'

'Well and good, then. Ye gods! Another war in Cerrgonney!'

'Now, now!' Affyna paused for a sly smile. 'The king never says war. It's a rebellion, according to him.'

'And when did the Boar clan swear fealty to the royal Wyvern?' Nevyn said.

'Oh, according to our present king's father, it was round about 962 or so. Gwerbretion, he called their lords, and how could they be gwerbretion if they hadn't sworn to him?' Olnadd rolled his eyes heavenward. 'We can't doubt the king, can we now? He had it on the best authority – his own.'

They all shared a laugh but a grim one. In truth, Cerrgonney had been an independent kingdom for the past hundred and thirty-odd years, though kingdom was perhaps too grand a word for that rocky land filled with feuds, factions, and petty hatreds. The High King's vassals, however, would support a war more readily if it were presented as putting down a rebellion rather than outright conquest.

'And of course his scribes will write down what he tells them to,' Affyna said, 'and the royal bards sing the correct verses.'

'Indeed,' Nevyn said. 'But ye gods, another war with the cursed Boars. I wonder if we'll ever see the end of them?'

'Now here!' Olnadd gave him a grin. 'I was hoping you could tell me.'

'I can't, alas. The dweomer tells a man what he needs to know and little else.'

That night Nevyn retired early to the small spare guest chamber to work an elaborate piece of dweomer. As much as false omens and pretentious glamours annoyed him, he knew that he'd need them. He'd worked too hard on the opal talisman to have the king accept it lightly, and if he simply gained an audience and handed it over, the king most likely would underestimate its importance. Many years before, Nevyn had successfully used a certain kind of magical trick to shorten a rebellion against the current king's grandfather. Quite possibly he could use it to benefit the grandson as well.

Nevyn lay down on the bed, slowed his breathing, and visualized the sigils that would lead him out to the etheric plane. In his mind he saw the blue light gather; then suddenly it flooded the room. The walls, dead things, turned black, while the air and its spirits pulsed around him with a sapphire glow. To travel on this plane he would need his body of light, but he had worked this dweomer so often that it came to him almost automatically. He'd created from the etheric substance a body, solid blue against the flux, shaped like a man wearing brigga and a shirt, though lacking detail, and joined to his solar plexus by a silver cord. Nevyn transferred his consciousness into it and looked down at his physical body, lying inert and apparently asleep on the bed below. He rose up higher, slipped out of the house, and hovered in the air. Above him the stars gleamed, great silver whorls and streaks against the night sky.

Down below, flickering in the silvery-blue etheric light, the houses and streets of Dun Deverry spread out, black and sullen with stone and tile. Here and there a garden or a tree gleamed with a reddish vegetable aura. Here and there as well the bright ovoid auras of human beings and animals hurried through the streets or disappeared behind dead wooden doors. Yet in an odd way the city itself did seem alive. Its history was so long and so troubled that images from the astral plane had spilled over, as it were, into the etheric, so that Nevyn could see superimposed pictures from all its times of violence and hope.

The tangle of images formed a dense flood, rising and swelling – the streets shrinking, changing place, broadening, disappearing altogether; houses rising, aging, and falling; fires raging through the streets; ghostly crowds of those who'd lived and suffered here rushing to and fro, then disappearing, leaving the desolation of the Time of Troubles, when a tiny village huddled inside shattered walls, only to swell again as the prosperity of peace returned. In the midst of the swirling flood of images, a few unchanging points stood out – the huge temple compound of Bel on one hill, the smaller temple of the Moon Goddess on another, each glowing under a silvery dweomer-shield created by the priests and priestesses. Yet always, under the mutating images, the city, the Holy City, shimmered with power, the soul of the kingdom simply because so many thousands of people believed it so.

In the centre of the city, in the heart of the glowing, surging magical web stood the king's dun, a cluster of tall towers on the highest hill. With barely an effort Nevyn drifted towards it through the rippling etheric light. He had been born on that hill well over three hundred years ago. All the history that had taken place since his birth rose up in a second wave of images and lapped over the dun, then swirled back to allow his memories to flood over it in their place.

Once again Nevyn could see the brochs of his youth with their rough chambers and crude furnishings. In that torch-lit chamber of justice he'd infuriated his father and so set in motion the terrible mistake responsible for his unnaturally long life. With a flicker of light the image changed into the larger, more polished royal compound he'd visited as a simple herbman, then he watched the buildings crumble as rebellion and strife broke out among the great clans. In the civil wars he had installed a new king in a dun that was half in ruins from the long years of siege and betrayal.

Among the images of place he saw the empty simulacra of persons long dead, what ordinary folk call ghosts. He saw his father striding through the ruins, shouting soundless orders to vanished servants. His mother ran after, begging mercy for her unfortunate son. The Boars of Cantrae appeared, all swagger and rage. Prince Maryn and his tragic queen, Bellyra, walked through a translucent great hall. Branoic the silver dagger, Maddyn the bard, Councillor Oggyn – shadows of their forms rose up as if to greet him once again.

Among these images drifted one that Nevyn hadn't expected to see: Lord Gerraent of the Falcon clan. The set of his broad shoulders, his easy warrior's stance, the falcon-image embroidered on his shirt – the image was true in every detail, so much like Gerraent that Nevyn felt his old hatred for the man well up. He had been tangled with this soul's wyrd for three hundred years, yet he would have assumed that any image seen here would have come from a much later incarnation, Owaen for instance, the captain of Prince Maryn's personal guard. Another surprise: rather than dissolving into the general drift, this image lingered, pacing back and forth over a red glow like a carpet of fire. Finally Nevyn realized the truth, that he was seeing no mere memory-ghost, but the actual Gerraent, or rather, his soul reborn in a new body.

Nevyn dropped down through the blue light and hovered a few inches above the ground. This close he could see that the red glow emanated from a lawn, enclosed in the dead black of a stone wall. Off to one side a cluster of pulsing orange resolved itself into rose bushes, swelling with the astral tides of spring. Nevyn could see Gerraent – or whatever he was called in this life – in the midst of his aura, a typical young warrior, his sword at his side even in the midst of the king's gardens, blond, tall, heavily muscled and every bit as arrogant as always. His aura was shot through with blind rage, a blood-coloured crackle of raw energy that Nevyn found sickening.

Nevyn's sudden disgust seemed to touch Gerraent's mind. He stopped his pacing and whirled around, his hand on his sword-hilt as he peered through the night. In puzzlement his aura shrank, then swirled around him. Nevyn marked him well so that he could recognize him again, then let his body of light drift upward. He was high above the ground when he saw another gold aura entering the garden, this one glowing softly around a female body. When Gerraent hurried forward to greet her, Nevyn lingered just long enough to confirm that she was no one bound to him by wyrd, then glided away.

Not far from the garden stood the heart of the king's dun, four towers joined to a central fifth like the petals on a wild rose. In the bottom floor of the tallest tower, open windows glowed with torch light. Nevyn swung himself through one of them and found himself inside the great hall. The last time he'd seen this room it had been filled with shabby furniture, its walls hung with faded, torn tapestries, its huge hearths filthy with ash and refuse. Now the walls had been plastered and decorated with bright banners, one for each of the great clans, hanging between each pair of windows. The tables and chairs at the honour hearth shone with polish, and light winked on silver goblets. Over on the servants' and riders' side of the hall, the furniture was stained and old, but serviceable. Neatly braided rushes covered the entire huge floor.

Nevyn took himself over to the honour hearth, where noble lords sat drinking and a bard sang, his voice sounding oddly hollow and distorted to Nevyn's etheric ears. Although no one sat at the king's table, that is, the one closest to the fire, Nevyn saw a page leaving the hall with a flagon of mead on a silver tray. He followed the lad up the spiralling stone staircase, then along a familiar corridor to the king's apartments.

Fine Bardek carpets covered the floor; elaborately carved

furniture sat upon them. On a long, narrow table, candles flamed in banked silver candelabra, but they sent out as much etheric force as light, making it hard for Nevyn to see in the chamber. Looming out of the golden mist, a man with dark hair but green eyes stood by the empty hearth. His linen shirt, stiff with embroidery, displayed the red wyvern of the royal clan, and he wore brigga in the red, white, and gold royal plaid of Dun Deverry. The page set the flagon down on a little table, then bowed and walked backwards to the door. With one last bow he let himself out.

Nevyn remained, floating near the candles, and considered Casyl the Second, King of all Deverry and Eldidd. Casyl poured himself mead into a golden goblet, then sat down in a cushioned chair and stretched his long legs out in front of him. Finding the king alone was such a rare bit of luck that Nevyn decided to take it as a good omen. He moved closer still to the candles and began gathering both their etheric effluent and their smoke, winding it round his hands with a motion like that of a woman turning loose yarn into a proper skein. Although he couldn't speak from the etheric, he could send thoughts to the king's mind that to him would seem to be speech.

'My liege,' Nevyn thought to him. 'A faithful servant stands ready to aid you.'

Casyl leapt to his feet so fast that he nearly spilled his mead. He set the goblet down on the tablet and began looking around him. With a wrench of will, Nevyn tossed his skein of smoke and effluent around the head of his body of light. Casyl yelped and stepped back. At that Nevyn knew he'd been successful – a ghost-like shape had come through to visible appearance.

'Sometimes great gifts come from no one at all,' Nevyn went on. 'Remember this jest well in days to come.'

Casyl's aura shrank so tight against him that it was barely more than a skin of light hanging around his body.

'Your most honoured grandsire knew who no one was,' Nevyn said. 'The blood royal has its friends.'

With that Nevyn broke the vision. He allowed the candle smoke to disperse, scattered the effluent, and let his body of light drift towards the open window. The working had tired him badly. Casyl never moved, merely stared open-mouthed at the spot where Nevyn's image had appeared.

Time to get back, Nevyn thought, and with that thought he felt something nearly as tangible as a pair of hands tugging at the silver cord. In a dizzying swirl of motion he swept back to Olnadd's house, where his physical body lay, calling him back with a force his exhaustion couldn't resist.

Yet, tired though he was, Nevyn lay awake for a while that night, thinking about Gerraent. If his old enemy were here, perhaps he would also find the woman who had shared their original tragedy, Brangwen of the Falcon, Gerraent's sister and Nevyn's betrothed, back in that far-distant time when he'd been a prince of the blood royal himself. He hoped and prayed to the Lords of Light that he would find her. If only he could make restitution to her for his fault, he would at last be allowed to die. *If it's meant to be,* he told himself, *I'll see Gerraent again, and no doubt he'll lead me to Brangwen – if she's here.*

Whether by chance or wyrd, Nevyn saw the reborn Gerraent early the next morning, when Nevyn and Olnadd went together to the dealer in books to buy Petyc's bribe. As they were walking back to the priest's house, they heard the clatter of hooves and the chime of silver bridle rings. Horsemen were trotting straight for them. All the nearby townsfolk ran for safety, darting into doorways or down alleys, plastering themselves against the walls of the houses. Silver horns blew; men shouted, 'Make way in the king's name! Make way!' Nevyn and Olnadd found a safe spot in the mouth of an alley just as twenty-five riders on matched grey horses trotted past. At their head, unmistakably arrogant, rode Gerraent, his blond head tossed back, his blue eyes narrow and cold. Nevyn pointed him out to Olnadd.

'Do you know who that captain is, by any chance?'

'Only by name,' Olnadd said. 'He's something of a hero, you see, but I truly don't remember his tale. His name's Lord Gwairyc, and he did somewhat or other in the war a few years ago that won him King Casyl's favour. You'll have to ask Petyc about it. I don't keep up on the court gossip. I'll send him a note asking him to join us tonight.'

Directly that evening, after dinner, Petyc arrived at Olnadd's house. He may have been the head of the royal scriptorium, but his god held higher rank than his king, and as he remarked to Olnadd, he couldn't refuse the summons.

'Not that I mind answering it,' Petyc said with a smile.

The scribe was a lean man, hollow-cheeked and balding, with deep-sunken dark eyes that flicked this way and that around the room, as if he were looking for hidden enemies. After they seated themselves at Olnadd's table, the priest introduced Nevyn simply as a friend and scholar of strange lore. Petyc looked him over with a half-smile.

'Nevyn?' Petyc said. 'It's an odd name, Nevyn. You seem too corporeal to be no one at all, though that's what the name might mean.'

'It does mean no one, and it was a nasty jest of my father's,' Nevyn said. 'No doubt you've never heard it before.'

'Oddly enough, our liege the king was consulting with me about it this very morning.'

Nevyn smiled and waited.

'Petyc keeps the royal archives, you see,' Olnadd put in. 'So many a strange question comes his way.'

'No doubt,' Nevyn said. 'And did our liege find the answer to his question?'

'He found an answer of sorts.' Petyc paused, quirking an eyebrow, then continued. 'But whether the answer applies to you, good sir, I couldn't say. It seems that in the reign of our liege's grandsire, King Aeryc, there was talk of a mysterious secret order of priests – or somewhat of that sort – who all bore the name Nevyn. A certain Nevyn paid King Aeryc a great service in the matter of the Eldidd rebellion.'

'Ah,' Nevyn said. 'An interesting tale.'

Olnadd suppressed a smile and studied the ceiling. Petyc considered them both, as nervous but as eager as a stray cat who approaches a bowl of scraps laid out by a farmer's wife.

'May I ask you somewhat?' Petyc had gathered his courage. 'If I pry, then tell me, but do those old tales of other men named Nevyn have somewhat to do with you?'

'They do. What made you guess, besides the name, of course?'

'The name, mostly. Some of the records discuss a clan – I suppose you'd call it a clan – of sorcerers, always headed by a man called no one. I take it you're sworn to aid the king?'

'Him, too, but we do our best to offer our aid to anyone who needs it, whether prince or bondman.'

Petyc considered this in some surprise.

'Matters of history have always interested me.' Nevyn decided to change the subject. 'It's a great honour to meet the keeper of the King's archives. Olnadd tells me you understand their importance, unlike so many scribes.'

With this sort of opening, the conversation could turn to the safe and pleasant matters of scholarship. As Petyc talked about his chronicles, his intelligence became obvious. He carefully selected what to record with a clear view of what granted an event importance.

'Some of the ancient annals we have would no doubt amuse you,' Petyc said. 'They record with great solemnity every two-headed calf and dragon-shaped cloud seen in the kingdom, but omit to tell us anything about the king's councils.'

'You seem quite interested in ancient times.'

'I am, truly.' Petyc nodded in Olnadd's direction. 'His holiness here was the first to show me how fascinating the past can be. I was just a lad, then, sent to him once I'd been taken on by the dun. He taught me that there was more to books than the shaping of their letters.'

'You were a quick pupil, one of the best I ever had.' Olnadd glanced at Nevyn. 'Petyc has an interesting library, some twenty volumes in his own personal collection.'

'That's an amazing number, truly.' Nevyn took the hint and the opening. 'I have a volume with me, actually, that might interest you, Petyc.'

Nevyn brought out the bribe, a copy, some eighty years old, of the anonymous saga of Rwsyn of Eldidd, a king who'd ruled in the fifth century. When Petyc exclaimed over it, Nevyn could easily press it upon him as a gift without the word 'bribe' ever coming near the surface of conversation. With the saga duly accepted, Nevyn mentioned that he'd always wanted to see King Casyl from some better vantage than as a bystander to a formal procession.

'That could be arranged,' Petyc said. 'I'd be most honoured, anyway, if you'd visit my humble quarters and look over some of the other books we've been discussing.'

'And I should be most honoured to see them. May I visit you sometime soon?'

'Come tomorrow afternoon, by all means. I'll speak to the chamberlain about your audience with our king, but I fear that the chamberlain will tell you that he's much too distracted these days. The Cerrgonney war, you know. I mean, rebellion.'

'Oh no doubt. But perhaps I can impress the chamberlain with my sincerity.'

On the morrow, wearing a clean shirt for the occasion, Nevyn presented himself at the massive iron-bound gates of the dun. When he announced his business, the guards looked him over suspiciously, but they allowed him into the ward while they sent a servant off to fetch the scribe. Petyc appeared promptly, then escorted him inside the rearmost tower of the conjoined brochs. As they were walking down a corridor, a pair of the king's riders came swaggering along, shoving them out of the way and walking on fast. Petyc made a sour face at their broad backs.

'That reminds me,' Nevyn said. 'Do you know anything about one of the King's captains, a man named Gwairyc?'

'I do. Now, I've only met him most briefly and formally, but his liege requested I enter a tale about Gwairyc into the annals for 980. It marked an event important in itself, but as well our liege meant it as a mark of honour to the captain. To give the man his due, it was splendidly brave. I suppose.'

'An event of warfare, then?'

'Just that.' Petyc paused by a big wooden door. 'Come in, and I'll show you the very annal itself.'

Petyc led Nevyn into a long low-ceilinged room, well-lit by a rank of windows. Four long wooden writing tables stood by the windows, and at the nearest, a pair of young scribes were making copies of a royal decree. Petyc spoke to each of them, checked their work, then led Nevyn into a smaller chamber, lined with wooden shelves, where leather-bound codices exhaled a faint smell of dust and old parchment. Most of the volumes seemed to be household accounts and bound correspondence, but Nevyn was gratified to see a fairly new copy of Queen Bellyra's history of Dun Cerrmor.

'A most interesting compendium, isn't it?' Petyc nodded in its direction. 'She also left part of a manuscript about Dun Deverry itself.'

'Ah, it's survived, then.'

'It has. The original's down in Wmmglaedd, but we have copies here. Let me get you the annals we were speaking of.'

Petyc squatted down in order to ferret about on a low shelf. Eventually he brought out a splendidly bound book, its wooden cover engraved with interlace and painted in red and gold. He thumbed through it and found the passage at the end.

'You will forgive my humble style, of course.'

'Oh, but the lettering's splendid. The proportions are most just and fluid.'

Petyc allowed himself a small smile. Nevyn read over the passage while Petyc watched amazed, simply because Nevyn was one of the few men in the kingdom who could read silently rather than aloud.

'The most sorrowful death of Prince Cwnol was nearly deflected,' the passage ran. 'But his wyrd came upon him, and no man could turn it aside, not even Gwairyc, son of Glaswyn. When the foul traitors closed around the prince on the field, Gwairyc thrust himself forward and fought like a god, not a man, attempting to save his prince. He slew four men and carried the prince alive back in his arms, but alas, the wounds were too deep to bind. In honour of his bravery, Prince Casyl counted him as a friend from that day on and commends his memory to all who might read this book.'

'Nicely phrased.' Nevyn closed the book and handed it back. 'Did he truly slay four men by himself?'

'So Casyl told me at the time – Prince Casyl, as he was. His father was still alive then, of course. I've never seen a battle, myself.'

'You may count yourself quite lucky. Is Gwairyc still in Casyl's favour now that Casyl's king?'

'He is.' Petyc looked briefly sour. 'He's one of the many younger sons of the Rams of Hendyr – do you know them? A fine old clan, truly, but perhaps a bit too prolific for their own good. Gwairyc got himself into the king's warband because of his skill with a sword, and now that he has his chance at royal favour, he sticks closer to the king than wet linen.'

Nevyn was about to ask more when the chamberlain came bustling in. A stout man with flabby hands and neatly trimmed grey hair and beard, Gathry made Petyc's earlier prediction come true.

'Alas, good Nevyn,' he said, 'the king is much distracted these days. The Cerrgonney wars and all.'

Petyc thoughtfully turned his back so that Nevyn could slip Gathry a velvet pouch of coins. The councillor patted his shirt briefly, and the pouch disappeared.

'But you know,' Gathry continued, 'I do believe that our liege might have a few free moments this very afternoon. Allow me to go inquire.'

The chamberlain bustled out again, only to return remark-ably fast with the news that indeed, the king had a few moments to give one of his subjects. Nevyn followed Gathry up a long staircase and through a door into the central tower, where they went down a half-flight of steps to a pair of carved double doors. Gathry threw them open with a flourish and bowed his way inside. Nevyn recognized the half-round chamber; it had been the women's hall when Maryn was king.

All of Bellyra's cushioned chairs and silver oddments had long since been replaced. On the stone walls hung tap-estries of hunting scenes and hunting weapons – boar spears, bows and quivers of arrows, a maul for cracking the skulls of wounded game – displayed on iron hooks. The furnish-ings consisted of one long rectangular table and a scatter of benches. A pair of much-faded banners appliqued with red wyverns hung on the flat wooden wall, and in front of them in a half-round carved chair sat the king.

Thanks to the royal line's dubious inbreeding, Casyl looked much like Aeryc: the same squarish face, the same wide green eyes and tight-lipped smile, but his shock of hair was a dark brown, not blond like his grandfather's. His long, nervous fingers played with a jewelled dagger. When Gathry started to kneel, the king pointed the dagger at him.

'Leave us. Come in, my lord Nevyn.'

Bowing, Gathry hurried out backwards and carefully shut the doors behind him. When the king nodded at a nearby bench, Nevyn sat.

'Very well, ' Casyl said. 'This is one of the few places in the dun where we won't be overheard. I trust you'll forgive the lack of ceremony.'

'Ceremony means little to a man like me, your highness.'

'So I thought.' Casyl ran his thumb along the dagger's hilt. 'My scribes tell me many an interesting thing about men named Nevyn. Are they true?'

'Do you doubt it after seeing me in the candle-flames?'

Casyl's hand tightened so hard on the dagger hilt that his knuckles went white. Nevyn said nothing. In a moment, the king glanced at his belt, took his time sheathing the dagger, then finally looked up.

'King Aeryc was a very long-lived man,' Casyl said. 'I had the privilege denied to most men of knowing my grandfather. He made a point of telling me when I was a little lad never mock the dweomer.'

'Aeryc was wise. My master in magic told me much about him.'

'I'm honoured that you'd seek me out. But tell me, does this mean some great trouble coming to me and mine?'

Nevyn almost laughed. He'd forgotten that most men saw the dweomer only in terms of dark and portentous warnings of doom.

'Not in the least, my liege. I've only come to give you a gift, one that I hope will prevent such troubles.'

At that, Casyl smiled, but his eyes stayed wary.

'I've brought you a gem, a dweomer-stone,' Nevyn went on. 'And I'll beg you to guard it as the greatest treasure you have and to pass it on to your son when the time comes. Will you promise me that, my liege, as one man to another?'

'Gladly. Here, I never dreamt there truly was such a thing as magical jewels.'

'They're quite rare, your highness, as well you can imagine.'

Nevyn brought out the pouch and unwrapped the opal, laying it onto the long table. Before he could offer to bring it to the king, Casyl got up and strode over for a look. When he saw the perfect opal gleaming among its silks, he gasped aloud. He reached out his hand, then stopped.

'May I touch it?'

'By all means, your highness. If it pleases you, do look into it. I'd be most interested in what you might see there.'

Gingerly, as if he were approaching a wounded wild animal, the king picked up the gift, silks and all, and cradled it in the palm of one broad hand. The opal glowed with flame-coloured veins set against its misty white depths. While the king gazed into it, Nevyn silently called upon the Kings of the Elements, who ruled the spirits attached to the talisman. He directed their minds to the king and announced that he and his heirs were the rightful owners of the stone. Casyl felt their presence. Nevyn could see it by the way he shuddered, turning uneasily as if he felt a draught of cold air.

'By the gods,' Casyl whispered. 'Never have I seen a gem like this one.'

'Well, your highness, I'd wager high that you'll never see its like again, so treasure it well. May I ask what you see within it?'

'A golden sun. By the hells, am I going daft?'

'You're not. You've merely proved yourself a true king, if you can see that inner sun.'

Casyl looked up, his lips half-parted in awe. In truth, any person of good will who looked into it would see the same sun, but Nevyn knew from long experience that flattery and fine words worked more wonders than dweomer when it came to influencing royalty.

'You may use this stone as a test of honour,' Nevyn went on. 'If ever you gaze upon it, and the sun has set, some evil will have beset your heart. Undo the evil you have done, and the sun will rise again.'

'A mighty gift indeed! May I never betray it!'

'So I would hope, but truly, it's the men who might come after you that trouble my heart. Everyone knows that you're the soul of honour.'

'You flatter me, but you have my thanks. I hope that I remain worthy of this marvellous gift.'

'You're most welcome, your highness, but remember that it's just a gem, though a mighty one, and I'm just a man, though a highly skilled one. Now listen well! This is the Great Stone of the West. Remember that name, but tell it to no one but your legitimate sons. Show the stone to no one but them. Tell the eldest that no one must see it but his heirs, and so on down the long river of Time. Guard this stone like the mighty treasure it is, but if harm ever comes to it, I or my successor will appear to rescue it. When it comes time for me to appoint a successor, he too will be another Nevyn, as my master was before me.'

'Well and good, then,' Casyl looked into the stone again and smiled. 'It's passing strange. Just looking at this gem, just holding it – I've never felt like this before. It brings peace, but a peace that's alive, not like dropping off to sleep or suchlike.' Casyl laid a fingertip gently on the stone. 'Is there anything I should do to tend it?'

'There's not, but the keeping of it secret and the honouring of it.'

'A marvel indeed. Here, why would you give me such a thing?'

'Because you're the king, and the king is the shield of his people. Through you I can help bring them safety.'

Casyl nodded, turning solemn, staring into the opal's depths for many a long moment. Finally he looked up. 'Come now, good Nevyn. Surely you'll let me give you a good price for this stone.'

'I won't, your highness. The dweomer asks no price for its aid to good men. It's a gift to you and the kingdom.'

'Then you shall have a gift in return.' Casyl grinned, abruptly boyish. 'Anything in my kingdom you desire is yours. Well, except my wife.' He laughed aloud. 'I've never had such a splendid gem before! Name what you desire, good Nevyn – I truly mean it, anything at all.'

Olnadd's right, Nevyn thought. *The king does like the grand gesture.*

'Fine horses, other jewels, gold, land,' Casyl went on. 'Have you ever desired a vast demesne? Here, the tieryn of Buccbrael has just died, and he has no heir but a daughter. Shall I apportion his lands and the lass to you?'

'Your highness, I honour your generosity, but my craft leaves me no time for ruling lands and marrying young wives.

I want nothing at all. Your gratitude is the greatest reward an old man's heart could have.'

'Oh, but there must be somewhat. Here, it would be dishonourable of me to let you go away empty-handed. How can I be dishonourable to the man who's given me the very jewel of honour's soul?'

Nevyn was about to make another self-deprecating reply when he felt a cold touch of dweomer-warning down his back. He knew in the strange wordless way of the dweomer that there was something he was supposed to have from Casyl.

'Your highness, I'm most touched and overwhelmed. May I think about this for a bit? A king's boon is too rare and splendid to be spent upon a whim.'

'True spoken. Think on this boon carefully, and –' Casyl paused, thinking. 'In three days, when the sun's marking out the same hour, I shall receive you in the great hall. Come to me then.'

'My humble thanks.' Nevyn bowed to him. 'Done, then.'

'Splendid! Now, let's go down to the great hall. Let me give you a goblet of mead to accompany my thanks.'

'My thanks, your highness, but I'd prefer dark ale.'

Before they left the private chamber, Nevyn taught Casyl how to wrap up the opal in its silks. Even though he'd bound the stone over to the king, he preserved one link back to himself, so that he could tell if the stone should somehow be endangered. He had no desire to see all his hard work wasted.

The king personally escorted Nevyn to the great hall and sat him down at the honour table. A young page brought the ale, but Casyl himself filled Nevyn's tankard. As he sipped the good strong brew, Nevyn was aware that every single man and most of the women in the hall had stopped whatever they were doing to stare at him, this shabby old man that the king treated like a long-lost grandfather. When the time came for him to leave, Nevyn could feel their gazes following him the entire way out of the hall. Walking outside into the cool of late afternoon made him feel as if he were tossing aside a burden, the weight of so much envy.

A company of the king's horsemen came trotting through the gates. Nevyn stepped back out of the way as the men dismounted and grooms rushed forward to take the horses. Most of the riders were laughing, shouting jests back and forth and talking about ale and their dinner, but Lord Gwairyc stood alone and watched them with a small contemptuous smile. Or was it truly contempt? More of a shield, that smile, against the contempt of other men. Before Gwairyc could notice him, Nevyn went on his way, but at the dun gates he stopped to speak with the two guards, who bowed to him. Apparently the news of his sudden high standing had spread fast.

'Tell me somewhat,' Nevyn said. 'Lord Gwairyc, there, who just rode in. Do you know him?'

'Well, my lord,' one guard said, 'Everyone knows *of* him. He wouldn't have much to do with the likes of us.'

'They say he's splendid on the field,' the other guard put in. 'He's got no more fear in him than a ravening wolf. And you'd best not cross him, either, my lord. Touchy, he is, and I swear he'd kill a man for one wrong word.'

'Ah, I see. Does he have any close friends?'

'The king honours him, my lord.' The first guard thought for a long moment. 'I can't think of anyone else.'

In gathering twilight Nevyn walked back to Olnadd's house. Around him, merchants and craftsmen were hurrying home to their dinner. In open windows lanterns glowed, and the smell of cooking drifted in the warm evening air. A group of little children were laughing and tossing a leather ball back and forth while they waited for their mother to call them in for dinner. Nevyn suddenly felt that he understood Gwairyc, cut off like him from normal life and easy companionship. Once he finished his work in the city, he might never see Olnadd again, since he went where the dweomer led him, not where he wished to. Gwairyc would dine in an honoured place in the great hall and sleep in a crowded barracks, but that little smile – Gwairyc was lonely, Nevyn realized. A younger son, a man with an empty rank and no prospects, he'd found the only way to gain a position and honour, by endlessly risking his life until the day he died young in his king's service. *Of the two of us, he's got the harsher wyrd,* Nevyn thought, *no matter how weary I grow.*

This idea brought with it the first real pang of sympathy for Gerraent that Nevyn had ever felt. The sympathy seemed to grow of its own accord. At dinner, as he told Olnadd and Affyna about his day, an idea came to him, so strange that at first he refused to consider it. Affyna unwittingly gave it to him when he told them about the king's offer of a boon.

'I can't accept some expensive gift, of course,' Nevyn said. 'I see what you mean about the grand gesture, Olnadd. Turning him down would be like snubbing a child who offers you his favourite toy, some grubby wooden horse or suchlike. You don't want it, but how can you say him nay?'

'But here, Nevyn,' Affyna broke in. 'If you took a gift that would help someone else, I'm sure it would be honourable enough.'

'Now that's true spoken. There's plenty of poor folk in the kingdom who can use the king's gold.'

Nevyn considered the boon in this new light. *Somewhat I could sell, and then give the proceeds to the poor,* he thought, *or maybe another jewel to make a second talisman.* He was going to miss having regular work to give meaning to his long days.

'Oh, I meant to ask you,' Affyna said. 'Did you find out about that captain who interested you?'

'Gwairyc? I did. Petyc knew his tale.'

'Oddly enough, I met him once. I have a friend, Ylaenna, who has the prettiest daughter. Oh, she's a beauty, that lass! Well, somehow or other, she met this Gwairyc, and he was sniffing around her good and proper until Ylaenna's husband put a stop to it.'

'I take it Gwairyc has little honour around lasses.'

'Well, now.' Affyna considered for a moment. 'No doubt he doesn't, but you know, I thought there was more to the lad than anyone would allow.'

'You have the best heart in the world,' Olnadd said, grinning. 'I swear, you'd find something good to say about a murderer or suchlike.'

'Oh come now, the lad's not that bad!' Affyna said. 'But I suppose you're right enough. It's a short life that the royal horsemen lead, but there's a good heart in Lord Gwairyc, if only someone could bring it out in him.'

'I doubt me if it was his heart that Ylaenna was worrying about,' Olnadd muttered.

'Oh!' Affyna made a mock-slap in his direction. 'There's no need to be coarse!'

Her opinion of the captain brought Nevyn first a feeling, then a thought, that he did his best to argue out of existence. Why should he do one cursed thing for Gerraent? Why should he put himself out a jot for that arrogant soul? *Because he's another human being*, Nevyn reminded himself, *one of the race you've sworn to serve.* Late that night, as he was meditating in his chamber, his mind continually brought up the memory image of Gwairyc's lonely little smile. Perhaps Affyna was right, and a good man lay under that surface, if someone could find and release him.

Nevyn groaned aloud. Transmuting Gerraent's soul promised to be a much harder job than his fifty years of work enchanting the opal. He did have one perfectly legitimate reason to let Gwairyc be. Lilli, his apprentice, would take all his time once he found her. *Surely she's been reborn by now!* Nevyn thought with some irritation. He had several days to see if indeed, she was alive somewhere in or near Dun Deverry. If not, then he could worry about Lord Gwairyc.

Over the next two days, he wandered the city in search of her. He even made a point of meeting the reputedly lovely daughter of Affyna's friend, just on the off-chance that she might be Lilli reborn, but though she was undoubtedly beautiful, she was not his former apprentice. At night he both meditated upon Lilli and her harsh wyrd and actively hunted for traces of her soul upon the astral plane. He found nothing.

On the third day, when he was to return to the king to claim his boon, Nevyn woke to a realization. His old chains of wyrd, the tragedies over many lives that bound him to Gerraent and those other souls who had participated in his original fault – they would always take precedence in his life. Lilli had great talent for the dweomer, and most likely she would catch the attention of some other dweomermaster. If not, then he would find her when it was his wyrd to find her, and not a moment before.

Late in the warm and muggy day, Nevyn puffed back up the hill to the royal dun. The guards ushered him in with bows, and a page came running to greet him.

'His highness told us to look for you, my lord,' the page said. 'He's in council at the moment, but he begs that you'll not be offended, and that you'll wait for him in the great hall.'

'I shall be honoured,' Nevyn said. 'Lead on.'

As they walked together across the ward, Nevyn noticed that Lord Gwairyc's contingent of horsemen had just ridden in. The men were dispersing while the grooms were leading their mounts away. Near the broch Lord Gwairyc was standing and speaking with another nobleman. As they passed him, Gwairyc glanced Nevyn's way. For a moment, their eyes met, only briefly, but what Nevyn saw there shocked him: no recognition, no hostility, nothing, really, but a cold indifference. Always before, Gerraent reborn had recognized him, as an enemy perhaps, but still, he had recognized him.

The page, Nevyn noticed, seemed terrified of the captain. In a moment he saw why. The groom leading Gwairyc's dappled grey gelding had one hand on the horse's bridle; with the other he held and idly swung the reins like a whip. Just as they were passing Gwairyc, the groom swung them too vigorously and clipped the startled horse across the nose. Gwairyc took two long strides, grabbed the groom by the shoulder, and hit him across the face so hard that the fellow yelped and staggered back.

'I'll take him in myself,' Gwairyc snarled. 'He's twice as valuable as you are, and don't you ever forget it.'

The groom pressed one hand over his bleeding nose and ran off, stumbling a little, without looking back. The page who'd been attending to Nevyn caught the old man's sleeve.

'Let's go inside, my lord,' he whispered.

'By all means,' Nevyn said. 'We don't need ill-temper coming our way.'

They hurried into the great hall, a cool refuge from the heat of the day as well as from Lord Gwairyc. Riders and servants were gathering at their hearth, while across the hall a few courtiers had already come in to sit together and gossip. At the table of honour Lord Gathry was waiting. He personally pulled out Nevyn's chair for him, then sat down beside him.

'Here, page,' Gathry said. 'Run and fetch mead and goblets. No doubt our guest is thirsty.'

The boy nodded and trotted off.

'My thanks,' Nevyn said, 'Tell me somewhat, good sir. Do you know Lord Gwairyc?'

'As much as any man can know him, I suppose. He's part of the royal household now.' Gathry paused for a twist of his lips. 'There's some talk that our liege will make him an equerry.'

'Indeed? This idea seems to displease you.'

'Oh, not at all, of course. If our liege chooses to do so, of course I have no objection.' Gathry glanced around, turning to look behind him as if he expected Gwairyc to crawl out of a crack between the stones in the wall. 'A good man, truly. Most devoted to our liege.'

'Ah, I see. May I ask you just how devoted?'

For a moment, Gathry looked puzzled by the question; then he considered.

'Now, truly, there are some at court who don't care for Gwairyc and talk against him, but I must give the man his due, my lord. I think he'd walk into a fire if our liege asked him. The lords who grumble against him feel shamed. Their own allegiance runs a bit thinner than that, if you take my meaning.'

'Oh, indeed I do, and my thanks.'

Nevyn turned in his chair and looked back at the doors. Gwairyc was standing alone, his arms crossed tight over his chest, his face utterly stripped of all feeling. No one spoke to him when he walked in and took his place at the head of one of the riders' tables. A handful of men at a time, the king's riders clattered in, laughing among themselves. Nevyn watched, and while he saw many men nod to Gwairyc or even bow to him, no one seemed to say a friendly word, nor did Gwairyc ever say one in return. Nevyn began to think of him as a soul standing on the edge of some abyss, just as when a man, all unmindful, strolls along the sea-cliffs to take a bit of air at night and cannot see the dirt crumbling just a few inches from his foot. A man so cut off from his fellows risked falling into evil ways, maybe not in this life, with his devotion to the king to guide him, but in his next the cliff edge might give way beneath him and let him fall into the darkness that recognizes nothing but its own wants and whims.

I truly can't get out of this, Nevyn thought. *He always was an irritating little bastard, so I don't know why I'm even surprised that he'd be a nuisance now.*

The sunlight streaming in through the windows had turned gold with the sunset by the time that the king's private door opened. There was a blare of silver horns, two pages marched through, and everyone in the hall rose and knelt as Casyl came striding in with a pair of black-robed councillors. Casyl smiled and raised a hand in greeting to his court, then strode over to the honour table and took his place at the head. In a clatter of chairs and benches the assembled company sat down again, yet no one spoke more than a few whispers. Nevyn realized that almost every person in the great hall had turned to stare at him, that mysterious shabby old man, back again.

'Greetings, my lord,' Casyl said to Nevyn. 'And have you come to tell me what you desire for your boon?'

'I have, my liege.'

'Splendid!' Casyl rubbed his hands together like a merchant who's just made a good sale. 'The gift you gave me grows the more wondrous the more I study it. Speak. Tell me your wish, and if it's in my power to bestow, then you shall have it.'

'Your highness, my thanks.' Nevyn paused for effect. 'I want Lord Gwairyc to be my servant for seven years and a day, to serve me as faithfully and scrupulously as he would serve you.'

The men at the honour table gasped aloud; those at the nearest ones leaned forward, all of them desperate to know and unable to ask what had been said. Casyl frankly stared, eyes narrowed in confusion, as if he thought Nevyn were jesting.

Nevyn smiled briefly. 'Do you think that Lord Gwairyc will comply with your wishes in this matter, my liege?'

'No doubt. But with all the splendid things I can offer you, why do you want him?'

Nevyn leaned close to whisper.

'For reasons of the dweomer's and my own. I don't care to reveal them, my liege. I swear it will be to your friend's benefit and ultimately to yours.'

'Done, then. Page, run and fetch me Lord Gwairyc.'

It took the page some while to thread his way through the crowded hall. He reached Gwairyc, said a few words, then stood back and allowed the lord to make his way back across alone. By the time he did, the human patience of the courtiers had been stretched beyond breaking. First the king's servitors began to whisper about Nevyn's strange request. The knowledge spread with the servants who'd been pouring mead and laying out baskets of bread. Once the warbands heard it, muffled oaths and loud talk overwhelmed the polite whispers. Gwairyc was forced to make his way to the king's side through a clamour, all centred on what lay ahead of him. Silently Nevyn cursed himself — he should have requested the boon privately, but it was too late now.

Gwairyc knelt before the king, who turned in his chair and laid a hand on his shoulder.

'My Lord Gwairyc,' Casyl said, 'once you swore to serve me and follow me to the death if need be. Is that vow still true?'

'More true than ever, your highness.' Gwairyc's voice was soft and dark. 'Do you doubt me?'

'Never for a moment. You must have heard what's transpired.'

'I did. I just didn't believe it.'

'Alas, it's true.' Casyl waved in Nevyn's general direction. 'I promised Lord Nevyn any boon he desires. He's asked me for you, to be his servant for seven years and a day, and to serve him the way you'd serve me.'

Gwairyc swung his head around like a striking snake and stared at Nevyn for a long poisonous moment before returning his gaze to the king. 'Your highness,' he whispered. 'You'd send me away?'

'Not willingly, but how can I go back on my promise? What kind of man would I be, to promise a boon and then haggle like some merchant? Here, my friend, I'll miss you.'

Gwairyc slumped and stared at the floor. 'Well, my liege,' Gwairyc said at last. 'A vow's a vow, and whatever Lord Nevyn says, I'll do it as willingly as I can.'

'Well and good, then. And when the seven years and a day are over, I beg you to return to me.'

'I will, my liege.' Gwairyc's voice came close to breaking. 'I swear it.'

Casyl glanced at Nevyn to give him permission to speak. 'My thanks, your highness,' Nevyn said. 'Now, my lord,

I'm staying at the temple of Wmm in the city. Tomorrow at dawn, come to me there. Bring a horse and gear for a long journey.'

'I will, my lord.' Gwairyc hesitated, looking up at him with stunned eyes. 'May I ask how I am to serve you?'

'You may, but not here,' Nevyn said. 'On the morrow I'll tell you more. I'm a herbman, though, and we'll be travelling the roads all summer.'

The eavesdroppers snickered. Gwairyc's face became a mask of shrouded feeling. Everyone else in the hall began to whisper among themselves, a vast susurrus of 'what did the old man say?' When the king threw up his hand, silence came promptly.

'Gwarro, my friend,' the king said. 'Serve this man as you would serve me. That's all I'd ask of you.'

'Then that's what I'll do, your highness.' Gwairyc rose and bowed to him. 'If you'll give me leave to go?'

Casyl nodded his agreement. The great hall sat stunned as Gwairyc turned and strode out. No one spoke, no one followed him, but here and there, Nevyn noticed, at other tables, courtiers smiled as slyly as if they'd just seen an enemy slain.

Nevyn took leave of the king as soon as he could. He walked back to Olnadd's along streets that lay in shadow from the setting sun, even though the sky above still shone blue. *Well, Lilli,* Nevyn thought, *someday mayhap we'll meet again, but it won't be this summer.*

'Gwarro, it's just too awful,' Sagraeffa said. 'I've been weeping for hours.'

Around her swollen eyes ran little streaks of Bardekian kohl, witnesses to the truth of her tears. She'd taken off her headscarf as well and dishevelled her hair, which hung like thick dark ropes around her full face.

'I just hate this,' she went on. 'You can't go!'

'I don't have any choice, do I? By the black hairy arse of the Lord of Hell, do you think this gladdens my heart?'

Sagraeffa snivelled and twisted her handkerchief tightly between pale fingers. Lady Sagraeffa, wife to Lord Obyn of the White Wolf, was a lovely woman, with raven-dark Eldidd hair and cornflower-blue eyes to match. For months, Gwairyc had been stalking her, flattering her, courting her, and now, just when he had a chance at the prize, disaster had ended his hunt. He felt like strangling her for putting him off for all these months. As if she read his temper, she shrank back into the corner of the window-seat.

'I shall miss you so,' she said. 'Don't you even know where that awful old man is going?'

'I don't. The hells, for all I care.'

Sagraeffa gave a small delicate sob and twisted the handkerchief tighter. With a muttered oath, Gwairyc got up and began pacing around the chamber, which was stuffed with cushioned furniture and little knick-knacks. He picked up a silver basket of glass flowers from Bardek and considered heaving it into the gilded mirror above the hearth.

'Gwarro, what are you doing?' Sagraeffa snuffled. 'Come sit down. We don't have very long, and I want one of your kisses.'

Gwairyc paced back, but he stood over her rather than sitting down. She leaned against red velvet cushions and smiled wistfully at him.

'How long will your cursed husband be gone?'

'How should I know?' Sagraeffa pouched her full lips into a moue. 'He's so tedious when he gets to talking with Lord Banryc.'

'Good.'

When Gwairyc sat down next to her, she smiled, offering him her hand, then pulling it back again. She wanted some more fine words, he supposed, all that courtly drivel that she ate up, like a chicken pecking seed as he trailed it out in front of her.

'My heart aches at leaving you, my love,' Gwairyc said. 'It's the worst thing of all.'

Sagraeffa smiled, moving a little closer and letting him catch her hand.

'Ah by the hells, how can the gods be so cruel?' Gwairyc went on. 'They show me the love of my life, then tear me away from her.'

'Well, they've done the same to me. That beastly old man! Oh, Gwarro, it's going to be all tedious again without you.'

Gwairyc pulled her close and kissed her. With a sigh, she slipped her arms around his neck and let him take a few more kisses, but when he laid his hand on her breast, she giggled, pulling away and glancing at the door. Admittedly, her stupid husband could come in at any minute, but Obyn was a man who liked his habits, and one of those habits was having three games of carnoic with Lord Banryc every other night. He estimated that they were just finishing the first one.

'Now come along, my love. It's our last night together. Are you going to be as cruel as the gods and send me away without even a splendid memory of your love?'

Sagraeffa caught her lower lip under her front teeth and stared up at him, honestly frightened. All at once, Gwairyc realized that she'd never had any intention of sleeping with him.

'Obyn might come back.' Her voice shook.

'So what? I've already been banished, haven't I? And do you think that dry stick of a husband of yours has the strength to beat you? I'll wager he doesn't. He won't be back anyway.'

'But I –'

Gwairyc caught her face in both hands and kissed her hard. When she squirmed away, he caught her by the shoulders and kissed her again. For a moment she struggled with him, then went satisfyingly limp in his arms.

'You told me you loved me. Do you or not?'

Sagraeffa looked up at him with tear-filled eyes, a pleasant sign of weakness. This time, he kissed her gently, letting his mouth linger on hers. She laid a trembling hand on his arm and caressed him. He knew cursed well that she wanted it as badly as he did. He decided that this time, she wasn't going to put him off.

'Tomorrow I'll be gone. Who knows if we'll ever see each other again? Please, my love? My heart aches with wanting you so badly. There's never been another woman who could make me feel this way.'

This brought a wary smile to her slightly swollen lips. Gwairyc had one brief thought for her husband – what if he did leave early? Then he kissed her again, kept kissing her until she gave in and let him caress her.

'Let me take you to your bedchamber.'

Sagraeffa went stiff in his arms and turned her head away.

'Oh by the hells!' Gwairyc snapped. 'We're running out of time!'

'Don't be so beastly, Gwarro! You're just not as nice tonight as you usually are.'

'Ah, curse it! What do you expect? I've been flayed alive, and I'm supposed to mince around?'

'Well, you don't need to be mean to me.'

Gwairyc felt his temper snap like a rope pulled too tight. He grabbed her, kissed her, and threw her down on the window-seat, falling half on top of her to kiss her again. She screamed, but only feebly, a little yelp carefully calculated to stay in the chamber. This time, when she surrendered to his caresses, he gave her no chance to change her mind. He picked her up, slid off the window-seat and laid her down again right on the floor.

When they were finished, Sagraeffa lay still on the carpet for a long time and stared at him. Her face was flushed, and when he caressed her, he could feel her nipples, as hard as Bardek almonds. Gwairyc gave her one last kiss, then got up, pulling up his brigga and lacing them.

'You're such a brute,' she whispered.

'Oh am I now? Those noises you made – it didn't sound to me like you were screaming for help.'

Gasping in rage, Sagraeffa sat up, pulling down her dress and glaring at him. Gwairyc picked up his sword belt from the floor and began buckling it on.

'And I suppose you're just going to leave me now,' she said.

'You're the one who was worrying about your blasted husband. I don't want to leave. I'd rather spend all night in your bed.' He gave her a grin. 'Admit it – you'd like to have me there.'

Sagraeffa got up, then stood glaring at him while she tried to smooth down her skirts with nervous fingers. He liked seeing her this way – dishevelled, flustered, utterly weak before his superior strength. He took her by the shoulders and gave her a kiss, which she took meekly, leaning against him.

'Oh ye gods, what if I have a baby? Obyn will know it isn't his.'

'Indeed? Then maybe you'd best do something to stiffen his, um, resolve.'

With a snarl, Sagraeffa pulled away and slapped him across the face. Her soft hand barely stung on his cheek.

'Get out of here! I hate you!'

Gwairyc dodged another slap, made her a hasty bow, and ran for the door. As he let himself out, he heard her weeping. With a shrug, he slammed the door and hurried down the corridor. He had no more time to waste on her. The worst part of this last night lay ahead of him: going back to the barracks to face his men.

The king's riders were housed in five separate barracks. Each warband had its own standard and blazon in addition to the royal wyvern. Gwairyc's band, the Falcons, were housed in barracks closest to the broch complex. As he hurried across the dark ward, Gwairyc was brooding about the other four troops. During the winters, when they lacked real enemies, all five of them were bitter rivals. No doubt the Falcons were in for a lot of jests about the wyrd that had fallen on their captain. When he reached the door, he paused, summoning courage. Then he flung open the door and strode in, bracing himself for jeers.

Instead, the men merely looked at him, glancing his way, then turning silently back to dice games or polishing gear as he walked the long way down the row of bunks to his own small chamber at the far end of the barracks. He slipped in, barred the door behind him, then let out his breath in a long sigh of relief.

The room sweltered from a fire his page had lit in the small hearth. Gwairyc lit a pair of candles from the coals, set them on the mantel, then spread and smashed the fire to dead ash. For a long time he leaned against the wall and watched the candle flames dance.

'Ah ye gods! How can you do this to me?'

The gods didn't deign to answer. With a sigh, Gwairyc unbuckled his sword belt and laid it down carefully on the bed. He had better pack up his gear, he decided, what there was of it, enough clothes and the like to fit into two pair of saddlebags and little more. At a timid knock on his door, he opened it to find a small group of his riders clustered behind red-haired Rhwn, who generally acted as his second-in-command. Rhwn was holding out a big silver pitcher and a clay cup.

'My lord?' Rhwn said. 'Me and the lads bribed a kitchen lass and got you some mead. Figured you'd need it.'

'My thanks.' Gwairyc steadied his voice by force of will, then took the mead. 'Do you hold this to my shame?'

'How can we? I tell you, my lord, me and the lads are as vexed as the Lord of Hell with boils on his cock! It's not going to be the same, riding behind some other captain.'

The men behind him all nodded their agreement.

'Well, my thanks,' Gwairyc said again. 'I never knew I had such a blasted strange wyrd in store for me.'

'No man knows his wyrd,' Rhwn said with a shrug. 'Here, my lord, who is that old man? He can't truly be some old daft herbman. The King himself called him a lord.'

'Then he's a daft old lord who turned herbman, maybe.
Ah horseshit, I'm going to find out, aren't I?'

Rhwn nodded with a long sad sigh, then herded the other
men away to leave Gwairyc his privacy. Gwairyc barred the
door again and returned to stuffing his material wealth into
his saddlebags. By the time he'd done, he'd drunk half the
mead. He finished off the rest of the pitcher fast, drinking
it down like physick, then passed out fully dressed on his
bunk.

Waking brought torment, a headache like a sword cut, a
stomach that roiled like a winter sea. Rolling up his blankets gave him a foretaste of the seven hells. Gwairyc had a
brief thought of suicide, decided it would be acknowledging
defeat in a battle not yet begun, and grimly got his gear
together instead of slitting his own throat. Just as dawn was
brightening the sky, he led his grey gelding, a personal gift
from the king, out of the dun gates. When he mounted, the
effort made the buildings around him sway and wobble. He
let the horse pick a slow way out into the city streets.

Only a few townsfolk were out this early: a housewife
sweeping off her steps, a servant emptying a chamber-pot
into the gutter. Gwairyc found the temple of Wmm by luck
as much as memory. He dismounted, wondering where exactly
Nevyn might be. When he touched the locked gate, the
geese charged, hissing and flapping.

'If you didn't belong to a priest,' Gwairyc said, 'I'd wring
your ugly white necks.'

He led his horse around to the mews he'd noticed behind
the priest's house. Sure enough, Nevyn was just tying a
saddled riding horse to a hitching rail.

'Ah, there you are,' the old man said. 'I'm still loading the
mule.'

The gate was just broad enough to let Gwairyc's horse
follow him into a small dusty yard behind what seemed to
be a stable. Nevyn was standing beside a pair of large canvas
packs, while his mule stood head-down and sulky nearby.

Gwairyc made an uneasy bow to his new master. Nevyn was a tall man, slender and remarkably strong-looking with a vigour that belied his untidy shock of white hair and his wrinkled face, dotted with the brown spots of advanced old age. He was dressed in a pair of dirty, much-mended brown brigga and an old shirt without any blazon on the yokes. A tattered brown cloak hung over the horse's saddle.

'Well, here I am,' Gwairyc said. 'Do you want me to load that mule for you?'

'In a bit. You look ill. What did you do, drink yourself blind last night?'

'Just that.'

'I thought you might, so I saved out a few herbs for you. Here, sit down. I'll just fetch a bit of hot water from Affyna's kitchen.'

Gwairyc sat down on the ground. His head was aching so badly that it was hard to think, but he wondered if he hated the old man. It seemed that he should hate someone for this indignity. What by every god did this daft old bastard want with him, anyway? Nevyn came back with a clay cup and handed it to him. A drift of sweet-smelling steam came up from a murky greenish liquid.

'Drink all of it, lad,' Nevyn said. 'You'll feel better in a bit.'

Gwairyc managed to choke the sweet stuff down. For a moment, he felt sicker than before, but remarkably quickly, his headache began to ease and his stomach to settle down.

'Ye gods!' He handed the cup back to Nevyn. 'You could make a fortune with this brew.'

'Indeed? Well, I've never wanted a fortune. It's a pity you had to drink yourself sick.'

'Can you blame me?'

Nevyn caught his gaze and looked at him, merely looked, but all at once Gwairyc turned cold. He felt that the old man was looking through his soul, seeing old secrets, old faults, old crimes that he couldn't even remember committing.

'Listen, lad.' Nevyn's voice stayed free of any feeling. 'What

I'm doing with you is for your benefit. I know you won't believe me at first. Hate me if it makes you feel better. Just do as I say, and remember that I'm doing this for your benefit.'

The gaze from ice-blue eyes bored holes through his very soul.

'I will,' Gwairyc said, 'but it's for the king's sake, not yours.'

'Not your own?'

Gwairyc tried to answer, found no words, then handed back the empty cup, the only gesture he could think to make.

'Well, that was unfair of me.' Nevyn turned away and released him. 'Just remember what I told you. Now. I've bought you a new shirt and a cloak. Pack those fine ones away. You might be doing this for the king's sake, but you won't wear his blazon again for a good long while.'

The shirt turned out to be plain rough linen, and the cloak the coarse brown of farmers' clothing. Once Gwairyc had changed, he loaded the mule while Nevyn went inside to say farewell to the priest of the temple. By the time they left the mews, the townsfolk had started their day, bustling along the streets or standing gossiping in front of one house or another. When Gwairyc started to mount up, Nevyn caught his arm.

'We're walking to the gates. Too crowded to ride.'

'The common folk can just get out of our way.'

'Common folk? Those are proud words from a herbman's servant.'

Gwairyc had to bite his lip to keep from swearing at him.

Once they were clear of the city walls, they mounted and, with Gwairyc leading the mule, took the west-running road. Nevyn set a slow pace, letting his horse amble along in the hot summer morning. On either side of the road, the rich green fields of Casyl's personal demesne rolled off to the horizon. Gwairyc felt sick to his heart: soon the army would ride north without him. All the bitter splendour of battle – his one real love, his whole life – had been stolen from him by an old herbman's whim. He began to have thoughts of murdering Nevyn and leaving his body somewhere beside the road. *But what then?* he told himself, *You could never go back to court.* For the sake of the king he worshipped, he was going to have to play this bitter game out to the end.

Gwairyc urged his horse up beside Nevyn's. 'May I ask where we're going?'

'West. I never have any particular place in mind when I travel. There are sick folk all over the kingdom.'

'I suppose there must be, truly.'

'But we'll spend part of the summer in the old forest. It still covers plenty of ground once you get off to the west.'

'The forest, my lord?'

'Just that. I have wild herbs to gather, you see.'

Gwairyc couldn't stop himself from groaning aloud. Off in the forest, all alone with this cursed old man, not even a pretty wench to use for a bit of comfort!

'What are you doing?' Nevyn said. 'Cursing the very day you were born.'

'Somewhat like that.'

Nevyn laughed and said nothing more.

That first day they headed south, skirting Loc Gwerconydd, then turned west. Gwairyc soon learned that travelling with Nevyn meant meandering from village to village at a comfortable walking pace for the horses. In each village the inhabitants clustered round to buy Nevyn's herbs and ask his advice on their various aches and pains. Much of the time Gwairyc himself had little to do but tend the horses and the mule. He began to wonder if he'd die of boredom before his seven years were up. As they usually did when he was bored, his thoughts turned to women.

Most of the village lasses struck him as dirty and bedraggled, but one evening a finer prize came to the bait of Nevyn's herbs. She was young but full into womanhood, with high breasts set off by a tight kirtle, and she wore her long chestnut hair pulled back from her heart-shaped face. Unlike those of the usual village lasses, her face and her hands looked well-washed. While Nevyn dispensed advice and sold herbs, she lingered at the edge of the crowd. Gwairyc caught her eye and smiled at her. He was hoping for a smile in return or at least a blush, but she looked straight past him.

Maybe she's near-sighted, he thought. When her turn came to consult the herbman, Gwairyc stood right behind him and smiled again. Again, he might as well have been made of glass for all the response he got. After she bought her herbs, he took a step in her direction, but she held her head high and walked off fast.

'Well, well,' Nevyn said. 'I take it she wasn't interested.'

'I should have known you'd notice. She wasn't, at that.'

'You're just a herbman now, lad. The lasses won't be fawning on you like they did with one of the king's own captains.'

Gwairyc opened his mouth to say something foul, then shut it again rather than give the old man the satisfaction of having riled him. Nevyn laughed anyway and turned away to begin packing up the unsold herbs.

Some ten mornings after, they stopped at a farm. Behind an earthen wall stood a round, thatched house, a tumble-down barn, a pig sty, and a chicken house. The pigs lay in stinking mud, but the chickens were out scratching and squawking in the dirt yard. When Nevyn shoved open the gate, a pair of scruffy black dogs rushed out of the barn, but they barked and wagged in friendly greeting. Right behind them came a stout woman in a torn brown dress. A leather thong tied back her greasy black hair. Her thick fingers and her hands were as calloused and scarred as a blacksmith's. When she opened her mouth to talk, Gwairyc saw that she was missing half her teeth.

'Oh Nevyn, Nevyn,' she stammered out. 'Oh ye gods, this is an answer to my prayers, I swear it!'

'Here, Ligga, what's so wrong?'

'Our lad's sick, cursed sick. I've been praying and praying to the Goddess to help us.'

'Well, maybe She made me decide to stop by. Gwarro, unload the mule's packs. Take those horses to the barn.'

Gwairyc tied the horses up in the stinking cow-barn, then carried the canvas packs inside the house. He found himself in a big half-round room, set off from the rest of the house by a filthy wickerwork partition. Under a smoke hole lay a pair of blackened hearthstones where a low fire burned. A little girl, wearing a clean if stained brown dress, was standing by the hearth and stirring soup in an iron kettle perched over the fire on an iron tripod. She gave Gwairyc a terrified glance and pointed at the far side of the room.

Gwairyc shoved aside the much-mended grey blanket that served as a door and carried in the packs. He found Nevyn and Ligga standing by a big square bed. A little boy lay on coarse dirty blankets. Snot and tears mingled on his fever-red face. Gwairyc could smell him and Ligga both, a reek of sweat, dirt from the animals, and in the boy's case, excrement.

Nevyn gestured at Gwairyc to put the packs down, then sat on the edge of the bed next to the lad, who promptly turned his head away.

'Come along, Anno. It's old Nevyn. I want to make you feel better.'

Anno shook his head in a stubborn no.

'Your mouth hurts, Mam says. Let me have a look.'

Anno whimpered and flopped over to bury his face in the blankets.

'Anno, listen,' Nevyn said. 'I'm going to look at your mouth whether you want me to or not. You're very sick, lad. You don't even know what you're doing, do you? Come along – you know I won't hurt you if I can help it.'

When the lad began to sob, Nevyn caught him and pulled him into his lap. After a brief struggle, Nevyn took the lad's jaws the way you'd take a horse's and pried them open. Anno moaned and pissed all over himself and the old man. Nevyn barely seemed to notice.

'Thank the gods, it's just a bad tooth. I was afraid you had the clotted fever in your throat, lad, but it's just this nasty tooth. You'll be all better once we have it out.'

'Don't!' Anno screamed. 'Mam!'

'You've got to!' Ligga said. 'You listen to your elders! Forgive us, Nevyn, I –'

'Hush, hush! It's not his fault. The gum's gone so pussy that he's fevered and half out of his mind. The tooth's loose, anyway, so it won't be a hard thing to do. Then we'll work on the fever. All of his humours are out of balance, you see, with a superfluity of the hot and moist.'

This sonorous explanation seemed to comfort Ligga, even though Gwairyc doubted if she knew what it meant. When Nevyn started to let Anno go, the lad tried to slither off the bed. Nevyn caught him and hauled him back.

'Gwarro, come sit down. Take him and hold him still while I get the things I need.'

Choking on revulsion, Gwairyc took the skinny little lad in his arms. He sat down on the edge of the bed and wondered if it had bugs. Anno squirmed, tried to bite his wrist, then began to cry. The urine and the pus both reeked. *I promised the king*, Gwairyc reminded himself. *I swore a vow to the king* – he made himself repeat the thought over and over. It seemed to take Nevyn forever to get out a pair of forceps, a bottle of spicy-scented oil, and some scraps of cloth. For the operation itself, Gwairyc pressed the lad's shoulders down on the bed; he was forced to watch while Nevyn deftly pulled a broken stump of tooth from his jaw. An ooze of green pus came with it.

'You see the green material, oh apprentice of mine?' Nevyn said. 'It's the perturbed hot humour combined with an excess of the moist. Teeth are of course ruled by the cold earth humour in crystalline form, and their natural enemy is the moist.'

Gwairyc tried to speak, but he could only swallow – hard, and several times.

'You look pale, lad,' Nevyn said to Gwairyc.

Gwairyc bit his lip and looked away. In the doorway, Ligga was quietly sobbing to herself. *She must love the stinking little brat*, he thought. *Well, cows watch over their calves, too.*

'We'll stay here tonight, Ligga,' Nevyn said. 'I'll tend that fever with herbs.'

'My thanks.' She pulled up the hem of her skirt and blew her nose on the frayed and stained brown cloth. 'Ah ye gods, my thanks.'

Gwairyc silently cursed him. He'd been hoping they'd get free of the farm straightaway and camp somewhere clean.

After several doses of herbs, Nevyn finally got Anno to fall asleep. The old man changed into a fresh pair of brigga, handed the soaked ones to Gwairyc, and told him wash them out.

'And you'd best do yours while you're at it,' Nevyn said. 'You've got a spare pair, haven't you?'

'I have.'

'There's a stream out back,' Ligga said. 'Here, I'll get you some soap.'

A scrap of soap in one hand, the dirty clothes in the other, Gwairyc strode out of the house into the relatively clean air of the farmyard. Ligga followed him out and pointed. 'Go straight out the back gate. You'll see my pounding rocks on the stream bank.'

'Pounding rocks?'

'Now, here, haven't you washed clothes before?' She gave him her half-toothless grin. 'Get them wet first. You work the soap in good, then put them on the flat rock and beat the soiled bits with the round rock.'

Cursing under his breath, Gwairyc took the brigga down to a tiny streamlet, meandering through wild grass. He found the rocks, knelt down, and tried to follow her instructions. His rage built and flamed until he could barely see what he was doing. How could he be here, him, the hero of the Cerrgonney wars, washing some farm-brat's piss out of a pair of old brigga? He considered waiting till dark and running away, but a bitter truth stopped him. If he broke his vow, he'd have nowhere to go, unless of course he wanted to sink to the level of a silver dagger. Even being a herbman's servant would be better than that.

All at once, he realized that he was weeping, a final blow of shame. He threw the wet brigga onto the grass and sobbed aloud until he heard footsteps rustling through the grass. He wiped his face on his sleeve and looked up to see Nevyn, standing there with his hands on his hips.

'Oh here, lad. This is a good bit harder on you than I thought it'd be.'

The old man's sympathy delivered the worst cut of all. Gwairyc wanted to kill him. *I'm doing this for the king,* he reminded himself. With a sigh, Nevyn sat down next to him in the grass.

'The lad's going to live. Do you care one jot?'

'I don't. Ye gods, how can you do things like this? With your skill, you could be the king's own physician or suchlike.'

'There's many a man who wants to physic the king. How many want to help folk like these?'

'Well, and why should they? This lot is hardly better than bondfolk.'

'I treat bondfolk who need me, too.'

Gwairyc stared at him. *Daft and twice daft!*

'I'll admit to being surprised when you looked so ill,' Nevyn continued. 'After all, you've ridden to many a battle. You must have seen the dead and dying, the wounds and suchlike.'

'I don't understand it, either. You're right enough about the things I've seen.' Gwairyc thought for a moment. 'But you expect that, in a battle. You're used to it. And you don't let yourself dwell on it, like. This –' He paused and suddenly saw the answer. 'In battle, you're fighting for your clan or your king. So much hangs on the outcome of a war. So all the death and the cuts and suchlike – they're in a good cause, like. They matter.'

'And this lad doesn't matter?'

'Why would he? Folk like these – one dies, there's always more. They breed like rabbits.'

Nevyn cocked his head to one side and considered him for a long moment. Although the old man's face displayed no particular feeling, Gwairyc began to wonder if he'd somehow shamed himself.

'Well, um, mayhap, they're more like horses.' Gwairyc tried again. 'You appreciate a good one, but if you lose him, you can get another.'

Nevyn blinked a few times, quickly.

'It's shameful!' Gwairyc burst out. 'I'm noble-born, but now I might as well be a farrier or a stablehand.'

'Ah. Treating the sick is shameful.'

'Well, not for you.'

'But for you it is.'

'Of course. You're not a noble-born man.'

'You're quite sure of that?'

Gwairyc suddenly remembered the king, pouring the old man ale with his own hands. In a kind of panic he tried to speak but found he could only stammer.

'It appears you see the flaw in your argument.' Nevyn smiled in a twisted sort of way, then stood up. 'You might think about all this a bit. Now, wring the water out of those brigga. Then spread them out flat on the grass to dry. I'm going back to the house.'

Once the brigga were drying, Gwairyc returned to the cow-barn. He unsaddled the pair of riding horses and unloaded the mule. He found a reasonably clean spot in a corner to pile up the gear, then looked over the various stalls. He had no idea if these folk brought the cows in at night or left them out. A skinny youngish man with a weather-beaten face and cropped brown hair, slick with grease, came into the barn.

'Be you Nevyn's apprentice? I'm Myrn. Ligga's man.'

'I'm Gwairyc.'

Myrn nodded in what might have been a greeting. 'I'll put them horses up for you. My thanks for saving my lad.'

'That was Nevyn's work, not mine, truly.'

Myrn nodded again and took a pitch-fork from the floor. Gwairyc hurried out and left the horses to him.

On the morrow, Anno seemed to be recovering, but Nevyn left various packets of herbs for his care just in case. When Ligga tried to offer him her few saved coppers as payment, Nevyn refused. That gesture Gwairyc could understand. Taking coins from folk like these would be as ignoble as stealing a hunting dog's food.

They left the farm and took up their slow road west again. Mile after mile, village after village, farm after farm – Nevyn seemed to know every commoner in the kingdom, and all of them were, in Gwairyc's opinion, filthy. Gwairyc saw more injuries and illnesses than he'd ever known existed, with disgusting symptoms all: cuts gone septic, clustered boils, fevers, vomiting, loose bowels, swellings, foul dark urine, and dropsies, to say naught of the ever-present diseased teeth. He tried at first to shut the symptoms out of his mind, but the sights and smells haunted him. At times he dreamt about them. *It's the shame of the thing*, he told himself. *Why else would they sicken me so much?*

Yet one afternoon, as they rode down a lane between two fields pale green with sprouting wheat, he remembered the first battle he'd ever seen, or rather, its aftermath, the dead men, the dying horses. Once the battle-rage had worn off, he'd felt a stomach-churning disgust far stronger than any of Nevyn's patients aroused in him. He'd been not much more than a lad, then, and he would rather have died than let any of the men around him see his feelings. And in time, he'd learned how to armour his soul. *I'll grow used to this, too,* he told himself. *After all, I've got no choice.*

Late one hot afternoon, when rain clouds were boiling up from the south, they came to a sprawling village on the banks of a broad but shallow stream. The place was too small to offer an inn, but the tavernman, who knew Nevyn well, let them shelter in his hayloft. After Gwairyc stabled the horses and mule, Nevyn bought them each a tankard of ale. They sat outside the tavern on a little bench across from a market square, empty except for a couple of brown dogs, lying near the public well. In the stiff wind the poplars growing all round the town shivered and bowed.

'We're in for a storm, all right,' Nevyn pronounced.

'I'd say so, my lord. I hope to the gods that the stable roof doesn't leak.'

Nevyn nodded his agreement and had a sip of his ale. With the clatter of hooves and the jingle of polished tack, a squad of five horsemen came trotting down the village street and up to the inn. As they dismounted, Gwairyc saw the swords at their sides and the blazon of a red hawk on their shirts.

'Must be the riders of our local lord,' Gwairyc said.

'Just so. I don't remember his name.'

The lads tied their horses up at the side of the tavern, then came strolling around to the door. Gwairyc envied them. Once he'd been free to enjoy a tankard in the company of men who understood him, men who were true companions and fellow-warriors. One of the riders paused, looking Nevyn over.

'Good morrow, sir. You look new to our village.'

'Just passing through. I'm a herbman, you see.'

The rider nodded pleasantly and went inside with his fellows. In a bit, Nevyn finished his ale and handed the tankard to Gwairyc.

'Take this back in. One's enough for me, but buy yourself another if you'd like, lad.'

'My thanks. I will.'

Gwairyc took the copper for the ale from Nevyn and carried the tankards back to the tavernman. While the tavernman was dipping him a second tankard from the barrel, Gwairyc realized that the Red Hawk riders were looking him over.

As Gwairyc started back outside with his full tankard, a beefy
blond fellow got up and blocked his way.

'What are you doing with a sword, lad?'

'What's it to you?' Gwairyc said.

'You're naught but the servant for that moth-eaten old
herbman. You've got no right to carry a man's weapon.'

Gwairyc threw the tankard of ale full into his face. With
a howl of rage, the fellow staggered back and swatted at the
ale running and foaming down his chest. Shouting, the other
lads jumped up, hands going to their hilts. Gwairyc drew
and dropped into a fighting stance. He could ask for naught
better than a chance to kill someone and wash away his
shame with blood.

'What's all this?' Nevyn yelled. 'Stop it!'

No one paid him the least attention. The nearest two
riders drew, dropping into their stance, and edged cautiously
for Gwairyc. Gwairyc waited, judging distance. All at once
a crash and crackle like thunder boomed around him. Blue
fire leapt up, surrounding his enemies in one enormous
flame, blinding him as well as them. He heard the lads yelling
and cursing as another fire came with the thunder close
behind.

'Get out!' Nevyn's voice said calmly. 'All of you – out now!'

Still half-blind, Gwairyc staggered back, shaking his head
in a vain attempt to clear his sight. He could just barely see
the Red Hawk riders, equally blind, stumbling as fast as they
could, shoving each other to be the first out the door. In the
corner the tavernman was laughing in long peals while he
hugged his own middle. Nevyn strolled over to Gwairyc and
pulled the sword from his limp hand.

'Did you do that?' Gwairyc heard his voice squeaking like
a lad's.

'And who else would it have been?' the tavernman broke
in. 'Ye gods, Nevyn, you're a marvel, you are – and at your
age, too.'

'Oh, the old horse can take a jump or two yet,' Nevyn

said, grinning. 'Now listen, Gwarro. I won't have you killing anyone. Do you understand me?'

'I think I finally do understand you, my lord. You're dweomer.'

'Just that. What did you think I did to earn the king's favour? Lance his boils?'

Shaking too hard to speak, Gwairyc leaned back against the tavernroom wall. Nevyn looked at the sword.

'You won't be carrying this from now on. Take off that sword belt, lad, and hand it over. I'm not giving it back to you until I see fit.'

For a moment Gwairyc's rage flared up like dweomer-fire. Taking his sword away was the worst dishonour in the world. Nevyn's cold blue gaze caught and pinned him to the wall. Slowly, silently cursing himself for doing it, Gwairyc unbuckled his belt and handed it to the old man, then turned and ran outside rather than watch another man sheath his blade. He threw himself down on the bench and watched the clouds darkening the sky while he trembled so hard he could no longer tell if the cause were rage or terror.

The rain clouds had turned as dark as cinders when Nevyn came out to join him. He stood, his hands on his hips, in front of the bench and look Gwairyc over. 'Well?' Nevyn said.

'Well what?'

'What have you made of all that?'

'The blue fire and the like? I've not made anything out of it, except you called it down from wherever it came from. Isn't that enough?'

'Most likely. Do you remember what I told you that very first day at the temple of Wmm? There was a thing I told you to remember.'

Gwairyc thought for a long moment. 'You told me you were doing this to benefit the king.'

'I didn't.' Nevyn suddenly grinned. 'I told you I was doing it to benefit you.'

'Ye gods! That ran right out of my mind.'

'I thought it might have.'

'But how by all the ice in all the hells – I mean, benefit me how?'

'Only you can know that.'

'What? I –'

'If I explained, you'd only miss it.'

Gwairyc thought up a nasty reply, but the memory of the blue fire leaping through the tavern stopped him from voicing it.

'I'm not talking in riddles to tease you,' Nevyn continued. 'Some things truly can't be made clear.'

'Well, since it's dweomer, I'd be a fool to argue.'

Gwairyc had the rare pleasure of seeing Nevyn taken utterly aback.

'Come to think of it,' the old man said at last, 'I would have thought you'd be alarmed at the very idea of dweomer, but you're not.'

'I'm one of the Rams of Hendyr, aren't I? Most lords mock the dweomer. Can't be true, they say. But not us, and we won't let anyone of our rank or below mock it in our presence. It's one of the things that makes us Rams. That's what my father and my grandfather tell all of us.'

'Indeed?' Nevyn considered this for a moment. 'May I ask why?'

'Of course, you being what you are. It's because of Lady Lillorigga of the Ram. One of our ancestors, she was, back in the Time of Troubles.'

'I've heard her name, truly.' Once again Nevyn looked startled, and Gwairyc began to enjoy the effect he was having. 'Go on, lad, if you don't mind.'

'Not at all. She was a sorceress, and the bards have passed down the tale. She made a prediction of some sort, I think it was.' Gwairyc paused, frowning over details – he'd not heard the story for a good many years now. 'They'd been loyal to the cursed Boars, but thanks to her, The Ram recognized the true king in the nick of time and went over to his side.

It's all a bit muddled in the tales, my lord, when it comes to exactly how she did it, but she did, and that's been good enough for us.'

'As well it should be. And now we'd best get inside, because it's starting to rain.'

By the morrow the weather had cleared, and they took up their slow travelling west again. At intervals Gwairyc would think about Nevyn's words. Try though he did, the only benefit he could see was that he wouldn't die in this summer's fighting, which was a coward's benefit and beneath contempt.

On the longest day of the year they reached Matrynwn, a proper town near the headwaters of the Vicaver. From the dusty village square they could see mountains, rising squat and rocky off to the west.

'They mark the Eldidd border,' Nevyn told him.

'Good,' Gwairyc said. 'That relieves my heart.'

'Of what?'

'The fear of meeting some lord I know. I've never been this far west in my life.'

'Ah, I see. Well, we could easily travel on to Eldidd.' Nevyn paused, thinking. 'I've got friends off to the west.'

'What about the herbs you were looking for? In old forest, I think you said.'

'I did say just that, and truly, old forest's easy to find in western Eldidd. Done, then! Let's ask around about the road ahead of us.'

Matrynwn turned out to be the last town on the only road that would lead them through the mountains. Thanks to its position it sported several proper inns, each with fenced pastures for the horses and mules of the caravans that came through. After a little asking around, Nevyn found an inn that was sheltering a caravan heading west. Its master, a Cerrmor man named Wffyn, considered himself lucky that a herbman wanted to join them. He was a burly fellow, with a sandy beard streaked with grey and a scatter of grey hairs on his mostly bald head. Judging by the heavy muscles of his long arms, though, he could still wield a quarterstaff if he had to. And sometimes, or so he told them, you had to.

'You never know who's lurking about the mountains, but you'll be safe, riding with us,' Wffyn said. 'I've got ten men who can fight as well as tend the mules. By all means, good sir, you and your apprentice will be most welcome.'

Wffyn had an apprentice of his own, of sorts – very much of sorts, Gwairyc decided. Tirro was a skinny lad, probably no more than fifteen summers old, with the bright blue eyes and high cheekbones of a Cerrmor man, though red pimples dotted those cheekbones and clustered around his mouth. His hair – actually, he seemed to have none, because he wore on his head a little linen cap, all stained with some sort of grease – but his eyebrows were blond, as you'd expect of someone from the south. When Gwairyc first met him, Tirro refused to look him in the eye. Every now and then, while their two masters discussed the trip ahead, Tirro would stick a skinny finger under the cap and scratch viciously, to the point where he eventually made himself bleed.

'Ye gods,' Nevyn said. 'What's vexing you so badly, lad?'

'Ah, well, uh.' Tirro kept his gaze on the floor.

'Ringworm,' Wffyn broke in, 'and come along, lad, you're not supposed to scratch it. Get some more salve if you need it.'

'I will, master.' Tirro stood up. 'My apologies.' He turned and ran out of the tavern room.

'What kind of salve is it?' Nevyn said.

'I don't truly know. The apothecary in Cerrmor made it up for him. Ceruse, he called it, in emollients.'

'Ah,' Nevyn said. 'Ceruse is the calx of lead, that is, whitened lead.'

'Lead? Now that I know.' Wffyn nodded sagely. 'It does seem to be working, when I can get him to stop scratching.'

'Good. Is he bloodkin of yours?'

'He's not, and I thank the gods for that. An unfortunate

sort of lad, Tirro. I'm taking him along as a favour to his father, naught more.'

'I see,' Nevyn said. 'Giving him a taste of the merchant life?'

Wffyn started to speak, paused, had a sip of ale, frowned into his tankard, started once more to speak, then sighed. 'Well,' he finally said, 'I didn't mean to go telling tales, but truly, I wouldn't mind a little help with keeping an eye on the lad. He had to leave Cerrmor, you see, and sudden like.'

'Stealing?' Nevyn said.

'Worse.' Wffyn hesitated briefly. 'He's somewhat of a lori-cart, if you take my meaning.'

'I don't,' Nevyn said. 'Cerrmor cant-words are beyond me.'

'Well, now, I've heard this sort of man called hedge creepers in other parts of the kingdom, or lobcocks.'

'I've heard those, too.' Gwairyc cleared his throat and spat into the straw on the floor. 'He means men who fancy little children.'

'That,' Nevyn said slowly, 'is truly disgusting.'

'It is all of that,' Wffyn said. 'There was a lass name of Mella, a pretty little thing but not more than six summers old, and Tirro got a fair bit too friendly with her, if you take my meaning. Her father and her uncles were going to beat the cursed wretched young cub to a bloody pulp, but fortunately they saw reason when I said I'd take him away on caravan.'

'I gather there was no doubt that the lad was guilty.'

'None. On top of everything else, he gave the poor child his ringworm.'

Nevyn made a profoundly sour face. 'But you'll take him with you?'

'Well, now, I wouldn't have lifted a finger to help him, but I owed his da a fair bit of money, if you take my meaning.'

'I see. So he's erased the debt now?' Nevyn said.

'He has,' Wffyn glanced at Gwairyc. 'But if you see Tirro hanging around some little lass during our travels, tell me, will you? I can't be everywhere at once.'

'Gladly,' Gwairyc said. 'Have no fear of that.'

Wffyn raised his tankard in salute and smiled his thanks.

'What's going to happen when you get back to Cerrmor?' Nevyn asked.

'Tirro will be shipping out for Bardek,' Wffyn said. 'His father has a friend with a ship, you see, but he'd left harbour before this thing happened – the ship's captain I mean, not the father. He'll come back late in the summer and then make the last run over to winter in Bardek. Tirro will be going with him, and good riddance.'

'I see,' Nevyn said. 'Exactly where is the ship going, do you know?'

'Myleton.'

Nevyn nodded, as if merely acknowledging the information, but by then Gwairyc knew him well enough to see that something had troubled him. Later, when they were alone, he asked the old man about it.

'Bardek is a very strange place,' Nevyn said. 'There are men there who share Tirro's particular vice, and some of them are rich and even powerful. They pursue their prey in the shadows, because most Bardekians are decent folk, but at the same time, in the larger towns, there are brothels where they can satisfy their wretched cravings in safety.'

'That's loathsome!'

'Indeed. So I was wondering if I could send a message to some friends of mine there, to suggest they tell the archons to keep an eye on this unfortunate cub. Alas, they live on Orystinna, nowhere near Myleton.'

'A pity. This Orys-whatzit – it's another island?'

'It is. Most likely Tirro will alert the archons to his presence on his own, by doing some wretched thing too openly. He strikes me as more than a little dim-witted. I wish I could prevent it, but alas, like our good merchant, I can't be everywhere at once.'

'Indeed.' Gwairyc shook his head in disgust. 'Ye gods, if the lad was as hard up as all that, he could have gone after a sheep. It would have been cleaner.'

'True spoken.' Nevyn managed a twisted smile at the jest.

Gwairyc realized that for this moment at least he and his master, as he always thought of Nevyn, had found a common bond of sorts in their disgust. It would be a good time to bring up a matter very much on his mind.

'There was somewhat else I wanted to ask you,' Gwairyc said. 'About these bandits, my lord. I can't defend the caravan with my bare hands.'

'Ah. You want your sword back, do you?' Nevyn considered, but only briefly. 'Very well. I'll give it to you. Just don't go drawing it on anyone but the bandits.'

'I won't, I swear it.'

The return of his sword raised Gwairyc's spirits more than anything else could have, except perhaps the chance to kill a bandit or two with it. Unfortunately to his way of thinking, though not to anyone else's, the ride through the mountains proved hot, tedious, and uneventful – except for a strange accident.

It happened on the steepest part of the road up to the main pass. In the sticky summer heat the caravan made slow progress that day and camped early when they found a reasonably flat area off to one side of the dusty trail. Lined with some sort of shrubby tree that Gwairyc couldn't put a name to, a muddy rivulet ran nearby, flowing out of the forest cover and heading downhill. The hot day had exhausted everyone. The stock had to be tended and fed, exhaustion or no, but no one spoke more than they absolutely had to. With his share of the work done, one of the muleteers pulled off his boots, rolled up his trousers, and trotted off to soak his aching feet downstream from their drinking water. Gwairyc had just turned Nevyn's mule into the general herd when he heard the man scream. Without thinking he drew his sword and ran just as a second agonized shriek rang out to guide him.

In the spotty shade the muleteer was lying sprawled with one leg held high in the air. It was such an odd posture that it took Gwairyc a moment to notice the blood sheeting down the muleteer's leg. The fellow had stepped into a wire snare and tripped it. Now the thin wire was biting ever deeper into his unprotected ankle as he flailed his arms and screamed.

'Hold still!' Gwairyc put all his noble-born authority into his voice. 'You'll be hurt worse if you don't.'

The fellow looked his way, sobbed once, and fainted. Gwairyc trotted over and considered the wire. He had no desire to blunt his blade by trying to cut it. His inspection showed that the thin strand forming the noose had been knotted repeatedly over a much thicker wire, reinforced with rope, that formed the long portion of the snare and anchored the whole contraption to a nearby sapling. By then another muleteer and Wffyn himself had come at the run. With a cascade of foul oaths the muleteer set to work untwisting the strands whilst the merchant supported the injured man's leg.

'I've never seen such a cursed strong snare,' Wffyn remarked. 'What was the hunter after, I wonder? A bear?'

'That thing would never take a bear's weight,' Gwairyc said. 'A deer? Not likely, either.'

'Huh.' Wffyn's face was beginning to turn pale. He looked away from the muleteer's blood-soaked leg. 'Makes you wonder if that trap was set to catch a man. Guarding somewhat, like, close by here.'

'It might be.' Gwairyc sheathed his sword. 'I'll get Nevyn. Our friend here should thank the gods that the old man's nearby.'

Indeed, whether it was the gods or luck, the fellow would have lost his foot and perhaps his life as well if it weren't for Nevyn. Still, the process of getting the embedded wire out of the wound and the whole mess washed clean and stitched up was painful enough to watch, much less experience. The poor fellow would keep coming round only to faint again the moment Nevyn touched the leg. Gwairyc busied himself with heating water in an iron pot for steeping herbs while the rest of the caravan stayed strictly elsewhere. Only Tirro stuck close to them.

'I could help,' Tirro said. 'I can look for firewood if you need to brew herbs.'

'That's not a bad idea,' Gwairyc said. 'Go to it, but be cursed careful where you put your feet.'

'I will, sir.'

With a little bow of his head Tirro hurried off into the underbrush. In but a little space of time he came back with a good supply of dead branches. By then Nevyn had begun to stitch the wound. Tirro glanced at the muleteer's leg and went decidedly pale.

'Just feed some wood into the fire,' Gwairyc said. 'Don't look.'

'I won't, sir.' Tirro hunkered down by the fire.

The pot of water hung from a tripod. Tirro concentrated on breaking up branches and feeding bits into the fire underneath. He was doing well until the muleteer came round from a faint and began moaning. Tirro straightened up and looked at the leg just as Nevyn started pouring warm herb water over the wound, releasing a flood of clots and bits of skin. At that the lad turned dead-white and rushed away to vomit among the bushes.

By then Gwairyc could see even worse sights without feeling sick. Instead he merely felt shamed, as if he'd sunk even lower in the world by simply knowing enough herbcraft to act like the apprentice he nominally was. Still, once the muleteer was lying on a pad of blankets with his ankle wrapped in clean bandages, and his pain eased with one of Nevyn's herbal mixtures, Gwairyc had to admit a certain admiration for the old man's skill. When they were sitting by their own fire and eating a delayed dinner, Gwairyc told him so.

'I wish we had chirurgeons like you with the army,' Gwairyc said. 'There must be naught that you can't cure.'

'My thanks, but I only wish that were true, lad. There's

many a foul illness that baffles my herbs, wasting diseases of the lungs, strange fevers from Bardek, and the like.'

'I see. I've never been down on the southern coast, but I've heard about those fevers. Doesn't make me want to go there.'

'Well, even in Bardek the fevers are not what you'd call common.' Nevyn paused, glancing away in thought. 'Strange ills can strike a man down anywhere. In fact, my master in herbcraft told me once about a very strange disease that someone contracted not far from Dun Deverry. The patient – one of the king's own riders – had been wounded in a fight against bandits. They'd finally cornered the bandits in an apple orchard, of all places, one where the trees had gone untended for years, and –'

'Wait a moment,' Gwairyc interrupted. 'There haven't been any bandits near Dun Deverry for a cursed long time.'

'True spoken. This incident happened when my master's master was young, or so he said.' Nevyn paused to count something out on his fingers. 'It must have happened not long after the Civil Wars, now that you mention it.'

'Ah, now that makes more sense.'

'Anyway, this fellow was a fine swordsman, but he and the warband had never had to dismount and fight among trees before.'

'That's doubtless why the bandits made a stand there.'

'Doubtless, but would you let me finish?'

'Apologies, my lord. Go on.'

'So he was too used to trusting his skill. He was an arrogant lad, all in all, but he had reason to be, I suppose. He rushed in and got himself severely wounded. Well, my master's master managed to stop the bleeding, and the fellow was a strong man, so he assumed that the captain – he was the captain of the king's personal guard, you see –'

'Silver daggers, weren't they?'

'That's right. You've heard about them, then?'

'Many a time.'

'Well and good. That'll shorten the tale. So just when this captain should have been starting to recover, a truly strange thing happened to his wound. It turned foul and corrupted, but in a way the chirurgeons had never seen before. The flesh turned black at the edges of the wound, like a bit of parchment held too close to a candle. The blackness spread, and the stench was truly horrible. Had he been wounded on an arm or leg, they could have amputated and saved him, but it lay on his thigh too close to the body for any such thing. It must have been a sickening thing, to see the corruption spreading through the captain's body with naught anyone could do to stop it. Finally he died, so mayhap the blackness reached the heart. My master didn't know nor did his master. The rest of the silver daggers called it evil sorcery, and for all I know, they were right.'

Gwairyc shuddered. The tale affected him far more deeply than it should have. He'd seen many a man die in battle and others die from wounds afterwards, but none like this, from some black rot that crept along, conquering new territory on a man's body. It seemed to him that he could almost smell it, just from hearing the description, a rank acid smell like rotting meat. *Well, it was rotting meat* – the thought nearly made him gag.

'Are you all right, lad?' Nevyn was studying his face.

'I am, my lord. My apologies. It just touched my heart somehow, hearing about Owaen dying like that. Or – wait – was that his name?'

'Owaen? It was indeed, and oddly enough, his device was a falcon, just like yours.'

'That's a horrible wyrd for a man to have!' Gwairyc paused for a cold shudder. 'And here he was, the survivor of all those battles and years of war.'

'He'd survived many, indeed. You must have heard about him in a bard song or the like.'

'I must have, truly. I –' Gwairyc realized that he could call up no memory of having heard so much as the name. 'Well,

I don't remember him turning up in the bard songs, but he must have. How else would I know his name?'

'Indeed.' Nevyn smiled, just briefly. 'How else, truly?'

Yet for the rest of the evening, Gwairyc felt troubled, wondering how he knew so much about this Owaen. He was sure, for instance, that the Silver Daggers' captain had originally been an Eldidd man. That fact suddenly rose in his mind along with the sound of a voice lisping at the beginning of words like gwerbret. Werrbret, they would say in Eldidd. He knew it, and yet there was no way he could have known it. Finally he managed to put the matter out of his mind, but that night he had a confused dream, flashing by in fragments, about fighting with a red wyvern on his shield.

In the morning light Gwairyc, Tirro, and a couple of the muleteers searched the area around the snare. They found only a single trace of the man or men who might have set it. Tirro suddenly stooped and reached into a pile of dead leaves to pull out some small shiny thing.

'It's a coin,' he announced. 'A Bardek coin.'

'A what?' Gwairyc held out one hand. 'How can you be sure?'

'It's just like the ones my da's friends bring home from Myleton.' Tirro gave it to him. 'They call it a sesture.'

The coin proved to be barely big enough to cover one of Gwairyc's fingernails, but its green tarnish showed that it contained at least some silver. Gwairyc could just make out a few foreign-looking letters. When they brought it to Nevyn, the old man rubbed it clean on his sleeve.

'It's from Bardek, sure enough,' Nevyn said. 'Do you see the device upon it? A man's head in profile. It must one of their archons, as they call their leaders, but I've not the slightest idea which one.' He handed the coin back to Tirro. 'You've got sharp eyes, lad.'

'I'm sorry about yesterday, sir, really I am.' Tirro stared at the ground. 'I didn't mean to.'

This outburst seemed to make Nevyn as puzzled as

Gwairyc felt. He considered the lad for a moment with his head cocked to one side.

'Um, what?' Nevyn said finally.

'The way I looked after you told me not to. Isn't that what you just meant by mentioning my sharp eyes?'

'Naught of the sort! I was complimenting you, as a matter of fact.'

Tirro blushed scarlet, started to speak, then merely bolted, running back towards the camp before either Gwairyc or Nevyn could say a word.

'What by all the ice in all the hells was that about?' Gwairyc said.

'I don't know,' Nevyn said, 'but I'd guess that his father was given to making cruel remarks, and frequently to boot.'

'Oh.' Gwairyc shrugged the problem away. 'Anyway, that coin is the only thing we found, other than trees and a cursed lot of rocks. The banks of the stream are low and damp, but the only tracks we saw were made by deer and then some sort of small creature, a badger, most likely.'

'How very odd,' Nevyn said. 'The snare had to be fairly new, because it hadn't rusted. Well, we can't stay here to keep hunting. Wffyn and his men are ready to move out, and we'd best join them.'

'Well and good, then. What about the injured fellow?'

'They shifted the load of one of the mules to the other packs and tied him to the saddle instead. This way, if he faints, he won't fall. He'll have to stay behind, though, once we get to a town.'

It took the caravan most of a day to travel down from the mountains. Towards sunset it reached a prosperous-looking farm, where Wffyn stopped to barter with the farmwife for peaches and cabbages to freshen up the communal meals. After the haggling, the merchant described the accident his muleteer had suffered.

'Do you know who might have set that snare?' Wffyn said. 'It was a cursed dangerous thing to do.'

The farmer and his wife exchanged a glance, but their eyes showed no feeling at all.

'I don't,' the man said at last. 'You're right enough. It's too close to the road for someone to be setting snares.'

'Let me get you a sack for them cabbages.' Without looking at any of the men, the wife turned away and hurried into the farmhouse. Wffyn raised one eyebrow but said nothing.

Once they were back on the road, Wffyn manoeuvred his horse to ride next to Gwairyc and Nevyn.

'What did you think about those people?' the merchant said. 'It looked to me like they knew plenty about that snare.'

'To me, too,' Nevyn said. 'I wonder what they're after, up in the wild hills.'

At the next village, when Wffyn told his story in the local tavern, the men there responded with honest bewilderment. After some discussion, however, the local miller remembered that you could find small grey hogs up in the hills.

'Pigs, they get loose now and then,' the miller said. 'Go wild, they do, breed amongst themselves. There's a right proper herd of swine by now, I'd wager. Our local werrbret hunts them now and again, but he don't claim them or nothing, so the pork's free for the taking.'

Werrbret. Gwairyc was so startled by the man's accent that he nearly gasped aloud. He covered the sound with a quick cough. 'Hogs, eh?' Wffyn turned to Nevyn and lowered his voice. 'That farmer and his wife – why would they act so strange, like, if they were just hunting wild pig?'

'Indeed. I wonder – I've heard rumours about slavers landing their boats in the wild places along the coast. No doubt there are ways of finding out where, if you have some-what to sell.'

'Gods!' Wffyn spat on the straw-covered floor. 'You could well be right, good sir.'

'I'd rather be wrong, truly. Come to think of it, why would they risk maiming the merchandise? That snare was a dangerous thing.'

'Well, if someone were wearing boots and hadn't rolled up his brigga, either, it wouldn't bite very deep.'

'True spoken.' Nevyn frowned down at his tankard. 'Even a good thick wrap of rags would protect the leg to some degree. On the way home, tell your men to keep their boots on.'

'Oh, I don't think I'll need to tell them.'

Nevyn agreed with a smile, then turned to Gwairyc. 'You look like somewhat's troubling you, lad. Is it about these slavers?'

'What? It's not. I was just wondering why the Eldidd folk speak a fair bit different than we do, with their werrbret and all, and then the way they roll their R's around.'

'I'm surprised you'd notice such a thing.'

Gwairyc shrugged in feigned indifference. *Someone must have told me about it*, he decided. He refused to believe anything else, despite a voice from deep in his mind that persisted in whispering: *you remember*.

Tirro's scalp was beginning to sprout a blond fuzz, marred by a few small circles of ringworm. Nevyn had him sit on a bale of goods in the strong morning sun and turn his head this way and that just to make sure that the spots were on the verge of disappearing. As he worked, he was also inspecting Tirro for something entirely different. He'd begun to suspect that he'd known this unfortunate little scoundrel before, during one of Tirro's earlier lives, someone with a nature equally flawed. He would have to find some excuse for staring into Tirro's eyes before he could be certain. At the moment Wffyn stood nearby and watched the inspection.

'Very good,' Nevyn announced. 'You can burn that ghastly linen cap, lad, but keep putting salve on those spots.'

'I will, sir,' Tirro said. 'Thank you, sir.'

'One more thing.' Nevyn pounced on the white lie that suddenly occurred to him. 'I don't like the appearance of your left eye. Getting a trace of this particular salve in your eye can be a very bad thing. Here, tip your head up and look me right in the face.'

Tirro caught his breath with a small gulp of fear.

'Go on,' Wffyn snapped. 'Do what the herbman wants.'

Tirro gulped again and caught his shaking hands between his knees. *So!* Nevyn thought. *He's got some reason to fear me, has he?* Tirro raised his head, glanced at Nevyn, and immediately looked down again.

'Come along, Tirro,' Nevyn said. 'I won't bite.'

Once again the boy raised his head. This time he did manage to look at Nevyn for a few beats of a heart – enough. *Brour!* Nevyn thought. *That slimy little renegade!* Aloud, he said, 'Ah, splendid! The eye looks fine. I thought I saw a swelling, but it must just have been some trick of the light. You can go now.'

Tirro jumped up and ran, heading for the herd of mules. Nevyn watched as he disappeared among them.

'I've been meaning to ask you.' Wffyn stepped forward. 'Will you be travelling on with us a-ways? A man as good with his herbs as you are, Nevyn, is welcome everywhere.'

'That's very kind of you,' Nevyn said. 'I'm thinking of going all the way west to Aberwyn or thereabouts.'

'We'll certainly be going that far and beyond, since we're going to trade with the Westfolk.'

'True spoken. Where are you planning on crossing the Delonderiel?'

'A good distance north of Aberwyn, actually, just north of the Pyrdon border. Now, some will tell you that's the long way round, but I've found better horses up in the Peddroloc region than I have at the southern trading grounds nearer to Aberwyn. Is that too far out of your way?'

'It may be. We'll stay with you till you reach the Gwynaver, though. We can always turn south from there.'

Not long after, however, an old friend gave Nevyn a reason to travel the entire way with Wffyn. Some hundreds of years before, Nevyn had taken on a young apprentice in the dweomer, Aderyn by name, who had gone to live among the Westfolk. Over the years, Nevyn had kept in touch with his former apprentice, now a master in his own right. At night when both of them were near a fire, they could reach each other's minds through the flames.

Since he needed only a few hours of sleep a night, Nevyn generally was the last person awake when the caravan camped. That particular evening he was sitting up by the dying fire, tending the glowing coals and watching the salamanders leaping and playing among the last of the flames, when he felt someone tugging at his mind. The contact strengthened so readily that he knew it had to be Aderyn, and sure enough, his ex-apprentice's image built up as if his face floated on fire.

'It's good to see you,' Nevyn thought to him.

'And the same to you. In fact, I'm hoping to see a fair bit more of you.' Aderyn's image smiled at him. 'I was wondering if you were planning on riding our way this summer.'

'Not planning on visiting you, precisely, but I'm in Eldidd at the moment. There's no reason I couldn't ride a little further.'

'Excellent! One of my former students has joined my alar – Valandario her name is. Have you met her?'

'Not that I remember,' Nevyn said. 'Which means naught, of course. I may well have.'

'She'd heard about your work with the Great Stone of the West, and so she –'

'Wait a moment. How did she hear about it? It's not precisely a secret, but I don't want a lot of talk, either. Did you tell her?'

'You know, I don't think I did.' Aderyn's image frowned in thought. 'I don't know where she did learn of it.'

'Ask her if you get a chance, will you?'

'I will. Val's always had a special affinity for gems. Now just recently, at the summer festival, I happened to meet her. She wanted to know if she could ask your advice about a particular gem.'

'Can she speak through the fire? I'll be glad to talk with her. I learned a fair bit about gem dweomer in Bardek.'

'She can certainly try.' Aderyn sounded and looked more than a little doubtful. 'It's not one of her stronger gifts, though she's learning. But we wondered if you might actually come out here, or if we could meet you perhaps in Eldidd. She thinks you'll need to see this stone for yourself.'

'Well and good, then. I'm travelling with a merchant who's bound for your trading grounds. I'll continue on with him.'

'Splendid! I'm truly glad to hear it, and I'm sure Valandario will be, too. Come to think of it, maybe you can also help me with a little problem I've run into.'

'I'll most assuredly try. How's Loddlaen these days?'

'Doing well.' Aderyn's image turned expressionless, but since they'd joined minds through the fire, Nevyn could feel his anger. 'I don't know why you'd assume —'

'My apologies, my apologies. What's the real trouble, then?'

'Oh, well, mostly, my grand scheme's not going as well as it should.'

For a moment Nevyn quite simply couldn't remember what Aderyn's grand scheme was. Aderyn felt the lapse and smiled.

'My compilation of dweomerlore,' Aderyn said, 'trying to piece together the ancient elven dweomer by filling the gaps with our own lore.'

Nevyn's memory creaked into life at last. 'Of course, the dweomer system the Westfolk lost when the cities were destroyed. We've talked about it many a time. Ye gods! I cannot tell you how aggravating it is, not being able to remember things the way I used to. Next I'll be forgetting my own name.'

'Well, you have a great deal more to remember than most men. Three hundred years' worth, isn't it now?'

'Somewhat like that. Your own memories stretch a fair way back.'

'Ah, but life out here is simple. You've always managed to complicate matters for yourself.'

'That's one way of putting it, I suppose. But about that problem –'

'I've gathered together every shred I can, but there are large stretches of territory still missing from my mental map, as it were.'

'I like that figure of speech.'

'My thanks.'

'Do you have any idea of what was in that missing province?'

'Some important thing at the very centre.' Aderyn's mind radiated frustration. 'I do know that the masters of the seven cities studied dweomer for very different reasons from ours. Their ultimate goal wasn't to help their folk, though they did that, too, but to – well, to do somewhat that I can't fathom, some grand result.'

'No clues at all?'

'Only an unusually elaborate schema of Names and Calls. When I first came to the Westlands, there were still a few dweomerworkers alive who had studied with a teacher who'd been taught in the lost cities. Unfortunately, that teacher was young by elven standards, and only a journeyman. The masters among the dweomerfolk stayed to fight till the end.'

'And so the lore was lost with them?'

'Just that. But one thing that did survive was a list of names of certain areas of the Inner Lands. These names, or so I was told, were all that survived of a twice-secret lore. Apparently you had to prove yourself worthy before you were allowed to study it.'

'Secrecy has a bitter price in evil times.'

'Just so. But I'm looking forward to telling you what little I've gathered, once we can talk face to face.'

'I'm looking forward to it, too. We'll be there as soon as we can.'

'We?'

'I've acquired a rather odd apprentice. I'll tell you more once you've met him.'

The Westfolk lands lay a good month's journey away, out beyond the western border of the kingdom. Wffyn the merchant's ultimate goal was to trade iron goods for Westfolk horses, but rather than pack the heavy metalwork all the way from Cerrmor, he'd brought Bardek spices and fine silks to trade for it in Eldidd. As they made their slow way north from market square to market square, Nevyn had ample time to sell his herbs and other medicinals as well as collect more in the meadows and along the roads.

Nevyn also made a point of treating Gwairyc as the apprentice he supposedly was. He taught him herblore, trained him in the drying of herbs, and used him as an assistant when he performed the few simple chirurgeries he knew how to do. When it came to procedures, Nevyn found that having a large, strong assistant was very useful indeed, since the various anodynes available in those days lacked the power to render the sufferer unconscious. Over the years Nevyn had learned how to dodge the sudden fists or teeth of a patient driven mad enough by pain to attack the man trying to help him. Gwairyc, however, could hold them down and occasionally administer an anaesthetic of desperation by clipping the patient hard on the jaw. That part of the work he seemed to enjoy.

When they worked together in less trying situations, Nevyn studied the apprentice as much as the patient. Once, over three hundred years before, Nevyn had been a prince of the royal house, as arrogant as Gwairyc – *if not more so*, he reminded himself. Yet studying herbcraft with his teacher in the dweomer had opened his eyes and his heart. Once he'd seen how the ordinary people of the kingdom lived, and in particular the bondfolk who were at that time little better than slaves, he'd wanted nothing more than to end every moment of suffering that he could. He'd been hoping that this similar exposure to the ills and suffering of the common folk would open Gwairyc's heart as well, but he saw on his apprentice's face only the flickers of disgust and annoyance that would, occasionally, break through a mask of utter indifference. *You weren't a warrior*, he told himself. *You never had to temper your soul like iron.*

Only once did Gwairyc take any interest in a patient. In a village called Bruddlyn, they met the local lord, a certain Corbyn, who brought them to his dun to treat his small son, also named Corbyn, for spotted fever. Fortunately, the boy's mother had kept him in a dimly lit room, away from the sunlight that might have blinded him. Nevyn brewed one type of herbwater to lower the fever and a second as a soak for compresses to ease his itching skin.

'Our lordship didn't have much coin,' Nevyn told Gwairyc afterwards, 'but he did give us a silver cup that belonged to his own father. It has the name 'corbyn' inscribed on the bottom, but still, we should be able to sell it somewhere, for the silver if naught else.'

'I take it the lad's going to recover,' Gwairyc said.

'He is.'

'Good.' Gwairyc smiled in sincere pleasure at the news. 'He's the only son of that clan, the only one yet, anyway, and I'm glad they won't lose their heir. But here, do these lords always name their first-born Corbyn?'

'So it seems. Why?'

'There's somewhat odd about Eldidd, foreign-like.' Gwairyc frowned at nothing in particular. 'And that's another thing that I just can't . . .' He let his voice trail away.

Nevyn waited for him to go on, but in a moment Gwairyc merely said that he'd saddle the horses and walked away.

Eldidd may be strange, Nevyn thought, *but I begin to think Gwarro matches it! And what am I going to do with the lad, then?* His first course of treatment for the illness in Gwairyc's soul was failing, and badly. With a sinking feeling around his heart, he realized that he didn't have a second.

It wasn't until they'd almost reached their destination that Nevyn saw Gwairyc respond to the sufferings of a common-born soul, and even then, the circumstances were decidedly unusual. He received his first omen of that future event, and a hint of just how complex the days ahead might be, when he contacted Aderyn again.

'Here's a question for you,' Nevyn said. 'How will I be able to find you once we get to the grasslands? The trading grounds are quite large, as I remember them anyway.'

'They stretch a good hundred miles, yes, north to south.' Floating over the campfire, Aderyn's image smiled at him. 'I've arranged an escort for you and your merchant.'

'Splendid! Where do I find this escort?'

'In Drwloc. The fellow's a bard, Devaberiel by name, and he's going there to fetch a little son of his.'

'What's an elven woman doing living in Pyrdon?'

'She's not elven, though I suspect there's elven blood in her clan – somewhere. She looks human, and her kin certainly act that way.' Aderyn's image scowled into the flames. 'Her brother's done naught but berate her since the day she had to tie her kirtle high. A bastard in his clan! Oh, the shame of it! To hear him rant, you'd think he was the high king himself.'

'I see. The child's better off with his father's people, then. We're not far from Pyrdon. How soon will this bard get there?'

'Around the next full moon. We – my alar, that is – are on our way to the border now.'

'Good. Well, my thanks. This will make things a fair bit easier. Huh, I've not seen Dun Drw since King Maryn was young.'

'The place must hold plenty of memories for you.'

'Doesn't everywhere?'

'True enough.' Aderyn's image turned solemn. 'But oddly enough, Drwloc holds some memories for me as well, bitter ones. I think I told you about this – the young lad who died of consumption because of that poor twisted spirit-woman. Meddry, his name was. I feel responsible for his death. I should never have left his side for a moment.'

'Well, don't be too harsh on yourself. I – wait. Ye gods! Meddry died only a few years ago, didn't he?'

'He did.' Aderyn paused, thinking. 'Maybe ten, maybe less. Time truly loses its meaning out here on the grass, and so I don't remember precisely when.'

'That's good enough. It makes me wonder who else might be living in Drwloc or roundabout.' Nevyn paused for a morose sigh. 'And here I am, bringing Gerraent with me.'

A few more days of travelling brought them to the gwerbret's own town, Drwloc, a much grander affair than Lord Corbyn's village. The town sported a proper stone wall, sheltering nearly two hundred round houses arranged around a big market square. Among them Wffyn found a good-sized inn, which sat beside a stretch of grass pasture and near the local smithy as well.

'Excellent!' the merchant said. 'We'll be able to get our stock reshod before we start for the trading grounds.'

A crowd of villagers gathered round to watch the caravan tether out its stock on the pasture. The muleteers would camp there with the horses and mules, just in case Drwloc included a horsethief among its denizens. Nevyn and Wffyn, however, rented themselves a chamber, little more than a loft, above the tavern room.

'Well, this is quite the day!' the innkeep's wife announced. 'Here's a caravan come through, and we're having a market fair as well.'

'That's a bit of luck for me, too,' Nevyn said. 'I'll just go down to the market, I think, and let everyone know that there's a herbman in town.'

'I'll do my trading later with that blacksmith,' Wffyn said. 'You go on, and I'll keep an eye, like, on things here.'

Nevyn opened his mule packs, filled a sack with bundles of various remedies for common ills, then handed it to Gwairyc to carry. They followed the curving street to the open square in the centre of town and the market, which turned out to be a straggling line of farmers, selling fresh produce, eggs, and chickens out of the backs of wagons. Here and there a peddlar spread out his wares on a blanket:

pottery, soap, embroidery threads, all manner of small port
ables brought up from the more prosperous coast. The
villagers stood around gossiping or strolled along, looking at
the various offerings, or hunkered down to bargain when
they saw something they liked.

'We'd best buy some more food for the last bit of our
journey,' Nevyn said. 'Usually there's someone selling cheeses
at these village markets.'

As they made their way through the confusion, they came
upon a young woman, walking some paces in front of them.
She was so short and thin that at first he thought her a young
lass. She carried a child in her arms. Her dark hair, however,
was combed straight back into a clasp at her neck in the style
of an unmarried woman. While her overdress of undyed linen
looked clean and well made, there was nothing fancy about
it. She wore another strip of plain linen around her waist as
a kirtle. *A nursemaid,* Nevyn thought. The child in her arms
twisted around to rest his chin on her shoulder and look back.

'Ye gods!' Nevyn said. 'There's a beautiful little lad!'

Perhaps two years old, the boy had enormous grey eyes and
hair as pale as winter sunlight on snow – Westfolk blood in
his veins, Nevyn decided. When he realized that Nevyn was
looking at him, the boy smiled so cheerfully that Nevyn had
to smile in return. The boy giggled and said something in his
nursemaid's ear. She stopped and turned round.

She would have been a pretty lass, if it weren't for the
witchmark that split her mouth. During his long years as a
physician, Nevyn had seen plenty of harelips and cleft palates
– normal disfigurements, he was tempted to call them at that
moment, because this unusual blemish sat well off-centre.
Although it revealed the pink upper gum, a couple of stained
teeth, and a twist of dark pink scar, it looked more like a
healed wound than a harelip, so puzzling a feature that it
took Nevyn a moment to notice her eyes, deep-set and cornflower blue. He caught his breath. He recognized her: his
Brangwen reborn again.

She set the boy down, then caught his hand to keep him close. For a moment she studied Nevyn as intently as if she saw a puzzle in his eyes. He could guess that she recognized him without knowing how or why she did. Maybe, at last, he would be able to bring her to her true wyrd, the dweomer, and free himself of the rash vow he'd sworn so many hundreds of years earlier.

'Good morrow, good sir.' She spoke with a pronounced lisp, a moist thickening of many consonants. 'I see you're new to our town.'

'We are,' Nevyn said. 'My name's Nevyn, I'm a herbman, and this is my apprentice, Gwairyc. Forgive me for seeming to follow you. Your young lad there caught my attention.'

'Oh, no harm done. My name is Morwen.' When she smiled, the scar tissue curled her lip into an animal snarl that matched the lack of good humour in her eyes. 'A herbman's always a welcome thing. He's not my lad, though, but my sister's.'

'Well, your sister's a lucky lass, then.'

Her eyes filled with tears, and she looked sharply away.

'My apologies!' Nevyn said. 'What did I –'

'Forgive me, good sir. My sister doesn't think she's lucky in the least. She'll be sending our Evan away soon to his father's people.'

'And you've been his nursemaid?'

Morwen nodded. Evan leaned against her skirts and stared at Gwairyc, who'd been listening to all this with a sullen kind of patience. Nevyn suddenly realized just who this child had to be.

'The lad's father?' Nevyn said. 'Is his name Devaberiel, and he's a bard of the Westfolk?'

'He is. Fancy you knowing that!'

'Well, actually, I rode here to meet up with him. He's a friend of a friend of mine. We were going to ride west together.'

'I see.' The tears were back in her voice. 'That means he'll be here soon, doesn't it? Dev, I mean.'

'Well, it does, truly.'

The silence hung between them, awkward and painful. Evan picked up her mood and whimpered, holding out his arms. When she picked him up, he buried his head in her shoulder.

'Morri,' he said. 'My love you.'

'I love you too.' She nearly wept, then forced out her twisted smile. 'Well, we'd best be getting home. Your Da should be riding in ever so soon, and your Mam will want to know that.'

With the child clutched tight in her arms, Morwen hurried off, head held high.

'That's a pity,' Gwairyc said.

'It is, truly,' Nevyn said. 'Poor lass! The child's probably the light of her life.'

'That too, I suppose. I meant the witchmark.'

Nevyn didn't bother to answer. His mind was racing with plans, to return to Drwloc as soon as possible and win Morwen's confidence. *The dweomer will provide plenty of light for her life*, he thought, *if I can only make her see it*. As Morwen passed by, some of the market people turned away. Others frankly stared. She ignored them all, doubtless from long practice, but a gaggle of boys, farm lads judging by their much-mended clothes and dirty faces, proved harder to ignore. The four of them followed her, taunting and laughing.

'Here, ratface!' one yelled out. 'Witch lass! Too proud for a word with us, are you?'

When she walked a little faster, they ran after and surrounded her. The two largest lads planted themselves firmly in her path.

'That's enough!' Gwairyc muttered.

Before Nevyn could say a word, Gwairyc took off running straight for the lads. He grabbed one from behind by the shirt, swung him round, and punched him so hard that blood poured from the lad's nose. With a yelp the lad sank to the ground. One of the others broke and ran at that, but two remained game – at least until Gwairyc hit one back-handed and split his lip. With a shriek the coward fell to his knees. Gwairyc had saved the largest lad for last. Him he grabbed by the shirt and punched him in the stomach. The lad sank to the ground and vomited cheap ale all down his front. By the time Nevyn trotted up, the fight, such as it was, had finished.

'All right, you dogs!' Gwairyc snarled. 'Now you're a fair bit uglier than this poor lass is. Get out of my sight!'

The two who could still walk grabbed the vomit-covered lad by the arms and hauled him up and away. Their more cowardly but wiser friend was hovering nearby. With his help they broke into a shambling trot and disappeared in the crowd. It had all happened so fast that little Evan seemed barely troubled. He did pop his thumb in his mouth, then twisted in his nursemaid's arms to watch her assailants run away. Morwen herself was staring wide-eyed at Gwairyc.

'My thanks,' Morwen said in her thick, moist voice. 'But you needn't have troubled yourself. I'm used to this sort of thing.'

'Mayhap so,' Gwairyc said. 'But it griped my soul, somehow, seeing you mocked.'

'You're the first man I've ever met who felt that way.' Morwen seemed less pleased than thoughtful. 'I do appreciate it, good sir. Don't think that it didn't gladden my heart to see them bleed.'

Gwairyc laughed, briefly. After a nod in Nevyn's direction, Morwen turned and walked off, carrying Evan. This time, no one bothered her.

'Very good,' Nevyn said. 'I'm glad to see you have a bit of pity for someone beneath you in rank.'

Gwairyc shrugged, then began examining his bruised knuckles. Nevyn merely waited. At last Gwairyc looked up and spoke. 'I'm not sure I'd call it pity,' he said. 'Everyone says that a harelip means a person's been cursed by the gods.'

'Everyone?' Nevyn raised an eyebrow. 'And cursed in the womb, before the poor baby even sees the light of the sun?'

'It happens in the womb?'

'It does.'

'Well, then, that's a bit different, isn't it?' Gwairyc turned to look off in the direction that Morwen had taken. 'Seeing her mobbed like that, it just somehow griped my soul.'

'Unfair odds, if naught else.'

'That's it, truly.' Gwairyc turned to him and smiled. 'That's what touched my heart, then, the unfair odds.'

Nevyn was profoundly disappointed. He'd hoped that Gwairyc was feeling some compassion at last.

That evening, after a long afternoon selling herbs and sundries, Nevyn learned a great deal more about Morwen and Evan from the innkeep's wife. After a dinner of boiled beef and bread, Wffyn went off to bed. As mere apprentices, Tirro and Gwairyc would sleep on the straw-strewn floor. They spread their blankets out in the curve of the wall at a good distance from one another, then lay down and were soon snoring. The innwife dipped Nevyn a tankard of dark ale, then took a cupful for herself and sat down opposite him at table. She was a thin-lipped, narrow-eyed, skinny woman, wearing a greasy pair of green dresses. A little woad-blue scarf, stained with sweat, bunched around her wattled neck.

'Well, since you asked about Morwen's sister, good sir,' she began, 'it was ever so great a scandal, but they always say that great beauty is better than a dowry any day, and they're right enough when it comes to Varynna – that's Morwen's sister, Varynna. As beautiful as the moon in the summer sky, or so the lads all call her. Well!' She paused for a sip of ale, then dropped her voice to a conspiratorial whisper. 'And that Westfolk man of hers could see it as easy as anyone. So there she is, big with child, and her not married, so oh, she's had her comeuppance, all right!'

'Comeuppance for what?' Nevyn said.

'The airs she gave herself, good sir, ever so high and mighty she was until her belly started to swell. Now, there are some as say that Varynna was but following in her mother's footsteps, like, because Varynna doesn't look much like her sister and brother, if you take my meaning.' She paused for a wink. 'And that name! Not a usual sort of name, is it?'

'It's not, truly.' Nevyn managed a polite smile.

'A bit of the Westfolk, eh? So, anyway, Varynna did nurse the little lad, but for everything else, she handed him over to her sister, and I doubt if she's touched the lad since he was weaned. Goes to show how wretched a mother she is, giving her lad to a witch lass to raise!'

'Now here, Morwen seems to be taking good care of the lad.'

'Oh, I suppose she's fond of him. She'll never have a child of her own.' She paused for a ladylike sneer at the very thought. 'Well, as to Varynna, her brother was ever so angry, having a bastard in the family, but he could do naught about it thanks to the will.'

'Hold a moment. What will?'

'Tsk, you're so easy to talk to, I keep forgetting you're not from around here, good herbman. Their father's will. You see, he died of a fever, so he knew he was going, like. So he called in the priest of Bel and a few other men of good standing to hear his will. The farm went to the brother but only on the condition that he provided for his mother and the two sisters.'

'Ah, I see.'

'So brother Dwal was stuck, like, with the three of them. The mother died not long after her husband, though. She'd not been quite right since Morwen was born.' She tapped her forehead and winked. 'It was the shame of it, I suppose.'

'Now here, why blame her?'

'It must have been her doing, producing a deformed get like that. No doubt she stepped over a crack or killed a hare or suchlike when she was carrying the child. That's the way these things always happen.'

'Not truly. It's much more likely to be the effect of malefic lunar influences on the four humours, you see, early in the pregnancy. The moist humour is particularly susceptible.'

'It is? Well, fancy that!' She looked utterly unconvinced. 'But, truly, we were speaking of our haughty little Varynna. So anyway, this spring all the old gossips had a fair bit more to wag their tongues about. A merchant and his son came in, all the way from Abernaudd, they were, and come to look for Westfolk horses. And the son was fair taken with Varynna, turned quite daft he was. But the father, well now, he had more of a head on his shoulders, and he wasn't too pleased to find that his son's new ladylove had a bastard. Back and forth they went about it, yelling and pounding on the table right here in my inn, and finally the old man relented. As long as the bastard never darkens my door, says he, you can marry her and take her away.'

'Ah, I see,' Nevyn said. 'And now Evan's father is coming to collect the little lad.'

'Just that.' The innkeep's wife finished her cup of ale in one long swallow. 'And Dwal's fair pleased to be rid of both of them, I tell you. He's planning on finding a wife himself now.'

'Poor little Morri! Losing the lad seems to be aching her heart, and badly.'

'I suppose it is.' She shrugged the issue away. 'Her nose-in-the-air sister wants the child far away from her, as far as he can get, and truly, the Westfolk live on the edge of nowhere, and so that's that.'

Late that evening, after the innwife had gone to bed, Nevyn stayed by the glowing coals of the dying fire and considered Morwen's strange situation. The unusual harelip was a clear example of repercussion, as the dweomerfolk call it, where some mark or wound from a particularly violent death carries over to the victim's next life. The victim's flood of ancient emotion marks the budding etheric double of the child in the womb, which in turn influences the physical body. Yet since such repercussions rarely last more than a single lifetime, Morwen's scarred lip indicated that this incarnation was her first since Branoic's horrible death all those years past.

And she's so scrawny, Nevyn thought. No doubt she'd had a difficult time eating as a baby and a small child. Most children with harelips did. Once she'd grown older, most likely her kinsfolk had begrudged her food. Nevyn realized that he wouldn't need some complicated scheme to take Morwen away from her family. Most likely her brother would be glad to see her go if Nevyn could convince her to leave.

On the morrow Nevyn left his stock of medicinals in Wffyn's care and went with Gwairyc to Morwen's brother's farm, which lay not far beyond the town wall. It was a prosperous-looking place, three round houses joined together in a cluster, all of them white-washed and roofed in new thatch. They sat on a square of green grass, protected by an earthen wall from the cows and horses grazing in a large pasture out back. Beyond the pasture lay wheat fields.

By the front door Morwen was sitting on a little bench in the sun while she watched Evan playing with a leather ball. When Nevyn hailed her, she got up and walked over to the gate. Two big black and tan hounds accompanied her, tails wagging.

'Good morrow, good sirs,' she said in her moist lisp. 'What brings you to me?'

'I was wondering if you'd seen any sign of Devaberiel yet,' Nevyn said. 'He might arrive today, you see.'

'I've not.' She looked away, fighting tears for a long few moments. 'Ah well,' she said at last, 'I'd invite you in to wait, but my brother takes it ill when I have guests. He's always afraid I might offer them a bit of his ale or bread.'

'Ye gods,' Gwairyc said. 'From the look of your farm there's no call for him to be so miserly.'

'There's not, and he's not, except when it comes to me.'

'I see.' Nevyn had long since got out of the habit of making small talk, but now he badly wanted to linger. 'Do you have many guests?'

'Me?' Morwen paused for a short bark of a laugh. 'Hardly, good sir.'

'What? No friends or suchlike?'

'There was only one lass in our entire village who ever dared befriend a maimed creature like me, and she –' Morwen paused for a quick intake of breath that might have been a sigh or a choked back sob. 'She died but two years ago. Lanmara, her name was.'

Nevyn felt the brush of an omen's wing across his mind. Might this Lanmara have been someone he would have recognized? 'That's very sad,' he said aloud.

Morwen nodded. She might have told him more, but the front door swung open, and a young woman stepped out. *Westfolk blood, indeed,* Nevyn thought. *The innwife was right enough about that.* Tall, slender, with moonbeam pale hair that matched little Evan's, she walked with such innate grace that she might have been floating over the grass. But she possessed one trait that he'd only seen once among the Westfolk: an utter indifference to her child. When Evan came running, carrying his ball, she gave him a look of such contempt that he stopped and took a step back.

'Don't shove that nasty thing at me.' Varynna pointed to the ball. 'It's dirty.'

Morwen hurried over to claim Evan and the ball both. Nevyn took the opportunity to reach over the gate, unlatch it, and let himself and Gwairyc into the garth. Varynna deigned to glance their way.

'Good morrow,' Nevyn said. 'I just stopped by to tell you that Devaberiel's on his way here. He might arrive this very day.'

'Then my thanks for the news. I'll be glad to see the last of him.' Varynna left it unclear as to whether she meant the bard or his son – perhaps both, Nevyn supposed.

Morwen caught her breath and raised a quick hand to wipe the tears from her eyes.

'Oh, will you stop snivelling?' Varynna said. 'It's not like he's really your child.'

'Then he's nobody's child,' Morwen said. 'Because you're not a fit mother for a pig, much less a little lad.'

'You!' Varynna raised a hand as if she'd slap her sister, then hesitated, doubtless because Nevyn and Gwairyc were watching. 'You malformed get! It's no wonder the gods cursed you.'

In a rustle of dresses, her head held high, Varynna swept into the house and slammed the door behind her.

'Your sister needs a good spanking,' Gwairyc remarked. 'Or mayhap two.'

'I only wish I could see it, good sir. Or do it myself. With a horsewhip.' She turned a little away and rolled the ball across the grass. With a giggle Evan went toddling after it.

'And what will you do,' Nevyn said, 'once Evan's gone with his father?'

'I don't know.' Morwen's face turned slack with grief. 'My brother can't turn me out, but I'm half-minded to go to the Temple of the Moon. The holy ladies told me I'd be welcome should I wish to join them. It's not a bad life.'

'Well, it's not, truly, but –'

'I've been studying the lore,' Morwen went on as if she hadn't heard him. 'It's an odd thing, but it seems to come to me naturally, like.'

'Well, don't be too hasty,' Nevyn said. 'Let me think about this. There might be somewhat I can do to make things a bit better for you.'

'Huh! Unless your herbs can grow me a new face, good sir, I don't know what that could be.'

'I'll think on it.' Nevyn smiled at her, then glanced at Gwairyc. 'Well, we might as well wait back in town and spare our proud Varynna the sight of us.'

As they were walking along the dirt road back to town, Gwairyc seemed preoccupied. Finally he gave one of his dismissive shrugs and came out with it. 'A question for you, my lord,' Gwairyc said. 'The land out here's not as rich as that around Dun Deverry, is it?'

'The soil's rocky in places, truly. I'm surprised you'd notice that.'

'And isn't half the fighting in the kingdom to see who'll have the best land? Between the great clans, I mean.'

'True spoken.'

'But anyway, I was just remembering that pissing brat with the rotten tooth and his stinking family. Why is Morwen's farm so wealthy-looking and theirs so poor?'

'Myrn and Ligga, you mean? It's not the farm that's poor. It's them. The reason? The closer you get to Dun Deverry, the more the noble-born take in taxes. Myrn and Ligga have the misfortune to live close to court.'

Gwairyc turned to look at him in open-mouthed amazement. 'Misfortune?' he said at last. 'It's an honour to be close to the king's own city.'

Nevyn felt like grabbing him by the shoulders and shaking him. Instead, he said, 'Not for them. Their local lord takes most of their crop, and they rarely have enough left to sell for things like cloth and furniture. If they can't make it themselves, they don't have it.'

'Well, but don't Morwen's kin pay their lord taxes?'

'Of course, but here in Pyrdon we're close to the border. The lords know they need the loyalty of their folk. And beside, the lords here only go to court once a year, and not even that for some of them. They don't need to cut a fine figure there, so they're not as greedy as the courtiers.'

'Greedy?' Gwairyc blinked several times, as if he were trying to see something that lay beyond his vision. 'If you're going to stay at court you have to dress well, and entertain, and the like. The noble-born don't have any choice about that.'

'Um, well, no doubt they think they have no choice,' Nevyn said. 'Ah, here we are, back in town! Let's go to the tavern room. I need a tankard of our innkeep's darkest ale.'

With the market fair over, Nevyn had no customers that afternoon. He sat with Wffyn in the tavern, deserted except for them, their two apprentices, and the innkeep's wife. Some flies circling round and round in the middle of the room provided the only distraction.

'Uh, Gwairyc?' Tirro said. 'I was wondering if, well, if you'd like to dice for straws. It would be somewhat to do.'

Gwairyc considered for a long moment, while Tirro waited, his shoulders so tense he was nearly crouching on the bench.

'Oh, why not?' Gwairyc said at last. 'Here, let's move to one of those empty tables.'

Tirro smiled so broadly that he might have been given some expensive gift. 'Splendid idea! Here, let me stand you a tankard. Please? I got my wages yesterday.'

'Very well. My thanks.'

Nevyn watched while they set up their game and took their tankards, then leaned forward to speak softly to Wffyn. 'He's a sad creature, your apprentice. Desperate for a little friendly conversation.'

'He is that,' Wffyn murmured, 'but I still wouldn't trust him with anything I valued.' He raised his voice to a normal level. 'I wonder what he'll think of the Westfolk? We'll be there a fair bit of time, a good fortnight I was thinking.'

'That long?'

'That long. You see, I've got a grand scheme in mind.' Wffyn smiled, and his eyes sparkled. 'The Westfolk never sell us anything but geldings. That way we can't breed their golden horses for ourselves. But I've brought some very special goods along. I'm hoping to find an opening, like, to persuade someone to part with a mare or two. If I can, then maybe next trip I can go to a different part of the trading zone and get a golden stud. No more of these long tedious trips, then!'

'Indeed. Do you think you have a chance?'

'I do. It's all a question of finding the right goods to trade, the right temptation, if you will. The Westfolk are an odd-looking lot, but they're human enough. Greed, my dear herbman – it's a merchant's true friend. Find the right bait, and the fish will swarm to the hook. I could be properly rich, I could.'

'True spoken.' Nevyn bit back his own temptation to point out that greed seemed to have become Wffyn's mistress rather than a mere friend.

'Now,' Wffyn continued, 'when shall we leave? I was thinking on the morrow, assuming that Devaberiel's got himself here by then.'

'You never know with the Westfolk, truly,' Nevyn said with a sigh. 'They come and go as they please and when they please and not a moment before.'

Wffyn nodded sadly. At their table Tirro and Gwairyc were still gaming, throwing the dice as grimly as if the fate of kingdoms depended upon their luck. Across the broad round room, the innkeep's wife was swabbing out tankards with an old rag and rinsing them in a wooden bucket of well water. A few of the more industrious flies circled around her. Nevyn got up and strolled over to hand her his empty tankard.

'I happened to speak with Morwen,' he remarked, 'when we went out to warn Varynna that her child's father was on his way.'

'I'll bet you got a scant welcome from both of them.' The innkeep's wife tossed her grey and fraying rag into the bucket.

'From Varynna, certainly, but I had a bit of a chat with Morwen. She mentioned a friend of hers, Lanmara. That's an unusual sort of name.'

'She wasn't your usual sort of lass.' The woman frowned in thought. 'Now, don't take me wrong, good sirs. Lanni was a decent lass, the blacksmith's youngest, and very well brought up. The whole village was shocked that she'd befriend a witchmarked lass. Some people even said truly nasty things, that mayhap the two lasses were entirely too close and familiar with each other, if you take my meaning like, but I never believed that.'

'Oh? Why not?'

'Because Lanmara was too well brought up, that's why, to even think of such! Though she did say some truly odd things, now and again, and I swear she had the second Sight.'

'Truly? Why?'

'She and Morri had a game they played when they were little lasses, all about the Wildfolk. They were pretending, like, saying they'd seen this one or that one, or pretending they were talking to some of them.'

'Well, here,' Nevyn said. 'Most children do like a good tale about the Wildfolk.'

'True spoken, good sir, but these two, well, they never grew out of it. Or at least, Lanmara never did. She was old enough to marry and still babbling about them.' The innwife glanced around her, then dropped her voice to a conspiratorial murmur. 'And I swear, she saw somewhat, sure enough. You'd see her eyes moving, like, but there'd be naught there. A bit touched, she was.' She tapped her forehead with one finger and winked. 'But then she foresaw her own death. It gave us all a fair turn, that.'

'No doubt! What happened?'

'She caught a fever a few winters back, and it was a nasty thing that settled in her chest. Coughing up blood she was, poor lass! With the spring it went away, but she told her mam plain as plain that it would return with the winter, and that she'd die. Her mam told her she was just ill and imagining things, but by the Goddess herself, come the first snow, the fever comes with it, and Lanmara was dead in four nights.'

'The poor lass!'

'Truly. It's a pity you weren't here with your herbs.'

A pity in more ways than one, Nevyn thought. *Lilli, mayhap?* She'd died of a consumption of the lungs, after all. Since that particular trouble had an etheric component, it might well have followed her from life to life. He had no way of knowing for certain, but the omen he'd felt earlier returned with a touch of ice along his spine. He went back to Wffyn, who was half-asleep at the table.

'I'm just going to take my mule to the blacksmith,' Nevyn said. 'His shoes aren't as new as they might be, and I don't want to take any chances.'

The blacksmith, a short but heavily muscled fellow, had no other customers that afternoon. After he trimmed up the mule's hooves and fitted him with new shoes, Nevyn bartered him various preparations of herbs in lard to treat skin burns and paid the rest in coin. For a few moments they stood chatting while Nevyn considered an opening for the questions he wanted to ask. Fortunately, the blacksmith's young son came out to the forge to see what his father was doing.

'You've got a healthy-looking lad there,' Nevyn said.

'I do, and I thank the gods for it,' the smith said. 'We've got an older daughter, too, and she seems to be a strong lass, so again, may the gods be praised.'

'I don't mean to pry, but it sounds like you've had illness in your family before.'

'Terrible illness, good sir. My poor Lanni!' He shook his head with a sigh. 'Our first-born, but she died of a consumption of the lungs, and her just old enough to marry.'

'Truly, that saddens my heart!'

'Her mother's not got over it yet. It was just two winters ago, you see.'

'Recently, then. Was there a fair bit of fever in the town?'

'There wasn't. It came on her sudden-like.' He paused to frown, and his voice tightened with old anger. 'I'll wager that wretched witch lass had somewhat to do with it, too. A friend of my daughter's, good sir, if you can call a deformed get like her a friend. I told our Lanni to stop seeing her a hundred times if I told her once, but here she was sneaking round to see her on the sly!'

'Did this lass have the consumption, too?'

'She didn't. She's healthy to this day, which is why I'm sure as sure she cursed Lanni somehow. I wanted to go to our local lord and have the ugly little creature dealt with, but my wife, she talked me out of it. She was afraid the witch would curse us, too.' He spat onto the ground. 'Women!'

Naught more to learn here, Nevyn decided. He bade the smith farewell and led his mule away.

The Westfolk arrived just as the innkeep was serving yet another meal of boiled meat and stale bread. Nevyn, Wffyn, and their two apprentices were eating at a table near the hearth when three men strode into the tavern room. Gwairyc looked up from his plate, glanced at the men, and stared, his table dagger forgotten in his hand. They were tall and slender, as most of the Westfolk men seemed to be, all blond as well, and they moved with an easy grace even though they carried bedrolls and travellers' bundles. One of them had a longbow slung across his back and a quiver of arrows at one hip; another carried an elaborate leather case that could only contain a small harp.

'That must be our bard,' Nevyn said.

The putative bard was looking around the crowded tavern room. Finally he spoke to the innkeep, who pointed at Nevyn. The bard smiled and led his two companions over to their table. As they came close, Nevyn heard Gwairyc swear under his breath, and Tirro gasp in surprise. The Westfolk looked much like ordinary men, except for their ears, as long and delicately curled as a flower petal emerging from a bud, and their deep-set eyes, marked by vertical pupils like a cat's. A gaggle of gnomes materialized to dance around them, but those, of course, no one at the table but Nevyn saw.

'Good morrow,' Nevyn said. 'Are you Devaberiel?'

'I am.' The bard smiled pleasantly. 'And this is Jennantar and Yannadariel. Here, let us pile these things up somewhere, and then we'll join you at table.' He glanced at Wffyn. 'And a good eve to you, too, good merchant. There'll be an eager crowd waiting for you at the trading ground.'

'I'm glad to hear it,' Wffyn said. 'I've got many a fine thing to show you all.'

With a bard in the tavern room, the evening went by fast and pleasantly. He may have been tired from his long ride, but Devaberiel, like any true bard, couldn't pass up a willing audience. He knew songs in Deverrian as well as in the Westfolk's own language, and he'd barely finished the first one before the tavern room began to fill up. The news and the music had spread through the village. When the room could hold no more, townsfolk stood outside the windows and at the doors, so quietly that it seemed they barely breathed. No one moved until at last Devaberiel begged fatigue and began to loosen his harp strings.

In a swirl of talk and laughter, the crowd began to clear out. As Devaberiel made his way back to Nevyn's table, the villagers pressed coins into his hands, which he took with murmurs of thanks and good-natured smiles. The innkeep brought a tankard of dark ale to the table and waved aside a proffered coin.

'Not needed,' the innkeep said. 'Ah, it's been a long time since we've heard you sing!'

Devaberiel smiled pleasantly but said nothing. This was the last time he'd sing here, Nevyn supposed, without his son to draw him. Some of the villagers began calling for ale, and the innkeep bustled away. Devaberiel took a good long swallow from his tankard, then wiped his mouth on the back of his hand.

'So, good Nevyn,' Devaberiel said. 'Our wise one is looking forward to seeing you again.'

'And I feel the same about him,' Nevyn said. 'It's a bit of good luck that we could travel together.'

'It is at that. You know, Aderyn told me that he travelled all over with you when he was but a little lad. Would it be an imposition to ask your help after I've claimed my son?' Dev's smile faded. 'The poor lad! I don't have the slightest notion of how to care for him, either on this journey or at all.'

Nevyn suddenly saw the obvious.

'Well, you know, he has a nursemaid already.' Nevyn kept his voice casual by force of will. 'The thought of losing him has been aching her heart.'

'Of course! Poor little Morri! Do you think she might be willing to come with him?'

'I certainly can't see why she'd want to stay on her brother's farm.'

'Now that's most assuredly true spoken! It'll be a good thing for both her and Evan if she comes along, then.' Devaberiel stifled a yawn. 'If you'll excuse me, good sir, I've got to get some sleep – and strength, just in case my son's mother turns nasty on the morrow.'

Early on the morrow morning, Wffyn began to organize his caravan for departure. Devaberiel's two friends would leave with the merchant, while Nevyn, the bard himself, and Gwairyc rode out to the farm to collect little Evan. They would catch up to the caravan on the road, since men on horseback could travel faster than a line of burdened mules led by muleteers on foot.

The news of the bard's arrival had apparently reached the farm ahead of them. When they dismounted at the gate, they saw Morwen and Evan waiting for them on the little wooden bench. Evan was wearing a clean, unpatched pair of grey brigga and an embroidered shirt – his best clothes, no doubt, for the occasion. When Gwairyc reached over the gate to open it, Morwen stood up. She took Evan's hand in one of hers, and in the other picked up a small sack that seemed to be full of clothing. As they strolled over Nevyn could see that her eyes were red and puffy, though she put on a brave smile. At the sight of the horses and the tall strangers, Evan let out a wail. He stopped walking and began pulling on her hand as if to drag her back.

'Now, come along, Evan,' Morri said. 'You remember your da, don't you?'

'Don't.' Evan pulled his hand free and dodged behind her skirts.

Devaberiel motioned to the others to stay back, then knelt on one knee near the boy. 'You've not seen me in a while,' he said softly. 'But I'm your father, lad. You're going to come home with me today.'

Evan threw his arms around Morwen's legs and clutched. When Devaberiel held out his hand, Evan shook his head in a vigorous no.

'Don't you want to come visit your brother and sister?' Dev said. 'We're going to ride on the pretty horses. We'll go a long way.'

Evan stared at him for a moment, glanced at the horses, then back to him – and burst into tears. Apparently he'd understood enough to know he disliked what he'd heard.

'My apologies,' Morwen stammered. 'You'll be thinking I did a bad enough job at raising him.'

'What?' Devaberiel got up, then turned to her. 'Not at all. I want to hire you as his nursemaid, in fact. He'll need someone better than me to care for him. Would your kins-folk let you come with us?'

Morwen stared at him for a long moment, then began to weep herself, but out of relief, apparently, because she was also smiling.

'There, child.' Nevyn stepped forward. 'I told you I might think of somewhat to make things better, didn't I?' He fumbled in his brigga pocket and found a reasonably clean rag to offer her.

Her tears stopped. She handed Nevyn the little sack she'd been carrying, then took the rag and wiped her face. Before she spoke again, she stooped and picked Evan up. The bewildered child stopped weeping, but he threw one arm around her neck and clung to her while she wiped his nose.

'Why should I care what my brother thinks?' Morwen said at last. 'Doubtless he'll be glad to be rid of the burden of feeding me. Will you really let me come with him?'

'Let you?' Devaberiel paused for a brief laugh. 'It would gladden my heart if you'd come along. Now, in all honesty, I have to tell you that it won't be an easy ride for you, and life out on the grass is going to strike you as passing strange, but if you hate it or suchlike, Nevyn here can bring you back when he leaves us.'

Morwen smiled, and even though her split lip curled round its scar as always, she looked as triumphant as a warrior. 'I'd like naught better,' she lisped. 'And I'd ride to the Hells for my baby if I had to.'

'Well and good, then.' Devaberiel laid a gentle hand on

his son's back. 'We're going home. Your Morri's going to come with us. You won't have to leave her here.'

Evan looked only at Morwen.

'It's true,' she said. 'I'm coming with you. We'll have a nice ride with your da and his friends. Now, I'm going to pack up my things. Come along. You can watch.'

'I suppose I'd best tell your sister,' Devaberiel said.

'Why? She'll not care, and no more will my brother. They won't have their ugly little witch lass spoiling Varynna's fancy wedding this way. Nevyn?' Morwen turned to him. 'My thanks. My humble thanks, indeed! I'll be forever grateful for this. I lacked the courage to ask to come with him, though truly, I was wishing for it.'

'Well, then.' Nevyn smiled at her. 'It's all worked out quite nicely.'

Morwen picked Evan up and carried him towards the house. Once the door shut behind her, Gwairyc muttered a few choice curses under his breath.

'And what's that for?' Nevyn said.

'Her kin,' Gwairyc said. 'Particularly that sister. Cold as ice and twice as sharp, if you ask me. She reminds me entirely too much of a woman I used to know entirely too well.'

'I'm glad to hear it,' Devaberiel said. 'It means I'm not the only man here with poor taste in women. Misery loves company and all that.'

Not counting her bedding, everything Morwen called hers fitted into one cloth sack, but she decided that her kin owed her a few things towards her new life since she'd cost them so little in the old one. With Evan clinging to her skirts she went through the house and took a good kitchen knife and a steel to sharpen it, a table dagger, a pair of her brother's old brigga for riding, and a winter cloak. She rummaged through the cook house as well and filled another sack with food for the journey.

Evan still seemed bewildered, especially when they went

back to the draughty little shed that had served as their bedchamber. Since she'd already handed his few possessions over to Nevyn, he wandered around as if he were looking for them. When she put the brigga on under her dress, he laughed at the sight.

'We're going riding,' she said, 'with your Da and his friends.'

He smiled and clapped. 'Horses,' he said. 'Pretty horses.'

'They are that,' Morwen said. 'Riding them will be much nicer than riding our old mule.'

'Mama coming with us?'

'She's not. Does that sadden your heart?'

He merely shrugged as if he'd not quite understood the question.

Once Morwen was dressed for the journey, she rolled up her blankets and tied them neatly at both ends with scraps of cloth, then slung them over one shoulder. She picked up her two sacks of belongings, one in each hand, and shooed Evan ahead of her. Together they marched out into the sunshine. Devaberiel and Nevyn had already mounted their horses, but the herbman's apprentice stood waiting. He took her sacks and bedroll.

'I'll tie these on behind my saddle,' he said. 'We'll put them on a mule when we catch up with the caravan.'

'My thanks,' Morwen said. 'If Evan rides with his da, I can walk.'

'No need for that. You can't weigh more than a hundred-weight, lass, and my master's a thin stick of a man himself. His horse can carry the pair of you.'

Nevyn kicked one foot free of its stirrup to allow her to mount. With Gwairyc's help she settled herself behind him on the horse.

'You can hang on to me, if need be,' Nevyn said. 'I won't mind.'

'My thanks,' Morwen said. 'Here, I was just wondering how I should say your name. Should I call you sir or my lord?'

'What? Neither! Whatever for?' Nevyn paused for a laugh. 'I'm naught but an old herbman.'

'You may be that, but you've done me the biggest favour of my life.'

'Huh. Only because your life's been short up for favours. Don't trouble your heart about it.'

'I won't, then. But you'll have my gratitude forever.'

As they started off, Nevyn took the lead. Morwen kept looking back to make sure that Evan was behaving himself. Every time she did, he would smile and wave to her. Apparently the novelty of riding on such a beautiful horse had made him forget his earlier fears. His father occasionally sang to him, as well, odd little songs that he was probably making up as he went along. Morwen felt like singing herself. Not only did she still have Evan, but she was free of the farm and her wretched kinsfolk, free of the contempt of the town. The only thing she'd miss about either, she realized, was her regular ritual of putting flowers on Lanmara's grave. Still, at moments she was frightened, wondering if she'd jumped out of a tree only to land in a thorn bush, but during Devaberiel's visits he and his Westfolk friends had never once stared at her lip or so much as mentioned it. She could hope that the rest of their people would treat her the same way, even though she'd heard that every single one of them was beautiful. *After all*, she thought, *I'd be ugly anywhere, so it won't make any difference.*

Soon enough they caught up with the slow-moving caravan. Since the Westfolk had brought an extra horse with them, Morwen had her own mount, a sturdy dapple grey and easily the finest animal she'd ever ridden. When Evan began whining, she took him from his father.

'Here, now, you're tired, little one,' she said. 'You've not had your nap. Gwairyc, if you'll lead my horse, I can hold Evan while he sleeps for bit.'

'Done, then. Toss me your reins.'

Finding a way to settle Evan into her lap took some ingenuity, since she'd never tried to hold him on horseback before.

He fussed until he could rest his head on her shoulder, as he was used to doing when they were sitting on their bench with her back firmly against a wall. Eventually he got his chubby little legs around her waist, and she held him securely by wrapping her arms around his midsection. It only took a mile or so for her arms and back to start aching, but it never occurred to her to disturb him and insist he sit some other way. In her entire life only two persons had ever loved her, Lanmara and Evan, and he was now the only one she had left. Her comfort on that long day's ride meant next to nothing compared to his.

That night they made a camp on the edge of the wild forest that had formerly marked the boundary of Morwen's life. Devaberiel put together a shelter for her and the child by tying a long rope between two trees. He then draped extra blankets over it and weighted down the corners with rocks to form a triangular tent of sorts.

'It's a bit of privacy for you, anyway,' Dev said. 'Albeit not of the best.'

'It will do splendidly, my thanks,' Morwen said. 'I can get Evan to go to sleep much more easily if he feels set apart, like, from everyone else.'

After the evening meal, and after the men had drawn lots to see who would stand a watch to guard the mules and horses, everyone but Nevyn went to their blankets. Morwen lay down next to Evan until he fell asleep. She'd been planning on going straight to sleep herself, but her mind kept scurrying around the events of the day, gloating at one moment, bringing up fears the next. Through the open end of the shelter she could see Nevyn, sitting in a pool of light from a little campfire. She found the sight oddly reassuring. Finally she crawled out of the shelter and went to join the old man at the fire.

'Can't sleep?' Nevyn said. 'I would have thought you'd be exhausted after a day like today.'

'So did I.' She stopped herself just in time from adding a

'my lord'. 'But I'm used to hard work and the like. I used to have plenty of chores to do besides tending Evan, so I'd be up at dawn every day.'

'Ah, of course. The work on a farm's never done.'

'Just so.'

They shared a companionable silence, watching the fire, occasionally feeding it with twigs and small branches, while Morwen gathered her courage to ask Nevyn the question that always haunted her. *He seems truly wise,* she thought. *Mayhap he'll know.*

'Nevyn?' she said. 'Do you know why the gods cursed me? I mean, not so much why they cursed me as me, if you take my meaning, like, but why they curse people with the witch-mark.'

'They don't,' Nevyn said. 'That's naught but superstition, and a silly one at that.'

'But everyone says —'

'Huh! That "everyone" is very often wrong. Now, I don't pretend to understand exactly what causes a harelip, mind, but the gods have naught to do with it. Some of the learned physicians of Bardek attribute it to certain influences of the moon upon the baby in its mother's womb. Others think that too little food or too much ale might weaken the mother's humours and unbalance those of the womb, allowing the watery humours to take precedence over the earthy. Such a precedence might produce a split in solid flesh, just as a river cleaves the land. There are other theories, but those are the two that sound the best to me. The cause might even be a combination of both.'

In utter shock Morwen could only stare at him.

'Either way,' Nevyn went on, 'you're not in the least to blame, no matter what the old hags and gossips in your village told you.'

Morwen tried to speak, couldn't, and wondered if she'd ever speak again.

'It will take you a while to digest what I've told you,' Nevyn said with a smile. 'But do think about it.'

She nodded her agreement. Nevyn suddenly yawned and clasped a quick hand over his mouth to stifle it.

'Here, you're doubtless tired.' Morwen finally found her voice. 'And I'd best get some sleep myself.'

'Indeed. And we'll have plenty of time to talk about such matters during our journey.'

Morwen returned to the shelter and the sleeping Evan, but for a long time that night she lay awake. *You're not to blame.* Nevyn had spoken so calmly, so quietly, that she believed him beyond her simple wishing his words to be true. Her old pain had been like clutching the handle of an iron pan only to find it burning hot – in her shame at the gods' curse she'd been unable to either let go of it or to carry it. Now she felt as if she'd plunged that charred hand into cold water at last. *If only I could tell Lanni!* That regret was the only blemish on her new-found wondrous freedom. *If only Lanni were here to share it!*

In the morning, she woke to find most of the camp up before her. The thought woke with her: *it's no fault of mine.* It accompanied her, too, like a cheerful friend, while she fed Evan and got him ready to ride with his father again. Yet during the morning's journey, when she had plenty of time to herself for thinking, the good cheer faded away. She remembered another phrase of Nevyn's, 'old hags and gossips'. Little did he know just how horribly the women in question had treated her as a child, how they had refused to let their own children play with her, how they had taught those children to taunt and tease her.

And then at home her sister and brother teased her as well. Worse yet, they fell into the habit of hitting or pinching her, just casually, every time they passed by. She had taken it meekly, sure she'd deserved every sting and bruise because neither her mother nor father had intervened. And all along, it hadn't been her fault, nor her shame, nor her curse, not in the least. *If I could only go back,* she thought. *Just back for one day, oh, what I'd do to them!*

She imagined how her brother would look if she rose up after one of his insults and hit him in the head with an iron cooking pan – hit him hard, so his skull would crack and the blood run down. And dear Varynna – her beauty would vanish before the sting of a hot coal from the fire. Morwen could imagine it clearly, the skin blackening, the hiss of burning, the stench of charred flesh. As they healed, the scabs would crack and peel, leaving huge scars upon those rosy cheeks.

The village women deserved even nastier fates. She imagined their deaths in detail, by dismembering, drowning, scalding with boiling water. Too much detail – suddenly she saw her revenge fantasies so clearly that the pictures began to take on a life of their own. She could watch them unfold as if she were dreaming, and yet she was awake, aware of the horse under her, the hot sun on her back, Dev's voice as he sang to Evan. She watched with inner eyes as her dream-self rampaged through the village, stabbing, clawing, flailing around her with any weapon that came to hand. Blood flowed, flesh split and bruised, and always she saw more blood, bubbling from wounds.

'Oh stop!' She'd spoken aloud in a great sob of words. 'It's too horrible!'

The world around her snapped back into reality. Morwen felt herself trembling, and her face burning with shame, but when she glanced around, she realized that no one had heard her little outburst or noticed her dreamy condition. Best of all, no one could read her thoughts; no one else had seen her horrifying visions. *How could I? Just how could I? What am I, a fiend who just looks like a human being?*

Up at the head of his caravan, Wffyn yelled for a halt. She'd never heard a voice as welcome as his at that moment, calling her to human company.

'Let's have a meal, lads,' he bellowed. 'Time to rest the stock.'

Morwen nearly wept at the relief of knowing that she'd be free of her own thoughts for a while.

The caravan stopped in a long grassy meadow, dotted here and there with the dead stumps of cut timber, at the edge of the forest. The muleteers unloaded their stock to let them roll, then set them out to graze along with the riding horses, which the Westfolk men had tended.

'It'll be two days before they get fresh fodder again,' Nevyn told her. 'We'll rest here for some time before we push on into the forest.'

'Well and good, then,' Morwen said. 'Evan and I can chase his ball around for a bit. Maybe he'll sleep better this afternoon than he did last.'

'I had a thought about that. The Westfolk women use a sort of sling made from a long bit of cloth to hold their children when they ride. It saves the back, they say. I'll get a length of linen from Wffyn's trade goods for you. He owes me somewhat for tending one of his men after an accident. Jennantar says he'll help you rig it up.'

'My thanks! That truly would be a comfort.' All of a sudden Morwen felt tears rise in her throat. She turned sharply away.

'What's so wrong?' Nevyn said.

'Naught. This is just the first time in my life that anyone but my friend Lanni put some thought into helping me.' Morwen snivelled back the tears and tried to smile. 'It took me by surprise, like.'

Using the sling did indeed ease much of the strain on Morwen's back, because she no longer had to clutch Evan tightly to keep him from falling. He fussed about it at first, but once the caravan started down the well-shaded road through the forest, he drifted off to sleep. After Morwen's scant rest of the night before, she turned drowsy as well. It took an effort of will, but she was determined to keep any more ghastly blood-soaked daydreams at bay. Fortunately, once they'd ridden deep into the trees, a new surprise brought her wide awake.

Wildfolk popped into manifestation and thronged around the caravan. Sprites hovered in the air. Gnomes raced back and forth under the horses' legs or rode on the mule packs.

When they forded a shallow stream, undines rose up to splash water on the gnomes and giggle among themselves. Morwen hadn't seen so many Wildfolk since Lanmara's death, and for a moment, remembering how her beloved would have enjoyed the sight, she wept a few scattered tears of old grief, until she noticed how Devaberiel and his two friends reacted to this sudden swarm. Not only did they seem to be watching the Wildfolk's antic, but Devaberiel held out his hand to a sprite, who settled upon it just like a tame sparrow.

I won't have to hide it any more, she thought. *They see them, too.* She felt like throwing her head back and howling with delight, but the presence of the human men, who obviously saw nothing at all, kept her silent. All day the Wildfolk came and went, hovering around the Westfolk men. At night, when the caravan made its camp in a forest clearing, salamanders appeared to play among the flames in the Westfolk campfire. Evan had always been able to see the Wildfolk, and now he pointed them out to his father.

'Manders, Da,' he said.

'Salamanders,' Morwen corrected him. She glanced at Dev. 'They've always been his favourites. I realized that he'd started to crawl when he nearly went right into the fire after them.'

'Well, I'm glad you pulled him back in time,' Dev said, smiling. 'Here, Evan. I'll tell you a story about salamanders. You can lie down on my blankets right here to listen.'

Once Evan had fallen asleep with his father to watch over him, Morwen got up and moved away from the smoky fire. To a farm woman like her, a day spent riding was a day free of real work. Since she wanted to exhaust herself in the hopes of having a sleep free of violent fantasies, she decided to walk around the edge of the camp a few times.

Out behind the tethered mules and horses she saw someone moving through the trees – one of the muleteers, she assumed, but when she came closer, she saw a Westfolk woman. She was dressed just like the men, in leather leggings with high boots and a loose shirt belted at the waist, but she wore her thick honey-blonde hair in a single long braid down her back. In one hand she carried an unstrung bow, and at her hip hung a quiver of arrows. She smiled at Morwen and beckoned her over.

'Forgive me for sneaking around like a thief,' the woman spoke in a whisper. 'But I can't let the men see me here.'

'Indeed?' Morwen kept her voice low in return. 'Why not?'

'I'm looking for the man who stole my daughter. The child riding with you – he's a little lad, isn't he?'

'He is, truly. Devaberiel's his father.'

'Ah.' The woman nodded slowly. 'Well, then, he can't be my daughter, can he now? My thanks!'

She turned, took one step, and vanished like a puff of smoke in the wind. Morwen felt the hair rising along her suddenly cold arms and the back of her neck. She ran all the way back to the light of the fire.

The bard was lying asleep next to Evan. Morwen considered waking him to tell him about the strange woman, but her life had taught her that no one but Lanmara had ever cared about what she may have seen or done. Besides, her stories about the Wildfolk had got her beaten for a liar too many times as a child to risk telling a peculiar story now that she'd finally found people who treated her decently. Evan looked so comfortable that she decided to try leaving him with his father. She lay down on her own blankets and fell asleep straightaway, but she woke at intervals, listening for Evan. Somewhere in the middle of the night she heard him just starting to cry. As soon she got up and fetched him, he quieted right down.

Much to her great relief, she had no dreams of maiming and killing all night long. In the morning when she woke, she remembered the woman, but the more she thought about the experience, the more it seemed to her that she must have dreamt it. No one but Lanmara had ever cared about her dreams. She put the incident out of her mind and set about feeding Evan his breakfast.

*   *   *

Gwairyc found himself painfully confused by the Westfolk. At first they had seemed utterly alien, but as the caravan made its slow way west, he began to accept them. As they talked at the evening campfire or helped him tend the horses and Nevyn's mule, he would begin thinking of them as ordinary enough men, merely with some odd details, like their ears. Yet just when he'd decided he'd got used to them, they'd come out with some idea that made them seem stranger than before.

For instance, there was Devaberiel's attitude to his son. Although he left the actual work to Morwen, such as feeding Evan and cleaning him up afterward, Devaberiel doted on the boy. He told him little stories, sang him little songs, and began teaching him the Westfolk language with every evidence of enjoying the process enormously. Gwairyc had never seen a man treat his son that way before. In fact, he'd never paid much attention to children at all. In his mind they fell under the rubric of women's work and thus no business of his, either to like or dislike them.

'Dev seems cursed glad to have an heir,' Gwairyc remarked to Jennantar one evening.

'Heir?' Jennantar said. 'Not truly. Not as you Deverry folk think of heirs, anyway.'

'Well, a man needs someone to leave his property to.'

Jennantar laughed, but pleasantly. 'You'll understand more once we get out on the grass,' he said. 'None of us have property, exactly, not as you'd think of it.'

Gwairyc found he had no comment to make on such a bizarre idea, so he merely smiled.

Gwairyc got his biggest surprise, however, when they reached the trading grounds. He'd been expecting a town of sorts with a seasonal market, just as he'd seen so many times on their journey west, that is, a rural place, and certainly isolated, but a town nonetheless. Instead, they rode free of the forest one sunny day to see a green sea stretching out ahead of them – a sea of grass, rippling with wind-blown waves, and dotted at some distance with a cluster of white tents like ships.

'Ah, there they are!' Nevyn rose in his stirrups and pointed at the tents. 'There's quite a crowd waiting for our merchant.'

'That's it?' Gwairyc said. 'That's the Westfolk town?'

'They don't have any towns.' Nevyn sat back down into his saddle. 'They don't farm, either, you see. They wander with the seasons out here with their herds of horses and flocks of sheep. They trade wool, lambs, deerskins and the like to border farmers for some of the things they can't make themselves, but their real wealth is the horses. Look at Wffyn, come hundreds of miles to acquire a few.'

Gwairyc shook his head in amazement. 'Wandering around – that's the strangest life I've ever heard of,' he said at length. 'What about their king? Does he go with them?'

'He does, but truly, he's not much of a king by our standards.' Nevyn thought for a moment. 'To tell you the truth, I've never even heard his name. I do remember being told they have one, though.'

'Ye gods, what a cursed lot of savages!' Gwairyc shook his head again. 'No wonder I've never heard of them before.'

Devaberiel and his friends rode straight for the tents, but Wffyn halted his caravan at what looked to be a regular camp site for traders. Beside a stream where willows and tangles of hazel wands offered shade and some shelter from the wind, someone had built three stone firepits, about twenty feet apart and each large enough to roast an entire sheep, assuming of course that the cook had enough fuel to do so. Gwairyc had noticed Wffyn's men cutting up extra deadfall wood during their forest camps, and now he understood why they'd carried it with them. *Naught but grass out there*, he thought, and he shivered with a toss of his head.

Some of the muleteers began unloading the mules while others rummaged through the packs and brought out tether ropes and pegs. Wffyn wandered around, shouting orders, then stood talking to Nevyn. Gwairyc was waiting for Nevyn to tell him where totake their horses and mule when he noticed Morwen, standing at the edge of the confusion and staring out to the west. She was holding Evan's hand, and the child was leaning against her as he too looked out onto this alien grassy sea. Gwairyc paused for a word with her.

'How come you're still here?' he asked. 'I thought you'd be over at the Westfolk tents.'

'Dev wanted to tell his people that I was coming first,' Morwen said. 'Nevyn told me he'd take Evan and me over in a little while.'

'I see.' Gwairyc gestured at the view. 'It's more than a little strange, isn't it?'

'It is,' Morwen said. 'I heard Dev and his friends talk about the grass, when they came to our village, I mean, but I never knew how vast it is! It chills my heart, somehow.'

'You can always ride back with us when we leave here.'

'My thanks, but ride back to what? I'd have to leave Evan, and I'd be twice cursed before I'd go back to my wretched brother. It would have to be the Temple of the Moon, and truly, I don't know if I could bear being shut away like that for my whole life.'

'Well, mayhap you'll get used to the life out here.'

'So I can hope.' She pushed out a brave little smile. 'And no doubt I can.'

Back at the encampment, Wffyn's men were busily raising tents and hauling the canvas mule-packs into them. Nevyn owned a tent, too, a shabby affair of much-mended canvas and ill-assorted sticks. It would protect their trove of herbs and other medicinals if it rained, but it wouldn't keep one man dry, much less two of them.

'You know, my lord,' Gwairyc said, 'we've done well this summer. Mayhap you could buy some new canvas if we go to a proper town when we leave here, one where we can find someone to lash a tent together, that is.'

'That's a good idea,' Nevyn said. 'Don't bother to set the old one up here. We'll be sheltering with my friend Aderyn in his tent among the Westfolk.'

'That gladdens my heart. I've slept wet many a time on

campaign, but I can't say I liked it. Should I tether our stock over with theirs, too?'

'Just that. You know, I'm pleased to hear you say "we" in that casual way. I've been wondering if one morning I'd look around and find you gone.'

'What? I promised the king I'd be at your beck, didn't I? And truly, riding around like this, it's not much worse than being with the army.'

'Not much, eh?' Nevyn smiled briefly.

'And you know –' Gwairyc paused, surprised at his own thoughts. 'In a way, my lord, you've become a friend of mine.'

'Truly? I never thought I'd hear you say that.'

'No more did I, when we first left Dun Deverry. You know, it doesn't pay to make friends in a warband. You tend to lose them sudden-like, if you take my meaning. And the other lords at court – huh. They might flatter you to your face, but they'd put a dagger in your back if they could. But truly, it's not a bad thing, having a friend.'

'Most assuredly it's not.' Nevyn's smile grew broader. 'After all, we rode all this way so I could visit one of mine.'

Gwairyc met this friend of Nevyn's not long after. Devaberiel returned on foot to collect Morwen and Evan. Leading their horses and mule, Gwairyc and Nevyn followed them over to the Westfolk camp. Waiting for them about halfway between the encampments were two men. One, a short, slender Deverry man, had deep set dark eyes, oddly large for his face, and grey hair that swept back from his temple in two peaks. He stood with his shoulders slightly hunched, allowing his arms to dangle at his sides. All in all, he reminded Gwairyc strongly of an owl. Nevyn tossed Gwairyc the reins of the horse he'd been leading and hurried to meet him.

'Aderyn!' he called out. 'Ye gods, it's good to see you.'

'And it's good to see you,' Aderyn answered, smiling. 'It's been too long.'

They turned and began walking towards the camp, talking

all the while so rapidly that Gwairyc had little idea of what they might be saying. The other fellow came forward and gave Gwairyc a friendly smile. At first Gwairyc thought him one of the Westfolk, because he had hair as pale as moonlight, but although his ears had a definite point to them, they were human-sized. His eyes were human as well, despite their dark violet colour. *A half-breed, most likely*, Gwairyc thought.

'I'm Loddlaen,' he said, 'Aderyn's son.'

'And I'm Gwairyc, Nevyn's apprentice.'

'So I thought. Here, I'll help you with your horses. You'll be sharing my father's tent, or so he told me, so let's unload your gear first.'

'Very well,' Gwairyc said. 'Do you live with your father?'

'I don't. I've got a small tent of my own.' Loddlaen smiled, but his eyes seemed to flare with terror. 'I'm somewhat of a solitary soul.'

As they led the horses across to the Westfolk camp, Gwairyc could look Loddlaen over. He had a thin face and large eyes like his father's, and during the moments when he was silent, his eyes grew haunted, always open a little too wide, always darting back and forth as if he expected trouble to spring out of the grass. Gwairyc had seen similar expressions before, usually in the eyes of old men who'd lost kin and home to the wars and the reiving of the Cerrgonney rebels. They had looked upon events that no man should ever have seen – their daughters raped, their sons killed, their homes burnt – and they would never forget those sights. Gwairyc assumed that Loddlaen had lived through some great tragedy himself.

The Westfolk stitched their circular shelters together out of deerskins rather than proper canvas. Loddlaen showed him into one of the largest tents. Inside, Gwairyc could clearly see the wood frame under the skins, an ingenious arrangement of crossed sticks that would fold in key places when the time came to travel. Loddlaen helped him pile his

gear and Nevyn's near the door, then escorted him out to
the horse herd. Although Gwairyc had often seen Western
Hunters, as Deverry men called the Westfolk horses, he'd
never come across an entire herd before.

For some moments he stood gazing upon them in utter awe.
The smallest of them stood at least eighteen hands high and
had deep chests and strong legs. They moved with grace, like
ripples on water, long manes and tails flowing, heads held high
as they surveyed the shabby-looking pair of mounts and the
mule that were being turned into their ranks. They had delicate heads with slender muzzles and large eyes, deep set and
dark, that watched the men with some intelligence. And the
colours of their coats – silver, dun, rich blood bay, pure glossy
black, and of course, the gleaming golden tan that Deverry lords
coveted more than real gold – it took Gwairyc's breath away.

'They are beautiful, aren't they?' Loddlaen said.

'Truly beautiful,' Gwairyc said. 'I can see why old Wffyn's
come all this way to get them.'

'Indeed. And these are only the geldings and a pair of old
bell mares. We never bring the breeding stock to the trading
ground.'

'That's wise of you. Any Deverry lord would sell his
bloodkin for a golden stud and a couple of golden mares.'

Loddlaen laughed, a sharp almost painful bark. 'True
spoken,' he said. 'We won't need to hobble your stock. They're
doubtless glad to be among their own kind, and we've got
mounted herdsman keeping watch, too.'

In Aderyn's tent, Nevyn was waiting for them. The old
man gave Loddlaen a pleasant smile and held out his hand,
which Loddlaen shook as weakly and briefly as possible.

'Dev's taken Morwen into his own tent,' Nevyn remarked.
'There really isn't anywhere else for her, I gather, but he
wanted to make sure that everyone realized she was a nursemaid and naught more.'

'Why would anyone have thought otherwise?' Gwairyc
said. 'Ugly little mutt as she is.'

'Ye gods!' Nevyn rolled his eyes in disgust. 'She's a human being, lad, not just a face.'

Gwairyc turned to Loddlaen to ask his opinion on the matter, only to find him gone. 'By the hells!' Gwairyc said. 'That lad can move fast and quietly when wants to.'

'Indeed.' Nevyn looked abruptly troubled.

'What's wrong?'

'Tell me somewhat. What do you think of Loddlaen?'

'All I can offer you is a first impression.'

'That's what I want to hear.'

'Well and good, then. Somehow he makes me pity him, but I'd never let him into any warband I captained.'

'Why not?'

'He'd get himself killed in the first scrap we fought. You can see that in a man's eyes, when he's had enough of life but doesn't know it yet. The trouble is, he usually takes some other lad with him.'

'I see.' Nevyn considered for a long moment. 'Another problem – Tirro. It's going to take Wffyn a good long time to barter all his trade goods away. Keep an eye on that miserable creature, will you?'

'Have no fear of that! There'll be temptation all around him out here.'

Gwairyc had noticed the Westfolk children, who were all as beautiful and graceful as their parents, especially the little lasses. They ran wild through the camp, either in groups or pairs, playing games with various leather balls or running here and there with their packs of mongrel dogs. They seemed to lie down to sleep wherever they felt tired, and he noticed them begging for food from one adult or another whenever they felt hungry. Standing guard over all of them would be impossible, leaving him no choice but to keep his watch over Tirro instead. Sure enough, on their second morning at the trading grounds, a pair of silver-haired little girls with violet eyes came with their mother to look over the iron goods. Gwairyc saw them leaving the Westfolk camp and followed,

an impromptu guard. While the mother asked Wffyn ques-
tions about some bone-handled knives, Tirro began joking
and talking with the lasses, who knew some Deverrian.
Eventually he got them to come for a little walk with him.
When they were about twenty yards from their mother,
Gwairyc strode over and intervened.

'You!' Gwairyc pointed at the girls. 'Go to your mother.'

Their laughter stopped. They stared wide-eyed at Gwairyc
for a moment, then glanced at each other.

'Now!' Gwairyc pointed at the mother. 'Go!'

At that they took off running. Gwairyc turned his attention to Tirro. 'Listen, you! While we're here, you'd best behave
yourself around these little ones.'

'And what do you mean by that?' Tirro drew his scrawny
self up to his full height. Gwairyc was tempted to grab him
by the throat, but fear of ringworm stopped him.

'As if you didn't know, you slimy little loricart,' Gwairyc
said. 'If I see you make one wrong move towards any little
lass, I'll kill you. I can't put it any more plainly than that.
Do you understand?'

Tirro went dead pale and raised a shaking hand to his
throat. He gulped several times, then nodded his agreement,
staring all the while at Gwairyc's face.

'Good.' Gwairyc smiled, but grimly. 'You Da's not here to
buy me off, and I wouldn't take one cursed copper from him
even if he was.'

Tirro nodded again. He reminded Gwairyc so strongly of
a rat paralysed by a ferret's gaze that Gwairyc was tempted
to slit his throat and be done with him there and then. As
if he read the thought Tirro yelped and broke, racing off
towards the caravan's tents. *Good*, Gwairyc thought. *If he
doesn't fear the wrath of the gods, at least I've got him to fear
mine.*

'What's all this about the merchant's apprentice?' Aderyn said.
'One of the women was down at the trading grounds this

morning, and she told me that your Gwairyc seems to hate the lad.'

'There's good reason for it,' Nevyn said, 'but I gather that Gwarro has the situation well in hand. Little Tirro is entirely too fond of very young lasses.'

Aderyn stared, speechless for a long moment.

'I doubt if anyone among the Westfolk shares that vice,' Nevyn went on.

'Not that I've heard of.' Aderyn paused to make a sour face. 'We value our offspring far too highly.'

'As well you should. It does happen now and again in Deverry, especially down in Cerrmor. It's a poisoned legacy from the Dawntime. The ancient Rhwmanes and Greggyns saw naught wrong with such nasty practices. It's no wonder that our ancestors rebelled against their swinish ways.'

'Just so.' Aderyn shook his head sadly. 'It's a terrible thing for someone to force himself upon a child. They can't defend themselves against someone twice their size.'

'True spoken, but that's not the worst of it, of course.'

'Indeed? Um, I don't recall the subject ever coming up during my apprenticeship.' Aderyn smiled with a wry twist of his mouth. 'And it gladdens my heart, too, that we never saw any such thing on our travels.'

'Quite so,' Nevyn said. 'Well, you see, it's the balance of etheric forces, or the complete lack of the balance, I should say, that should take place between two lovers. A child can't possibly absorb or return any of the etheric energies released by sexual acts. So those floods of magnetic force burn the astral body the way fire will burn a child's slender little fingers, and they leave the same sort of scars – deep ones, for life.'

'Ah. It's even more loathsome than I thought, then.'

'Unfortunately.'

'I'd best warn everybody.'

'I wonder about that.' Nevyn hesitated, thinking. 'If I thought one child here would suffer the slightest harm, I'd do the telling myself, but I don't think it's necessary. Tirro's terrified of Gwairyc, and with very good reason. Gwarro's threatened to kill him at the least sign of trouble.'

'I'll wager that Gwairyc would, too, without a moment's thought.'

'He would indeed, and Tirro knows it. I find this odd of me, but I rather pity Tirro.'

'Ye gods, how could you? Why?'

'Haven't you noticed the way he grovels the moment a grown man says a harsh word to him? He's always flattering the men around him, too, as if he's frightened and will do anything to propitiate them. I suspect that when he was young, someone did foul things to him. As long as he works no harm, I'd rather he not be humiliated.'

'Humiliation might be the best physick for his disease.'

'Not truly. With some men, especially the honour-bound, being shamed is their worst fear. Prince Mael made a good comment about that in one of his books: 'the threat of shame turns an honour-bound man into a paragon of virtue.' With weak souls, though, humiliation drives them to worse evils. They'll do anything for revenge, anything to make themselves feel powerful and beyond humiliating again.'

'I'd not thought of it that way.' Aderyn was silent for some moments. 'Tirro strikes me as a very weak soul indeed.'

'He strikes me the same. Besides, he'll be leaving soon.'

'True spoken. Well, I won't say anything to the alar unless it's absolutely necessary. I'll keep an eye on him myself, though, just in case he outfoxes Gwairyc.'

Nevyn and Aderyn had spent the afternoon strolling along a stream away from camp. They'd been discussing a far more pleasant subject than Tirro, namely Aderyn's attempt to restore the lost dweomer system of the seven cities, those fabled places in the far western mountains where the Westfolk's ancestors had lived in civilized splendour. When the Horsekin swept down from the north, destroying everything they found, the refugees who managed to reach safety on the plains had been common folk, mostly farmers and herders. Only a handful of learned persons had come with them, and of those, only a few had studied dweomer. When Aderyn had come to the Westlands, some hundreds of years earlier, he had found dweomer workers who knew only a tattered body of lore, complete in a few areas but utterly torn and gone in others.

'Still,' Nevyn told Aderyn that afternoon, 'you've done a truly impressive job of bringing together the fragments. It's a fine piece of work.'

Aderyn blushed scarlet, and for a brief moment, despite his silver hair and deeply lined face, he looked like the young apprentice Nevyn remembered so well. 'My thanks,' he said at last. 'I'm still missing some important elements at the core, but at least I can teach what we have. The more who learn it, and the more students who write it down, the better chance we'll have of preserving it.'

Their stroll had taken them close to the Westfolk tents. A soft evening breeze brought them the smell of roasting lamb. In an unspoken understanding, they began walking briskly back. Even the greatest dweomerworkers grow hungry at dinnertime. At the camp's edge, they came across Evan, playing with a little lad about his own age. The two children were sitting on a stretch of grass and rolling a leather ball back and forth. Morwen stood nearby, smiling a little as she watched them. The lads were giggling and chattering in Deverrian and Elvish both.

'It won't take Ebañy long to learn our language,' Aderyn said. 'He's just at the proper age.'

'So he is, if you mean Evan.'

'I do. Ebañy's as close a name to his old one as Devaberiel could think up. It means 'winter wind', a bit harsh, mayhap, but he recognizes it as his name already.'

Morwen looked up and saw Nevyn, then waved to him and smiled. Nevyn strolled over to chat with her, but before he could say a word, a swarm of older boys came racing up

to the two little ones. Most of them ran right by, but a lad
with night-dark hair and pale yellow eyes gave the ball a
good kick, sending it flying far away among the tents. Both
little ones began to cry.

'You!' Morwen reached out and grabbed the back of his
shirt. 'Bring that back!'

For someone so small, she was remarkably strong, a legacy
of all those hard years of farm work. The lad choked on the
neckline of his own tunic, and, gasping, stopped in his tracks.
Morwen gave him a good shake, then let him go.

'Bring the ball back,' she said. 'Look! You've made them cry.'

'Huh!' The boy wrinkled his nose at her. 'So what? One
of them's a stinking Round-ear brat, and you're ugly as a
dead frog.'

Morwen hauled off and hit him so hard across the face
that he staggered. He yelped and flung up both hands to
defend himself as Morwen closed in, swinging again, smacking
him even harder. Blood spurted from his nose and upper lip.

'Morri, stop it!' Nevyn made a grab at her, but she danced
away from him. He caught a good look at her face and saw
that her eyes had turned as blank as any berserker's.

With a shriek the boy's mother came running, yelling in
Elvish, pointing at Morwen and gesturing to Aderyn, who
yelled back, apparently trying to calm the mother down while
Nevyn dealt with Morwen, though why he thought screaming
at the top of his lungs would be calming was beyond Nevyn's
power to guess. He made another futile grab at Morwen just
as the outraged mother stepped in between her and the
weeping boy. She raised a hand to slap back, and she was
easily a foot taller than Morwen.

In an odd sort of calm Morwen ducked the slap, then
charged, striking up from below with a fist and hitting the
Westfolk woman precisely on the point of her chin. The
woman staggered once and dropped to the ground. Morwen
stepped back and came to herself. She'd woken from the
berserker fit, which drew its power, Nevyn knew, from deep

memories of this soul's earlier lives. She clasped both hands over her mouth and stared at the prostrate woman. Aderyn flung himself down on his knees next to the victim, who groaned and turned over onto her back.

'She'll be all right,' Aderyn said in Deverrian. 'But let's not move her just yet.'

More shrieks, more screaming – the entire camp seemed to have come running to watch. Both little boys were weeping in terror. Fortunately, the mother of Evan's playmate was right at hand. She scooped up her child, paused to hurl insults at the prostrate elven woman on the ground, then carried her son away. Nevyn started to fetch Evan, but Loddlaen came trotting over and picked the boy up.

'Let me, Wise One,' Loddlaen said. 'I'll get Morwen out of here.'

'My thanks,' Nevyn said. 'I'd best stay and soothe the situation.'

'Oh, don't let it vex you.' Loddlaen settled Evan on one hip. 'Doubtless the bitch and her pup both deserved it.' He grabbed Morwen's arm with his free hand and strode off, leading her away.

Utterly speechless, Nevyn stood staring after them. From behind him he heard someone laughing. He turned to see Gwairyc, his hands on his hips, shaking his head in amusement.

'Ye gods, our Morri's not a lass to cross, is she, my lord?' Gwairyc said. 'Who would have thought that she had so much fire in her soul? Good for her!'

'I'm not so sure how good it's going to be,' Nevyn said, 'if it loses Morwen her place as Evan's nursemaid.'

'Oh, it won't do that.' Aderyn walked over to join them. 'This sort of thing happens all the time among the Westfolk.' He glanced back at the Westfolk woman, who was sitting up, still groggy, in the midst of friends. Some of them were grinning. 'Morri will fit right in.'

* * *

Morwen followed Loddlaen almost blindly. Still carrying Evan, he took her to a small tent at the edge of the encampment and sat her down by a little fire, then put the boy down beside her.

'Your hand could use some tending,' Loddlaen said. 'Look at it, blood all over the back.'

He ducked inside the tent. Morwen stared at her bleeding knuckles and wondered why they didn't hurt. She was still shaking with rage and barely able to think, but slowly, as the berserk fury left her, the pain arrived.

'Morri hurt,' Evan said. 'Poor Morri!'

'Stupid Morri,' Morwen said. 'Ye gods, I don't know what came over me!'

Loddlaen came out of the tent with a packet of herbs, a brown pottery bowl, a waterskin, and a small iron pot. He put the pot right into the coals, filled it with water, sprinkled in the herbs, then added a few more twigs to the fire.

'We'll let that heat up a bit,' Loddlaen said. 'Then you can soak your hand in it.'

'A thousands thanks!' Morwen said. 'I feel like such a fool. I don't know why you'd help me, after I've shamed myself in front of your whole clan.'

'What?' Loddlaen paused for a laugh. 'I don't consider you shamed. Dangerous, truly, but not shameful. I doubt if anyone else does, either. You don't understand the Westfolk yet. Little scraps and arguments flare up all the time. Once they've died down, no one bothers to remember them.'

'Truly?'

'Truly.' He smiled at her.

'Well, that's a relief, then.'

Loddlaen tested the water in the kettle by sticking his finger into it. 'Still too cold,' he announced. 'Frankly, I admire you for putting that harridan in her place. Ebañy, you're a lucky lad. You've got someone to stick up for you.' His smile turned brittle. 'I didn't, when the little beasts tormented me.'

'Why would they do that?' Morwen said. 'Look at you, as handsome as a prince in one of those bard songs.'

'You think so, maybe.' The bitterness in Loddlaen's voice
shocked her. 'You were mocked as a child, or so my father
told me, because of your lip. Well, so was I, for my eyes and
ears. The other children called me Roundear and Squinteye.
At night they'd make little traps because they could see in
the dark, but I couldn't. I was forever falling over stretched
ropes or stubbing my toes on rocks. Once a pair of them
even laid an ambuscade behind a tent and scared the wits
out of me.'

'I never would have thought you'd have suffered such.'

'Most people wouldn't. But I did.'

'Why didn't your father put a stop to it? Everyone seems
to respect him.'

'Oh, I was supposed to be strong, you know, and just
laugh and ignore them. They'll stop teasing you if you just
ignore it, Da kept saying. I was a Wise One's son. Why wasn't
I just as wise as he? No matter that I was but a little lad!'

'And I don't suppose their mothers ever stopped the little
beasts from hurting you.'

'Oh, they did try. I'll give them that. The women were so
kind, treating me like I was a half-wit. Now don't hurt
Loddlaen, they'd say. He can't help being like he is. Ever so
kind of them!' Loddlaen paused for a deep breath. 'Ah well,
that was all a long timeago. Here, there's a breath of steam
on that water.' He tested the herb brew again, then used a
forked stick to lift the pot by itsmetal handle. 'It'll sting at
first, but then it'll soothe.' He poured the herb water into the
bowl, then set the pot down on the bare ground near the fire.
'Ebañy, don't you dare touch that kettle! It's hot hot hot!'

Evan drew his hand back fast.

'Good lad,' Loddlaen said. 'Try it, Morri. Just one finger
at first.'

The herbwater did indeed sting, but in a remarkably short
time the sting receded and took the pain with it. Morwen
sighed in something like wonderment. Someone was tending
her, making her feel better. Someone had gone out of his

way to take her part in a squabble, someone who had suffered in the same way as she had.

'A thousand thanks,' she said. 'These herbs are marvels. I truly appreciate your aid.'

'Well, now,' Loddlaen said, 'who wouldn't do as much for a friend?'

They shared a smile, but Morwen felt as if she could weep from joy. A friend. First Nevyn, now Loddlaen – she had friends, a splendid luxury that she'd always thought beyond her station in life. Lanmara, after all, had been so much more than a friend that at times loving her had been almost painful, almost a burden.

Once the herbs had done what they could for her hand, Morwen went back to Devaberiel's tent. She found Dev inside, taking a pair of wooden bowls out of a tent bag.

'I'll fetch us all some dinner,' he said. 'Evan – I mean, Ebañy – come with Da. Morri needs to rest.'

When he left, Evan toddled along eagerly after him. Morwen spent a moment looking around the tent. Her shabby blankets lay by the door, while Dev had placed his own on the other side of the hearth, which amounted to a collection of flat slates under the smoke hole in the roof. A collection of brightly coloured tent bags hung on the walls, and a scatter of leather cushions lay on the painted floor cloth. Even though she'd already spent one night there, still it struck her as gaudy and strange. *But it's a fair bit nicer than my old shed*, she thought. *Thank the gods for that!*

It was also, at the moment, stuffy after a long summer's day with the scent of dust and sun-warmed leather. Morwen went outside to wait for Dev to return. She had just sat down in the grass outside when Nevyn joined her.

'I hope I didn't shame you,' Morwen said.

'Not at all,' Nevyn said. 'I was startled at first, and then I was afraid you were going to be hurt. I see that my fear was quite unnecessary.'

'Well, I truly don't know what came over me, except I absolutely hate seeing Evan cry. I – Oh wait, here's the little troublemaker coming now.'

The dark-haired boy with the yellow eyes walked towards them, but he stopped a safe distance away and stared at the ground. Red and purple bruises blotched his face. He was carrying Evan's ball.

'I brought it back,' the boy said in Deverrian. 'And I'm sorry I called you ugly, and Ebañy doesn't really stink.'

'It gladdens my heart to hear you say so. I'm sorry I hurt you. I don't know what came over me.'

'Well and good, then. I've got to go apologize to Danalaurel now.' He tossed her the ball, then trotted off.

'Danalaurel?' Nevyn said.

'That's Evan's little friend,' Morwen said.

'Ah, I see. Well, it looks like Loddlaen did exactly the right thing for your hand. It's swollen, but not half so much as I expected.'

'It was very kind of him, truly.'

'It was, and I'm a bit surprised. He can be sullen at times, that lad, and moody, but then, his life didn't get off to the best of starts.'

'Indeed. He told me how the other children teased him. Is that what you mean?'

'Partly. When he was new-born, his mother had very little milk, and he went hungry for a while until she found him a wetnurse. And then –' Nevyn hesitated for a moment. 'Well, I shouldn't be telling tales.'

'Oh come along!' Morwen smiled at him. 'I'll not be repeating anyone's secrets. I've had to keep my thoughts to myself for my whole life.'

'Very well. Loddlaen's mother was a Wise One, too. Or is, I suppose I should say.' Nevyn thought for a moment, frowning. 'I assume that Dallandra's still alive somewhere, at least in some form or another. She went off with the Seelie Host, you see.'

Morwen crossed her fingers in the sign of warding. Everyone knew that the very mention of the Host brought danger.

'The whole affair was very sad,' Nevyn went on. 'But it was her wyrd and work to go. Perhaps she never should have tried to marry and live like an ordinary woman of her people, not that I realized it at the time. Aderyn's never truly recovered, and you can imagine the effect on her son.'

'I can indeed. Naught good, for a certainty. Is that why Loddlaen looks so troubled now and then?'

'Partly. The lad's seen other trouble in his life, too, but truly, that's not a tale I can tell you.'

'Well and good, then. I shan't pry.'

It wasn't until much later that Morwen remembered Nevyn saying 'it was her wyrd and work to go'. *What did he mean by that?* she wondered. It was, she supposed, just another of the many strange things she'd have to learn here in her exotic new life. She thought about asking Loddlaen, but she had no desire to cause him the pain of remembering a lost mother, a pain she knew too well herself.

In the morning a new alar rode into the trading grounds, and with them came Aderyn's former apprentice, Valandario. Whilst the others in her group unpacked their travois and tended the horses, the young dweomerworker joined Aderyn and Nevyn in front of Aderyn's tent. In those days Valandario was more gaunt than slender, mostly because her studies engrossed her so thoroughly that she often forgot to eat. Her pale blonde hair fell down her back to her waist in a messy tangle because she refused to spend the time to braid it in the usual manner of the Westfolk. Since she'd learned Deverrian quite recently, she spoke with an oddly careful diction.

'Good morrow, Master Aderyn,' she said, 'and a good morrow to you, Master Nevyn. My heart is gladdened to see both of you.'

'And mine to see you,' Aderyn said. 'I trust you had a safe journey?'

'We did indeed.'

'Good, good. So, I'm assuming you've got that mysterious gem of yours. When shall we have a look at it?'

'To be honest, I have not yet received it. It should however arrive soon.'

'Someone's bringing it, then,' Aderyn said.

'That is so. You see, many nights ago I received a message from Javanateriel. He and his companions had travelled west a fair ways, so he felt they could not yet journey to the trading grounds until more time had passed.'

Aderyn nodded sagely.

'Um, may I ask why not?' Nevyn said.

'Because of the plague that killed off the Horsekin invaders,' Aderyn said. 'Or to be more precise, the fear of it. It's somewhat of a rule among us Westfolk, that anyone who rides too far west can't return to the main camps until he's sure that he's not carrying it.'

'Wait a moment. You must mean the plague that raged during the destruction of the elven cities in the mountains. That was a thousand years ago.'

'Oh, I know, and it's probably an unnecessary precaution. By all accounts the illness sprang from tainted food.' But Aderyn sounded doubtful. 'Still, you never know. Better safe than sorry.'

'Truly spoken.' Valandario took up her tale again. 'So, on his way home, he met some distant herders. They in turn passed his message to me, that he had a marvellous gift he wished to give me. He wanted us to meet at the trading grounds.'

'So,' Aderyn said, 'he told you he was bringing you a jewel of some sort.'

'He did not, just that he was bringing a gift. But I dreamt about it, which is why I know the gift to be a gem.'

Nevyn felt like heaving a deep and weary sigh. It was just

like the Westfolk to ask someone to travel a hundred miles
out of their way on the strength of a dream alone. A fortnight, a month or two – those measures of Time had the
same importance to them as an afternoon would to a human
being.

'He also told me,' Valandario continued, 'that he had found
a gift for you, Master Aderyn. But I dreamt not about that
one. Gems call to me, as you know, but naught else does.
However, Jav should be here soon. Now I'd best go help my
alar set up the tents.'

With a cheerful wave she trotted off, heading back to
camp.

'Soon, is it?' Aderyn gave Nevyn a twisted sort of smile.
'My apologies. Let's hope the wretched thing truly is a gem.'

'Oh, don't be embarrassed. It's good to see you, so I'm
glad I made the trip, no matter what this mysterious gift
turns out to be.'

Much to Morwen's relief, none of the Westfolk mentioned
her fight as she and Evan walked around the camp on the
morrow morning. Since she had a reason to look for them,
she noticed other squabbles that broke out quickly and died
even faster. She made a point, however, of avoiding the woman
she'd knocked unconscious. She also noticed that none of
the other children teased Evan nor Danalaurel, either, when
the two little ones set about playing with Evan's ball.

Not long after the noon meal, Loddlaen sought her out.
She was returning to Devaberiel's tent to put Evan down for
a nap when he walked up behind her, so noiselessly that she
nearly yelped in surprise when he spoke.

'How's the hand today?' Loddlaen said.

'Ye gods, you startled me!' she said, laughing. 'It's a fair
bit better, my thanks. I can close my fingers now without it
hurting.'

'Good. Tell me somewhat, will you? What do you think
of Gwairyc?'

'I'm not sure. At times he's pleasant enough, and at others he frightens me. Why do you ask?'

'He's a cursed strange apprentice for a herbman.'

'Well, that's certainly true.'

'I was wondering if you knew why he seems to hate Tirro. I went down to look at Wffyn's goods, and I saw Gwairyc treating Tirro like a dog. Some of the women here in camp told me that he follows the lad around and yells at him for the least little thing.'

'I saw him do that on the way out here, too, but I don't know why. You could ask Nevyn.'

'I'd rather not.' Loddlaen looked away, his eyes wide with fear. 'He might tell Gwairyc I asked.'

'So?'

'What if he challenged me? Gwairyc's the kind of man I've always hated, a swaggering bastard of a warrior. They usually hate me, too.'

'Why would they do that?'

'I've no idea.' He made a sharp bark of sound that might have been a laugh. 'But be that as it may, there's somewhat else I wanted to ask you. Would you like to have dinner with me tonight?'

'My thanks, I would.'

'Come at sundown, then.'

Loddlaen looked as if he was about to say more, but Evan began whining in a wordless sing-song and pulling on her hand.

'I've got to get him to sleep,' Morwen said. 'I'll see you at sundown.'

When the time came, Devaberiel offered to take care of his son so Morwen could have a little time to herself. She took the offer, but reluctantly. Since Loddlaen's tent stood a fair distance away from the campground proper, she enjoyed being so far from its noise, but at the same time it vexed her to be away from Evan, even though she was leaving him with his father and Nevyn as well. *He'll be perfectly safe,* she kept telling herself. *And he'll have to grow up and grow away from me sooner or later.*

When Morwen arrived at Loddlaen's tent, she was surprised to find Tirro there. Morwen disliked the merchant's apprentice, but since Loddlaen was the host, she decided that it wasn't her place to argue about the other guest, especially as Tirro had sweetened his welcome by bringing a basket of griddle cakes with him to supplement the meal. The Westfolk seemed to eat mostly meat, along with various raw leaves, dressed with oil and herbs, and wild fruits, a diet she was finding difficult to digest. The three of them sat down on the ground cross-legged by a fire burning in a circle of stones. Loddlaen had sliced chops from a lamb slaughtered the day before. They cooked them on a flat stone slab of the sort that a Deverry woman would have used for baking bread, then laid them on top of the griddle cakes.

'These are delicious, Tirro,' Morwen said. 'I miss bread ever so much.'

'Well, we do trade with Deverry farmers for grains and flour,' Loddlaen said. 'But bread and porridge and the like are for the winter camps. When it's damp and cold they fill you up.'

'You live so differently than people do in Deverry,' Morwen said. 'I'm still getting used to it.'

'No doubt. I've often wondered what it would be like, living there, but I've never quite got the courage to go try it.'

'Well, you'd fit in better than most of your folk. You could be a herbman like Nevyn.'

'Truly,' Tirro joined in. 'You don't even look that much different, and Loddlaen sounds like a Deverry name to me. Some of the names around here would twist your tongue, they would.'

'True enough, but Loddlaen's just a nickname. I was named after my grandfather, Alodalaenteriel.'

'I'm not even going to try to say that. Tirro's not my real name, either. It's Alastyr.'

'Much grander,' Morwen said. 'Tirro suits you, though.'

Tirro glanced her way with a scowl, then smoothed the expression away.

'So tell me, Tirro.' Loddlaen intervened quickly. 'Are you going to be a horse trader the rest of your life, like Wffyn?'

'I am not.' Tirro put ice into his voice. 'I'm marked for greater things, I am. Once we get back to Cerrmor, I'm going to sail to Bardek and learn to be a proper merchant. I want to deal in exotic spices and silk and precious gems, not frying pans and knife blades.'

'What's Bardek like?' Morwen said. 'I've never heard anything about it but the name.'

'You wouldn't, up in Pyrdon.' Tirro thought for a moment. 'Um, well, I've not been there yet, mind. But lots of Bardek folk come to Cerrmor.'

'I've heard they're black as pitch,' Loddlaen said.

'What? That's just one of those silly things people say. Some have dark skin, truly, but most are just brown or tan, and a few look no different from Deverry folk.'

'That's truly interesting.' Loddlaen leaned forward. 'I've often wondered what it would be like to go to Bardek.'

'When I'm a rich merchant with my own ship, you can come with me.' Tirro paused to smile. 'Well, assuming I truly do get rich and own a ship some day. There's a bit of work ahead of me twixt now and then.'

They all laughed. Loddlaen proceeded to ask a good many questions, keeping Tirro talking about the Bardekians and his own city of Cerrmor, too, a place that seemed as exotic to Morwen as those foreign islands far across the Southern Sea. They finished the dinner, and Loddlaen brought out a skin of mead, something Morwen had never tasted. Since it was made from honey, Morwen was expecting it to be sweet; its dry sharp taste surprised her, and she took only a couple of small sips for the sake of politeness.

Loddlaen and Tirro talked on, passing the skin back and forth, while Morwen let her mind wander, worrying about Evan despite her best efforts to enjoy herself without him. She was just thinking that she might as well leave when she suddenly felt she was being watched. She turned around to look.

By then night had fallen, and they sat in a pool of fire-light on the edge of darkness. Behind her the grassland stretched out seemingly forever, half-seen in the faint starlight. *There's naught there,* she told herself, but in the instant she had the thought, she saw and recognized the elven woman she'd seen on the journey west. She was standing just beyond the light. In one hand she carried an unstrung bow, and a quiver of arrows hung at her hip.

Morwen got up and walked a few steps to greet her. The woman smiled at her, but her eyes were pools of sadness.

'Have you found your daughter?' Morwen said.

'I've not, but it's very kind of you to ask.'

'It saddens my heart to think you've lost her.'

'Does it? Then my blessings upon you, child.'

At that moment the woman began to change. She grew taller, grew huge, towering above Morwen, smiling down at her as she stretched out one hand to bless her. Her hair now hung around her face in a shining golden mane, decorated with jewels. Her clothing, a medley of greens, shimmered and rustled as if she stood in a private wind. Her bow gleamed with gold, and gems studded her quiver.

From behind her Morwen heard Tirro yelping in surprise and the sounds of the two men scrambling to their feet.

'The nine in one,' Morwen whispered. 'All goddesses in one vast soul.'

'Not her, but myself alone. I am Alshandra.' The woman's voice sounded like a silver gong, struck for each word. 'I am the huntress from the edge of the stars.'

She floated free of the ground, then hovered for a moment, smiling upon them all. All at once she vanished, leaving Morwen shaking and cold.

'The goddess.' Tirro was trembling, too. He stretched out his arms to the sky. 'The goddess came to us.'

'I'm not so sure of that,' Morwen said.

'What?' Tirro's voice squealed indignantly. 'How would you know?'

'I've studied at the temple, that's how. She didn't have the right attributes, and besides, she claimed she wasn't – well, I can't tell you that bit of lore. It's secret.'

'Oh how very convenient for you! I say she's a goddess.'

'She's not. I don't know what she was, mind, but she wasn't the goddess I've gone to worship at the Temple of the Moon.'

'Oh very well, another goddess, then!' Tirro turned on her with a snarl in his voice. 'What does it matter? A goddess appeared to us. Didn't you see? Have you lost your wits, Morri?'

'I've not, but you have.' Morwen stamped a foot. 'I tell you, I know lore, and that wasn't any true goddess.'

'Lore? Huh! What, then? Tell me why you don't believe her.'

'I can't tell you. I swore a vow to keep things secret.'

'I'm supposed to believe you instead of my own eyes, and you can't offer me any proof. I –'

'Whist! That's enough!' Loddlaen stepped forward. 'I'll wager Morri's right. She's studied the lore, and we've not. I believe her.'

Tirro hesitated, looking back and forth between them. His expression reminded Morwen of Evan's when he'd been denied some treat he wanted, a disappointment utterly pure because so childlike.

'Well, I –' Tirro said at length. 'She was so beautiful, so strange. I've never seen anything so lovely.'

'Lovely she was,' Loddlaen said, 'but there are plenty of beautiful spirits, and I wouldn't trust a one of them. My da told me about them – he knows lore, too – and they'll lure you and then betray you. Ask him about it. He's the Wise One in this camp.'

The snap of bitterness in his voice made Morwen realize he was speaking of his absent mother. Tirro stared at the ground and considered this, his mouth working. Finally he looked up with an artificial smile.

'I'm going to pray to Alshandra from now on,' Tirro said. 'If she answers my prayers, we'll know she's a goddess. And if she won't, then we'll know she's not.'

'That could be very dangerous,' Morwen said. 'She might be one of the –'

'Oh stop it!' Tirro turned his back on her. 'Loddlaen, my thanks for the dinner. I'd best get back before Gwairyc comes after me.'

Tirro turned and bolted into the darkness. They could hear his running footsteps until he disappeared into the camp.

'Do you think he'll ask your da about spirits?' Morwen said.

'I doubt it,' Loddlaen said. 'He's a craven little soul. Maybe I can help him.'

'That's kind of you, truly.'

'I want to be a good healer one day, whether it's here or in Deverry. And Tirro seems to have some sort of wound deep in his soul.'

'True spoken.' Morwen considered staying, but the apparition had taken the bloom off the evening, somehow. 'You know, I think me I'd best get back to my duties. I wonder if Dev's managed to get Evan – I mean Ebañy – to go to sleep?'

'Probably not.' Loddlaen grinned at her. 'He's probably talking as fast and loud as the winter wind and wondering why his lad's not nodding off.'

'That's like him, truly, but he's one of the best-hearted men I've ever met.'

'Most bards are.' Bitterness crept back into Loddlaen's voice. 'Why shouldn't they be? Everyone grovels in front of them and heaps praise upon them and gifts and the like.'

'Well, I suppose they do.' Morwen suddenly felt uneasy, though she was at a loss to know why. 'My thanks for the dinner. I truly must be getting back.'

As she walked off, Morwen glanced back to see Loddlaen

sitting down by his fire, his shoulders slumped, staring into the flames. At moments, she realized, he frightened her. *Ye gods,* she told herself, *who's the craven soul now?*

When she returned to Devaberiel's tent, she found Nevyn sitting by the fire in front of it. The bard and his son were inside, where Dev was still trying to get Evan to sleep. She could hear the child wail that he wanted his Morri, which brought an immediate song from his da.

'I should go in,' Morwen said.

'It won't hurt Evan to learn how to go to sleep for someone else,' Nevyn said. 'Soon enough he'll have to learn how to go to sleep on his own, after all.'

'Well, that's true.' Morwen joined him on the ground. 'Besides, there's somewhat I want to tell you about. A truly strange thing happened at our dinner.'

Nevyn listened to her account of Alshandra's appearance with intense interest. She told him as well about her encounter with the same being on their trip out to the Westlands.

'I thought later I must have been dreaming,' Morwen finished up. 'Which is why I didn't tell you then.'

'I can understand that.' Nevyn took his chin in his hand and rubbed it while he stared into the fire. 'I quite agree. That was no goddess.'

'Was she one of the Seelie Host, then?'

'I think so. The Westfolk call them the Guardians, because, or so I gather, they've done the folk many a favour in the past. But I wouldn't trust them.'

'No more I, never fear.' Morwen made the sign of warding with crossed fingers. 'I didn't want to say the name at first, there in front of Loddlaen, because of his mother and all, but I did wonder. We heard about those spirits in the temple lore.'

'Did the lore say if they sometimes masquerade as gods? Or can you even tell me?'

'Oh, that bit wasn't secret. They do, or so the high priestess told me. I wanted to warn Tirro, but he wouldn't listen, and then he ran off.'

'I suspect that Tirro's had a very painful life. This Alshandra creature must have looked splendid to him.'

'He said she did, truly. I hope he doesn't come to any harm.'

'I hope so, too. If he gives me a chance, I'll talk to him about it.'

'Splendid! I wager he'll listen more to you than to me.'

As far as Morwen could see, however, Tirro was determined to avoid both Nevyn and Aderyn as much as possible. During the days that followed, the apprentice had his work to do down at the merchant camp, and in the evenings, he took to sticking close to Loddlaen, if for no other reason than Gwairyc seemed inclined to ignore him as long as he was in Loddlaen's company. Occasionally, when Devaberiel wanted some time alone with his son, Morwen would join the pair of them. She still found the Westfolk too alien to try to make friends among them, though she repeatedly told herself that eventually she would have to. Tirro never mentioned Alshandra again. Nevyn told her that he was probably afraid that she'd talk him out of his belief.

'Some men are so hungry for god lore,' Nevyn remarked, 'that they'll eat chalk if they can't get cheese.'

Loddlaen eventually offered Morwen a glimpse of an even more exciting type of lore. After some five days of camping in the same spot, their horses and the caravan mules had eaten down the best fodder. The entire market fair, Wffyn and Westfolk alike, moved upstream some five miles to a new campground on the southern tip of a small lake. While the horses had plenty of flat grazing ground to the west, just to the north lay a low semi-circle of rocky ridge that provided shelter for the tents from the endless winds off the grasslands.

Loddlaen as usual pitched his tent some distance from the rest, close to a tumble of big granite boulders at the foot of the ridge. In mid-afternoon Morwen took Evan out of the way of all the unpacking and joined him. He'd already gathered wood for a fire and was laying out kindling and tinder in a circle of stones.

'It's so warm,' Morwen said, smiling. 'Surely you're not going to light a fire now.'

'I'm not,' Loddlaen said. 'I just like to have one ready. I hate the dark. You never know what might sneak up on you out of it. Come sit down, though. I've made some honey-water and put in some spices from Bardek. You'll like it better than mead.'

He brought out two crudely glazed pottery mugs and filled them with a sweet-smelling drink from a pottery jug. Morwen had never tasted cinnamon before, and she loved it immediately. So did Evan. Since the mugs were too heavy for him to hold safely, she gave him sips from hers, but each sip turned into a long gulp.

'Careful now,' Loddlaen said to him. 'You don't want to get a sour stomach.'

Evan merely grinned and wiped his sticky mouth on the back of his hand.

'How do you like the life of the camps so far?' Loddlaen said. 'I'm afraid my folk can be wretchedly noisy.'

'Oh, I don't mind that!' Morwen paused to smile at him. 'It's splendid, compared to the life I had before. I've not had to scrape out a henhouse or pull rocks from a field or carry in hay for weeks now.'

'I hadn't thought of it that way. They must have worked you like one of the mules.'

'Everyone works on a farm. Even my nose-in-the-air sister had her share of the hard jobs. Life here seems a fair bit easier, though, truly, Dev did warn me that the winters can be miserable. Well, they weren't any better in Pyrdon, when the snow came up over the windows and the food ran low.'

'At least we can take the herds south where it doesn't snow much at all. I was just wondering if you found us all strange.'

'Different, but not strange in a bad way.'

'Good. But if you have any questions or the like, just ask me.'

'Well, here's a thing I don't understand. Why do your people call Nevyn and your da "Wise Ones"?'

Loddlaen hesitated for several long moments. 'Because they have dweomer,' he said finally.

'Oh here! Now you're teasing me. Seriously, why do they?'

'It's no jest. They have dweomer, and they studied long and hard to get it, too, so they deserve to be called wise.'

'I truly do hate being teased like this.'

'So do I, and that's why I'm not teasing you. Why do you think I am?'

Morwen was about to snarl and demand he stop, but he looked so honestly puzzled that she refrained. 'I've always been told,' she said instead, 'that there's no such thing as dweomer.'

'Oh.' He paused to grin at her. 'I should have known that Roundears would be so stupid.'

'Are you truly telling me that there's such a thing?'

'See for yourself.' Loddlaen pointed at his fire circle, then called out a few words in Elvish.

Two salamanders appeared on either side of the tinder and kindling. Evan squealed in delight as they rose up on their hindquarters; one even waved a steaming orange paw in his direction, and its flat broad mouth gaped in what might have been a smile. She heard Loddlaen snap his fingers. The bits of grass suddenly burst into flame. When Loddlaen snapped his fingers a second time, the flame went out.

'The salamanders will light fires for you,' he said. 'If you know how to ask them. Learning how is part of the dweomer.'

From behind her a masculine voice suddenly swore. She twisted around to see Tirro staring, as open-mouthed as the salamander. Loddlaen jumped to his feet.

'What are you doing here?' Loddlaen snapped.

'I'm sorry.' Tirro took a step back. 'My master let me have

a little time to myself, a reward, like, for helping move camp. I'm sorry. I'll go away.' Tears came to his eyes.

'What? Don't!' Loddlaen said. 'You just startled me, and you're not supposed to see things like this.'

'I won't tell! I promise. I truly truly won't.'

'It's all right, then. Here. Come sit down.'

Like a dog who fears a beating, Tirro walked up one slow paw at a time. When Loddlaen gave him an encouraging smile, he sat down a few feet farther from the fire circle than Morwen and Loddlaen. His eyes still glistened with tears, but he seemed to have forgotten about them in his awe at the blackened tinder.

'Did I really see you light a fire without anything?' Tirro whispered. 'No flint, no steel, naught?'

'Well, the Wildfolk are the ones who actually did the lighting,' Loddlaen said.

'Oh, of course they did!' Tirro grinned at him. 'But it doesn't matter. I can see why you don't want to tell me how you did it.'

'I already did tell you,' Loddlaen said with a sigh. 'But no matter, indeed. Please – I can't say this enough – never ever let my da know what you saw here. He'd have my hide on the wall of his tent. We're never supposed to let outsiders know about dweomer.'

'I shan't say a word.' Tirro suddenly looked so sad that he seemed to have aged fifty years. 'You're lucky, Morwen. You belong here now. You get to see the marvels.'

'So I am.' All at once she felt sorry for him. 'Well, though, who knows? Maybe there are marvels for you somewhere else.'

'Where?' Tirro spat out the word. 'In Bardek? Not beastly likely!'

'From what you've told us, just being in Bardek will be a marvel in itself,' Loddlaen said. 'Let me get you a mug and somewhat to drink. Mead or honey-water?'

'Mead, and my thanks, if you can spare a bit.'

When Loddlaen got up, Evan leaned against Morwen and stuck his thumb in his mouth. He was watching Tirro with his pale brows furrowed in a little frown.

'You look tired, sweetheart,' Morwen said to him. 'It's time for your nap. Let's go to Da's tent.'

Instead of whining, Evan merely nodded agreement. *He doesn't like Tirro, either,* Morwen thought. *I always knew my lad was a smart one!*

As they were walking back, Morwen was wondering if she should tell Nevyn what she'd seen. The old man seemed so wise, and he knew the Westfolk so well, that he might be able to explain more about this mysterious dweomer. She could simply never mention Tirro and so protect Loddlaen. Yet fear stopped her. Tirro had said that she now belonged to the Westfolk. She wanted it to be true, but deep in her soul she felt that she'd never belong anywhere. If she caused any more trouble, they might cast her out, or so she feared. Her mother had always told her, 'when the bucket's full, don't swing it around and spill the milk'. *Good advice,* she thought. *I'll just wait and see if Loddlaen will tell me more.*

In among the tents she met Gwairyc, striding along with a grim look on his face. He paused and hailed her.

'Have you seen Tirro?' he said.

'I have. He's with Loddlaen, over by the rocks.'

'Ah. Good.' The grim look softened to his more usual neutral expression. 'I'll just make sure he's not up to some wrong thing.'

'And just what that might be?'

Gwairyc considered her for a long cold moment. 'You never know,' he said at last, then strode off, heading for the rocky ridge.

Gwairyc was keeping so strict a watch over Tirro mostly out of boredom. Stuck out here, so far away from the war in Cerrgonney, he was finding the days long and tedious. Even the royal court intrigues, which he'd always hated, would have been more interesting than watching the Westfolk trade horses for Wffyn's ironware.

When he found Tirro and Loddlaen, they were passing a skin of mead back and forth and laughing at some jest. At the sight of Gwairyc, however, Tirro's laughter died with a squeak.

'Having a bit of fun, are you?' Gwairyc said.

'We are,' Loddlaen said. 'What's it to you?'

'Does my master want me?' Tirro said. 'I'll come. I'm sorry.'

'Nah, nah, nah!' Gwairyc said. 'Go ahead, lads. Enjoy yourself. Drink all you want, Tirro. There'll be plenty of work on the morrow.'

Bewildered, Tirro stared up at him. Gwairyc gave them both what he assumed was a pleasant smile, then turned and walked off again. *Get howling drunk, you dog,* Gwairyc thought. *It'll keep that ugly little cock of yours limp.*

The children that Gwairyc was so assiduously protecting had mothers, of course. Once he got used to their strange eyes and even more peculiar ears, Gwairyc found them beautiful. They didn't return the opinion. Every time he smiled at a woman or tried out the few Westfolk words that he'd picked up, she would politely but firmly turn her back or walk away with some muttered excuse in Elvish that, of course, he couldn't understand. Later he'd often overhear these same women speaking perfectly good Deverrian to Wffyn or Nevyn, but if he tried to pursue the acquaintance, they would avoid him ever after.

After some days at the camp, Gwairyc found one woman who let it slip that she knew Deverrian. When he asked her name in the most pleasant way he could manage, her eyes grew wide in something like fear. She crossed her fingers in a warding gesture, backed away, and ran off. Gwairyc swore under his breath and turned around to find Nevyn grinning at him.

'By the black hairy arse of the Lord of Hell!' Gwairyc said. 'What is this, my lord? Have I grown pusboils all over my face or suchlike?'

'Naught of the sort,' Nevyn said. 'But you're from Deverry. Westfolk women think that all Deverry men are household tyrants and wife-beaters.'

'I see. Well, then, it's no wonder they're so cold to me. Here I thought that mayhap there was somewhat wrong with me.'

'Perish the thought.' Nevyn rolled his eyes skyward.

Had Nevyn been a man of his own rank or just somewhat below it, Gwairyc would have challenged him right then and there. As it was, though, Nevyn had dweomer, and with that, or so the Ram lords always said, there was no arguing.

'Somewhat very odd happened to Morwen,' Nevyn said. 'One of the Guardians appeared to her, or at least, I think Alshandra's a Guardian.'

'She is,' Aderyn said, 'and a very nasty one, at that.'

'That's unfortunate. Morwen told me that Alshandra was scouting out the camp, like, looking for her stolen daughter.'

'Stolen daughter?' Aderyn frowned, thinking. 'I wonder what she means by that? I don't know, but I'll wager it's an evil omen.'

The two dweomermasters had walked out into the grasslands, mostly to get away from the noise of the Westfolk camp, but also to take advantage of the warm sunshine while it lasted. On the northern horizon clouds were piling up in huge white drifts, gleaming in the sun for the nonce but threatening rain later.

'Morwen also told me,' Nevyn continued, 'that Tirro saw her and decided she was a goddess.'

'Did he now?' Aderyn made a wry face. 'Maybe she'll do us all a favour and spirit him away.'

'That thought doesn't become you.'

Aderyn shrugged and walked a little faster. Nevyn would have said more, but he heard someone calling Aderyn's name. When he looked back towards the camp, he saw Valandario, pushing her way towards them through the waist-high grass.

'Master Aderyn,' she called out, 'the merchant needs your help to settle an argument. Two of our men are squabbling over one piece of his goods. I am uncertain what the trouble may be, but they're not far from drawing their knives.'

'Bad trouble, then.' Aderyn glanced at Nevyn. 'I'll be back as soon as I can.'

Aderyn hurried off, heading back towards the camp and the trading ground beyond. Nevyn and Valandario followed more slowly. The young journeywoman kept her gaze straight ahead, as if she were afraid to look at Nevyn.

'Has there been any news of your mysterious gift?' Nevyn said.

'There hasn't,' Valandario said, 'but I feel in my heart it will be soon. Um, Master Nevyn, may I be so bold as to ask you a question?'

'Certainly.'

'My thanks! Well, actually, I have a good many of them.' Valandario paused for a shy smile. 'But I know your time is precious.'

'Not particularly precious at the moment. It's clear that you're very interested in gem lore.'

'I am, and that constitutes my first question. Is it a proper sort of study for a journeyman, or journeywoman, I should say? I know not why, but I feel so drawn to gems and crystals. It's as if they have a scent as beautiful as roses, and I can smell them or suchlike. That sounds daft, does it not? Or perhaps, they seem to have auras, and I can feel them even though I cannot see them. It's very hard to explain.'

'Not daft at all. Gems aren't alive like an animal or a plant, but the powerful ones have within them the germs or seeds of life. They don't have minds, of course. Those seeds do produce some effects on the astral and etheric, and events on those planes can affect them in turn.'

'Ah, I see. And they attract spirits, do they not?'

'They do. Elemental spirits feel a certain affinity with them. That's why some workings can attach spirits to the right sort of gems. Notice I say "attach", not "bind". Trapping and binding spirits into gems is an evil practice.'

'I'd never do that, Master Nevyn! But would you say that gems have a certain sensitivity to events in the physical plane?'

'In the right circumstances, most assuredly.'

'And then it's possible that some people have a strong sensitivity to them?'

'Very possible.' Nevyn smiled at her. 'I take it that by the "some people" in question, you mean yourself.'

Valandario blushed. 'I do,' she said. 'I thought I must be sensitive in such a way when I had that dream about the stone. It was as if it were sending some sort of astral perturbation ahead of it. And when I woke up, I wondered if such a thing could happen.'

'It can, certainly. You seem to have found your proper calling within the wider realm of the dweomer, I'd say.'

'Oh, my thanks! My heart is gladdened to hear you say that, Master Nevyn! When I heard you were riding our way, I was so pleased. You see, I heard that you were coming on the very day after I had that dream.'

'Indeed?' Nevyn paused, struck by the odd coincidence – if indeed it were just a coincidence. 'Just who is this young man? Is he anyone I might know?'

'I am not sure. His name is Javanateriel, and he is Loddlaen's foster-brother. His mother nursed Loddlaen after Dallandra left us, and so he knows Aderyn awfully well.'

'Has he ever studied dweomer?'

'He has not.' This time her blush turned deep scarlet. 'I believe that he is merely in love with me.'

'Then he has good taste in women. He has some tenuous connection with the dweomer, however, through you and his mother. I wonder if we have a confluence of forces at work here. You receive the message from your young man, you have the dream, you hear that I've created the Great Stone of the West – which reminds me. How did you hear about my work with the opal?'

'Loddlaen mentioned it,' Valandario said. 'I suppose he heard it from his father.'

'No doubt. Here, don't go mentioning it to anyone else, will you?'

'Of course not. I told Loddlaen at the time that he'd best hold his tongue, too.'

'Ah, my thanks! If you've got no more questions, I think I'll just tell him again myself as well.'

'Oh, I could talk about gems for days and days, so it would be better to let you go now.'

As soon as they returned to the Westfolk camp, Nevyn took his leave of Valandario and began to look for Loddlaen, who was nowhere in evidence. Finally Nevyn saw a lad he knew named Farendar, kneeling on the ground with three others. As he walked up, he noticed that they'd spread out a painted doeskin to play an elaborate game of dice. At his question, they laid the dice aside.

'I'm not sure,' Farendar said. 'I did see him walking with Morwen, Wise One, and that shifty-eyed little apprentice merchant was tagging after them.'

'Oh. You know, I think Loddlaen must have moved his tent. I went by there, but all I saw was a worn patch on the ground.'

'He does that now and again.' Farendar let his lip curl. 'It's our noise. He's too good for the rest of us.'

'That's not it, and you know it.' Another lad scowled at him.

'Just so,' the third said. 'Wise One, don't listen to Far. Loddlaen does keep to himself, but by the Star Gods! there's plenty of room out in the grasslands for a man who needs a little peace and quiet.'

'Ah, I see,' Nevyn said. 'Do you know why he needs it?'

'Loddlaen's just Loddlaen.' The lad got up and shaded his eyes to look around the campground. 'Ah, I think they're down near the stream, past the herd, do you see? By the two willows. It's a fair distance along.'

'My thanks. My old eyes aren't as sharp as yours.'

By following the lad's directions, Nevyn did find Morwen, Tirro, and Loddlaen sitting on the grass in front of the newly placed tent. Evan lay asleep beside his nursemaid. Every few moments Morwen would brush the flies away from the child's face with a whisk she'd woven from strands of dry grass.

A great crowd of Wildfolk swarmed around them, but as he watched, Nevyn noticed that while Loddlaen and Morwen could see them, Tirro seemed oblivious. He'd often make a gesture with his hands or move to a more comfortable position without noticing that he'd nearly sat upon a gnome or swatted a sprite, a lack that surprised Nevyn. Brour might have been a shifty little thief, but he'd had undeniable dweomer gifts. In this life, apparently, he had none.

Loddlaen glanced up and smiled. 'Good morrow, Master Nevyn,' he said.

'And a good morrow to you,' Nevyn said, 'I want a word with you, lad.'

Loddlaen's pale face turned a little paler. For a moment he froze, then scrambled up as quickly as he could. They walked along the stream out of ear-shot of the others.

'Valandario mentioned that you told her about the Great Stone of the West,' Nevyn said. 'I hope you've not told anyone else.'

'I've not, I assure you.' Loddlaen arranged a brittle smile. 'I only mentioned it to Val because of her own gem dweomer.'

'There was no harm in telling Val. It's not precisely a secret, but I don't want it bruited about, either. There are evil men here and there who might covet the thing.'

'True spoken. I shan't say another word to anyone.'

'Good lad!' But Nevyn hesitated. He had a feeling that Loddlaen was lying, but it was only a feeling, and a weak one at that. 'That's all I wanted to ask, so I'll leave you to your friends.'

Loddlaen's smile turned genuine with relief.

Javanateriel brought his gifts for Valandario and Aderyn

into camp the next afternoon. Nevyn and Aderyn were sitting in front of Aderyn's tent when they heard a shout from the general direction of the horse-herd. Aderyn stood up and shaded his eyes as he peered into the distance.

'Someone's arrived.' Aderyn sat back down.

Not long after, Valandario came running. 'It *is* a gem!' she called out. 'I've not seen it yet, but Jav told me that much. My dream was a true one.'

Eventually Javanateriel and his friend, Albaral, joined them at Aderyn's tent. They were both typical Westfolk men, blond and impossibly handsome, but Albaral carried a long scar down one cheek. Aderyn ushered them inside, along with Nevyn, and of course, Valandario. They all sat down in a rough circle around the patch of sunlight coming through the smokehole.

'What about Loddlaen?' Nevyn said.

The two young men exchanged a quick glance.

'I don't know where he is,' Aderyn said with a rueful smile. 'I looked around the camp, but no one seems to know where he went.'

'I saw him walking over to the merchant's camp,' Nevyn continued. 'But that was some while ago.'

'What a pity.' Valandario sounded profoundly relieved. 'He will doubtless be gone for a long while.'

'Ah, too bad,' Aderyn said. 'Now then, Jav. Where did you find these mysterious treasures?'

'First of all,' Jav said, 'Albaral came with me. We rode west on a dare, you see. Just along the coast, though I was half-minded to see if we could get all the way to Rinbaladelan.'

'Half a mind is about right,' Albaral muttered.

Jav ignored him and went on. 'We'd ridden for eight days along the cliffs, following the line of the beach. It's desolate out there – ye gods, at night you can hear the ghosts, drifting back and forth, mourning the lost cities.'

'The sound of the sea on the rocks,' Albaral interrupted again.

'Some of us have more imagination than others.' Jav glared at him. 'Will you hold your tongue and let me finish?' He turned to Valandario. 'It was the thought of you that gave me the courage to go on.'

Albaral pressed one hand to his stomach and the other to his mouth as if he were going to vomit.

'But we found a marvel long before we reached the ruined city,' Jav continued, 'a toppled watchtower.'

'A what?' Aderyn leaned forward, all attention.

'A tower, Wise One, built of fine pale stone. It must have been as tall as a Deverry broch when it was new, but they'd built it right on the edge of the cliff. Those big storms we had this winter past? A big chunk of cliff had eroded and fallen, taking the tower with it. It was spread out along the beach, pointing towards the water.' Jav gestured with his right hand as if he were strewing a line of dice. 'We poked around the stones a bit.'

'He nearly toppled one big stone onto his own foot,' Albaral put in. 'It was balanced on another, you see, and –'

'It's a cursed good thing I did, wasn't it?' Jav turned and scowled at him. 'That's where we found first box.'

'Ah,' Aderyn said, 'the point of this story at last.'

'Just that, Wise One,' Jav said. 'I brought the whole box with me, because oddly enough, it looks new, when you'd think it would have rotted away by now. There must be some sort of dweomer upon it.' With a flourish Jav pulled a wooden box out of a saddlebag and handed it to Aderyn. 'Your gift is inside.' He glanced Valandario's way and smiled. 'Rank before beauty, I thought, even beauty as great as yours.'

Her only answer was a blush. Albaral made a gagging noise.

The narrow box, about a foot and a half long, bore a design of spirals and bands of interlace on its top. From where Nevyn sat, it looked like a nice bit of oak.

'This is an Eldidd-made box,' Aderyn pronounced. 'It's not a question of dweomer in the least. It's quite new, actually. A couple of years old at most.'

Javanateriel's triumphant smile disappeared into a slack mouthed disappointment. Albaral snickered.

'Wise One,' Jav said, 'we truly did find it where I told you it was.'

'Oh, I'm not saying you didn't, lad. The question is, how did it get there?' Aderyn frowned down at the box for a moment, then shrugged and opened the lid. His expression changed to something like awe. 'Now this,' he said softly, 'must be very old indeed.'

Nevyn leaned forward to look. Inside the box lay a scroll written not on parchment but on Bardekian pabrus, a thin, flexible material made from reeds. Pale brown stains and small rips disfigured this particular example, but Nevyn could distinguish a line of faded writing in the elven syllabary.

'I think I'll wait to try unrolling this,' Aderyn said. 'But Jav, you have my heart-felt thanks.'

Javanateriel grinned in sheer pride. Albaral kept quiet.

Aderyn put the lid back on the box. 'Well, bring out the gem you found.' he said. 'We've made Val wait long enough.'

Jav rummaged through the saddlebag and came out with an object wrapped in a scrap of Deverry-made linen tied up with blue ribands. 'It was sitting on top of the box in a shred of rotting cloth. I wrapped it in fresh,' he said to Val. 'I only wish I had fine Bardek silks, all tied with a cord of the purest gold, for you deserve naught but the beautiful.'

Everyone leaned forward to watch while Valandario unwrapped the bit of rough linen. She gasped, let the scrap fall, and held up a truncated pyramid of obsidian, about six inches high, with a base that fit neatly on the palm of her hand. Nevyn had often seen obsidian before – dwarven traders regularly brought pieces to northern Deverry – but he had never seen a cut stone like this. In the bright sun it glittered with reflected light, but it seemed that the light itself turned black as it recoiled from the touch of the gem – an impossible effect, of course, but more witnesses than Nevyn vouched for it.

'The Black Sun,' Aderyn whispered. 'I think I finally understand what that oath means, "by the Black Sun herself". This
thing shines with one of her rays.'

Valandario nodded, staring into the depths. 'Master Nevyn,
is this an evil thing? I feel no harm coming from it, but still,
it glows with darkness!'

'Give it to me.' Nevyn held out his hand. 'I'll test it out.'

'My thanks.' Valandario put it on his palm. 'I am very glad
you're here.'

'Then it's passed the first test.' Nevyn smiled at her. 'If
you'd been unable to part with it, even for a moment – well,
that would have been a sign of great evil.' He paused, shutting his eyes to let his impressions of the obsidian pyramid
fill his mind. 'I feel no harm, either, but I do feel dweomer,
sure enough.' He opened his eyes, then handed the stone
back to her. 'I don't have the slightest idea of what kind of
dweomer, mind. Finding out is going to be your task, not
mine, I think, and it won't be an easy one.'

'I can't think of a better way to spend a few years.' Valandario
turned to Jav and gave him a smile so warm and soft that he
leaned towards her, seemingly without realizing he was doing
so. 'Thank you, I thank you. I am overwhelmed. This is the
most beautiful gift that anyone has ever given me.'

'Then every moment it took me to find it was worth the
trouble, ten times over.' Jav glanced at Albaral. 'Oh just hold
your tongue! I know you're thinking it wasn't worth yours,
but didn't I promise you that golden colt from my herd?'

'I'm glad to see you remember,' Albaral said. 'Saves me
the trouble of badgering you for it.'

'Huh.' Javanateriel stood up. 'Let's go get him now, then.
I suppose you expect me to give you a halter, too.'

Albaral got up and followed him out of the tent. For a
moment Valandario smiled after him, then with a sigh she
brought her attention back to the two dweomermasters.

'I traded for scraps of Bardekian silk last year,' Valandario
said. 'It's lucky I have them. A stone like this deserves a

beautiful wrapping. They are lavender. Is that an appropriate colour, Master Aderyn?'

'It is indeed,' Aderyn said. 'May I have a closer look at the stone?'

'But of course!'

For a long while that afternoon the three dweomerworkers puzzled over the obsidian pyramid. They all could tell that it possessed dweomer; the question was, what kind? The answer eventually came from an utterly unexpected source, when little Evan – or Ebañy, as Nevyn reminded himself – came crawling into the tent.

'Well, well,' Nevyn said to him. 'What brings you here, lad?'

Ebañy shrugged, popped his thumb in his mouth, and stood looking around him. When he noticed the stone, he took the thumb out and smiled.

'Pretty,' he said. 'Pretty stone.'

'It is, truly,' Nevyn said.

Ebañy toddled over and plopped himself down into Nevyn's lap without so much as a by-your-leave. Nevyn put one arm around the lad and held the black stone up to give him a look at it.

'Shiny,' Ebañy said, then laughed aloud. 'Look, island! An island in there.'

'Indeed?' Nevyn worked to keep his voice level. 'So, you see an island inside the stone, do you? Do you see anything else?'

'Water all around. Tall house. Boat with a funny head on it. Lizard head.' Ebañy leaned closer, his eyes suddenly wide. 'And a man, a funny man. Yellow hair.'

'Yellow like Valandario's hair?' Nevyn kept his voice low.

'Not. Yellow buttercups. Blue eyes, funny blue eyes.'

'Does he live on the island?'

Ebañy shook his head no. 'Island all gone. The funny man's got somewhat in his hands.'

'Can you tell me what the somewhat looks like?'

'A flat thing, a flat white thing, and a black lizard. A lizard on it. Not a lizard. A bird.' Suddenly he frowned and shook his head. 'Clouds, and now it's all gone.'

Valandario had been watching wide-eyed. 'Well,' she said, 'I think our Dev has fathered a very remarkable child.'

'I'd say so, too,' Nevyn said.

Aderyn nodded his startled agreement. Outside the tent a frantic female voice began calling Ebañy's name.

'Morri.' Ebañy slipped off Nevyn's lap, then stood up. 'My go to Morri.'

'By all means,' Nevyn said. 'Let's not make her worry.'

Ebañy launched himself into a flat-footed run and barrelled out of the tent. They could hear Morwen laugh in relief and call out to someone, 'I've found him! I'll just give him some dinner.' The voices moved off slowly.

Valandario ran her fingers over the stone. 'A very remarkable child indeed,' she said, 'and he seems to have some kind of kinship with a very remarkable crystal.'

'Indeed,' Nevyn said. 'You're too young to take an apprentice, but then, Ebañy's too young to study the dweomer. When his time comes, you'll be ready.'

She looked up sharply, her lips half-parted.

'It's part of the work,' Nevyn went on. 'Passing on the lore, that is. We don't want to see it lost again. Remember the bitter price of secrecy.'

'True spoken. I only hope I'm good enough to teach him when the time comes.'

'I have a feeling you will be.' Nevyn paused for a smile. 'And now we know what this bit of obsidian is: a showstone.'

'Indeed. But what is it showing us? I wonder who that "funny man" is, for instance.'

'Evandar.' Aderyn spat out the name like a curse. 'There's only one creature it could be. This whole thing is doubtless another one of his blasted riddles.'

'How odd!' Valandario said. 'Little Ebañy seems to be the only person who can see into the stone. Could Evandar have planned that?'

'I wouldn't be surprised if he did, even down to the names. Evan and Evandar, I mean – he might well have intended us to see the resemblance.' Aderyn paused for a grimace. 'Oh, who knows the all of what the Guardians can or can't do? Or why they do it, either. I suppose the lizard that might be a bird is a dragon.'

'Ye gods!' Nevyn said. 'So the Maelwaedds of Aberwyn are mixed up in this?'

'So it would seem,' Aderyn said. 'I wonder if I'll ever forgive Evandar? I wonder even more if I should bother.'

'Of course you should,' Nevyn said wearily, 'but for your own sake, not his. Hatred binds a man to what he hates, and I think me you need to be free of him.'

For a brief moment, rage flared in Aderyn's eyes. Then he managed to smile, a twisted wry smile, but a smile nonetheless. 'True spoken. Well, this certainly explains why that box is so new.'

'It does indeed,' Nevyn said. 'Evandar must have put both the stone and the scroll there when he saw your lads riding west.'

'I wonder why the slimy little – I mean, I wonder why he left the scroll?' Aderyn looked down at the box in his lap. 'No doubt he never meant it to come to me.'

'I'm sure he meant just that,' Nevyn said. 'From everything you've told me about him, I'd say he thinks in a very primitive way. A bride-price, or part of one, is my guess.'

Aderyn swore under his breath in Deverrian.

'My apologies, Master Aderyn,' Valandario said, 'but I do not know those words you just used.'

'Good,' Aderyn said. 'You don't need to. Now, as for this scroll, we probably won't know what Evandar intended until we open it. I don't want to do it right in the middle of camp, just in case there's some foul spell or suchlike on it.'

Nevyn sighed aloud. 'Oh come now! Wouldn't I have felt the resonances if it were some evil thing?'

'Um, truly, you would.' Aderyn had the grace to look

embarrassed. 'But you never know about the Guardians.' He glanced at Valandario. 'Nevyn and I will take a look at this first, some distance away from camp. Later we'll tell you what we've found. I don't care to take chances with your well-being.'

'As you wish, Master Aderyn.' Valandario stroked the gem with two loving fingers. 'I shall have plenty of work to occupy me on the morrow as it is.'

After the evening meal, Nevyn decided to look in on Wffyn. As he walked across the strip of neutral ground twixt the merchant and his prospective customers, he could see the horses that Wffyn had already acquired in trade, a beautiful herd of some twenty head, mostly blacks and dapple greys, but here and there he saw a golden horse with a silvery mane and tail. Around their campfires the muleteers were laughing and joking with each other as they passed around a skin of elven mead.

Wffyn himself was sitting cross-legged on the grass and unloading some hammered steel knife blades from one of his canvas packs. He laid a scant selection of blades and other small bits of ironware out on a blanket big enough to hold three times as many. Firelight winked and danced on the polished metal.

'Nevyn, and a good evening to you!' Wffyn called out.

'And the same to you,' Nevyn said. 'It looks like you've sold most of your wares.'

'I have, and truly, I've done well enough, I suppose.'

'You sound mournful.'

'I am, but it's my own fault for reaching too high. I've been trying to acquire a stud and a couple of brood mares, as I believe I told you some while past. No one would sell me anything but geldings. I tried offering gold, I tried gems, but naught did I get in return but scorn.'

'Ah.' Nevyn wasn't in the least surprised. *The Westfolk aren't stupid!* he thought to himself. Aloud, he said, 'That's a pity.'

'True spoken, good sir! Well, soon we'll be heading back to Pyrdon. Will you and your apprentice be coming with us?'

'I doubt it. I've not seen Aderyn in many a year, and we still have much to talk about.'

'What about little Morri? Is she going to settle here, do you think?'

'Most definitely. She told me she'd never been so happy in her life.'

'No doubt that's true. The poor lass!' Wffyn paused to look around him. 'I wonder where Tirro's got to.'

'Gwairyc probably knows. I'll ask him to send your wandering prentice back to you.'

For some days Morwen had been waiting for a chance to question Loddlaen about the dweomer. He seemed willing enough to discuss it, but every time they started a conversation, it came to an abrupt end. Either Ebañy would wake and demand her attention, or someone from the Westfolk camp would innocently interrupt, or Tirro would appear, all ears. Once, when Loddlaen had been telling her about dweomer gems, they'd caught Tirro hiding in the rocks above Loddlaen's tent. Loddlaen had scolded him for it, too, but Tirro had grovelled and wept his way into forgiveness.

On the evening of the day that Javanateriel returned, she left Ebañy with his father, and she and Loddlaen retreated to his tent site, well out of earshot of the noisy camp. They'd just started talking when Tirro trotted up and sat himself down at the fire without so much as a by-your-leave. He'd brought them a basket of bread and a honeycomb, wrapped in fresh leaves, to drip onto the slices.

'Morri, I thought you might like somewhat other than meat,' Tirro said.

'Well, that does look lovely, and my thanks,' Morwen said, but she was thinking that she would rather have had the privacy.

Tirro passed the bread and honey around, talking all the while, but he saved his real news till the last.

'We're leaving tomorrow,' Tirro said. 'It'll sadden my heart to go, truly.'

'Well, once you've become that rich Bardekian merchant,' Loddlaen said, 'mayhap you can return.'

Tirro tried to smile, but he suddenly looked like a small child, lost in some strange place but determined not to cry.

'Or maybe sooner than that,' Morwen said. 'From what you've told us, Bardekian goods should do well out here. Spices for the meats, carpets for the tents, that sort of thing.'

'That's true!' Tirro tried another smile. 'And I won't have to be rich to get together a shipment of little things like oil lamps and glass beads.'

'Well, there you go, then!' Loddlaen saluted him with a slice of bread.

They'd nearly finished eating when a second uninvited guest showed up: Gwairyc. He strode into the pool of light from the fire and pointed a finger at Tirro.

'You,' Gwairyc said. 'Have you been here the whole time?'

'I have, truly.' Tirro said.

'Good, but now your master wants you. He says you're to go back to camp. There's packing to be done, lad.'

Without another word Tirro got up and followed, leaving the last of the bread and the basket both. Morwen waited for their footsteps to die away into the darkness before she spoke.

'Poor Tirro! Gwairyc truly does treat him like a dog.'

'Gwairyc treats everyone like a dog – well, except for Nevyn and my Da, of course,' Loddlaen said. 'What I wonder is why Tirro puts up with it.'

'Tirro's terrified of him.'

'True spoken, but why?' Loddlaen was silent for a long moment as he thought something through. 'You know, I'd like to have a talk with Tirro before they go. Once he's finished his work, his master shouldn't mind. I'll take this basket back for an excuse, like.' He glanced into it. 'You can have that honeycomb for Ebañy.'

'He'll enjoy that ever so much. But Loddlaen, about the dweomer, do you have to be born with it, or can you learn it?'

'Both. You have to have the gift, but then you've got to study for years and years. It's not some simple thing.' He looked away, and for a moment he looked as sad as Tirro had earlier. 'I've got the gift, but it's a slender one. I keep trying to study, but I'll never match my Da.'

'You can't be sure of that. He's a fair bit older than you, isn't he? So he's years ahead. Besides, to have even a small touch of dweomer – oh, it seems so wonderful!'

'Does it?' All at once Loddlaen laughed aloud. 'You know, for years I've been thinking of it as a burden, and here you are, all amazed! My thanks, Morri. You see things more clearly than I do, I think.'

'Oh, I doubt that. I wish I had a gift for dweomer.'

'But you must. You're a Deverry woman but you see the Wildfolk. The only Roundears who can see them all have dweomer gifts.'

Morwen caught her breath, too stunned to speak.

'Now, how much of one I couldn't say,' Loddlaen continued. 'You won't know that till you start learning to use it.' His voice fell to a bitter whisper. 'They let you see the treasures, sometimes, then snatch them away.'

Morwen barely heard him. Her mind was galloping like a half-tamed horse towards the freedom of an open gate.

'Do you truly think I could study dweomer?' she said.

'Why not? It's the only way to find out how great a gift you have.'

'I'm afraid to ask Nevyn or your da. They'll think it's presumptuous of a cripple like me, I'll wager. Whenever I wanted anything, you know, it got snatched away from me, one way or another.'

'Truly?'

'Truly. I remember finding a copper in the marketplace when I was a little child, and how my brother took it from me. He pried my fingers open to get it, while my da just laughed. I made myself a doll out of straw, and my sister snatched it, and no one would make her give it back. Well, those were silly little things, I know, but it was always like that.' Morwen paused on the edge of tears, thinking of Lanmara. 'Everything I ever loved got taken away. Except for Evan – Ebañy I mean. I nearly lost him, too, and I would have, but for Nevyn.'

Loddlaen was watching her solemnly with his head tilted a little to one side. 'I'm so sorry,' he said. 'I thought I had a wretched time as a child, but I can see that yours was worse.'

'Oh, maybe, maybe not. I'm surprised that all those little things still matter so much. But you see, I'm afraid that if I asked Nevyn or your da to teach me about dweomer, they'd just laugh. That would be so horrid.'

'I can understand that.' Loddlaen reached out and caught her hand in a sympathetic squeeze. 'But I could teach you what I know.'

'Would you? Will you truly?'

'I will.' He smiled at her. 'It'll be our secret until we see how strong your gifts are.'

'Our secret?' Morwen hesitated, feeling a stab of doubt. 'Shouldn't we tell Nevyn at least?'

'And have him stop us? He might, you know. The masters are really jealous of their precious lore. They don't want to share it with anyone they don't think is worthy of it.'

If ever a person fell under the heading of 'unworthy', Morwen supposed, it would be her, with her nasty temper and well-stewed resentments, to say naught of her ugly face. Loddlaen – handsome, kind Loddlaen – smiled a little as he leaned towards her and touched her hand.

'Oh do come on, Morri,' he said. 'It'll be grand, having a secret that's ours alone.'

'So it would. Well and good, then, and my thanks.'

They talked until late that night, while above them the stars wheeled in a brilliantly clear sky. Somewhere well past midnight Morwen realized that she was in danger of falling asleep where she sat, and Loddlaen kept yawning. She gathered the remains of the honeycomb up in the leaves and hurried back to Devaberiel's tent.

Fortunately Ebañy slept late the next morning. Apparently his father had kept him up far longer than Morwen would have. It was the middle of the morning before she woke, only to find Ebañy just beginning to stir. He was wet, of course, since he'd slept so long. She fed him, then took him down to the stream, where she washed out his blanket. Ebañy was singing to himself and playing some elaborate game with shiny pebbles when Loddlaen came hurrying up to them.

'Morri?' Loddlaen said. 'I'm going down to talk with the merchant about Tirro. Why don't you come with me?'

'What's Tirro done?'

'Naught, naught.' Loddlaen smiled at her. 'I had a long talk with the lad early this morning, and we hatched a plan. I could use a bit of support.'

'I'll come then, of course. Let me just finish cleaning Ebañy up. He had that honeycomb with his breakfast.'

Honey and dirt smeared his face from ear to ear, but a twist of grass and some stream water soon solved that problem. She spread his blanket out to dry on clean grass before they left. Hand in hand they walked with Loddlaen across the empty stretch of meadow between the Westfolk and the merchant's camps. Morwen felt as if she were crossing a real border, twixt the Deverry world and the Westfolk world, and that by going over to the Deverry side she'd gone among strangers rather than back to her kinsfolk. *We've not been here long,* she thought, *but oh, it's been so lovely!*

They'd just reached the merchant's camp when someone hailed them from behind. Morwen glanced back to see Gwairyc trotting after them.

'Oh ye gods!' Loddlaen muttered. 'What does he want, I wonder?'

Gwairyc told them when he caught up. 'I just thought I'd have a last word with Tirro.'

'It might not be the last one,' Loddlaen said. 'Wait and see!'

'What?' Gwairyc snapped. 'What do –'

Loddlaen chuckled under his breath. 'Wait and see,' he repeated. 'We might be having a bit of a surprise.'

In Wffyn's camp the muleteers were trotting back and forth. Some were carrying packs and packsaddles out to the herd to set beside the mules, who were still grazing; others were haltering the Westfolk horses and roping them together. Wffyn was standing in the midst of all this confusion while Tirro knelt at his feet, putting the last pieces of ironware into a canvas pack. When he saw Loddlaen and the others coming, Tirro got up.

'Master,' he said, 'I want to ask you somewhat.'

'Do you?' Wffyn said. 'Well, ask away.'

Tirro took a deep breath. His eyes shone – it was the first time she'd ever seen him look truly happy, Morwen realized. 'I want to stay here with the Westfolk,' Tirro said. 'I spoke with Loddlaen about it, and he said I could. It will save Da a fair bit of coin if I never come back, and he won't mind.'

'Well, by the gods!' Wffyn said with a laugh. 'This is a bolt from a clear sky, lad.' He glanced at Loddlaen. 'Do you truly think your father would allow him to stay?'

'I do, sir.' Loddlaen stepped forward. 'There's one good thing about living as we do out here. We always have room for another person. Tirro's been truly unhappy in Cerrmor, and he told me that he'd got into some sort of trouble, but out here, in the wild country, he would –'

'Some sort of trouble?' Gwairyc turned to Tirro. 'Did you tell him what?'

Tirro went dead-pale.

'I see you didn't,' Gwairyc said. 'Here, Loddlaen, this is a horse you don't want running with your herd. He was thrown out of Cerrmor for raping a little lass, no more than six summers old, she was.'

'I did not rape her!' Tirro burst out. 'I truly loved Mella, and she loved me. I never would have hurt her.' He froze for a long moment, then winced and clasped both hands over his mouth, as if he could shove the confession back in.

For a moment Morwen feared that she was going to vomit and disgrace herself. 'You horrible foul swine,' she said. 'You disgusting lump of –' Words failed. She grabbed Ebañy, picked up him, and stepped back a few paces to put distance twixt him and the creature she once had pitied.

Tirro turned to Loddlaen and held out both hands, but he could say nothing, apparently, judging from the way he gulped for air.

'You've got children in your alar,' Gwairyc continued. 'Do you truly want this piss-poor excuse for a man riding with you?'

'I don't.' Loddlaen was very nearly whispering. 'You have my thanks, Gwarro. I had no idea.'

Tirro spun around and raised balled fists at Gwairyc. 'I hate you,' Tirro burst out. 'I'll hate you forever for this.'

'Will you now?' Gwairyc hooked his thumbs in his belt and looked the lad over. 'Am I supposed to be frightened by that?'

Tirro's face turned dark red. 'You wait,' he snarled. 'I'll get you for this. I swear I will.'

Gwairyc laughed. Tirro spun on his heel and took one stride as if he were planning to break into a run, but he nearly collided with Wffyn. He began to cry, moist sobs so loud, so violent, that he could barely stand upright.

'Oh ye gods,' Gwairyc said wearily. 'I should have slit your throat and thrown you out for the ravens. You snivelling little coward!'

At last Tirro managed to control his sobs and haul himself upright. Panting for breath, he set his hands on his hips. 'Sneer all you want,' he said between gasps. 'I'll get you for this one fine day. I swear it. I shall have my revenge.'

'Such fine words! There's green snot all over your lip, by the by.'

Morwen burst out laughing, a shrill little cackle of mockery.

Tirro began to sob, his skinny little face so pale that she thought he might faint, but Wffyn grabbed him by one arm.

'Come along, you,' Wffyn said. 'It's time to ride to Cerrmor. That ship bound for Bardek will be waiting for you.'

Tirro pulled his arm free, shook himself, and tried to muster a haughty expression. For a moment the expression held, but only for a moment, before he began to weep again. Wffyn hauled him off, still sobbing. No one spoke until they were out of earshot.

'In a way,' Loddlaen said, 'I feel sorry for him.'

'How could you?' Morwen snapped.

'Well, he's another human being, isn't he?' Loddlaen hesitated, thinking. 'Some evil thing must have made him the way he is.'

'I suppose you're right.' Gwairyc's eyes showed a brief flicker of remorse. 'But this should teach him that he'd best mend his ways.'

'We can ask your da,' Morwen said. 'About what made Tirro the way he is, I mean.'

'Oh, I don't think we'd better.' Loddlaen's voice trembled. 'I don't want my father to know about this.'

'And why not?' Morwen said.

'Because I nearly let Alastyr into the alar. I feel like such a cursed fool now, trusting him. I even kind of liked him. I don't want Da to know how stupid I was. And then there's Nevyn. I can't tell you how much I admire him. I don't want him to know, either, how close I came to making a wretched rotten mistake.'

'I do see what you mean.' Morwen glanced at Gwairyc. 'What do you think?'

'Doesn't matter to me.' Gwairyc shrugged. 'I won't mention it if you'd rather I didn't.'

'I do wish,' Loddlaen said. 'Please, let's just not let anyone know.' His voice dropped to a whisper. 'They all hate me enough already.'

*   *   *

Nevyn and Aderyn, meanwhile, were sitting in the sweeping shade of a willow tree, upstream a good long way from both encampments, where they could examine Jav's gift privately. Before he opened the box, Aderyn made a warding circle around them, the scroll, and the trees, too, for good measure. Once the pentagrams shone clearly at the cardinal points, he sat down again and took out the scroll. In the dappled shade he spread it out, revealing it to be only a few feet long and torn off towards the end as well. Rows of dark brown symbols marched across the tan-coloured pabrus, whilst all round them in the margins someone had scrawled more symbols in red.

'That red ink intrigues me,' Aderyn said. 'It hasn't faded like the other, older writing. I'm guessing, anyway, that the main body of writing was black to begin with.'

'No doubt,' Nevyn said. 'Now, that red – they make it in Bardek, but it's a guild secret.'

'That's a pity. Perhaps I can get one of the merchants to bring me some next year. I'll wager it's for sale in Aberwyn, what with Wmmglaedd so near. Maybe the pabrus is, too. But be that as it may, the style of the brown writing is much older than the red, so I'm assuming that the scroll was annotated long after it was copied.'

'That's reasonable. Do you know by whom?'

'I don't.' Aderyn laid a fingertip on one of the red scrawls. 'But it must have been by someone with dweomer. This note tells us that at least one word is missing from this formula, because it, and I quote, gave no result.'

'Fascinating! One of these days I must learn to read Elvish.'

'Well, the actual formulae aren't Elvish. They just use the same syllabary, but there's an Elvish translation given for each one. Let me sound out a bit for you.'

When he read out loud, Aderyn kept his voice deliberately conversational; he even at moments paused to break up the flow of sound. Neither he nor Nevyn wanted to find some powerful being standing in front of them, evoked by accident and furious about it.

'Bah-zoad-em ay-loh ee-tah,' Aderyn began, 'Pee-rip-so-noo obla-noo. Noh-zoad-ak-vah bay-hay – Well, you get the idea.'

'Ye gods!' Nevyn said. 'I've never heard anything like that in my life. What does it mean?'

'According to the translation, it means: the mid-day, the first, is like the third of the highest, made of twenty-six purple –' Aderyn hesitated briefly '– purple pillars. Sorry, the Elvish word the glossor used for pillar here is quite archaic.'

'I'm not surprised. Read out some more of the originals, if you don't mind, and let me see what impressions I receive.'

As Aderyn continued reading, one careful syllable at a time, Nevyn allowed himself to sink into a shallow trance. Even though the words sounded like utter nonsense to him, his mind began to form images in response to the sounds. He began to see pieces of buildings and quick flashes of bizarre landscapes, lit by peculiar light. Very occasionally he got a brief impression of a spirit or a being moving through the image.

Aderyn paused to rest his voice and drink from the water-skin he'd brought along. Nevyn shook himself and slapped his hand upon the grassy ground to earth out any trace of the forces they might have invoked.

'Those are incredibly powerful formulae,' Nevyn said. 'I don't know a word of that language, but it had its effects upon me nonetheless.'

'I was hoping it would.' Aderyn's eyes gleamed, like those of a farm lad who sees a market fair spread out before him after long months of hard work. 'This scroll was truly a splendid gift. It must have come from the ruined cities.'

'It's lucky it survived. I wonder why Evandar gave it to you?'

'Well, you know, from time to time he has done favours for me. I suppose you're right, and the wretched creature is trying to pay me a price for my wife.'

'He may be honestly remorseful.'

'Hah! He's not evolved enough for that.'

'Are you certain?'

'Of course I am!' Aderyn had snarled the words, but he caught himself and took a deep breath. 'My apologies. I'm grateful for this scroll, mind, no matter what Evandar may have had in mind.' He stroked the box lid as if it were a pet cat. 'I wouldn't be surprised if these evocations lead me right into the centre of the lost lore.'

'No more would I,' Nevyn said. 'If I were you, I'd study them most carefully before chanting any of them.'

'Have no fear of that! I'm not given to sticking my hand into fires, either.'

One by one they worked through the formulae on the scroll. Aderyn would read the original words; Nevyn would consider them and mouth a few to see what images they evoked in his mind. Aderyn would do the same, and then they would compare the images, only to find in every case but one that they matched. At that point Aderyn would read the translation. They found that the images consistently bore some relation to details in the translation of the formula as well. The one exception was, of course, the formula with the missing word or words. Somehow or other each formula was putting them in contact with an exactly designated part of the inner planes.

By the time they'd finished reading the last evocation on the scroll, the sun was hanging half-way between noon and sundown. Nevyn felt a little dazed, even though they'd both taken care to remain in normal consciousness.

'We need to eat,' Aderyn said. 'I should have brought food with us, but somehow it slipped my mind, I was so eager to take another look at the scroll.'

'Well, I didn't think of it either.'

'Huh, we should both start taking some of our own herbs. Do we have any that help the memory? I don't remember.'

They shared a laugh.

'Which does remind me,' Nevyn said. 'I promised you

some medicinal brimstone. I'd best fetch it before I forget again.'

Wffyn's caravan was long gone by the time they reached the Westfolk camp. While Aderyn went to find someone to cook them dinner, Nevyn ducked into Aderyn's tent to fetch the medicinals and found Gwairyc there, napping on top of his blankets with his saddle for a pillow. He sat up with a yawn.

'No need for you to get up, lad,' Nevyn told him.

'Oh, I don't mind being roused, my lord. I was just bored, not truly tired. In a way, I'm going to miss Tirro. Guarding the little bastard gave me somewhat to do.'

As soon as Nevyn opened his mule pack, he realized that Lord Corbyn's silver cup was missing. He remembered that he'd tucked his supply of brimstone into the cup for safe keeping, because the dwarven alchemist from whom he'd bought it had packed the yellow powder into short lengths of sausage casing, tied off at each end with thread, an efficient but vulnerable container. He eventually found the brimstone, but not the cup.

'Tirro, I wager,' Gwairyc said.

'Well, we don't know that for a certainty,' Nevyn said, 'but I wouldn't be surprised if he was the thief.'

'If one of the Westfolk wanted it badly enough, he'd have come right up and asked you for it.'

'That's true, isn't it? Ah well, it's not worth riding after Wffyn to fetch it back.'

'No doubt, my lord, but it vexes me.' Gwairyc shook his head as if trying to shake off the frustration. 'It's just too cursed easy to steal things out here, with everything lying around on the ground, like, and people coming and going from everyone's tents.'

'You have a point, truly.'

Nevyn laid a tube of sulphur on top of one of Aderyn's sacks of medicinals, then left the tent. He found Loddlaen standing right outside, staring down at the ground. When

Nevyn spoke to him, he looked up fast and took a step back, then laughed.

'You startled me, sir,' Loddlaen said. 'Is Da in there?'

'He's not,' Nevyn said. 'He's off looking for food.'

'Well, it's not truly important. Val was just showing me her new gem, and I was wondering what you and he thought of it.'

'Both of us found it very impressive, not that we could tell much about it. It seems to be a showstone of sorts, though.'

'I thought it was marvellous. It radiates an odd sort of power, doesn't it?'

'It does, but what sort of power? That's what I don't know. Here, did Val let you look into it?'

'She did. I saw a light moving in it, but it might just have been a reflection from the sunlight. It's a crystal, after all.'

'So it is. But the light moved?'

'Back and forth, as if it were the end of a rope someone was swinging. When I told Val that, she got excited, but she doesn't know what it means.'

'Well, no doubt she'll figure it out. She's got quite an affinity for gems.'

'She certainly does. Well, my thanks. I'll find Da sooner or later, no doubt.'

Loddlaen turned and walked away. Nevyn watched him till he disappeared among the tents and general clutter. *I've got to do somewhat for that lad*, he told himself. *But I wonder if his father will let me?*

On the morrow, Aderyn's healing work occupied him until mid-afternoon. When it came time to leave the disorder of the camp in order to work with the scroll, Valandario joined them. Aderyn insisted on Loddlaen coming along as well. Nevyn decided against arguing the point, mostly out of respect for his friend, but also because he wondered just how much of a dweomer gift Loddlaen might show.

The four of them returned to the spot in the shade of the

willow trees and settled themselves in the grass. As before, Aderyn paced out a protective circle. The blue light built up the pentagrams even faster and more solidly than it had the day before. Nevyn could feel power flowing from Valandario to contribute to the ritual, but from Loddlaen, nothing. Once they started working with the scroll, however, Loddlaen read off several of the red marginal notes and had information to add.

'This one here, number seven,' Loddlaen said. 'The note says that ra-as corresponds to our word van-el, the East. Whoever wrote it didn't realize that there's an older Elvish word for east, ra-san-ah. I wonder if the two are related.'

'That's very interesting,' Nevyn said. 'Where did you hear it, ra-san-ah, I mean?'

'In one of Dev's songs, the one he does at the day of remembrance for the Great Burning. He learned the song from an older bard who learned it from a man who'd been alive at the time.'

Nevyn began to think that indeed, he'd judged the lad's gifts too harshly, but once they began reciting the formulae, it became obvious that Loddlaen's knowledge came from the intellect, not from the deeper levels of the mind that need to resonate with dweomer workings if the workings are to have any effect.

'Rah-as ee Sal-mah-noo par-ah-de-zo-od.' Aderyn was reading from the seventh formula. 'Oh-ay Kah-ree-mee Ah-ah-oh.' He paused and turned to Loddlaen. 'What images does that evoke for you?'

'Images?' Loddlaen said. 'I don't see any. Is it some sort of description?'

'It is. Well, let's try the next one.'

As Aderyn continued to read from the scroll, Loddlaen's response was always the same. He saw nothing, felt nothing from hearing this alien tongue. Finally, after Aderyn had read five separate formulae, his disappointment began to show in his voice. Loddlaen began to describe images, but they had nothing to do with the text or with the work Aderyn and Nevyn had done on the previous day.

'You're just making those up, aren't you?' Aderyn said finally. 'You're not really trying at all.'

'Da, I am trying.' Loddlaen kept his gaze on the grass in front of him. 'I'm sorry.'

Aderyn set his mouth in a little twist of a scowl.

'You look tired to me, lad,' Nevyn said briskly. 'Sometimes simple weariness interferes with dweomer work, particularly speculative work like this.' He turned to Aderyn. 'I think he's done enough for one day. Apprentices need to build their stamina slowly.'

'Perhaps so,' Aderyn said. 'Loddlaen, are you tired?'

'I am, Da. I'm sorry.'

'Oh, no need to apologize!' But Aderyn sounded down-right peevish. 'Did you want to just go back to camp?'

Loddlaen smiled in evident relief. He got up, looked at Nevyn, mouthed a 'thanks', then turned and hurried off as if he were afraid his father would change his mind and insist he remain. When Nevyn glanced at Valandario, he found that she'd carefully arranged her face to reveal nothing at all. He wondered how often she'd witnessed similar scenes.

It was Valandario's turn to try working with the images. Although her responses were never as clear or strong as those of the two dweomermasters, she did receive impressions that matched the translations, especially when one of the formulae mentioned a gem.

'Well,' Aderyn said at last. 'That's enough for one day, I think, but we're on to somewhat grand, if you ask me. We need to consider what these images might have meant to the dweomermasters of the old cities.' He rolled up the scroll and put it into its box, then handed it to Nevyn. 'Why don't you keep the scroll with you for a while? You're quite skilled at picking up impressions from objects like this. I'd like to know more about the original copyist and glossor.'

'Me too. I'll see if I can find anything out.' Nevyn hesitated, choosing words. 'But you know, that work requires a partic- ular kind of silence and privacy.'

Aderyn laughed with a toss of his head. 'You're telling me that you'd like to move out of my noisy tent,' he said. 'Tactfully, of course.'

'Of course.' Nevyn returned his smile. 'It's not so much the noise, mind, as the etheric traces. People come in and out of your tent all day long. They're usually either sick or troubled in mind, after all, and they leave disturbances behind them.'

'True spoken,' Aderyn said. 'I feel them myself, especially during the winter, when I can't get outside much. But be that as it may, we'll have to see about getting you a tent made.'

'Master Nevyn?' Valandario leaned forward, and her cheeks flamed scarlet. 'You could have my tent. You see, I'll be moving into – well, into another one.'

'Aha!' Aderyn grinned at her. 'So, Jav finally convinced you?'

'He did. We were going to move my things this afternoon, when I returned, and I honestly did not know what to do with my tent. It's quite well-made, Master Nevyn, though you'll want to have your apprentice beat the floor cloth. I fear me that I do little in the way of keeping things clean.'

Valandario looked so happy that Nevyn couldn't bring himself to voice his doubts, not so much for her, but for Javanateriel. Would he someday be as bitter as Aderyn when his woman left him for her true work? *None of your affair!* he told himself sharply. Besides, since Jav had not the slightest trace of dweomer gifts about him, their bond would be an ordinary one, not the iron clamp around two souls such as Dallandra had shared with Aderyn. *It might be the best thing for Val*, Nevyn thought. *Maybe he can get her to eat more often, if naught else.*

When they returned to camp, Nevyn set Gwairyc to moving their possessions over to their new tent. It was small, though big enough for two men, and well made indeed of new panels of deer hide, painted on the outside with a tracery of flowers. They pitched it some distance away from the camp itself. While Gwairyc took the filthy floor cloth away to beat out the dust and bits of ancient food, Nevyn sat just inside the door and enjoyed the relative silence. He'd been feeling a growing sense of irritation with the noise, the clutter, and the daytime disorganization of a Westfolk gathering.

'This will be much better,' Nevyn said to Gwairyc when he returned. 'Sometimes I wonder if these people ever tire of making noise.'

'No noisier than the king's dun, my lord,' Gwairyc said. 'It's a fair bit quieter at night than Dun Deverry.'

'Well, that's true. They do train their children to sleep in utter silence. That's one good thing I can say for them.'

'And the men don't snore. Huh, an odd thing, that.' Gwairyc suddenly grinned. 'I wish I could teach my men back home that trick. The sound of a night-time barracks would probably drive you daft.'

'Oh no doubt! It's good thing I never wanted to ride with a warband.'

Every evening, once Ebañy was asleep in his father's care, Morwen would join Loddlaen to learn more dweomer. She was surprised to find that she already knew the first elements of the lore. Since the priestesses of the Moon had always assumed she would someday join them in the temple, they had taught her how to visualize images and chant prayers in the proper voice, a deep vibration of sound. Instead of prayers, Loddlaen taught her how to use that voice in the small beginning rituals of dweomer. He also told her what she was supposed to be visualizing when she meditated.

Thanks to the Holy Ladies, she already knew that the universe had more levels than the physical plane, but Loddlaen had surprised her when he'd told her that every creature, human and animal alike, had several bodies. For

some days now she'd been learning how to visualize a body
of light so that she could eventually see some of those levels
for herself.

'You really are making splendid progress,' Loddlaen said
that evening. 'I'll wager your gifts are much greater than mine.'

'Oh come now!' Morwen said. 'It's because you're a
splendid teacher.'

'Well, my thanks. I suppose that's somewhat to the good.'
With a sigh he looked away. 'I wish I had that black stone
of Val's.'

'Why?'

'Every time she lets me touch it, I feel –' He frowned,
thinking hard. 'It's hard to put into words. I feel like it's
giving off power, like the sun gives off light. I can absorb it
the way you'd sit in the sun on a chilly morning to warm
yourself. So if I had it with me, I'd finally be powerful enough
to learn dweomer the way my Da wants me to.'

'Why don't you see if Val will trade it to you? You were
saying the other night that you've got lots of extra horses.'

'What a sensible idea!' Loddlaen grinned at her. 'Morri, I
don't know what I'd do without you. Here, let's get back to
our lesson, but first thing on the morrow, I'll ask Val.'

Valandario, however, had no intention of trading away the
obsidian pyramid. Morwen accompanied Loddlaen when he
went to see if she'd bargain, but her answer left no doubt.

'Not for all the horses in the world,' Valandario said
solemnly. 'It fits too well with my work, you see. If it were
an ordinary gem, I would give it to you in return for that
silver colt of yours, but it's not. It's the key to a great many
things I'm studying.' She shot a nervous glance Morwen's
way. 'Studying about jewellery, I mean.'

That's right, Morwen told herself. *I'm not supposed to know
anything about dweomer*. Aloud she said, 'It must be very
difficult to cut black firestone like that. Doesn't it shatter?'

'It does,' Val said brightly. 'That is the reason I need to
study the pyramid. Someone managed to cut it.'

Loddlaen kept quiet during this exchange. When Morwen glanced his way, she saw that his face had gone pale. At his temple a vein stood out and twitched repeatedly. She laid a soothing hand on his arm, but he shook it off, then turned and strode away. Morwen stared after him.

'He does so hate it when people say him nay,' Valandario said softly. 'Though his temper has improved just recently. You are good for him, Morri. It gladdens my heart to see him more at ease.'

Morwen realized with a sense of shock that Val thought she was Loddlaen's lover. *As if he'd want an ugly thing like me!* she thought. That someone would entertain the idea, however, was surprisingly pleasant.

'Oh, we're just friends,' Morwen said, 'but we do have some nice long talks.'

'Ah, I see.' Val winked at her. 'But you never know what may happen, do you?'

'I suppose not. Um, I'd best go find Ebañy. He's playing with his little friend Danno, and they're probably running Danno's mother ragged.'

That evening, when she arrived at Loddlaen's tent for her dweomer lesson, Loddlaen had returned to his usual self. Still, when she considered asking him about his afternoon's fit of temper, some feeling from deep in her mind warned her off. She concentrated on that evening's lesson instead. By the time she left him, he'd made several small jests and seemed in a very good mood indeed.

In the long hot summer afternoons, Nevyn, Aderyn, and Valandario fell into a routine. After a scant meal they would walk upriver away from the noisy camp and work with the dweomer scroll, trying out the various incantations and discussing the results with one another until the images held steady in everyone's mind. Loddlaen generally managed to find one excuse or another to skip these sessions. Much to Nevyn's relief, Aderyn eventually stopped asking him to join them.

At first Val brought her obsidian gem along, but whatever its mysterious dweomer attributes might have been, working with the scroll was apparently not one of them. While either Aderyn or Nevyn intoned an invocation, she would study its various surfaces, but she saw nothing of any value.

'Every now and then,' she said in her careful way, 'I see a flash of light, but it reveals naught. It comes and goes at random, not in response to any words.'

'Very well then,' Aderyn said. 'Apparently Evandar's two gifts aren't related. It was a good guess that they might be, however.'

'I shan't bring it any more,' Val said. 'It will be safer in my tent. I should hate to drop it or suchlike.'

The danger lying in wait for the stone, however, had naught to do with chips and cracks. Late one afternoon, after the three dweomerworkers had returned to camp, Nevyn and Aderyn were sitting in front of Aderyn's tent, taking the last of the sun and saying very little. They heard, above the usual noise and bustle, a piercing high shriek of mingled rage and fear that could only have come from a woman's throat.

'That's Val!' Aderyn sprang to his feet. 'Ye gods!'

Nevyn got up and followed him as Aderyn ran through the camp. They found Val standing in front of her tent, fists clenched, tears running down her face, while Javanateriel held her in his arms and murmured soothing words in Elvish. When Aderyn spoke to them in the same, she answered him with a burst of fury that made him step back.

'Val?' Nevyn spoke in Deverrian. 'What happened?'

'My pyramid is missing, Master Nevyn.' Val gulped for breath. 'I know Loddlaen stole it, and no one wants to believe me.'

'Val, beloved,' Jav said, 'we can't accuse someone without a shred of evidence.'

Aderyn crossed his arms tightly over his chest and pinched his lips together.

'I suspect that Val and her gem are linked strongly enough that she knows where it is,' Nevyn said. 'But "steal" is rather a harsh word. I suggest that we simply go and ask Loddlaen if he wanted a look at it.'

Both Aderyn and Valandario relaxed into smiles and nods. Javanateriel let his breath out in a long sigh of relief. They all trooped off to Loddlaen's tent at the edge of the encampment, where, to Nevyn's surprise, Morwen and Ebañy were keeping Loddlaen company. Ebañy was sprawled on a patch of grass and playing some elaborate game with sticks and pebbles, while Morwen was stirring a kettle of soup at Loddlaen's fire.

'Ah, there you are, lad,' Aderyn said. 'Val seems to be missing her black gem, and I was wondering if you'd seen it.'

Loddlaen got up slowly, his face a mask. 'Why would you think I had?' he said.

Morwen stopped her stirring and turned to look at him. Loddlaen abruptly shoved his hands into his pockets. Nevyn had the nasty suspicion that they were shaking and he was trying to hide them.

'Well, no real reason –' Aderyn began.

'I know it's in there!' Val pointed at Loddlaen's tent. 'I can feel it call to me, and it's in there.'

'It is not!' Loddlaen snapped.

'Don't lie!' Jav stepped forward. 'Don't make it worse!'

Valandario moved so fast that Loddlaen could only make a futile grab at her as she dashed by. She ducked into the tent, and when Loddlaen tried to follow, Javanateriel stepped in front of him and blocked his path. Val made an inarticulate cry of triumph and ducked out again, the black stone cradled in both hands. Loddlaen turned pale.

'It was sitting right on top of his blankets,' Val said. 'I told you so.'

Loddlaen said something in Elvish that made Jav grab him by the shirt with both hands and shake him, then answer in the same. They began shouting at each other while Aderyn tried to separate them. Nevyn glanced at Morwen and saw tears in her eyes. She swung the kettle off the fire, then grabbed

Ebañy and picked him up. For a moment she hesitated at the edge of the raging argument, then turned and marched off back towards the encampment. Nevyn hurried after her.

'What's wrong?' he said.

'I don't understand how Loddlaen could do such a thing!' Morwen said. 'My heart's sore troubled, Nevyn. I've come to think of him as a friend, but if he's a thief –'

'Well, he may not have meant to steal it. He may have just wanted to study it privately.'

'Do you truly believe that?'

'Let's just say I'd like to believe it, and it's possible. It's difficult for Loddlaen to – to –' Nevyn hesitated, thinking. 'To do things in the most direct manner, I suppose I mean. He might have been afraid to ask Val for a long look.'

'I'll try to believe that.' Morwen paused to set Ebañy down. 'Oof! You're getting heavy, my love.'

'Tell me, Ebañy,' Nevyn said. 'Do you like Loddlaen?'

'I do,' the child said. 'The funny man don't.'

'Doesn't,' Morri interrupted. 'What funny man?'

'The man in the stone.' Ebañy frowned and looked away. 'I saw him.'

'When was that?' Nevyn said.

'Just now. In the tent.' He looked at Morri. 'You see him, too?'

'I didn't. You don't mean Tirro, do you?'

Ebañy wrinkled his nose and shook his head. 'The funny man,' he repeated, 'with the yellow hair.'

'I think I know what he means,' Nevyn said. 'Someone from his Da's tales, I suspect.'

Morwen nodded, accepting the white lie. Nevyn wanted to question Ebañy further, but not in front of Morwen. Unfortunately, by the time he got a moment alone with the child, Ebañy had forgotten the incident.

Nevyn would have explained more about Loddlaen if he'd thought that Morwen could understand. He knew that the priestesses had taught her some of the preliminary knowledge

that they shared with dweomerworkers, but at the stage of
knowledge that he was assuming she possessed she never
could have comprehended the truth about that strange breed
of incorporeal beings, the Guardians, or as Deverry men called
them, the Seelie Host. Besides, as he had to admit to himself,
he didn't completely understand what had happened to
Loddlaen's mother, Dallandra.

Somehow the Guardians could keep a person alive indefin-
itely on the astral plane. In Dallandra's case, Evandar – Ebañy's
funny man – had turned her physical body into an amethyst
crystal, or perhaps it was only the semblance of a crystal wrought
in some substance of which he had no knowledge. At will they
could release her from the crystal, sending her back to the
physical world, or entrap her again to bring her back to their
astral country.

But inside her body, when first she'd gone off with them,
had lain the beginnings of another body, and with it, the soul
destined to become her son. It was time, Nevyn decided, to
ask Aderyn a few questions.

Nevyn had to postpone his talk with Aderyn, however,
because that morning Valandario announced that she and
Javanateriel were leaving. They'd gathered a new alar and
were going to head north to the far grazing for the rest of
the summer.

'I truly did think it was best, Master Aderyn,' Val said, 'if
I took the black gem away.'

'Perhaps so,' Aderyn said. 'It seems to spread an evil influence. Apparently it makes some people jump to conclusions
and make false accusations.'

Startled, Val glanced at Nevyn. He smiled and slipped his
arm through hers. 'I'll walk you back to your horses,' Nevyn
said. 'Come along.'

Aderyn made no move to follow as they left. Nevyn waited
to speak till they were well out of earshot.

'You'll never get Aderyn to think ill of his son,' Nevyn said.
'Surely you know that.'

'I do, but –' Valandario hesitated for a long moment. 'This time it seemed so obvious.'

'Have there been other times when he's stolen somewhat?'

'Oh, never that! He tells lies, though, and then there's his nasty temper.' She paused again. 'Maybe he truly didn't mean to steal the gem. I'll try to think that, anyway.'

'It's all we can do. Now, as you work with the gem, you can reach me through the fire if you have questions. If naught else, I'd love to know what you discover about it.'

'My thanks, Master Nevyn. I'm honoured.'

Nevyn returned to Aderyn's tent. They sat down outside the door, idly watching the life of the camp swirl around them. One of the women brought them a basket of wild redberries, which they shared as they talked.

'How long, exactly,' Nevyn said, 'was Loddlaen's soul trapped with Dallandra in that amethyst crystal?'

'As we reckon time?' Aderyn said, 'Or as the Guardians reckon it?'

'As we do. Loddlaen most assuredly has either a human or an elven soul. Had he been one of the Guardians' flock of spirits, the experience wouldn't have scarred him so deeply.'

'I don't know why you keep insisting he's been scarred.'

Nevyn wanted to scream, *Just look into his eyes, you wretched doting fool! Are you blind?* Instead, he said, 'Well, how could it not have? Trapped like that, half-born but not truly alive, aware of only himself and the gem around him?'

'Oh, I doubt if he was truly aware. After Dallandra came back to us, it was a good many months before she gave birth.'

'How many?'

'I don't remember.'

Nevyn decided against pointing out just how obvious it was when Aderyn lied.

'But as for your other question,' Aderyn went on, 'it was close to two hundred years.'

Nevyn shuddered, his blood abruptly cold in his veins.

'I do see your point,' Aderyn said. 'If he'd been truly aware, it would have been agony. But he wasn't, he couldn't have been, not for all of those years, or he'd be stark raving daft.'

'Well, he's not that, certainly.'

'I suppose you've brought this up because of the misunderstanding over Val's obsidian gem.'

'I have. You're convinced it's a misunderstanding?'

'He just wanted a look at the thing. He wasn't stealing it. It is true, though, that he's never been good at explaining himself, or at telling others how he feels. Maybe you're right about those years in his mother's womb, now that I think of it. No doubt they would have had some effect.'

'Imph,' Nevyn said. 'Let's hope that he slept in the darkness of his mother's body, at least for most of the time.' *May the Lords of Wyrd have been merciful enough for that, at least.*

Aderyn stood up, staring off into the distance. 'I see there's a new alar riding in. I'd better go tell them the merchant's already left.' He walked off without a glance back.

Nevyn stood and looked for himself, shading his eyes. Indeed, in the far distance he could see the tiny figures of horsemen riding through the billowing grass. They would have found out for themselves soon enough that they'd missed the trader, but Nevyn couldn't begrudge his old friend the excuse.

Every day more and more Westfolk brought down their tents, cut their horses out of the herd, and struck out into the grasslands. Morwen and Ebañy would watch them go until they disappeared, sinking into the grass, or so it seemed, along the far horizon, dancing with heat. With fewer people in camp, it became harder and harder for Morwen to avoid Loddlaen, and finally, one sunset hour when she went to the stream to draw water, he caught her alone.

'Morri, please,' Loddlaen said, 'won't you even talk to me? I didn't steal that gem, truly I didn't. I just wanted a chance to study it.'

His voice ached so badly that she felt her heart softening.

She put down the heavy water jug and turned to look at him. Tears glistened in his eyes.

'You could have asked Val first.'

'I know, but I figured she'd never let me have it even for a day, and I just couldn't concentrate on it when she was standing right there.'

Morwen looked away. The setting sun gilded the stream among the grey rocks. In the thick-growing rushes frogs were croaking their evening song.

'Please, Morri?' Loddlaen's voiced dropped to a whisper. 'You're the only real friend I've got, you know. Don't you remember telling me how things got taken away from you? Let's not let our friendship get snatched away from us.'

He'd said the perfect thing to melt her resolve. 'Oh, very well,' she said. 'But if somewhat like this happens again, you'll ask first, won't you? I'll help you if you need me to.'

'Then I will. I promise.'

She turned back to find him watching her, his eyes as large and solemn as a child's.

'Besides,' Loddlaen said. 'Don't you want to go on with your lessons?'

'I do, truly. I've missed them dreadfully.'

'Them but not me?'

He reminded her so much of a small boy at that moment that Morwen had to smile. 'You, as well,' she said.

He grinned at her. 'Here, let me carry that jug for you. It's heavy when it's full.'

'So it is. My thanks. When it's dark, and I've got Ebañy to sleep, shall I come to your tent?'

'Please, and we'll have one of our talks.'

Aderyn and Nevyn both felt Valandario's absence, but they continued to work with the dweomer scroll. After they'd studied it for some weeks, Aderyn began to wonder about its place in the overall dweomer system developed in the ancient elven cities.

'The language of the calls intrigues me,' Aderyn said. 'Some of the words have an oddly Bardekian flavour to me, but others are just simply odd.'

'They are that, for certain!' Nevyn said. 'I wonder if it's an artificial language.'

'It could well be. Some of the old tales that have come down from the Great Burning mention sages who supposedly could talk in a great many strange tongues. Unfortunately, no one remembers exactly what they were.'

'Well, if the names were invented, they'd be hard to remember, I suppose.'

'Good point. And of course, they had that wretched obsession with secrecy.' With a sigh, Aderyn stood up, stretching. 'Shall we go back to camp?'

Nevyn got up and joined him. Twilight was just beginning to darken the sunset sky, and a soft wind made the tall grass bow down before it. When Nevyn looked towards the camp, he could see fires glowing between the tents and hear music as the Westfolk sang at their evening's work.

'Addo,' Nevyn said, 'before we go back, we've got to have a talk.'

'I suppose you mean about my son?' Aderyn said. 'I've noticed the way you look at him, as if you're studying him like a disease.'

'Not like a disease. I worry about the lad.'

'You don't like him, do you?' Aderyn crossed his arms over his chest and turned to face his old master.

'Actually, I do like the lad,' Nevyn began. 'Besides, it's not a question of like or dislike. It's a question of –'

Aderyn went straight on as if he'd not heard Nevyn's words. 'We all have our faults, don't we? But I'm his father, and fathers do forgive their children. Well, the good ones do.'

'I'm not asking you to condemn him. Quite the opposite. I'm asking you to stop teaching him dweomer. Or trying to.'

'Just what do you mean by that?'

'That he's learned what he's going to learn, that's all.

He doesn't truly want it, for one thing. He wants to please you – that's the only reason he keeps trying.'

'He just tires easily. You said that yourself when we were first working with the scroll. He's done better at other times.'

'Mayhap, but he's got a very slender dweomer gift. The dry lore is one thing – anyone can learn that – but actually working dweomer is very different.'

'Oh come now! He can form the body of light and travel on the etheric – quite easily in fact. If that's not working dweomer, I don't know what is.'

'Certainly, but what does he have to balance it? Of course he can split the levels of his being. That's the result of what those wretched Guardians did to his mother when she was pregnant. I've been studying the lad. Open your sight! You can see his etheric double hanging around him like an ill-fitting cloak. His various bodies have never properly knitted together, Addo. I'm surprised he managed to get fully incarnated.'

'Naught of the sort! I –'

'You can see it, can't you? You just don't want to admit it to yourself.'

Aderyn let his arms drop and hang limply by his sides, but his hands clenched into fists.

'It aches my heart to be so blunt,' Nevyn softened his voice.

'Oh? And what about yourself, then? You think you see so clearly while I'm blind, do you? How wrong you are!'

Nevyn stared at him, utterly taken aback.

'I mean Morwen.' Aderyn brought out the name with a tight little smile. 'That poor lass! Do you truly think you can teach her dweomer? I don't care how many oaths you swore. She's been scarred by her horrid childhood. Can't you see it? She can no more control her rages than lightning can stop striking the earth. It means she's been twisted inside by the ghastly way she was treated. Do you truly think she's fit to learn dweomer?'

For the briefest of moments Nevyn considered swearing at him – how dare he insult his old master this way? But a cold sick feeling in his stomach stopped him. 'You're quite right,' he said instead, 'I hadn't seen it before this moment, but you're right.'

Aderyn's smug smile vanished. He started to speak, choked it off, half-turned away, then turned back. 'Well, I –' Aderyn's voice was barely audible. 'You may be right about Loddlaen as well.' His voice grew stronger. 'At least in part.'

'Just think about it, that's all I ask. As for Morwen, well, there's naught I can say to that.' Nevyn had to pause and collect himself. A strange grief threatened to force tears.

'She'll stay here with little Ebañy for some years at least,' Aderyn said. 'Mayhap I can help her lay aside the bitterness in her soul. She's part of my alar now, and it's the least I can do.'

'My thanks. From time to time I'll ride your way and see how she's faring, if I may.'

'Of course you may! Ye gods, there's no reason for you to ever leave, for that matter.'

'Of course there is.'

'Your duty to Gwairyc?'

'That too.'

Aderyn tried to smile, then let it fade. 'I see what you mean,' he said. 'I – well, forgive me. Loddlaen's the only thing I have left of Dalla.'

'I know that. But he's a man now, not a thing, any more than –' Nevyn forced himself to go on. '– any more than Morwen is Brangwen.'

'That's true spoken.'

'I brought the matter up out of concern for Loddlaen as much as for you. He'll make a splendid herbman and healer, if only he's free to study that body of lore.'

'I suppose.' Aderyn's voice dropped in exhaustion. 'Truly, perhaps so.'

Nevyn tucked the scroll box under one arm, then held

out his hand. Aderyn clasped it in both of his for a long moment before he released it. It seemed that he would speak again, but he turned on his heel and walked away fast, heading for the camp, which glowed with the light of little cooking fires against the darkening sky.

For a little while Nevyn stayed out in the grass and watched the stars come out until the Snowy Road hung full and bright in the sky. Normally the sight soothed him, but that night it seemed ominous, as if the stars were sparks from a fire that might drop to earth and set the grasslands burning. Although he tried meditating upon the symbols that this feeling presented to his consciousness, he could find no concrete reason for it, not in vision nor in the vague hints that the Lords of Wyrd at times manage to give dweomer-masters. Finally he decided that he was picking up traces of the past from the scroll, memories of ravaging Horsekin burning the Seven Cities of the Far West. When the wheel of stars showed that the night was approaching its zenith, he walked back to the tents.

At breakfast the next morning Nevyn told Gwairyc that they'd be leaving soon to return to Deverry.

'That gladdens my heart, my lord,' Gwairyc said, and he smiled in sheer delight. 'Will we be going back to Eldidd?'

'Most likely. Has being out here troubled you?'

'To some extent.' Gwairyc considered for a moment. 'A man feels more comfortable, like, among his own kind, though if I could speak their blasted language, I might have liked them better.'

'I can see your point.'

'But you know, my lord, in a cursed strange way I'm grateful that you brought me here. The world's a fair bit wider than I thought it was, and that's always good for a man to know. Eldidd was only a name to me, too, and now I've seen it.' Gwairyc paused again. 'I've been thinking about the things you said, back in Dun Deverry, about your taking me away, I mean. You said it would be to my benefit, and it has been, at that.'

'Well, that gladdens my heart to hear.'

Before they left, however, Nevyn wanted to gather some medicinals. On the morrow Nevyn and Gwairyc were working along the bank of a stream, hunting for young green willow withes, a remedy for sore teeth, when Morwen brought Ebañy out to see what they were doing. Ebañy was particularly interested in the little silver sickle that Nevyn used to cut herbs whose virtue lay in the watery humours. As he showed it to the boy, he noticed that Morwen and Gwairyc were chatting while they watched, and after Morwen took Ebañy back to camp, Gwairyc mentioned their conversation.

'She was asking me about Loddlaen, my lord,' Gwairyc said. 'Did I think he was trustworthy.'

'Indeed?' Nevyn said. 'What did you tell her?'

'That it depended on what she was trusting him for. If he made some small, easy promise, no doubt he'd keep it. I wouldn't trust him to do anything of grave import. He'd want to keep the promise, but ye gods, he's so miserable, it would be hard for him to do.'

'I'd say that's a very good judgment.'

'My thanks, then.' Gwairyc paused, glancing back at the elven camp. 'The poor lass! You know what she reminds me of, my lord? When I was but a little lad, my sister had a favourite hound. And one day the blasted dog got its paw stepped on and crushed by a horse out in the stable. The kennelmaster was minded to slit its throat and put it out of its misery, but my sister begged so prettily that our clan's chirurgeon took the paw off instead and bound up the wound. It healed, though she had a three-legged hound ever after.'

Gwairyc had never even mentioned before that he had a sister, Nevyn realized. He smiled to encourage him further. 'And Morwen,' Nevyn said, 'reminds you of your sister?'

'What?' Gwairyc looked sincerely puzzled. 'Not my sister. The hound.'

Nevyn felt the smile freeze on his face. Apparently Gwairyc noticed. 'Well,' Gwairyc went on, 'that harelip's turned her into a wild thing, hasn't it? She's never going to lose her vile temper.'

By the hells, even Gwairyc sees it! Nevyn thought. *Has everyone noticed but me?* 'Never is a very long time, lad,' he said aloud. 'It won't be easy for her to heal, certainly. It'll take a fair bit of help.'

'No doubt. If she's even worth it, ugly little mutt that she is.'

For the first time in some hundreds of years, Nevyn felt like smashing someone's face with his fist. He could feel the Wildfolk swarming around, offering to lend their energy to the blow. Fortunately his rigorous training in controlling his emotions kept him from doing so, and Gwairyc never realized how close he'd come to a broken jaw. Nevyn found himself remembering Ligga and her little son. *They breed like rabbits,* Gwairyc had said about farm families, then compared them to horses. *Now, be fair*, Nevyn thought. *The king's riders value horses above the men of their own class, too.*

'I'm beginning to wonder,' Nevyn told Aderyn later, 'if I can ever get Gwairyc to see the common-born as human beings rather than animals.'

'I wonder, too,' Aderyn said. 'Probably the only way he's going to see it is to live poor himself. Mayhap he'll be reborn one day as a farmer or a servant.'

'Mayhap, indeed. Who knows what the Great Ones will decide?'

'You know the old proverb: you can load a manger with hay but you can't force your ox to eat it.'

'And an excellent proverb it is! I'll meditate upon all this.'

'It always helps.' Aderyn paused, and he seemed to be gathering his strength. 'I've been doing the same, you see, about Loddlaen.'

'Ah. My apologies once again for being so blunt. I –'

'No need to apologize. You're right. I was wondering if you'd take him on as apprentice.' Aderyn hesitated, then smiled. 'In the healing arts, that is. I know you have Gwairyc on your hands now, but once you've sent him on his way, like.'

'I'd be glad to, truly glad.'

'A thousand thanks, then. I'd been planning on teaching the lad more dweomer this winter, but I'll stick to herblore instead.'

'Splendid! Whether I come back alone or with Gwairyc, I'll be visiting you and Morwen next spring, and Loddlaen and I can discuss his apprenticeship then.'

That evening Nevyn went off alone to meditate. He realized that while Gwairyc had expressed his pity for Morwen in an arrogant and condescending way, he'd at least felt pity. He'd changed in other ways, too, during his time on the road. *Perhaps I've done all that I can do,* Nevyn decided. *The gods all know that I can think of naught else!*

Despite his decision to leave, Nevyn ended up lingering for a few days more, because, as he knew deep in his heart, he hated the idea of leaving Morwen. Not that he saw much of her these days – she and Loddlaen always seemed to be off alone somewhere. Like everyone else in camp, he assumed that they were having a love affair, the best medicinal he could have prescribed for the bitter loneliness in her heart.

'It should be good for Loddlaen, too,' Nevyn remarked to Aderyn.

'Indeed,' Aderyn said. 'You're not jealous?'

'Only of his youth.'

They shared a laugh, then returned to their study of Aderyn's mysterious scroll.

Somehow, Morwen knew, her dweomer studies caused the strange way she was feeling about Nevyn. She liked him, she had many reasons to be grateful to him, and yet she found herself avoiding him. For a reason beyond her understanding, she felt profoundly guilty every time she saw the old man.

'I truly should tell Nevyn what we're doing,' she said to Loddlaen.

'Why?' Loddlaen said. 'I think it's splendid, having our secret. Why spoil it?'

'I don't know, exactly. I just feel that he should know.'

'Well, we'll tell him together, but in a little while.' Loddlaen smiled at her, his open grin that reminded her so much of Ebañy. 'He'll get a splendid surprise, won't he? You're making such fast progress, Morri. It'll be our gift to him.'

'So it will. Well and good, then. I'll let things be.'

Morwen had learned how to go into trance at will. In that state she could conjure up a body of light as well, but she was having trouble transferring her consciousness over to it.

'It's just a matter of practice,' Loddlaen told her. 'Once you get the hang of it, it's quite easy.'

'Huh! You may find it easy! I most certainly don't.'

As the nights passed, Morwen kept practising. Loddlaen had told her enough about the marvels of the etheric plane that she longed to see them for herself. When Nevyn mentioned that he would be leaving the Westlands soon, she became more determined than ever. She wanted to give him the gift of the secret she and Loddlaen shared before he left.

Finally, and almost by accident, she succeeded in reaching the etheric plane. She and Loddlaen were lying in the grass in front of his tent as usual for her lesson. She went into trance, built up the image of the body of light, and attempted the transfer over. Suddenly she heard a peculiar noise, a rushy sort of click, too distinct for a buzz, too soft for the sound of metal on metal – and she was looking out of the simulacrum's eyes. Her shocked delight thrust her right back into her normal body again, but she sat up with a laugh and a shout of triumph.

'I did it! Oh Loddlaen, I truly did it!'

'I know.' He was smiling at her. 'I was there and saw you. What a splendid job, Morri. It should come easier from now on. Try again.'

Just as he said, when she returned to the trance state, she found her body of light waiting for her. She thought herself into the image and again heard the click, again found herself seeing with other eyes. When she glanced around, she saw Loddlaen, hovering over his physical body. All around them the world had turned strange in a shimmering silvery blue glow. The grass shone with a reddish glow, the distant trees shimmered orange. The dead things – the tent, the boulders, and the like – were pitch black.

'You're here.' Loddlaen's voice seemed to sound inside her mind. 'This is my true home, Morri. This is the only world where I feel I belong.'

'It's so lovely!' She thought the words back to him.

'Then let's have a look at it.'

He began to rise slowly into the air. A mere thought let her follow him as if she had wings. Behind her the silver cord joining her to her body paid slowly out of its own accord. She kept her sight fixed on his shimmering gold body of light as they rose higher and higher.

'Look at the stars,' he said.

She transferred her gaze up and saw above her enormous swirls of silver in the glowing blue night. Since she'd put her attention into following what she saw, the sight of them drew her upward. She felt herself streaking upward fast, faster, beyond her power to stop, as if she were falling upward as fast as a stone falls down when thrown from a high cliff.

'Morri!'

The sound of his thought caught her like the jerk of a leash on a running hound. With a wrench of will she forced herself to look down, but she'd lost track of his position in the billows of silver light. She looked this way and that, and with every transfer of attention she moved, swooping up, down, swinging from side to side, utterly out of control. She could hear him calling to her, but he must have been flying after her, because no matter which way she looked, she never saw him.

'Down!' he screamed. 'Come back down!'

Flailing with etheric arms Morwen managed to invert her body of light. She began falling, plunging, again fast, faster, far too fast. She saw her body looming in front of her, a vast mountain of flesh, draped with avalanches of clothing. She tried to turn and fly upward, but she felt the silver cord hauling her closer and closer, as if her body were a fisherman hauling a reluctant coracle onto shore.

'Loddlaen!' She tried to cry out with her thoughts, but the momentary distraction snatched away her only chance at safety. The silver cord snapped taut, then yanked her down, slamming her etheric double into her body. Pain like burning swept over her. She rebounded, momentarily free, with the silver cord trailing broken behind her. The pain turned to a gold mist, suffocating her, then into golden light. She was floating in light, drifting this way and that, head down and motionless as if the light were water. She saw someone floating towards her in the light, a vaguely human shape of silver, and he was followed by giant beings who had no bodies but golden flames.

Only then did she realize that she was dead.

Even though he was sitting on the far side of the camp, Nevyn heard Loddlaen's panicked scream. He jumped to his feet just as Devaberiel raced over, panting, his face dead-white even in the reddish glow from the little fire.

'It's Morri,' he gasped. 'Loddlaen's killed her.'

Nevyn swore and took off running through the camp. A small crowd had gathered on the edge of the meadow. As he pushed his way through he saw Aderyn and Loddlaen. Aderyn had grabbed Loddlaen by the shoulders and shoved his face up close to the terrified lad's to berate him, speaking Elvish so fast that Nevyn couldn't understand two words together. Morwen lay on the ground, her arms and legs akimbo, her head twisted to one side so violently that he knew her neck was broken. Jennantar crouched at her head, and Farendar knelt at her feet, on guard over her body. Nevyn snapped his fingers and summoned a ball of silver light. In the garish glare he could see that her face, her neck, her arms and hands were a mass of red and purple bruises.

'I didn't mean –' Loddlaen spoke in Deverrian, but he was sobbing too hard to finish. He twisted free of his father's hands and tried to bolt, but Devaberiel grabbed him and hauled him back. Nevyn strode over and looked him in the face.

'What happened?' Nevyn could hear his voice twist into a snarl. 'What were you doing to her?'

Loddlaen began to tremble. 'I – I was showing her – I mean, I was trying to teach her, just a little, about – well, dweomer.'

'You wretched young dolt!'

Nevyn dropped to his knees beside her body and laid a hand on her face. Instantly he knew that her etheric double had already separated from the dead flesh. He crouched low over her to hide his face and slipped into trance. When he raised his Sight to the etheric, he saw only the billows of the blue light – not so much as a trace of her. He returned to normal consciousness and sat back on his heels. Loddlaen was staring at him, his eyes tear-filled in a dead-pale face.

'Let me guess,' Nevyn said. 'You decided to show her how to travel on the etheric. You forgot that she had no idea of how to stay there or get back safely.'

Loddlaen threw back his head and howled in grief and terror both.

'I thought so.' Nevyn got up. 'There's naught I can do for her. She's dead.'

'Morri!' Loddlaen screamed the name, then whispered. 'Morri, Morri, Morri.'

Loddlaen wrenched himself out of Devaberiel's grip. He raced off into the darkness beyond the dweomer light's circle of glow. Dev took two steps after him, then sighed and let him go.

'I doubt me if he meant to harm her,' Dev said.

'I doubt it, too,' Nevyn said. 'If I hadn't, he'd have gone to join her.' Slowly he rose and turned to face Aderyn, who stood nearby, silently weeping.

'I warned you,' Nevyn said – then hated himself for saying it. *I might as well have fetched him a blow across the face,* he thought. 'My apologies, oh ye gods, I don't know what made me say that. I should never have – a thousand apologies!'

'I deserve it,' Aderyn whispered. 'I know.' His voice choked on the tears.

'By the Dark Sun!' Devaberiel said abruptly. 'Ebañy! He'll be waking up!'

The bard took off running, heading back into the camp.

With a wave of one hand Jennantar caught the attention of the Westfolk who had clustered around the two dweomer-masters.

'Someone go fetch a blanket,' he said. 'We should wrap the poor lass up properly, anyway, and we don't want any of the children in camp seeing her like this.'

'Let's take her into a tent,' Farendar said. 'I'll help carry.'

'Good idea,' Jennantar said. 'The Wise Ones will handle – well, handle the rest of this.'

Between them they picked up Morwen's body in as digni-fied a manner as they could, then hurried off. Aderyn sank to his knees, slumped forward, and stared blindly at the grass. Nevyn sat down next to his friend and waited while Aderyn struggled to compose himself. Nevyn was surprised at his own feelings, or rather, at their odd absence. He felt so detached that he realized he'd been expecting a tragedy such as this, yet another evil thing that would tear his Brangwen from him once again.

'I can't.' Aderyn raised his head and looked at some distant point. 'Talk just yet, I mean. Could we –'

'Discuss this later? Of course. I just want to ask you again to forgive me for that remark, and now I'll go back to camp.'

Among the tents subdued children sat on the grass and watched him go by without speaking. Farendar was standing at the door of his tent, waiting for him. When he beckoned, Nevyn joined him. He could just see a white-wrapped bundle lying on the floor cloth inside.

'Shall we bury her in the earth?' Farendar said. 'Or give her to the fire?'

'The earth, I think,' Nevyn said. 'As her people do. A deep grave, a stone over it. Bury some prized thing with her, perhaps, if she brought any with her.'

'Very well. We'd follow our own rites for her if you thought best, but the way of her folk, well, that sounds proper.'

'When –'

'As soon as possible. We want to take her a good distance from camp, you see, so little Ebañy won't have to watch.'

'Ah, the poor little lad!'

Farendar wasted no time organizing the funeral. He found Albaral, and the two of them dug a grave near the merchant's camp but not in it – a place between her new people and her old, as Far put it. Since she was as light as a child, Jennantar carried her body over and laid it gently down into the raw earth. Next to her they put the sack of goods she'd brought with her, her few pieces of clothing and the kitchen knife.

'Will you say a few words, Wise One?' Jennantar said.

'I'll try.' Nevyn could hear how damp and choked his voice sounded. 'Go to the Light, little one. We'll all miss you.' His voice broke, and he turned away.

'That's enough,' Jen said softly. 'My thanks.'

Nevyn found it too painful to stay and watch them fill in the grave. He went back to camp and sought out Devaberiel, who was sitting in front of his tent, his harp slack-stringed beside him. When Nevyn knelt down near him, the bard acknowledged him by raising one weary hand.

'How does Evan fare?' Nevyn said. 'Ebañy, I mean.'

'I finally got him to sleep.' Devaberiel turned to look at him. 'I've not told him she's dead. He wouldn't understand.'

'That's true enough.'

'I told him that she had to go away and that she'll be back in a while. I'm hoping he'll just forget her.'

'In time no doubt he will, but do you think it's wise to lie to him? He'll have to know sooner or later.'

'Later is soon enough. Ye gods, it's a hard thing to admit to your son that you failed him so badly.'

'You failed him? How –'

'Don't you understand?' Dev's voice shook in a ghastly blend of grief and guilt. 'She was my guest. I should have seen – should have known – should have made that cursed little wretch leave her alone. Loddlaen! He's always been the wormy sheep in the flock. He should have been turned out long ago, truly, but that decision wasn't mine to make. It was my duty – my sacred duty – to protect my guest and my son's nursemaid. And I failed.'

'Here, then I failed as badly as you.'

'Nonsense! You've been trying for years to make Aderyn see the truth about his son. Has he listened? Not to one word, I'll wager.'

'He's listening now.' The voice sounded so exhausted, so old, that at first Nevyn couldn't place it. Then Aderyn stepped into the pool of firelight. 'What can I say? You were right. I was wrong. I never should have taught the lad the first thing about dweomer.'

Devaberiel rose to his feet. 'Here, come sit down, Wise One. Forgive my harsh way of speaking, will you? I'm half-torn apart by this, but I'm a father, too, and I know how hard it must be when your son does –' he paused briefly, '– somewhat like this.'

Aderyn hesitated, then took Devaberiel's outstretched hand and clasped it. 'He was all I had left of Dalla,' Aderyn said. 'I couldn't say him nay about one little thing.' With a sigh he let go of the bard's hand and sat down next to Nevyn. 'I'd like to blame her, of course, but I can't. She left him with a wetnurse who loved him and a father who loved him more. He shouldn't have come to harm. I'm the one who spoiled him.' Aderyn covered his face with both hands, but he neither sobbed nor spoke more.

Devaberiel sat down opposite them. For a long moment the silence grew, as discomforting as the summer's humid air, thick around them all.

'Where is Loddlaen now?' Nevyn said at last.

'Gone.' Aderyn was staring into the darkness. 'He took his gear and some of our horses and fled. I've no idea where he's going. Some other alar will take him in. We'll meet again in good time, no doubt.'

No doubt, Nevyn thought. *And will you forgive him, then?* Abruptly Aderyn got up. He paused for a moment, looking at Nevyn, then with a shrug turned and walked away, heading in the direction of his tent. Nevyn rose too and took his leave of the bard, but he went to his own tent. Out in front of its door Gwairyc was sitting by a tiny fire, feeding it twigs to keep the light burning.

'I see you waited up for me,' Nevyn said.

'I did,' Gwairyc said. 'I thought I'd ask if you wanted me to track down Loddlaen and slit his throat for him.'

'I don't. If it would bring Morri back, I'd take your offer gladly, but it won't, and I'd not add to Aderyn's grief. We'll be leaving on the morrow, by the by. Staying would only pour vinegar in Aderyn's wounds.'

'Fair enough. Well, the poor lass! But in a way, she's better off. No one can ever mock her again, but you know, my lord, I'm sorry now that I didn't keep a better guard over Morwen. I didn't realize she needed guarding.'

'Neither did I. I feel like a fool! I never realized that Loddlaen was teaching her dweomer lore.'

'No doubt he made sure you didn't know. But I've been thinking. She was an ugly little mutt, but I liked Morri. I didn't much realize that I did, mind, and just as a friend, of course, but I wish I'd seen that she was in danger. It gripes my soul, somehow, that she was finally happy, and then it all got snatched away from her. Ah well. Too late now.'

'So it is.'

But not too late for you, my friend! Nevyn realized that Gwairyc had just given him the signal he'd been waiting for. For the first time in their journeying together – most likely for the first time in his life – he was voicing a genuine concern for and a regret over the welfare of another human being. Gwairyc no longer stood on the edge of that crumbling cliff of isolation that might have plunged him into a sea of evil far below. Somehow or other, Nevyn had managed to drag him back to solid ground. Soon it would be time to free him from his king's rash vow.

Nevyn waited until they'd ridden back to Eldidd to have his final talk with Gwairyc. They travelled south till they reached the sea, just west of Wmmglaedd, then followed the Eldidd coast. By the time they'd worked their way to Abernaudd, near the Deverry border, the days had grown short, and frost nipped the nights.

They took shelter in an inn that catered to sailors and merchants. Although the port was half-deserted at this time of year, they did find a crew that would be returning to Cerrmor from their last trading run of the season. Nevyn took it as an omen. That evening, while they ate hunks of mutton and turnips fried in the mutton grease, they sat at a table close to the fire for its warmth. Gwairyc apparently had been thinking about the weather.

'Where will we be wintering, my lord?' Gwairyc said. 'If you don't mind me asking.'

'I'm going back to Cannobaen,' Nevyn said, 'but you're not. Return to your king, lad. I'll give you a letter that tells him I've released you. I'll give you half of our coin, as well. That should be enough to pay your passage to Cerrmor on that merchantman in the harbour and then get you back up the Belaver to Dun Deverry.'

Gwairyc dropped his table dagger in surprise. He broke into a broad grin and began to stammer his thanks.

'No thanks needed,' Nevyn said. 'It's time, is all. Just try to remember what you've learned from me, and I don't mean only the herbcraft.'

'I will do that, my lord,' Gwairyc said. 'Ye gods, it'll be good to see my men again! Huh, I wonder how many of the Falcons lived through the summer? Well, I'll pray it's all of them, and I'll be finding out soon enough. Although, truly, it would be good to see you now and again. Do you think you'll ever come back to Dun Deverry?'

'I doubt it,' Nevyn said. 'I think I'll stay in Eldidd for the last few years left to me. I've got friends here as well as among the Westfolk, you see.'

'Oh, here, my lord! You're in such good health that I wager you'll live to be a hundred.'

'Well, you know, you might be right at that.' Nevyn managed to keep from laughing. 'And I'll hope the same for you.'

And yet, as common sense would predict, Gwairyc's life ended far short of that hundred years. The Cerrgonney wars dragged on and on, and many a good man died in battle, as Gwairyc did some five years after his trip to the Westlands, when a squad of Boarsmen cut him off from the main body of the king's riders. Before the end came, practically everyone at court had remarked that he was a changed man, more courteous and far more pleasant company. Still, the only person at court who honestly mourned him was King Casyl himself.

Thanks to the link he'd forged between them, Nevyn knew what had happened the moment that Gwairyc died. He felt a stab of grief, and one that lingered. *May he have better in his next life!* Nevyn would think whenever Gwairyc came to mind. He wondered, as well, if he and Gwairyc would meet again. Only the Lords of Wyrd would know the answer to that question – not that they would ever have told any mortal foolish enough to ask. Nevyn would remind himself that after all, with a man like Gwairyc, news of his death in battle had hardly come as a surprise.

The next sad death that he heard of, however, shocked him to his very soul.

It was a good many years before anyone in the Westlands saw Loddlaen again. One spring day, he turned up on the seacoast riding a decent horse and leading a mule loaded with fancy trinkets and oddments from Bardek, which he proceeded to give away to whomever fancied them. He'd gone there to study physick, he told everyone, and done a little trading to support himself while there. Valandario heard the news some days later.

'He must have done well,' Javanateriel said. 'I hear that he brought back real glass beads and some silver ones as well.'

'That's nice,' Valandario said. 'Um, wait – who?'

'Loddlaen. Didn't you hear what I said?'

'My dearest love, forgive me! I was brooding about my wretched apprentice again.'

Javanateriel rolled his eyes and sighed with a shake of his head. They were sitting in front of their tent, sharing a roast rabbit and some Deverry-style flatbread that Jav had cooked for their dinner. Around them the noisy life of an evening camp eddied and swirled – harp music, yapping dogs, the whining of overly tired children, singing, laughter, and the occasional angry argument all mingled together.

'Where is Ebañy?' Javanateriel said.

'I don't know,' Valandario said. 'That's the problem. I suspect he's gone off to Deverry again. I wish his father didn't expect so much from him! Every time Devaberiel starts nagging him about his progress in the dweomer, off he goes.'

'Tell Dev to stop.'

'I have. He doesn't listen. Bards don't.'

'That's true, unfortunately.' Javanateriel paused to lick a greasy finger. 'But about Loddlaen. Danalaurel told me that Loddlaen wants to see you.'

Valandario stopped in mid-bite and laid her piece of rabbit down on her wooden plate.

'What's wrong?' Javanateriel said. 'An omen-warning?'

'Nothing so strong. I just simply don't like the fellow.'

'Well, maybe we can just avoid him. The grass stretches a fair long way, after all.'

'He's got enough dweomer to scry me out.'

'Oh.' Jav scowled at their campfire. 'I forgot about that.'

'Besides, it would be better to simply confront him and get it over with. I'm not going to sneak around the grasslands just because of him.'

'You know, in some ways you're the bravest person I've ever met.'

Javanateriel was smiling at her in such open admiration that Valandario blushed. 'No,' she said, 'you're braver than I. You've got the courage to live with someone like me.'

He laughed, then got up, wiping his hands down the side of his trousers. 'Want some honey water?' he said. 'I made some earlier.'

'Yes, please, I do.'

Javanateriel brought the drink in a pair of wooden cups that he'd carved when she'd first agreed to share his tent. He'd sanded them down until they were almost as smooth as glass, then engraved their names around both rims. With the passing years the wood had polished up further into a rich dark patina. Valandario liked to think that their love had deepened the same way, domestic yet beautiful at the same time.

'In a way I'd like to see Loddlaen again,' Jav said. 'He's my foster-brother, after all.'

'That's right,' Val said. 'Well, maybe he's changed for the better, if he's learned physick. It'll give him a place in the world.'

Two days later, on an overcast afternoon, Loddlaen arrived at their alar's camp. Danalaurel came running to tell Valandario that he'd arrived.

'He's asking to ride with us, Wise One,' Danno said. 'Do you think that's a good idea?'

'I won't know until I talk with him,' Valandario said. 'So I'd better go do just that.'

Loddlaen was waiting at the edge of the alar's horse herd. He stood next to his riding horse, a grey Western hunter, and he held the lead ropes of two jenny mules, each carrying half-empty canvas packs. He looked much like the same old Loddlaen with his haunted eyes and nervous hands, twisting the ends of the lead ropes this way and that as he watched her approach. What interested Valandario the most, however, was not his physical being but his aura. She opened the Sight just enough to see it clearly – his usual trembling pale gold, hanging far too loosely about his physical body – the same old Loddlaen, indeed. She closed the Sight down again.

'Well, and a good morrow to you,' Valandario said. 'We've not seen you for a good long while now.'

'Yes, I've been in Bardek.' His voice sounded steadier, even a little deeper, with a new confidence. 'I managed to apprentice myself to one of their physicians.'

'Excellent! How did the training go?'

'Oh, very well indeed.' Loddlaen smiled, again with a confidence he'd lacked before. 'I learned a lot of valuable lore, though it mostly applies to Roundears. So, actually, Val, I'm planning on returning to Bardek before the winter. The only reason I've come to the Westlands is to visit my father.' His voice suddenly reverted to its old jittery self. 'If he'll even see me, that is. I came here to ask you if you'd help me – if you could sound him out first, I mean.'

He was looking at her with a desperate hopefulness that touched her heart.

'Of course,' Valandario said. 'I'll get a couple of the men to help you pitch your tent. Turn your horse and mules into the herd.'

While Loddlaen was settling into the camp, Valandario contacted Nevyn to give him the news. She wanted his advice on how to approach Aderyn, as well.

'Be direct,' Nevyn said. 'Tell him straight off why you're contacting him.'

'I will, then. My thanks, Master Nevyn I hope I'm doing the right thing by letting Loddlaen ride with us.'

'Here, have you felt an omen against it or suchlike?'

'Nothing so dire! I've just never really liked him. But he looked so pathetic when he asked for my help that I couldn't turn him away. I suppose I'm just afraid that he'll end up causing trouble. He always seemed to before.'

'Well, let me know straightaway if he does.'

Since she wanted to get her thoughts in order, Valandario waited till later that day to reach Aderyn through the fire. He responded immediately.

'I have news for you, Master Aderyn,' she said. 'Loddlaen's returned from Bardek. He wants to see you, and he asked me to ask you if you wanted to see him.'

A flood of emotions rushed into her mind from his – joy, remembered anger, a tinge of fear, and a grief centred around Dallandra rather than their son. She waited, watching the flames crackle in her little campfire, until his mind returned to its usual steady calm.

'Tell him yes,' Aderyn said. 'I do want to see him. No matter what he did, all those years ago, he's still my son. Tell him that too.'

'I shall indeed! Where's your alar now? We're about two days ride north of the southernmost trading ground.'

'We're about five days ride east of it and heading that way. Why don't you ride straight there? We'll join you as soon as we can.' Aderyn's image grinned at her. 'And here I thought I'd never see him again!'

When Valandario relayed the conversation to Loddlaen, he wept, turning fast away to bury his face in the crook of his arm – tears of joy, she assumed.

'My thanks, Val,' he said.

'You're very welcome.' She patted him on the shoulder.

He wiped his face on his sleeve, then turned back to give her a smile – an odd smile, in a way, nervous, forced, and brief. Yet Loddlaen had always displayed such peculiar mannerisms that she thought little of it.

'It'll take us two days to get down to the coast and the trading ground, right?' Loddlaen said.

'That's right,' Valandario said. 'And your father should be there three days later. I'm sure he's going to hurry his alar along, so it won't be more than that.'

Loddlaen nodded and pursed his lips, looking away as if

he were counting something out. 'My thanks again,' he said
finally. 'I'm very grateful.' With a last nod her way, he walked
off, heading for his tent, which he'd pitched, as usual, some
ways away from the rest of the alar.

When they reached the trading ground, they found two
Deverry merchants who'd set up shop with iron goods, grain,
and a general supply of threads, woven cloth, soap, and other
small necessities difficult to produce out on the grass. This
particular site lay close enough to the Eldidd border to attract
merchants who were willing to take raw fleece in trade for small
items, rather than dealing only in the more valuable horses.
When several other alarli rode in the day after they arrived, the
trading became a market fair, though in the Westfolk manner.

Everyone cooked their favourite food; everyone else was
welcome to sample it. Here and there little groups of musi-
cians gathered. Since they rarely bothered to play the same
tunes as the other groups scattered through the encampment, music rang out in a pleasant cacophony. Children,
dogs, and Wildfolk raced through the camps, dodging cooking
fires, tripping over tent ropes, yelling and laughing as they
invented games on the spot.

As a Wise One, Valandario found herself in demand for
advice and omens both. The People brought her all manner
of questions, a few of which she felt incompetent to answer.
'Aderyn will be here soon,' she would tell the askers, and
they would smile and agree to wait. Despite his new-found
knowledge of healing, Loddlaen kept to himself as much as
always. He had brought no medicines with him, and whenever anyone asked him for advice, he would repeat that he
only knew Roundear lore, nothing that would benefit the
People. He too would suggest they wait for Aderyn.

The night before Aderyn was due to arrive, the music and
the feasting went on late into the night. Out in a meadow
lit by small fires the People danced in long lines. One of the
other alarli had invited everyone in camp, including of course
Valandario and Javanateriel, to their central fire. When

Javanateriel suggested to his foster-brother that he come with them, Loddlaen said no.

'I hate crowds, Jav,' he said. 'You know that. It's the noise and suchlike. I might even take a long moonlight walk or suchlike, just to get away from all this confusion.'

'All right, then,' Jav said. 'I didn't want you to feel left out.'

'The way I always was before, when we were children?' Loddlaen's smile grew tight. 'Ah, that was a long time ago! But I remember things, you know, maybe more than other people do.'

'You always did.'

'Yes.' His voice sank to a whisper. 'Yes, I always did.'

As they walked off, Val glanced back to see Loddlaen standing alone, watching them with his hands shoved in his pockets.

When they arrived at the gathering, Val counted roughly eighty people in attendance. Loddlaen would have hated it, certainly. Some of the guests stood near a firepit and watched their host carving up an entire roast lamb; others sat in the grass behind the tents and watched the dancing out in the meadow. Javanateriel and Valandario found a good place to sit among the others. Women brought them plates of the choicest foods, happy to wait upon the Wise One and her man.

Although Val had no taste for strong drink, Jav had never said no to any skin of mead that came his way, and that night plenty of them arrived. While most Westfolk men could drink mead like water all night, for some reason Javanateriel had always been susceptible to strong drink, and he felt shamed that he was. The full moon was still high in the sky when Val realized that he had drunk more than enough. Someone passed him a full skin, and while he managed to get a good squirt into his mouth, he also sprayed mead across the front of his shirt.

His drinking was the only thing they ever argued about. Among strangers as they were, she tried to ignore his lapse, but she knew that her silence was growing colder and colder. Finally he spoke first.

'You're angry, aren't you?' Jav said.

'Well, you promised me you wouldn't get staggering drunk tonight.'

'I'm not staggering.'

'Not yet.'

'What makes you think I will be?'

'Past experience.'

'Oh come on, Val! If you'd have a sip or two yourself –'

'I don't care to get muddled, thank you very much.'

'Oh, so now I'm muddled!'

'That's not what I meant!'

Some of the others at the gathering were watching them, Val realized. She took a deep breath and let it out as a long sigh.

'Our squabbles always end the same way,' she said. 'I'm sorry I said anything, all right? I won't say another word.'

He stared at her, his mouth twisted into a wry smile. She thought the matter settled, but after a little while he abruptly spoke.

'You're saying I can't hold my drink. That's insulting.'

'I didn't mean that.'

'Oh? What else does staggering drunk mean?'

Val found herself tempted to scream at him, but she choked the impulse back. Maybe a smile would soothe his temper? She tried laying a loving hand on his arm as well, but he shook it off.

'Very well, then,' Jav said. 'If you're going to mock me, I'll go home.'

Javanateriel stood up, took a staggering step to restore his balance, then walked off, heading in the direction of their tent. Valandario started to get up to follow him, but one of the other women caught her arm.

'You're the Wise One, but I'm a good bit older than you,' she said. 'It's best to let the men just sleep it off.'

'Maybe so.' Val sat back down. 'If I go after him now, we'll only fight some more.'

The woman smiled, nodded, and hurried away, disappearing among the tents. Valandario returned to watching the dancing, but something nagged at her. As she thought about it, Val realized that she'd never seen her before – a tall woman with honey-blonde hair, darker than usual for one of the People. She turned to a man sitting nearby.

'Who was that?' Val said.

'I don't know,' he said. 'She must have come with some other alar. She's not a part of yours?'

'No. It's odd. I can't even picture her face, and here she just spoke to me.'

The dweomer cold seized Valandario in claws of ice. She got up, trembling and gasping for breath. The fellow she'd been speaking with rose, too, caught by her alarm.

'Wise One?' he said. 'Are you all right?'

'Yes,' Val said, 'but Jav's not.'

She turned and ran, dodging through the crowd. Dimly she was aware of other people following her, of shouts of alarm, of cries that the Wise One needed help. All she could think of was Jav, off alone somewhere – *our tent*, she thought. *He said he was going home.* By the time she reached her alar's part of the campground, she was panting for breath and soaked in the cold sweat of sheer terror. Their tent stood in the midst of others. She dodged her way around and through. As she ran up, Wildfolk appeared in swarms, gnomes at her feet, sprites in the air, clustering around her, drenching her and the tent flap in silver light.

Valandario flung back the tent flap and ducked inside. Jav lay sprawled on his back, his mouth open, his eyes staring at nothing, his shirt soaked not with mead but blood from the dagger wounds stabbed into his chest. All around him lay tent bags and their contents, spilled and kicked this way and that. Val took a few steps and flung herself down beside him, too out of breath to scream. She could hear the others, swearing, yelling back and forth, but their words made no sense at all.

'Jav?' she whispered. 'Jav?'

She grabbed his right hand – still faintly warm – but she knew he was dead. She dropped into trance as fast as she could, found her body of light waiting, and transferred into it. All around her the Wildfolk shone and sparkled, lines of light and crystalline shapes in a multitude of colours, their true appearance on the etheric. In this glimmering crowd she rose up to the tent roof. She should have seen Javanateriel's etheric double still hovering around his body, but she only saw the dead flesh and the blackness of the objects scattered around him. She rose higher and sailed through the tent's roof out into the night sky, where the blue light billowed around her. Far above the moon shone like an enormous silver scowl.

'Jav!' She sent her thought out in a scream of pain. 'Jav! Think of me so I can find you! Call my name!'

Someone was approaching her through the blue, but it was the simulacrum of a woman, an abnormally tall woman with honey-blonde hair. She wore the semblances of leather leggings and an elven tunic, and she carried a golden bow in her right hand, while a golden quiver nestled at her hip.

'I took him to the lavender meadow and sent him across the white river,' the woman said. 'He interrupted us.' She sent out an exhalation of regret like bitter perfume, then disappeared, completely and suddenly gone.

Only Valandario's long years of training saved her from joining Jav there and then. A lesser dweomerworker would have screamed and raged and flown this way and that until her silver cord broke behind her. Instead, Valandario slid down the cord back to her body, transferred her consciousness over to the flesh, and banished her body of light with the proper ritual. Yet when she opened her eyes, she saw that she'd fallen forward into the pool of drying blood on Jav's chest. She screamed, screamed again, could not stop screaming and sobbing, reached up to claw at her hair and face with her fingernails. Hands caught hers and stopped her.

'Val, Val!' It was Enabrilia's voice. 'No! Don't hurt yourself! He wouldn't want that.'

She turned blindly towards her old friend and wept. Enabrilia threw her arms around her and pulled her close. Other women clustered round, murmuring, and helped them stand.

'Come out of the tent,' Enabrilia murmured. 'Let's go outside.'

Without their support Valandario never would have been able to walk those few steps. They half-led, half-carried her into Enabrilia's tent while she wept, trembling with it, choking on her grief, gasping down air only to weep again. They helped her sit, then huddled around her, while the sprites hovered above and wrung tiny hands.

A man's voice cut through her tears. 'I thought maybe Loddlaen could help, but none of us can find him,' he said. 'His horse and mules are gone. His tent's here, but it's empty.'

Rage flared and burned into the grief. Valandario choked down her tears and looked up. 'Was it him?' she whispered to the sprites.

They nodded, then winked out like blown candles. She realized that Danalaurel was standing in the doorway.

'Was it Loddlaen who killed him?' Danno's voice trembled as badly as hers, but with rage. 'His own foster-brother, and he killed him?'

Valandario nodded. Words lay beyond her.

Danno turned and shouted to someone outside. She heard answering shouts, then Danalaurel turned and ducked out, yelling about fetching horses.

'Why?' one of the women said. 'Why would he do –'

'Thievery, most likely,' another woman said. 'Didn't you see how everything was all thrown around in there? Everyone knows that Val carries a lot of gemstones with her.'

A memory began to rise in Valandario's mind. Gemstones, Loddlaen wanting –

'The black pyramid!' she said. 'I've got to go back to the tent!'

'Not just yet.' Enabrilia grabbed her by the shoulders. 'Let the others –' She hesitated briefly. 'Let the others finish what they're doing in there.'

'Do what?' Val whispered. 'You mean taking Jav away.'

Enabrilia nodded. Valandario began to weep again, hugging herself and rocking back and forth like a child. When another woman brought in a clean tunic and leggings, Enabrilia helped Val out of her blood-soaked clothing and into the clean as if she really had been a child.

'I've got to tell Aderyn,' Valandario said. 'He can't just ride in and hear about this.'

'Yes, he can,' Enabrilia said. 'I think it'll be kinder, actually, to tell him about it to his face. We can all try to comfort him that way. It's not long before dawn, anyway, so he'll be here soon.'

No one slept that night. Two and three at a time, the men rode back to camp to relay messages, then rode out again to resume searching. By dawn they'd all returned with the bad news that the search was hopeless. Although they'd sent out parties in all directions, Loddlaen and his stock had vanished, apparently without leaving a single hoof print on the ground.

'He has dweomer, doesn't he?' Danalaurel said. 'It's no wonder we can't find him.'

With the pale light of day Valandario's first flush of grief had spent itself. Danno's remark reminded her that she had dweomer herself, more powerful than Loddlaen's, and she tried scrying for him. She could see nothing, no matter how hard or how carefully she focused her inner vision.

'He might have taken ship again,' Valandario told the others. 'I wonder if someone was waiting for him down at the coast. It's only a few miles away.'

At daybreak Valandario, Enabrilia, and two other women returned to her tent to sort through the tent bags and other possessions scattered around. Since Valandario couldn't bear to remove them, the others packed up Javanateriel's clothing and possessions. Val searched through the scattered goods left behind. As she worked, she carefully repacked each tent bag and hung it in its usual place to force her mind to do something besides mourn. She found that Loddlaen had left two handfuls of gemstones behind – a small fortune in gems, in fact – but sure enough, the black obsidian pyramid had disappeared with him.

'Everything else is here,' Valandario said at last. 'As far as I can tell, anyway. My mind – I just can't seem to think.'

'Of course,' Enabrilia said. 'Do you think you can sleep?'

'I doubt it, but I'll try.'

Despite her doubt, as soon as she lay down, Valandario did fall asleep. She dreamt of Javanateriel. She saw him walking towards her, laughing at the jest he'd played on her. She berated him for pretending to die, but when he caught her hands, she forgave him – only to wake and remember that no, he truly had been murdered. She sat up, feeling that she might be sick at any moment, sure that the smell of his blood still lingered in the humid summer air. Enabrilia was sitting near by, watching her.

'It's noon,' Enabrilia said. 'Do you feel like coming outside?'

'Yes,' Valandario said. 'I've got to have some fresh air.'

They walked outside to find the camp oddly quiet. Children stayed close to their parents, who stood or sat in little groups, talking in subdued voices. Even the dogs had picked up the mood and lay near the tents with barely a wag of a tail or a whine.

'They never found him,' Enabrilia said. 'Ah by the Black Sun! I wonder what his mother's going to think of this, if we ever see her again to tell her about it, anyway. Dalla was my closest friend, you know, when we were girls. Thinking that her child – ah gods.'

Distantly, at the edge of the camp, someone howled out the word 'no', followed by a long shriek of mingled rage and grief. Everyone turned to look in that direction.

'I'll wager that's Aderyn,' Valandario said. 'Someone must have told him.'

Aderyn came striding through the tents, his silver hair swept back from his face, his eyes dripping silent tears, his mouth set and grim. Everyone turned to watch him without speaking a word. When he saw Valandario, Aderyn stopped, then drew himself up to full height and hurried to meet her.

'My poor child!' Aderyn said. 'My heart aches for you!'

When he held out his arms, Valandario ran to him. She felt like a child, indeed, that young, frightened apprentice once more. Aderyn held her close and stroked her hair with one hand while she wept against him.

'Forgive me,' he said. 'Please forgive me.'

'It's not your fault,' she said through her sobs. 'I don't blame you.'

They wept together while all around them the People stood watching. On the edge of the crowd someone began a mourning song, and slowly, a few at a time, the others joined in, until the entire camp chanted its grief.

In the hot weather, the death ground at the Lake of the Leaping Trout lay too far north for his alar to take Javanateriel there for the last rites. The Deverry merchants and their men gave them every stick of firewood they'd brought along with them for the funereal pyre. The women in the alar wrapped Jav in a linen sheet and laid him on the pyre, then poured flasks of olive oil from Bardek over him and the wood. Before they lit that final fire, Valandario brought out the pair of wooden cups and tucked them one into each flaccid hand.

The fire burned much of the night. With the dawn, when the ashes had cooled, Valandario let them scatter in the rising wind. As she watched them drifting away, she knew that she would never love another man, no matter how long the life ahead her.

On a late afternoon that threatened rain, Nevyn was digging up comfrey roots out in a fallow pasture when he felt Aderyn's mind reaching out to his. He lay down his trowel, sat back on his heels, and used the gathering grey clouds as a scrying focus. When Aderyn told him about the murder, Nevyn was so shocked, so bitterly surprised, that for a moment he could say nothing at all. Finally he found words.

'I never ever thought Loddlaen would do such a thing,' Nevyn said. 'Never in a thousand years!'

'I can't tell you how it gladdens my heart to hear you say that,' Aderyn said. 'I've been berating myself, thinking I should have known what he was capable of.'

'Don't! The Loddlaen we knew wasn't capable of it. Besides, do you really think he intended to kill Jav? It sounds to me like he panicked when Jav came into the tent.'

'So I thought, too. From what Val told me, one of the Guardians was mixed up in this as well – Alshandra, most likely.'

'Worse and worse! Why would she have wanted the obsidian piece?'

'I have no idea. The message from Evandar in it, mayhap? Or maybe to allow one of her worshippers to travel in her country the same way Dalla did, all those years ago.'

Nevyn felt old grief troubling Aderyn's mind. It took some time before Aderyn could continue.

'If only I had seen,' Aderyn said. 'If only I'd seen what you saw, all those years ago.'

'You couldn't have. Now, look, you told me that Val doesn't blame you. Well and good, then. Don't you blame yourself, either.'

'My thanks.'

The words reached Nevyn on a wave of sincere gratitude. With them he felt the breach between him and Aderyn, caused all those years ago by Morwen's death, finally close and heal.

'What hurts me the most,' Aderyn continued, 'was the way he wormed himself into Val's trust, telling her he'd come to see me, and all the time he was planning on stealing the gem. I suppose he dragged me into it in order to punish me somehow. I was so happy, thinking he'd come home at last.'

'I was wondering about that, not that I wanted to say it first.' *That little viper!* Nevyn thought to himself alone. *If I ever get hold of him –*

'Well, now he's gone,' Aderyn said. 'Probably to Bardek. Doubtless I'll never see him again.'

'Oh, don't believe that,' Nevyn said. 'He'll come back to

Deverry one day. I'm sure of it. He's set forces in motion that will drag him back, and he'll want to take out his rage on you again, if naught else.'

'Perhaps so. If he does, it'll be up to me to deal with him, too. I'm torn in half, hoping he does come back but wishing he'd stay away forever.'

Aderyn sounded so exhausted that Nevyn said nothing more that afternoon but comforting platitudes. He mulled the situation over in his mind for days, however. He knew with the wordless surety of a great master of magic that dark dweomer lurked somewhere on the fringes of Loddlaen's life. Exactly where and how he couldn't know – not yet. He could only watch and wait for him to come back to Deverry. *His own kind will draw him*, Nevyn thought. *Ai! None of us ever dreamt that there was so much hatred in the lad!*

From time to time during his unnaturally long life, Nevyn had to leave whatever place he'd been living in and relocate somewhere else. If he stayed in one home too long, the local folk would have noticed that he was living for far too many years. That summer, after the murder, Nevyn left Cannobaen. He travelled north-east, heading for Cantrae province and his hidden dwelling in Brin Toraedic. He stopped in Cerrmor, however, when he received an obscure hint from the Lords of Wyrd that someone of great interest happened to be there.

Although the Lords of Wyrd were once ordinary human beings, they have evolved so far, and live on such an exalted plane of existence, that communicating in words lies beyond them. All they can do is send hints, intuitions, odd twists of feeling and thought – the sort of thing men call omens – down to the dweomermasters who live so far below. Nevyn interpreted this particular omen as meaning that Lilli or Morwen had been reborn in Cerrmor. Unfortunately, he'd misread the intent, though not the impulse.

On his second day there, Nevyn turned onto a street leading to the docks and noticed a stout fellow walking ahead of him

– a successful merchant, judging by the brightly checked wool of his brigga and the heavy embroidery on his fine linen shirt. At a tavern door the fellow turned in, pausing to glance back. Nevyn received the impression of a typical Cerrmor man, with a broad face, blue eyes, and thick pale hair, but the impression was all he got, because the fellow blanched, ducked, and practically leapt into the tavern. Nevyn glanced behind him and saw no one on the street. *It must have been me who frightened him*, Nevyn thought. *I wonder who he is?* He hurried over to the tavern door, but when he looked in, he found no sign of the fellow except the swinging of the back door, as if someone had rushed out and flung it closed behind him.

Nevyn trotted through the tavern and out the back, but he saw only empty ale barrels and a dungheap in the narrow alley. With a shrug he went on his way, but for the rest of his time in Cerrmor, he kept on guard in hopes of seeing the mysterious merchant again. He never did, and no more could he place the fellow among the crowded memories of his unnaturally prolonged life. Once he even remembered Tirro, the shifty-eyed little wastrel of a merchant's son, but he never equated the two – which was a great pity, because many years later, that sight of a grown, prosperous, and utterly corrupt Tirro, or Alastyr to give him his full name, would have stood him in good stead.

Eventually his search for those souls to whom he owed debts of wyrd made Nevyn forget about the mysteriously frightened stranger. After wandering the kingdom for some years in the hopes of finding Lilli and Morwen reborn, he returned to Eldidd and the small town of Cannobaen. He decided he'd stay there, too, until the Lords of Wyrd sent him an omen that indicated otherwise. Not even such a powerful dweomermaster as he could realize, however, just how right his choice was, nor could he know that hundreds of years later he would be reborn on the western border at a time when its folk would stand in the gravest peril they had ever faced.

PART II
The Westlands
1159

The spiral, not the circle, is the key to the fulfilment of Wyrd.

The Secret Book of Cadwallon the Druid

I n a pair of old man's hands, the black stone glittered. They sat inside a tent, and soft voices talked incomprehensibly as Evan – he knew his real name was Evan – stared into the stone. In the black glow a man with daffodil-yellow hair and cherry-red lips held out a white flat thing with a picture of a black lizard upon it. Or was it a raven?

Salamander woke suddenly with the dream vivid in his mind. He sat up on the bed and ran his hands through his sweaty hair while he stared at the braided rushes covering the floor. He reminded himself that he was sitting in a chamber in the Red Wolf dun, not in a Westfolk tent. After a few good yawns, he rose and went to the window. Down below in the ward servant lasses were carrying baskets from the cookhouse into the great hall. On the far side of the ward he could see grooms leading horses to the watering trough. The dun had woken for the day.

Salamander dressed, ready to go down for breakfast, but he lingered in the chamber, thinking over the dream, trying to dissect its residue. The obsidian pyramid was calling to him. He could understand it no other way than that the stone was trying to reach him. He sat down on the bed and considered the stripe of sunlight while he let his mind reach out to the stone.

In vision he saw the obsidian pyramid standing upon an altar beside an oil lamp. The pyramid glowed with its strange black light – a spirit, he suddenly realized, was indwelling the gem. Nothing else would explain the glow and the bright black sparks that occasionally flashed from its surface. What sort of spirit? With the Sight as his only tool the answer lay beyond him. He widened the vision. He could clearly discern the stone altar, the oil lamp, and behind both, a painting of

Alshandra in the Bardek manner. Beyond, he saw only a misty void, hiding the rest of Alshandra's Inner Shrine.

Scrying out Zakh Gral made him think of Rocca. Instantly his vision jumped to daylight and the Outer Shrine. Rocca was leaning over the rough stone outer altar, scrubbing it with a handful of rags. On the ground beside her sat a bucket of water. The job would make every muscle in her torso ache. She'd be glad of the pain, he supposed, because she'd see it as yet another sacrifice to her goddess. Nearby stood one of the Gel da' Thae priestesses, waving her hands while she spoke. Rocca paused in her cleaning to listen, her face grave, almost troubled. Salamander wished for the thousandth time that he could hear while scrying, but only the greatest masters of the dweomer could manage that.

Rocca began talking. The Gel da' Thae woman listened intently, then suddenly smiled, showing her teeth, filed to sharp points in the Horsekin manner. She seemed deeply relieved about whatever problem had brought her to her fellow priestess. Rocca patted her on the shoulder, as if to comfort her. The other woman nodded, then walked away. Rocca returned to her work.

And Sidro – where was she? The Sight took him flying upriver to the forest edge. Rocca had led him out of the forest at just that point, or so he remembered, following the same road that Sidro now walked in the opposite direction. She was trudging along in her painted leather dress with a blanket tied around her waist for a skirt and a bulging sack of supplies over one shoulder. She walked with her head down as if she were already profoundly weary with the journey just begun.

In the sunlight her cropped hair shone like a raven's wing. He noticed for the first time that the back of her neck bore a string of green tattoos. Those and the width of her shoulders, her oddly round eyes, the strong modelling of her features – *ye gods!* he thought. *I'll wager there's Horsekin blood in her veins!* He focused in closer and saw that she was weeping. She raised her head and looked up at the sky while tears ran down her cheeks, a gesture that cost her when she stumbled over a rock in the path. She stopped, dropped her sack, and covered her face with her hands while she sobbed, her shoulders shaking from the pain of bare flesh meeting stone.

He pitied her. His involuntary stab of compassion surprised him so badly that he nearly lost the vision then and there, but he managed to stay focused for a few moments more, until she suddenly lowered her hands and twisted around to look behind her. Her tear-streaked face showed panic as she looked this way and that, just as if she knew someone watched her.

Salamander broke the vision fast. He sat still for a few moments, staring out at nothing, then tried to stand. The chamber swelled and swirled around him so violently that he nearly lost consciousness. Eventually his physical sight steadied down, but the stones of the chamber seemed to be breathing, a hundred swellings and flattenings of little lungs.

'Star goddesses help me!' he whispered aloud. He wanted to contact Dallandra, but he was suddenly afraid of using any dweomer at all.

A sound struck the chamber door from outside. He cocked his head to one side, puzzled, but when it sounded again he realized that someone was knocking.

'Who is it?' Salamander called out.

'Neb. Are you ill or suchlike?'

'I'm not. The door isn't barred. Come in.'

Neb pushed open the door and walked in, stood looking down at him with his hands on his hips. 'You look ill,' he said.

'Do I? Well, most likely it's just the heat of the summer's day. I didn't sleep well last night.'

'Then you'd best get out of this chamber, hadn't you? It's sweltering in here.'

'Splendid idea! Have I missed breakfast?'

'You've not. The lasses are just setting it out.'

After a bowl of porridge and a chunk of fresh bread and butter, Salamander felt his normal self. Still, he reminded himself that Dallandra had been right as usual. He needed to

limit his scrying and to refrain from any other dweomer workings – unless some crisis demanded them.

The Northlands rise into a wilderness maze, cut up by streams
and rivulets that tumble down to join one or another of the
south-flowing rivers. At the time of which we speak, primeval
forest covered its hills and clustered at the bottom of canyons
and valleys. Even those who travelled through it regularly
would have been lost after a few days if it weren't for the
existence of a secret pathway. Alshandra's initiates had devised
a set of symbols that, carved high up on tree trunks or chipped
into boulders, marked an east-west route leading to northern
Deverry and the little villages and farms of those Deverry
folk who believed in the goddess.

Although she'd been a priestess for some years now and
thus should have trusted in Alshandra, Sidro still feared the
forest road. She'd been born and raised in Taenalapan, one
of the towns the Gel da' Thae had built among the ruins of
an ancient city. In her view, stone walls meant safety and
comfort, while every crack of a branch or rustle of leaves
and bracken in the forest signalled bears and wolves,
searching for a tasty two-legged meal.

The damp woodland smell frightened her even more. She
had enough Horsekin blood in her veins to pick up scent-
marks too faint for a merely human nose, but she lacked a
gamekeeper's knowledge to identify their makers, so to her,
the leavings of the smallest weasel reeked of as much danger
as those of a big black bear. When night fell, she climbed
into the cleft of a tree and twisted her blanket into a rope
to tie herself to a branch. She drowsed, clutching her sack,
rather than slept, until at last the sun rose.

As chief acolyte in Zakh Gral, Sidro had been free of
missionary work and its long treks through wild places. Her
humiliation over the matter of Evan the gerthddyn and his
supposed miracle had lost her that high position in the order.
As she trudged along, her mind rehearsed grievances beyond

her power to stop it. *Rocca worked that very well, the scheming shrew!* she would think. Now Rocca held the post of chief acolyte and the favour of the high priestess while Sidro found herself back as a simple traveller for the goddess, the lowliest rank in their order, Alshandra's Elect. *I know he was a fraud, but they'd never let me tell them why!* That thought brought her a scatter of tears.

Late on her third day out of Zakh Gral, Sidro came to a narrow strip of meadow crossed with a stream of clear water. In the sunlight she felt safe enough to rest. She laid her sack of supplies and her blanket on the grassy bank, then considered the shallow stream. Although by the rules of their order the priestesses of Alshandra scorned such comforts as bathing, Sidro had never been able to break herself of the desire to be clean.

She pulled off her leather dress, laid it on the grass, and, still dressed in her linen shift, stepped into the cold mountain water. Gasping and splashing she sank into a shallow pool, then knelt on comfortable white sand to let the water run over her back and shoulders. Without soap she could do little more than rinse off loose dirt and old sweat from skin and linen both, but even that little felt like luxury.

'Alshandra forgive me,' she murmured, several times over.

She was scooping up water and splashing it onto her face when a shadow swept across her. Overhead a raven circled, an enormous raven, so large that she knew exactly what – or rather who – it had to be. She rose and climbed onto the bank just as the raven landed with a flurry of shiny black wings, which he folded before he spoke. Although he used the Horsekin tongue, his rigid beak distorted his speech so much that she understood him only because she'd known him since childhood.

'Turn away!'

Sidro did as he asked. A sudden shimmer of blue light cast a brief shadow onto the grass in front of her. When she turned back, Laz Moj sat cross-legged and naked on the grass, holding a single raven feather in his long fingers. His mach-fala, that is, his mother-clan as the Gel da' Thae call their extended families, had mingled human and Horsekin blood for a good many centuries. He was as tall and heavily muscled as a typical Horsekin, but he wore his brown hair cropped short and slicked straight back, as sleek as the raven's feathers. His dark brown eyes dominated his face and its slender nose, thin lips, and sharp jawline – a face like a knife-edge, or so most people described it. Between the welter of blue tattoos on his face, neck, and shoulders, his skin was tanned, not the pure white of Horsekin skin, though his chest and stomach were pinkish-pale from a lack of sun.

'I'm surprised to see you,' Sidro said.

'Why?' Laz said with a bird-like dip of his head. 'Sisi, my only love, I long for you still. Your scent haunts my dreams.'

Rather than respond, she took a few steps back.

'Whether you long for me or not,' Laz continued, 'I've come to warn you. You're in real danger.'

'I thought so! There are bears and wolves around here, aren't there?'

'Oh, worse than bears, worse than wolves. The silver dragon has come a-hunting me and thee.'

Sidro caught her breath. For a moment the meadow seemed to rise up above her like a green wave. She dropped to her knees and let the world steady itself while Laz watched with a twisted grin.

'Why?' she whispered. 'I only wish I knew why he hates me so much. I'd suppose it's because I'm a priestess, and he belongs to Vandar, but he's never tried to kill the others.'

'And needless to say, I've never been a priestess,' Laz said, 'and yet he's made it quite clear that he thinks I belong in the land of the dead right along with you.'

'He hasn't found Zakh Gral, has he?'

'Oh yes he has. You daren't go back. He'll find you there. I know you hate the forest, but you'll be safest here with me and my men.'

'Your criminals and blasphemers, you mean. Your idola-
ters.'

'Why do you keep calling them that? I may not believe
in gods, but they all keep the old faith. I encourage them to
do so, you know. It keeps them obedient.'

'Then you're murdering their souls. When you die —'

'I know, I know, when I die I'll go to Vandar's horrible
country in my raven body, and he'll be plucking my feathers
for all eternity.' Laz was grinning at her. 'He'll doubtless roast
me every night and serve me with some kind of nasty sauce
to his fellow demons. And every morning, we'll start all over
again.'

Sidro set her lips tight together. She'd been trying to make
him see reason on this subject for years, but all he ever did
was mock.

'What's this?' Laz went on. 'It's not like you to have no
interest in discussing theology.'

'Not with that loathsome dragon nearby,' Sidro said. 'If
he's found the fortress, we're all in danger.'

'We? Your pack of holy fools may well be in danger. You
and I are not, as long as we stay in among the trees.'

'They're not fools!'

'No? Think, Sisi! Only fools believe themselves safe when
they have enemies. Only fools throw away their best weapons
against those enemies, too. That Evan — we know how he
managed to fly away. Would they have believed you if you'd
told them? Oh no, they would have killed you just because
you know mazrak lore.'

And now Rocca has her fake miracle, Sidro thought, *the
filthy little sow!* Aloud, she said, 'Evan's been scrying me out.'

'You're sure of that?'

'Yes, very sure.'

'And I suppose you don't dare tell your ever-so-holy high
priestess that, either.'

'Don't insult Lakanza! I shan't stand for it.' All at once
she felt weary. 'But we've argued all this out a hundred times.

Yes, when it comes to sorcery they're utterly irrational, but they're still my people.'

'And I'm not?' He paused to quirk an eyebrow in her direction. 'You loved me once.'

'Who took me in when you deserted me?'

'I never meant to desert you. I was afraid to claim the child. I thought my mother would order him killed. You agreed with me, didn't you? If you'd given me a girl, it would have been different, but with two bastard sons in the mach-fala already – my dear mother, miserly old hag that she is, would have begrudged every mouthful he ate.'

'Of course, of course. I'm sorry, Laz. We've chewed on this old bone too many times, and I should let it drop.'

'Bury it once and for all, will you? I would have claimed you both if I could have. Don't you believe me?'

She ignored the question and glanced up at the sky, half-expecting to see Vandar's white dragon stooping for the kill. 'What's wrong?' Laz said. 'Are you ill?'

'No, you dolt, I'm terrified. First Evan, now the silver wyrm – I've got to go back to Zakh Gral. The silver dragon is one of Vandar's servants in this world. What if he tells the prince of Vandar's spawn or one of those Lijik Ganda rakzanir, the gwerbrotz, whatever they call them, about Zakh Gral? I've got to warn the fortress.'

'Are the holy ladies going to believe you? "And how do you know about this dragon?" they'll say. "Oh, a mazrak told me," you'll say.' Laz tossed the feather away. 'The rakzan of the fortress would have you raised on the long spear before you could scream Alshandra's name.'

'Hold your tongue!' She heard her voice shaking. 'I'll tell them Alshandra sent me a vision.'

'They won't believe you. You've just been disgraced. Why would your goddess deign to warn you and not them?'

'How do you know about that?'

'I watched, of course, from way up high. The raven has sharp eyes, my love, and even sharper ears.' He grinned at her. 'And here you are, smelling of despondency, with all your lovely hair cut off, turned out onto the road to go wipe the spiritual arses of your believers over in Slavers' Country, and a stinking lot of rabble they are at that. Your dear friend Rocca must be strutting like a bell mare in a herd of geldings.'

Sidro felt tears gather. She raised her hands and covered her eyes, trying to hide the tears, to force them back, to wipe them away, but they spilled between her fingers. She heard Laz getting up, walking over – a danger of another sort. She was only half-dressed, he naked, just as on that day so long ago when his mother had ordered her into the First Son's chamber. She could remember walking in and seeing Laz lounging naked on his bed. She had known then what her duty would be, and she'd been so glad of it.

Glad then. Not now. Laz knelt in front of her and laid a gentle hand on her cheek. He took a deep breath, soaking in her scent. She knocked his hand away. With a soft laugh he sat back on his heels.

'Ah yes,' he said, 'your holy vows.'

'Don't torment me. Please, Laz, don't.'

'Well, I didn't come here to cause you pain. Don't you remember when you were a slave in my mother's house? I set you free then. I'm trying to set you free again now. Please, won't you even look at me?'

He was smiling, but sadly, his brown eyes strangely shadowed as he leaned closer. She looked into his eyes and found herself unable to look away. All at once she yawned with a convulsive shudder. *I'm exhausted*, she thought. *I hardly slept last night.* Laz kept staring into her eyes.

'Come with me, Sisi,' he said. 'I want you to come with me.'

'I can't. I swore a vow to my goddess.'

'But I've got something I want to show you, something very special. It's a crystal, a crystal with sorcerous powers.'

'The goddess comes first. I've got to go warn her people.'

'There's no need of that. They're safe. That dragon – he wants to kill us, not them. Come with me so I can keep you safe.'

His eyes seemed to have become great drifts of dust, blown in a hot summer wind around her. His scent enveloped her.

'But Evan, he'll tell someone.' Sidro suddenly found it hard to remember just who Evan was. 'Word gets around. Those lords of theirs. Lijik Ganda, I mean.'

'Why should they care what happens so far west?' Laz leaned closer still. 'Zakh Gral's perfectly safe. No one will harm it. It's hidden, it's secret.'

Sidro yawned again. The dust clouds returned, dancing and swimming around her. 'Secret,' she whispered.

'Yes, we have our secrets, don't we, Sisi? Don't you remember them? Come with me. I've learned so many new secrets since we were separated. Don't you want to share them?'

'I suppose.'

'Don't suppose. You know you want to learn them.'

'I want to share them.'

'You want to come with me.'

'I want to come with you.'

The clouds turned black as smoke, and she fainted. When she woke, she lay decorously on her side in the grass. Laz was sitting cross-legged nearby. She sat up and looked around. Long shadows fell across the meadow from the western verge of the forest. In among the shadows something moved. As she watched, a Horsekin man emerged from the trees, leading a saddled horse.

'Do you feel better?' Laz said. 'You needed that little nap.'

'I must have, yes.' Sidro sat up, yawning. 'Who's that over there?'

'A friend of mine. I summoned him while you slept. The horse is for you, to spare your poor swollen feet the walking. Ah, my love, I can't tell you how joyful my heart is, that you've agreed to come with me.'

'Mine is too.' Yet for a moment she felt utterly muddled. When had she agreed? She couldn't remember, yet she was sure that somehow, she had indeed done so. *And I won't have to walk in the forest alone,* she thought. *My dear Laz! Alshandra must have sent him.*

When Laz's friend arrived, Sidro noticed that the horse – a black mare with a white off-fore and a white diamond on her forehead – followed him without the benefit of a lead rope, though she wore a leather halter. The Horsekin nodded at Laz, then bowed to Sidro, but said nothing. He was slender, short for one of the 'Kin at about six feet tall, with their typical milk-white skin between the welter of blue tattoos on his face, neck, and hands. Across his left cheek blue letters in the Horsekin alphabet spelled KREN, the goddess of wild things. He wore a loose green shirt and a pair of buckskin leggings, ordinary enough clothing.

His black hair, however, marked him as someone beyond the typical. Most Gel da' Thae men let their hair grow long and brushed it straight back or kept it in waist-length braids. This fellow had cut his hair very short except for a wide stripe down the middle of his skull, which he'd done in a row of narrow braids so that it fell to one side like a horse's mane. When he bowed to her, the metal charms tied into the braids jingled and caught the light with a glint of silver.

'I'll transform and fly over the forest, my love,' Laz said to Sidro. 'I'll see you at our camp. It's not very far.'

Sidro's shift had dried enough for her to put the dress on over it. Laz waited to leave until his friend had helped Sidro mount the horse. He handed her the blanket and her sack.

'Don't watch,' Laz said.

She looked away, but once again she saw the flash of bluish light. From the saddle she glanced back to see his human body gone. The raven took a few steps, then bunched his muscles and sprang into the air with a drumbeat of wings. The mare ignored him; she must have been part of his herd for a good long while. Laz circled over the meadow once, croaked a farewell, and headed north-east.

The Gel da' Thae nodded to Sidro, then clucked to the mare and strode off in the same direction. His long braided

mane bobbed and swayed as he walked. The mare followed
right along, switching her tail in a parallel rhythm.

'What's your name?' Sidro said to him.

'Pir.'

'You must be a horse mage.'

'Yes.'

She waited, but he volunteered not a word more. She
considered asking more questions, but once they walked into
the forest all her attention went to ducking low-growing
branches and clinging to the saddle-peak. The trail they were
following twisted uphill and down, dodged around boulders
and sudden ravines. The black mare plodded after her leader,
only breaking stride when she needed to pick her way around
some obstacle.

The sun hung so low that shadows filled the forest, though
overhead the sky still shone blue, when Sidro first smelled
the camp: a stink of men, old cooking, some sort of ale-like
brew, and the inevitable results of the last two. Another
quarter mile on, and she saw it.

Scattered among the trees stood wooden shelters, made of
rough planks supplemented with deer hides and laced together
with thongs and bits of rope. She counted sixteen of them,
more lean-tos than cabins, with their slant roofs and empty
windows, but she could just make out a few more, half-hidden
by the forest. Pir led the horse to the largest, which unlike
the others sported four proper walls and a plank roof, though
it seemed oddly squat and low. He clucked to the mare, who
stood perfectly still while he helped Sidro dismount.

'Welcome,' Pir said. 'Here come the others.'

She turned to see a sizeable number of Horsekin men
walking out of the forest cover, at least two dozen by her
rough count, dressed in a rag-tag assemblage of clothing:
leather leggings, wool trousers, linen shirts, wool shirts, all
of them dirty and torn. They kept their weapons, however,
sparkling clean, since the last of the sunlight was glinting
off spear points and the blades of long knives. They formed

a semi-circle around her, Pir, and the horse, then knelt, bowing their heads. At a rustle behind her she glanced round and saw Laz, free of the raven form but still barefoot, standing in the doorway. He wore loose grey trousers in the Slavers' Country style and a once-white shirt, belted at the waist. On the belt he carried a bone-handled hunting knife in a dark leather sheath.

'Welcome and three times welcome,' Laz said. 'Come in, come in, my love! Men, this woman owns my heart and all my joy. Protect her as you'd protect me.'

With a shout the men hefted their spears in salute. Sidro raised her hands to acknowledge them, then turned away and joined Laz. He led her inside, down three steps to the sunken floor of the cabin. It proved to be one large room with a floor of rushes. In the corners, heaps of green pine needles filled the air with a cool, clean scent, a profound relief after the stench outside. A square plank table with two cut tree stumps for chairs stood in the middle. In one corner lay a straw-filled mattress with reasonably clean blankets upon it. Diagonally across from the bed stood a perch made of branches. She pointed at it.

'For the raven, I assume,' she said.

'Yes, it makes the transformation easier,' Laz said. 'I wish I had a fine house to give you. Do you remember my mother's?'

'Of course.' She tossed her blanket onto the bed, then sat down on one of the stumps and laid her sack of belongings on the table. 'It was all so beautiful and clean. And the floors – there were so many colours of marble it was like you walked across flowers. I didn't even mind scrubbing them.'

'Someday perhaps you'll be the mistress of a fine house like it. I'll do my best to provide one. If of course your holy fools don't kill me first. They would, you know. And Pir the horse mage – why do you think a man with his gifts is willing to live here in this filthy stinking camp? They'd kill him, too, if they got their claws into him. Well, wouldn't they?'

Sidro saw no reason to argue, since he was speaking the

truth. 'What about your other men?' she said. 'Do they have gifts, too?'

'A few of them. Most, alas, are the criminals and renegades you called them. Those who know wizardry help me and Pir control the others.'

For a moment Sidro sat yawning, looking around the cabin, while she tried to remember – tried to remember – what had happened, why she was there, what he'd told her – tried to remember. A detail swam to the surface of her mind.

'You told me you had something to show me,' she said.

'I do indeed.'

Laz went between the wooden perch and the far wall, then stooped down with his back towards her. For a moment he scrabbled through the rushes on the floor with both hands. She heard something metallic click and creak. In a moment he stood up and returned to the table carrying a plain wooden box. He sat down opposite her and opened the box, brought out a dirty wool pouch, opened that and took out a smaller pouch of sleek gold fabric.

'What's that made of?' Sidro said.

'It's called silk,' Laz said. 'It comes from the Black Islands, ultimately, but I got it in the Slavers' Country. Here's what it's covering.'

With a flourish he pulled a glittering object out of the pouch and set it on the table. It proved to be a narrow pyramid cut from white quartz, about six inches high with a base that fitted comfortably in the palm of a hand. Its point had been sliced off at an angle.

'Alshandra protect!' Sidro whispered. 'It's like our altar gem, just white to its black. I told you about that, didn't I?'

'You certainly did,' Laz said. 'Which is why this caught my eye in a marketplace, when I was languishing in exile. Some dolt of a jeweller thought it was a little bauble and nothing more.'

Sidro had always been able to tell when he was lying, mostly because he did it so often.

'No,' she said. 'Tell me where you really found it.'

He laughed with a toss of his head. 'Having you with me is going to be challenging. Still, tis worth it. I'll tell you in good time, my love, all in good time.'

'I'm not surprised you worship Vandar. He loves lies and riddles, too.'

'I do not worship Vandar. I wish, my dear Sisi, that you could disabuse yourself of that notion. I can't worship Vandar because he was only a sorcerer, not a god, no more than Alshandra was a goddess.'

'She *is* a goddess.'

'No, she's dead, just like Vandar.' Laz grinned at her. 'Think, Sisi! Hundreds of our people saw her torn apart over Highstone Tor down in the Slavers' Country. The chronicles make it quite clear. They –'

'That's all lies. You have to see with the eyes of faith, not believe everything some crazed bard recited to some corrupt old-god priestess.'

'The eyes of faith!' He rolled his in mockery. 'You can't convert me, you know. If I could be converted, Mother would have done it years ago.'

'Oh, probably so! But how do you know that the chronicles aren't lying?'

'Why would they? Besides, I remember it.'

'You dreamt it, you mean. You've been having those dreams and calling them memories for as long as I've known you.'

'No, I recovered this memory in trance.'

Laz spoke so quietly, and he looked at her so steadily, that she held her tongue. He sat down on the other side of the table and leaned forward. Between them the white pyramid glowed for a brief moment, as if it had caught a random wink of sunlight.

'It's a true memory,' Laz said. 'I tested it with all the sigils. I stood on a ridge near Highstone Tor and watched Alshandra die. It happened over a river ford. Her form was like seeing a picture in clouds – you know, thinking you see a tower or a palace of cloud, but then the wind springs up and tears it apart. Pieces fall away, the illusion breaks up. Her arms went first, then part of her torso. She screamed, one last horrible scream, and –'

'Stop! I don't want to hear it! One of your nightmares, that's all.' Sidro realized that her hands were shaking. She laid them into her lap to hide them.

'No, a memory! I was a soldier in that life, an officer of some sort, so I suppose I died soon after. There was one last battle the next day, the chronicles tell us, but our men were so demoralized they could barely fight.'

'They were fooled by some ugly trick, that's all. There's no use in arguing about it.'

'Why? Because you're losing the argument?'

For want of a decent retort, Sidro made a sour face at him. Her head seemed to have turned to stone or perhaps lead. She leaned forward, braced her elbows on the table, and rested her head in her hands.

'What's wrong?' Laz's voice snapped with urgency.

She found herself unable to answer. He got up, strode around the table, and knelt on the floor beside her. When she turned her head to look at him, she nearly fainted. His eyes narrowed.

'My apologies.' Laz caught her gaze with his. 'Keep looking at me, my love.' He raised one hand and sketched a sigil in the air. 'There!'

Her head cleared. The memories came back, tumbling into her consciousness. In one smooth motion she slid free of the stump and stood up.

'You reeking scum!' Her voice shook with fury. 'You ensorceled me!'

'I'll confess.' Laz got to his feet. 'I knew you wouldn't come with me otherwise.'

'You were quite right. I'm not going to stay, either.'

'Yes, you are.'

Sidro grabbed her sack from the table. Laz stepped around

the stump and caught her by the shoulders. Although she struggled, she could do nothing against the strength in his arms, so
heavily muscled from raven flight. She could smell that their
brief battle had aroused him. The scent made her hesitate. It
had been so long since they'd – resolutely she forced her mind
away from the memories. When he tried to look into her eyes,
she focused her gaze on the bridge of his nose.

'You *are* clever,' he said.

'You taught me that trick yourself. You caught me off-guard
in the meadow, but it won't happen again. Laz, let me go!'

'No.'

'Why not? Do you think I'd betray you? Don't be stupid!
Of course I won't.'

'I know that. I won't let you go because of two things.
First, I need your help to work with the white crystal. Second,
I want you to stay.' He bent his head and touched her lips
with his. 'Please.'

She turned her head away and tried to twist free. For a
brief moment he let her go, but only so he could fling his
arms around her and pull her close. His sexual scent strengthened till it seemed to drift around them like a mist. Her
heart began pounding as one strong hand slid down to her
buttocks and caressed them. She felt herself gasp for breath.
His scent filled her lungs. The cloth sack slipped from her
fingers and fell to the floor.

'It'll be dark out soon,' he said. 'You can leave in the
morning.'

'I've got to leave now.' But she could hear doubt shaking
her voice.

'No. Stay with me. Please?'

This time when he laid his mouth on hers she opened
her lips and let him kiss her. His grip relaxed. She slipped
her arms around his neck and kissed him again. He laughed
and picked her up to carry her the short few steps to his
bed. In his arms she could forget everything but his scent
and his touch.

But much later, when he lay naked and asleep beside her, she remembered her goddess and her vows. She felt every muscle turn rigid as shame rose like vomit into her mouth. Her sudden rush of tears shocked her. *I've betrayed Alshandra,* she thought, and the thought made her sob aloud. Laz woke, rising up on one elbow in the darkness.

'What's wrong?' he said.

'What's wrong?' She could barely force out the words. 'I've broken my holy vows. I –' She was weeping too hard to finish.

She heard Laz sit up. A golden ball of light suddenly appeared, gleaming on the table in the middle of the room. By its glow she could see his knife-blade face, smiling at her.

'I'm glad you did break them,' he said. 'You can't go back now, you know. Some of your holy ladies are full-blooded Gel da' Thae, aren't they? They'll smell the difference in you, and then they'll throw you out of the order. You'll only have to come back to me, so why bother leaving?'

Sidro sat up and turned her back on him. The tears were slackening. With one last sob she forced herself into a tight-strung composure. When he ran his hand down her naked back she wrenched herself away, then stood up, grabbing her shift from the floor as she did so. Her hands shook too badly for her to put it on. Behind her he laughed under his breath.

'I suppose you think this is all a jest,' she said. 'You love to mock, don't you? It's not a jest to me.'

For a moment he was silent. 'Sisi, Sisi, I'm sorry.' He did sound contrite. 'I didn't realize it mattered this much to you. I thought – I don't know what I thought. Forgive me.'

She heard him get up, felt his hands touch her shoulders, but lightly, gently. 'Forgive me,' he repeated. 'I've hurt you. I never meant to hurt you. I thought you'd throw off that asinine vow like a cloak.'

The power to speak seemed to have deserted her. She stared at her shift, shaking in her trembling hands.

'But you know,' Laz went on, and he sounded positively cheerful, 'I'm all you have now. You might as well stay.'

With a gulp for breath she found her voice. 'Did you seduce me just to make sure I couldn't go back?'

'Of course not! I seduced you because I wanted you. Haven't I always, from the very day Mother bought you? But I have to confess, that particular consequence of breaking your vow did cross my mind.' His voice changed back to contrition. 'But somehow I didn't realize how much it meant to you. For that I'm sorry.'

'Laz, I've never truly believed you love me, not for all these years.'

'I know. We all have our blind spots. I suppose this has only made things worse.'

'No. I do believe it now. I believe that you love me as much as you're capable of loving anyone, but that's not very much.'

He made an indignant sound so much like a squawk that she spun around, expecting to see him in raven form. A man still stood there, his hands on his hips as he scowled at her. Sidro took a deep breath and realized that she'd stopped trembling. She saw that she had two choices: pretend to give in to him and kill him when he slept, or merely give in. At the moment she hated him, but she'd hated him in the past, and the feeling always, sooner rather than later, deserted her. *I'm still his slave,* she thought, *no matter how long it's been since he freed me.* She realized that she was still clutching her shift. She slipped it over her head and pulled it down.

'I suppose we'll go to Vandar's hell together,' she said.

'If there were such a place we would. However, there's not.' His scowl disappeared, and he laughed. 'But even if it were real, it wouldn't be hell, then, would it? If we were together.'

'Perhaps not for you. To lose Alshandra's country – that's hell enough for me.'

'Then you'd best find what joy you can now.' He glanced

at the table, where the white pyramid glittered under the wizard light. 'It wouldn't hurt to find what power you can to go with the joy, either. I suppose you're determined never to use your gifts again.'

'They're not gifts. They're curses.'

'According to your pack of holy fools, not to me. Why? I cannot understand why they're so adamant about condemning sorcery. Unless – the chronicles tell us that sorcery's what destroyed Alshandra, there at Highstone Tor. It certainly looked like that to me, in my memory not dream.'

'That's ridiculous! You weren't there. It was a dream. She wasn't destroyed.'

'Oh? Then why –'

'The teaching on the subject's simple enough. Vandar uses sorcery to spread evil in the world, and so Alshandra's people are forbidden to use it.'

'They weren't in the early days, you know. Those old chronicles you scorn, they tell us a great many interesting things. The first worshippers knew sorcery, and they used it, too. For just one example, Nag-arshad, the First Priest, owned a staff that could evoke blue fire.'

'So? It probably wasn't forbidden yet. The goddess didn't reveal her will all at once. We had to work towards the revelations.'

'That is utter nonsense, and I'll wager you know it.'

Sidro crossed her arms over her chest and glared at him. He merely smiled, and went on smiling with the gleam in his eyes that she could never quite resist.

'But I'll admit,' she said, 'that I sometimes wonder if the rakzanir are just simply afraid of sorcery, and that's why they're so eager to stamp it out. I haven't stopped thinking altogether.'

'Good.' Laz emphasized the word with a sharp nod. 'If you're right, it means they're all cowards as well as fools. I suppose, then, you'll deign to look into this crystal for me?'

'I certainly won't.'

'Why not?'

'I swore a vow. I've already broken one. I don't care to break another.'

Laz shrugged, then walked over to the table and leaned on it with both hands so that he could stare into the crystal pyramid. With the wizard light gleaming on his naked body, she realized that he'd changed. His shoulders and upper arms had grown so heavily muscled that they were out of proportion to the rest of him.

'You've been spending more and more time in the raven form, haven't you?' Sidro said. 'That scroll our teacher gave us – it said it was dangerous to use the animal body too much. Fly only for that space of time when the moon is full or nearly so, I think it said.'

'Did it?' Laz sounded profoundly indifferent. 'You know, I think this gem is a showstone. Huh! Look at that.' He leaned closer, mouthing a few silent words. Despite Sidro's intentions, her curiosity began to battle with her last unbroken vow.

'I don't suppose it would hurt,' she said, 'if you told me what you were seeing.'

He looked up and grinned. 'No, I won't,' he said. 'You'll have to come look for yourself.'

'Damn you, Laz!'

'I'm already damned, according to you.' The grin grew broader. 'So curse away!'

'Will you put that thing back in its box, then? I'm tired, and I want to sit down.'

'Come sit. You don't have to look. Turn your back to it. But I'm a wretchedly bad host, aren't I? My poor love, you must be starving. Here, let me dress, and I'll go get us some food.'

He pulled on his trousers, laced them up, then sat on the stump to put on his boots. When he stood up, he glanced back at the white pyramid. 'Huh,' he said. 'Evan the minstrel.'

With a vague smile in her direction he walked out without putting the crystal away. Sidro thought of lying down on the

mattress again, but if one of his men should come in –
besides, her back hurt her – and she might fall asleep – her
mind produced so many reasons to sit at the table instead
of on the bed that she knew she'd already lost her battle
with curiosity. *I'm damned, too*, she thought. *Nothing matters
any more.* She walked over to the table, sat down on one of
the cut stumps, and looked into the crystal.

At first she seemed to be peering through a crack in a
wall and seeing a very small painting on the other side. All
at once the vision widened. She was seeing a painting, indeed,
the picture of Alshandra hanging over the altar in the Inner
Shrine, although the colours were oddly dull, and the details
hard to distinguish, as if she were looking through smoke.
She sobbed aloud as her broken vows stabbed her conscience.
The gesture changed her focus. She was looking through
deep smoke or mist at the interior of the shrine. Rocca knelt
before the altar. Her lips moved as she stared directly into
the smoke.

'Sow!' Sidro spoke aloud. 'Ugly sow!'

Rocca raised her head fast and drew back in shock. The
vision wavered, then disappeared, leaving Sidro staring into
the clear depths of a piece of rock crystal, sitting on a table
in Laz's cabin. That smoke – of course, she'd been seeing the
shrine through the obsidian of the black pyramid. The white
had somehow or other linked her to its black twin. Rocca
must have been working the ritual devoted to the holy witness
Raena, which entailed staring into the obsidian crystal.

As Sidro thought about it, she remembered the times that
she'd worked that ritual herself. In most instances she'd seen
nothing but obsidian, though now and then she'd picked out
a murky form or an indistinct shape that might have been
a face. Had she been seeing Laz here in this cabin? And
how had Laz seen Evan in the white crystal? Maybe that
loathsome viper of a minstrel had returned to Zakh Gral.
Maybe he had the gall to enter the holy shrine itself.

She took a few breaths to calm herself, then sent her mind

looking for Evan. Occasionally she could scry people out. Before she'd always attributed the power to Alshandra's favour, the goddess's reward for her chastity. Thanks to her broken vow Sidro was expecting to see nothing, but much to her surprise, the vision built up more strongly than it ever had before.

She seemed to be hovering in the air above a vast round room where Lijik Ganda men and women sat at wooden tables and drank from pottery mugs or metal tankards. On a table near a cold hearth Evan was standing and talking, his hands moving gracefully as he mimed his way through some sort of tale. Her heart fluttered at the thought that he might be describing Zakh Gral, but he reached up and appeared to pluck an egg out of the air.

Suddenly he dropped it, and everyone in the round room laughed. A marketplace trick like that would have no place in any serious recital. Her heart steadied itself.

Behind her the cabin door opened with a thump and a kick. She turned around to see Laz carrying a big pottery bowl in both hands. Behind him came a skinny Horsekin boy whose skull sported the thin dark fuzz of his first hair-growth. He carried a basket in one hand and a pitcher in the other. She smelled burnt bread and venison stew.

'This is Vek,' Laz said. 'He has the unfortunate habit of going into trances and mumbling omens, so he had to flee Taenalapan for his life.'

The boy gave her a watery smile and set his burdens down on the table. With a nod towards Laz, he turned and trotted out of the cabin. Laz put the bowl of stew down in front of her, then picked up the white stone and began to wrap it in its various sacks.

'What did you see in it?' he said.

'The black pyramid on our altar back in the shrine.'

'What?'

'Just that. It was like I was looking out of the black stone and seeing the shrine. You said you saw Evan, but I don't understand how you could have.'

'No, no, I must confess something. I was just guessing. I saw some sort of figure, but it's very cloudy to me, that crystal, so I didn't know who it was.'

'It was Rocca. I wish you'd stop lying to me.'

'I wasn't lying. Merely guessing.'

She decided against starting an argument. In the basket lay thin rounds of soda bread, blackened along one edge. They would do, she supposed, for spoons.

'I have some cheese in that sack,' she said, 'and some apples. They're still a little green, but they're ripe enough.'

'We'll save those for our breakfast.'

The stew contained carrots, onions, and turnips as well as chunks of venison, and though luke-warm, it tasted half-way decent and safe enough to eat. Sidro scooped up mouthfuls with the bread, then ate the scoop when it grew soaked with cold gravy. She'd refrained from eating meat for so long that she could only manage a little before she felt disgustingly full.

'Where do you get all this food, anyway?' she said.

'Raiding,' Laz said. 'Where else? We hunt for the deer, though.'

'Raiding? You mean stealing from farmers.'

'Who else raises food?' He paused to wipe his mouth on his sleeve.

'I suppose you kill anyone who objects.'

'Of course. We're not Gel da' Thae any longer, Sisi. We've reverted to our savage tribal roots. We're outlaws, you know, and that's what outlaws do. Why should we stay civilized when our fellow citizens would like to torture us to death? And in the public square, too! The gall! If I'm going to be forced to scream and moan and piss all over myself, I'd at least like to do it in private.'

'I've heard about those raids on the Lijik border. They get blamed on Alshandra's men.'

'Most of them are done by Alshandra's men, that's why. I happened to witness a particularly nasty incident myself earlier this summer, when I was flying over a farming village.

They killed all the men in cold blood, just lined them up and cut them down. Then they dragged the women away – to sell, I suppose, in Taenalapan and Braemel.'

'As if your pack is any better!'

'But we are. If the farmers don't object, we don't kill them, and we only steal what they can spare. Farmers who starve to death plant no crops. Besides, we don't take slaves – hence our lack of hard coin to pay the farmers with. I've come to the conclusion that taking slaves is a very bad thing.'

'What?' She was honestly shocked. 'Why? Everyone keeps slaves, well, except for Vandar's spawn.'

'I wish you'd stop calling the Ancients Vandar's spawn. The name is meaningless and really rather stupid, given as he fathered none of them.'

'But –' She choked the words back. The sacred teaching no longer mattered, she reminded herself, now that she was damned.

'As to why,' Laz continued, 'consider yourself, born into slavery and utterly incapable of living free even though I made you legally free. As soon as we had our difficulties, what did you do? You joined a cult of fools and madmen who ordered you around, and why? Because you were so accustomed to being ordered around. You couldn't stand being free, could you, Sisi? You didn't know how. That's a horrible thing to do to someone, like pulling the wings off a butterfly.'

Sidro felt as stunned as if he'd struck her in the face. Laz flashed her a brief grin and returned to eating his dinner. She took another piece of griddle bread, had one bite, then merely crumbled the rest between her fingers while she tried to bring to heel the yapping pack of thoughts that Laz had awakened in her mind.

Every evening after dinner, Salamander would entertain the great hall with his patter and sleight-of-hand tricks. Gerran enjoyed them as much as anyone. At Tieryn Cadryc's insistence, during these shows he stayed with the noble-born at the table of honour. He was thus close enough to see Salamander's slip that evening. The gerthddyn was prattling away as usual when he reached up and plucked an egg out of mid-air – only to drop it. His audience laughed, thinking he'd done it on purpose, but Gerran noticed how troubled he looked. For a moment Salamander stared out at nothing. While it was hard to be sure in the uncertain candlelight, Gerran thought he turned a little pale.

'Ye gods!' Salamander recovered himself with a sickly grin. 'My apologies, one and all! I seem to be oddly clumsy tonight, and now I've quite forgotten what I was saying.' He jumped down from the table that he'd been standing on. 'If you'll forgive me?' He bowed to the tieryn and Lady Galla, then strode off to the staircase without another word.

In a stunned silence everyone watched him hurry upstairs. Finally Cadryc shook his head and shrugged.

'And what was all that about, I wonder?' Cadryc said. 'He looked so startled that I thought mayhap he was seeing a ghost stroll in the door.'

'This dun's too new to have ghosts,' Galla said. 'I hope he's not been taken ill.'

Neb swung himself free of the bench and stood up with a half-bow in her direction. 'I'll go see, my lady,' he said, 'with your permission of course.'

'You have it,' Galla said, 'and my thanks.'

Neb returned some while later with the news that Salamander was suffering from a headache. 'Councillor Dallandra left me some medicinals,' Neb told Galla, 'so I gave him some willow bark to chew upon.'

'That should help, certainly,' Galla said. 'Don't tell me you're a herbman as well as a scribe.'

'I'm not, my lady, not yet. Those books she sent? One of them's a herbal, so I've been studying.'

'A very accomplished young man!' Galla favoured Neb with a smile.

Gerran, however, had the uneasy feeling that Neb was hiding

something about Salamander's condition. If so, he suspected that dweomer, not headache, lay at the root of the gerthddyn's strange behaviour. Late that evening, when the great hall was clearing out, he had a chance at a private word with Neb.

'Did the gerthddyn truly have a headache?' Gerran said.

'He didn't,' Neb said with a slight smile. 'You've got good eyes, Gerro.'

'Dweomer?'

'Just that. I'll explain more if you like.'

'No need, no need! Don't trouble yourself.'

'Answer me somewhat. Why are you fighting men so troubled by talk of dweomer?'

Since it was a serious question, asked with no hint of mockery, Gerran considered his answer. 'I don't know,' he said at last. 'But I'll wager it's because we don't understand it, and we can't understand it, no matter how hard we try. It doesn't seem real, because we can't see it or touch it, and yet it *is* real. How can a man fight an enemy he can't even see? It creeps my flesh, it does.' All at once he grinned. 'Besides, if we can't use it to slash someone to bits or bash his head in, well, then, what good is it?'

'Ah. That makes it perfectly clear.'

They shared a laugh.

On the morrow, the first lords and their warbands arrived for the muster. Cadryc's vassals showed up first. Each brought as many men as he could spare from guarding his own holdings, generally five to ten. Although the noble-born slept in the broch, with so many guests expected, their riders ended up camping out in the meadow behind the dun. Next came Cadryc's allies, among them Branna's father, Tieryn Gwivyr, who brought twenty-five men and provisions for sixty days. When Gwivyr rode in, Branna dutifully went out to greet him. They spoke briefly, an odd pair, with him so tall and stout, her young and slender, though she'd obviously received her yellow hair from him. He patted her on the head, then strode past her into the great hall. With a shrug Branna followed him in, but as far as Gerran could tell, she seemed neither pleased nor distressed.

Later that day, Gerran came across Gwivyr down by the dun wall. The tieryn stood with his hands on his hips and scowled at the bundles of hay leaning against the stones. Gerran stopped and greeted him with a pleasant 'good morrow, your grace'.

'Same to you, my lord.' Gwivyr jerked his thumb at the bundles. 'What are these supposed to be, targets?'

'Just so. Goodman Gwervyl's archers need practice.'

'I don't like it, all these cursed archers. What would our ancestors say about noble-born warriors fighting behind a shield of common folk? It's dishonourable!'

Gerran realized an unexpected advantage to having been ennobled. He no longer had to keep a polite silence around lords like Gwivyr.

'Is it, your grace? What about letting the commoners face Horsekin raids without weapons to defend themselves?'

'Well, true spoken, that would be a graver dishonour. But for a thousand years and more we noble-born have fought like men, facing our enemies sword in hand. Why bring these common-born archers to battle with us?'

'Why?' Gerran paused to consider how to keep his answer in the bounds of courtesy. 'Because they can kill some of our enemies, your grace, while we kill the rest.'

Tieryn Gwivyr stared at him for a moment, then laughed, a long braying bellow.

'A good answer, my lord,' Gwivyr said, still smiling. 'But come now, doesn't it ache your heart? You're the greatest swordsman in the Northlands, but some oaf with a longbow could put an end to all that skill from a hundred yards off.'

'That's true spoken. I can't say it gladdens my heart. You're right about another thing, your grace. That thousand years you spoke of? It's coming to an end, whether we want it to or no.'

Gwivyr's smile disappeared. He raised one hand in a strangely clumsy wave, then turned on his heel and strode off.

Gwivyr's heart would be a cursed lot more troubled, Gerran thought, *if he knew about the dweomer mixed up in this*. He thought of Neb, discussing dweomer so calmly and at times drawing upon it the way Gerran would rely on his sword. *Better him than me!* Yet he felt in an odd way that dweomer had somehow touched him and stained his thoughts. He was sure – though he tried to dismiss it as mere superstition – that in the coming battle he would find his father's killer and face him. *It was sixteen years ago!* he reminded himself. By now that Horsekin warrior was most likely dead, or too old to be posted to a frontier fortress, or just simply living elsewhere. Yet deep in his soul he felt – no, he knew – that he wouldn't merely face the killer. He would recognize him.

You're going daft! he told himself. With a shake of his head he turned back to the broch. Out of habit he started to go in by the servants' door, then caught himself and walked around to the honour side. Lady Solla was just coming out. At the sight of him, she broke into a grin, then hastily stifled it into a decorous little smile.

'And a good morrow to you, Lord Gerran,' she said.

'The same to you, my lady.'

They stood facing each other in an awkward silence. There was so much that Gerran wanted to say, all of it leading to 'will you marry me?', but he hesitated, not out of fear that she'd say him nay, but its opposite. If they became betrothed now, and he were killed, she'd be a widow in men's eyes, and have no chance at a good marriage. As she waited for him to speak, her beautiful hazel eyes grew troubled, and she arranged an utterly false smile. He had to say something, he knew, or he'd wound her.

'My lady,' he said, 'I have the greatest respect for you.'

'And I for you.' She sounded puzzled – not a good omen.

'Will you hold me in your prayers while I'm gone to war?'

'Of course.' The smile began to look natural.

'I suppose you women folk will have plenty do while we're gone, your spinning and suchlike.'

'Oh, we certainly will! The sewing's eternal.'

'Do you think I could presume to ask you a favour? The tieryn owes me a new shirt as part of my maintenance, but these blazons —' Gerran touched the Red Wolf embroidered on one yoke.

'They're not right, are they?' Solla smiled again. 'I can work you a shirt with a pair of falcons easily enough. Those wolves look like they're going bald, don't they? That shirt's so old.'

Gerran grinned at her. 'So it is, but good enough for war.'

'I suppose so. The new one will be waiting when you return.'

'Let's not tempt the gods, my lady. *If* I return. And if I do, I uh er, well, there'll be um somewhat I want to discuss with you. A matter of great import for both of us.'

He felt that the sunlight had suddenly turned her face to gold, she looked so happy. She'd understood, and he thanked every god.

'It's not the time now,' he went on. 'What if I don't come back?'

'I'm not even going to think such a thing possible!'

'But it is. Here, you're a warrior's daughter. You know what war means.'

'So I do.' She looked away, the smile gone. 'Well and good, then. But may I give you a token to wear? To the others it'll mean naught more than that I favour you.'

'Then I'd like naught better.'

Solla turned and hurried into the broch. He followed more slowly and paused in the shadows by the door as she hurried up the staircase. The great hall stood mostly empty, except for a pack of dogs snoring in the straw out in the middle of the room and a pair of ragged lasses gossiping over by the servants' hearth. In but a few moments Solla returned, carrying a narrow scarf, which she laid across his hands when he held them out. It had once been beautiful, he supposed, a blue strip of fine Bardek silk, embroidered with roses at either end, but long years had faded and frayed it.

'It's not grand, but it's the best I have,' she said. 'My brother begrudged me the coin for finery.'

Gerran stopped himself just in time from calling her brother, Gwerbret Ridvar, a mingy little bastard. 'Well, this suits me,' he said instead. 'I'm not much of a noble lord, either.'

He folded the scarf up and slipped it inside his shirt, settling it against his belt to ensure it stayed there. For a long while they stood staring into each other's eyes until they heard Tieryn Cadryc and his guests talking and laughing as they strode towards the door.

With the dun so full of noble lords, Neb and Branna took to spending as much time as possible up in their chamber. They would sit on their bed and take turns reading to each other from the books Dallandra had sent them. Of course, at times their newly-wed feeling for each other took over, and they'd get no reading done of an afternoon. But they kept on, memorizing page after page, until sundown made reading the faded writing impossible. They drilled each other on the tables of correspondences and the lists of peculiar names until they could rattle off the various planes and levels of the universe, the beings who lived upon them, and all their various attributions and characteristics.

'I suppose this is all going to make sense one day,' Branna remarked late one afternoon. 'In those dreams I had, everything was so easy and glorious, not like this at all. It's almost as tedious as spinning.'

'Well, the memory work leads to the other,' Neb said, 'or so we've been told. You know, I'm finding that book about physick almost as interesting.'

'I've noticed you studying it.'

'It's because of the sickness that killed my father and sister and half of our town, too.' Neb glanced away, his eyes brimming with remembered mourning. 'I want to understand it. I know that if a person's humours are unbalanced, then the person will get sick. But how can an entire town's worth of people get unbalanced humours all at once?'

'When you put it that way, it sounds ridiculous.'

'Precisely. So some evil thing, a poison or suchlike, must have disrupted the humours in the first place, somewhat in the town wells, mayhap, or in the air, or . . .' Neb let his voice trail away. 'There had to be some agent of corruption; a thing that could somehow spread itself through the town. I don't know what it could be.'

'I'd guess that it spread through the air.'

'That was my thought, too, because of the bodily spirits.'

'Spirits in the body? Wildfolk or suchlike?'

'Not in the least.' Neb grinned at her. 'That's just a name for the subtle vapours that –'

Someone knocked on their chamber door.

'Who is it?' Branna called out.

'Salamander, escaped at last. Are you decent?'

'What? Of course we are!'

Without waiting to be invited, a pale and weary Salamander opened the door and slipped in, shutting it firmly behind him. 'If anyone comes looking for me,' he said, 'I'm not here.'

'What's happened?' Neb said, grinning. 'You look like Lady Adranna's been trying to poison you or suchlike.'

'Poison would be a relief.' With a groan Salamander flopped into the only chair. 'I've been slaving away in the great hall, performing tricks and telling tales for the noble-born until my poor throat's practically stripped raw.' He flapped one hand in Branna's direction. 'Your uncle's going to owe me a winter's maintenance at least.'

'Oh, I'm sure you'll be welcome, but it'll mean telling more tales.' Branna picked up the herbal, which had been lying next to her on the bed. 'Let me see, Bardek wine's a good remedy for an aching throat, but I don't think Cook's got any left. Perhaps I can find somewhat else.'

'Horehound,' Neb said, 'the whole herb, minced, steeped, and reduced to syrup with honey water.'

'Aha!' Salamander said. 'You've been studying.'

'We have. Branni, do you think Cook has any horehound?'

'She should. It's blooming in the meadows, or at least it was, if all those horses haven't eaten it. Gods, there's a lot of them! And the men, too, and the servants –' Branna shook her head in wonder. 'It's almost as many people as live in Cengarn, isn't it?'

'A few less.' Salamander grinned at her. 'Which reminds me. I've been scrying, and the army should arrive soon. Ridvar's left Cengarn.'

Branna felt a stab of grief, so sick at heart that she nearly wept.

'What's wrong?' Neb reached over and clasped her hand.

'I'm frightened. My uncle, and Gerran, and my father – all the men, really. Who knows what will happen to them?' She took a deep breath to steady her nerves. 'Neb, you'd best start spending time with your brother.'

'He's going to the war?' Salamander sounded astonished. 'He's but eight summers old!'

'He's Gerran's page now,' Neb said. 'Where his lord goes, he goes. That's one reason I wanted to go with the army, to look after Clae.'

'I'll do the looking after, then,' Salamander said. 'I shall be you, scribe and brother and all.'

'My very great thanks,' Neb said. 'Truly, that's most generous of you.'

'I just hope he won't take it amiss.'

'I'll tell him that he has to listen to you.'

'Well and good, then.' Salamander paused, thinking. 'What about Matto? They must be taking him along, too. He's the prince's hostage, after all.'

'They're not,' Branna joined in. 'Voran sent a message about that, asking Mirryn to stand surety for the lad.'

'Good. He'll doubtless be happier after Gerran and I are gone. If naught else, at least he'll be willing to take his meals in the great hall.'

'No doubt,' Branna said. 'When do you think the army will get here?'

'Soon. A couple of days. I'll tell you if I see anything un-
toward.'

Perhaps the strangest thing of all, Branna decided, was
how normal and ordinary it seemed to have a master of
dweomer discussing an event happening far away. Only a
few short months ago she would have laughed in scorn at
anyone who'd tried to tell her that a person could know what
was happening forty miles off. Now she knew that the world
was not only bigger, but far stranger than she'd ever believed.

That night, she stood at her chamber window looking out
at the stars. Where was the silver dragon lairing, she
wondered, on such a fine night? Surely not in some squalid
cave. *Someday*, she told herself, *I'll have a chance to speak
with him.*

'Oh do come lie down!' Neb already lounged on their bed.
'Are you thinking about that wretched dragon again?'

'I am, truly. He's just such a puzzle to me. I know Jill
made a vow to free him from his evil wyrd. Getting himself
turned into a dragon must be the evil, wouldn't you think?'

'I would.'

'I'm assuming that I'll have much to say to him when we
finally meet, but I don't know what it would be.'

'Well, since we're not going with the army, you'll have
plenty of time to think, so don't worry about it now.'

'You're right.' She turned to smile at him. 'Do you want
the shutters open or closed?'

'Open, I think. It's such a warm night. Now, come lie
down. I mean, please?'

With a laugh, Branna joined him, and for the rest of that
night, she never thought about the silver dragon, not once.

The dwarven contingent had reached Cengarn on the day
before Gwerbret Ridvar was planning to leave it. After a
single night's rest, therefore, they set out again for the Red
Wolf dun, though they found the trip less than gruelling.
Travelling with an army of Deverry men turned out to be a

much slower business than travelling with Mountain Folk alone. What was normally two days' journey to the Red Wolf dun took three full and a bit over.

Kov, in his role as dwarven envoy, used the time to get to know as many lords and captains as he could, although he spent most of it with Gwerbret Ridvar and Prince Voran. The prince, a younger son of a younger son of the royal house, was an ordinary looking fellow at first acquaintance, with his brownish hair, thinning a bit on top, large ears, and a generous mouth that made his grin border on the froggy despite the attempt of his full moustache to hide it. But the intelligence gleaming in his grey eyes impressed Kov. When someone spoke to him, the prince would listen intently, his eyes shrewd and focused as he weighed the words being offered him.

Ridvar, on the other hand – Ridvar had inherited the rhan because both his father and his older brother had died in battle. He was a good-looking lad, dark-haired and hazel-eyed, but an arrogant child, in Kov's opinion, though he did his best to keep the opinion to himself.

'Just how old is he?' Kov asked Blethry one noontide.

'Not quite fifteen,' Blethry said. 'But a married man withal, and one who's fought and fought well in a couple of scraps against the raiders.'

'Very admirable of him, truly.'

Blethry raised an eyebrow. Kov smiled blandly back. In a moment Blethry changed the subject.

As the army travelled south, it gathered men and lords along the way, both those who owed fealty directly to Ridvar and those vassals of his tierynau who happened to live along the route. The gwerbret's allies sent messengers, announcing that they were raising men and marching with all possible speed for the Red Wolf dun. Yet despite all the musters, by the time the army reached Cadryc's, it numbered just over twelve hundred human men. Cadryc had a hundred waiting to add to the total. Without the dwarven sappers and miners, the chance of victory would have been slim indeed.

The dwarves set up their camp in the meadow behind the dun along with the majority of the army. Cadryc's lady and his elderly chamberlain put forth a superhuman effort and managed to house the noble lords in the dun itself. Kov and Brel found themselves classed with the nobility. Lord Veddyn, the chamberlain, offered them a small chamber near the roof that gave every sign of having been hastily vacated by someone else.

'By the stone gods!' Brel muttered. 'I'd rather sleep in the meadow than turn someone out of their bed.'

'Indeed, my lord,' Kov said to Veddyn. 'We have a comfortable tent in one of our wagons. Why don't you return this chamber to its owner? We'll camp in the meadow.'

'Ah, your wagons.' Veddyn's rheumy old eyes briefly gleamed. 'I've heard they contain many an interesting thing.'

Kov smiled and said nothing. *Ye gods!* he was thinking. *What do they think we're carrying? Gems and gold and such?* Considering the reputation of the Mountain Folk, he supposed, they might indeed have been thinking just that.

When, therefore, Kov saw Lady Branna studying the mysterious carts, Kov assumed that she too was wondering about the rune-marked crates, but her reason turned out to be atypical.

'This new kind of wheel – it's awfully clever,' she said.

It took him a moment to realize that her comment was sincere. 'It is that. You'll be seeing more of them, I'll wager. Every cartwright in Cengarn took a good look at them. Your woodcutter did, too, here in this dun.'

'Horza? He's a marvel when it comes to making things, truly.'

One of the dwarven carters was leaning over, hands on knees, and frowning at the cart's left rear wheel. He muttered a few foul words, then knelt on one knee and began pulling something free of the strakes.

'A lot of the wheels have tangled stuff on them,' Branna said. 'I noticed it earlier, when your men were lining the carts up.'

'It's the long grass,' Kov said. 'There's one big problem with this new device. The strake edge can cut dry grass, and if it does, it gathers it up and spins it right round the wheel. It'll be a cursed nuisance when we're travelling over the grasslands.'

The look on Branna's face surprised him – a sudden wondering, then a grin. Without a word to him she trotted over to the cart and watched the servant pulling the long stalks free. The action of the strake and its nailheads had twisted them into a messy sort of rope. Puzzled, Kov followed her.

'Uh, is somewhat the matter, my lady?' he said.

'Not in the least!' Branna looked up, and her grin turned even broader. 'Here, good envoy. Surely your men have brought a lot of extra wheels along, haven't they? Do you think I might have one of them? I don't have any coin to pay you with, but I do have a bit of jewellery you might fancy.'

'My dear lady! It would be an honour to present you with one as a gift, but um er, might I ask why?'

'I've got an idea, that's all. I wonder if one of those wheels or somewhat like it would spin wool as well as it tangles grass.'

Kov had never felt so bewildered in his life, but his master Garin's long training in courtesy saved him. 'Very well,' he said. 'Here, let me find you one. I think our head carter's just over there.'

Once Branna had her straked wheel, she thanked him profusely, then carried it up to the dun. He heard her calling for Horza as she ran through the gates. *I don't know why I'm so surprised,* he thought. *Our women do love their contrivances, too.* After all, he reminded himself, it was just such a womanly love of devices that had led to the secret carried in those wrapped and rune-marked crates.

No one, however, could spare much time to wonder about mountain secrets. That very afternoon Prince Voran called a council of war. Since Cadryc had no proper chamber of justice – he judged local crimes and disputes right in his great hall – the prince, the gwerbret, Brel, and Kov met in

the prince's bedchamber, a smallish shabby room in Kov's
eyes but obviously the best in the dun. Servants had set up
chairs near the window; a low table sported a map of Deverry
that Ridvar had brought with him from Cengarn. Kov was
expecting that Cadryc would be invited to sit in on the council
out of courtesy's sake, him being the lord of the dun, but
he never appeared.

In the curve of the wall sat a young brown-haired scribe
– Neb, Kov thought his name might be, though he'd not
heard it clearly – and an oddly handsome fellow with hair
as pale as moonlight and slightly pointed ears. At first Kov
thought this Westfolk half-breed an apprentice scribe, since
Neb was showing him how to write upon waxed tablets with
a stylus, but he turned out to be a fair bit more important
than that.

'Cadvridoc Brel, Envoy,' Prince Voran said, 'this is
Salamander the gerthddyn, the man who discovered the existence of Zakh Gral.' He abruptly frowned. 'Here, lad, you
must have some better name than Salamander.'

Salamander handed his pair of tablets to the scribe, then
rose to a kneel. 'I do, your highness,' he said, 'Evan of Drwloc.'

'Much better! Very well, Goodman Evan,' the prince
continued. 'I had you brought here to tell us about the terrain
around Zakh Gral once again. Neb, I'm hoping to you can
take what he tells us and make some sort of picture of it on
the back of this map.'

'I'll do my best, your highness.' Neb glanced at Evan. 'You
talk, and I'll make a sketch on the wax tablet. Then you tell
me if it's correct before I do it in ink.'

'Good idea,' the prince said. 'Proceed.'

By the time that the gerthddyn had finished his description, and the scribe's drawing was done, Kov and Brel were
exchanging grim glances. The Horsekin obviously knew a
thing or two about siting a fortress. Zakh Gral sat at the edge
of the grasslands, where the plateau began to rise into the
foothills of the fabled mountains of the far west. To the north

lay broken tableland, set off by a rise of cliff that, the Mountain Folk knew, marked the old coastline of the landmass back in ages so old that no one remembered them but the Wildfolk. The northern heights had spawned a river, running straight south to the sea, which Goodman Evan had crossed close to its source.

'It might be called the Galan Targ. We travelled by such a roundabout route, your highness,' the gerthddyn said, 'that I was thoroughly confused by the time we left the forest. Thank the gods for sending us the dragons! They'll see more than I did.'

Dragons? Kov thought. *We have dragons?* Brel caught his glance, then rolled his eyes heavenward as if to say, 'worse and worse'.

'Very well,' the prince said. 'So you followed this river south to the fortress?'

'We did, your highness,' Evan said. 'Zakh Gral must have been at least twenty-five miles south of the ford. We walked for nearly a day and a half to reach it. The road runs by the river at first, but as it flows south, the river gets faster, and the canyon grows deeper.'

Much deeper, as it turned out – Evan estimated that the river lay thirty feet below the fortress, perched on the west bank cliff above. Brel began to stroke his beard in thought. The one hopeful thing about the description, Kov decided, was the nature of the cliffs – red sandstone, easily shattered by good steel picks, assuming, of course, that the sappers could reach the bottom of the gorge in the first place.

'The hard question,' Brel said, 'is how we're going to get the army across that river.'

'I was hoping your men could build us a bridge,' Voran said. 'Everyone knows how clever the Mountain Folk are at such things. I have great faith in your – '

'Flattery's all very well,' Brel interrupted, 'but does timber grow around there, enough for the building of a bridge?'

Everyone looked at Evan, who smiled in a sickly sort of

way. 'The hills to the west of Zakh Gral are wooded,' he said, 'but on the east side of the river, I saw only scrub and grass.'

Brel muttered a Dwarvish oath foul enough to make Kov glad that he was the only one there who understood it. The young gwerbret looked back and forth between Brel and Voran.

'Well, your highness,' Ridvar said. 'We can cross at that northern ford easily enough.'

'We can,' Voran said, 'assuming they don't learn we're coming till we're across it. If they do, we can still cross at the ford, but it won't be easy in the least.'

Neb the scribe, who'd been studying his map, suddenly looked up and shuddered, as violently as if snow had just slid down his back. Voran laughed, one sharp bark.

'Geese walking on your grave, lad?' the prince said.

'I'll hope not, your highness,' Neb said. 'My apologies.'

Kov felt his stomach clench. He preferred to disbelieve in evil omens, but he couldn't stop himself from thinking that he'd just seen one arrive.

With the muster complete, the army would stay only a single night at the Red Wolf dun. Dinner among the noble-born that night, a feast laid on to honour Gwerbret Ridvar and Prince Voran, presented such a challenge that Branna was glad that they'd all be leaving soon, despite her fears for the safety of her clansmen. As lord of the dun, Cadryc kept his usual place at the head of the table of honour, while the prince sat at his right and the gwerbret at his left. Since the tierynau in attendance filled the rest of the seats, leaving no room for Cadryc's family or lesser lords, Lord Mirryn headed the next table over. Branna, who sat at the far end to share a trencher with Gerran, could overhear the conversation at the honour table. Neb found himself banished to the servitors' table once again, some distance away.

At the various honour tables, conversation proceeded slowly, in spurts, making eavesdropping even easier. Branna assumed at first that the men going to war were wrapped in their own thoughts, but when the servants were clearing away the last of the roast pork, Gerran pointed out the truth.

'Keep an eye on your uncle.' He leaned close and dropped his voice to a murmur. 'He was never invited to that council today. If he starts to go off, can you pretend to faint or such-like? Anything to cause a distraction.'

Branna followed his glance and realized that Cadryc had turned red in the face. He was glaring at Gwerbret Ridvar over the rim of his tankard while Ridvar smiled blandly out at nothing in particular. Prince Voran slid to the edge of his chair and leaned forward, ever so slightly.

'I'll try,' Branna whispered. 'But I'm not very good at fainting.'

Ridvar made some remark that she couldn't quite catch, but she did hear him say the name 'Matyc.' At that Cadryc slammed his tankard down. His bellow carried quite clearly.

'He's up in the women's hall with his mother, your grace. Since he's but a little child, he can still eat there. You needn't be afraid of him.'

Ridvar flushed red, then went dead-white. Hampered by her skirts, Branna took several moments to get free of the bench. Fortunately Prince Voran could move faster. He was on his feet and standing beside Cadryc before Ridvar could say a word.

'Your grace,' Voran caught Cadryc's arm. 'You promised me a look at that Western Hunter in your stables. The air in here's so hot and stale that I'd very much like to go see him right now.'

Cadryc blinked in utter confusion, but Voran hauled him up bodily by one arm. Left with no choice, Cadryc allowed himself to be dragged away toward the door out. Branna darted forward and sat down in her uncle's place before half the great hall even knew what had happened. She turned to Ridvar and smiled.

'Oh, your grace!' Branna mustered her best simper. 'I know this is just awfully discourteous of me, but I really had to ask about your delightful wife. One of the servant lasses told me that she might be with child.'

Ridvar opened his mouth and shut it several times, then glanced around on the edge of anger, but he did finally answer. 'Not that I know of, Lady Branna, though such would be a great blessing, of course. Otherwise, she fares well.'

'She must be so happy, married to a handsome lord like you.'

Ridvar blushed, but he did smile and stay where he was.

Branna managed to chatter for some brief while, long enough for Prince Voran and her uncle to return. As soon as she saw them in the doorway, Branna got up with one last piece of flattery for Ridvar. A much subdued Cadryc took the chair that had formerly held the prince, while Voran seated himself in the tieryn's, directly next to Ridvar, and looked at the gwerbret in a way that managed to be bland and frosty at the same time. Branna hurried back to her place beside Gerran, who gave her one of his rare smiles.

'Well done,' he said. 'If Ridvar forces Cadryc into rebellion, the war's over. The Horsekin can finish their cursed fortress in peace.'

'It gladdens my heart that you'll be travelling with my uncle, you and Salamander both.' Branna grabbed his tankard and helped herself to a long swallow of ale. 'I'll pray for you.'

The rest of the evening passed without further trouble. After the women had retired to their own hall, Prince Voran's body servant appeared at the door with a note, written on the finest scraped white leather, from his master for Branna. It said simply, 'my thanks,' but Branna tucked it into her kirtle to save, not because it came from a prince, but because she could write upon the back.

After a hasty breakfast eaten in grim silence, the noble-born allies and commanders began leaving the dun to rejoin their men in the meadow. The Red Wolf warband began to get itself ready to ride. Out in the ward, pages and servants rushed back and forth, carrying sacks and campaign chests and wicker baskets of gear and supplies. Grooms led out the horses and began to saddle them.

Through the midst of this confusion Branna and Neb went looking for Clae. They found him eventually down by the dun gates. He was standing on a crate beside Gerran's dun riding horse in order to reach its saddle. He'd already attached his lord's saddlebags to the cantle; now he was struggling to hang the shield, which Neb had recently painted; on a white-washed background a yellow falcon spread its wings, done in paint made from the local clay for lack of gold for gilding.

'Well, now,' Neb said. 'I've come to bid you good luck.'

'My thanks.' His task finished, Clae jumped down from the crate. 'Don't look so grim, Neb. It's not like I'll be fighting or suchlike.'

'Still, a war's a dangerous place to be. You be careful now, won't you?'

'Of course.'

'Do you remember what I told you about Salamander?'

'I do. And Lord Gerran won't let any harm come to me.'

Not if he can help it, anyway, Branna thought to herself.

'True spoken.' Neb managed to smile.

'It must ache your heart, not getting to go.'

'Oh, I'll get over it. So fare you well.'

'And the same to you.' Clae glanced around, distracted. 'It's time for me to lead my lord's horse into line.'

The Red Wolf warband were forming up their marching order. Branna and Neb got out of their way and went to stand by the entrance to the great hall.

'Does it truly ache you're heart that you're staying behind?' Branna said.

'Of course it doesn't,' Neb said, 'but I didn't want to be telling Clae that. Here, I'm going inside. I know that my brother's an apprentice of sorts now, and that he's gone from my care, but blast it all, I can't stand to watch him ride to war!' He turned and strode off before Branna could say a comforting word.

As her father and uncle left the broch, Branna bade farewell to them, then stood to one side with Solla while the warband finished getting itself organized. The men led their horses into line, then stood waiting for the order to mount. Gerran had a brief word with Tieryn Cadryc, then walked down the line, looking over every man, checking his gear, and making the occasional remark, before returning to its head, where Clae was holding the reins of his horse. Before he mounted, Gerran reached inside his shirt and took out a strip of blue cloth, which he gave to Clae, and said a few words.

Branna stood too far away to hear the order, but Clae handed him the horse's reins. Gerran held them in his right hand while the page tied the strip around Gerran's upper left arm. Solla caught her breath. Branna glanced her way.

'That's your scarf, isn't it?' Branna said.

'It is,' Solla said. 'Just a little token. For luck.'

'Of course. Just a little token. Of course.'

They shared a smile, but when Gerran mounted and gave the signal for the warband to do the same, Solla's smile disappeared into a tight-lipped determination to show no feeling at all. Branna suddenly felt selfish, that her beloved would stay behind, in safety. *If we are safe,* she thought. When she glanced up at the sky, she saw no sign of the raven mazrak. With a yell and a wave, Tieryn Cadryc led his men and his noble-born allies and vassals out of the gates at the trot. On Gerran's arm the blue scarf fluttered like a pennant.

While the army assembled out in the meadow, the women of the dun climbed up to the catwalk to watch and wave farewell. Branna was about to join them when she felt a tug at her skirt. The grey gnome stood beside her, his pointy little face screwed up in anxiety. His mouth gaped, and he waved his hands.

'What is it?' Branna whispered. 'What's upset you?'

The gnome turned and dashed a few yards away, then paused, flapping its hands at her. When she followed, it darted around the side of the broch. A man was just leading a horse from the stables, and despite the warmth of the day, he wore a cloak with the hood up around his face in a futile attempt to hide his identity.

'And what are you up to, Mirro?' Branna said. 'Going to sneak off and follow the army?'

'Blast you!' Mirryn pushed the hood back; sweat beaded on his forehead and cheeks. 'I suppose you'll run straight to my mother and tell her, too.'

'I won't have to. She's up on the walls with the other women, and she'll see you ride out. Did you really think you could bring this off? You could wear ten cloaks, and your womenfolk would still recognize you.'

'Ah by the red scabby balls of the Lord of Hell!' Mirryn pulled the cloak off and threw it onto the cobbles. His horse snorted and danced a few steps back. 'Hold and stand, you mangy mule!'

As if it knew it were being insulted, the horse laid its ears back, but it did stand.

'You might as well take him back to his stall,' Branna said. 'Besides, you promised the prince you'd stand surety for Matto, didn't you? How can I let you sneak away from that?'

'You wretched little tattle-tale!'

Branna started to retort, but all at once an omen took over her mind and mouth. She could hear her own voice, cold and hollow, speaking beyond her power to stop it.

'Much evil would come from your riding, more than you can know, Lord Mirryn. It's a right thing that your father bade you stay. Soon, at the turning of next year towards spring, your time of war will come, and your glory will travel the kingdom.'

The omen left as suddenly as it had taken her, leaving her cold and trembling. Mirryn was staring open-mouthed.

'What was that?' he whispered.

When she staggered, he grabbed her arm with one hand and her opposite shoulder with the other. Gratefully she let him steady her.

'Mirro, please, stay here. You've got to, you've just got to.'

For a long moment he hesitated; then he nodded. 'Maybe I'd best do just that. I've heard you say strange things before, Branni, but this takes the prize at the tourney!'

'It's an omen, that's all.'

'That's all? What do you mean, that's all?'

'I don't know.' She held up a shaking hand. 'Mirro, I've got to get somewhat to drink. My mouth's as dry as a bone.'

Mirryn took her into the great hall and brought her a pitcher of water and a cup. Branna gulped the first cup down, then sipped the second while he hovered nervously by her chair. 'Ah,' Mirryn said suddenly. 'Here's the gerthddyn.'

'What?' Branna turned on the bench and saw Salamander strolling in the door. 'You didn't ride with the army?'

'The army's still milling around the meadow.' Salamander walked over and made her a bow. 'It takes a long time to get that many men on the road. They can't all start moving forward at the exact same moment, you know. I'll ride near the end of the line, so I've time to come say farewell.' Abruptly he leaned closer. 'Are you ill or suchlike?'

'Just tired. I had an odd dizzy spell out in the ward a moment ago.'

Mirryn started to speak, then merely gave the gerthddyn a vacant smile.

'Truly?' Salamander hesitated for a moment. 'Well, I'm glad Neb will be staying here. Between his lore and that herbal Dalla sent you, he should be able to tend you if you need it.'

'I don't,' Branna said. 'Now, you take care of yourself, will you? I do worry so.'

'Oh, I have no intention of getting anywhere near the fighting, I assure you!' Salamander glanced at the door. 'I'd best leave. My lord Mirryn, fare thee well.'

'Same to you, gerthddyn,' Mirryn said. 'And may the gods speed you all to the war and bring you all home again as well.'

Salamander bowed, then hurried out to the ward. Branna went to the door and looked out just as he was mounting his horse. He waved to her, then clucked to the horse and trotted out of the gates. *May the true Goddess watch over you.* The thought brought her a peculiar sense of knowledgeable dread, one that she could only explain as dweomer. Someone else was on the watch for Salamander, someone female, and whoever she was, she meant him no good.

Sidro often did try to scry for Evan the minstrel, as she thought of Salamander. Every now and then she received a faint, momentary impression of him but naught more. Those moments always seemed to come just after sunrise and sundown. Mostly, though, she could only sense, rather than clearly see, some sort of sphere or shield glowing around him. Of his whereabouts she could see nothing.

'He's probably building a sphere of light around himself,' Laz told her when she asked. 'Master Hazdrubal showed me that trick after you left us.' He sighed in a sudden melancholy. 'Ai, our poor teacher! I miss him still.'

'How could you?' Sidro snapped. 'He was a disgusting old man. Eating raw meat like that! I never trusted him around young boys, either. He kept staring at their bottoms.'

'In his personal habits, most assuredly disgusting, but a good teacher of wizardry nonetheless. Besides, no one deserved to die the way he did.'

Once, Sidro realized, not so very long ago in fact, she would have told him that Hazdrubal had deserved his death because he'd defied Alshandra's laws. Once.

'Well, I have to admit it was horrible,' she said. 'I couldn't bear to watch.'

'No? I should have thought you'd have gloried in it. Your pack of holy fools did.'

'Not Lakanza! She ran into the temple with me, and we prayed that Alshandra would stop them. Those weren't our people, Laz, not at that moment. They were like animals,

that mob. I mean, tearing a man apart with their hands . . .'
Memory pictures rose and made her stammer. 'Horrible.'

'They came for me next. Did that frighten you, Sisi? To
think of your old love being torn to shreds by the fingernails
of the faithful?'

'No.'

He looked at her gape-mouthed, his eyes brimming with
hurt.

'Because I knew you'd get out of it,' Sidro went on. 'I have
perfect faith, Laz, that you could talk your way out of
anything.'

He tipped back his head and laughed in prolonged delight.
'And so I did,' he said at last. 'Though it took a bit of help
from my mother. Huh. I was surprised then and I still am
now that she cared enough to hide me.'

Sidro reached up and tapped with her fingertip on the
blue spiral tattoo in the centre of his forehead. 'You were
First Son.' She brought her hand down. 'What she thought
of you didn't matter, compared to that.'

He winced. 'I suppose it was silly of me to hope for a
flicker of maternal love in her dry and stony heart.'

'She had her heart set on your becoming a rakzan, that's
why. It dried up because she was so disappointed –'

'– that I turned out to be a coward? That's how she saw
it, you know. I was supposed to want to throw my life away
for the mach-fala's glory. The very first rakzan to come from
a mixed-blood clan! What an honour! I didn't want it.'

'I thought you made the right decision.'

'Which is another reason I love you.' Laz paused for a
dramatic sigh. 'But be that as it may, do you want to learn
how to make a protective sphere around yourself? I don't
like the idea of Evan scrying you out.'

'I don't like it, either. Please do show me.'

Since she'd already broken her vows, Sidro returned to
the dweomer studies she once had shared with Laz with
some of her old passion. Since she was damned, she would

think, she might as well revel in her damnation. Yet, every time she tried to scry in the white pyramid, she would see the Inner Shrine through the smoke-coloured crystal of its twin upon the altar. The sight made the shame of her broken vows rise up and choke her until she wept, shaking her head in pain like a dazed animal. Laz finally put the crystal back in its locked box and told her to leave it alone.

In their first days together, Laz never left the camp and only rarely left their cabin. Their long years apart had left them greedy for each other. Their scent surrounded them, permeated the blankets, the bed, the very walls, or so it seemed to her. Laz forbade any of his men to enter, for fear that the scent would make them lust after her, too. When they needed food or water, he went and fetched it.

While he was gone, she would stand at one of the cabin's two windows and look out at the forest, on one side, or the camp, on the other. Occasionally Pir or one of the other men would stop to chat with her, but only briefly, and always from a decorous few feet away. Only young Vek, the boy who would have grown up into a prophet of the gods, had the old gods still held sway in Taenalapan, dared come close. He missed his mother badly, he told her one day.

'But I had to run away,' he said. 'The priestesses would have killed me.'

'Alshandra's people, you mean?' Sidro said.

He nodded, his eyes full of tears. *A child*, Sidro thought. *How could they have wanted to kill a child?* She was getting a different view of her beloved Alshandra's Elect, here among exiles.

She came to know the other men by sight as they went about various errands: gathering firewood, bringing home game or fish, cleaning weapons, talking among themselves. Most were full-blooded Gel da' Thae – thieves and political exiles both – but she counted five obvious half-breeds, three mostly Horsekin in appearance, two who could easily have passed for Lijik, just as she and Laz often did. The unofficial

leader of the mixed blood men was Faharn, who had the
thick black mane and welter of tattoos of a Horsekin man
but whose blue eyes told of slave blood in his background.

If Pir was Laz's friend, then Faharn was his disciple. Laz
had taught him magic when they both lived in Taenalapan
and continued the lessons when Faharn had followed him
into exile. At first, Sidro tried to talk with Faharn as she did
with Pir, just a pleasant chat as they got to know each other,
but if he answered at all, Faharn spat out short words only
and ended the conversation as fast as he could.

'Why does he resent me so much?' Sidro asked Laz.

'You've interrupted his training,' Laz said. 'It's too bad that
he doesn't have much of a gift for magic. He wants to learn
it very badly. But there's no need for him to blame you for my
obsessive lust.' He grinned at her. 'I'll have a word with him.'

After that, Faharn made an obvious effort to be civil to
Sidro, but she still caught him watching her at times with
a weary resentment.

She worried about Faharn's ill-will, but not half as much as
she feared Movrae, a full-blooded Gel da' Thae who, according
to Laz, had joined the band not because he had magical gifts,
but because he'd deserted his military unit. Had he stayed in
the towns, they would have found him easily, since he wore
his regiment's name and number tattooed across his face.
Whenever Movrae saw Sidro at the window, he would stand
and stare at her from a distance, narrow-eyed and so grim that
she had no idea whether he felt lust or some strange rage. She
would leave the window until Laz or Pir chased him away.

On a sultry afternoon Sidro was standing just to one side
of the window, so she could get some air while staying out
of Movrae's sight. She heard Laz talking in an irritated near-
whisper, but she couldn't quite discern what he was saying.
Pir's answer, however, she heard quite clearly.

'She'll have to know sooner or later,' the horse mage said.

They moved away, but when Laz came back inside, Sidro
told him that she'd been eavesdropping.

'And just what is it that I'll have to know?' she said. 'You might as well tell me sooner rather than later.'

'Oh, it's nothing, really. Just another sign that we've sunk to the level of savages. I'm thinking of having Movrae killed.'

For a moment she was shocked enough to believe him. He shrugged and turned away, but he was looking back at her out of the corner of his eye, and she could see the barest twitch of a smile on his mouth.

'Don't lie!' she snapped.

'I'm not lying.' He turned back. The child-like innocence on his face convinced her that indeed, he'd lied. 'The way he stares at my woman bothers me. Don't savage tribal chiefs always kill men who covet their woman?'

'I don't have the slightest idea, but I do know you're a liar.'

'Then I won't say anything.' He grinned at her. 'But I'm not going to tell you the truth, either. Don't bother to try to pry it out of me.'

'Laz –'

'Although –' He hesitated briefly. 'Now that I think of it –' He turned and walked out without another word.

Sidro ran to the door and yelled insults after him until she realized that Faharn stood within earshot. She stepped back in and slammed the door shut, then stood fuming in the centre of the cabin. As her anger receded, she noticed that trouble seemed to be brewing outside. She heard men's voices shouting in anger. Over them rang Laz's laughter, a shrill croak like a raven's call. She hesitated, afraid to go to the camp-side window, then got an idea.

Since the cabin floor lay below ground level, she found it easy to slip out of the forest-side window. The rough wall of the cabin proved easy climbing, too, with its untrimmed logs providing steps and handholds. She squirmed onto the roof, then lay on her stomach to look down.

In the centre clearing of the camp sat a big fire-pit, cold and empty at the moment. The men had gathered in the bare ground around it. They stood silently, spears in hand but held upright, as if they were merely waiting for trouble. Thanks to his horse's mane of hair, Sidro could pick out Pir easily, standing right next to the stone circle. He had a protective arm around Vek's shoulders. Faharn paced back and forth at the front of the mob. Even from her distance Sidro could catch the scent of his fear – fear for Laz's sake, no doubt, because some yards apart Laz and Movrae stood facing each other, both of them yelling challenges.

Next to Movrae Laz looked slender, even weak, but while Movrae had the trained soldier's muscle, Laz had speed. Movrae struck first; he launched a flat-handed slap at his leader's face. Laz ducked under, but the blow caught him on the side of the head and made him stagger. Movrae rushed in and swung hard to keep his advantage, but Laz had recovered enough to dodge to one side. For a moment they circled; then Laz darted forward and struck back with two quick blows, one a clip on the face, the other a fist thrown hard into Movrae's stomach. The bigger man staggered and doubled over. Laz chopped him hard on the side of the neck with the side of one hand. He fell, grunting, to his knees.

Faharn dashed forward. He carried leather thongs, and he bound Movrae hand and foot while Laz watched, breathing hard and rubbing his bleeding knuckles. The other men moved back out of the way as Faharn dragged Movrae to the fire-pit and slung him in like a log.

The wind sighed through the surrounding trees as if in pity, but none of the men said a word. Laz stepped into the pit, stood looking down at the bound man, then knelt. He drew his knife from its sheath at his belt with his right hand and grabbed Movrae by the hair with his left. Movrae screamed, yelled, twisted as he tried to get free. Laz yanked him back by the hair, then struck. Movrae lay still. Blood soaked Laz's sleeve and flowed from the Horsekin's throat into the sand and ashes of the pit, a scarlet trickle in the sunlight. Laz wiped his knife clean on Movrae's shirt, then stood up, looking at the assembled men. They looked steadily back and said nothing.

Sidro let out her breath in a sob. Her pulse fluttered in her throat, and sweat beaded her breasts – whether from revulsion or excitement, she couldn't say at that moment. She slid backwards to the edge of the roof, then climbed down. For a moment she stood outside the window and stared at the dark forest, looming over her like a wave of shadows. She considered escaping into it and trying to make her way back to Zakh Gral, but she lacked the courage to face the wilderness alone. She climbed back in through the window and sat down on one of the tree stumps by the table.

With shaking hands she pushed her sweaty hair back from her face. She had just watched Laz kill a man for looking at her in the wrong way. He had told her the truth about one thing, that the scholarly First Son had disappeared, hidden somewhere inside a savage tribal chief. The door swung open. She got to her feet and involuntarily laid a hand at her throat when Laz stepped in. His shirt sleeve had turned stiff and rust-brown.

'I saw you watching.' He shut the door. 'If you were a savage tribeswoman, you'd be as pleased as a mare with a new foal.' He paused, studying her face. 'I take it you're not.'

'Part of me is. Part of me feels sick to her stomach.'

'That's the trouble with our mixed blood.'

'No, it's got nothing to do with that. We could be full-blooded Horsekin, and I'd still feel torn in half.'

Among the tattoos on the left side of his face a purple bruise was rising into a swelling. She touched it with her finger tips.

'It hurts, but not too badly.' Laz pulled off the blood-stained shirt and tossed it onto the table. 'Do you realize that the sun is a long way past its zenith, and I've not taken you back to bed yet?'

'I don't want –'

He caught her by the shoulders and drew her close. 'Yes, you do,' he said. 'I can smell it on you.'

The horrible truth, she realized, was that he was right. She found herself remembering the silent way his men had done nothing to save Movrae. None of them had dared to cross Laz, their commander, their dominator. The memory rose of Movrae, twisting in terror, and of Laz, so quick to strike, and the blood, that flash of scarlet in the sun. Something deep in her soul had responded to the sight. Something was responding now, revelling in the memories like a dog rolling in carrion.

'No,' she whispered. 'Alshandra help –'

Laz kissed her before she could finish the prayer. He pulled her close, kissed her again, then walked her backwards until they fell together into the tumbled blankets, soaked in their scent. The world shrank to his body and his bed, as it always did once he had his hands upon her.

As the drowsy days passed, her years in the temple began to seem like a story she'd told herself rather than memories of a time when she'd been happy. Even her worries about damnation receded into the distant mist of the future. Yet she had a new fear. How would he react when she got pregnant again? Laz had his own view of what had happened the last time, a much rosier picture than her memories of his temper tantrums and sulks. When, after an eightnight, her moon flow began, she danced around the cabin in joy.

By Gel da'Thae custom, that flow marked her as forbidden to him. The dangerous blood reminded men that women came and went as they wished, not as the men wished, and that men must wait for what they wanted from their women. For the first four days Laz shared Faharn's shelter, and while she was secluded, he flew. She looked out of a window on the first morning to see the raven swooping up from the clearing and heading for the open sky beyond. *The dragon! What if the dragon sees him?* The thought filled her with such terror that for a moment she laid a cold hand over her heart and gasped for breath. Yet he'd flown off so confidently – the fear vanished in a stab of anger. He'd lied to her, no doubt, about the silver dragon, when he was trying to persuade her to come away with him.

'Why do I ever believe him?' she whispered.

Laz returned safely that evening. She saw the raven land, and in a while he came to the door in his man's shape. He brought her a carefully packed basket of food, setting it down outside, then retreated while she brought it in. From the doorway she saw Faharn, waiting some yards away and smiling as Laz walked over to join him. For these few days, at least, he would have his teacher back.

With Laz gone, the sexual scent in the cabin air slowly cleared. Sidro began to realize how much his raw smell had intoxicated her, trapped inside as she'd been. It had muddled her thoughts far worse than any ale or mead could have done. She began to remember various odd things that she'd accepted without much of a struggle. What had Pir meant, anyway, that she'd have to know sooner or later? And where had Laz found the white crystal? Where did he go when he flew as the raven? She decided that from then on she would spend part of the day outside or at the least, at the window. The stinking air of the camp seemed preferable to losing her reason for days on end. After what had happened to Movrae, none of Laz's men would dare accost her. She could be sure of that.

To occupy her time apart, Laz had opened the locked box and given her a pair of thick books, written on pale leather. Even though she'd been born a slave, Sidro had been taught to read. In the Gel da' Thae view, reading helped set themselves and their slaves apart from the savage tribes of the far north as well as from the farm slaves who fed the cities. During the day she sat at the table and read bits and pieces of magical lore from the *Pseudo-Iamblichos Scroll,* a book bound in black leather and decorated with a white dragon on its cover. Laz himself had translated it from the language of the Black Isles into the Horsekin tongue.

Inside its plain green binding, the other book held a copy of the chronicles he'd mentioned on her first day in the camp, an account of the War at Highstone Tor in Slavers' Country and its aftermath in the Freeland city of Marshfort. The latter tale she knew well. In Marshfort the holy witness Raena had died, slain by the man known as Rhodry Aberwyn, whom Vandar had then transformed into the silver dragon. Laz saw the chronicle of these events as a weapon to destroy her faith, Sidro knew, and at first she left it unopened. But curiosity – *it's your besetting sin, Sidro,* she told herself. *That and lust.*

Finally, on the fourth evening, after she'd eaten the dinner Laz left outside the door, she surrendered to her sin and opened the chronicle. By dweomer light she read until her back was cramped from leaning over the book and her swollen eyes could read no more. She dragged herself away from the table and leaned on a windowsill to look through the trees at the night sky. Judging by the wheel of stars, the dawn lay close at hand.

'He's not the only liar in the world, is he?' she said aloud.

For a moment she wept, then returned to the table. She banished the dweomer light, shut the book, and turned away to fall upon the mattress, exhausted. When she woke to a sunny room, Laz was sitting at the table and smiling at her. The book lay open in front of him.

'Are you hungry?' he said. 'I'll sleep over at Faharn's again tonight, but I figured it was safe for me to be here during the day.'

'Yes, I suppose it is. I'm barely bleeding at all.'

He touched the tips of the fingers on his right hand to his forehead, a sign of submission and warding both. She sat up and considered him.

'For all that you love to mock,' she said, 'you still cling to the old ways.'

'In some things.' He grinned again. 'I brought you a couple of buckets of wash water. I'll go get some food.'

Once he left, Sidro took off her dress and shift, then

considered the buckets of water. There were prayers to be said while she purified herself, but she'd have to choose between two sets, the ancient ritual she'd learned as a young girl, and the new ritual that Alshandra's priestesses had devised to replace it. She'd not used the ancient set in years. For a moment she considered chanting the prayer to Alshandra. Perhaps the chroniclers were wrong. Perhaps *she* would answer and forgive her priestess her broken vows. Sidro hesitated, then remembered Laz, touching his fingers to his forehead in a gesture as old as the Horsekin race.

'Rinbala, goddess of the sea,' she began. 'Wash me clean now that my blood time is ending.'

When she finished the chant, she gathered up the bloody rags she'd been using. Later she would go into the forest and wash them in running water. When that time came, she knew that she would pray not to Alshandra, but to Kanz, goddess of the moon.

Sidro wasn't the only person wondering about the whereabouts of the two dragons. Salamander was beginning to worry about their absence. The army, led by Maelaber and his escort, had been making its slow way west into the roadless grasslands for nearly a fortnight. With so many men and horses to tend, making and breaking camp took hours out of the day's travel. Much to the frustration of the dwarven carters, the long grass kept catching and winding itself around the strakes on the cartwheels. The army would have to pause while the swearing carters removed it. The old-fashioned wooden wheels of the Deverry carts broke just as often as they always had, and again, the army would have to stop. On three different days it rained, forcing the army to huddle in its tents.

Salamander felt that they were crawling, not marching. Every now and then the raven mazrak would fly overhead. Salamander worried constantly that he'd flap off to warn Zakh Gral.

'I wish that wretched dragon would get herself back here,' Salamander said to Gerran.

'Where is she, anyway?' Gerran said.

'Looking for Rori — the silver dragon, that is.'

'Oh, I'll not be forgetting him. Don't trouble your mind about that!'

'Well and good, then. He was supposed to have joined us long ere this.'

Gerran started to say more, then stopped, glancing away, biting his lower lip as if he were chewing over some difficult thought. Salamander waited. They were standing at the edge of the camp on the morning of their twelfth day on the road. Although the sun was already a good distance above the eastern horizon, the servants and pages had just begun to load the carts for another day's march. The men of the warbands were bringing in the horses from pasture and saddling them.

'Tell me somewhat,' Gerran said at last. 'About Rori, now. He truly is your brother, isn't he?'

'He is. I'd not lie to you about a thing like that.'

Gerran let out his breath in a sharp puff, but his expression remained perfectly calm.

'What made you change your mind?' Salamander said. 'I know that you thought me daft for saying he was my brother.'

'Well, all this cursed dweomer. What else? I've learned it truly exists, and you hear all those old tales about dweomer turning men into frogs, so what's to stop it from turning someone into a dragon?'

'A good point, but, I hasten to add, it was only the greatest dweomermaster in the world who managed that particular trick. And, if I remember the tale a-right, working the transformation killed him.'

'Well, that's some comfort, then. I didn't like the thought of waking up one morning covered with scales and sprouting wings.'

'Fear not! You're perfectly safe from such a fate.'

Salamander had the somewhat crazed thought of confessing

that he could turn himself into a magpie, just to see Gerran's reaction. Fortunately, common sense took over, and he held his tongue.

Arzosah returned to the army late on the same day. She circled high above the camp, then headed east to land about a quarter of a mile away, far enough to keep the horses from panicking at her scent. Salamander made his way through the waist-high grass and joined her. She'd used her long tail as a scythe of sorts to cut and beat down a circle in the green. In the midst of this clearing she sat with her front paws tucked at her chest and her tail laid neatly against her shiny black haunches while she looked up, studying the sky. When he approached, she lowered her head and contemplated him with her copper-coloured eyes, slit vertically like elven eyes to reveal a deep green pupil.

'Greetings, oh perfect pinnacle of dragonhood!' Salamander said in Elvish.

'Same to you, oh maudlin minstrel of many words,' Arzosah said. 'Flames and fumes! Your army travels so slowly that it's enough to drive one daft. I've been waiting for you out here for days.'

'It's driving me daft, too. The Roundears can't seem to unpack so much as a saddlebag without it taking forever.'

'How like them! Now, as for me, I've tracked Rori down.'

'That's grand news! Is he willing to join us?'

'Oh yes. As soon as I mentioned slaughtering Horsekin, he became quite tractable.' She sighed with a lift of a wing. 'He really is splendid, when he's himself, anyway.'

'Is that wound still troubling him?'

'Oh yes. He wants revenge for it, he tells me, and so do I, after having to live with it all these years. There have been times I've felt like biting him, just to make him stop all his licking and worrying at it! Let's hope Dallandra can heal it.'

'I shall hope indeed. Where is he?'

'Off to the west, scouting the fortress. Your description of its whereabouts was more than a little vague, you know.'

'Well, I was confused when I arrived there and even more so when I left.'

'Your natural state, no doubt. Now, I'm going to chase after Rori when I leave here, but we'll both return and join you once you meet up with the Westfolk muster. It's quite near.'

'Splendid!'

'Keep a watch for us. We'll fly overhead and then land some decent distance away.'

'It'll probably be easier for Rori to meet with us without everyone watching.'

'Do you think so?' Arzosah cocked her head to one side and considered this. 'You're quite possibly right. For now, however, I'm off to look for my dinner.'

'Very well. I'll go back to camp and get my own.'

Salamander waited until the camp had quieted down later that evening before he tried contacting Dallandra. As soon as his mind touched hers, he knew she was deeply troubled.

'I heard from Niffa earlier,' Dallandra told him. 'Cerr Cawnen won't be sending us any troops. They need every man they've got to stay home and guard their walls.'

'Are the Horsekin prowling around?'

'Not yet, but messengers rode in yesterday from Braemel. The council there has broken its alliance with Cerr Cawnen.'

'Ye gods! What does Grallezar say about that?'

'I haven't been able to reach her.'

Simple common sense frightened him as much as any dweomer omen might have. 'Do you think she's dead?' he said.

'No. I'd feel that. She's merely too upset about something to hear me. She's more angry than frightened, though, which gives me hope. Her adoptive mother was the one who forged that alliance, you know.'

'I didn't know, actually. But no wonder the daughter's furious.'

'Just so. But the evil thing is, there's no use counting on

troops from Braemel, is there? Ebañy, I have to go. Here comes Prince Dar, and he needs to know about Cerr Cawnen.'

She broke off contact before he could answer. *Worse and worse*, he thought. *That's two allies lost. Thank all the gods for the Mountain Folk!* And how was he going to tell this news to Prince Voran and Gwerbret Ridvar? He quite simply couldn't, he realized, because even if he could convince them that dweomer could send messages, they would never believe that he possessed it. He'd played the babbling fool too long and too well.

On the morrow, the army reached the elven muster. Around noon, Salamander was riding just ahead of the baggage train when he heard shouting up at the van. Slowly the sound and the news travelled back along the length of the army – Westfolk tents ahead! Salamander turned his horse out of line, rode some hundred yards out to get free of the dust the army was raising, and saw like tiny clouds on the horizon the white peaks of elven tents. He nudged his horse to a trot and rode on ahead of the army.

Salamander had never seen a Westfolk camp so large or so organized. What with the archers, the swordsmen, the horse handlers and others who'd volunteered to act as servants, the packhorses and the travois loaded with supplies, it spread out as widely as a small Deverry town. Herds of horses grazed round the edge of the camp under the guard of mounted archers. Inside this ring ditches stood open for garbage and other leavings; they also provided a certain amount of protection, Salamander supposed, should there be an attack by Horsekin cavalry. In the middle of the area, tents marched in even rows.

Salamander dismounted and hailed the guards, who let him through. Leading his horse, he made his way through the camp. Everywhere he looked, swordsmen were coming and going with purposeful strides. Archers sat on the ground, straightening arrows, repairing fletching, testing bowstrings. He eventually found Prince Daralanteriel's tent, painted with its distinctive roses, in the centre of a tight ring of other tents.

'Ebañy!' Dallandra hailed him. 'Over here!'

She was standing in front of Calonderiel's tent, one of the central ring. Two men and two women stood around her – healer's assistants, Dallandra told him. One of them took his horse's reins and led it away.

'I'm counting on your help, too, once the battles start,' Dallandra said.

'Whatever I can do, I will,' Salamander said. 'I can fold bandages if naught else. But I shan't be able to camp with you once the two armies start moving again. I have to stay with the Red Wolf. I've been sharing a tent with Gerran and young Clae.'

'Ah yes, you're Cadryc's scribe now. I'm so pleased that Neb isn't with the army.' Dallandra glanced around, then pointed to a plain grey tent set a little apart from its neighbours. 'Valandario's still with us. She'll be part of the alar – well, the military escort, really – that's going to take Carra and the children down to Mandra. All of the women archers will go with them. Cal says they're more accurate than the men, you see, so they'll make every arrow count if they have to. The entire contingent will stay close to the town for the duration.'

'Near the ships, you mean?'

'Just that.' Dallandra's eyes turned grim. 'Just in case. If Dar dies, Rodiveriel's the prince of the Westlands. They've got to keep him safe, even if it means heading out to sea. We have a treaty with the gwerbret of Aberwyn, and he'll shelter the boy if it's necessary.'

'It's just as well to plan for the worst, I suppose, but I doubt me if the Horsekin force at Zakh Gral is large enough to threaten Mandra.'

'Oh, so do I, or I'd be a gibbering madwoman out of sheer terror.' Dallandra smiled briefly. 'I've got herbs to sort. Do you want to go talk with Val?'

'I most certainly do. I've been vexing myself about that

obsidian pyramid. If anyone knows anything about that most peculiar, bizarre, and just plain odd crystal, it will be Val.'

Salamander found Valandario in her tent. A dweomer light hung in the air to supplement the sunlight filtering in from outside; the silver glow gleamed on her silk scrying-cloths and sparkled on the gems spread across them. Valandario herself was sitting cross-legged on a leather cushion behind the array. When he came in, she looked up and smiled without a trace of surprise, as if perhaps she'd not noticed he'd been gone for weeks.

'Val, I know you'll be leaving soon,' Salamander said. 'So I need to ask you a question. My apologies for interrupting.'

'You're not really interrupting, actually. I was just studying a fine point from yesterday's omens.' She waved at another cushion on the other side of the cloth. 'Sit down and ask away.'

Salamander sat down as carefully as he could to avoid disturbing the arrangement of gems.

'When I was at the Horsekin shrine,' he began, 'I saw some objects they keep as holy relics. One of them was a crystal, and I thought you might know something about it and why the wretched Horsekin would value it. It was a piece of obsidian in the shape of a pyramid, but the top point, the peak, as it were, looked as if it had been lopped off at an angle.'

For a long moment Valandario stared at him, her eyes wide, her lips half-parted.

'Uh,' Salamander said, 'is it at all important, or is this an utterly stupid question?'

'Not stupid, no, merely painful. So that's where it went.' Val set her lips in a thin line of grief. 'That wretched awful gem.' Her voice wavered. 'I was so glad to get it, too. When I think what it brought with it —' She caught her breath and steadied her voice. 'What I wonder now is how did the filthy Horsekin get hold of it? It suits their nature, I suppose, a wicked little morsel like that.'

'I take it you know what this thing is.'

'Well, there might be more than one of them, but I doubt it. Don't you remember it? It's the gem that Loddlaen was stealing when he murdered my beloved.'

Salamander let out his breath in a sharp puff. Val looked away, her face set, her delicate hands clenching into fists.

'I was off in Deverry when the murder happened.' Salamander made his voice as soft as he could. 'So I only heard about it much later. I'm sorry I've reminded you of it.'

Valandario shrugged, then let her hands relax. Still, it took her a moment more before she looked at him. 'About the gem itself, though.' Val's voice had steadied again. 'It's a show-stone of sorts – very much of sorts. You were the only person who could ever see anything in it. I honestly don't understand why Loddlaen wanted it so badly.'

'I was? I don't remember ever looking into it.'

'You were a very young child at the time. Let me think.' She paused, her mouth a little slack as she considered her memories. 'You saw a book with a dragon on it, and a man who turned out to be Evandar.'

'By every god!' Salamander whispered. 'I've got no memory of that at all!'

'I'm not surprised. You were just learning to talk at the time. What you told us was all very choppy and scant.'

'No doubt. Why didn't you have me look in it again later? When I was older, I mean.'

'It would have been too dangerous – dangerous to you, that is. I consulted with Nevyn, and he agreed. It's terrible to let an untrained child mess about with dweomer devices. In fact, one apprentice of his died young because some unscrupulous fellow exploited her gifts before she was ready to control them. It weakened her etheric double, and she came down with consumption. Lilli, I think her name was.'

'I remember that story, yes.'

'So we decided I should wait till you'd completely mastered scrying. But by then the stone was gone.'

'I see.' Salamander felt a stab of guilt. *If I hadn't kept running away, if I'd only worked harder, maybe I could have seen the message years ago.* Valandario was looking at him with a grim frown that made him wonder if she were thinking the same thing.

'Uh, well.' Salamander came up with a quick question to change the subject. 'What about the spirit indwelling the stone? Do you know what it is?'

'Spirit? There wasn't any spirit when I had it. Someone else has been working with the thing.'

For a long moment they stared at each other in surprise.

'It might have been Evandar's doing,' Salamander said at last.

'That's true, it might have,' Val said. 'You know, you can never ever tell Dallandra I said this, but the Guardians positively make my flesh creep. How she could have run off with one of them, I'll never know.'

'Jill made similar remarks.'

'No doubt! Now, Evandar was at least less irrational than most Guardians. If he put a message in that stone, it must have been something important.'

'Maybe it's still there. If we do take Zakh Gral, I'll be able to recover the pyramid and look into it again.'

'If it isn't destroyed in the battle. I wonder how the Horsekin got hold of it? After Loddlaen's death, Aderyn looked for the stone, but he couldn't find it. No one knew what had happened to it.'

'It seems to have travelled a long way west.'

'Yes, and I wonder how. Now, if you get the thing, look into it, write down what you see, and then smash it to pieces.' For a moment her voice touched upon an animal growl. She laid a hand on her throat and coughed before she spoke again. 'Look into it more than once, of course, if you need to. But when you feel there's no more good to be got out of it, destroy it for me. Will you do that? I'd love to know it was gone forever.'

'I'll do that. I promise.'

'Thank you.' Valandario smiled, back to her usual composed and golden self. 'You know, I'd best put these gems away and start packing for tomorrow. Princess Carra wants to leave at dawn.'

'Well, then, may you all have a safe ride down to the coast.'

'Oh, we will.' Valandario pointed to her scrying array. 'It's the rest of you I worry about.'

Salamander pushed out a weak smile, then rose and left. He had to admit that even though he'd received no sinister omens, he was worried himself.

He found Dallandra and her cluster of helpers packing up for the march as well. Behind Calonderiel's tent lay a welter of pack panniers, which the assistants were filling with medicinals, bandages, kettles for brewing herbs, and the like. When Salamander joined them, Dallandra gave some orders to her chief assistant, Ranadario, a young woman with raven dark hair and deep purple eyes. Since she had no dweomer apprentice at that time, Dallandra had taken on two young men and two young women who wanted to learn healing and herbcraft. Dallandra led Salamander some distance away, where they could speak privately.

'What did Val have to say about the obsidian pyramid?' Dallandra said.

'A very great deal,' Salamander said. 'Let me tell you.'

By the time he finished, Dallandra was frowning in thought.

'The thing that bothers me,' Dallandra said at last, 'is the presence of that spirit. I wonder who bound it? Evandar never would have done such a thing. I doubt me if it was someone who followed the path of light.'

'I'd wager on your nasty bitch of a Raena,' Salamander said, 'or beg pardon, the holy witness Raena. The other objects on the altar supposedly belonged to her.'

'I know the wyvern dagger did at one point. But you know, I met Raena, and she didn't have the power to bind spirits.

She only knew the most elementary things about dweomer. All her dweomer acts derived from first Alshandra and then Shaetano working through her.'

'Then someone must have done it before it came into her hands.'

'Well, there's Loddlaen.' Dallandra pronounced the name carefully, slowly, as if it pained her. 'But I doubt if he had the skill to do a binding like that. I'm just judging from what Val's told me, over the years, though. I don't know for certain.'

'Maybe someone got hold of it after he – um, ah, no longer had the crystal.'

Dallandra flinched as if from a blow.

'I'm sorry to bring this all up,' Salamander said. 'We don't have to discuss it.'

'Yes, we do. It could be important. Does Val know what happened to the stone after Loddlaen died?'

'No. She told me that no one knows.'

'Then he probably didn't have it when –' She let her voice trail away.

Salamander waited.

'I've really got to go back to my work,' Dallandra said abruptly. 'We can talk more later.'

Before he could answer, she turned on her heel and strode off to rejoin her assistants.

Although Princess Carra led her contingent out just after dawn, the army lingered to allow the army from Deverry to rest their horses. Some of the Westfolk archers had fought at the siege of Cengarn, as had some of the dwarven axemen, and they spread out among the Deverry men to tell them what they knew about the Horsekin they'd faced in battle. When Salamander walked through the camp, he saw the fighting men standing in small groups and talking urgently together.

Around noon, the two dragons flew over just as Arzosah had promised. Salamander and Dallandra had been waiting at her tent with a sack of medicinals. They hurried through the camp as fast as possible – not very, with the clutter and crowding of tents, men, horses, and wagons all around them. The dragons stayed high, drifting on the wind, then slowly led them off to the north about half a mile before they settled to ground. As the two Westfolk pushed their way through the high grass, Salamander could feel his heart pounding, but not from the physical effort.

'You look anxious,' Dallandra said.

'I am,' Salamander said. 'What does one say to a brother who's been turned into a dragon?'

'What does one say to an old lover who has?'

'Aha! That's why you never wanted to discuss him with Branna.'

'Well, yes. You have to admit that it's all a bit complicated.'

'Complicated?' Salamander found himself on the edge of laughter but pulled back. If he gave in to the impulse, he knew, his laughter would become a hysterical giggle or perhaps even a shriek.

Apparently Arzosah found the situation distressing as well. The two wyrms had beaten down a good-sized circle in the grass, but well before Dallandra and Salamander reached it, Arzosah sprang into the air and flew, a black glint against the sky like a spark from the obsidian pyramid. Rori sat alone at its centre, lounging on one side, his front legs outstretched like a Bardek lion at ease. From a distance he looked as majestic, too, with his massive silvery head, touched along the jaw and the lines of the skull with a glistening blue. Although he'd folded them, his huge silver wings shimmered with a rainbow pattern where they caught the light.

As they approached, however, Salamander saw the wound in his side, barely a foot long but black with crusted blood and morbid flesh. It stank so badly that they could smell it through the normal vinegar scent of wyrm.

'By the Black Sun!' Dallandra murmured.

'Indeed.' Salamander nearly gagged as he spoke. 'It must be dweomer-cursed.'

Dallandra shook her head no. By then they were close enough for Rhodry to overhear. When they stepped into the circle, he lifted his wings, just very slightly before he folded them again, yet enough to show that he felt like taking flight. Dallandra marched straight up to him.

'That wound!' she said in Elvish. 'Rori, you've got to let me look at it.'

Her flat matter-of-fact voice worked like dweomer on Salamander's nerves, and apparently on Rhodry's as well.

'Why do you think I'm here?' His voice had a breathy rasp at its edge, but it sounded like the voice Salamander was remembering as his brother's, merely magnified. 'Dalla, I have to say one thing straight off. I should have listened to you, that day in Cerr Cawnen.'

'You know, I never thought I'd live to see the hour when I'd hear you say that – about anything.'

The dragon rumbled, and Salamander laughed, a normal laugh that matched Dallandra's grin.

'But there was the little matter of the town's safety,' Dallandra went on. 'With Arzosah threatening to destroy it, what choice did you have?'

'To die and let Evandar control Arzosah. He could have taken her elsewhere in a beat of the heart, somewhere too far away for her to harm the town. Eventually she would have come to her senses. I realized that when it was too late.' He tossed his head with a glitter of light off silver scales. 'Or no, that's less than honest. At that moment I wanted what I have now. I refused to think clearly. If I hadn't wanted it, Evandar never could have worked the transformation.'

'Rori, you were dying!' Dallandra said. 'How can I hold it to your shame, that your mind wasn't perfectly clear and calm?'

He was silent for a moment, then nodded. 'I can't tell you how much that eases my heart.' His voice dropped to a whisper that was almost a hiss. 'The shame of it's been eating me worse than this wound, that I'd not seen what might happen.'

'We've all been wondering what was so wrong.' Salamander stepped forward. 'I've been trying to find you, but it seemed that you'd fly off the moment I spotted you. I gather you didn't want to speak to me.'

'My apologies. I did feel shamed, but you see, I've also been patrolling the Northlands.'

'For Horsekin, I assume.'

'Just that. I found some raiders earlier this summer. I was too late to save the villagers they killed, but I did manage to give the hairy bastards the scare of their lives.'

'So that was you!' Salamander said. 'I thought so.'

'Were you there?'

'No, but I rode that way later with the warband sent to chase them off.'

'Ah, I see. It's just as well you weren't. They've got a new kind of sabre, the Horsekin do. It curves like a scythe blade. They rode down the men fighting on foot and swung down with the blade. It wasn't a pretty sight.' Rori lifted his head and looked around him. 'Where's Jill? I know her name's not Jill in this life, but you know who I mean.'

'Yes,' Dallandra said. 'Her name's Branna, and she's not truly Jill. You've got to remember that. We refused to let her come with the army. She's only a young lass, and she's married to the lad who once was Nevyn.'

'Good.' Rori nodded in approval. Before he spoke again, he looked this way and that, peering into the grass as if he thought someone might hide among the stalks. 'I've also been looking for Raena.' He lowered his voice to a near-whisper. 'I guessed that she'd be reborn among the Horsekin, and I was right.'

'Sidro the priestess?' Salamander said.

'The very one. I'm going to kill her if I can get at her.'

'Rori, no!' Dallandra said. 'That's what got you into this wretched mess in the first place, isn't it? Wanting revenge?'

Rori swung his massive head around and blinked at her as if he was puzzled. 'If I hadn't killed her,' he said, 'Carra and the child would have had no peace.'

'That war was mine to fight, not yours. Besides, we can't know what would have happened had Raena lived. For one thing, the Alshandra people would have lacked their most important witness, as they call them. Her death heaped tinder on the sparks of the cult.'

The dragon growled under his breath. Dallandra set her hands on her hips and considered him, her eyes as cold as his, their two heads close together, his so massive, hers so delicate — but he looked away first.

'I hadn't realized that.' His voice was as mild as a dragon's voice is capable of being. 'I don't know, Dalla. I don't know anything any more, who I am, what I am. The one sure thing in all my days is my Lady Death. I've not stopped longing for her. I'd say she's set a task for me, to send her as many Horsekin as I can before she deigns to release me.'

'Lady Death?' Salamander said. 'Do you mean Alshandra?'

'Of course not!' Rori rumbled with laughter, then spoke in Deverrian. 'My Lady Death, my own true love, she whom I served all my years as a silver dagger and a warlord both. They're the same, truly, aren't they, my brother? A warlord talks and talks and talks some more about his honour, but in the end, doesn't it always come down to death? He's merely paid in a different coin than the silver dagger.'

'Well, that it does. But why do you —'

'Don't you see?' Rori raised himself up on his front legs. 'If I don't serve my lady, she'll never take me. I'll live a dragon for hundreds of years. My only hope is to send her tribute.'

Salamander took an involuntary step back. The dragon rumbled and lowered his bulk to the ground again.

'What about Raena, then?' Dallandra returned the conversation to Elvish. 'I suppose your Lady Death demands her, too.'

'No. I'm the one who wants her dead, and Tren as well.'

'Tren?' Dalla said. 'Who's Tren?'

'Matyc's brother. The one I killed in front of Cengarn.'

Salamander's bewilderment deepened. The only Matyc he

knew was Branna's young nephew. Rori seemed to sense his confusion.

'Matyc was a traitor lord I killed in a trial by combat,' the dragon said. 'His brother Tren tried to avenge him, but I killed him during the battle in front of Cengarn.'

'Oh,' Dallandra said. 'I do remember that, just vaguely.'

'He's returned to torment me as well. They're like the wound, those two. They eat at me. I've been searching for them. I forget them for a while, but then I remember, and I have to search for them. If I kill Sidro, maybe the wound will heal. I don't know Tren's new name, but he's a shapechanger, and he's cursed me.'

'No, he hasn't!' Dallandra snapped. 'Killing her won't heal you, either. Rori, I'm willing to wager high that they don't even remember you. They've died and been reborn since then. For all I know, they may even have had two new lives. Do you remember the talk we had, standing in Cengarn's dun? I told you then that most people become someone new when they return.'

'They're still my tormentors.'

'No, they're not.' Dallandra strode up next to him and laid a hand on his massive jaw. 'They are no longer who they were. Why would they torment you? Please believe me!'

Rhodry looked as if he would speak, then lowered his head and rested it upon the ground to allow her to reach his face. She stroked him as if he were a pet dog, and slowly his mad fit eased. Salamander felt tears rising beyond his power to stop them. When he caught his breath in a sob, Rhodry's eyes flicked his way, cornflower blue and shaped like human eyes, with their round irises and dark dot of pupil, not dragonish at all. Through them, despite their size and the taint of madness, he saw his brother looking back at him.

'Go fetch Calonderiel, would you?' Rhodry's enormous voice became oddly gentle. 'I've much to tell him.'

Salamander glanced at Dallandra, who mouthed a single word, 'go'.

'I'll do that, then.' Salamander turned and shamelessly ran before they could change their minds and call him back. After a few hundred yards he was gasping for breath. He slowed down to a trot. Around him the grass blurred and shimmered through tears.

By the time he reached the camp, he'd managed to stop weeping. He found Calonderiel, gave him the message, and saw him on his way, then sat down on the ground in front of the banadar's tent. The smell of dragon lingered on his clothes, or so he felt, like a poison, forcing him to remember his brother's misery. Clae found him there some while later – how long a while, Salamander was unsure – with a summons from Tieryn Cadryc.

'His grace wants to send letters home while he can.'

'Well and good then.' Salamander hauled himself to his feet. 'That gladdens my heart.'

Clae shot him a puzzled look.

'It will be somewhat to think about,' Salamander went on. 'Somewhat other than the silver wyrm.'

Towards sunset, long after the messengers had got on their way, Salamander saw Rori flying over the camp, heading west, so high that for a moment he looked like a white bird, gleaming in the slanting light of late afternoon. Salamander walked back out to meet the returning Dallandra and Calonderiel.

'He found Zakh Gral,' Calonderiel said. 'I've got to go call a council of war.'

Calonderiel rushed off, racing down the path of broken grass leading back to camp. Salamander and Dallandra followed, but slowly, and he stayed silent, letting her collect her thoughts. Finally she glanced his way.

'I may be able to heal that wound,' she said, 'but it's going to take leeches, if indeed leeches will eat dragon flesh and drink dragon blood.' Her voice rose sharply, but she took a deep breath and resumed in a normal tone of voice. 'I may be wrong, but I really don't think it's a dweomer curse, Ebañy.

That would be too simple. He's done it to himself, licking it and biting at it, over and over for nearly fifty years now. It was starting to heal, he told me, but it itched, so he began licking it, and then of course it got worse again. Now it's horribly septic. There's dead flesh all along its edges, too.'

'Has the rot spread into his blood?'

'I doubt it, but I don't know. If he were a man, and the rot had spread that far, he'd be dead. But he's not, he's a dragon, and I don't know the first thing about healing dragons. I do know that I'll have to clean up what he's done to it.'

'Where are we going to find leeches?'

'Out here? I have no idea. Look for slow-moving water, like you'd see down in the Delonderiel's estuary.'

'If we can't find any nearby, it's a long way down to the coast.'

'Yes, it is. It's all so horrible.' Her voice trailed off.

Salamander decided that silence was the only appropriate comment. They reached the encampment and made their slow way through to the Red Wolf's sector. Gerran was sitting on the ground in front of the tent he shared with Salamander and dicing for splinters of kindling with Kov, the dwarven envoy. The envoy's staff lay on a folded blanket right beside him. Dallandra paused to speak with Gerran, who rose to a kneel and made a half-bow to Dallandra.

'What news, Wise One?' Gerran said.

'Listen to you!' Dallandra was trying to smile. 'You're turning into one of the Westfolk.'

'It would be an honour, truly, but I was wondering —'

'Cal will tell you everything later,' Dallandra interrupted him. 'I'm not sure if I understood all the details. But Rori told us that it's impossible for us to mount a surprise attack on Zakh Gral.'

'Oh, I assumed that, my lady,' Gerran said. 'If naught else, they should be able to hear an army this size coming from miles away.'

'I see. Here I was thinking it was a terrible setback.'

'Not truly. What counts is when they learn about us. If they're warned, we'll end up fighting the first battle at the ford.'

'The first battle.' Dallandra repeated the words as if she could think of naught else to say.

'Well, they're not going to sit behind their walls and wait for us to invest them.'

'Truly, I suppose they wouldn't.' Dallandra sounded so faint that Salamander caught her elbow to steady her. Dallandra glanced at Salamander and spoke next in Elvish. 'You've gone white in the face.'

'I feel sick, that's why.' Salamander answered in the same.

'It's truly ghastly, isn't it? Everything, I mean.' She turned back to Gerran and spoke in Deverrian. 'My apologies, Gerro, and you too, Envoy. I don't mean to put you both off, but I'm very tired.'

'Then I should apologize to you,' Gerran said. 'I shouldn't have kept you standing here. No doubt I'll hear all I need to know later.'

'And I apologize as well,' Kov said. 'Please, my lady. Do go rest.'

When Dallandra turned to walk away, Salamander started to follow, but she swung around and held up one hand to stop him. 'I can't talk about Rhodry any more just now,' she said in Elvish. 'I don't want to talk about anything. Can you understand?'

'Oh yes,' Salamander said. 'I can understand very easily indeed. But please, could you tell me just one more thing? What of Sidro?'

'I don't know if he'll leave her alone or not.' She cocked her head to one side and considered him. 'I suppose you want her dead, too.'

'No. I've come to pity her. That's why I asked.'

'Well, there's one of you sane, anyway.' Dallandra smiled briefly, then turned and strode away. Salamander sat down to watch the dice game. In but a few moments, Clae came running with the news that the princes were summoning

Kov to the council of war. The dwarven envoy scrambled up, grabbed his staff from the blanket, and trotted off after the page. Gerran scooped up the dice in one hand and held them out to Salamander.

'I doubt me if I can think clearly enough to count the pips,' Salamander said.

Gerran nodded and put the dice away in a leather pouch. Far above the army's tents, the sky shone an opalescent blue, touched here and there with clouds turned gold by the setting sun. Salamander stared at the sky but barely saw it. The memory of Rori's human eyes, staring desperately from a reptilian head, filled his inner vision.

Without an army and bad weather to hold them back, the messengers – two men, their horses, and a pack mule – made good speed back to the Red Wolf dun. Dusty, sweaty, and exhausted, they walked into the great hall some hours before sunset, when Neb, Branna, and Lady Galla were sitting at the table of honour. With a sigh of relief Daumyr knelt by the lady's side and pulled a silver message tube out of his shirt.

'Took us just four days, my lady,' Daumyr said. 'We pushed it a fair bit, of course. We had two horses a-piece, you see, so we could change back and forth.'

His companion, Alwyn, raised an eyebrow and gave Neb a weary grin.

'Well, lads,' Lady Galla said. 'You'll sleep well tonight, and we'll give you fresh horses in the morning. Go get somewhat to eat and drink.'

'My thanks, my lady.' Daumyr got up, staggered, and steadied himself by grabbing the corner of the table. 'A tankard will be welcome just now.'

Alwyn nodded his agreement and got up as well. Together they hurried over to the servant's side of the hall, where the men of the fortguard were waiting for them. Neb pulled the letters out of the tube and looked them over.

'All the news is good so far, my lady,' he said to Galla.

'In fact, there's not much news at all, except that the silver dragon's joined the black one and pledged his help.'

'I suppose that gladdens my heart,' Galla said. 'Everything's turned so strange lately that I'd not be surprised if one of the gods came to the door and announced that he'd like to join us for a meal or two.'

'No more would I, my lady. We seem to live in peculiar times.'

'Does it say anything more about the dragon?' Branna put in. 'The silver one, I mean.'

'It doesn't, just that he's joined his mate.' Neb suddenly realized that he felt jealous of this Rori creature. Why was Branna always so interested in him, anyway? *You're going daft,* he told himself. *Jealous of a wild animal, ye gods!*

Neb spent the rest of that evening first reading the letters to the noble-born, then writing their answers. On the morrow, Daumyr and Alwyn, with their fresh horses and a fresh mule laden with supplies, stood by the gates while Neb handed them the messages and told them which tube went to which lord.

'Are you going to be able to find your way back?' Neb said,

'Don't trouble your heart about that,' Daumyr said, grinning. 'The army's left a trail of ruts and filth behind it as broad as a river.'

With the messengers on their way, Neb returned to his work in the herb garden. The Red Wolf cook had planted a few table herbs: sage, thyme, mustard, and rosemary. The mustard would also make a useful rubefacient. Neb searched through the meadows and hedgerows around the dun until he found more medicinals: coltsfoot, comfrey, feverfew, horehound, and, out by the fence in a fallow cow pasture, valerian. When he was digging up the valerian to transplant, its disgusting smell brought with it a faint whisper of memory. He used to slice this root with a miniature silver sickle, he realized, though he couldn't quite remember why. Jill's book

of physicking, his guide in these matters, never mentioned
the sickle, either.

'I suppose it was buried with Nevyn,' he remarked to
Branna.

'I think it was,' Branna said. 'He didn't want grave goods,
but Jill couldn't stand it, just dumping him into a bare grave.'

They were up in their chamber. Branna was sitting on the
floor, reading by the light of two candles set on her dower
chest, and Neb was scrubbing his dirty hands in the wash-
basin by the window. He used up their scrap of soap before
he got them clean enough to satisfy him.

'I don't understand why you're working so hard in the
garden,' Branna said. 'One of the servants could do the digging
for you.'

'Oh, I've got to do somewhat to fill my time. You spend
most of your days with your cousin and the children, after all.'

'Do you want me to stop?' She sounded alarmed.

'What? I don't, truly. They need you, just as the garden
needs me.' Neb was concentrating on rinsing his hands.
'Besides, I don't want to eat at the tieryn's table without
earning my keep. Being your husband is a joy, not gainful
labour.'

She laughed, pleased, or so she sounded. He shook his
hands dry, then turned to smile at her. For the briefest of
moments she looked like a stranger. He was expecting Jill,
who was taller, thinner, her hair heavily streaked with grey.
Why weren't they sitting together in their home deep within
Brin Toraedic, laughing at the antics of the Wildfolk? Then
he remembered when and who he was.

Those moments, when the past would take over his
consciousness, happened regularly enough that they'd
stopped frightening him. Working in the garden, the regular
rhythms of physical labour, the heat of the sun, the smell of
the herbs – they all combined to thin the barrier in the mind
that separates conscious awareness from deep memories and
dreams. While he worked, he also would meditate upon the

figure of the raven mazrak, as Salamander had suggested. This he found difficult. His mind kept wandering, or so he thought of it at first. The image of the young priest who'd escorted him and Clae down the Great West Road after the death of their parents kept rising in his mind and spoiling the meditation.

'I don't understand it,' Neb told Branna one evening. 'I don't think about that priest when I'm doing anything else, just when I'm trying to concentrate on the wretched mazrak.'

'Well, maybe that's a clue,' Branna said.

'Maybe he's connected in some way with the mazrak, you mean?'

'Just that. You told me about that head priest in the northern temple, the one whose cows Arzosah stole. Didn't he know a little dweomer? And didn't you and Dalla wonder who taught him?'

'Ye gods.' Neb felt like an utter fool. 'Of course he did. And truly, this fellow – he said his name was Tirn – didn't strike me as your usual priest of Bel. He had quite an eye for the lasses, for one thing, and then there were the tattoos.'

'Tattoos? I've never heard of a priest of Bel having tattoos.'

'Exactly my point, my love. These were blue and all over his face, and down his neck as far as I could see, too. He told me that they covered scars from burns he'd got as a child.'

'Could you see scars under them?'

'I never really looked. My mother had just died, and I wasn't thinking very clearly.'

'My poor love! You've suffered so much.'

'So did half the people in Trev Hael. I've no reason to pity myself.' Neb shrugged with a shake of his head to banish the grief. 'But those tattoos – they looked like writing. Ye gods! I didn't realize it then, but they looked like characters from the Westfolk syllabary. Meranaldar wrote it out for me during the siege of Honelg's dun, you see, just to pass the time.'

'Now that's significant.' Branna spoke slowly, thinking. 'Ask Mirryn, will you? It's a thing he told me a long time ago.'

Lord Mirryn did indeed know the meaning of tattoos that featured Westfolk letters. 'Horsekin,' he said. 'The Horsekin put those all over themselves.'

'But this fellow was human,' Neb said. 'Or at least, he looked human, except for the tattoos.'

'Well, they've been taking slaves for centuries, haven't they? I'd imagine that the women have little choice about whose bed they warm.' Mirryn wrinkled his freckled nose in disgust. 'Savages, they are, the Horsekin.'

'They are all of that,' Neb said. 'Though to be fair, our ancestors weren't much better, or so my father told me once, when it came to bondwomen.'

'Well, maybe so. You know, I think we'd better tell Lord Oth up in Cengarn about this. A Horsekin half-breed in Bel's priesthood? He's most likely a spy or suchlike.'

'True spoken, my lord. I'll go get my pen and ink. Lord Oth probably can't smoke him out till the gwerbret returns, but he should be warned. Though you know what's odd? I never saw this fellow in the temple when I went there with the prince and Gwerbret Ridvar. I was looking for him, too, because I wanted to thank him.'

'That *is* odd. Maybe he wasn't a real priest of Bel at all. I suppose if you shaved your head and put on that tunic they wear, who would argue with you about it? Giving a priest trouble is a good way to get the god he serves angry with you.'

'You're quite right. Challenging him would be too risky. If it turned out he was genuine –' Neb shuddered to finish the point.

It was several days before Neb saw the raven mazrak again. Neb worked all morning in the sunny herb garden until his shirt was soaked through with sweat and he felt dizzy from the lack of moving air. He hauled up a bucket of water from the well and poured it over himself, then hauled up another and used the tin cup chained to the bucket to scoop up a good long drink. Once his head cleared, he climbed up the ladder to the catwalk near the top of the dun wall, where the Red Wolf pennant flapped, promising a breeze. Neb breathed in the cleaner air, then sat down on the catwalk and leaned back against the cool stone wall.

Down below he noticed Branna, walking across the ward with Horza the woodcutter. Branna held a big sack of the sort in which she stored carded wool. Horza was carrying an odd contraption – a dwarven straked wheel mounted on a very short axle supported on four little legs. He'd added wooden pegs to the wheel's rim as well. They disappeared into his workshop with Branna talking all the while. For a moment Neb wondered what they were doing; then he remembered Branna talking about making a device she called her wool-spinner.

The idea held little interest for him. He leaned back, glancing up, and saw the raven mazrak, drifting in a circle high above the dun. Slowly, keeping his back to the stones of the wall, Neb slithered up rather than stood. The raven completed his circle and began another. Neb slid his hand into his pocket and very slowly, standing in shadow, pulled out his leather sling, then froze. The raven finished his second drifting circle and began a third. Equally slowly Neb reached into his other pocket and pulled out a smooth round stone. All at once the raven croaked in alarm. Rather than flying off, he merely climbed higher, out of the sling's range, and began another circle. Neb had the sudden odd feeling that he'd heard the raven speak, then realized that he was perceiving an attempt to reach him with thought alone. He put the sling and stone back into his pockets. The raven dropped down lower again.

'Do you want to parley?' Neb called out.

The raven croaked, then began to lose height, circling and following the line of the dun wall. In a flurry of wings he landed on a crenel, swaying and flapping until he got his balance. Intelligence peered out of his round eyes, an abnormal – for a raven – brown. With a clack of beak, he spoke or tried to speak. He could only manage a series of croaks and clicks that sounded, faintly, like words.

'I can't understand you,' Neb said.

The raven tried again, his beak working hard as he formed a few ungrammatical Deverrian words, 'ihr yhdoh een anavod ki.' Or at least, as far as Neb could tell, he might have said, 'I know you.'

'I know you, too,' Neb said. 'You called yourself Tirn, last time we met.'

Neb was merely guessing, but his guess hit home. The raven bobbed his head in acknowledgement and spoke again, a few words that seemed to say, 'my name is —' What the name might have been, Neb couldn't decipher.

From down in the ward a woman's voice shrieked in anger. Neb glanced down to see Branna, a stone in her hand. Before he could call out to her, she swung around in a half-circle and let the stone fly. The raven squawked and leapt into the air, flapping hard to gain height. The stone sailed just under his feet. A second stone followed but fell short.

'Branna, stop it!' Neb yelled. 'He's trying to parley.'

Too late — the raven was flying away as fast as his huge wings could take him. Neb watched until his form dwindled to a black speck against the sky, then climbed down the ladder to the ward. Branna was waiting for him with her hands on her hips.

'Parley, indeed!' she snapped. 'He was probably going to try ensorceling you.'

'Oh.' Neb considered for a moment. 'I hadn't thought of that.'

'Well, was he that priest you told me about?'

'He was Tirn, all right. Here, did anyone else see him on the wall?'

'I doubt it. It's so beastly hot today, everyone's inside.'

'Good. You know, you could well be right about his wanting to ensorcel me, but truly, I could have sworn he just wanted to talk. I couldn't understand him very well. It's the beak, I suppose. It must be blasted hard to form words.'

'It must be, indeed. But —'

'He walked miles and miles out of his way to see me and Clae to safety. Why would he harm me now?'

'I don't know.' Branna hesitated, her anger gone. 'I suppose it was stupid of me, then, to lob stones at him. But when I saw him, I don't know what came over me. You traitor! I thought. And I was so angry I couldn't think.'

'Here! Did you truly think I would betray you?'

'Not you! Him. He was the traitor. Whoever he was.' She let her words trail away into a puzzled silence.

'So! You knew him in our other When. I hope to every god you dream about this tonight.'

Unfortunately, when she woke the next morning, Branna had no dreams of past lives to report. As Dallandra had warned her earlier, now that her mind had actively engaged with studying the dweomer, those easy memories had stopped rising.

When the messengers Mirryn sent to Cengarn returned, an answer from Lord Oth came with them. He was sending men to the temple of Bel to inquire about the tattooed priest, but he doubted if Govvin would co-operate. 'Govvin the Stubborn', he called the head priest of the temple, and Neb could only agree. Still, he supposed, the gesture would have some effect. If naught else, it would put Govvin and Tirn, if Tirn still dwelled in that temple, on notice that the gwerbret's men were watching them.

'Those Lijik women are savages,' Laz said. 'I swear, she would have dashed my brains out with those rocks.'

'What brains?' Sidro snapped. 'I can't believe you actually landed on an enemy wall like that. Why?'

'I wanted to talk with young Neb, of course.'

'But the Lijik men are vicious killers.'

'The women are, too, apparently. Neb himself is not the murderous sort, but that girl!' Laz shuddered and lifted his arms with a little shake, as if he were remembering spreading raven wings. 'She has a good eye, too. She barely missed me.'

'My heart aches for you,' Sidro said in Deverrian, 'you dolt!'

'My humble thanks,' Laz said in the same, then switched back to their own tongue. 'Oh, very well! It was stupid.'

They were sitting at the table in their cabin, where they'd been eating cold spoon bread and a sort of porridge made from barley and old gravy. When young Vek had brought them a bowlful, Sidro had decided that it would be better not to ask too many questions about the contents. On the table between them lay a red-brown pottery plate, stolen from some farm family, a crude pottery stoup, and a wood-handled kitchen knife, Laz's entire store of dinnerware.

'Why did you want to talk to this Neb person?'

'I'm not sure, really.' Laz got up, stretching his back. 'I rather liked him when I travelled with him in the Slavers' Country.' He stood and stretched his arms behind him. 'I'm tired. Even with the astral gates, it's a long way to fly.' Laz flopped onto the mattress and settled himself on his side. 'Aren't you going to come lie down and comfort me? I've been gone for an entire day, after all.'

'No, I'm not.' Sidro stayed on her tree stump, on the far side of the table from the bed. She crossed her arms over her chest and glared at him.

'Ah.' Laz sat up. 'You're vexed with me.'

'How perceptive you are.'

With a sigh he got up and joined her at the table. 'What have I done now?' he said.

'Going off without telling me. Flying when the dragon's nearby. Landing on that Lijik rakzan's wall. How reckless are you, Laz? Or were you lying about the dragon?'

'I was most assuredly not lying about the dragon, or dragons to be precise. The mated pair are both out here in the Northlands, though fortunately the little ones seem to have stayed at home in their nest or whatever it is dragons have. I flew over the forest so I could duck into the trees if I saw them.'

'What good would the trees —'

'Sisi, the wyrms are huge, at least thirty feet long, I'd say.

How are they going to fly into a forest? They couldn't wedge themselves between the trees. Besides, the forest reeks of animal smells. Dragon noses are keen, but nothing like ours. They'd have a hard time smelling out a single person. An army of Gel da' Thae, yes. One me, no.'

'Very well. I suppose you're right.'

'Of course I am. What else is vexing your soul?'

'I want to know where you got the white crystal pyramid.'

'I found it in the ruins of Rinbaladelan.'

'Do you really think I'll believe that? Laz, I am so tired of your lying to me.'

'No, it's true. Rinbaladelan, Sisi. I've been there.'

Before she could answer, they heard shouting outside, the deep voices of Horsekin men, and a high-pitched scream that sounded as if it might come from a human throat. Someone pounded on the cabin door.

'Laz, get out here!' Pir called out. 'A thief's been prowling around our horses.'

With her thoughts full of dragons, Sidro felt her heart flutter in her chest, but when she followed Laz out, she saw a young Lijik man kneeling on the ground between two of the spearmen. Pir stood nearby, his horse-mane of hair glittering with charms in the bright sun. The Lijik man's clothes were filthy and torn, his hair so matted with dirt and leaves that its colour was impossible to discern, his face smeared with mud and discoloured with bruises. He trembled as he looked this way and that, but when he saw Sidro he broke into a grin.

'Priestess,' he whispered in Deverrian. 'Blessed Sidro.'

She'd heard his voice before, Sidro realized. She stepped forward and peered into his face. His eyes were pale blue and again, familiar.

'You do come from Lord Honelg's dun,' she said in the same language. 'Be you one of his riders?'

'I was. My name's Bren. I'm the last left alive. My lord had given me leave to visit my father, you see, so I was out of the dun when the siege began.'

'Siege? What –'

'The gwerbret found out we worshipped our goddess. He called us traitors. Holy one, he took our dun. Everyone's dead but me.'

Sidro could find the air neither to speak nor breathe for a long moment. She laid a shaking hand over her heart to steady both.

'Worse news yet,' Bren continued. 'He's marching on Zakh Gral. It was the gerthddyn that told him. They've gathered an army.'

Behind her Laz squawked raven-like in cold rage. He pushed past her, drawing his knife. With a yell, Bren tried to draw his own knife and stand up in the same motion, but Pir stopped him with a well-placed kick to his chest that sprawled him in the dirt. Bren moaned and coughed, scrambled to his knees, then reached out to her with both arms.

'Holy one! Don't let them kill me! I've got more to tell you.'

Knife held low but wicked in his fist, Laz strode forward, his gaze fixed on Bren's face. Sidro stepped in front of him and grabbed his right arm. She had the sudden definite sensation that someone was standing directly behind her – one of the men, she supposed – but she refused to break concentration.

'Leave him alone!' she snarled.

Laz froze, then slowly raised his head and looked at her, his mouth half-open from sheer surprise. Sidro dug her fingernails so hard into his arm that blood welled. He flinched but never made a sound.

'Leave him alone,' Sidro repeated. 'By all the holy gods of our people, Laz, leave him alone!'

She caught his gaze and held it, then released her grip on his arm. He shrugged, sheathed the knife, and stepped back. Pir was watching her, she realized, with a faint trace of a smile. 'Pir, feed this man.' She pointed at the kneeling rider. 'He doesn't speak a word of our language, and as long as no one tells him who we are, he'll think we worship Alshandra like he does. He's no threat.'

'No, he's not.' Pir glanced at Laz. 'I'm going to do what she told me.'

'Please do,' Laz said with another shrug. He hesitated a moment, then turned on his heel and strode into the cabin.

Who stood behind her? She spun around and saw no one, saw in fact that the nearest onlooker stood a good ten feet away. Vek, however, had dropped to his knees, bowed his head, and stretched out both arms in her direction. The hair on the back of her neck rose.

'Who did you see, Vek?' Sidro said.

'Kanz,' he whispered without looking up. 'She came to you and overshadowed you, holy one.'

Sidro wanted to scream at him, 'Never call me that again.' Bren was looking up at her in awe, his eyes full of tears. For his life's sake, she supposed, she had best let the others think her a true priestess. She laid a hand on his filthy head.

'May Alshandra protect you always,' she said in Deverrian, then spoke in the Horsekin tongue. 'All of you, listen! No matter what Laz says or does, keep this man safe.'

The gathered outlaws nodded, murmured their agreement, and bowed to her in a ripple of respect. Feeling like the worst fraud in the world, Sidro turned away and followed Laz inside.

By then she was shaking so hard with rage that she could barely speak. Laz put his hands on his hips and watched her. His mouth twitched on the verge of a smile that only infuriated her more. On his right arm the cuts from her fingernails looked like crescent moons tattooed in red.

'That's what you didn't want me to know, isn't it?' Sidro found her voice at last. 'You told me Zakh Gral was safe, but you were lying.'

'I don't see any reason to deny it. Now.'

'You want them destroyed, don't you?' She paused to gulp for breath. 'You lied to me because you didn't want them warned.'

'That's exactly right.' Laz grinned at her. 'I want that stinking fortress and its preposterous shrine reduced to rubble. It's bad enough that the holy fools have taken over my city and infected Braemel. I don't want them spreading their madness any further.'

Sidro grabbed the kitchen knife from the table and threw it at him. He dodged with a quick laugh, then sprang forward as she picked up the red-brown plate.

'No no no.' Laz grabbed her wrist with one hand and the plate with the other. 'Pottery's a rare thing out here in the woods. If you hit me with it, you could break it.'

For a moment she struggled, but he twisted her wrist so hard that she yelped and let go of her improvised weapon. He set it down on the table. As soon as she felt his grip relax on her wrist she pulled her hand free. For a moment she pretended to calm herself, then dashed around him and ran for the door. He came after, grabbed her by the arms from behind, and dragged her to a stop.

'What's this?' he said. 'Surely you're not going to try to warn the fortress.'

'Let me go, you filthy depraved sorcerer!'

'Shan't.' He began to walk backwards, hauling her with him away from the door. 'I can't deny that I'm both depraved and a sorcerer, but I'm quite clean, at least in summer.'

She kicked backwards and caught him on the shin with her much-calloused heel. He squawked, but his grip on her arms stayed strong.

'Think!' he snapped. 'How are you going to get back, Sisi? Do you know precisely where you are? Can you find your way back to Alshandra's road?'

'I've got to try.'

'Even though you'll likely wander in the forest till you starve? Or worse yet, what about the silver wyrm? You'll have to leave the forest to reach Zakh Gral. We may not know why he hates you, but he undeniably does, and what if he's waiting for you? Snap snap! No more Sisi.'

Sidro felt herself go limp, sincerely this time. Laz released her and stepped back. She turned to face him and began rubbing her aching arms.

'It's Lakanza,' Sidro said. 'She's been so good to me. How can I just let her die?'

'Do you think the army's going to kill an old woman? If she were a man, now, or a young woman, who knows what they'd do to her, but Lijik warriors have a sentimental streak when it comes to crones.'

Sidro considered him. He set his hands on his hips, cocked his head to one side, and looked straight at her, so openly that she knew he was telling the truth for a change.

'They might not kill her on purpose, perhaps,' Sidro said. 'But in a battle –'

'Well, there you have a point.' Laz paused for a smirk. 'But I thought all of your holy fools were eager to die for Alshandra. What's that you call it? Witnessing?'

'Just that. But now that I know –' Sidro caught herself on the verge of an admission she hated to make.

'Now that you know what?' His smirk vanished. 'What were you going to say?'

'Oh, I don't know. Something, I forget what.'

'This time you're the one who's lying. Now that you know what?'

Caught by a wave of exhaustion, Sidro leaned back against the edge of the table. 'Now that I know Alshandra's not a goddess,' she whispered. 'Damn you, Laz! You've destroyed everything I loved so much, my vows, my faith, and now Zakh Gral.'

'Don't blame me for Zakh Gral! The Lijik Ganda are the ones trying to bring it down. What makes you so sure they're going to succeed?'

Hope – one sweet note of it – sang in her heart. 'That's true, isn't it?' she said. 'They've not finished building it yet, the fortress I mean, but we've got enough men there to stand a siege. More are supposed to arrive, too, though I'm not sure when. The rakzanir were always talking about reinforcements coming from Braemel.'

'And surely they've got sentries out east of the river. I'm only a filthy depraved outlaw, but even I know enough to have my men keep a watch.'

'That's true, isn't it? Of course they do.'

'You see? You've been wallowing in unnecessary despair. Don't mourn Zakh Gral just yet, Sisi my love. It's quite capable of defending itself. Unfortunately.'

She grabbed the plate and slung it straight for his head. He ducked, twisted, and caught it with his right hand. With a wince and a curse he dropped it onto the bed.

'I hope that hurts,' Sidro said. 'I hope I broke half the bones in your hand.'

'Very nearly.' Laz was concentrating on examining the hand in question. 'But not quite.'

'What a pity!'

'I've never seen you so angry before.' He looked up with a twisted grin. 'Which is odd, considering how often you've raged at me over the years.'

'You get more infuriating the longer I know you.'

'Ah, I see. But you know, just because I do love you, I'm not going to tie you up to keep you here. If you want to go back to Zakh Gral, go. I'll have Pir take you back to Alshandra's road, while I stay here, moaning and rubbing ashes in my hair to mourn your imminent demise by dragon fang.'

'Oh hold your rotten tongue, will you? How can I go back now, knowing what I know? If it weren't for Lakanza, I wouldn't even want to, I suppose. I wish I could beg Alshandra to keep her safe, like I used to, when I believed.'

'Are you going to weep? You'll feel better.'

'I can't even do that. I'm too tired.' With a sigh she sat down on the nearer tree stump.

Laz knelt beside her and laid a gentle hand on her thigh. She laid her hand over his, but she found it too difficult to look him in the face.

'Tell me something, Laz. If Alshandra wasn't a goddess,

what was she? There are all those old stories of miracles. Surely they can't all be lies. Was she just a sorceress?'

'No. As far as I can tell, she was a kind of spirit. The Ancients call them Guardians. Vandar was another one. They're as mortal as you and I, but they have power beyond anything we'll ever be able to command.'

'There are more than just the two, then.'

'A good many more, or so Hazdrubal told me. I remember a few of them. There's a man with a stag's head, and then someone the Ancients call Our Lady of the Beasts. They're both forest spirits. There was a half-fox, half-man, too, who seemed more malicious than powerful. And oh yes, some sort of furred sea creature, a male, and another female the Ancients call Our Lady of the Waves. They're all rather grotesque, living on the astral as they do. Apparently they try to look like creatures on the physical plane, but they're not terribly good at choosing their illusions.'

Sidro grimaced and shuddered.

'Sisi, what's wrong?'

'A grotesque spirit and a mortal, and I was ready to die for her.' She turned her head to look at him. 'I feel so shamed.'

'I'm sorry.' He was watching her without a trace of a smile or a glint of mockery in his eyes. 'You look so sad,' he went on. 'I wish I could do something to make you feel better.'

'The only thing that would help would be warning Lakanza somehow, and that's impossible.'

'Yes, but – wait! I wonder. We know that the white crystal links with the black. Were you the only priestess who used to look into the black one?'

'No. We were all trying to see if we could feel the presence of the holy witness Raena through it. There was some sort of legend that she'd left a message in the stone.'

'Maybe it was more than a legend. I might be able to send them an omen.'

'But you want them dead. Why would you even want to warn them?'

'Only out of love for you.' Laz frowned, staring down at the floor. 'It's a vast thing, the love I bear you.'

Sidro felt like screaming at him, her usual shriek of 'oh don't lie!', but he looked up with eyes so full of genuine warmth that she held her tongue. She'd seen him look at her with lust a thousand times, and with affection almost as often, but never with such a depth of feeling. When she reached out to stroke his hair, he caught her hand and kissed her fingers.

'Let me think about this,' he said. 'There's something about omen crystals in the *Pseudo-Iamblichos Scroll*.'

While Laz studied the book, Sidro left the cabin. She was planning on talking with Bren the Lijik rider, but she saw Faharn standing some yards from the cabin door.

'You can't go in,' Sidro said, 'Laz is studying.'

Faharn turned on his heel and strode off without a word. Sidro felt like yelling something nasty at his retreating back. Instead, she resumed her search for Bren.

She found him sitting on a log bench with Pir and eating cold porridge with his fingers from a cracked bowl. She could tell he'd washed, because his brigga were sopping wet, his hair was clean, and his wet shirt hung from a tree branch nearby. She could have counted his ribs had she wanted, proof that he'd wandered in the forest for a long while. When Sidro walked up, he started to set the bowl down, but she bade him go on eating.

'There be no need on you to kneel or suchlike,' she said in Deverrian. 'But eat not too quickly and too much, or you risk a foul stomach after so much starving.'

'True spoken,' Bren said. 'Holy one, do you despise me for not dying at the dun?'

'I do not, because in your own way you be a true witness to our goddess.' *How could you, Sidro!* she was thinking. *You slimy deceiver!* 'What other news have you for me?'

'I managed to hide until they took the dun,' Bren said. 'Then I pretended to be one of the servants. You see, there were a lot of noble lords in the siege army, and they'd all brought servants, so if anyone asked me who I served, I'd just pick a lord's name and say I was new to his dun. I had to hide my sword, though, and then I never managed to fetch it back before I left. So anyway, I heard the fortguard talking. The gwerbret's sent messages to the high king of all Deverry and to the Mountain Folk as well as his own vassals and allies. The lords say Alshandra's men have been killing farmers out on the border, so they have the right to bring down Zakh Gral. They're lying, aren't they? About the raiding?'

'I wish in my very soul that they did lie,' Sidro said, 'but they do not. Some of our men have gone mad, I do think, slaying the innocent, stealing their women for slaves. Our lords do wish to slay the Westfolk, too, and steal their lands. All those of us here in this camp do decry such things and the false notions some priests spread among the faithful. We be exiles therefore.'

Bren sobbed deep in his throat, just once. For a long moment he stared at the ground, then slowly raised his head. 'I was going to try to warn the fortress,' he said, 'and if you order me to, I will. But I'll be doing it with a cold heart.'

'Nah nah nah! I do have another charge for you.' She turned to Pir and spoke in the Horsekin tongue. 'Can we outfit this man with weapons and a horse?'

'Easily. Movrae won't be needing any of his gear in the Deathworld.' Pir considered Bren for a moment. 'Movrae had the new sort of sabre, but Bren will get used to it with practice.'

'With luck he won't need to swing it.' Sidro returned to Deverrian for Bren. 'Now heed me well! First, there be a need on you to rest and eat. When you be strong again, I shall give you a horse and a sword and send you with messages to the men of the Boar. Ken you them? They do dwell east and north of Lord Honelg's dun, but a short way over the Deverry border.'

'I've heard of them, holy one,' Bren said. 'Are they loyal to our goddess?'

'They be so. There be a need on us to warn them. Will

you ride that message? I shall show you how to see the markings of Alshandra's holy road. It will take you there.'

'Well and good, then.' He smiled, one weary twitch of his mouth.

'Return to your meal,' Sidro said. 'My blessings upon you.'

When Sidro turned to go, Pir got up and followed her. He waited to speak until they'd gone too far for Bren to overhear. 'That were well-spoken.' He used Deverrian. 'He should make trouble for none now.'

'What?' Sidro spoke in their own language, then paused for a laugh more startled than amused. 'I had no idea you spoke the Lijik tongue!'

'Oh, I've tried to learn everything I need to know.' Pir sighed and glanced away. 'Over the years and all.' Without another word he turned and ambled off to rejoin Bren.

Sidro returned to the cabin to find Laz still sitting at the table. He'd set the white crystal pyramid under a wizard light beside the open book of the *Pseudo-Iamblichos* text. Leaning on folded arms, he appeared to be studying both at once, his eyes narrowed, shadowed, so intent that the tattoos around them stood out, as thick as embroidery on his face.

Sidro sat down opposite him, folded her hands in her lap, and waited. Her years as a priestess had taught her patience if naught else. Every now and then Laz would turn a page in the book or mouth a few silent words. Outside the windows the light slowly faded until they sat surrounded by darkness in a pool of silvery glow from the wizard light, but still he read, his knife's edge of a face all concentration. Suddenly he threw his arms in the air and laughed, a long croaking rasp of triumph.

'I think I understand now,' he said, grinning. 'Sisi, look into the showstone. Tell me when you see one of your holy fools looking back.'

Sidro leaned forward on to the table on folded arms and stared into the crystal. She could see through the smoky glass of the black pyramid into the shrine back at Zakh Gral.

Two oil lamps burned on the altar, a sign that someone had come into the shrine to pray. Laz, sitting opposite her, mirrored her pose and stared into the crystal from the other side. For a long while they waited under the silver wizard light until at last she saw a woman's shape moving towards her. Rocca walked up and knelt before the altar. Her mouth moved in the salutation to the holy witness Raena.

'Now, Laz,' Sidro said. 'Rocca's looking into the black pyramid.'

Laz murmured a few words, then let his head drop onto his arms. He had slipped into full trance with his eyes wide open and his mouth slack. The ease with which he could work magic, whether he was transforming himself into the raven or merely translating his consciousness to another level of being, had always frightened her. In the beat of a heart, he could stop being Laz, the man she loved, and turn into someone or something else – so quickly that it made her shudder at the edge of nausea.

When she returned her focus to the white crystal, she realized that she could no longer see Rocca or the shrine. A silver whorl, flickering like a candle flame in a draught, blocked her view. Across from her, Laz lay so still, slumped half across the table, that she feared him dead, but he moaned under his breath and his lips moved to form a few silent words. In a moment he blinked, grinned at her, and sat up, stretching his back as if it pained him.

'Now look into it,' he whispered.

Sidro could see Rocca again, her eyes wide with fear as she rose and saluted the altar. She seemed to be calling out, then turned and rushed away out of the smoky view.

'She saw something, certainly,' Sidro said. 'She's badly frightened.'

'Let's hope it's what I wanted her to see. I sent an image of the Lijik army at the ford.'

'You what? You know what this army looks like?'

'Of course. I've been flying over it for weeks now.'

'So that's where you've been going when you fly, and that's why you haven't wanted to tell me.'

'Yes. They're heading north for the ford.'

'You're sure?'

'Sisi, dearest, how else are they going to cross the river?' Laz started to get up, staggered, and sat down again. 'Ye gods, I'm soaked with sweat, and curse it all! I've drooled all over my sleeve.'

'Shall I bring you some water?'

'Please.' His voice cracked and croaked on the word.

Sidro got up and fetched the bucket of clean water she kept on the windowsill, then found their one cup. He drank greedily, smiling at her between gulps, his face softened by sheer exhaustion.

'You need to sleep,' she said.

'Quite right you are. Let's hope your holy fools interpret the omen correctly.'

He stood up more easily this time and staggered over to the mattress. As soon as he lay down he was asleep, flopped on his back with one arm flung over his face. Sidro doused the wizard light, took off her dress, and lay down next to him.

As she was falling asleep, she remembered Laz telling her that he'd found the crystal in the ruins of Rinbaladelan. *As if I'd believe that!* she thought. All at once she was wide awake, wondering if he'd actually sent a warning to Zakh Gral. Why would he? 'Only out of love for you', he'd told her, a dull spur when it came to urging him to forgive the people who'd tried to kill him. She remembered how he'd looked at her so lovingly. She desperately wanted it all to be true. Was that why he'd said those particular words and given her that look, to ensure she'd believe him?

But what then had frightened Rocca so badly? Sidro lay awake for a long time that night, trying to resolve in her own mind what Laz might or might not have done, and whether or not he'd ever tell her the truth about it. Finally she realized that whether he said yes, he'd sent it or no, he hadn't, she couldn't believe him. Zakh Gral and Rinbaladelan merged in her mind until, that night, she dreamt about a city drowned in forest like breaking waves and saw the raven, drifting high above an army marching to destroy it.

'Ebañy, wait up! If you'd be so kind, I mean.'

The voice belonged to Kov, the dwarven envoy, speaking Elvish with a guttural accent. Salamander turned around and saw him, staff in hand, dodging his way through the noisy Deverry camp. The army had halted for the night's rest not long before. Servants and fighting men swarmed around, putting up tents, clearing grass and digging firepits, rushing this way and that with rations and bedrolls. Salamander waited in a clear spot by a wagon for Kov to catch up.

'I'd like to speak with the Wise One, Dallandra,' Kov said. 'Do you think that's possible?'

'Certainly,' Salamander said. 'Would you be offended if I ask why?'

'No, no, not at all. It's about this staff. It has some very ancient runes on it, and I thought maybe a learned woman like her would know what they meant. I realize it's a trivial matter.'

'Ancient runes are never trivial.'

They found Dallandra supervising her helpers as they set up the healers' tent. When Salamander hailed her, she left the job to her chief apprentice, Ranadario, and came over to join him. After a few moments of shouting at one another over the noise of an army making camp, Dallandra led them inside to the relative quiet of the tent, which smelled of herbs and roots, a spicy blend in the hot summer air, from the packets of medicinals lying stacked on the floor cloth. They stood under the smokehole to catch the last of the sunlight.

'It's about this staff.' Kov waggled it in emphasis. 'I was wondering if you knew anything about the runes upon it. It's very old, at least a thousand years old, in fact.'

'May I?' Dallandra held out her hands.

When Kov handed it over, she spent some while studying the twelve runes, then turned the staff so Salamander could get a good look at them.

'I recognize Rock and Gold,' Kov said, pointing. 'Those two there. This third one might be a very old form of Dust. And of course, there are two Deverry letters at the very beginning.'

Dallandra nodded and continued studying the staff. Her lips moved as if forming words. With a shake of her head, she handed the staff back.

'Two of the symbols are from an ancient version of our syllabary,' she said. 'I recognize them from a scroll that Aderyn left me as a legacy when he died. The one that looks like Dust to you is actually the elven Cloud, and this fourth one is Sky.' She pointed to the runes with a fingertip. 'Two are Gel da' Thae, but there are others that I can't sound out.'

Kov caught his breath, and his eyes grew wide. Dallandra continued to study the runes. 'So, we have twelve marks,' she said eventually. 'Two are in the Mountain language, two in Elvish, two in Gel da' Thae, two from Deverry, and then there are four others that I can't decipher. Tell me, if Rock and Gold stood alone, what would they mean?'

'Earth,' Kov said. 'Earth in the elemental sense, that is.'

'Good, because Cloud and Sky together mean air. These Gel da' Thae marks – well, I can speak something of their tongue, and while I can't read it, I did see an explanation of their writing once. If I'm remembering it a-right, this pair means fire. The Deverry letters –' She glanced at Salamander.

'It could mean Aethyr,' Salamander said. 'The actual word has four letters, but if you say the names of those two aloud, you get eth err.'

'Hah!' Dallandra's eyes gleamed. 'So the symbols that we don't understand should mean water – in some language or another. Bardekian, could it be?'

'No,' Salamander said. 'Their writing is almost the same as the Deverrian, and their word for water is much longer than two letters. Dragonish?'

'A good guess, not that there's much watery about dragons. Kov, when Arzosah returns, you could ask her.'

'I could?' Kov's rose several intervals. He coughed and brought it back down. 'I mean, why, yes.'

'I'll go with you.' Salamander managed to keep from grinning. 'Don't worry. She's quite safe around people she views as useful.'

'Then I'll hope she finds my presence of some benefit. There's a legend about these runes, that they spell out an ancient dweomer spell. Silly, isn't it, how these superstitions spring up?'

'Do you think so?' Dallandra quirked an eyebrow. 'I'd say that it must have some kind of dweomer upon it. The wood should have rotted away by now, if it's as old as you say.'

'What?' Kov frankly stared. 'I never – I mean, I – ye gods, you make a very apt point, Wise One. I, uh, well, um.'

Salamander suppressed another smile. Kov hesitated, looking back and forth between them. Finally he bowed to Dallandra. 'My thanks, Wise One. I very much appreciate your help.'

With a second bow, Kov backed a few steps away, then turned and strode off, his staff over his shoulder. Salamander started to make some pleasantry, but a yawn interrupted. Dallandra looked at him with narrow eyes.

'How much have you been scrying?' she said.

'Too much. I should have known I couldn't hide it from you, oh mistress of mighty magicks. The problem is, I can't see Sidro.' Although he wasn't telling the entire truth, what he was telling was true enough to pass Dallandra's muster, or so he hoped. 'I can find her, but she's built some kind of shield around herself, so I spend a great deal of time trying to break through her defence.'

'If she's using dweomer, she can't still be a priestess.' Dallandra said. 'I wonder where she learned that trick?'

'From our raven mazrak, mayhap? He was following her when last I saw her clearly.'

'You told me, yes, that she'd left the temple and met up with him.'

'Well, now she's living in a forest. She herself is mostly a patch of fog, the clot-of-wool sort you get hanging over Cannobaen in the summer, but I've had glimpses of trees and shadows around her. The raven might well hide in the forest.'

'Just so! Isn't this interesting? Curse it all, I wish I'd seen her in the flesh so I could scry her out. Rori's convinced she was Raena in her last life, or at least, in some life, so she must have a certain amount of dweomer talent.'

'I suspect that all the priestesses do. They merely won't admit it. Rocca can summon the Wildfolk of Aethyr to make a dweomer light, for example, but she insists that Alshandra's sending it to her, and that she herself has naught to do with it.'

'Raena said the same, but in her case, it was accurate enough, though she could work a little dweomer on her own. I suppose Sidro has gifts in this life because of Alshandra's meddling in her last one. But that's only a guess on my part.'

'It sounds reasonable to me. Perhaps you'll meet up with her one fine day, and then we'll know.'

When he returned to his tent, a question of a different sort waited for him. Gerran had been telling Clae what he knew about the Horsekin, and something odd had occurred to him.

'When we were still back at the Red Wolf dun, gerthddyn,' Gerran said, 'you told us a tale about the burning of the Vale of Roses.'

'I did, indeed. It was a translation of a long poem my father recites now and then. I didn't put it in rhyme though, that lying beyond my modest powers.'

'Well, somewhat just struck me. In the tale, you said the Horsekin were small, like demons or suchlike, clinging to their horses' necks.'

'I didn't say that. The tale did. And now that you mention it, I wonder why. The Horsekin are anything but short.'

'Think that scribe of Prince Dar's would know the answer?'

'Most likely. Shall we search him out?'

'Let's go.'

They found Meranaldar sitting near Prince Daralanteriel's tent. When he saw them coming, the scribe rose and bowed to Gerran, then favoured Salamander with the briefest possible nod. He did, however, listen carefully while Salamander explained their question.

'Naught happened to make them grow,' Meranaldar said. 'They've always been large. Making them small was just a poetic convention.'

'I don't understand –'

'Well, they were enemies, so of course they had to be described as ugly and despicable, as their name, Meradan, that is, demons, also indicates. They certainly couldn't be portrayed as the equals of the People, could they?'

'Why not?' Gerran broke in. 'It would have given us a picture of them, and that would have been cursed useful when they showed up again.'

'Ah.' Meranaldar blinked at him for a moment. 'Your lordship, I'd not thought of it that way. But you have to admit it makes for a better tale.'

'Hang the tale! What we needed was hard fact.'

'The sagas present things symbolically. How could those horrible bloodthirsty beings be as tall and graceful as we are?' Meranaldar laid a hand on his own chest. 'Inwardly their souls are shrunken and hairy, so the poets made them consistent, that's all.'

'That's all?' Gerran snapped. 'You mean they lied.'

'No, they were depicting an inner truth.' He turned to Salamander. 'Here, you're a gerthddyn. You know tales. You must see that the poem's better the way it is.'

Salamander saw nothing of the sort, but the point hardly seemed worth arguing. He caught Gerran's eye. 'We've got our answer, don't you think?'

'So we do.' Gerran said. 'My thanks, good scribe. We'd best be getting back to our quarters.'

Late that night, Salamander felt too tired to sleep at the same time as he wanted nothing more than to sleep. He went for a walk through the camp, then left it for the sake of silence. The new moon, close to setting in the clear sky, tempted him too badly for him to resist using it as a focus. He scried for Rocca and saw her sleeping, lying in straw heaped on a stone floor. And what was she going to say to him, he wondered, if they met again? *If she lives*, he thought. *If they let her live*. The prince would no doubt give the women of the fortress the chance to leave unharmed, but would the rakzanir let them take it? He could do nothing but wait and see.

'Laz,' Pir said, 'the only thing worth eating in this camp is meat. The men are starting to grumble. I sent the last of the horses' grain off with Bren for his mount. He won't reach the Boar dun without it. You've got to go raiding, and you've got to do it soon.'

'So we do,' Laz said. 'There's that big farming village north of here. We've not paid them one of our visits since the spring.' He glanced at Sidro. 'I don't suppose you'd care to join me and the fellows?'

'I most certainly wouldn't,' Sidro said. 'It's bad enough knowing I'm eating stolen food. I don't want to watch you steal it.'

'Suit yourself. Pir will stay here, being of much the same noble turn of mind as you. I'm surprised he didn't end up in a temple like you did.'

The horse mage gave Laz a look that Sidro found hard to interpret. Annoyance, most likely, at the tease, but something else flickered in his dark eyes. Contempt, perhaps?

'Vek never goes with us, either, but mostly because he's too young,' Laz went on. 'We'll be gone several days. Don't worry about me, Sisi. This lot won't give us any trouble.'

Although Faharn would officer the raiding party on the ground, Laz would fly ahead and lead them in his raven form. The magical raven always frightened the villagers into obedience, or so he told her. Sidro supposed that the fifteen

Horsekin spearmen he was bringing along would frighten them a fair bit more, but she refrained from pointing that out. Pir accompanied them when they left the camp, but only to help them with the packhorses, which he pastured during the day in forest clearings.

Now that she'd left Alshandra's worship behind, Sidro had returned to the scrupulous cleanliness that she'd learned as a slave child. First she took Laz's clothes and her own linen shift down to a stream and pounded them clean, then hung them from low-growing branches to dry. Next she set work on the cabin, despite the way her leather dress chafed without the shift under it. First she made a broom of twigs and swept the filthy rushes and pine needles out of the cabin. Down by the stream fresh rushes grew in profusion. She pulled big armfuls of them, then spread them out in front of the cabin to dry.

For the pine needles she'd need an edge sharper than the kitchen knife. She searched through the camp until she found an axe and a big basket, then returned to the forest and cut a number of slender branches. Trimming the needles from the pitch-sticky twigs proved difficult. She was struggling with the job when she heard someone walk up behind her. With a yelp, she spun around, clutching the axe, but it was only Pir, returned from seeing the raiders on their way.

'I'll do that for you if you like,' he said.

'Thank you.' She handed him the axe. 'You're doubtless better with this than I am. Do you have a spare shirt I can wash in return?'

'No.' He leaned the axe against a tree, then pulled off the shirt he was wearing. Soft dark hair rippled on his chest and arms and down his back. 'But I'd appreciate it if you could do something with this one. It, um, well, stinks, not to put too subtle a word upon it, as Laz would say.'

Stink it certainly did. Sidro hurried to the stream and immersed it straightaway to soak, weighted down with stones. The cloth, once sturdy farm-spun wool, had worn so thin in places that she hated to pound it clean. *What are we all going to do in the winter?* she wondered. *None of us have cloaks or anything but old blankets to keep us warm.* When she realized that she'd started thinking of the band of outlaws as 'we', she nearly wept.

Once the shirt was as clean as she could get it, Sidro hung it to dry with the others. She sat on the ground and watched Pir strip branches of their needles against the edge of the axe.

'Been meaning to ask you,' Pir said. 'Could you do the coming of age ceremony for Vek? His hair sprouted months ago, but we didn't have a woman with us to work the rite.'

'I don't see why not. Do you believe in the old gods, Pir?'

'No, nor in the new one, either.'

'Yet you want the ceremony done?'

'I don't. Vek does. He was brought up to expect it.'

'So he was. Very well, then. Do you remember much from your own ceremony?'

'Yes, most of it, if you want me to be the sponsor.'

'If you would. You know that Laz won't do it. He'll only mock and sneer.'

Pir smiled, just a twitch of his mouth, but for him it amounted to a smile. For a few moments he concentrated on his work.

'There's something else Vek asked me,' Pir said, looking up. 'He told me that he wants to become a true prophet of the old gods. I pointed out that no one wants to listen to his kind of prophecies any more, but he insisted it doesn't matter. Do you know how to perform the prophet's rite?'

'No, I certainly don't! It would be too dangerous anyway, out here with no healer for miles and miles. What if something went wrong?'

'I did ask him that. He said he was willing to risk it.'

'Does he know how much it's going to hurt?'

'Oh yes. He told me all about it.' Pir's mouth twisted in distaste. 'Having a slit cut into your – well, imph – manhood, and then a stone put into the cut, and all the rest of it. It makes me sick to think about it. But Vek told me that he has to become both male and female or the goddesses won't accept him.'

'Well, luckily for him, I can't help him do it.'

'I suppose it's lucky. Sometimes I envy Vek. He's lost his mach-fala, his home, his city – everything he ever had in life. But it doesn't matter to him. He has his gods, and he's determined to serve them. And he says that it's enough.'

'I used to feel that way. Once.'

'But now you know the truth about your Alshandra.'

'Yes. It's a very bitter thing, that truth. I suppose I was happier with the lies, but truth is always better than falsehood.'

'Is it?' Pir frowned at the basket of needles. 'I begin to wonder. Consider our rakzanir. Will they ever become Gel da' Thae, true Gel da'Thae, I mean, without Alshandra or someone like her to believe in? All they did before was fight among themselves. Now at least they're fighting someone else.'

'Oh yes. They're planning on slaughtering the Ancients and taking their land. I don't see where this is a step away from savagery.'

'Ah. You're quite right, now that I think of it. Um, well. Yes. Um.' With a sigh Pir stood up. 'Here's the first basketful. I'll cut more if you'll take these back.'

That night Pir lit a bonfire in the ashy pit where Movrae had died. The men who'd stayed in camp gathered around, spears in hand, to welcome Vek into their ranks when the moment came. The ceremony itself was simple and short. Pir brought the boy forward and told him to kneel before the priestess. Sidro combed Vek's hair with her fingers, found a bit long enough to braid, and tied into it one of Laz's old charms that she'd discovered in the detritus on the cabin floor.

'You have left the arms of your mother,' she said. 'Where will you stand in the ranks of men?' She whispered under her breath. 'Turn and look at Pir now.'

When Vek followed her order, Pir stepped forward. For the

ceremony he'd washed himself to match his clean shirt
and combed and re-braided his mane as well. It hung in a
splendid cascade over one side of his head, revealing the
close-cropped hair on the rest of it. In the leaping firelight
his face gleamed like the charms tied into the braids. Long
glints of light flew from his hunting knife when he drew it
and held it point up.

'Answer the truth,' Pir said. 'Or die.'

'I will,' Vek said. He smiled in such sweet delight that, Sidro
assumed, he was seeing some deity behind the actual man.

'Will you walk in the ranks of warriors?' Pir said.

'Never!'

One at a time, Pir named the choices a man might make
at this ceremony. Vek answered 'never' to each on the brief list.

'What then will you do?' Pir finished.

'Serve the goddesses and gods all my life,' Vek said. His
voice choked on tears although he kept smiling. 'And die
when they wish me to.'

'So be it!' Pir grabbed the boy's left hand and scratched
its back with the point of his knife. 'Blood and fire have
witnessed your vow.'

Vek raised his hand and let the blood run down his arm
for all to see. The men in the surrounding circle lifted their
spears and cried out, 'Hai! Hai! Hai!' Vek rose, still smiling
as if he saw a thousand delights spread before him, and
turned to Sidro.

'Walk as a man from now on,' she said. 'Ride as a man
always.'

Once again came the ancient chant, 'Hai! Hai! Hai!' Sidro
stamped her foot three times, and the ceremony had ended.

Although she'd fretted enough about the ritual cut to bring
a scrap of cloth for a bandage, Pir had managed to keep the
scratch shallow. By the time Sidro examined it, the blood
had already stopped running. She bound it up anyway to
keep the ever-present camp dirt out of it, then sent Vek off
with the rest of the men. Pir lingered with her at the fire.

'Very nice,' he said.

'Thank you. I have this awful feeling I forgot a speech in the middle, but the ritual pleased Vek, and that's the main thing.'

'That speech was boring, anyway.' Pir thought for a moment. 'I don't remember much about it. The priestess droned on about never betraying your mach-fala, but um well, he's already done that, hasn't he? Betrayed them, I mean, by having magic.'

'Perhaps they've betrayed him, rather, by hating him for it.'

'Ah.' Pir looked at her sharply. 'Hadn't thought of it that way.'

Sidro met his glance, then forgot what she was about to say. She found herself wondering what it would be like to stroke his close-cropped hair, to run her fingers through the hair on his chest. He stared back at her, unsmiling, silent, but she knew that he too felt the sudden attraction between them, because his scent began to change. Horse mages, however, learned to control their scents. After that first unmistakable waft of sexual desire, his returned to the normal smell of a man who's stood close to a fire on a warm night. He started to speak, swallowed the words, then turned and strode off. Sidro stayed where she was until two of the other men came back with shovels to smother the bonfire.

As she walked back to the cabin, she was wondering what her own scent had revealed. *It's the ceremony*, she thought. *Somehow we worked magic together*. She'd never thought of the coming of age ritual as sorcery. As she mulled it over, she realized that Vek's presence and his deep-rooted magical gifts had brought power into what was usually a mere social occasion. The power had caught her and Pir both unawares until that moment by the fire. That night she dreamt of the horse mage, but if he'd done the same about her, he gave no sign of it when she saw him in the morning.

Laz led the raiding party back into camp late that day. Whooping in triumph, the men who'd been left behind rushed to unload the booty from the packhorses. The raven landed at the cabin door, then hopped and fluttered his way inside to his perch. Sidro stayed outside, watching Pir collect the horses, until Laz strolled out in human form, dressed in the clean shirt and brigga she'd washed for him, his brown hair roughly combed, like feathers ruffled by the wind.

'My thanks,' he said, patting the linen over his chest. 'But I could have washed it myself.'

'It gave me something to do while you were gone,' Sidro said. 'I gather everything went well.'

'Yes, it did. I managed to extort some linen cloth for you, by the by, from a fairly well-off woman who, or so the farmers told me, is the local miser and deserves it.' He smiled with an odd twist to his mouth – covering not a lie but an apology. 'I have a small spark of moral sense left, I suppose.'

'Well, thank you. I have to admit that I need something to wear besides this shift. I don't suppose you thought to steal me some needles and thread.'

Laz swore under his breath.

'That means no, I take it,' Sidro said. 'Oh well, maybe you can find a peddlar in the woods and waylay him.'

'Ah, a jest! Your good humour returns at last. I can whittle you a bone needle. This cloth looks like a very loose weave to me.'

'That will do, most likely. I can pull some of its own threads or lace it with thongs.'

'Good. But you know, I did see something very odd in the woods, though not a peddlar, alas. When I was flying home, I spotted a small party of our Gel da' Thae compatriots, on foot, coming down from the north.'

'You didn't summon your men to rob them, too?'

'I considered it. They were leading a mule that looked pretty well loaded down. But I recognized their leader, so I decided to leave them alone.'

'What? Who was it?'

'The Most Exalted Mother Grallezar, head of the Braemel town council.'

For a moment Sidro found it impossible to speak. 'In the forest?' she said at last. 'Not on the Braemel Road?'

'Stumbling around among the trees, yes. Hiding from someone, I'd say.'

'Do you know what that must mean?'

'Your holy fools have taken over Braemel.'

'Just that. It pains me to admit this, but I'm horrified.'

Dallandra had learned of Braemel's fate from Grallezar herself, when the Gel da' Thae leader finally reached her mind to mind and begged her for help. With an escort of thirty mounted archers, Dallandra rode out to find her just below the cliffs at the forest verge. Her archers led extra horses, because Grallezar had warned her that two of her four loyal men were wounded, one badly from a spear thrust to the ribs, and the other with an arm broken in a good many places from a blow with a heavy club. When they saw the elven party approaching through the grass, the Gel da' Thae stopped walking and merely stood, heads bowed, to wait. Grallezar herself could barely stand. She leaned against a laden mule who looked as weary as she did.

With a shout, the Westfolk men surrounded them, then dismounted and hurried forward to help the men. Dallandra swung down from her saddle and rushed to greet her friend. Like the average Horsekin woman, Grallezar was taller than many Deverry men, and as well-muscled, too, but at that moment she looked frail. The dust of her frantic journey smeared the green tattoos covering her face. Somewhere in the forest she'd lost the leather cap that usually protected her shaved head, which had sprouted a brownish stubble in compensation. Her dress, once the finest buckskin, had rips and stains all over it. When Dallandra put her arms around her in greeting, she could feel Grallezar trembling.

'Thank every god you're alive!' Dallandra said.

'I suppose I'm glad, for all the good it is,' Grallezar said. 'I left Braemel with over twenty loyal people and as many horses. These four men and the mule are all that survived.'

'Ah, gods!'

'We had to fight our way free,' Grallezar went on. 'We managed to kill all the attackers. May the Light be thanked, I can scry out those filthy priest-dogs. I saw them waiting for their soldiers to return. By the time they realized they weren't coming back, we were long gone.'

'I cannot tell you how glad I am that you escaped.'

'Dalla, they were going to burn our books. Every scrap of the dweomerlore we've put together with so much work over so many years – they wanted to burn it all.'

'And you with it, I suppose.'

Grallezar shrugged her own danger away. 'We saved it, though.' Her voice broke, but she steadied it again. 'Every book I had I brought, and I had copies of everything.' She turned to stroke the mule's nose. 'He's carrying them all.'

'Good. Let's get you and your men back to camp so I can treat the wounded.'

When they reached the encampment, Dallandra took Grallezar to her own tent to eat and rest, then did what she could for the two injured men. Both would recover, as she told Grallezar later that day, when the Gel da' Thae leader woke after a long afternoon's sleep. Since they were alone, they could speak in the strange mixture of Elvish and the Horsekin tongue they'd developed on their various visits.

'The army will camp here tonight, so we won't have to move them immediately,' Dallandra said. 'We're waiting for scouts to return.'

'I see.' Grallezar paused to rub her face with both hands. 'Dalla, we're really here, aren't we? I'm not just dreaming this or meeting you on the astral or some such thing, am I?'

'You're not. You're safe in my tent.'

Grallezar looked up with a long sigh. For a moment she stared out at nothing, then sighed again. 'It's an evil day indeed,' she said, 'when my city would open its gates to savage tribesmen.'

'Is that what happened?'

'Yes. The Alshandra people got themselves elected to the council, you see, then voted an alliance with the northerners – those are the people who settled Taenalapan. When I objected, they stirred up their mob against me.' But Grallezar suddenly smiled, revealing her long teeth, filed into points like fangs. 'My city may be lost to me, but I'll pray that Zakh Gral pays the price for it. I hope to every god that your army razes it to ashes. I hope they kill every man in it.'

'Oh, if they can, they will. Have no fear about that.'

Dallandra had some hard questions to ask Grallezar, but the leaders of the army were as eager to talk with her as she was. A page came with a polite summons and interrupted their talk. Dallandra accompanied her to Prince Voran's peaked tent, where Gwerbret Ridvar, Prince Daralanteriel, Warleader Brel and Envoy Kov stood waiting. In the rising evening wind their banners, carried by the heralds who stood behind each man, snapped and fluttered with their devices, the gold wyvern, the red rose, Cengarn's blazing sun, the dwarven axe. At the sight Grallezar caught Dallandra's hand and squeezed it.

'Courage!' Dallandra murmured. 'They won't dare harm you, not with me here.'

Indeed, Prince Voran behaved like the flower of courtesy. He had his canvas stool brought for Lady Grallezar, as he called her, and a stoup of Bardek wine as well, which he personally handed to her. Yet Dallandra was aware of the other lords eyeing the Gel da' Thae women with a mixture of awe and suspicion, the way they might view some huge Bardekian lion brought to them in a cage. Even Daralanteriel – Dallandra stored up a few choice words to say to him later.

Prince Voran knelt beside Grallezar's chair with a friendly smile. Someone must have told him that she spoke a dialect of Deverrian, because he addressed her in that language.

'My lady, if you've rested enough, it would gladden my heart if you'd tell us your tale.'

'My thanks,' Grallezar said. 'It be a familiar tale, here in the Northlands, but no doubt not one you hear off to the east. Once there were six cities of Gel da' Thae, though Taenalapan and Braemel were the largest. Now there be six towns ruled by Horsekin savages. Braemel, it were the last to fall to these loathsome dogs of priestesses and prophets. The price they did pay for those towns, it were high, a price of blood, not that these madmen count death as a peril.'

'These savages,' Voran said, 'are they your northern tribes, then? We've heard about them.'

'Some are, but their leaders, they be bred inside town walls as Gel da' Thae. In the end they did prove themselves as brutal as any northerner, and all in the name of their goddess. This Alshandra poison, it did well up among the tribes, but then it did spread to the cities. One by one they fell to Alshandra's people. Mine, it were the last. Their leaders did corrupt our troops and win them over.'

'They have well-armed regular troops, then?'

'They do, officered by our own rakzanir, driven mad by dreams of loot and pasture land, all promised by the false prophets who think this Alshandra creature still lives.'

The men listening glanced at one another with expressionless eyes, their faces as grim as stone.

'I don't suppose, my lady,' Voran said, 'that you'd know how many of these troops they have.'

'Why would I not know? Were I not once the commander of those men Braemel could summon to war?'

Voran grimaced at his gaffe and bobbed his head in her direction. 'My apologies,' he said. 'Your ways are still new to me.'

'No doubt.' Grallezar tried to soften her remarks with a smile, but the sight of her pointed fangs made the prince wince again. 'Each town, it did support a thousand men at arms, to say naught of the citizens who would muster to fight in times of war. But that were before town upon town did turn on its fellows and battle them. Many have died, your highness, and the rakzanir, they did strip their garrisons for the building of Zakh Gral.'

'Thank every god!' Ridvar muttered. When Kov shot him a warning glance and shook his head in a no, Ridvar had the decency to blush. Grallezar pretended to take no notice, but Dallandra saw her glance flick the young gwerbret's way and back.

'Let me trouble you for one last question,' Voran said to her. 'The northern tribes, will they be riding to Zakh Gral's aid?'

'They be here already, your highness. Once a town did go over to the worship of Alshandra, its leaders did bring men from the north to swell the ranks of its armies, fresh and ready to conquer the next town should it hold out for the old ways. So the armies now, they be led by men who ken the ways of fighting, but the men they lead, some ken little but rushing into the enemy ranks and laying about them with whatever weapon they have to hand.'

'I see.' The prince got up and bowed. 'You have my humble thanks, my lady. Please, go back to your friend's tent and rest yourself. In the morning, come tell me what you wish to do next, whether to remain with the Westfolk or take refuge in Deverry.'

'Refuge in the Slavers' Country?' Grallezar rose from her chair and smiled again, all fangs. 'Refuge in the Slavers' Country! Those words, they be ill-matched in my mind, your highness.'

'No doubt, considering the ill will between our two peoples in the past, but I'd gladly offer you shelter in Dun Deverry itself. I think me that my father, the high king, would consider lending you an army to see you rightfully restored to your city.'

'Would he now?' Grallezar, just the same height as the prince, was looking straight at him with a faint smile hovering around her fanged mouth. 'Among my folk the children have a little toy. Mayhap your folk do whittle somewhat like it. On the end of two sticks there stands a tiny wooden warrior with a spear. The children may push the sticks up and down and see the warrior fling his arms about and wave his spear. It be a clever thing, but truly, your highness, never have I wanted to be one.'

Voran opened his mouth and shut it again. Dallandra risked a quick glance at Kov and saw him grinning in open admiration.

'My friend Dallandra did offer me shelter, your highness,' Grallezar continued. 'I shall take that. No doubt I can find honourable work tending her horses.'

Grallezar dropped the prince a curtsey, then turned and strode off. Dallandra had to run to catch up to her. As they walked back through the camp, Grallezar kept her gaze firmly on the ground in front of her. All the men, whether they were Westfolk, Mountain Folk, or Deverry bred, stared as she went past. Dallandra felt like screaming at all of them to mind their courtesies.

Once they'd regained the safety of the tent, Grallezar sank onto a pile of leather cushions. Dallandra sat cross-legged on the floor cloth. She had crucial questions to ask, and all of them distressed her. They sat in silence until Dallandra realized that she needed to be blunt.

'I absolutely have to ask you something,' Dallandra said.

'I know what it is,' Grallezar said. 'Why didn't I tell you years ago about the savages in Taenalapan?'

'That's one question.'

'I was afraid your men would raise an army and come destroy it. They barely accepted the existence of us Gel da' Thae as it was. If they'd known that the northerners were moving south, they would have wanted to destroy all of us.'

'That might have happened, yes.'

'Besides, when Mother Zatcheka made the alliance with your people and with the men of the Rhiddaer, all those years ago, Taenalapan was no more than a town, a small town at that, not a city at all. It wasn't till some years ago that I realized how big it had grown.' Grallezar leaned forward, all urgency. 'It's the tribes, Dalla. Some thousands of them settled in Taenalapan about twenty years ago. They brought slaves to do the farming, and horses to trade, and bit by bit, they took the town over.'

'Just like they did to your city.'

'Yes. Now I wish I had told you.' Grallezar paused and looked away, stark-eyed. 'I wish your men had come and burned Taenalapan to the ground. If I had had the omen-gift, if I'd seen what would happen, I would have led my own city's troops out and helped them.' Grallezar's voice quivered and nearly broke. 'Too late now.'

'Tell me something else,' Dallandra said. 'Why have your folk turned to Alshandra like this? Oh, I know that it's a comfort, thinking you'll go to some wonderful country when you die, and the rakzanir want lands to conquer, but surely that can't be all.'

'It isn't, of course. Do you want the truth? It may pain you.'

'There are a good many things in life that pain me. So far I've survived them all.'

'Very well, then. Do you remember when we first met, all those years ago in Cerr Cawnen? My people then thought you were the children of the gods, and they were terrified of you and yours. Prince Dar made things worse by humiliating that rakzan, whatever his name was – I've forgotten.'

'Krag, Kraal, something like that. I do remember how your mother's men kept kneeling to us. Your stepbrother Meer used to do that to me, too, no matter what I told him.'

'Well, after that meeting in Cerr Cawnen, the truth spread fast. Yes, our people had done a horrible thing to yours, but you were mortals such as we, not gods, not favoured by the gods any more than we were. The Great Burning was a terrible burden of guilt, Dalla, a burden we carried for a thousand years. The priestesses had built all our rituals, our prayers, our sacrifices, around that guilt. And suddenly we threw the burden down.'

Dallandra felt the hair on the back of her neck rise in a dweomer chill.

'Ah,' Grallezar continued, 'You're beginning to understand, aren't you? I can tell by your shiver.'

'Let me guess. The priestesses of the old gods looked like liars and fools.'

'You're precisely right. What had happened in the past all looked new again, and we began to remember how we had suffered, not at your hands, but from the Lijik Ganda.'

'And now your people want revenge on them?'

'Right again. Oh, the rakzanir have worked everyone up so cleverly about those old horrors. A thousand years old and more, those stories, but oh so useful! After the great revelation, we'd begun to call your people the Ancients rather than 'children of the gods'. We all thought we should respect you, until the rakzanir saw that you stood in the way.' Grallezar paused for a fanged smile. 'And of course, they also saw that the way you were standing in happened to cross good grazing land. Suddenly we began hearing about Vandar's spawn. Those so-called holy women – oh ye gods! Can't they see how they're being used? They talk about Alshandra's love, but they're nothing but weapons to the rakzanir.'

The dweomer-chill deepened around Dallandra so badly that she shivered. 'I'm going to have to tell Cal all of this,' she said. 'I hope you realize that.'

'Why do you think I'm telling you? I couldn't bring myself to tell him or that sly little Lijik prince, but you can.' Her smile vanished. 'And that's another reason why I couldn't tell you about Braemel. I knew where your loyalties lay. I never dreamt that mine would someday lie with yours.'

Again, grief trembled in Grallezar's outspread hands. In silence she waited for Dallandra's judgment. As Dallandra thought back over the last ten years or so, she could remember all the times that Grallezar had seemed distant, evasive, but she could also remember hints that something might be wrong, little clues and allusions that Dalla might have followed up, might have asked her to clarify, if only she had realized how important they were, as if her friend were hoping that she'd demand the truth.

'Well, the past is past,' Dallandra said at last. 'You're forgiven.'

Grallezar let out her breath with a sharp sigh. 'Thank you.'

They clasped hands, but both found it too hard to smile.

'What now?' Grallezar said. 'For me, I mean. My men want to fight in your army, but I'm too old. My hair gets more brown in it every time I let it grow. I know very little healing lore, but surely there's work I can do. I'm willing to tend your horses, as I told the prince.'

'That will hardly be necessary.'

'But if naught else, you'll have to let me do any lifting and hauling of heavy things.'

'Um, why?'

'Don't you know?' Grallezar sniffed the air, thought for a moment, sniffed again, then nodded as if affirming something to herself. 'You're pregnant.'

'Oh no! Not now! Oh no no no!'

'The goddesses are never convenient, are they?'

'Apparently not! I can't think of a worst time. Here, please, don't tell anyone, will you? Cal will try to send me away, and I've absolutely got to be here for a great many reasons.'

'Very well.' Grallezar gave her a tentative smile. 'Your men really don't know their place, do they?'

Much to her surprise, Dallandra found she could laugh, and Grallezar joined her.

'You're not far along,' Grallezar paused for another sniff. 'It's too early to tell whether it's male or female. How long do your folk carry your babies?'

'A full year, and sometimes a moon beyond that.'

And thank the gods for it, too, Dallandra thought. *There's no reason for Cal to know yet.*

At dawn the next morning Arzosah and Rori flew back to the army with the news that the Galan Targ lay close ahead. Dallandra realized with a coldness around her heart that the battles for Zakh Gral were about to begin.

As the army made its slow way towards the ford of the Galan Targ, the two princes, the avro and the gwerbret rode together, talking back and forth, at the head of the line of march. Lesser lords, such as Gerran, rode some distance behind, out of earshot, though Gerran could see that some kind of argument was talking place. He noticed as well that Kov, Grallezar and Calonderiel rode just behind the commanders, close enough to lean forward and shout things into the conversation. Around noon, when the army came within sight of the river, the commanders called the usual halt to feed their men and rest the horses, then sent the dragons ahead to scout.

Gerran and Salamander walked a few hundred yards away from the camp to a low swell of ground from which they could see the ford. At this point the river stretched broad and shallow, maybe fifty yards across but not more than four feet deep. Big grey stones marked out a safe route across.

'Someone made this ford, I'll wager,' Gerran said. 'They must have widened the channel to let the water spread out.'

'It does look like that,' Salamander said. 'The hard work was doubtless all done by slaves.'

Gerran snorted in disgust.

On the other side of the river scrub grass and weeds covered an area of uneven ground that stretched towards the west for about a hundred yards. Beyond lay scruffy second-growth forest. This weedy terrain, as far as Gerran could tell, rose to heavily wooded hills at some middle distance. In the heat of the summer's day, the river murmured, and insects swarmed along its banks. Otherwise nothing moved, but the hair on the back of Gerran's neck rose. Someone was watching him. He looked up, shading his eyes with one hand, then laughed. Salamander caught the gesture and did the same.

'It's just a raven,' Gerran said. 'I've seen one following us now and then.'

'It's a raven, all right.' Salamander sounded so alarmed that Gerran shot him a puzzled glance.

'Ravens do follow armies,' Gerran said. 'They always seem to know when a feast's on its way.'

'Oh, true spoken!'

Salamander's tone struck Gerran as oddly brittle, but his face gave nothing away. Gerran looked back up and studied the raven – a strangely large bird, he realized. All of a sudden the raven croaked and flew, darting away as fast as its wings would work and heading north to the forest cover. Gerran heard a sound like a distant drum, coming closer.

'The bird's got good ears,' Gerran said. 'It doesn't seem to like the dragon's company.'

'Sensible, I'd call it,' Salamander said, grinning. 'Shall we go back to camp?'

The dragon turned out to be Arzosah, returned with the news that Rori was scouting out the fort itself and would bring back information shortly. Gerran overheard Kov ask Salamander for an introduction to the black wyrm. Since he'd always wanted to meet her, he followed them out to the sunny spot where Arzosah was resting. She greeted them all graciously and listened with attention when the envoy showed her its staff.

'None of those runes are Dragonish,' Arzosah said. 'Those four peculiar ones, though – I did see somewhat very much like them once, cut onto rocks up in the north country.'

'You don't think they're a different form of Horsekin writing, do you?' Kov said.

'I don't, because that far north none of the Horsekin know how to read and write. It's a Gel da' Thae trait, writing. Let me think – where was – by a river. That's all I can remember, alas. It was in the wilderness somewhere, a big river that was flowing south. Not very helpful, I'm afraid.'

'Still, my humble thanks for allowing me to impose upon you,' Kov said.

'Ah, what nice manners!' Arzosah swung her enormous head towards Salamander. 'That banadar person could take lessons.'

'What counts now,' Salamander said, suppressing a grin, 'is crossing the river we know and see. We'll have time later for worrying about the rivers we know not, if the gods kindly allow us all to live long enough.'

In the event, the army crossed the ford without incident. Although the Mountain Folk grumbled about the depth of the water, they eventually got their carts across dry by hoisting them up, six men to a cart, and carrying them. By the time everyone had crossed and reformed the line of march, the sun hung low in the western sky. The army found, running parallel to the river, a decent road of gravel and hard-packed earth mixed with some sort of binding substance that none of the Deverry men or Westfolk had ever seen before. Envoy Kov, however, knew exactly what it was.

'Rhwmani stone, we call it,' Kov told Gerran. 'I don't know why, but that's its name. We make it, too, but I'm shocked to see that the Gel da' Thae know the secret.'

The Rhwmani road turned out to make travelling a fair bit easier for cart and horse alike. The army, however, had marched for only a mile or two when the silver dragon re-appeared, circling high over the line. One massive paw dangled under him.

'Is he hurt?' Gerran asked Salamander.

'He's not,' Salamander said. 'He's carrying somewhat. His dinner, most like.'

Rori came to earth a decent distance away among the brush and scrub growth off to the west. When the order came down the line to halt and make camp for the night, Salamander dismounted and called to Gerran that he was going to speak with the dragon. Gerran swung down from the saddle, tossed his reins to Clae, and followed the gerthddyn out of simple curiosity.

As they approached, Gerran realized that the dragon's prey

was no deer or cow, but a Horsekin warrior, lying sprawled on the ground in front of the silver wyrm. Blood oozed from the corner of his mouth and stained the sides of his pale tan brigga. A few drops spattered his linen shirt as well. Salamander hurried forward and in Elvish spoke to the dragon, who was sitting on his haunches like a giant cat, tail wrapped around his front paws.

'Is he dead?' Gerran was speaking to Salamander, but the dragon answered in perfect Deverrian.

'He's not,' Rori said. 'Fainted dead away, but not truly dead. You'd best disarm him while he's still out.'

The Horsekin carried a sword on a baldric rather than on his belt. The peculiar scabbard, lozenge-shaped and re-inforced with strips of brass along its edges, hung across his lap, an odd angle for a weapon. When, however, the Horsekin stood or rode upright, Gerran realized, it would lie to one side but horizontally, the hilt near the rider's hand, the point safely free of leg and stirrup. He unbuckled it, laid it down next to him, and pulled the man's dagger from his belt as well. He looked up to see the dragon watching him.

'You are?' Rori said.

'Gerran of the Gold Falcon. My honour, I'm sure, to meet you.'

Rori's cornflower-blue eyes considered him – sadly, Gerran realized. 'You won't remember me,' Rori said. 'Ah well. Take a look at that blade, Gerran. You're in for a surprise.'

When Gerran drew the sabre from its scabbard, he swore aloud. 'I've never seen anything like this,' he said.

The weapon, about four feet long overall, had a hilt that was more of a handle – a squared-off loop of steel decorated on one corner with a horse's head in silver. The blade was not only curved, but towards its point it swelled to a sharp angle before tapering again. When Gerran laid a cautious finger-tip on the edges, he found it dull on the outer but razor-sharp on the inner. He slipped his hand in to the loop and gave the sabre an experimental swing. Thanks to the extra weight near the tip, it snapped around with extra force to match. If you rode a fleeing man down, Gerran realized, then swung at his neck, his head would come half off his shoulders with one smooth stroke.

'It be called a falcata,' Grallezar said from behind him. 'Nasty little things. Very effective from horseback.'

Gerran rose, his hands full of the falcata and Horsekin dagger, and made her an awkward bow. Dallandra had accompanied her; she nodded at Gerran, then hurried past him to kneel down beside the wounded Horsekin, who was just coming around with a few mumbled words.

'A scout,' Rori said. 'The others got away. I wanted you all to have a close look at that sabre. Arzosah's off hunting, so she'll keep a watch on the enemy camp.'

The Horsekin moaned and tried to sit up. He looked around him, saw Dallandra and the dragon, and fainted again.

'He's lost a lot of blood,' Dallandra said. 'Your claws, I assume.'

'I tried to keep from killing him, but without thumbs, it's wretchedly hard to be delicate.'

'Well, he'll live. He won't be trying to escape, either.'

'I suppose that gladdens my heart.' Rori sighed in a melancholy way. 'I never appreciated thumbs before, I'm afraid. The things one learns too late!'

Although Gerran had certainly believed Salamander, that the dragon had once been a human being, he hadn't truly understood what that might mean to the dragon himself. He did then, and bile rose in his throat. He covered the feeling by turning away and calling to Salamander.

'The princes will want to see this falcata,' Gerran said. 'I'm cursed glad we know what we're facing. Can you take it to them?'

'The princes and the gwerbret are on their way here to listen to Rori's report,' Dallandra said. 'Gerran, Ebañy, you'd best leave those weapons with Grallezar and go back to camp.'

At sunset, the commanders summoned every lord of the

rank of tieryn, as well as Calonderiel and Brel Avro, for a council. It was long after sunset when Cadryc returned to the Red Wolf camp and squatted down next to Gerran at his fire. While they talked, they kept a look-out for the gwerbret or any of his men.

'They're ready for us, all right,' Cadryc said. 'They had a good scatter of scouts posted. The black dragon saw two men riding like the Lord of Hell was chasing them. They reached the fortress just after dawn today. Not long after a small army rode out. They're marching up from the fortress towards our position. They were some ten miles away, the last Rori saw of 'em.'

'I'm not surprised, your grace,' Gerran said. 'You can't hide an army this size under a blade of grass.'

'True spoken. That arrogant cub Ridvar was surprised, or he pretended to be. He had the gall to suggest we might have a traitor in our ranks.' Cadryc snorted profoundly. 'Looked right at me, too, the ill-got little –' He swallowed the last word and snorted again. 'The dragon put him right, he did. Said he'd never known the Horsekin to be either blind or stupid, and especially not both at once.'

'We bested Ridvar over your grandson. It's the honour of the thing that won't let him drop it. Eventually the prince and his councillor will talk some sense into him.'

'So we may hope. Cursed if I know how I'm going to get through the next few years with him as my sworn overlord.' Cadryc paused to chew on the ragged ends of his moustache. 'Be that as it may, lad, there was a blasted lot more shouting than sense at that council. It boils down to this. If we insist on riding to battle, the dragons can't join in. How can they spook the Horsekin mounts without doing the same to ours, eh?'

'We'd best fight on foot, then.'

'Just so, but some of the lords cursed near shat at the very idea. Gwivyr was the worst, prattling about the honour of true-born noblemen and how only peasants walk and suchlike.'

'Did you see the falcata?'

'I did.' Cadryc turned grim. 'That was the one point in Gwivyr's favour. If we're unhorsed, and the dragons can't disrupt the Horsekin cavalry, well then! We'll all be eating at the Lord of Hell's table, eh? If we're not carved up as the main dish.'

'Most likely. So what do we do, your grace? Wait for them, or go to meet them?'

'Both. In the morning, we move the camp a few miles south, fortify it with ditches and the wagons, then draw up our lines beyond it and wait. We'll have the horses in reserve, the banadar tells us. His men know how to bring them up to the front lines in a hurry.'

The camp woke with the dawn and made a short and hurried march south. While the Mountain Folk and the servants did the hard work of assembling what fortifications they could between the wagon train and the approaching army, Prince Voran and Gwerbret Ridvar walked through the Deverry camp, telling those who would fight where they would be in the line of march and where they would stand. Prince Dar and Calonderiel did the same for the Westfolk.

Gerran saw many a noble lord shaking his sceptical head once the commanders had turned their backs. In the end, Tieryn Gwivyr got something of his way; he would lead a mounted squadron held in reserve. Either it would swoop in at the end of the battle to cut down any Horsekin stragglers, or else it would guard the Deverry retreat. Although Gwivyr grumbled about missing most of the fight, even he had to admit that he'd talked himself into his position.

The black dragon returned around noon with evil news. The Horsekin had made a forced march late into the yester-night. Now they'd drawn up their ranks much closer than anyone had expected.

'Not more than two miles away, Arzosah tells us,' Cadryc said. 'Ready or not, lads, the fight's on.'

None of the Deverry men in the army had ever walked

to war before, nor had the Westfolk swordsmen. When the time came to leave camp, they formed up in pairs in a more or less straight line, but by the time they came within sight of the Horsekin, they had bunched up into a straggling mob. The dwarven axemen, far more disciplined, marched in good order behind them, while the Westfolk archers ambled along to either side of the main body in no particular formation. Gwivyr's mounted squadron brought up the rear from a good quarter of a mile back. With him rode the two princes, Warleader Brel, and Gwerbret Ridvar, but Gerran noticed Banadar Calonderiel walking with his swordsmen.

On a slight rise of rocky ground the enemy waited, their ranks formed into a narrow front between the river on the Gel da' Thae right and the scrubby woodland to their left. Front and centre stood lines of spearmen, arranged so that the oval shield each man carried on his left arm provided some protection for the right side of the man next to him. They held their spears at a slight angle, a glittering hedge of death. At a quick estimate Gerran guessed that there were about five hundred of them, mostly human beings – the famous slave soldiers of the Gel Da' Thae. To either side, wings of heavy cavalry sat on their horses, circular shields on their left arms, falcatas drawn and ready in their right hands. Gerran had no time to count them or even to estimate their numbers.

Some fifty yards from the Gel Da' Thae front line, the Deverry swordsmen stopped walking to form up ranks as best they could. A few spearmen chuckled at what appeared to be this messy excuse for an army across from them; others took it up; the chuckles blossomed into full-blown howls of laughter when the cavalry joined in. In the midst of their scorn they apparently never noticed the dwarven axemen pivoting off under cover of their taller fellows and heading into the forest to the west.

Gerran heard the men around him muttering in rage, but they held their places as they'd been ordered to do.

He himself smiled, just briefly. The Horsekin had made a mistake by enraging the Deverry ranks. Among the enemy sour brass horns sounded. The Horsekin spearmen held their position, but the cavalry began to move forward. Apparently their commander had decided that they might as well charge this disorganized bunch of human bumpkins and Westfolk deer hunters and get the battle over with.

From a distance came the sound of two enormous pairs of wings, beating the air. The cavalry horses tossed up their heads, sniffed the wind, and began to prance and tremble. The Horsekin laughter stopped. Gerran looked up, looked around, and saw the dragons flying up from the south. On the Horsekin side horns sounded again. The spearmen began to close ranks and move forward as the cavalry tried to turn away or back their mounts to the flanks of their army, but they were caught twixt cliff and woodland. The horses were rearing, tossing their heads and fighting for the bit while their riders fought just as hard to control them.

With a roar that split the sky the dragons swooped down in a long arc. The horses went mad, kicking, plunging, throwing their riders, bursting forward into the ranks of the spearmen where they kicked and bit anyone in their way. The spearmen began to curse and yell; some turned out of line to avoid the plunging hooves. Here and there a man screamed as he went down to be crushed by the out of control cavalry. The dragons flew some yards above the spear points of the infantry, swooped up and away, then turned for another plunge down, this time from the north. Some of the mounted men got their horses under control just enough to allow the spearmen to get free of them, but the infantry's rear ranks had been pushed out of position.

While the dragons were turning, the Westfolk loosed their first volley of arrows. The shafts hissed as they rose into the air, then whistled down in a long arc of death, piercing the cavalry's mail, striking their unarmored horses. Horses screamed and reared, only to fall, throwing their riders. The

Gel da' Thae spearmen flung up their shields in a well-practised manoeuvre to protect themselves. *They'll be our part of the job*, Gerran thought, *us and the Mountain Folk.*

Over the screaming of Horsekin and the agonized neighing of their horses, brass horns blew desperately, signalling – what? Gerran had no idea, but the riders seemed to be trying to reform their ranks. Unfortunately for them, the dragons had completed their turn. The rain of arrows stopped. The two great wyrms swooped down again and destroyed the last bit of the cavalry's morale. The few men still horsed gave in to their struggling mounts and let them run downriver. The silver dragon banked sharply, changed direction with a flapping of huge wings, and took off after them, while the black dragon scattered the few horses that remained on the battlefield. She flew too far above the spearmen for them to do more than shake their weapons in her direction.

Over the screams and shouting, Prince Dar's silver horn sang out. The black dragon swung off and flew up high to let the Westfolk loose flight after flight of arrows. The unhorsed cavalrymen were trying to shelter under their small shields and at the same time get themselves into some kind of order among the infantry. Once again Dar signalled. Yelling warcries, the Deverry and Westfolk swordsmen trotted up the rise and charged into the disorganized mob that had once been an army. With shrieks like demons from hell the dwarven axemen burst out of the forest and fell upon the enemy from their flank.

Caught between two attacks, the spearmen lost the discipline that their lives depended upon. They'd been trained to hold ranks to defend against an equally well-drilled enemy. Now from one side they faced men with long axes that could sweep up from below and cut through their greaves. From the other side, swordsmen, both human and elven, charged in with their own shields held ready to turn aside – or to trap – their spears. The entire contingent of spearmen broke ranks, a fatal mistake.

Some swung round to face the dwarves, only to be engaged from the side by swordsmen. Others tried to make a stand against the Deverry charge only to have their legs slashed out from under them by the dwarves. Another silver horn – Gwivyr and his squad slammed into the battle. All around the edge the Westfolk archers prowled, loosing shaft after shaft whenever they had a clear target.

At first Gerran found himself shut out from the real fighting. With the archers he prowled like winter wolves around a stone-walled sheep fold, desperate to get in, unable to find a breach. At last an unhorsed cavalryman came running his way, his shield gone, his cap-like helmet and breastplate intact, both of them heavy leather studded with bronze. Gerran stepped into his path, feinted, then dodged to one side.

His enemy's clumsy swing showed Gerran that he'd learned to use his falcata on horseback, not on the ground, but he still stood a good head taller. Gerran dodged to the enemy's left; the Horsekin turned and swung again, his blade parallel to the ground. The weighted tip of the falcata pulled him a little farther than he should have gone. Gerran flung up his shield to catch the blow and sliced in from behind to hit him hard just beside the breast plate. His sword cut into the leather below. The leather split. So did the flesh under it, and blood ran.

With a yelp the Horsekin spun back towards Gerran and swung his falcata up from below. On its trailing edge the falcata was as dull as a club, but if it had hit its mark, Gerran would have fallen with a crushed jaw. He sprang back barely in time. Bleeding, out of balance, the Horsekin stumbled, flailing his arms like a dancer. His head for a brief moment bobbed to the level of Gerran's chest. Gerran swung up from below and slashed him across his eyes. With a scream the Horsekin fell to his knees and grabbed at his face with both hands.

Gerran stabbed him in the throat, then jumped back, on guard, searching for enemies, but by then Horsekin horns were screeching commands that could only mean one thing:

retreat. Unhorsed cavalrymen were already running for the lives, easy victims for Westfolk arrows. The spearmen threw their shields and ran with them, heading downriver.

Half of the elven archers pulled back to turn and run for the horses the Deverry army had left behind them. Others held their ground and sent flights of arrows racing after the retreat. Men screamed and fell. Some rolled wounded into the river and drowned. Others bled to death where they lay. The Deverry men and the Mountain Folk followed, killing the wounded enemies as they passed, facing off with the few men who turned to make a stand with their backs set against one another — two or three spears against a mob of swords and axes.

When Gwivyr's mounted squad galloped forward to harry the retreating men, the remaining Westfolk pulled back. Gerran heard Calonderiel yelling orders in both Elvish and Deverrian. 'Leave the bastards to the others! The horses are coming!' Prince Voran appeared on horseback, screaming more orders as he rode among his men and the Mountain Folk.

'Pull back, pull back! To me! To me!'

The unmounted swordsmen slowed, stopped, began milling around the prince. Gwivyr and his men turned their horses and swung back to join them. Among the fleeing cavalrymen, one suddenly spun around and flung a long dagger like a javelin. It struck Gwivyr full in the back so hard that he dropped his sword and slumped forward. Although the horse reared, the tieryn managed to cling to its neck, but two spearmen sprang forward. As the horse came down, a Gel da' Thae stabbed his spear with desperate force into Gwivyr's back. With screams of rage the tieryn's warband surrounded the attackers like hounds around a fox. Gerran could assume they'd cut them to pieces, just like the fox as well. Two men rode up to their lord's horse, grabbed the reins and led him onward. Just as they passed Gerran by the spear worked its way loose with a gush of blood and fell, bouncing over the horse's rump to the ground.

'Get him back to the chirurgeons!' Voran yelled.

Gerran glanced upriver and saw the horses coming – each mounted archer guided his horse with his knees while he led two riderless mounts. Another danger point: if the Horsekin rallied and charged back while the Deverry men were trying to mount up, they could reverse the tide of the battle. The Mountain Folk rushed forward to provide a barrier against a counter-charge, but none ever came.

Gerran grabbed the reins of the first horse he could reach and swung himself into the saddle. He could see Tieryn Cadryc nearby, safely mounted and swinging a bloody sword as he yelled orders. Prince Voran did the same, and the freshly horsed Deverry men formed a living wall around their position.

'The dragons are harrying them!' Newly mounted, Calonderiel rode back and forth, yelling the news at the top of his lungs. 'Hold and stand!'

Gerran rose in his stirrups and looked downriver. He could see a distant cloud of dust and above it two flying specks that repeatedly swooped down and rose again. In but a few moments the specks became too small to see. When Voran blew his silver horn, Gerran sat back down and turned towards the prince.

'Back to camp!' the prince yelled. 'We need to collect our wounded from the field.'

Their losses turned out to be light, not that the news surprised Gerran. Fresh orders spread through the camp, to get ready to move out south, where they'd fortify a new camp. Although a good many men grumbled at the thought of digging more ditches, Gerran understood the prince's reasons and told them to every grumbler he overheard.

'We're a cursed long way from home, lads,' he said. 'We've got nowhere to retreat to if we lose our baggage train.'

Like dweomer the grumbling stopped.

It was near sunset before the army had dug itself into its new position some six miles closer to Zakh Gral. Although they found a good stretch of flat ground and some grazing for the horses, by that point the river bed had deepened into a gorge which hemmed them in on the east side. To the west, however, the scrubby forest had disappeared, replaced by a welter of recently cut stumps and debris — lopped branches, piles of leaves, the scrap wood trimmed away from felled logs, sheets of bark, dead brown ferns and shrubs, all left to lie in a carpet of decay.

'They had to clear-cut a lot of timber to build Zakh Gral's wooden walls,' Salamander remarked. 'At least the Horsekin can't hide in the forest.'

'True spoken,' Gerran said, 'but their infantry can mount a flank attack from all this open ground. We've got nowhere to go on the other side but down to the water.'

Salamander grunted in disappointment.

'We're not going to have a pleasant little ride to Zakh Gral,' Gerran went on. 'Keep those Westfolk eyes of yours open every step of the way.'

That night, the dragons promised to lair somewhere close by. With so many dead horses left behind by the fleeing cavalry, they had no need to go hunting for food. *Just as well*, Gerran thought. The first battle had gone too easily, as far as he was concerned, which left him suspecting that the Horsekin had some sort of plan or sneak attack in mind. Something nagged at him, some sort of present danger that so far at least, everyone had overlooked.

Apparently Prince Voran agreed with him, because he set a ring of sentries around the camp, made up of pairs of swordsmen, one Deverry, one Westfolk. As he usually did, Gerran volunteered for the worst watch in the middle of the night. Much to his surprise, Calonderiel appeared to stand it with him.

'I didn't think a banadar would have to stand a watch,' Gerran said.

'He doesn't,' Calonderiel said. 'Neither does a noble lord, but here we are.'

That night the moon shone nearly full, but in the gauzy

light Gerran could see only a short way beyond their position. Calonderiel, of course, suffered no such limits. With
his drawn sword he pointed towards the south.

'According to Lady Grallezar,' Cal said, 'a couple of miles
along we'll meet a road that runs west to Braemel. If any
reinforcements are on the way, that's where they'll arrive.'

'If we're between them and the fortress,' Gerran said, 'we'll
be pinned.'

'Exactly. The dragons will be flying sweeps to the west,
and I thank the Star Goddesses for that, too. But we'll need
some sort of a plan if they do see another army coming.'

'Just so.' Gerran turned to the west and took a good look
at the broken field of stumps and litter. In the dim light he
had trouble distinguishing one lump from another. *If I had
a torch,* he thought, *I —.* 'Oh horseshit!' he snarled. 'So that's
what's been bothering me.'

'What are you talking about?'

'Tinder and firewood, banadar. There's a nearly a mile of
tinder and firewood right next to our camp. What if the
Horsekin drop a torch or two into it?'

Calonderiel let fly with a string of Elvish oaths, then pulled
his silver horn from his belt. 'A good point,' he said mildly,
then raised the horn and blew the three harsh notes of the
alarum, over and over until the camp woke, shouting.

Cursing and muttering, men rolled out of their blankets,
pulled on boots, grabbed weapons, and came running. Each
time a couple of men arrived, Calonderiel expanded the ring
of sentries. Westfolk he sent ahead, swords or longbows at
the ready, while the Deverry men stumbled along behind.
Warleader Brel collected his axemen and headed downriver,
fanning out as they did so into the wooden rubble. Since his
vision was so limited, Gerran stuck close to Calonderiel as
he trotted back and forth along the crescent-shaped line. At
last the sentries reached the edge of the dead wood and took
up posts that looked into green, damp forest.

Gerran and Calonderiel had just returned to the road after

walking the newly placed sentry ring when, ahead to the south, shouting broke out, the deep voices of the Mountain Folk and a sudden scream that might have come from a human or Horsekin throat. Calonderiel began yelling in Elvish, a cry that brought archers and swordsmen both racing to him. They all took off running down the Rhwmani road so fast that Gerran was hard-pressed to keep up. He was gasping for breath by the time they reached the Mountain Folk.

In the moonlight Gerran could see a shallow river or large stream flowing from the west, parallel to another Rhwmani road leading west towards the mountains – towards Braemel, he assumed. The water crossed their path and plunged down over the canyon's edge to join the Galan Targ below. The road itself made a sharp turn upstream, away from the cliff edge, to cross a wooden bridge, swarming at the moment with Mountain Folk. With a couple of barked orders Calonderiel sent archers to join them. Two Mountain Folk appeared out of the mob in the road and hurried over to the banadar. It wasn't until they came close that Gerran recognized Brel Avro.

'Good thinking, banadar,' the warleader said in Deverrian. 'We caught some of the Horsekin trying to fire that bridge. The sparks would have spread north quick enough.'

'Thank Gerran here.' Calonderiel jerked his thumb in Gerran's direction. 'He's the one who realized we were sleeping next to enough wood to roast the lot of us.'

'Good lad!' Brel said to Gerran. 'I'll see that the princes know your name.'

'No need for that,' Gerran said. 'I would have roasted along with everyone else.'

'True spoken. I'll tell them anyway.' Brel turned his attention back to Calonderiel. 'But we've run into a difficulty. Do you think this rubbish heap runs all the way down to the fortress?'

'Most likely and beyond as well,' Calonderiel said. 'They must have wasted a lot of wood building the thing. Why?'

'You'll see when it's time.' Brel started to walk away, then looked back over one shoulder. 'I need to talk things over with our envoy.'

From the west came the drumbeat of dragon wings, flying fast towards them. Gerran glanced up to see the silver wyrm circling far overhead, the size of a white bird in the moonlight. Rori dropped down closer, roared out a few Elvish words, then headed south.

'He's going to scout the fortress,' Calonderiel said. 'Just to make sure they don't have any other clever ruses on hand.'

Since returning to sleep was impossible, the army moved its camp downriver to the Braemel road. Just as the sun was rising, they dug into a new position to the north of the bridge, where they could guard it and the Braemel road without being pinned between it and the fortress, should fresh Gel da' Thae men-at-arms come marching down that good Rhwmani road. Rori returned soon after, and the commanders gathered around the dragon to wrangle out plans.

Gerran walked through the camp until he found Salamander, who was helping Dallandra with the Westfolk wounded. As she went from man to man, Salamander followed along behind, carrying a basket of clean bandages.

'Here, gerthddyn,' Gerran said to him, 'why didn't you tell us about that bridge and the road?'

'They weren't there before,' Salamander said. 'The priestess and I splashed across that little river upstream. It's so shallow it's easy to ford, though a bridge is doubtless easier for troops to cross. They must have brought in more men and slaves. I was here some months ago, you know.'

'But you haven't seen it since then? By dweomer, I mean.'

'You don't understand about scrying, Gerro. Running water makes it nearly impossible. I can explain –'

'Oh, don't bother,' Gerran said hastily. 'Quite all right.' He turned Dallandra's way. 'Wise One, do you know how Tieryn Gwivyr fares?'

'He's still alive,' Dallandra said. 'Which amazes me.'

'I see. Well, then, I'll hope for the best.'

By then the weary army wanted nothing more than sleep, but everyone knew that the Horsekin would rather attack a sleeping army than a ready one. Men kept their armour on, and with weapons close at hand they sat on the ground, dozing until the horns cried out for battle. Close to noon Arzosah came winging back to camp with the news that Horsekin infantry – and only infantry – were heading north along the cliff road.

'They've learned somewhat, lad,' Tieryn Cadryc told Gerran. 'The dragons won't be a cursed lot of help this time around.'

'Good,' Gerran said. 'We can fight mounted.'

'True spoken, and the princes have come up with a cursed clever idea.' Cadryc's mood brightened. 'We're going to cross the bridge and wait for them on the far side. This time, we're chasing them back to Zakh Gral.'

'What about the camp, your grace?'

'We'll be leaving a good many men behind to guard it. The dragon's certain we outnumber the army coming to meet us.'

After Cadryc relayed the commanders' orders, Gerran rounded up the Red Wolf warband and repeated them in as much detail as he could supply. In the midst of a swirling confusion of men and horses, Clae led over Gerran's battle-trained chestnut gelding, saddled and ready. Gerran mounted, reaching down to take the falcon shield from his page.

'My lord?' Clae said. 'When do you think I'll be ready to ride to battle?'

'Not for some years yet, lad,' Gerran said, smiling. 'And be glad of it. You stay back at the camp. Mount up and be ready to retreat if things go against us on the field. That's an order, by the by.'

'Well and good then, my lord.' Clae pulled a long face. 'I'll do what you say, of course.'

'Good.'

Gerran settled the shield on his left arm, then drew his sword to lead the Red Wolf warband out with a flourish.

They clattered across the bridge, where Tieryn Cadryc waited
on horseback in a little cluster of his noble-born vassals and
allies.

'Well and good then, lads!' Cadryc called out. 'Remember
your orders! Fight hard for Deverry and the high king!'

The warband cheered him.

Once the rest of the army had assembled, it set out down
the cliff-top road. The terrain here stretched reasonably level
from the cliff edge to their left all the way through the husks
and bones of a slain forest to their right – stretching close
to a mile in all, Gerran estimated, back to a rise of hills. He
no longer worried about fire. If the Horsekin set the rubble
alight this close to Zakh Gral, they would pay more heavily
than their enemies. The debris did provide another obstacle;
poor footing at the best and downright dangerous traps for
a horse's hooves at worst should the battle spread into it.
The archers, however, found it a blessing.

When the army reached a slight rise in the road, the
commanders called a halt. The archers, unmounted, spread
out into the debris fields. The Red Wolf and its allies took
their position near them on the right flank. Gerran had
noticed that each archer carried a small hatchet at his belt.
He'd assumed that it was a weapon, a last defence in case
of a defeat, but in fact, the archers used the blades to shape
stakes from dead branches. They then flipped the hatchet
over and pounded each stake into the ground in front of
them. Behind this waist-high palisade, they arranged themselves three men deep in a curving formation like an arm
reaching towards the enemy.

At the centre of the Deverry line a silver horn sounded.
Gerran rose in his stirrups and looked south along the road. A
column of dust rose in the air and moved steadily forward. He
sat back down in the saddle, then drew one of his three javelins
from the sheath under his right leg. He heard the rattle of
metal as the rest of the warband followed his lead. The dust
cloud came closer and resolved itself into a column of spearmen,

marching in tight formation some ten men abreast. Gerran could just make out the sound of brass horns, squalling orders. *They've spotted us*, he thought.

The column halted some hundreds of yards away, just out of bow range. Units from the Gel da' Thae rear ranks pivoted and swung to the flank, crunching into the debris field and wheeling around with a precision the more impressive for the uneven footing. Unit after unit fell into place until the line stretched from the road deep into the flat ground to the west. The spearmen stood some five ranks deep, raising their spears to form a hedge of metal points at an angle ready for a charge. With the Westfolk archers threatening on the flank, however, they held their position, just as the princes had expected they would.

For a brief while the stalemate held, giving Gerran time to look beyond the front ranks of well-armed and well-drilled Gel da' Thae troops. Behind them stood more spearmen, mostly human, and a pack of Horsekin armed with swords. Some of their shields were round, some oval, some almost square, a variety that made the Gel da' Thae style of shield wall impossible. These men, a good half of the army, stood in loose ranks, three or four men to a file. Gerran saw only leather armour, gleaming here and there with bronze strips and studs. Dotted among them were men in red surcoats carrying long whips – the Keepers of Discipline, the Westfolk had called them, the most important targets on the field.

On the Deverry side of the line, horses stamped and shook their heads. Men shifted in the saddle, muttering now and then. The Gel da' Thae spearmen held their position with scarcely a quiver or curse, but Gerran could see the Horsekin at the rear of the enemy formation growing restless, impatient even, as they moved back and forth. Some took a few steps forward only to jump back as the Keepers cracked their whips.

Prince Voran's silver horn rang out for the first feint. Screaming warcries, the front rank of horsemen spurred their mounts forward. They thundered down the rise towards the

Gel da' Thae, who set their spears to greet them. As he galloped towards the glittering spear heads, Gerran saw just how right the commanders had been – they would never have broken through the Gel da' Thae lines. He yelled once and threw his javelin as hard as he could, aiming over the regular ranks into the mob behind. The other riders threw theirs as well, then followed Gerran's lead as, some twenty yards from the Gel da' Thae line, he wheeled his horse around and rode back. They passed through the Deverry lines and took up a position at the rear of their fellows. The next rank of riders moved forward – and waited again, letting the Horsekin wait as well.

Twice more the Deverry and Westfolk riders made their feints, swinging close to the Gel da' Thae line, but hurling javelins into the Horsekin at the rear. After the third feint, which brought Gerran and his men back to the front rank of the riders, Gerran saw the Horsekin surging forward into the rear rank of the Gel da' Thae, only to be beaten back with whips and curses by the Keepers of Discipline. The Deverry horns rang out again. Gerran joined the rest of the front rank as they galloped forward and threw their second javelins. He caught a glimpse of one of the Keepers staggering with a javelin in his chest.

Behind him he heard yells and screams of rage following the fleeing riders. He spurred his horse on to rejoin the army, then turned and saw chaos breaking out in the enemy formation. The Horsekin had lost what discipline they had and were charging forward, disrupting the rear ranks of spearmen, pushing them into their fellows. The Gel da' Thae had no choice but to charge in order to stay clear of the mob behind them. Spears at the ready, they came running up the road into the range of the archers.

With a hiss and whistle the first flight of Westfolk arrows arced up and plunged down. The Gel da' Thae spearmen flung up their shields to protect themselves just as the second flight arrived, this lot aimed low to strike the men under their roof of leather and wood. The spearmen in the front rank began to crumple and die, disrupting their formation even more as the arrows flew again and again. Horsekin and Gel da' Thae both milled in the road, trying to get free of each other and charge the enemy.

Brass horns blared like frantic screams. All up and down the lines the Keepers, so obvious in their red surcoats, fell pierced as the archers picked them out. The men they could no longer control trampled them as the spearmen surged forward. Without them the Horsekin turned into an angry mob. The Gel da' Thae fell back and let their allies rush forward to meet the flights of arrows.

More Deverry horns, and the signal Gerran had been waiting for. He drew his sword, saw his men do the same, and paused until Calonderiel blew the final signal on an elven horn. The archers stopped loosing arrows, and like arrows themselves the riders charged. A Horsekin swordsman stood in Gerran's path. As his mount swerved to the Horsekin's left, Gerran leaned low over the horse's neck and swung his broadsword like a sabre. He caught the man hard across the neck, saw him go down, and swung his weight in the saddle to his left to catch a spear thrust on his shield. His horse followed the shift and turned, allowing him to attack the wielder of that spear from the side. He made a hard swing at the spear itself and snapped it in half. Its owner dropped the pieces and ran.

Gerran pulled up at the side of the road to let his horse rest. Among the dead and dying men, Gel da' Thae shields littered the road, only to be smashed under the hooves of the pursuing riders. Yelling and swinging, Deverry and Westfolk riders streamed past, cutting down Horsekin and Gel da' Thae both. The enemy were running full-tilt, gasping for breath in the hot sun, as the horsemen caught up with them. The riders swung and struck; blades flashed up bloody, then swept down again. The unequal slaughter turned Gerran's stomach, until he remembered the dead farmers of

Neb's village, laid out in a line for the ravens. He spurred his horse forward and joined the rout.

Still, the horses could only run so far, and the mob of riders began to spread out into a line, dangerously thin along the road. Here and there clusters of spearmen turned and gathered, back to back, to make a desperate stand. Silver horns shrieked, calling the Deverry and Westfolk men back to gather around their commanders. The remaining spearmen headed south again, running, walking, staggering towards the temporary safety of their stronghold. Gerran rode back to the army, spotted Calonderiel, and trotted his horse up to the banadar's mount.

'Can you see the fortress?' Calonderiel pointed south with a blood-streaked sword. 'Right down there.'

'I don't have Westfolk eyes,' Gerran said.

'Of course, my apologies.' He paused to catch his breath. 'The dragons are lurking down there somewhere. If the Horsekin cavalry rides out, they'll send them back in again.'

'Good. What do we do now?'

'Move the camp down. It's time to invest Zakh Gral.'

The archers changed their weapons to the curved hunting bows they could use from the saddle, then mounted up. Something occurred to Gerran as he watched them.

'The cursed Horsekin have got to have some kind of bow,' Gerran said. 'Why aren't they using them?'

'Good question,' Calonderiel said. 'My guess would be that they don't have a lot of arrows. You can always cut more shafts, but if you lose a fight, your points belong to the enemy. I'm willing to wager high that the Horsekin are hoarding theirs.'

Once the army had formed itself up into a decent marching order, it set out south along the river road. They passed the corpses of men who'd died in the retreat and saw wounded men who'd managed to crawl to one side to wait for death or capture. No one challenged them until they reached Zakh Gral. Even then, the challenges came from the top of the walls. The great iron-bound gates, wide enough for four horsemen to ride out abreast, stood shut against them.

Zakh Gral spread along the cliff edge, just as Salamander had described, but an outer stone wall, no more than five feet high, now circled the inner, wooden walls, made of whole tree trunks bound together and standing about twenty feet high. Next to the main gate stood another door, a mere sliver of a door compared to the massive construction next to it, though the builders had armoured it with metal strips to fend off an attacker's axemen. In an attack the defenders would doubtless block it with stone. Above the walls, Gerran saw three towers looming, one of wood, two faced in stone.

'We got here just in time,' Calonderiel said. 'Another eight-night, and those stone walls would have been finished.'

The wooden walls must have been fitted with inner catwalks, because Horsekin warriors stood along them at intervals. Gerran could just make out their heads and helmets over the barricade. Now and again he saw something that looked like the tip of a longbow as well. He pointed them out to Calonderiel.

'That's what they are, sure enough,' the banadar said. 'Well, we're going to find out how good they are. And soon.'

Just before sunset the baggage train, the servants, the wounded, and the chirurgeons caught up with the army, but they set up the encampment a safe distance from the fortress walls. While mounted riders guarded against a Gel da' Thae sally, in the last of the light exhausted men dug ditches and arranged wagons to protect the camp and the supplies. The sky hung so clear and warm above them that no one bothered to set up tents except for those that would shelter the worst wounded.

Salamander helped carry Tieryn Gwivyr into one of the elven round tents. Dallandra's assistants had bound the tieryn, lying on his stomach, to a platform made of two planks tied together with rope, then turned his head to the side so he could breathe. Gwivyr lay as limply a set of empty clothes, and he stank of blood and urine both. The spear thrust had broken his spine just above his kidneys, Dallandra remarked.

'He can't control his water,' she said, 'or anything else, either. If he lives, he'll never walk again.'

One of Gwivyr's eyes opened to reveal a bloodshot white around a clouded blue; then the lid drooped shut again. Had he heard? Salamander hoped not.

That night sentries ringed the fortress on both sides of its walls. The men slept with weapons and armour close at hand, but no sally came.

The morning brought with it mounted patrols, trotting back and forth in front of Zakh Gral. The rest of the men began to set up tents and dig more ditches at a further distance back from the fortress. Salamander crouched behind the chirurgeons' tents and hoped no one noticed that he was scrying. He could see inside the fort easily enough, at least when it came to the places that had existed during his brief visit there. Everywhere armed men stood in groups or paced back and forth, talking together or merely staring at the walls around them as if wondering how long they'd hold.

When Salamander turned his mind to Rocca, he saw her in dim light surrounded by stone. For the first time he saw most of the Inner Shrine, simply because she knelt in a crowd of priestesses and servant women, most of whom he'd physically seen. At the altar Lakanza stood, arms upraised before the picture of the goddess. Oil lamps burned on the dark altar stone, and the black pyramid glimmered with its sullen sparks.

'There he is!' Calonderiel's voice cut into his conscious-ness.

The vision wavered and disappeared. Salamander looked up to see Calonderiel hurrying towards him. Maelaber, carrying a staff wound with ribands, trotted after him.

'What's all this?' Salamander rose and met them. 'Mael, it looks like your father's decided you're a herald.'

'He's got the memory for one,' Calonderiel said before Maelaber could open his mouth. 'Ebañy, we need you to pretend to be a bard.'

'Uh, what?'

'Grallezar told us about a Gel da' Thae law,' Maelaber said. 'They can't hold a parley unless a bard's present. The gods only know if there's one in Zakh Gral.'

'The only other possibility is Meranaldar.' Calonderiel paused to spit on the ground. 'Not much of a choice at all. You'll have to do.'

'My most humble thanks!'

'Oh by the silver shit of the Star Gods!' Calonderiel set his hands on his hips. 'There's no time to stand on courtesies.'

'When you stand on them, they only get trampled anyway.' If he gave in to his heartfelt longing and punched Calonderiel in the mouth, Salamander supposed, he'd be broken into several pieces before he could land a second blow. 'How exactly do I pretend to be a bard?'

'I have no idea,' Calonderiel said. 'Figure something out.'

Smoothly Maelaber stepped in between them and raised the staff. 'Hold and stand!' he barked. 'Father, if you'd just leave this to me?'

With a shrug, Calonderiel strode off, heading back to the main camp. *Mael's going to make a good herald,* Salamander thought. *If we all live through this.*

'What are we parleying for?' Salamander said.

'The princes want to offer the women their protection and a safe passage out of the fortress.'

'Thanks be to the gods! For that I'll be glad to feign the bardic calling.'

'It should be simple enough. Grallezar told me about their bards. All you have to do is carry the drum I found and stand there looking grim, but if you could chant something impressive now and then it would help.'

'I can certainly – wait! Where is this parley going to take place?'

'Out in neutral ground.'

'Where the men on the walls can see me? What if they recognize me? I've been in the fortress before, you know. I don't want a well-placed arrow as a reward for my spying.'

'Oh.' Maelaber paused to chew on his lower lip in thought. 'Ah! I know! Do you remember how Danalaurel killed a wolf a couple of years ago? He was so cursed proud of doing it that he takes the skin with him everywhere. What if we put it on you for a head-dress? We could add a bit of cloth for a scarf if it doesn't cover enough of you.'

'That should do it. Very well, then. Will your father be coming with us?'

'Why would I want the parley to fail? Of course he won't.'

Salamander found the small hand drum easy enough to carry, but the wolfskin was hot, smelly, and itchy. The wolf's flaccid head, deprived of its skull, sat on top of Salamander's head, while the rest of it hung down his back. Maelaber tied the front paws together around his neck, then added a necklace of fancy Bardek beads that Calonderiel had once given Maelaber's mother. When Grallezar joined them, she announced that Salamander looked both convincing and well-veiled.

'I be coming with you,' she said, 'to ensure that someone attends who does speak the Gel da' Thae tongue. Prince Voran did decide to send a Lijik herald, you see, to do the speaking. Indar be his name.'

'He's a grand choice,' Salamander said. 'He's already talked one of Alshandra's lords into letting his women leave a siege.'

Together they rode out of camp and trotted the mile or so to the army's emplacement. Servants took their horses and brought them to the commanders, who were talking with Indar at the edge of the empty ground between them and the fort. They stood, however, well out of bow range. Indar acknowledged his reinforcements with a nod and a tight smile.

'Shall we go?' Indar said. 'Let's hope the commanders of

this fort are Gel da' Thae, not Horsekin. I've no desire to be spitted on an arrow before I open my mouth.'

As their small party approached the gates of the fortress, the two heralds held their staves high to let the wind catch the ribands and flutter them, an invitation to parley all across Deverry and the Westlands. Salamander was praying that the custom held in Gel da' Thae lands as well. When he looked up at the dark wooden walls, he could see the longbows in the hands of the guards. The four of them stopped walking some thirty yards from the gates, well within bow range. Helmets gleamed at the top of the palisade, looking oddly like shiny beetles scuttling back and forth as the men wearing them trotted from one position to another on the catwalks.

Inside the fortress a horn called out. The little door next to the main gates creaked open. Salamander beat a quick tattoo on his drum to cover the pounding of his heart. Two Horsekin, one carrying a riband-bound staff, stepped out. They were barely clear of the door when it slammed shut behind them. The herald, an enormous man with a coarse mane of bleached-red hair, decorated with charms and little scrolls, wore the common brown brigga and tan shirt of the Gel da' Thae infantry. A welter of blue and purple tattoos covered his face and neck.

The other, slender and young, wore a long leather shirt, fringed along the sleeves and yokes and painted in a variety of designs, over plain grey brigga. Under a short black thatch of hair, his milk-pale face sported only a single tattoo, Alshandra's bow and arrow on his left cheek. He carried a hand drum, wound round with blue ribands like the herald's staff. Scar tissue filled his eye sockets.

Grallezar murmured, 'The law says go meet them', and led her little delegation forward as the others approached. The Gel da' Thae herald stared at her, then bowed his head briefly and spoke in the Horsekin tongue. She answered in the same, then returned to Deverrian.

'Do you still ken the Lijik tongue, Minaz?' she asked him. 'Or do you scorn it by the laws of your false goddess?'

The herald's upper lip curled, and he made a growling sound deep in his throat. 'I do, Grallezar, and should you say to, I shall use it here. If, that be, you restrain your mockery of things you ken not.'

Grallezar snorted, then motioned to Indar. 'Do tell him, good herald, what the commanders wish him to hear.'

Indar stepped forward, as lean and bony as Minaz was stout.

'I come from the army of the two princes,' he began, 'to ask you in the name of mercy to set free the women you hold in your fortress. We see no need for them to suffer, and we promise them safe conduct and succour. They shall be free to return with us to Deverry should they wish or to return to your cities should they wish that.'

'Well and good, then,' Minaz said. 'What will you offer us in return?'

'We hold over seventy of their men, mostly Gel da' Thae spearmen. Some are wounded, but most can still fight. No doubt you'll need them to help defend your walls.'

Grallezar caught her breath in a sharp gasp. Minaz stared at his counterpart and blinked hard, as if he couldn't quite believe what he was hearing, but he composed himself in a matter of heartbeats.

'I shall tell the rakzanir of your most generous offer,' Minaz said. 'But be not surprised if they have no answer but mockery.' He barked out a few words in the Horsekin tongue to the bard, then turned and stalked off towards the fortress. The bard trotted after him. Together they slipped through the little door, which shut behind them with a clank and jingle.

'So much for that,' Salamander remarked.

'Indeed,' Indar said. 'I had a great deal more to say, about Alshandra's wishes for her priestesses and the like, but apparently they'd heard quite enough.'

Grallezar merely set her lips tight together and growled. They all trooped back to the Deverry lines, where the two princes, Gwerbret Ridvar, and Envoy Kov were waiting for them. When Indar told the commanders what had happened, Ridvar glowered, Daralanteriel swore under his breath, but Voran laughed.

'I'm not surprised in the least,' he said. 'Well, we need to do one of two things. Either convince them that our offer is the best they're going to get, or find some way to sweeten it.'

'Just so,' Indar glanced at Salamander. 'Tell me if I'm wrong, but it seemed to me that they felt they had good reason to reject it. I'm not sure if it was confidence or arrogance they displayed.'

'They may expect a relieving force,' Voran said before Salamander could answer. 'Braemel went over to their side not all that long ago. They may be thinking that the city will be sending them troops now that it has.'

'No doubt it will, your highness,' Salamander said, 'but that's not the reason they're so confident. They're expecting Alshandra to win the battle for them.'

'Ah.' Voran blinked rapidly several times. 'You may well be right, Goodman Evan. I tend to forget such things. Or there might be some other reason, one we don't understand.'

Everyone looked at Grallezar, who shrugged. 'My lords,' she said, 'had you told me of the terms you were offering before we did go forth, I could have saved us all much trouble. Among the Horsekin, a man who surrenders is no longer a man. Upon their return any hale and whole prisoners would be put to death on the long spear. Of what use would they be to their commanders? The grievously wounded would be forgiven, but again, of what use would they be?'

'Lady Grallezar, I apologize from the bottom of my heart,' Voran said. 'From now on, you shall be part of every council we hold.' He glanced at the others. 'I fear me we've started our haggling with a grave mistake.'

'I have to agree,' Daralanteriel said. 'My thanks, good heralds, and to you too, Ebañy.' Suddenly he grinned. 'You can take off that ridiculous wolf pelt, but if Danalaurel can bear to part with it, you'd best keep it handy in your tent.'

'My thanks, your highness,' said Salamander. 'The thing
itches like a plague of black flies.'

As soon as the heralds finished their report, Kov hurried
back to the dwarven encampment. He gathered Warleader
Brel and Weaponmaster Larn and led them out into the litter
of the cleared land, where they could talk without being
overheard. Here so near to the fortress only dead leaves,
scraps of bark, and slivers lay on heaps of dead bracken or
gathered, wind-blown, around a few stumps too large to pull.
Most likely the servants in Zakh Gral had collected all the
useful firewood long before. Kov kicked a few wood scraps
out of his way and surprised a nest of spiders. Larn swore
and jumped back.

'They don't look poisonous,' Brel said.

'The poisonous ones never do,' Larn said. 'How do you
know if they are or not?'

'Stop it!' Kov snapped. 'Do you want to hear what the
heralds said or not?'

They both scowled, but they did listen while Kov told
them about the princes' conference with the heralds.

'The lords want to hold the siege a while longer,' Kov
finished up. 'That's the upshot.'

'There's no use in sitting around out here eating every
scrap of food we brought with us,' Brel said. 'Why are we
waiting?'

'In hopes of getting the women safely out,' Kov said.

Brel snorted. 'They wanted to be there. They can take
their chances with the men.'

'Most of them are slaves.'

'Oh. Well, then, that's different. Do you think there's any
chance the stinking Horsekin will let them go?'

'No, I don't. We've already insulted them, and besides, if
they figure out that we won't attack the fortress while the
women are inside, why would they let them go?'

Larn nodded agreement, then kicked the debris lying

around his feet. When no more spiders appeared, he squatted down to pat the earth with both hands.

'What by the slavering trolls of Hell are you doing?' Brel said.

'Seeing how damp the ground is.' Larn got up and wiped his hands on his trousers. 'Not very. It can't have rained here recently.'

All three of them looked up at the spotless blue sky.

'When we fire the place,' Larn went on, 'it's going to be raining sparks. What we need is a short storm, just enough to water down this stuff here, but not enough to soak the walls.'

'By all means, ask the gods to send us what you need,' Brel said, grinning. 'They can fight it out with Alshandra.'

'Too bad we don't have a sorcerer or two handy,' Larn said.

All three of them laughed, but Kov found himself remembering the day he'd taken his staff to Dallandra to ask about runes. His realization that his staff would have crumbled away without some sort of spell upon it combined in his mind with all the old mountain folktales about the Westfolk and their skill with magic.

'What's wrong with you?' Brel said to him. 'You look like you bit into a peach and found a wasp there ahead of you.'

'Just an unpleasant thought or two,' Kov said. 'They're easy to have out here.'

'Now that's very true.' Larn had turned away to look over the stretch of debris. 'I suppose we could get every man in the army to pick up an armful of this tree dung.'

'And how long would it take to clear a wide enough area?' Brel said. 'We'd have to clean it up well past the encampment, wouldn't we?'

'Depends on the wind. If there was a wind blowing towards the camp, we couldn't get rid of enough of this rubbish in a month.'

All three of them took a few steps towards Zakh Gral. Up on the stone towers pennants fluttered. A huge banner

displaying the gold bow and arrows of the goddess hung
down the side of the wooden tower and occasionally flapped
in the rising breeze. The wind was coming straight up from
the south, as indeed it had been ever since the army had
arrived, blowing right over the fortress on its way upriver to
the army's encampment.

'One more idea,' Brel said. 'Tell me something, Weaponmaster.
Suppose we were on the other side of the river – the whole
army, I mean. Could you deliver a load of fire to the fortress
from there? I know the canyon's wide, but –'

Larn interrupted with a long peal of mocking laughter.

'Oh never mind!' Brel snarled. 'I suppose we could try to
send sappers and miners along the river. That sandstone
crumbles easily.'

'Not when you're trying to swing a pick from a boat,' Larn
said. 'The water comes right up to the canyon walls. It's fire
or nothing, Warleader.'

Kov's odd feeling was growing in his mind, turning into
an idea, an utterly improbable idea, an idea he found too
stupid to voice, but an idea all the same. He brooded over
it all afternoon until it became so insistent that he gave in
and went to find Salamander.

The gerthddyn was sitting in front of his tent with Lord
Gerran and Gerran's young page. Kov joined them, and for
a while merely listened to their conversation, which centred
around the care and breeding of horses – a common topic
among Deverry men, or so he'd noticed. Finally Salamander
turned to him.

'Is somewhat on your mind, Envoy? You looked troubled.'

'Well, there is, truly. We Mountain Folk have been thinking
about this siege, you see. We have somewhat with us that
could burn down the fortress, but if the wind carries the
sparks, we could roast our own army along with it.'

'Burn those walls?' Gerran leaned forward. 'You've gone
mad. Those logs won't catch like tinder. You'd have to build
a roaring blaze next to them, and the Horsekin would be

loosing arrows on you the whole time and throwing rocks, too, most likely.'

'True enough.' Kov allowed himself a grin. 'We've considered that little difficulty, my lord. What if we had a kind of tinder with us that stuck where it landed? Like pitch, say, but better.'

Gerran started to speak, then motioned for him to go on.

'The problem is the tents and suchlike. A chunk of burning bark hits a canvas roof – well, you lads can imagine the rest.' Kov glanced at Salamander out of the corner of his eye. 'It's too bad there's not some way to summon some rain, just enough to wet down all this clutter, like, that the Horsekin foresters left lying around when they cut down the trees. And to keep the tents damp, as well. We could do great things if only that were the case.'

Gerran's lips suddenly formed an 'O', and he too looked at Salamander. The gerthddyn was studying the fingernails of his right hand with great concentration. He polished them on his shirt, then looked up.

'What sort of great thing?' Salamander said.

'Well, suppose we set that wooden tower alight, just to start with, the one with the banner hanging from it.'

'I'd love to see that one burn.' Salamander heaved a wistful sigh. 'That's where they imprisoned me when I was spying out this place.'

'Indeed? Well, we can do it from our distance. Do you think that might change the fortress commanders' minds about another parley? Then the princes can come up with a decent offer to exchange for the women trapped inside.'

'It might be powerfully persuasive,' Salamander said. 'To say naught of a great encouragement, inducement, or even a lure to reopen negotiations.'

'I was wondering if the Wise One might have some thoughts on the matter,' Kov said, 'not that I'd be so rude as to trouble her with questions myself.'

'You know, we actually have two Wise Women in camp,'

Salamander said. 'The Exalted Mother Grallezar is said to
have some knowledge of the weather herself. Together they
might be able to um well, shall we say, predict when a rain
like that might fall?'

'It would certainly be grand if they could.' Kov found it
difficult to steady his voice.

Salamander smiled and got up, stretching his arms over
his head with a lazy yawn. Young Clae looked back and forth
between the men, his mouth slack with bewilderment. Gerran
quirked an eyebrow in his direction.

'My lord?' Clae said. 'Is this one of those things I'll understand when I'm older?'

'It is,' Gerran said. 'Don't trouble your heart about it now.'

Salamander smiled vaguely at everyone, then strolled off,
heading in the direction of the Westfolk camp. Kov rose and
took his leave as well. As he walked back to his own tent,
he felt as if two debating men shared his mind: the one smug
that his idea had been sound after all; the other convinced
that Salamander was only asking Dallandra about herbs to
cure madness in dwarves.

The debate settled itself in the middle of the night when
the rain started. Kov woke to the sound of water hammering
on the canvas roof of his tent. He stuck his head outside to
feel the cold drops on his face and ensure that the rain was
real. Since his tent faced in the general direction of the
fortress, he saw an even greater marvel and all unthinking,
got up and ran out, stark naked, into the rain for a second
look. Sure enough, over Zakh Gral the stars shone in the
night sky. The edge of the rain cloud, as sharp as a knife
cut, hung over the neutral ground twixt camp and walls.

That'll give them something to chew on! Grinning to himself
Kov hurried back inside to dry off. Although he tried to sleep,
he lay listening to the dweomer rain until dawn, when it
abruptly stopped. He started to drowse off, only to hear Larn
shouting his name. The weaponmaster threw back the canvas
door of the tent and stuck his head in.

'Did you hear that rain?'

'Oh yes,' Kov said. 'Did you see the cloud?'

Larn merely nodded, studying Kov's face with narrow eyes. Kov smiled blandly back until at last the weaponmaster shrugged and looked away.

'Might as well unload the carts,' Larn said. 'The walls are well within range, especially for our big girl.'

'Think you can hit that wooden tower?' Kov said. 'The one with the huge banner on it. Salamander tells me that the banner commemorates some event that the Gel da' Thae think is a holy miracle.'

'Let's see if we can send it up in miraculous flames, then. Good choice, Envoy! We want a single blaze, don't we? It might take a couple of throws, but we'll see what she can do.'

When the news went round that the Mountain Folk were at last going to unload their secret cargo, the princes and the gwerbret hurried to the baggage train to watch. A crowd of onlookers assembled, but Kov used his rank to shoo them away. Since the princes and the gwerbret, of course, were beyond shooing, Larn reluctantly agreed to let them stay. Kov did get them to stand well back, however, by stressing the dangers of this particular weapon.

'You'll see why I worry about your well-being, your high-nesses,' Kov said, 'once we begin.'

A team of sappers, led by an engineer named Grosh, dragged two of the carts to a position facing the wooden tower, well over two hundred yards away. The crates came out, and the sappers began to dismantle the carts, held together by iron pins. The slab sides they laid flat to level out the ground. The long wooden tongues, made of squared-off beams, provided the frame to support a long narrow wooden box, which Grosh pinned into place with one end aiming at the wood tower.

Kov still found the machine something of a mystery, because no one had ever bothered to explain it to him. When the noble-born pestered him with questions, he could honestly say that he didn't know the answers. What's more, the sappers and engineers were deliberately crowding around the weapon to hide the details from their eager onlookers. From their distance, Kov and the others caught glimpses of Grosh fussing over the frame and slider box, banging in pins and pegs and tightening down twists of rope. The other sappers handed him components as he called for them.

'Springs,' Kov said suddenly. 'He calls those twists of hair and suchlike torsion springs. I don't know what that means, though.'

The sappers drew up a third cart. Grosh brought out Big Girl herself, as they called her, a horn and sinew bellybow powered by the twists of hair and sinews tightened into the corners of the frame. Grosh laid her gently onto the slider box with a soft caress, then tied her down. Normally, the curved metal belt at the end of her shaft would go around an archer's belly to keep the weapon braced while he drew it. This belt, however, laced into the wooden frame.

'It's a splendid bow, your highnesses,' Kov said. 'Trouble is, she's so powerful that not even a pair of Mountain Folk can draw her. So we came up with this little device. She's strung with wire, and there's a hook that attaches to somewhat or other, and then a handle turns to pull back the wire, and well, that's really all I know.'

Larn hurried over to aim Big Girl at the tower. As he made his adjustments, everyone got a look at the bow itself, though not the full apparatus.

'Ye gods,' Ridvar whispered. 'She's beautiful.'

'Isn't she, your grace?' Kov beamed at him.

'The bolts she takes must be huge.'

'They are, your grace, and most unusual as well.' Kov considered just how much he could reveal without Grosh threatening to beat him into slime. 'They're hollow, and they hold a secret that I'm not at liberty to discuss. I assure you that soon you'll understand.'

Dwarven woman had invented the secret contents in their

perennial search to find something better than blue fungus in baskets to light the underground cities. This particular mixture – of bitumen, brimstone, rock oil, and tow for thickening – had proved entirely too illuminating. Experimenting with it had resulted in two deaths, in fact, before the warleaders commandeered it. So dangerous was it that they'd brought it to the war in sealed ceramic pots. Opening them to the air, Kov supposed, might result in disaster. He exerted himself, found enough courtesies, and got the commanders to move back another few feet.

'All ready,' Grosh said in Deverrian. 'Time to load up the bolts! Someone light a candle, but get well back before you strike any sparks. This stuff could blow us all to the clouds and back again.'

Kov and the commanders spontaneously moved off a few more yards. It had taken Grosh weeks of work to figure out the way to deliver this lighting material gone wrong. The flaming fuse often died, blown out as the missile soared on its way, unless the mix was allowed to take the fire before launch. Unfortunately, it often took too well. Larn had lost his beard and all of his hair to an early attempt, and Big Girl had needed repairs as well, after a day when the mixture exploded too soon. Now the long wood bolts, tipped in iron, had holes on their underside to allow air into the mix as they flew and several fuses embedded on top of the black, sticky mixture inside. In practice, at least, this had all worked splendidly. Kov refused to even consider the thought that it would fail to work now. While the engineer and the weaponmaster squabbled over the best way to aim Big Girl, Kov turned to look at the fortresses. Gleaming helmets lined the top of the wall as the men wearing them watched their enemies at work.

At last Big Girl stood ready. As Larn turned the handle on the slider box, the inner shaft turned as well, groaning and creaking. Sweat ran down Larn's face and soaked the collar of his shirt. With all his weight he leaned back, struggling to hold the handle steady. Grosh stepped forward and laid in a loaded bolt, lit it with a thin splint, then jumped back just as Larn let the handle go.

The shaft spun, the hook leapt off the wire, the first bolt sprang from the bellybow and arched up into the air. It whistled as it flew across and smudged the blue sky with black smoke, while the Gel da' Thae manning the walls turned their heads to watch. Larn began cranking up a second bolt as the first started its curve down, heading for tower window. Larn released the second bolt. Grosh positioned a third. In the fortress the Horsekin stayed dead-silent, as if they were puzzled rather than frightened. The first bolt struck the tower with such force that the wood structure quivered. For the briefest of moments nothing happened; then the mixture in the bolt exploded.

Little fingers of bright gold stroked the tower wall as the bitumen melted and ran, burning. First smoke curled, then flames leapt along the boards. The second bolt slammed into the flames and instantly shattered into a spew of fire. The last bolt flew and hit. With a roar the entire top third of the tower caught and burst into flames. An answering roar went up from the Deverry army as Alshandra's enormous banner flashed into a solid sheet of fire. Howls of panic from the Horsekin rose with the black smoke.

'Yes!' Larn threw both hands in the air and yelled in Dwarvish. 'It works! It works!'

'Well done, Weaponmaster!' Brel began to laugh for what must have been the first time in fifty years. 'Oh, splendidly well done! We'll avenge them all! Every last one of our dead! They'll be avenged!'

Inside the fortress brass horns squealed and squalled. Pieces of the tower broke free and fell, scattering flame as they went. More screams, more yells – Kov could imagine the panic inside: slaves running to and fro with buckets of water, others beating at the flames with shovels, the rakzanir milling around, screeching futile orders.

'It'll be hard work, dousing that fire,' Prince Voran said. 'But they have copious wells, unfortunately.'

'Let's hope they try to use water, your highness,' Kov said.
'The stuff just floats to the top, you see, and goes on burning.'

For a while it seemed that the entire fortress might burn
from this one attack. The princes and lords began shouting
at their own men to arm and get ready for a fight should the
Horsekin sally to escape the fire. The last chunks of the wooden
tower collapsed and crumbled below the level of the walls
with a belch of black, greasy smoke that streamed up and
arched over the river. Sparks flared, then died, within the
cloud. A few fell on the wet Deverry encampment, only to
hiss and go out. The cloud, however, enveloped them with
the stench of burning brimstone. Coughing and choking, the
princes and gwerbret ran to join their men.

The smoke began to clear almost immediately. The cries
of the horns and the shouts of the Horsekin died away. Kov
assumed that someone inside had figured out how to smother
the flames with dirt rather than aggravating them with water.
Up on Zakh Gral's walls the helmets of its guards returned,
black with ash.

The little door beside the gates swung open. Minaz the
herald appeared, waving his staff.

'Worked like a charm,' Brel muttered – then realized what
he'd just said. 'Luck, that's all that blasted storm was! Couldn't
be dweomer, just couldn't.'

Larn, Grosh, and the sappers ignored him – militantly.

Tricked out with his wolfskin and drum, Salamander hurried
after Indar and Maelaber as they went to meet the Gel da'
Thae herald. Minaz smelled of smoke, and a layer of ash
dusted his stiff reddish mane, but he stood proudly, his head
thrown back, as they greeted him.

'We have an offer to make your princes,' Minaz said. 'We
will give you all our slave women and a tribute of gold if
you'll withdraw from our lands. We have a hundredweight
of gold as you reckon weight. Load it upon your carts and
leave us in peace.'

'We don't want tribute,' Indar said. 'Your goddess wishes her devout women to live long lives so that they may spread her teachings. We are offering them the opportunity to do so because we believe that helpless women should not die for the sins of their menfolk. We offer your priestesses as well as your slave women refuge and life.'

'The priestesses perhaps might be persuaded to leave. And the gold? Is a hundredweight not enough?'

'We are not here for plunder. We ask you to flee Zakh Gral so we may finish burning it to the ground without burning you with it. And we demand you stop the raids on our farmlands.'

Maelaber stepped forward. 'Prince Daralanteriel adds this message: we will not tolerate a dagger laid against our throat. Zakh Gral must be the last fortress you ever build upon the Galan Targ.'

Minaz considered. The young bard drummed out a restless rhythm with his long fingers while he turned his eyeless face this way and that. Salamander broke into chant, reciting the few lines that he could remember, in Elvish, of 'The Burning of the Vale of Roses'. When Minaz raised his staff, Salamander fell silent, and the bard followed his example.

'I hear Ranadar's name on the lips of your bard,' Minaz said. 'The message is clear. I shall tell the rakzanir of your demands.'

Bard and herald retreated, a little too fast for dignity, back to the fortress. Both Indar and Maelaber glared at Salamander.

'The message, or so I'd guess, is that we want vengeance,' Salamander said. 'Their ancestors burned Ranadar's city to the ground and slaughtered everyone they could grab, too, women, babies, the lot.'

'The sentiment's appropriate enough.' Indar considered him with pursed lips. 'Next time, however, do warn me before you chant somewhat with so much meaning.'

They returned to their own lines and commanders. While Indar gave his report, Salamander stood off to one side with Grallezar.

'May I ask you somewhat?' Salamander said to her.

'You may, though I may not answer.'

'Minaz the herald — you knew him before?'

'I did. He were a man loyal to Braemel many years ago, and at that time he did court me. Almost did I marry him, but my mother, may she have rest in the Deathworld, did forbid it. At the time, I did weep, but I see now that she were right. He be a person of weak character, if he'd turn traitor to his city.'

When Indar finished, Prince Voran called Grallezar to his side to join the council. Salamander sat down on the ground, but he'd barely got comfortable when Minaz and the bard appeared in front of Zakh Gral and signalled for another parley. Once again the two heralds and Salamander hurried out to neutral ground.

'The rakzanir say that they will send out the women,' Minaz said, 'if your princes will let us fight and die like men. Take the women away. Then let us sally before you attempt to burn the fortress.'

'And the rest of the terms?' Indar said.

'Our rakzanir cannot speak for every Gel da' Thae warrior in our lands. If you win this battle, you may rest assured that none of the men here will ever raid your farms again. Never have I heard of a man coming back from the dead to swing his sabre once more. If you lose, then we shall see. The future is a very dark place, good herald. No man can peer into it and insist he has seen clearly what dwells inside.'

'That is very true.' Indar smiled with thin lips. 'I shall tell the princes what you've said here.'

Before the commanders and the rakzanir agreed on terms, the heralds went back and forth three more times. At last, when the sun hung well past its zenith, Minaz announced that the women would be coming out as soon as they could gather their possessions together. By then Salamander was trembling from the twin exhaustions of fear and hope. Soon he would see Rocca — if all went well, if the Horsekin refrained from some quick treachery. As he followed the heralds back to the front lines, he staggered and nearly fell. Maelaber grabbed him to steady him.

'Take off the wolfskin!' Grallezar ran out to meet them. 'The day's heat be troubling you. Your face, it be red as sunset.'

Salamander did just that, then allowed her to lead him, because he was nearly as blind as the Gel da' Thae bard from heat stroke. She fetched water in a leather bucket and handed him a dipper. He sat on the ground and drank as much water as he could get down, then poured the rest over his head. As his vision cleared, he looked around and realized that the men were arming and rushing past to saddle their horses.

'What is this?' Salamander said. 'Is the battle going to start right now?'

'Nah, nah, nah, or so we do hope.' Grallezar smiled, all fangs. 'Your princes, they be wise not to trust the rakzanir, so the army does go on alert. I think me, though, that the Gel da' Thae inside Zakh Gral will make the Horsekin keep their word.'

Salamander felt well enough to rejoin the heralds at the call for another parley. Maelaber was helping Salamander put on the wolfskin when a young Deverry man came trotting up to fling himself down to a kneel in front of Indar. A skinny lad, neither handsome nor ugly, with thick brown hair slicked back from his forehead, he wore no mail or helm, nor did he carry a sword.

'Please, good herald,' he said, 'a boon!'

'What's all this?' Indar said. 'Who are you?'

'My name's Tarro, my lord. I ride for Gwerbret Ridvar, but I disarmed so I could go with you – well, if you allow it. I think my sister might be one of the slave women. We lived out on the Great West Road, the village they burned early this summer.'

'I see,' Indar said. 'Very well, then, come along.'

'My humble thanks, my lord.' Tarro got up. 'I can't bear waiting. She's the only kin I've got left in the world.'

Salamander could understand how the waiting would eat at Tarro. He was feeling the same sharp teeth himself. Out in the neutral ground the two heralds stood with staves upraised until, after what seemed hours, the little door of the fortress swung open. Minaz stepped out, staff held high. As he walked to meet them, a long line of women followed, led by High Priestess Lakanza and the two Gel da' Thae priestesses, all of them as grave and stately as if they were leading some holy procession on one of Alshandra's festival days. But where was Rocca? Salamander rose on tip-toe, looking frantically up and down the straggling line of slave women in their dirty dresses.

All at once Tarro whooped in triumph and rushed forward. A brown-haired skinny girl broke out of line and ran to him, threw herself into his arms, and burst out sobbing. She was no more than a lass, Salamander realized, certainly no more than twelve summers old if that.

'I knew you'd come,' she kept saying, 'I knew you'd come for me.'

All Tarro could do was stroke her cropped-off hair as he wept with her. Minaz was watching the pair with a puzzled frown.

'His sister,' Indar said with some asperity. 'Do such kin ties matter among you?'

'They do, and most deeply.' Minaz paused to clear his throat. 'Did you think perhaps they did not? I merely wondered what relation the lass might be to him.'

Indar and his Gel da' Thae counterpart looked at each other for a long stony moment. The thin web of civility among heralds stretched close to breaking; then Minaz turned away with a shrug. 'These are all the women in the dun who would leave,' he said. 'Have you any messages for my rakzanir?'

By then the crowd of rescued women had hurried on past. Salamander spun around with Minaz's words burning in his soul: all the women who would leave. He saw no sign of Rocca anywhere he looked. He desperately wanted to run after them, to find Lakanza and beg her to tell him where Rocca might be, but he still had a role to play in the complex exchanges between the heralds. Although Zakh Gral's women might be safe, the lives of the men in both armies still stood at the edge of death's cliff. Honour demanded that terms be discussed, and threats exchanged, and more terms offered, even though every man there knew that words would never turn aside the battle.

By the time they'd finished, the sun hung just above the horizon. Salamander and the heralds hurried back to their lines to find the men still fully armed and ready, sitting on the ground beside their horses. While the heralds rushed off to talk with the commanders, Salamander lagged behind, wondering if he'd be required to stay. Wearing his mail shirt and sword belt, but carrying his helm, Gerran came to meet him.

'Go back to camp,' he said. 'I already sent Clae back. Take care of him if I fall, will you?'

'I will, but I'll pray you don't.'

They clasped hands for what might have been the last time. When a servant brought his horse, Salamander mounted up and rode off. A hundred yards or so away he turned in the saddle and looked back to see Gerran standing in the road, one hand upraised in farewell, his red hair like a beacon in the sunset.

Salamander reached the camp just as twilight was thickening into a hot summer night. Midges swarmed as he turned his horse over to servants and strode among the clusters of tents. Here and there little fires bloomed, and by their light he could see people eating or talking in low voices. Salamander searched until he found Clae, sitting by a fire with Grallezar.

'Ah, there you be!' Grallezar said. 'Come eat.'

'I need to go talk with the high priestess first.' Salamander's stomach growled audibly. 'Save me some bread, will you?'

'I will,' Clae said. 'They put the holy women in that big tent over there. I can tell the guards to let you in.'

'Better yet, ask one to come in with me,' Salamander said. 'These women have reason to hate me, after all.'

Inside the tent a cluster of candles stood on the hearth-stone underneath the smokehole. Among their little heaps of belongings, the priestesses and their maidservants sat huddled on the floor cloth, except for Lakanza. Someone had brought a wooden crate for the high priestess, who perched on top of a folded blanket placed on the crate to pad it. Near her feet sat a tall, rangy Deverry woman with dirty red hair. At the sight of Salamander and the guard, the Deverry woman rose to her knees and scowled. The rest of the priestesses got up and made a show of turning their backs on Salamander before they sat down again, as far away as possible. Lakanza leaned forward and laid a gentle hand on the red-haired woman's arm.

'It be all right, Mauva,' Lakanza said. 'I fain would speak with Evan.'

'Mauva?' Salamander said. 'Are you Neb's aunt?'

'Not any more. I was his uncle's wife, sure enough,' the red-haired woman said. 'Now I've got me a better life.' She glanced at Lakanza in wet-eyed adoration. 'Her holiness showed me the way.'

Lakanza leaned forward and murmured a few words too softly for Salamander to hear. Mauva nodded, then got up and went to join the other women at the far side of the tent. The guard stood by the door, one hand on the hilt of his sword, while Salamander knelt beside the high priestess.

'I came to ask you to forgive me,' Salamander said. 'I had to defend my people against your warleaders, or I'd never have betrayed you. We're not Vandar's spawn, your holiness. We're just mortals like you and yours. I swear it to you.'

Lakanza considered him unspeaking, her dark eyes bright and thoughtful despite the web of wrinkles that surrounded them.

'I can't find Rocca,' he went on. 'Why didn't she come out with the rest of you?'

'Truly, be you surprised?' Lakanza's voice wavered close to tears. 'All her trust she does put in Alshandra, to protect her and our holy relics both, or, if *she* wills it, then to die in the shrine. The two dragons be here, I see, and your dwarves do use evil magic against us, so methinks it be the last war at the ending of the world, just as prophecy do tell us.'

'It's not, your holiness. It's merely a strike by my people against those who've slaughtered our allies like sheep.'

'No doubt your prince of darkness told you such. There be no need upon it to be true. Now, you answer me somewhat. Since you be not taken to *her* country, how then did you escape the tower? Were it witchery?'

'It was, Your Holiness. There was no miracle.'

Lakanza said nothing, her wrinkled hands flaccid in her lap, and stared off into empty air. At length she sighed and shook her head. 'It does ache my heart the worst of all, that I were so unfair to our Sidro. She did try to warn me in hints and suchlike that you be a witchman, but in my pride I listened not. Be you a mazrak, then?'

'I am, Your Holiness. I tricked you into imprisoning me in the tower, and then I flew away.'

'Evan, Evan! End your evil ways, I do beg you, before it be too late. Be not asking me for forgiveness! Ask *her*, and *she* will give it. You'd not be here on your knees before me if in your heart you knew not how evil a thing this witchery be.'

'There's naught evil about the dweomer. That's not what aches my heart. It's that I betrayed you and Rocca both.'

'What of that omen in the black stone? Rocca did see a frightful vision there. A picture did appear of our goddess in the sky, but then she were torn to pieces by invisible beasts. She did die above a ford, while below the Lijik army did cheer and gloat. Were it you who did send it to torment us?'

'What? I didn't! Never would I mock you that way, never! Please believe me.'

'I do believe you.' Lakanza considered for a moment, then sighed. 'Who sent it, I know not, mayhap Vandar himself, but it gladdens my very soul that you be innocent of it. I do think me, Evan, that someday your true heart will speak, and then you'll be coming back to us, where you belong. I'll pray to our goddess to make it so.'

Salamander looked up at her face, at her dark eyes, so concerned, so genuinely kind, so deeply worried about him and his soul, despite the doom he'd brought to her people in the fortress – and to Rocca, as well. He tried to speak, then wept, sobbing like a child, while she laid both hands on his head and blessed him.

'Lakanza's safe in the Ancients' camp,' Laz said. 'I told you they wouldn't kill an old woman. So are your other sisters in Alshandra, as far as I could tell, anyway.'

'Well, if there are any gods, I thank them,' Sidro said. 'And if you're telling me the truth.'

'Sisi, I wouldn't lie about something like that.'

'Oh, wouldn't you? You lied when you told me you'd warned them that the Lijik army was coming. It crossed the ford without anyone there to stop it.'

'What? I told you, first of all, that I was working a complicated spell without ever having done it before. Second, even if the stone showed them what I wanted to show them, your holy fools had to interpret the omen. Don't blame me if they got it all wrong.'

'Well, that's true, isn't it? I'm sorry.'

He scowled at her, then continued. 'It was an interesting flight over Zakh Gral this time. I wasn't the only raven there, though the others were either ordinary birds or else very very small mazrakir.' He paused for a grin at his own jest. 'I'll wager on the former. Ravens always seem to know when the gods of war are going to feed them. Oddly enough, I didn't frighten them. Usually I do. It's my greater size, I suppose, or else they can tell I'm not a real raven. But the prospect of a nice bloody battle seemed to make them fearless.'

Laz stood watching her with his hands clasped behind

him, elbows cocked like wings, head tilted a little to one side. Sidro suddenly wondered if his sorcery would someday transmute him into a real raven. She could remember some odd warnings in the scrolls Hazdrubal had brought with him from the Black Isles, but the idea struck her as too grotesque to take seriously.

'What's wrong?' he said.

'Oh, nothing, really. It's just the thought of all the bloodshed.'

'Ah. Well, I'll hold my tongue about it and other morbidities, then. Here, I need to go talk with Pir. I'll be back shortly.'

As soon as he left, Sidro sat down at the table and scried for Lakanza. This time Laz had been telling the truth. She saw Lakanza sitting inside a tent, with a man kneeling in front of her — Evan! *That little viper*, Sidro thought. *How dare he speak to her!* She saw that indeed, the other priestesses sat near her as well, except for Rocca. When Sidro thought of her former rival, the image built up quickly: Rocca alone in the shrine, prostrate on the floor before Alshandra's altar as she prayed, her hands tight-clasped.

Get out of there, you fool! was Sidro's instant thought. Rocca apparently heard nothing. The black pyramid sat on the altar, high above her head. Although Sidro stared into its twin for a long while, Rocca never approached the gem. Without it, Sidro couldn't reach her mind. When she felt utterly unexpected tears in her eyes, she gave up trying.

'I don't hate her any more,' Sidro said aloud. 'I wonder why?'

Salamander slept little that night and woke well before dawn. He got up, grabbed his clothes, and left the tent to dress outside to avoid waking Clae. Although he knew that he could stay in the relative safety of the camp without anyone questioning his honour, he went out to the horse herd just as the eastern sky was turning an opalescent grey. He saddled and bridled his roan gelding, then led him back to the road.

'Sorry, old lad,' Salamander said to the horse. 'I can't sit here and wonder what might be happening to Rocca. Let's hope our friends win the battle, or we might both end up as Horsekin slaves.'

Salamander mounted up and headed back towards Zakh Gral. High overhead, the dragons circled, black and silver in the rising sunlight, like omens from a nightmare.

Just at dawn the army of the two princes woke, gobbled whatever food they could find fast, then armed. Since he'd been chosen to ride in the second wave, Gerran saddled up his horse. The commanders had laid out a simple enough battle plan. Let the Horsekin sally as promised, then let the dragons and the archers disrupt their cavalry while the Mountain Folk set fire to the fortress. After that – Gerran smiled at the thought. No one could predict what would happen after that, no matter how many commanders discussed the matter.

The archers set up a secure position behind their waist-high stakes off to the army's right flank. The Mountain axemen and the swordsmen, Deverry and Westfolk both, who would fight on foot ranged themselves in the front lines, facing Zakh Gral, while the men who'd fight on horseback took up a position well back from the field. Off to the left the dwarven engineers fussed over Big Girl and her little sisters, four more bellybows mounted on wooden stands, though these would shoot only ordinary bolts to defend their position from a Horsekin charge.

Inside the fortress horns sounded. From his distance Gerran heard them as thin cries, like puppies whining. He rose in the saddle and watched the huge doors of the fortress inch open. Between them he could see horses – riderless horses. He swore under his breath as he realized what was about to happen. From the fortress screams went up, shouts, the banging of drums and the clashing of sabres. Panicked horses plunged out of the fortress and galloped straight for the unmounted men in the front lines.

The archers loosed a flat volley into the herd. The lead horses reared, screaming, with arrows in their chests, and fell, kicking and writhing, but the rest leapt over their bodies and charged forward. Another flight of arrows hissed into the herd. As blood spilled onto the ground, horses slipped and went down, but still others carried the charge forward. Drums sounded overhead; the dragons swooped down from the side and roared. Horses scattered, turned aside, went plunging and neighing to the south and north as the dragons harried them.

A handful of massive warhorses still galloped straight into the scattering swordsmen. Men fell, crushed and broken, as the centre of the line broke. In the chaos came Gel da'Thae, advancing in lock-step, spears level, like some huge scythe aimed to mow down the broken ranks facing them.

'Ah horseshit!' Gerran screamed. 'Fuck the plans! Red Wolf, to me!'

He kicked his horse hard and headed for the battle. Howling warcries, the warband followed. They dodged through the retreating swordsmen and slammed into the flank of the Gel da' Thae line before the spearmen could wheel and reform their shield wall to face them. Gerran slashed, yelled, swung back and forth at every head or arm he could see. His horse reared, kicked out with its front hooves, came down hard on one fallen spearman. When his horse reared again, over the swirling mass of shields and spears, Gerran caught a glimpse of Mountain axemen, slashing in from the other flank. He could hear arrows, hoped they'd overfly him and his men, heard Ridvar's men shouting 'Cengarn! Cengarn!' behind him as the second wave of horsemen slammed into the breaking ranks of the spearmen.

A Gel da' Thae thrust his spear at his horse's neck. Gerran leaned, swung, cracked the spear just in time, then clubbed the man on the helmet with his backswing. The man went down under the hooves of another Deverry man's horse. In the welter of dying horses and dying men on the blood-soaked ground, the spearmen slippedand staggered. They'd lost any chance of reforming their shield walls, and with that loss they began to lose their lives as well.

Gerran kept cutting, leaning, fending off spear thrusts with his shield, while his horse kicked and bit, plunging onward. He saw the enemies only as faces and shoulders, the gleam of helmets and the spurt of blood as swords struck home. The warcries behind him told him that his men followed close behind him. Suddenly he smelled smoke – a lot of smoke – thick clouds of it eddied down, flecked with burning. The spearmen broke utterly, throwing shields, running for their lives, only to find themselves facing Mountain axes. The horsemen cut them down from behind as fast as the dwarves cut from the front.

Gerran broke through the line at last, nearly rode into a volley from Westfolk archers, and turned his horse barely in time. Here and there on the field Gel da' Thae spearmen had formed up into desperate clusters and squares. Horsemen rode around and around them, trying to break in while axemen shouted at them to get out of the way. Deverry and Westfolk swordsmen faced off with the near-berserk Horsekin, who screamed wordlessly as they attacked without the slightest thought or skill.

Behind it all Zakh Gral blazed. Ashes fell, swirling down upon the dying and the victors alike, white ash, black cinder, and here and there flecks of burning bark or scraps of cloth. Men swore as the burning kissed them. The wooden walls had turned into solid flame. Over the crackle and hiss of burning wood, Gerran heard the boom and crack of stones splitting under heat or falling as the beams that supported them burned through.

Almost over, Gerran thought, *and we've won*. At the edge of the battlefield he dismounted to rest his blowing, foam-streaked horse for the rout sure to follow, then took off his helm and padded cap to shake sweat from his hair. He heard someone moan and looked around. Nearby lay a pair of dead

horses, a grey killed by sword cuts, and a chestnut, who'd
fallen on top of the other, pierced with arrows. As he watched,
a Horsekin soldier stood up from behind this shelter, dragging
to his feet a wounded comrade, who moaned and staggered,
leaning on his friend, his broken right leg trailing. Blood ran
down his side.

The unwounded man stared at Gerran, his mouth working.
Gerran settled his helm and drew his sword, but the fellow
made no move towards him, merely stared as if he couldn't
believe what he was seeing. He'd lost his helm; a greyish-
brown colour streaked his tangled mane of hair, and the
tattooed skin around his eyes pouched in wrinkles. He wore
no breastplate, either, though Gerran saw the marks on his
leather jerkin that indicated where one had been.

'You come back,' the Horsekin said in stumbling Deverrian.
'You come back from Deathworld.' His voice failed.

'What?' Gerran was too surprised to say aught else.

'You come back,' he stammered. 'Red hair. I remember.'

Suddenly Gerran understood. 'You killed my father. I'm
the son.'

The Horsekin let his wounded comrade slide down to sit
behind the barrier of dead horses. He drew his falcata, took
a step back, stooped without looking away from Gerran, and
came up with a shield in his left hand. Gerran hoisted his
own shield down from the saddle peak and slid his left arm
into the straps. Every detail of the scene – the aging warrior,
the dead horses, the blood and the spill of horse guts across
the ground – glowed in a peculiar light, preternaturally sharp,
edges drawn like lines bitten into metal.

Gerran walked around the dead horses. The warrior spun
to face him, but he made no move to charge. Gerran hesitated
briefly – the man had no helm, no real armour – but in his
mind he heard his mother screaming over and over as men slid
the bundled corpse of his father down from his saddle. He
feinted in to the right side. The Horsekin turned, falcata ready,
shield up for a parry. Gerran feinted again, then risked a quick

dart forward. Just as Gerran hoped, the Horsekin stepped back, slipped in the spilled guts of his horse, and went down.

One quick stride, and Gerran stood over him, sword at the ready. The Horsekin tried to bring up his sword and drag his shield part-way over his chest, but Gerran kicked the shield away and struck, plunging his blade down into the man's chest. Leather split, cartilage cracked, blood gushed. The Horsekin's breath came in one last blood-flecked rattle.

'If you see my da in the Otherlands,' Gerran said. 'Tell him I avenged him.'

He swung around and with a backhand strike cut the throat of the Horsekin with the broken leg.

'And one for my mother,' Gerran whispered. 'Tell him that, too.'

Two menservants trotted up, slid the body of an unconscious man onto the wagon's tailgate, then trotted off again. Ranadario stepped forward to grab the man's legs and hold him down. A skinny lad, his brown hair plastered with blood and sweat, he lay so still that at first Dallandra thought he was dead, but his eyes flicked open, and his mouth moved with pain. His left arm lay at an impossible angle – two impossible angles, she realized, crushed twixt elbow and wrist, then mangled again twixt shoulder and elbow. She grabbed a knife from the array of supplies on the wagon bed and cut away the remains of his padded jerkin and shirt, both of them slippery with blood. Jagged pieces of bone stuck out of what was left of the muscles on his upper arm.

'The arm's going to have to come off,' Dallandra said, 'or you'll die.'

His mouth framed soundless words that she took as meaning 'well and good then'.

From close behind her she heard someone sob, just once, hastily stifled. She looked around and saw a skinny lass in a dirty dress staring at the wounded man.

'He's my brother Tarro,' the lass said. 'Can I help you?'

'Grab his good arm and hold it still,' Dallandra said. 'Think you can do that? You might get very sick from watching.'

'I won't. I saw lots worse, you know, when the raiders took our village.'

'Well and good, then. He's got to hold still.'

Her patient had fainted again, a blessing. Dallandra took her sharpest scalpel between her teeth and a threaded needle in her right hand and set to work. The joint lay mostly exposed by cuts from a falcata. She dug into it with the fingers of her left hand and found the pink tendons among the white cartilage. Tarro woke, screaming. He arched his back in agony, but Ranadario and the lass held on and hauled him down again. Dallandra leaned onto his chest with her left elbow to pin him further. He kept screaming and tossing his head from side to side, but the three of them could keep him motionless enough for her to work.

First she stitched the major blood vessels shut above the joint, then tossed the needle aside. She spit the scalpel into her hand, steadied it, and cut the tendons. With her fingers she separated the cartilage and cut again, disjointing his arm from his body much as she would have disjointed a leg of mutton, but she took care to leave a flap of skin all round. Blood oozed from tiny veins rather than gushed. Tarro fainted with one last scream.

Ranadario grabbed the remains of the limb and tossed it onto the heap of other dead flesh on the wagon bed, whilst Dalla held a thick linen pad to the wound with her left hand and pressed hard. With the right she grabbed a waterskin of herbal brew, then removed the pad and washed the joint and the flap of skin. A small hand gave her a fresh needle, threaded with a single linen strand. The sister seemed as composed as if she'd been a chirurgeon. She was in shock, more likely, but Dalla had no time to worry about her at the moment.

'Please don't die,' the lass whispered to her brother. 'Please, Tarro, don't die.'

'He won't,' Dallandra said. 'The bleeding's nowhere near

as bad as I feared it would be.' *Probably,* she thought, *because he's already bled half to death.*

But only half – once she'd stitched the wound, puckering the skin around his new stump like the end of a sausage, Dalla laid her hand on his face, cold and pale, but not deathly cold and bloodless, though his eyelids did have a bluish tint. If nothing more happened to the wound, if it stayed free of infection, he probably would live. She washed it all down again, then bound it with clean linen.

The menservants trotted forward. Dallandra turned to the lass. 'What's your name?'

'Penna, my lady. My thanks for helping him.' She ran off, following her brother as the servants carried him away.

Ranadario grabbed a waiting bucket of water and sluiced down the blood-soaked tailgate. Dallandra moved away from the gore flecked run-off and looked around. Head down, Salamander was striding along the lines of wounded men. She could guess whom he was searching for.

'Ebañy!' Dallandra called out. 'Rocca's not been brought in.'

'You're sure?' He raised his head to look her way. 'Of course you are. I'll go look in the fortress.'

'Not now, you howling dolt! It's too dangerous.'

Salamander ran off, heading for the battlefield.

'Shall I go after him?' Ranadario said.

'No.' Dallandra shrugged. 'He won't listen, and the wounded need you more.'

Salamander had been trying to scry for Rocca, only to have the smoke and the vast etheric disturbance of the battle defeat him. The etheric doubles of the men who had just died drifted helplessly across the field. Their spilled blood gave off life-stuff in waves of mist. The burning, too, filled the air around it with swirling vortices of astral energy. Finally Salamander gave it up. He could stand waiting no longer and went physically to the battlefield, where he crept around the battle's edge from the north.

Around him the fighting flared sporadically, just as a fire appears dead only to burst into flame when a servant stirs the ashes. Here and there Horsekin warriors made a stand, only to be cut down by Deverry men in twos and threes. An arrow whistled close by him – far too close, and Salamander began yelling out Prince Dar's name in Elvish to make sure the archers realized he was no enemy. Once he stumbled over a dying man and apologized without thinking before he hurried on again.

The wooden walls of Zakh Gral still blazed when Salamander reached them. The heat drove him back, a searing second wall, far more impassable than mere wood and stone. A memory from his brief time there surfaced. He ran down to the cliff edge on the north side of the fortress and found what he was remembering, a breach in a stretch of half-finished stone wall, probably left for a postern gate. The stone blocks now lay cracked and steaming, but he could pick his way through. The heat still clawed at him. He gasped for breath and pushed himself onward.

Once he got inside, he stopped running and considered his position while he panted for breath. Where would Rocca have gone? Eventually, she would try to flee, but he knew that she'd never leave without making sure the sacred relics were safe. He ran towards the little stone shrine, or rather, what was now the ruins of the shrine. The dwarven fire had burnt out the roof beams, and the roof itself had collapsed. Flames had cracked and blackened the fine stonework.

All around it lay dead and dying Gel da' Thae. They had tried to save their goddess's shrine and failed as Westfolk arrows rained down, killing the lucky ones outright. The others – the bitumen mixture had stuck like fangs to their flesh wherever it had struck them. Tiny flames still danced on blackened faces and arms turned to cinders. One man raised his charred head and called out to Salamander, 'Kill me, kill me! For *her* sake!' Salamander broke into a run and hurried past. Here and there an overturned bucket lay in a pool of water, but the black fire floated, still burning, in the puddles.

In the smoke and the dust, in the midst of shrieks of terror and cries of pain that hung as thick as the smoke and dust, Salamander finally found Rocca. Muffled in a shabby cloak she had wedged herself in to a corner of stone ruins, and she sat so still that he thought her dead, but when he knelt down in front of her, the cloak trembled as she moved an arm. In her lap lay a cloth sack, crammed full.

'It's Evan,' he said in Deverrian. 'Are you hurt?'

Slowly she raised her head and even more slowly lifted a hand to shove back the cloak's hood. Soot and grime caked her face, except where tears had embroidered a patten on each cheek. Blood crusted the hand that lingered beside her face.

'You *are* hurt. Tell me where!'

She looked up and smiled at him, a radiant burst of joy.

'Evan!' she whispered. 'You've come back. It be that you'll be bringing me to our goddess, isn't it?'

'Tell me where you're hurt.' He saw, then, the blood seeping through her cloak, a spread of crimson all down her side. When he folded the cloak back, he could see her blood-stained dress, half-torn away to reveal worse-torn flesh beneath. As far as he could tell, some heavy but sharp thing had fallen upon her, to do its worst damage when she struggled to get free. As carefully as he could, he picked her up. She cried out in pain, but he settled her against his chest. Staggering under her weight, he headed for the breach in the stone wall.

The smoke hung so thick that at first he feared he'd gone in the wrong direction. He could barely breathe, and her added weight made him gasp as he staggered onward in the parching hot air. One foot after the other – his world shrank to that, one foot after the other, until at last he saw ahead of them the opening in the stone wall. He was coughing and spitting, but he carried her through at last. He managed to get a few yards beyond the dying fortress before he could go no further.

When he laid her down she whimpered. He knelt down beside her and realized that he'd come too late. Blood soaked her dress and his shirt where she'd lain against him. Her face had turned a ghastly white.

'Will I see *her* soon?' She whispered the words.

'You will, truly.' *Even if I end up mad again*, he thought, *you will have that.*

Salamander summoned every bit of dweomer he had and thought of Alshandra, built up an image of her, vast, towering over them, but smiling, holding out her hands as if to greet her priestess. With a wrench of will he sent the image out from his mind. He could see it as if it hovered in the air over them. At first he feared he'd misjudged Rocca's latent dweomer talents, but all at once she smiled in her brilliant way and lifted one hand towards the image.

'Beloved,' she whispered. 'My life and hope.'

Salamander summoned his body of light, a silvery flame-shaped glow. He transferred over fast, too fast, but her etheric body had already separated from the flesh, and he had no time to spend on caution. Together he and Rocca floated in the blue light, high above the swirling storm over the battle-field. Before them the image of Alshandra towered, huge but smiling, and stretched out her hands to her worshipper.

'Go with her.' Salamander sent his thoughts to Rocca. 'Let us go with her to the river of life.'

With no dweomer training Rocca lacked the skill to send him coherent thought messages, but he could feel her joy, a pure thing like morning sunlight, as they rose together through the whirling indigo vortex that led inward to the astral. Ahead of them stretched the meadow of white flowers, pale under violet light, nodding in some intangible breeze. On the other side of the stretch of flowers Salamander could just make out the white river whose water has never flowed on land or into sea. He gave Alshandra's image a mental push that sent it floating towards the boundary of life and death. Smiling still, Rocca followed without his urging.

Pain struck Salamander like a razor cut. A tug on the silver cord wrenched him away from her. With a sound like the roar of a waterfall he plunged back into his body with a yelp of sheer agony as his etheric double slammed into bone and blood, muscle and skin. In his arms Rocca still breathed, but faintly, and for only a few heartbeats more. Her head flopped back, and her lungs emptied in a last rattling sob. He grabbed her shoulders and lifted her half off the ground.

'Rocca!' He howled out her name. 'Rocca!'

She had gone beyond answering him in any world. Gently he laid her down, then closed her unseeing eyes. When he looked up, the air seemed strangely thick and shimmering. Not madness, he realized, but tears. He bent his head and wept so hard that he was barely aware of the man running towards him, sword raised.

'Salamander!' Gerran shouted. 'Gerthddyn! You fool! Get out of here! The whole cursed field's on fire.'

Salamander grabbed the sack of relics, tried to stand, and nearly fell. Gerran seized him by one arm and hauled him to his feet. All around them fire crackled in the grass as it leapt from broken beams and walls. Greasy black smoke rose high in the sky. *At least she'll have a pyre*, Salamander thought. *There's naught else I can do for her.*

'Come on, move!' Gerran was yelling. 'Do you have horse-shit where your brains ought to be? Run!'

With Gerran hauling him along, Salamander managed to do just that. Together they stumbled through the spreading fire to the safety of the Red Wolf warband, waiting with horses on the edge of the battlefield.

'It's over,' Calonderiel said. 'Prince Voran and his men are chasing down the hairy bastards that managed to escape. The rest of our men are keeping the fire back from the camp.'

'Good,' Dallandra said.

'Is that all you can say?'

'Cal, I just finished taking an archer's leg off at the knee. He still might die anyway. I'm in no mood to sing your praises or whatever it is you want.'

Dallandra was sitting on the ground between two tents, taking a desperately needed rest. Calonderiel hunkered down in front of her. He reeked of sweat and smoke, and a mixture of the two smeared his face and neck. All down his right arm blood oozed through his mail.

'You're wounded,' Dallandra said.

'Not truly,' he said. 'I can still use the arm, so it can't be that bad. You look exhausted.'

'I am.' She watched as two Deverry men, supporting a wounded third between them, staggered past. 'That one's not that badly off. The chirurgeons can tend him.'

'Good.' Calonderiel pulled off his pot helm and pushed his sweat-soaked hair back from his face with both hands, leaving a smear of blood across his forehead. 'Why don't you go back to our tent and hide from all this? By now you've either treated the worst wounded, or they're dead.'

Dallandra allowed him to help her up. Although she was tempted to lean on him, she shook herself free of his offered embrace. 'I'm not that tired,' she said. 'I need to go back and see – Wait! There's Ebañy heading our way.'

Salamander trotted up, carrying a blood-stained sack. Blood crusted on his sleeves and soaked the front of his shirt.

'Your friend?' Dalla said in Elvish.

'Is dead.' Salamander tossed his head, then spasmed with a racking cough that ended when he spat up black rheum. He wiped his mouth on the back of his hand. 'Here are the so-called holy relics.'

Salamander shoved the sack into her arms, then trotted off, dodging among the other men. *He truly loved her, didn't he?* She watched him till she could see him no longer.

'Dalla!' Calonderiel grabbed her arm. 'You should go back to our tent.'

'I'll go back if you go.'

'You know I can't do that.' His mouth went slack, and he looked away. 'Too many of our men are dead. I've at least got to go speak to the wounded.'

'And I've got to do what I can for them. Let's go tend them together.'

Calonderiel had told her the truth about his wound. When she finally got a chance to examine his arm, she saw that a blow from the trailing edge of a falcata had landed with enough force to split the skin through his padding and mail, but the cuts were shallow and easily stitched. His mood, however, would take far more time to heal. He glowered and swore revenge for every dead man, for every wound any of his men had taken until he became a walking pillar of rage and little more.

With Calonderiel to worry over and so many wounded men to attend, Dalla had no chance to open the sack of relics that day or night. By then, with the fires beaten out, the army had chased down and slaughtered every Horsekin and human straggler from the fortress that they could find. In the morning, the various lords sent a pack of messengers off on their way back to Deverry with the news. Dallandra had already used dweomer to send messages from Prince Daralanteriel to Valandario and through her, to Princess Carra and the others at Mandra.

While Dallandra and the chirurgeons did their best to save the wounded, and the warbands buried the men they failed to save, the princes, the gwerbret, and all their lords held a long council of war. Calonderiel told her of their decisions that evening. They were eating a scrappy dinner of stale flatbread and mouldy cheese, augmented by a couple of chunks of stewed horsemeat, in their tent.

'The Roundears are probably still arguing,' Cal said. 'Prince Voran's come up with a splendid idea, but Ridvar doesn't like it. It'll cost him taxes.'

'Let me guess,' Dallandra said. 'The prince thinks Honelg's old dun is indefensible.'

'Right you are, my clever darling! He wants the Mountain Folk to take it over.'

'Now that I'd never have guessed. The Mountain Folk?'

'Why not? They maintain farming villages not all that far east of it. They could join those up with a dun or one of their underground fortresses and form a northern line of defence.'

'But what about Gerran and his new clan?'

'That's where the lost taxes come in. He'd become a vassal of Tieryn Cadryc and be given a new dun on the Melyn river somewhere. That area needs fortifying against raiders anyway. It would be to our advantage as well, having allies right there to call upon in the future.'

'So it would. Do you want some more of this bread?'

'I do, my thanks. So here's the thing that had Ridvar soiling his brigga. Voran wants Cadryc to change allegiance and become Prince Dar's vassal. And of course, all of Cadryc's vassals will come with him.'

'I can't imagine Ridvar allowing that.'

'He'll have to.' Calonderiel paused to grin. 'Otherwise, the high king will create a new gwerbretrhyn just to the south of Ridvar's – or so Voran says, at any rate. And that means a rival on our gwerbret's borders. Oh, he'll let Cadryc go, all right.'

Dallandra found that she could still laugh. 'Grallezar always calls Voran sly. It's a good word for him.'

'Yes, it is.' Calonderiel returned the grin. 'Now, tomorrow the entire army's pulling back to the place where that road to Braemel joins the river. Day after that, part of it will retreat further, across the ford and some miles east.'

'Only part of it?'

'Yes. We'll be sending the wounded back under heavy guard. The rest of us will stay and wait.' He paused to scrape green mould from a chunk of cheese.

'Wait for what?'

'The Horsekin reinforcements. The dragons killed a couple of men we missed who were trying to get back to their cities, but I'm certain that some will make it back, the ones with the wits to reach the forest. The dragons can't follow them there, and we can't ride in after them, either.'

'And when they reach the cities?'

'I can't believe the reserve forces won't march out immediately.' Calonderiel looked up with a sunny grin. 'This is our chance to deal them a blow they'll remember for years, Dalla. The more we kill now, the more time we'll have to fortify duns along the Melyn. If the People are going to survive, we have to have somewhere to retreat to if — no, when — these shit-ugly savages break out onto the grasslands again.' He stabbed the now-clean cheese wedge with his table dagger and gestured with it. 'And you know they will.'

'Yes, I suppose I do. Are you going to stay?'

'Of course. I'm the banadar.'

By sheer dint of will Dallandra managed to keep from shedding angry tears. With the fortress destroyed, she had thought the worst over, but the worst was refusing to end.

'I'll stay with you,' she said. 'Some of our men might well be wounded, and you'll need a healer here who understands the People. I can send two of my assistants back with the others.'

'Good. We'll need you.'

Her gratitude that he would say only the simple truth surprised her. Praise or fulsome thanks would have sickened her, she realized, but all of a sudden she lost her appetite, especially for tough, stringy horsemeat. She handed him the rest of her dinner to finish, then made a dweomer light and hung it near the smokehole.

'What's that for?' Calonderiel said with his mouth full.

'The holy relics from Zakh Gral. I haven't even looked at them yet.'

'You know, those might be useful. No doubt their wretched priestesses will want them back. They could give us something to bargain with in the future.'

'Perhaps. Some of them should be destroyed.'

Dallandra found the sack and sat down with it under the

light. She opened it and pulled out a lumpy bundle wrapped in the banner made of Salamander's old shirt.

'I can't believe they thought that prattling dolt had worked a miracle,' Calonderiel said.

'They wanted a miracle very badly, is why they believed it.' One fold at a time, Dallandra unwrapped the relics and laid them onto a leather cushion beside her. In the dweomer light the golden bow and arrow glittered with a normal metallic sheen.

'Now, these I won't mind turning over to you, if you think they'll be useful,' Dallandra said. 'They're just ordinary objects. So's this.' She picked up a wooden box inlaid with spirals and opened it to reveal the so-called wyvern knife. 'But here's Yraen's silver dagger.' Dallandra handed the box to Calonderiel. 'They shan't have that back. They stole it in the first place. Give it to Gerran, I'd say. None of us can touch the thing without it blazing like a fire.'

'Oh, it might come in handy on a dark night.'

'I doubt if you want to use it for a torch. I'm not sure how it affects us, but I suspect it sucks out life force to fuel the light.'

'Very well, out it goes.' Calonderiel was scowling into the open box. 'I'll see if Gerran wants it. A silver dagger's something of an insult among the Roundears, though.'

'It's too bad we don't know where Yraen's buried, or we could put it in his grave. Otherwise, I don't know what to do with it. One of the Mountain Folk might want it for the metal, I suppose.' She paused to hold up the bone whistle. 'Here's this hideous thing! I don't want it in Horsekin hands. It has an odd power over dragons. I'm planning on giving it to Arzosah to destroy. Huh. If they want Salamander's shirt back, they can have that, but I doubt very much that they will.'

Dallandra opened the last fold and found the black obsidian pyramid lying among the stains and frayed embroideries. It caught the dweomer light and glittered with sparks of what seemed to be black fire, edged with gold. Calonderiel leaned back as if he feared they would burn.

'It won't hurt you,' Dallandra said. 'That's just a manifestation of the spirit trapped in the pyramid. It's furious, I should think.'

'I would be, if someone trapped me somewhere.'

'I'm sure you would, but hush for a moment. Let me see if I can release it.'

Dallandra let herself relax to the edge of trance and opened her etheric sight. She saw a cage of blue light woven around the pyramid, the visible traces of the binding ceremony. Its builder, however, must have been an extremely powerful dweomerworker, because the lines of blue light ran through the obsidian as well, as if the cage had grown tendrils into the crystal. Deep in the black heart of the gem she could just make out a whorl of silver light, spinning around and around in a tiny cell – the trapped spirit.

Dallandra visualized a pentagram, then pushed the image out of her mind onto the etheric cage. Nothing happened. She returned her sight to the physical world with a toss of her head.

'May whoever did this rot!' she said.

'I take it you couldn't just let it go.'

'No, nothing so simple. Cal, would you go find Ebañy? I may need his help for this.'

'You're still so tired. Can't it wait?'

'And how would you feel, if the person who could let you out of prison decided to take a nap first?'

With a sigh Calonderiel got to his feet. 'I'll go look for him. No doubt someone knows where he is.'

Calonderiel ducked out of the tent, to return shortly with Salamander. Purple bruises under his eyes marked the gerthddyn's dead-pale face.

'Our most esteemed banadar told me you wanted my help,' Salamander said. 'Aha, behold the black stone!'

'Just that,' Dallandra said. 'I'm going to go up to the astral to try to free that spirit. I wanted you here in case something went wrong.'

'If naught else, I can channel vital force to you.'

'If you have any to spare. Ebañy, you look utterly drained.'

'Oh, it's only grief. No dweomer, nothing out of the ordinary.'

'Don't! I can't bear to listen to you try to joke it away.'

'No doubt. No more can I bear to listen to myself.' Salamander nearly wept, choked it back, then knelt on the floor near her. 'Are you going into full trance?'

Had it not been for the trapped spirit, Dallandra would have prodded him into the relief of tears. As it was, she said, 'Yes. The simple working I just tried failed miserably.'

Dallandra lay down on her back and set her hands on her chest. Salamander placed the black pyramid in her fingers, then knelt at her head while Calonderiel left to stand guard outside the door. Dallandra built up the image of her body of light, a glowing silver flame, then transferred her consciousness into it. Once she was free of her body, she looked down and saw the obsidian, shot through with lines of blue light, clasped between her pale hands. Unlike ordinary stone, so dead when seen on the etheric plane, the black crystal pulsed gold.

In this state she could work from above, as it were, upon the spirit trap. After an invocation to the Light that shines beyond all the gods, she focused her concentration upon the crystal. She could see the spirit as a golden line beating against the bars of its prison. Now and then it twisted into an agony of struggle.

'Hold still!' she thought to it. 'I come in the name of the Light!'

The golden line swelled in greeting, then shrank down to a point. Inside her flame-shape, Dallandra raised her etheric hands and began to gather force from the blue light billowing around her. She shaped it into the image of an axe, then grabbed the handle with both hands. With another call to the Light, she swung the axe up high and brought it down hard upon the bars of the spirit cage. They shattered into a shower of black sparks.

On a wave of joy the golden line darted from the crystal. As it rose, it grew until it reached a spear's length of gleaming metallic light. Trembling, it stood before her.

'You will have my thanks through all eternity,' the spirit thought to her. 'You are my deliverer. What may I do to serve you?'

Dallandra nearly lost her concentration in sheer surprise. She'd been expecting a fragment of mind such as the Wildfolk have, but this spirit belonged to a much higher order of being if it could send thoughts in the form of words.

'I ask nothing from you,' Dallandra said, 'but to serve the Light always.'

'That shall I do with great joy.'

'Tell me, who trapped you in this gem?'

'I know not his name. If I had, I should have cursed him thrice over. His image — look!'

The golden line flickered, swelled, and transformed itself into the blurry but recognizable image of a Deverry man — a typical Cerrmor man, Dallandra realized, with pale hair and high cheekbones. The illusion melted as fast as a sliver of ice on a hearthstone, leaving the spirit standing before her.

'I can show no more,' it said, 'but if you find that man, beware beware beware!'

'I shall indeed, and my thanks for the warning.'

'The man dripped evil. First he bought my prison from a murderer. He gave the murderer a golden coin for it. Then he built the cage and chased me until I could flee no more. When he trapped me, he mocked me, saying that the only being in any world who could release me was the murderer's mother. And so I raged, thinking I would be bound for all eternity.'

Dallandra felt such a stab of grief that it manifested. A long howl of pain, a keening wail, cut through the billowing blue light. She could feel the spirit's confusion as it swirled about her silver flame.

'You are my deliverer,' it said. 'I meant not to pain you by repeating that evil fool's lie.'

'It was no lie,' Dallandra said. 'I am that woman. I am the murderer's mother.'

The spirit turned into a rigid line of gold, pure force frozen briefly into form. For a moment it hovered in front of her, trying to comprehend, then like an arrow loosed from a bow it launched itself and flew, darting away into the billowing blue mists. Far more slowly Dallandra retreated down the silver cord to her body.

With a grunt of pain she woke to find herself still lying on her back with her fingers twined around the obsidian pyramid. Salamander reached over and took the crystal from her, then rose to call Calonderiel. She unfolded her hands and shook them to bring back feeling to them. She sat up just as Cal came hurrying back into the tent.

'No flopping around this time,' Calonderiel said. 'I can't tell you how glad I am, too.'

'So am I,' Dallandra said. 'I don't need bruises.' She looked Salamander's way. 'The spirit is free.'

Salamander smiled, but tears were running down his face. He handed her the pyramid and tried to speak. With a shrug, he stood up, then ducked under the door flap and left the tent.

'Sisi!' Laz said. 'Come look at this!'

He was sitting at the table with the white pyramid in front of him. Sidro sat down opposite and leaned onto the table to stare into the crystal. Her first glance made her gasp and lean closer. Instead of the Inner Shrine, she saw the smoky image of a woman of the Ancients sitting inside a tent. Golden light fell around her. The woman, silver-eyed and silver-haired, was talking as she pointed to the pyramid. The view changed and swooped so rapidly that Sidro felt momentarily ill. When it cleared, she saw the face of Exalted Mother Grallezar, peering into the smoky view. The Ancients woman had apparently handed the crystal to the Gel da' Thae.

'Rocca must have saved the holy relics somehow.' Sidro tore herself away from the image and looked at Laz. 'They wouldn't have the crystal otherwise.'

'That's true. She did one thing right in her benighted life.'

'Oh, hold your tongue! Don't mock the dead!'

'Why? Do you think she'll come back to curse me if I do?'

'Naught of the sort! It's merely an ugly stupid thing to do.' Sidro looked away, shocked at her own feelings. For years she'd hated Rocca, her rival and tormentor, but now Rocca was dead while she still lived. 'My sister in Alshandra,' she whispered. 'She really was, you know, in spite of everything, a sister. I shall miss her.'

Laz stared, uncomprehending.

'I used to envy her so much,' Sidro continued. 'Her faith came so easily, like a river in spate, where mine was a little trickle from a muddy spring. But now I see that she was mad, absolutely moon-struck. She'll never have the chance to learn the truth. I don't envy her any longer. I'm sorry she's dead, I really am.'

'I suppose I understand that.' Laz spoke softly. 'But I also suppose I don't need to understand.'

'No, you don't.' She managed a smile. 'Not in the least.'

He smiled in return, then lowered his gaze and contemplated the white crystal again. It glowed from within, as if celebrating its twin's release from the dark shrine.

'What I do want to understand,' Laz said, 'is this crystal. I wonder if I can make it show me other views. I want to know how it manages to convey images from one place to the next. And here's an answer very much worth knowing. If someone looks into its twin, can they see us?'

Sidro reflexively laid her hand on her throat.

'Not a nice thought, is it?' Laz said. 'Especially if that minstrel can see you. You'd best not look into it again, Sisi.'

'I won't, then. Maybe you shouldn't either.'

'I'll certainly put it aside for now. I don't want to cause Grallezar any more pain by forcing her to see my disgusting visage. But later, I'll come back to it. It intrigues me.' He picked it up in one hand and stroked it with the forefinger of the other. 'It has other secrets to show me. I'm sure of that.'

Sidro felt a ripple of cold run down her spine. *A wizard warning*, she thought, but she knew Laz too well to hope he'd stop pursuing a thing he wanted because of a mere omen.

Salamander's grief had finally forced him to see the obvious, that he'd been in love with Rocca. The bitterness of the realization haunted him, that he'd not seen how much he'd loved her until his treachery had killed her. He knew that he'd had no choice, that he'd had to protect his people from the Horsekin warriors no matter what the cost to himself or to her. *She was an enemy*, he would remind himself. *She wanted the Westfolk dead.* But always in his mind a traitor voice would answer, *I could have changed her, I could have shown her the truth.*

That night, when sleep refused to come to him, he slipped out of the tent without waking Gerran and Clae, then walked for hours at the edge of the sleeping camp. Now and then he would look up at the stars, so cold and far above him, and weep for her. At last, so weary that he could barely stand, he stumbled back to his blankets and fell into welcome darkness, only to have Gerran shake him awake at dawn.

'You've got to get up,' Gerran said. 'The army's pulling back this morning.'

Salamander mumbled a few unpleasant words under his breath and rolled out of his blankets. He pulled on his boots – he'd slept in the rest of his clothes – and staggered out of the tent to search for food. The servants had been busily packing up all the supplies, but he managed to talk one of the freed village girls into giving him some cold soda bread and half a greasy sausage, which he ate on his way to the horse herd to fetch his roan gelding.

While the rest of the army formed up into a rough marching order, Salamander sat on horseback and looked at the ruins of what had once been Zakh Gral. A breeze lifted wisps of ash and dust and sent them drifting before they scattered and fell. Somewhere in the cinders and shattered stones lay Rocca's ashes. The wind would scatter them, too. The rain would wash them into the river and down to the sea.

'Ebañy!' He heard Dallandra's voice so clearly that it took him a moment to realize he was hearing it only in his mind. 'Ebañy, get back here!'

'I'm on my way!'

Salamander turned his horse and jogged back in the direction of the army to find it already moving out. On her grey gelding, Dallandra was waiting for him. He pulled up next to her mount and turned in the saddle to face her.

'You had to do what you did,' Dallandra said. 'If Rocca had left with the other women, she'd still be alive. She chose to die, Ebañy. You didn't kill her.'

'I forced her into a position where she had that choice to make.'

Her silver eyes considered him in the same cool way that they would assess a man with a battle wound. 'You did?' she said at last. 'Ye gods, how vain are you? The will of the princes, your people, the Deverry lords, and the Deverry high king himself, to say naught of the rakzanir who decided to build that wretched fortress in the first place – none of them had a thing to do with it, did they? It was all you?'

Salamander had never felt so murderous in his life. Dallandra sat calmly in her saddle, though her horse tossed up its head as if it suddenly feared him.

'Well?' she said. 'Am I right?'

Salamander choked back a barrage of curses, then released his anger with a sigh that let him speak normally. 'Of course you are. I wouldn't be furious if you were wrong.'

'Ah, so you can see it. Good!'

'You're becoming as cold-hearted as Nevyn was, I hope you realize.'

'Maybe it's old age.' She smiled at him. 'Let's go catch up with the army. We can talk later.'

That day the army marched back to the west-running road leading to Braemel, a position about half-way between Zakh Gral and the ford. Dallandra and Salamander left the noise and confusion behind and rode a short distance west. Beyond the forested hills they could see the dark rise of the distant mountains. *Someday the People will have to go back there,* Salamander thought, *Horsekin or no Horsekin.*

'Do you feel a little better?' Dallandra said. 'About Rocca, I mean.'

'The guilt has not yet ceased to chew upon my heart, if that's what you mean,' Salamander said. 'But its teeth are shorter and duller. I still wish –' His voice clouded, and he stopped speaking.

'Grief takes its own time to heal,' Dallandra said. 'I'm so sorry you lost her.'

'So am I. Very sorry.'

When they'd gone about a quarter of a mile, they halted and dismounted beside a rivulet, trickling down to join the Galan Targ. They slacked their horses' bits and let them drink while they sat among the rubble from the clear-cut forest. Dallandra set the black pyramid down between them on Salamander's old shirt. With the spirit unbound, Salamander was expecting it to glitter in the usual way of gems, but a peculiar quality still marred its reflected light.

'It's staining the light that touches it,' Salamander said. 'Or withering it? No, that's not it, either. I don't understand.'

'I don't, either, not completely,' Dallandra said, 'but this pyramid isn't physically here in the way that an ordinary piece of stone is here in this world. It's the shadow of a thing that exists on a higher plane.'

'A what? I've never heard of that before.'

'Evandar explained it to me years and years ago. He gave Rhodry a knife that shared the same qualities. These things have their true being on another plane of existence – the lower astral in this case, I'd say – but they cast a shadow onto the physical plane. The shadow's made of matter.'

'It's like the Wildfolk, then.'

'Not precisely, no. When the Wildfolk manifest in our world, they're no longer in their own. They've travelled here, you might say. But with one of these –' Dallandra held up the obsidian pyramid, '– only the shadow is here. The real object's still in its proper world.'

'Yet it feels so solid.'

'It is solid, even though it's only the shadow. It can be held and used and carried around, but doing so has effects in its own world, ones we can't be aware of.'

'That must be why it could bind such a powerful spirit.'

'Exactly.' She paused, her eyes stricken. 'Loddlaen sold it to the man who trapped the spirit.'

'I see.' Salamander tried to think of some comfort to voice but found none. 'Who was he?'

'The spirit had no way of telling me that. It did show me an image of him, a very typical Cerrmor man, I'd say. The spirit used the words "he dripped evil".'

'Dark dweomer, then –' Salamander paused, thinking. 'There was a Cerrmor man who'd learned the dark dweomer in Bardek. He tried to steal the Great Stone of the West – Alastyr, that was his name. Nevyn drove him into a trap, and then the scum's own apprentice killed him. Nevyn told me that this Alastyr had some sort of link with Loddlaen.'

'And a great interest in dweomer gems, it sounds like. Well, it probably was him, then.'

Her face betrayed nothing, nor did her voice, but Salamander knew that hearing her son had trafficked with the dark dweomer must have stabbed her to the heart.

'Should we go back to camp?' he said.

'Not yet.' Dallandra turned calm eyes his way. 'The others

can tend the wounded. I want to sit where it's quiet for a while.'

'Shall I look into the stone?'

'Why not? I hope it'll finish giving you Evandar's message. You know, there was a time when I couldn't bear to say his name, just because I missed him so much, but now things are better, partly thanks to Cal, of course, but partly just because it's been so long. That's one of the gifts the People have, the time to let old loves slip away. The Deverry folk and the Gel da' Thae aren't so lucky.'

'And that's your message to me?'

She merely smiled for an answer.

Salamander picked the black pyramid up in both hands and stared into it through the clipped square of its tip, only to see what appeared to be a section of a wooden plank. When he leaned closer, the view widened just enough to for him to realize that he was seeing part of a rough-made table and the edge of a red pottery plate. Before he could tell Dallandra, the vision inside the crystal changed. With it memory came flooding back.

He saw the island once again, remembered seeing it before, remembered, even, sitting in Nevyn's lap and his bewilderment at the pictures that seemed to come out of nowhere. Now, as a man, he could focus his trained mind and understand what he was seeing.

'There's an island with a long wooden dock,' he said aloud. 'At the dock, a boat with a dragon head for a prow is bobbing at anchor. The island itself isn't all that large, and half of it's wooded. In the midst of the trees there's a tall square stone tower. I think there's a house of some sort in front of the tower. Someone's standing on the pier. Ye gods, it's Evandar, all right, yellow hair and turquoise eyes and all.'

Dallandra leaned closer. 'Is he holding something?' She kept her voice low. 'Val told me that he was carrying something when you saw him.'

'It's a book, bound in white leather. On the cover's a black figure of a dragon – it must be Arzosah! He's opening the book now, and I can see writing in it. It's the instructions for some sort of dweomer working. Blast and curses! The vision's fading. I can't read it.' He looked up from the crystal.

Dallandra was gazing into some far distance. 'Haen Marn,' she said.

'Um, what?'

'Not what. Where. That island and its lake are named Haen Marn. Rhodry told me about it, years and years ago. A woman he loved lived there at the beginning of the Cengarn wars. Her son, Enj, was the man who helped him find Arzosah, but when they returned to the place where the island had been, it was gone.'

'Gone?'

'Yes, disappeared, and its lake with it. It can move itself, apparently, in times of danger.' Dallandra turned back to look at him. 'And it certainly was in danger, with a Horsekin army heading for it. No one has the slightest idea of where it might be.'

'Which means no one knows where that book is, either.'

'Unfortunately, you're right. I wonder what that working was. Something important enough for Evandar to enchant this crystal with a message.'

'Why by all the hells couldn't he just say outright what he meant? Dalla, you've told me many a time that he loved riddles and jests and all sorts of tangled prophecies, but by the silver shit of the Star Gods, if I may quote your esteemed beloved banadar, why couldn't he just come straight out with his wretched predictions?'

'Because he was so afraid of being wrong.' Dallandra smiled, just faintly. 'He couldn't truly see the future, not whole, anyway. It took me years to understand that. He saw hints of the future – images, voices, bits of visions, nothing clear and nothing fixed. So he passed them along as riddles.'

'Riddles that he knew might have three or four possible answers.'

'Exactly. But that way he couldn't be wrong and mislead those he told them to.'

'And in a way, they *were* riddles, merely riddles to him as well as to the rest of us.' Salamander sighed and shook his head. 'When you consider it –' He stopped in mid-sentence.

In the obsidian pyramid an image was forming. When he returned his gaze to it, he thought at first that he was seeing his own reflection, because a pair of eyes looked straight back at him, but then he realized that the eyes were brown. Slowly the smoky image clarified until he saw the face in which the eyes were set, a sharp, slender man's face half-covered in blue tattoos. Salamander yelped in surprise and heard, very distantly, an answering squawk, very much like a raven's croak. The face disappeared. Salamander set the pyramid down.

'I think I've just seen the raven mazrak,' Salamander said, 'and he's as much human as he is Gel da' Thae.'

Dallandra grabbed the crystal and stared into it, then shook her head in frustration. She muttered an invocation under her breath, then revoked it and tried another, staring all the while into the black stone. Finally she set it down again with an oath so foul that she must have learned it from Calonderiel.

'Lost him,' she said, 'or more likely, he's covered his show-stone with a bit of cloth. I'm assuming he's got some sort of stone. It might be a mirror, of course, or some other object he can use for scrying.'

'I think that's a safe assumption,' Salamander said. 'He must be looking for me, or wait! He may be looking for this stone, if we're right and Sidro's with him. She knows what used to sit on the altar in the shrine.'

'So she does. Now, didn't you tell me that Valandario wanted the pyramid destroyed?'

'Eventually, yes, but she also told me not to do so until I'd learned everything I could from it.'

'That's sensible.' Dallandra weighed the crystal in her palm like a housewife judging a baker's loaf. 'If it really is a link to the raven mazrak, then it's going to be useful. Here's an idea! We'll study it until we meet up with Val. Then we'll hand it over to her and let her have the joy of smashing it to bits.'

'Now that sounds like a splendid plan, oh princess of powers perilous! I've no doubt that joy is exactly what she'll feel when she contemplates its shards.'

When Dallandra returned it to him, Salamander wrapped the stone back up in his old shirt, then wound and tied it with a leather thong to keep the pyramid from slipping out. He tucked the entire bundle into one of his saddlebags. If the stone had an inkling of the evil fate awaiting it, it gave no sign.

'They're going to destroy it, the frothing rabid idiots!' Laz looked up from the white crystal. 'They're planning on smashing the black twin to bits. They think it's evil.'

'If they do, it probably is,' Sidro said. 'They know as much wizardry as you do, and they have the pyramid in hand.'

'Sisi, I want that crystal. I want it very badly.'

Laz got to his feet and began to pace back and forth in what little space the cabin allowed him.

'Why?' Sidro said.

'What do you mean why?' He stopped pacing and glared at her. 'It's a gem of great and sorcerous powers, that's why.' The glare faded into confusion. 'But there's something more, even though I'm embarrassed to admit it. I'm suffering from the irrational conviction that it belongs to me. It doesn't, of course. I know that. But somehow or other, in my soul I feel it's mine. I gave over a small fortune for it, and I want it back. Don't bother to tell me I'm being stupid.'

Sidro slipped the white pyramid back into its multiple cloth bags and pulled the drawstrings tight.

'But it's also a very potent gem, and that's a rational reason to lust after it,' Laz went on. 'Don't you?'

'Laz, it's sitting in the middle of an army. What do you think we can do? Ride up and politely ask these sorcerers if we may have it since they've got no use for it? Sneak in past hundreds of armed men and steal it?'

He sat down opposite her at the table and leaned forward onto his elbows to prop his chin up in his hands. 'There's got to be some way to save it,' he said at last. 'It's so wretchedly unfair. I'm never going to be able to understand the white one if I don't have the black. Yes, of course, you're right. Stealing it's out of the question.' His eyes brightened, and he sat up straight to grin at her. 'Out of the question for a man, certainly, but what about the raven? After they cross the ford, they'll be close to the forest verge. I could build an astral tunnel, lurk there waiting for the right moment, and then swoop down.'

'You've gone mad! What about the dragons?'

'The dragons, my dearest love, are off scouting for the would-be avengers of Zakh Gral.'

'Have they taken all the archers with them?'

Laz's good cheer vanished. 'Ah yes,' he said. 'The archers.'

'Indeed. The archers.'

'I'll have to think about this.' Laz stood up and resumed his pacing. 'Surely I can come up with some way to get my claws on that spirit stone.'

That evening Gwerbret Ridvar issued his orders to those men directly under his command. His grace had decided that, since he himself would remain with the two princes, Tieryn Cadryc would take command of all the Red Wolf vassals and allies, including the Falcon clan and Salamander, to guard the wounded while they pulled back across the ford. With Clae trailing behind him, Gerran stalked through the camp until he found the tieryn.

'Why am I being sent off?' Gerran said. 'Doesn't his grace think I can fight as well as the next man?'

'Naught of the sort,' Cadryc said. 'It's because you're the

only lord the Falcon has. There's no use in bringing a clan to life only to kill it off straightaway.'

'Just so.' Calonderiel came striding up to join them. He was carrying a wooden box in one hand. 'A hundred of my archers will be riding back with you, by the by, and all of the Mountain Folk. None of them are insulted.'

'Besides –' Cadryc paused for a quick look around, then lowered his voice. 'If anyone should be insulted, it's doubtless me, and I'm not. No doubt the gwerbret's tired of looking at me. Hah! We'll be out of his grasp by Samaen.'

'And a grand thing that is!' Gerran suddenly remembered Solla, waiting for him at home. While he never would have admitted it to another man, thinking of her made him see some good in the gwerbret's decision. 'My apologies for the outburst, your grace.'

'Accepted,' Cadryc said. 'Now, banadar, what's that you're carrying?'

'Somewhat for Gerro,' Calonderiel held out the wooden box. 'A bit of booty if you want it. Dalla thought you might, but she doesn't mean to insult you, either, if you don't.'

'Why would she think I'd be insulted?' Gerran took the box and flipped the hinged lid open. 'A silver dagger! Now I understand, but no insult taken, tell her. Salamander mentioned somewhat about seeing a silver dagger on that piss-poor excuse for an altar.'

'This is the very one.' Calonderiel paused to spit on the ground. 'One of their not so holy relics.'

'May I see, my lord?' Clae said.

When Gerran handed his page the open box, Clae stared at the dagger for a long moment, then reached out a gentle finger and stroked the wyvern device engraved on the blade. Gerran could have sworn that the lad was near to tears, but Clae closed the box and forced out a smile.

'What's all this?' Cadryc said to him.

'I don't know, your grace,' Clae said. 'Seeing that dagger, it gave me the strangest feeling. I just don't know why.'

'Do you want it, lad?' Gerran said. 'The metal won't buy our clan much, and I'm certainly not minded to carry it.'

'I should think not, my lord!' Clae hesitated. 'You know, it's stranger and stranger, but I do want it. May I truly have it?'

'You may. Keep it as a reminder of the first war you ever saw. And if it ever looks like I'm going embroil the Falcons in a feud or suchlike, you bring that out and remind me of the cost.'

With a shy smile, Clae clutched the box to his chest and trotted off to stow it with his gear. Tieryn Cadryc shook his head in amazement.

'He's an odd lad, our Clae,' Cadryc said. 'Especially when you consider that his father was a scribe.'

'Well, he may come from a family of letter-writers, your grace, but he'll grow into the captain of the Falcon's warband, I think me, if the gods let both of us live long enough. There's iron in his soul.'

'And that's what a man needs these days, sure enough. Now, on the morrow, I'll be sending messengers home ahead of us. Where's that blasted gerthddyn? He might as well write the news down, since Neb's back in the dun to read it.'

'I last saw him with Lady Dallandra,' Gerran said. 'I'll go look for him.'

'I'll come with you,' Calonderiel said. 'I like to know where she is, especially if she's been off with that babbling fool.'

Gerran shot him a questioning glance.

'It's the danger we're in,' Calonderiel snapped. 'I can see it even if she can't.'

Gerran made a non-committal noise, but as he followed the banadar, he was wondering how Calonderiel could be jealous of the gerthddyn – and how anyone could think him a fool.

When Salamander and Dallandra returned to camp, servants took their horses, but he kept his pair of saddlebags with him. While he couldn't put the reason into words, he had the distinct feeling that the black pyramid needed guarding. With the bags slung over one arm, he escorted Dallandra back to the tents set up for the wounded. Grallezar joined them there. She'd been carrying Dallandra's medical supplies over from the wagons, an armload at a time.

'I've put them all in this tent here,' Grallezar said in Elvish. 'I've got one more load, so I'll just go fetch it now.'

Grallezar hurried off in the direction of the supply train. Before Dallandra could go inside, Calonderiel and Gerran walked up to join them. The banadar shot Salamander such a cold glance that he stepped back and arranged a foolish smile.

'There you are!' Calonderiel said to Dallandra. With Gerran standing beside him, he spoke in Deverrian. 'Will you be working with the wounded, my love?'

'I will.' Dallandra answered in the same. 'Some of the men might be able to ride tomorrow. They'll be far better off on horseback than jouncing around in the carts.'

'True spoken. Here, I've got to go talk with Prince Dar. It shouldn't take me long. Ebañy, Tieryn Cadryc wants you to write messages for him.'

'I'll go join him presently.' Salamander patted his saddle-bags. 'I've got to put these away first.'

Calonderiel grunted an acknowledgement, then, much to Salamander's relief, strode off without looking his way again. Gerran bowed to Dallandra.

'I hear, my lady,' Gerran said, 'that you'll be staying with the main body of the army. I won't be, and so I wanted to thank you now for the care you've given the Red Wolf men, and for sending me that silver dagger, too.'

'You're most welcome,' Dallandra said. 'It gladdens my heart that you took no insult from the gift.'

'I didn't. I hope you think no less of me because I'll be guarding the wounded.'

'What? Why would I ever do that? I can't imagine why you'd want to stay here.'

Gerran looked utterly taken aback. 'Well,' he said after a moment, 'I wouldn't mind another strike on the savage bastards. I'll never forget that prisoner they staked out, back near Samyc's dun. We should wipe them all out, the men, the females, the cubs, the lot.'

'Alas,' Salamander said, 'I fear me that a lot of my people would agree with that. I know Calonderiel does.'

'Oh, so they're the savages, are they?' Dallandra said. 'How do you dare say that, after what our men did to Zakh Gral's garrison?'

'That's war,' Gerran said. 'They'd have done the same to us.'

'Of course. That wasn't my point. You burned their fort and forced them into your lines like a forester smoking out badgers. Then you slaughtered every one of them. How is that more savage than what they've done?'

Gerran started to answer, then held his tongue.

'Besides,' Dallandra continued, 'you don't understand them. Do you know what the greatest fear of every Gel da' Thae is?'

'I don't,' Gerran said. 'Why should I?'

'Because they're your enemies, and you need to know them.'

'Well, true spoken. My apologies.'

'Accepted. They're terrified that they'll somehow slip back, lose the civilized life they've worked so hard for, and turn into those savages again.'

'They're not far from it. What about the way they stake out prisoners, and the long spear, and all of that? I can't call it anything but savage.'

'The priests claim that the gods demand it. Didn't your priests used to demand heads and sacrifices?'

'So the bards tell us, but —'

'But what?' Dallandra snapped. 'And how long has it been since your folk stopped taking heads? I gather that it still happens now and then. And what about drawing and hanging, like Ridvar wanted to do to the prisoners from Honelg's dun?

And he would have killed Cadryc's little grandson in cold blood if you and Neb hadn't stopped him.'

Gerran was staring at her open-mouthed. Dallandra caught his gaze and stared him down. With a shake of his head, Gerran looked away.

'Point taken.' Gerran's voice was perfectly calm. 'Ten of one, half-a-twenty of the other.'

'Well and good, then,' Dallandra said.

Salamander let out his breath in a long sigh of relief, then wondered why he'd been holding it. Had he really thought they might come to blows?

'I knew one of their bards once; he was a truly learned man,' Dallandra went on. 'And don't forget, I've visited Braemel. Most of their people live peacefully enough. They have craft shops and traders, they have law courts and temples.'

'I see.' Gerran paused briefly. 'Well, it's too easy, mayhap, to see your enemies as fiends from hell. Here, Salamander, what was it that scribe called them? The name your people have for them.'

'Meradan,' Salamander said, 'demons, that would be, in the Deverry tongue. The Gel da'Thae in turn call your people the Red Reivers, just by the by.'

Gerran looked honestly startled.

'Think on that,' Dallandra said. 'But I can't deny that the warriors can act like savages. They live for death, and they cling to their old ways. Horrible blood-thirsty ways, they are, too, including that awful ritual of the long spear.' Dallandra paused for a shudder.

'A question for you, Wise One,' Gerran said. 'If these ordinary townsfolk interfere with the Horsekin warbands, what then?'

'That's what Grallezar and her people tried to do.'

Gerran smiled, a brief twitch of cold lips. 'So I thought. We'll just kill as many of their warriors as we can.' He bowed to Dallandra. 'That'll be enough for me.'

With a cheerful little wave he strode off, leaving Dallandra staring after him with stricken eyes.

'I know what you're thinking, oh mistress of mighty magicks,' Salamander said in Elvish. 'But he's a good man in his way.'

'So's Cal in his.' Dallandra answered in the same. 'And he'd agree with Gerran down to the last word.'

When Dallandra went inside the tent, Salamander followed to leave his saddlebags and the black stone inside them in a safe place while he attended upon the tieryn. A heap of sacks and pack saddles waited, neatly arranged in a useful order, blankets and bandages to one side, herbs to the other, and in between such few tools as Dallandra had. When she'd done looking them over, she sat down with a long sigh. Salamander knelt down on one knee nearby and stowed his saddlebags behind the mule packs.

'It was good of Grallezar to do all this,' Dallandra said.

'Indeed,' Salamander said. 'I'm surprised that a person of her high position would, though, alas, she lacks any sort of position at the moment.'

'Do you know why the women are the leaders among the Gel da' Thae?'

'No, but I've often wondered.'

'It was after the Great Burning and the plague. When they realized what they'd destroyed by destroying us, the remnant left decided that from then on, the women would be their chieftains – their raz-kairen, as they called their leaders back then – because the men among them had failed their people.'

'I suppose they figured that women would be more naturally peaceful, more inclined to civilized things.'

'No, they weren't that stupid.' She softened the words with a smile. 'It was simply a question of replacing a group that had made horrible decisions with a group that hadn't. Besides, since the women wouldn't be riding to war, they'd live longer than the male leaders had.'

'Good reasons, then.'

'But it's true that when war comes, women have more to lose than the men.'

'Indeed? What?'

'Our children, of course. Who else does the fighting, but our children?' Dallandra's little smile suddenly froze, then disappeared. She flung up her hands to cover her face and wept.

Salamander sat stunned, then hesitantly laid a hand on her shoulder. 'Dalla?' he said. 'Should I go get Cal?'

'No.' She was fighting back her tears. 'He'll only make things worse.' She turned away and pulled over a saddlebag, brought out a linen bandage, and used it to wipe her face. 'I'm sorry. I don't know why I did that.'

'The times call for it, I suppose.'

'Yes.' She looked down at the bandage in her hands. 'Yes, I suppose they do.'

In the morning, the portion of the army that would be pulling back marched off north, heading for the ford. The last of the rearguard had just disappeared from sight when the dragons returned. The commanders rushed out to greet them and hear their reports. With the wounded gone, Dallandra had nothing to do but wonder what they'd discovered. Now and then she allowed herself a brief hope that no Horsekin reinforcements would appear, but she wasn't in the least surprised when those hopes proved foolish.

'They're on their way, all right,' Calonderiel told her. 'But the army's not all that large, and it's short on cavalry. Those heavy horses of theirs are hard to come by. We've killed a good many of them – too many. It's a pity, really, but that's war.'

'Are the dragons still here? I need to look at Rori's wound again.'

'Please do. It stinks as bad as burning wolf shit.'

Dallandra's assistants had all kept an eye out for leeches at every stream or pond they'd come across. Ranadario, in fact, had been hunting that very morning. When Dalla went to look for her, she found Ranadario out among the scrub, where a slow rivulet ran down towards the Galan Targ.

'Dalla, Dalla, look!' Ranadario hurried over, lugging a big pottery jar. 'I found some!'

At the bottom of the water in the jar lay what appeared to be a heap of grey slime. When Ranadario shook the jar, the heap uncoiled itself into several handfuls of fresh-water leeches, all of them hungry, judging by how pale their tubular bodies were.

'Wonderful!' Dallandra said. 'They're beautiful specimens. Now I need to fetch our dragon.'

Rori was quite willing to come and be treated. He followed her to the beaten-down area of grass where Ranadario was waiting with the jar of leeches, jars of herb water and wash water, and the various implements and salves they'd need.

'Lie down on your side,' Dallandra said. 'I don't want the leeches falling off into the grass.'

'Can they live out of the water?' Rori said.

'Not for long. We'll keep them moist while they're feeding. Well, if they will feed.'

Rori stretched out both pairs of legs and flopped over onto his side, making the ground tremble under her feet. While Ranadario held the jar, Dallandra fished out a leech with wooden tongs and laid it on top of a stripe of black-ened flesh at the very edge of the wound. The creature squirmed, then sank its larger mouth into the black flesh and attached itself with the smaller. In only a few moments its colour turned a faint pink. Dallandra sighed in relief. Apparently the leeches liked the taste of dragon well enough.

'Can you feel that?' Dallandra said.

'No,' Rori said.

'It's definitely morbid, then. Let's see how much this batch of leeches will eat.'

'There's lots more in the stream,' Ranadario said. 'When

I was collecting these, a really big one bit me, in fact, but I had to salt it and kill it to get it off.'

'That's too bad.' Dallandra dipped a rag in the jug of clean water and squeezed the moisture over the feeding leech. 'You keep doing this, and when this one looks ready to drop off, put it back in the other jar.' She handed her the tongs. 'Then put a fresh one onto the next bit of black stuff.'

Dallandra walked around to Rori's head so they could talk more comfortably. He opened his strangely human eyes and considered her.

'Owaen died of wound rot,' he announced. 'Is that what's wrong with me?'

'No, I'm glad to say. Who's Owaen? One of the men you fought with?'

'Yes, back in the Time of Troubles, that was. I was a bard then, a silver dagger's bard, but I could swing a sword when I had to. Owaen got a deep wound that went black, just like this one. I was wounded, too, but for some reason I survived. I remember lying there in a fever and hearing that Owaen still lived, but he died later that same day. I suppose Nevyn saved my miserable life, such as it was.'

'What? Rori, have you started remembering past lives?'

'A good many of them. Dragons do, you see, know their pasts, though they live so long that they only remember one or two old lives. They know a great many strange things, actually.' He was staring straight out in front of him. 'Some of them have come to me on their own. Others I suppose I'll learn some day.'

'Do you want to go on living as a dragon?'

'Do I have a choice?'

'As things stand, no, but we may be able to discover how to give you your proper form again.' Suddenly she remembered Evandar's message in the black crystal and the mysterious book. 'I think Evandar may have left us the key for unlocking his working, if we can find it.'

'Us? We?'

'Jill and I. Blast it, I mean Branna! Jill told me when she was still alive that she saw an omen about some evil that would befall you, you see, and she swore that she'd help you lift it. Since she died before she could, the vow's come to Branna.'

'Where is this key?'

'It might be in a book that seems to be on Haen Marn.'

'Then it's lost forever.'

'I wouldn't be so sure of that. The island may well return. Have you ever flown back to look for Enj?'

'Many a time. He still keeps his vigil in the wilderness in the summers and goes back to Lin Serr in the winters. He has more faith than I.' Rori abruptly raised his head and looked back to glare at Ranadario. 'Careful there, girl! I felt that.'

'My apologies!' Ranadario sounded terrified. 'But we've got to make sure the wound's stripped clean.'

'You may not eat my assistant,' Dallandra said. 'So be a good dragon and hold still.'

Rori growled, but he laid his head down again. His tail slapped the ground once, then quieted.

'That's better,' Dallandra said. 'Did you see any books when you were on Haen Marn?'

'I didn't, no, but that means nothing. Haen Marn showed me only what it wanted me to see.' He paused for a long sigh. 'Are you happy with Cal?'

'Yes.'

'Good. I knew he loved you. That's one reason I wanted to leave you and go back to Haen Marn. The other reason was Angmar, of course. Ye gods, I hope she never sees me this way.'

'Why not? From everything you told me about her, she's the one woman in all the worlds who'll understand.'

Rori stared at her for a moment, then laughed, a deep rumble that brought a howl of protest from Ranadario.

'You're shaking off the leeches,' Dallandra said. 'You need to lie still.'

Rori rolled his eyes in disgust, but he did stop laughing. 'How long is this going to take?'

'I have no idea,' Dallandra said. 'I've never treated a dragon before. Some days, I should think. If we can clear off all the infected bits, then the wound will have a chance to heal normally. I'll flush it out regularly with herb water, but I won't be able to stitch it. Your skin's too thick.'

'We don't have days. The Horsekin will reach the ruins long before that.'

'Then I'll do what I can now and finish it later. But the most important part of the cure is very simple. Stop licking it.'

'That's what Arzosah keeps telling me.'

'She's right. Stop! No licking, no clawing at it, or scratching, or biting it. If it gets dirt in it, come to me, and I'll wash it out properly.'

He growled under his breath and seemed to be studying the horizon.

'I can try numbing it down so it won't hurt as much.'

'It doesn't hurt, precisely. It burns and itches. But that's not the worst of it. It's the way it reminds me.'

'Of the transformation, you mean?'

'That, too. Are you certain that Raena didn't put an evil spell on that dagger?'

'Quite certain. She lacked the power and the knowledge both. The only spell on the dagger was the one that the silver dagger's smith put on it when he was forging it for Yraen.' She hesitated, remembering. 'You cried out that the wound burned when you got it.'

'It did.' He slipped into Deverrian, apparently without realizing it. 'I'd been wounded before, and badly at that, but none of them burned. They gave me pain bad enough to make me stagger and heave, truly, but not pain that felt like a burning brand thrust into my side. The wound's black as charcoal, too.'

'It is that. I thought of gangrene, when first I saw it, but it's not spread. If it were the true wound rot, you'd be dead.'

'More's the pity, then.'

'Rori, if you truly want to die, for the sake of all the gods, find some decent way to kill yourself.'

'Nah, nah, nah, it was only a jest, my lady. I do but jest to amuse both my ladies, you and my Lady Death. I'll tell you what the trouble is. How, pray tell, should I die in a decent way, were I so minded? Who's going to kill me? Who can?' He slapped his tail hard on the ground. 'Every fighting man who's ever lived has wished at one time or another that he was invulnerable. Well, I've got my wish, and ye gods, it aches my heart! Should I dive into the sea or a fire mountain and die without a shred of glory or honour? That's not a decent death. And so I keep on living, fighting for the high king as I always did, out here on the border.' He sighed in a soft roar of sound. 'It suits me, I suppose. It amuses me, at least.'

Dallandra found herself utterly speechless. He raised his head and looked at her.

'Is there really a chance you can unwind Evandar's dweomer?' he said.

'There is, but it's a small one.'

'That will do.' He began speaking Elvish again. 'Isn't that girl done yet with her slimes and worms?'

'Yes, I am,' Ranadario said. 'The leeches are all nice and fat and purple.'

'Good,' Dallandra said. 'Rori, we've brought some herbal water. Let me just clean up after the leeches, and then you can go for today.'

After he'd flown off, Dallandra remembered his saying 'that will do'. *Do for what?* she thought. *Most likely, for a reason to keep living.*

Arzosah returned late that day to give another report to the princes and the gwerbret. When she'd finished, Dallandra went out to show her the dragonbone whistle that once had lain on Alshandra's altar. When she held it up, Arzosah hissed long and hard.

'At last!' the dragon said.

'I take it you recognize it,' Dallandra said.

'Of course I do. It's made of my other mate's bones. I want to drop it into the melt of my fire mountain, so that at least a small part of him will have come home. Will you keep it for me until the war's over?'

'Gladly.'

'My thanks. Speaking of mates, I saw Rori. The wound looks a thousand times better. You have my thanks for that, too.'

'You're most welcome. I think I can cure it completely.'

'May all the gods of fire and steam be praised! If only he'd left that wretched Raena alone, but oh no, he had to have his revenge.' The dragon heaved a massive sigh. 'We both seem to have a penchant for unsuitable males, you with that disgusting Evandar first and now with the arrogant banadar person.'

'Here! Don't keep insulting —'

'It's obvious why, of course.' The dragon went on as if she'd not heard. 'We both like our privacy, and our time alone, and a suitable male would be underwing – well, under-foot in your case – all day long.'

Dallandra opened her mouth to argue but paused, struck by a sudden thought. 'You're right,' she said at last. 'There are advantages to wandering men.'

'I'm always right.' Arzosah yawned with a flash of fang. 'I flew over the other part of the army, by the by, on my way here. They've reached the ford safely. I did notice that some servants were digging a grave, but it looked big enough for just one man.'

'I was afraid that some of the wounded weren't going to live much longer. Well, I'll hope that whoever it was is the last to die.'

Tieryn Cadryc's contingent had made camp early that after-noon to bury Tieryn Gwivyr and let the other wounded rest.

After servants slung Gwivyr into the grave, Gerran jumped in to lay Gwivyr's sword on his chest and clasp his hands on its hilt. Salamander helped him climb out again, and together they watched the servants shovel dirt over the body.

'My heart aches for little Branna,' Gerran said. 'He was her father, after all.'

'So he was,' Salamander said. 'Well, he's not the only good man who's died in this war.'

'He won't be the last, either, if there are more Horsekin on the way to Zakh Gral.' With a shrug, Gerran turned away. 'Let's go draw our rations.'

Over by the horse herd, servants were handing out packets of food from an open wagon. As Gerran and Salamander walked up, Salamander noticed a skinny little brown-haired lass waiting patiently while men were served ahead of her.

'That's Tarro's sister.' Salamander pointed her out to Gerran. 'She was taken from Neb's old village. I suppose she's bringing food to her brother. I heard he was badly wounded.'

At Gerran's approach the other men stepped back to let him go to the head of the line, but Gerran gestured to the lass.

'What's your name?' he asked. 'And how fares your brother?'

'Penna, my lord.' She made a passable curtsey. 'He's healing as well as he ever will. He lost his left arm. I'm taking care of him, though, and so he'll get better.'

'Give him my sympathies.' Gerran turned to the servant. 'Give this lass what she needs right now, enough for both her and her brother. She's not safe, waiting around here with the men. From now on, give out her share as soon as she gets here.'

The servant looked shocked, but he answered politely enough. 'I will, Lord Gerran. As you wish, of course.'

Penna gave him a brilliant smile and curtsied again. Once she had the rations, she trotted off, disappearing among the tents.

'Tarro was one of Ridvar's riders,' Salamander remarked. 'The gods only know what will happen to them now.'

'They'll have a place in my dun if they want it.' Gerran gave him a smile twisted with irony. 'When, of course, I get a dun. I'll send Clae to tell them.'

Once they received their rations, much the worse for wear from their long journey, Salamander found he had little appetite. When he stowed his share of crumbling flatbread and rancid salted meat in his saddlebags, he noticed the bundle containing the black pyramid. Studying the gem would provide a splendid distraction from his grief. He carried the bundle a little ways away from camp, out in the grass to a comfortable spot not far from the forest verge, but he made sure that he stayed close enough to yell for help should there be any trouble. While he'd not received any dweomer omens, ordinary thoughts of mounted Horsekin attacks had occurred to him.

He unwrapped the banner made from his old shirt and spread it out on the ground, then sat down cross-legged and placed the crystal upon it. Once again he saw Evandar, standing upon the pier at Haen Marn, displaying the book, then fading away. Yawning, he leaned forward in hopes of seeing a different vision, but the sun was hot upon his back, and the events he'd just lived through had left him exhausted. He was half-asleep by the time he saw something move inside the pyramid.

He picked up the showstone, looked into it through the clipped apex, and saw brown eyes staring back. Dimly he could see the rest of the mazrak's face, as sharp-edged as he'd been remembering it. The brown eyes stared, wide and unblinking. *Ye gods!* Salamander thought. *He's trying to ensorcel me right through the stone!*

'It won't work,' Salamander thought to him. 'You've got to be close to someone's body to ensorcel them, you dolt!'

In his mind he heard the raven squawk. The eyes vanished. The mazrak had learned at least some of his dweomer by rote, Salamander could suppose, rather than from first principles.

Salamander wrapped the pyramid in his old shirt, secured the bundle with the thong, then laid it beside him on the grass. When he glanced at the horizon, he saw that the sun was perhaps an hour away from setting. What would Dallandra be doing? he wondered. He considered contacting her, but his stomach growled alarmingly, reminding him that he'd left his rations back at camp. He got up, then bent over to pick up his bundle. Just as he touched it, he heard the rush of wings behind him.

The raven mazrak slammed into him and sent him sprawling on his face into the grass. Salamander rolled over, got to his knees, and grabbed for the bundle, but the mazrak had seized it with strong claws. Flapping hard, he rose into the air. Salamander scrambled up, ran after, and leapt as high as could to snatch at the bundle. Not high enough – he fell flat on the ground. The raven shrieked in triumph and flew off, heading for the forest. Salamander got up and ran a few yards after him before he realized the chase was hopeless.

'You filthy scavenger!' he screamed after him. 'You foul and scabrous carrion crow! You – you –' He stopped and panted for breath. He could transform and fly after, he supposed, but by the time he stripped off his clothing and worked the dweomer, the mazrak would have such a long lead on him that he'd never catch up. He could only stand and watch while the raven dwindled to a black speck in the sky, then disappeared.

From the direction of the camp he heard a human voice yelling his name. He turned to see Gerran, running towards him with drawn sword.

'What in the name of the Lord of Hell was that?' Gerran called out. 'Are you unharmed?'

'Unharmed I am,' Salamander called back, 'except for my wounded pride. As to what – a thieving bird.'

Gerran stopped and sheathed his sword, then waited,

his arms crossed over his chest, for Salamander to walk over and join him.

'A bird, was it?' Gerran said. 'Biggest blasted bird I've ever seen.'

'Well, what else could it have been?' Salamander forced out a smile.

'That's what I'm asking you. It didn't look like a young dragon. Didn't smell like one, either.'

'How perspicacious you are, Gerro, clear of eye and keen of mind, astute –'

'That's enough blather, gerthddyn. What was it?'

'Oh very well! It was a dweomermaster who can turn himself into a bird at will, and he just stole an enchanted stone from me.' Salamander grinned when Gerran's jaw dropped in surprise. 'There! Now you know.'

Salamander stalked off, heading for the horse herd. In a few long strides Gerran caught up with him.

'What are you doing?' Gerran said.

'Fetching my horse. I'm going after him.'

'You're doing no such thing. It's almost dark, and you can't ride into an unknown forest in the dark. Get back to camp.'

'Who in all the hells are you to – don't you give me orders!'

'I happen to be the captain of Tieryn Cadryc's warband, and you're one of his servitors. You can take my order, or I'll knock the shit out of you and carry you back to camp.' Gerran's voice was perfectly mild, and his face showed not a trace of any emotion. 'Well, which is it?'

Salamander considered putting up a fight, dismissed the thought as a death wish, and took a deep breath to calm his nerves.

'Camp it is,' Salamander said. 'If dweomer could turn someone into a frog, though, you'd be hopping hard for the nearest stream.'

Gerran's mouth twitched in what might have been a smile. During the walk back, neither of them said a word. Although Salamander considered contacting Dallandra and telling her what had happened, he quite simply felt too embarrassed. The morning, he decided, would be time enough for yet another humiliation.

By the time Laz returned to the cabin, night had fallen. In his beak he carried the cloth bundle, dangling by its thong. Even though she'd scried him out earlier, Sidro felt a wave of relief at actually seeing him physically. He dropped the bundle onto the table, then hopped up onto the log perch.

'I'll turn around,' Sidro said.

She saw the flash of blue light and turned to see him jump down from the log, back in human form, and grinning in triumph, though his sweat carried the strong scent of exhaustion. He grabbed his brigga from the floor and put them on, then sat down on one of the stump chairs.

'Well,' he said, 'aren't you going to tell me I was stupid to take such a chance?'

'I'm just glad you're not dead.'

'I am, too, actually. The archers were too far away to loose a shaft at me, if indeed they even knew what was happening.' He grinned, then bent over to pull on his boots. 'Where's my shirt? I want to be properly dressed to savour this moment.'

With a weary shake of her head, Sidro tossed him the shirt. He finished dressing, then swung around on the chair to face the table and the odd-looking bundle. Beside it lay the white pyramid in its nest of sacks. He unwrapped the white first and set it down carefully on its silk pouch, then laid a hand on the bundle containing the black.

'It seems,' Laz said, 'that our minstrel friend has wrapped his treasure in an old shirt.'

'That used to be in the shrine. Rocca sewed it to a strip of cloth to make a banner. She insisted he'd worked a miracle and had joined the ranks of the holy witnesses.'

Laz rolled his eyes in disgust, then cut the thong with his hunting knife. Among the folds of cloth the black pyramid gleamed under the dweomer light.

'The spirit's gone,' Sidro said. 'It had a spirit bound in it when it stood on our altar.'

'One of the Ancients probably released it, then,' Laz said, 'and a good thing, too. Who bound it?'

'I have no idea. The holy witness Raena, maybe. It was always there as far as I know.'

'Ah, I see. Well, most likely it was releasing the spirit that brought the twins back to their full glory. Look at the sparks between them. You won't even need to use the Sight.'

With her ordinary vision Sidro could see a bluish flow, heavier than air but much less substantial than water, and flecked with silver, between the white pyramid and the black. When Laz pushed the white a little closer to the black, the flow increased and began to spit like a fire in green wood.

'I wonder what would happen if I touched them together?' Laz picked them up, one in each hand.

'Don't!' Sidro suddenly felt so cold and sick that she could barely speak. 'Laz, don't! It's dangerous. Look at them! Can't you see?'

He flashed her his knife-edge grin, then brought his hands together. The tips of the pyramids, a bare inch apart, began spewing silver flames like tiny fire mountains.

'Stop it!' Sidro hissed. 'Please –'

Too late. He touched the tips one to the other. Silver sparks exploded all around him. Blue light flashed, blinding her. A sound like thunder rolled around the cabin. She heard a woman scream, realized that the scream was hers, screamed again and again as she blindly groped for him. Her hands found only the table edge.

'Laz! Laz!'

She spun around, flailing open-handed. The air smelled oddly clean with the tingle of lightning. From outside she heard footsteps, men's voices, and Vek, howling as if in agony. The cabin door banged open. In a silver-tinged blackness she turned towards the sound.

'Sidro!' It was Pir's voice. 'What happened?'

'I don't know. Where's Laz? I can't see! Is he dead?'

'He's not in the cabin. What happened?'

The only thing that prevented her from collapsing onto the floor was her grip on the table. She began to sob, and the tears eased her vision. The darkness turned to a smear of reddish-gold light that floated in front of her like a mask. When Pir threw an arm around her shoulders, she turned to him and let her head rest against his chest while she wept, fighting to bring her tears under control. The red-gold mask shrank down to a point, freeing her vision at last. Pir let her go and stepped back, looking around him wide-eyed.

'What happened?' he repeated.

Men filled the cabin, she realized, staring at her. Faharn shoved his way through the mob and stood in front of her, his blue eyes narrow with rage.

'What have you done to him?' Faharn said.

'Me?' Sidro took a step back. 'Nothing! He's the one who –' The tears rose and drowned her words.

'Leave her alone!' Pir snapped. 'She's trying to tell us.'

Faharn crossed his arms over his chest and glared, but mercifully he stayed silent. Young Vek was shaking so badly that she knew he was close to having one of his seizures. Nothing else looked the least bit unusual. The wrappings for the two crystals still lay on the table among the remnants of their noon meal. Nothing had burned, nothing had broken, not one object had moved from its place. Except of course for Laz.

'I don't know what happened,' she whispered, then steadied her voice. 'It was the two spirit stones. Laz brought them together and touched them, tip to tip. Everything seemed to explode. He stood right here but a moment ago. Now he's gone.'

Faharn swore under his breath.

'Do you believe me?' Sidro said to him.

'Yes, yes, of course,' Faharn said. 'He's talked about nothing but those damned gems for days.' His voice wavered and threatened to choke. 'It's just like him, somehow, to do something like that.'

The men began to murmur, just a word here and there, and look slantwise at each other. A few laid their hands on their dagger hilts for the comfort of it.

'Do you think he's dead?' Pir asked Sidro.

'I don't know. I just don't know.'

Vek sobbed once, then choked, making a growling sound deep in his throat. Everyone turned towards him as his head began to sway from side to side. He threw his arms into the air, then his head suddenly flopped forward. He staggered and fell to his knees among the rushes.

'Alive,' he stammered. 'Alive but gone, gone. Alive but gone. Alive but –' He fainted, sprawling face down onto the boughs.

The two men nearest to him grabbed him and hauled him up. His head flopped back, and drool ran from his open mouth.

'Take him back to his shelter,' Pir said. 'And stay with him till he comes round.'

When they carried Vek out, the cabin began to empty. A few at a time, the men slipped out, whispering among themselves. Faharn lingered, tried to speak, then turned and ran up the steps and out. Sidro sat down on the stump and concentrated on keeping herself from weeping. Pir leaned against the table and considered her unspeaking until the last of them had left.

'You're our leader now,' he said. 'Until we find Laz, of course.'

'Of course? Do you truly think we can find him? Alive but gone, gone – what does that mean? What can it possibly mean?' Sidro held up her hands, noticed they were shaking, and tucked them into her lap. 'How can we even search with the dragons lurking right nearby?'

'The dragons? It's the Lijik men I'm worried about. Without Laz and his sorcery we can't hide if we stay here. We can't travel without leaving a trail they'd have to be blind to miss.'

'Ai, may every goddess help us! We'll need them all. How can I lead you? I'm all to pieces, I can't think, I —'

'Hush!' Pir held up a hand and let a scent flow out to her. 'I've been thinking about things.'

This scent smelled like horses, sharp, sweaty, and yet oddly calming. Sidro took a deep breath. Her hands lay still in her lap, and her thoughts steadied with them, though her grief still burned in her soul. *Laz, Laz, how could you desert me again?* A childish thought, ridiculous, even, she knew — yet she ached as badly as if it were true. Pir's voice shocked her out of self-pity.

'My idea is this,' Pir said. 'What if we surrendered to the Ancients in that army?'

'What?' Sidro stared gape-mouthed at him.

'Why are we here? Because the Alshandra people hate us. Why are the Ancients and their allies here? They hate the Alshandra people. They have sorcerers among them. Our sorcerer is gone. That black stone was theirs. They likely want it back. We want Laz back, and he likely still has the black stone.'

'They'll kill him if they find him.'

'Not if we strike a bargain with them.'

'They'll kill us if we try.'

'No, I don't think so. They're Gel da' Thae, not tribals, in their own way. The dragons obey them, you know. They could call them off.'

'What do we have to bargain with?'

'We hate their enemies, and we can tell them what happened to the stone. Besides, I can heal wounded horses.'

Sidro got up and walked over to the window that faced away from the rest of the camp. She leaned on the sill on folded arms and looked out, breathing the night air, the soothing scent of pine and fern, of running streams and a soft wind.

'I know a few weak little magicks,' she said. 'It's not enough.'

Pir walked up behind her. 'I know,' he said. 'We're going to need help to find him.'

'That's true, but it's not what I meant. I can't lead these men. Even though I'm a woman, I just can't. I don't know how, and they frighten me. A herd's not going to follow a weak bell mare.' She straightened up and turned around. 'Well, do you think they'll take my orders?'

Pir looked away, considering his answer for a long moment. 'They will at first, until you do something they don't like.'

'Something like suggesting we surrender?'

'Um.' Again he stayed silent, thinking. 'Something like that, yes.'

'The only person who can lead this wretched excuse for a herd is you.'

Pir looked down at the floor. Since he was standing with his back to the wizard-light over the table, shadow fell across his face and made it impossible for her to tell what he might be feeling. Finally, just as she was ready to question him, he looked up.

'You're right,' he said. 'Especially if they know you've passed the leadership to me.'

'I'll tell them, if you think they'll listen.'

'They should.' Yet Pir sounded doubtful.

Sidro wondered at her sudden fear. As a Horsekin woman despite her human blood, even as a Gel da' Thae slave, she had always been perfectly confident that men would never harm her sexually unless her owner, another woman, allowed them to – not that Borgren would have let them. She remembered Movrae and shuddered. These men were outlaws, fugitives from the Gel da' Thae world, as lawless as the savage tribes of the far north. She would need more protection than her weak magicks could give her. The ancient customs would have to provide it.

'You know that Laz will always be my First Man,' she said.

'Oh yes.' Pir's face showed no expression at all, but she could smell a change in his scent.

'I don't see why you couldn't be the Second. That should make everything perfectly clear.'

'I was hoping you'd say that.' He smiled, just briefly. 'I'm going to build a fire. The men need to know what's going to happen.'

Sidro stayed inside the cabin until she saw flames leaping from the firepit. The men had already assembled around it by the time she gathered enough courage to leave the cabin. Pir was talking fast, dramatizing his points with a shake of a fist here and a slap of his hands there. Many of the men were listening intently. A few at a time, they strode over to stand behind or next to him until some nine men had gathered on his side of the fire. The holdouts stood, scowling, behind Faharn.

Sidro took a deep breath to steady her nerves and walked over. Pir held out one arm, and she slipped into the comfort of his embrace. At that, four of the holdouts smiled and walked over to Pir's side of the fire.

'The rest of you can do what you want,' Pir finished up. 'You've got till the morning to, um, well, think about things.'

'Pir, I can't believe you'd come up with such a mad scheme,' Faharn said. 'Huh, Laz thought this woman loved him. Look at how fast she's deserted him! Or have you been scheming all along to take her away from him?'

'If I had,' Pir said levelly, 'I'd have come to you for help. You would have been happy to give it. You'd have done anything to have Laz all to yourself again.'

Pir's supporters whooped with laughter, and even the men standing with Faharn broke into broad grins. Faharn started to speak, blushed, scowled, tried again, then flapped his hands in the air and turned away. He strode off as fast as he could and retain his dignity. A few at a time, the men who were staying with him followed. Most nodded pleasantly enough as they walked away to disappear into the darkened camp. The loyal men clustered around Pir and Sidro for a last reassurance.

'I'll ride down to the Ancients first,' Pir said. 'If Vek's well enough, I'll take him with me. His omen-sense might come in handy.'

The men – his men, now – nodded their agreement.

'We'll arrange the surrender,' Pir went on. 'If it looks like they're going to be treacherous, then we'll leave. If Vek and I run into trouble, Sidro will know.'

'And we'll come after you,' one of the men said.

'No, don't! It won't be worth it. There's a wretched lot more of them than there are of us. Get Sidro somewhere safe. That's all I'd ask of you.'

They pledged him, hands on knife-hilts, with the ancient chant, 'hai! hai! hai!'

The men smothered the fire, then drifted away, talking among themselves. Pir took Sidro back to the safety of the cabin. Seeing the wizard-light still glowing where Laz had left it pierced her with grief like a spear. She stood staring at it while Pir watched, unspeaking, with shadowed eyes that revealed nothing of what he might feel. Finally she forced herself to turn away. She walked to the forest-side window and leaned out, breathing in the cleaner night air.

'Sidro?' Pir said at length. 'Should I go get my gear, or do you want to be alone tonight?'

'I don't know.' She turned to face him and leaned back, half-sitting on the windowsill for support. 'I'm so weary, but I'm afraid of being alone.'

'I'll tell you what. I'll go get my blankets, but I'll sleep outside, across the door. You need rest.'

'Yes, I do. I'm sorry.'

Yet once she was lying down, she could not sleep, even though she knew that she'd be safe with Pir right outside. Her thoughts swung back and forth between a certainty that Laz was dead and an equal certainty that he'd come back to her in the morning. Surely he'd be able to understand the magic of those two pyramids, surely he could think his way out of any danger. Couldn't he? Not if he's dead, her mocking mind would answer, and round she would go again. When she finally did manage to sleep, she dreamt of him floating in a lake, his unseeing eyes staring up at the stars, and woke screaming right at dawn.

She sat up in bed and clasped her hands over her mouth just as Pir, dressed only in his trousers, came rushing into the cabin.

'What is it?' he said. 'Nightmares?'

She nodded and forced her trembling hands away from her face. Pir stood yawning and rubbing his eyes with the backs of his hands.

'I'm sorry,' she said. 'You probably wanted to sleep longer.'

'No.' He paused for another yawn. 'I'm going to dress and then fetch Vek. It's time to ride down to the grasslands and see about that surrender.'

The sun was just rising when Salamander went down to the stream to scry. He knelt and stared into the sun-gilded water while he sent his mind out to the stone. Nothing. He felt nothing, saw nothing. Not the slightest trace of any sort of hint about the stone's whereabouts came to him. He scrambled to his feet and spun around, staring at the dark swell of the forest, like a wave on the northern horizon. Once again he reached out for the stone. Once again, nothing.

'How could I have been so witless, doltish, and in general, stupid? Ye gods, what am I going to tell Dalla?'

The stream ventured no opinion on the subject. Tieryn Cadryc, however, quite unconsciously saved Salamander from the grim task of admitting the truth by sending Clae to fetch him.

'The tieryn says we've got to ride out as soon as soon,' Clae said. 'He wants you to write a letter to go ahead with the messengers.'

'Splendid! I need to send a note to Branna myself about her father. Do you want to tell her anything?'

'Just that I'm dreadful sorry her Da's dead.' Clae's voice trembled. 'I know what that feels like.'

By the time Salamander had written the messages and seen them on their way, the wounded and their guards were ready to move out. They crossed the ford again without incident and headed east, following the trail of ruts, cropped grass, garbage, latrine ditches, and the like left from their journey to Zakh Gral. They made a short march that day, however, and set up camp some eight miles from the ford. They would wait there for the rest of the army to catch up. Salamander escaped from the general confusion and went out into the grass to scry.

The summer breeze rippled the long grass and turned it into the waves of a green sea. When Salamander used this focus to reach out to Dallandra, he could feel her presence immediately, but she never responded to his contact. He received quick impressions of her state of mind, a competent urgency. She was hurrying back and forth, giving orders, shoving away disgust and fear both.

'The battle's started,' he said aloud.

Salamander shifted his focus and opened his Sight. When he thought of Dallandra he could see her sluicing down a wagon gate with water in preparation for the patients sure to come. When he turned his mind to Calonderiel and the army, he saw archers, sending arrows in long arcs of death to fall among Gel da' Thae spearmen, whose ranks were on the point of breaking. The men milled around, their shields held high to fend off in vain arrows that plunged from the sky to split wood and leather. The arrow-rain paused as the dragons swooped down. Cavalry horses reared in panic, bucked out of control, throwing their Horsekin riders into the spearmen's ranks, plunging after them and kicking anyone and anything as they desperately tried to escape the huge meat-eaters swooping from the sky. Another volley of arrows fell. Horses and men both began to die.

Behind the archers, swordsmen formed up for the final charge. Salamander broke the vision. At any moment, he felt, he was going to vomit. He splashed his face with cold stream water until he could banish the images from his mind. He stood up, shaking water from his wet hair. Compared to what he'd just seen, the black crystal no longer seemed in the least important.

'The wretched thing has an evil wyrd anyway,' he said aloud. 'You're welcome to it, whoever you are, but I've no doubt it'll bring you naught but bad luck, bad cess, and general misfortune.'

He turned towards the forest verge to follow up his remarks with a few good imprecations. Before he could speak, he saw two Horsekin, a man and a boy, lead their horses down from the wooded plateau out into the open grassland. The boy carried a long straight stick with a dirty grey shirt attached to it for a surrender flag. Apparently they saw Salamander, because they headed straight for him. The man had cropped off most of his hair, leaving a short fur. Down the centre ran a long braided stripe like a horse's mane. Since his horse followed him without benefit of reins or lead rope, he cupped his hands around his mouth and called to Salamander.

'Be you Evan the minstrel?'

Salamander glanced back at the encampment. He stood close enough to yell for help if these Horsekin proved treacherous.

'I am,' he called back. 'What's all this?'

'Surrender. It be needful for us to parley and surrender.'

'Well, come ahead, then. I'll listen to what you have to say.'

As the pair walked up to join him, Salamander realized that they couldn't possibly be Horsekin soldiers. For one thing, the only weapon that either carried was the man's hunting knife. For another, their clothes were filthy and torn, their horses ordinary riding animals, their horse-gear patched together. Farm folk, he assumed, fleeing the war, but the man seemed not the least frightened of him. The boy watched him wide-eyed and wary, but again, he showed no particular fear.

'My name be Pir,' the man said. 'This be Vek.'

'Very well,' Salamander said. 'How did you know my name?'

'Sidro told me.' Pir smiled, ever so slightly. 'She did scry you out, too, and tell me where you'd be found. There be more of my people back in the forest. We be fifteen in all.

We all fled Taenalapan when the Alshandra folk did whip up the citizens against us. We did fear a slow death at the hands of their priestesses because of our gifts.'

'You're telling me you all have dweomer.'

'Not all, just some. The rest did come for their own reasons. But I be a horse mage, should you ken what that may be, and Vek here does see omens.'

For the first time in many years Salamander could think of nothing to say. He gawked at them, then mentally shook himself and caught Pir's gaze to determine if the man lied. When the horse mage looked steadily back, Salamander recognized him. After the long lapse of years, he could no longer remember the name of the miserable human being he'd once run across, the man whose instinctive dweomer gifts had ensorcelled Jill, but he knew him. Pir took a sudden step back.

'No need to fear,' Salamander said. 'You seem to be what you say you are.'

'I be not a man good at lying,' Pir said, 'unlike some among us. I did come first to ask of you, shall we be safe if we come to surrender? Sidro does have reason to fear your army's dragons, among other things.'

'It's only the silver wyrm who threatened her. He's already been told to leave her alone. Tell me somewhat – is the raven mazrak among your people?'

'He was, but he be there no longer, and therein lies a truly strange tale.' Pir shook his head in bafflement. 'He did vanish from the face of the world, as far as any of us do know. The black pyramid that he did steal from you? It did steal him in turn from us.'

Once again Salamander found himself at a loss for words. He longed to get Dallandra's advice, but of course the battle casualties would be engrossing her utterly. He would offer these refugees shelter, he decided, and wait till he reached her to do anything more. *But there's Gerran!* he thought. *He can be downright murderous.*

'Wait here,' Salamander told Pir. 'I want to ensure you'll be safe before I accept your surrender.'

'So be it. I'll let our horses graze while we wait.'

Salamander hurried back towards camp, but Gerran met him half-way.

'Now who's that?' Gerran said. 'More dweomermen?'

'They are, and they want to surrender.'

Gerran sighed with all the weariness in the world. 'More dweomermen,' he said eventually. 'And?'

'Will they be safe, Gerro? Or will the tieryn order them killed?'

'If he does, I'll bring him to his senses quick enough. Do you really think Cadryc would murder helpless prisoners or that I'd let him dishonour himself that way?'

'From the way you talked the other day –'

'Killing a man in battle is one thing. I'm ready enough to do that any time they offer me a fight. But killing someone who's given himself up?' Gerran's hand went to his sword-hilt. 'What do you think I am?'

'An honourable man, sure enough.' Salamander flung up both hands and stepped back fast.

Gerran laughed, the flare of temper gone. 'I'll go speak to them,' Gerran said.

'Good. There's fifteen of them – his folk, this fellow called them – still to come, but they don't all have dweomer.'

'Very well. Here, I've been meaning to ask you. Has the battle at the Braemel road begun yet?'

'Why do you think I'd know?'

Gerran looked at him with a sour twist to his mouth.

'Um, well, truly,' Salamander said. 'It has, and it appears that the army of the two princes is winning handily.'

'Well and good, then. I expected an easy victory. Those poor bastards had no idea of what they were riding into.'

They walked on and joined Pir and the lad. Nearby their horses grazed. Salamander noticed that both mounts wore rope halters rather than bridles. Gerran seemed to be studying them, and he had a sharp look for Pir's odd mane of hair, too.

'This is Lord Gerran of the Gold Falcon,' Salamander said.

'Morrow, milord,' Pir said. 'Be it that you be able to promise my people sanctuary in your camp?'

Gerran struggled briefly with the unfamiliar dialect. 'I can and I will,' he said at last. 'Salamander here told me there's more of you.'

'There be that, my woman among them.'

'How soon can you fetch them?'

'Before sunset, easily.'

'Done, then.' Gerran held out his hand. 'You have my word of honour that none of you will be harmed unless someone gives me cause.'

'I'll be leaving behind any of them that might give you cause, milord. The rest – I'll stand surety for them.'

Pir took the proffered hand and clasped it. Since Salamander felt not the slightest trace of omen warning, he considered the matter settled. He and Gerran watched the men mount up and ride off, heading for the plateau and the forest. Neither of them used any sort of rein.

'I've heard old tales about men like that,' Gerran said. 'Horse mages, aren't they called?'

'They are. We're about to learn more about them, I suspect.'

'Good. I wonder if he can teach our horses not to fear the dragons. It would be a handy thing, if he could.'

'Ye gods! I'd not thought of that. Very handy indeed.'

'We may be able to hold our own against these savages after all.' Gerran turned cheerful. 'In the long run, I mean.'

'Mayhap we will, then.'

At least until the Alshandra people finish converting all the savage tribes, Salamander thought, but that was a thought he kept to himself.

Dallandra had spent much of the day waiting for Westfolk wounded, but her only patient turned out to be an archer who had been accidentally pierced in the fatty part of the thigh by the man standing behind him. Rather than a flood, the wounded Deverry men arrived in a trickle that the chirurgeons could easily handle.

'The Meradan ran like rats, Wise One,' the wounded archer told her. 'The dragons did most of the fighting for us, especially the silver wyrm. You would have sworn he went berserk, dipping and swooping and killing the hairy swine right and left.'

'He does go berserk,' Dallandra said. 'Now hold still!'

She was just finishing up her work when Calonderiel joined her. The commanders had decided what to do with the Gel da' Thae priestess and those few prisoners of war who had survived their wounds.

'I suppose Ridvar wanted to kill the lot,' Dallandra said.

'Not the women,' Calonderiel said. 'Let's try to be fair to the lad. He heartily agreed that the women should be given horses and food for their journey back to Braemel.'

'I'm glad to hear it.'

'They'll take care of the wounded Gel da' Thae on the way. Voran's going to give them letters to take to Braemel's bunch of rabid priestesses and Alshandra rakzanir.'

'Letters? What for?'

'To give them our demands, of course. If they build this fortress again, we'll burn it again. It's as simple as that.'

'I see. Let's hope they see, too.'

'Grallezar did the translating. She told us she'd embellished them a bit, too.'

'With a few nasty remarks, you mean?'

'Just that. Not even Ridvar dared argue about it.'

Towards sunset Dallandra scryed for Ebañy. When she saw him sitting alone at the edge of camp, apparently studying the distant northern horizon, she sent her mind out to his. He responded immediately.

'There you are, oh princess of powers perilous! Is all well there?'

'As well as it can be,' Dallandra said. 'What about in your camp?'

'Uh, well, I've got something to tell you.'

Salamander's tale came across as garbled. His mind jumped back and forth from the lost obsidian showstone to Pir the horse mage and Sidro, with a fair bit of worry about the growing number of Gel da' Thae prisoners mixed in. Finally Dallandra interrupted him, as much to get a moment to think as for any other reason.

'If this Pir's surrendered to you,' Dallandra told him, 'then he's not precisely a prisoner. No, I don't think he'll lead some sort of revolt, so please stop worrying about that. Grallezar's made it clear to me that once a Gel da' Thae surrenders, he'll wait patiently to see what his wyrd may be – it's a point of honour with them. As for the showstone, somehow I can't say that I'm surprised you lost it. It's been ill-omened from the beginning.'

'Here! I didn't precisely lose it. The raven stole it from me.'

'It amounts to the same thing, doesn't it? It's gone.'

'Um, well, yes, I suppose it does.'

'The army's marching tomorrow for the ford. We should reach it easily, Cal tells me. The day after, we should join up with you. Please try to stay out of trouble until we do. As for today, one of the dragons will be carrying messages to Tieryn Cadryc –' Dallandra stopped, caught by a danger-omen. 'It's going to be Rori, and I only hope he's on his way back here before Sidro rides into your camp.'

'What are you going to do?' Sidro said.

'Stay in camp,' Faharn said, 'until Laz comes back.'

Although he was facing her, he was looking past her, his head held high, chin up, his blue eyes focused on some far-off thing.

'And if he doesn't?' she said.

'He will. Maybe you don't have any faith in him, but I do.'

'I'll hope you're right.'

He continued staring over her head. With a sigh Sidro walked away and rejoined Pir. He helped her mount the black mare, then collected the twelve men who'd accepted him as their new leader.

In a ragged line they rode to the edge of the forest, where they would wait while Pir and Vek rode down to the Ancients' camp. Pir left the men back at the camp a horse apiece, but he'd taken all the rest and the pack mule as well. Sidro had collected the few things she now owned – the books, the red pottery plate, the kitchen knife, the blankets, and the length of stolen linen – as much out of a desire to have some small reminders of Laz than because she valued them in themselves.

While they waited, Sidro kept to herself as much as possible. She found a fallen log a little ways from the clearing where the others waited, kicked it hard a number of times to drive out snakes and spiders, then sat down in the forest silence. At moments she scried for Pir; she saw him speaking with Evan. A second man appeared, but since she'd never seen him on the physical plane, his image blurred and wavered. He had red hair – that was the only detail clear enough for her to see. Her mind kept wandering away from the visions. She'd been attempting to scry for Laz ever since she'd woken, but she picked up not a trace of him beyond her untrustworthy dream.

Finally, when the sun hung low in the sky, Pir and Vek returned, waving and calling out in triumph.

'The surrender's arranged,' Pir said. 'Very well, men. If you have any doubts about this, leave now and go back to camp.'

None did. Sidro felt a last stab of doubt, but she realized that she had no real choice. Zakh Gral destroyed, Lakanza a prisoner, Laz disappeared, most likely forever – the fates had left her Pir and her life, naught else. When he strode over to her, she managed to smile at him, but she knew she was trembling. He caught her hand and helped her up.

'Can you really do this?' Pir said.

'Of course. We can't stay in the forest forever.'

'That's true. All we can do is hope for the best.'

With their ragged troop behind them, they led their horses down the cliff path, then mounted up when they reached the grasslands. Ahead of them the encampment rose out of the grass, like a billow of grey clouds among the green. When she glanced up at the sky, she saw a white bird, circling high above them – an omen. During the rest of their ride to the enemy camp, she felt danger pricking at her mind, but she thought she understood the sensation. Of course the situation was dangerous, turning themselves over to the Lijik Ganda! Some hundreds of yards away from the tents, Pir called a halt. Everyone dismounted and led their horses towards their surrender.

Men left the clustered tents and walked out to meet them – a lean fellow with thin grey hair and a thick grey mustache, the red-haired fellow she'd seen talking with Pir, and a man, who seemed to have both Ancients and Lijik blood, carrying a herald's staff. A gaggle of poorly dressed men she took for servants trailed after them. Sidro hung back behind Pir at first, then decided she was acting like a frightened child and hurried to walk next to him. He caught her hand in his but said nothing.

The herald trotted forward, staff in hand. 'Welcome,' he said. 'You know that Lord Gerran's sworn that he'll stand surety for your safety, but Tieryn Cadryc adds his pledge as well. In return, they ask you to give up your weapons, except of course for table daggers and the like.'

'Well and good, then.' Pir turned and repeated the request in the Gel da' Thae tongue. Some of the men grumbled, but Pir glared them into silence.

Slowly, reluctantly, the men unbuckled their baldrics and stepped forward to lay their falcatas or the older curved sabres down at the herald's feet. A few carried short swords and iron spear points in their saddlebags; they brought those out as well and added them to the growing pile. When they were done, the servants hurried forward and scooped them up. With the herald leading the way, they resumed their slow walk to the camp. Sidro let Pir go on ahead. She lingered behind for one last moment alone, one last look at the forest where, for that brief while, she and Laz had been so happy.

That lingering look back proved more dangerous than a thousand weapons. She heard a sound like an enormous drum, beating high above her, then the hiss of huge wings gliding from the sky. She looked up just as the silver dragon came plummeting down. Sidro screamed, unable to run, unable to think as he landed some twenty feet in front of her. With a roar that made her head ring with terror he folded his wings, then strode towards her.

'You!' he hissed. 'Raena, Merodda, you howling bitch!'

'Who?' Sidro stammered. 'I'm not! Why do you hate me? Please don't kill me!'

She fell to her knees and stretched out her arms in supplication. The vinegar smell of wyrm hung so thick in the air that she could barely breathe, much less think clearly. She heard Pir shout, heard men running towards her, but she knew that they could never prevent the dragon from striking. Sidro drew a deep breath and stopped trembling. She would face death bravely, she decided, the only dignity left to her. The dragon took another step towards her, lowered his head, and growled with a sound like an avalanche rumbling down a distant mountain.

'Get back!' Sword in hand, Lord Gerran charged in between them. 'You may not kill her.'

'What's it to you if I do or not?'

'I gave my word of honour that no one would harm her.'

'Do you think you can stop me?' The dragon's words turned into a long hiss.

'Of course not.' Gerran's voice sounded perfectly calm. 'But you'll have to kill me first to get hold of her.'

The silver wyrm raised his massive head and opened his mouth to reveal fangs the size of sword blades. Gerran waited, his sword held in front of him, the point touching the ground as if he were completely indifferent to the malevolence that faced him. In the sunlight, Gerran's red hair flamed. The dragon's scales glittered, as silver as a murderer's moon. Sidro waited, wondering if she'd find Laz in the Deathworld, for a moment that seemed to stretch to touch eternity. Suddenly the dragon sighed with so human a sound that she yelped in surprise.

'I could never harm you.' The dragon said to Gerran, then laid his head upon the ground. 'Well and good then. I shan't kill her, if it means that much to you.'

'Do I have your sworn word on that?' Gerran said.

'You do.' The dragon's voice turned into something very soft, very human. 'I swear it on a dragon's honour, Cullyn, since the man I was had none left.'

'Done, then!' Gerran sheathed his sword, then looked up, puzzled. 'What did you call me?'

The dragon rumbled with laughter. 'My apologies! He was another man I knew once, that's all. Before a fight, he held his sword much as you held yours, and so you reminded me of him just now. You have my sworn word, Lord Gerran, that I'll let the woman live. I'll take my oath on the fire mountain I call home.'

'My thanks,' Gerran said. 'And you have mine that she won't be doing you any harm – as if she could!'

The dragon bobbed his head in deference, then swung his massive self around and waddled away, as clumsy on the ground as he was deadly in the sky. His huge tail flicked from side to side. Sidro staggered to her feet, surprised that she could stand on legs that had all the strength of snow under a hot sun. Gerran was watching her with a slight smile. She could smell not so much as a trace of fear. He might have merely swatted away a fly who'd been circling around her.

'My thanks,' Sidro stammered. 'My heartfelt thanks! I know not how I may ever repay –'

'No repayment needed, your holiness.'

'Please call me not that. I be no priestess any longer.'

'Well and good, then, my lady.' Gerran bowed to her, then strode off, following the dragon.

Pir raced forward and flung his arms around her. She could feel him trembling and smell his fear, slowly ebbing. She pressed against him and ravelled in the warmth of his arms around her, a tangible safety. For a long while neither of them could speak. He stroked her hair, then kissed her on the mouth.

'We'd best join the others,' Pir said. 'The Ancients have taken charge of them.'

The Ancients seemed to be determined to treat their prisoners as decently as guests. Once they all reached the tents, the Lijik men drew back and let the Ancients lead Pir's band to a communal fire in the centre of their part of the camp. Since Sidro knew nothing of the Ancients' language, and they knew nothing of hers, they spoke together in the Lijik tongue. An archer with hair as pale as Evan's came forward and introduced himself as Danalaurel and the herald as Maelaber.

'Come eat,' he said. 'Do you drink mead? We've got some.'

'Not for me,' Sidro said, 'but it were kind if you did share with our men.'

'Gladly.' He turned to Pir. 'I understand that you're a horse mage. Come sit in the place of honour. My lady, if you'd accompany him?'

Pir shrugged and smiled his agreement. 'Um, well, this is a surprise,' he whispered to Sidro in their own tongue.

'Yes, it is,' she said. 'You've arranged the most successful surrender I've ever heard of.'

'I'll wager they want something from us. Let's not celebrate till we see what it is.'

As they walked through the camp, Sidro kept looking around her for Evan, even though she wondered why she would want to confront him. He'd lost her everything she loved – *no*, she told herself, *Lakanza's safe, Laz lost himself, and Alshandra never truly existed, did she?* Finally she saw him, standing off to one side. He hailed Danalaurel, started forward, then stopped, staring her way.

'Evan!' Sidro called out. 'Please, come speak with me!'

He hesitated, then slouched over, his hands in his pockets. 'Are you going to berate me, your — wait!' Evan said in the Lijik tongue. 'I hear you don't consider yourself a priestess any longer.'

'I do not, nor would the order consider me one, should I ever try to go back. Some days ago I scried that you did speak with Lakanza. I fain would know what she did say.'

'She forgave me, bizarrely enough. And she told me that it ached her heart that she'd not listened to you. She said she knew she'd been unjust to you and wished she could tell you so.'

Sidro's eyes filled with tears even as she smiled. 'That gladdens my heart,' she whispered. 'But never could I blame her.'

'Well, you were right, you know,' Evan said. 'I *am* Vandar's spawn, and a witchman, and all of it. I even was in love with Rocca, just like you thought.'

'Then my heart aches for your loss.'

'Does it truly?'

Sidro surprised herself, but she nodded. 'It does. Go in peace, Evan, and I shall do the same.'

'Done, then.' He reached out and touched her hand with his fingertips, then turned and strode away, disappearing among the tents and the growing shadows of twilight.

The Ancients gave them food as well as drink. After the meal, several men brought out harps. Pir and Sidro sat together and spoke but little, listening to incomprehensible songs swirling through the camp. The Ancients had parcelled out Pir's men to the campfires close by. At first Sidro worried about Vek, but Danalaurel told her that two healers had taken charge of the boy.

'One of Pir's men mentioned that Vek has fits now and then,' Danalaurel said. 'Our healers have herbs that might ease them.'

'That gladdens my heart,' Sidro said. 'I do worry that he might fall some time and badly hurt himself.'

As the evening wore on, Sidro first rested her head on Pir's shoulder, then leaned against him and fought to stay awake, until at last he told their hosts that she needed to rest.

'My apologies!' Danalaurel leapt up. 'Let me talk with our herald.'

At his call, Maelaber appeared along with a young Lijik boy, who told her his name was Clae.

'He'll take you to a tent,' the herald said. 'It's on the edge of the camp, where's it quieter. It's near Lord Gerran's.'

'You don't need to be afraid of anything,' Clae said. 'Not with Lord Gerran right there.'

'I see.' Pir smiled at him. 'You do honour Lord Gerran.'

'Oh, he's the greatest lord in all Deverry, but I don't suppose anyone but me knows it.'

'I'll tell you somewhat, lad,' Sidro said. 'I too know that he be so, and I will tell it to anyone who might ask.'

The tent proved to be a typical soldier's shelter, a prism shape of canvas pegged down and slung over stretched rope between poles, but it did offer privacy. Sidro spread out their blankets, which completely covered the floor cloth. Two people could sleep side-by-side, but should it rain, they would have to shrink back from the stretched canvas or let the water in. Sidro pulled off her leather dress, folded it, and laid it down for a pillow. In her linen shift she knelt on the blankets. Pir ducked inside and knelt facing her.

'You must be weary,' Pir said. 'The night's dry and warm. I can sleep outside –'

'No. I can't bear to be unfair to you.' The moment she spoke she regretted it. In the dim light filtering into the tent from the campfires outside, she couldn't see his expression, but she could hear him sigh clearly enough. 'That sounds so cold,' she said. 'I didn't mean it that way.'

'I don't see you like – well, like what? a meal you might owe me for tending your horses.'

'I know. I'm sorry. Please forgive me.'

'I'd best leave.'

'No.' She reached out and laid her hand flat on his chest.
'Pir, make me want you.'

'I can't do that. It's against every vow I ever swore.'

'No, it's not. I'm willing. That makes all the difference.'
She ran her hand down his chest. 'Please?'

He made no answer at first, then caught her hand and
raised it, kissed her wrist, then the palm. She could smell
his desire, smell Desire itself, or so it seemed, a flood of
scent that eddied around her, filling her lungs, sweeping over
her. In that mist of scent, he turned into the most desirable
man in the world. With a sigh of anticipated pleasure she
lay down on the blankets. He followed, settling himself next
to her on his side. She wrapped her arms around his neck
and pulled him down to kiss her.

It took the exhausted army a day and a half to join up with
the contingent waiting across the ford. Dallandra rode towards
the rear of the line of march to keep an eye on the recently
wounded. Two of them died on the way. The army stopped
each time to bury them as well as to repair the inevitable
broken wheels on the carts. When at last they saw the tents
of the encampment, like dirty flowers rising from the tall
grass, Dallandra felt she'd been given a promise of sanctuary,
though a treacherous one. No one knew how the Gel da'
Thae leaders in Braemel and Taenalapan would respond to
the demands of the two princes.

'They'll bluster,' Grallezar said. 'Truly, you may count upon
that, much blustering and threats. But as to acts of war –
well, I wager it were some time before they mount one again.'

'Let's hope you're right,' Dallandra said. 'A long long time.'

As soon as they reached the tents, Salamander came
running to meet them. Since they'd talked mind to mind
many times in the last few days, he had little new to tell
her, which didn't stop him from telling her the old news all

over again. Neither he nor Sidro, the upshot was, had been able to scry out the slightest trace of the black pyramid or the raven mazrak.

'I told Sidro you were coming,' he finished up. 'Do you want to meet her now?'

'By all means,' Dallandra said. 'I take it she can stand the sight of you?'

'Yes, and oddly enough it's because she was right about me.'

Sidro was sitting on the ground in front of the tent she shared with the horse mage, another person Dallandra wanted to meet. As they approached, she got up and stood waiting, her head held high, her hands clasped in front of her. Her raven-dark hair had grown out since her ritual humiliation to reach the neckline of her leather dress, painted with green and yellow designs, including a much-faded bow and arrow that looked as if she'd tried to scrub it off. As soon as Dallandra saw her, she recognized her: Raena, all right, but a changed Raena, one with dignity.

Although Dallandra had been expecting to recognize her, she'd not thought that Sidro would know her in return. Sidro, however, looked at her closely, then flung up a hand as if warding a blow and stepped back, only to blush and stammer.

'My apologies,' Sidro said. 'For a moment I did think I did know you, and it were not a good thing. But truly, we've never met.'

'Oh, it's quite all right.' Dallandra smiled at her. 'This summer's been hard on us all. I can understand why things seem strange.'

'True spoken, Wise One.' Sidro returned the smile. 'The Westfolk here, they do tell me to call you Wise One. Be that correct?'

'It is. Do you want me to call you priestess?'

'Never again!' Sidro shook her head in emphasis. 'I did worship a spirit and think her a god. Never again will I be cozened so.'

'I can understand that, too. May I speak with Pir?'

'He be out among the horses, but I shall fetch him if –'

'Don't trouble yourself. There'll be time later.'

Towards sunset, Meranaldar joined Dallandra as she made the rounds of the wounded men in her care. She'd had her assistants set up her tent near theirs on the edge of the Westfolk encampment. Most of those still alive would recover to various degrees, including the young Deverry rider, Tarro. When Dallandra squatted down by his bed of blankets, his sister helped him off with his shirt, then knelt at his head like a guard. Someone must have given Penna some soap, because she'd washed her brown dress and her hair both. Her short hair in particular gleamed, as thick and soft as fur upon her narrow skull, growing low on her forehead above her bushy eyebrows.

Tarro, Dallandra realized, shared the same thick hair and eyebrows. Although he was too young to raise a full beard and moustache, clumps of brown hair plumed at the corners of his upper lip. More to the point, though, he looked only a quarter of the way to dead, a definite improvement over half. While she changed the bandages around his shoulder, Dallandra was relieved to see that the flap of skin had avoided morbidity. In fact, it was already beginning to form scar tissue, incredibly soon for such a terrible wound.

'You're recovering,' Dallandra told him. 'Good.'

'It's because of Penna,' Tarro said. 'She's been tending me like a baby, and truly, I need it.'

'I won't let him die.' Penna spoke with calm certainty. 'I told him so, and I won't.'

'Well, there's no sign of infection,' Dallandra said to her, 'so you've done a good job so far. Tarro, what will you do, now that you can't ride in a warband?'

'Lord Gerran's offered me the post of gatekeeper in his new dun – when he gets one built, anyway. He said he won't let us starve in the meantime.'

'Excellent!' Meranaldar put in. 'This means that, ultimately, you'll be vassals of Prince Daralanteriel. Did you know that? Lord Gerran will swear to Tieryn Cadryc, and Cadryc will now be allied with the Westfolk as a direct vassal of the prince.'

'Whatever the lords decide,' Tarro said. He started to shrug, then winced in pain. The blood drained from his face. Penna leaned forward and placed her hands on his temples. His colour returned to normal so quickly that Dallandra gave Penna a good looking over. The lass stared back, calm but unsmiling, her luminous dark eyes utterly unreadable.

'Try not to do that again,' Dallandra said to Tarro, 'at least for the next fortnight or so. You'll get used to your loss eventually, lad.'

'I hope so,' Tarro said. 'Wise One, I can still feel the arm. It prickles, like, and sometimes it hurts, but when I go to rub it, it's gone, of course.'

'I'm afraid that's normal. In time, the sensation will fade away.' Dallandra glanced at Penna with a smile as casual as she could make it. 'Can you still see its shadow?'

'The blue glowing part, you mean?'

'Yes.'

'Sort of. It's shrinking, though.'

'Good. When it's all the way gone, he won't feel the arm any longer.'

Meranaldar looked as if he might gag on shock. Dallandra got up, slipped her arm through his, and steered him out of the tent.

'That girl!' Meranaldar said in Elvish, and he whispered for good measure. 'Is she human?'

'No, of course not! I don't know what she is, though, or her brother, either. I'll have to meditate on this. Farm folk, were they? I just wonder.'

Together she and the scribe strolled back to her tent. They were standing outside, talking idly, discussing bits of news from the princes' council, when Calonderiel emerged. He laid a hand on Dallandra's shoulder.

'There you are,' he said. 'I was wondering.' He turned to Meranaldar and frowned. 'You may go.'

'Oh, you think so, do you?' Meranaldar said. 'I was talking with Dallandra, not awaiting your orders.'

Calonderiel released his grip on Dallandra, stepped forward, and slapped the scribe so hard across the face that he staggered back and nearly fell. When Calonderiel slapped him again, from the other direction, he did fall, sprawling backwards, clutching his face with both hands. Blood oozed between his fingers. Calonderiel bent down and reached for him, but Dallandra grabbed the back of his tunic and yanked so hard that he choked and straightened up again.

'Stop it!' she snarled. 'Just stop it right now!'

Shouts, the sound of footsteps – men came running. Dallandra handed Calonderiel over to Danalaurel and two other archers. The three of them hedged him in while they murmured apologies, not to the scribe, but to the banadar for having to interfere. Calonderiel, however, had come to himself by then. He shook himself likea wet dog and glared at Meranaldar, who sat miserably on the ground, head tilted back as he tried to stop the bleeding of his broken nose.

'What's all this?' Prince Daralanteriel came striding towards them. 'Oh by the Black Sun herself! He's finally gone and done it, hasn't he? Cal!'

'My apologies,' Calonderiel said. 'Your highness.'

'It's not me you need to apologize to.'

Calonderiel crossed his arms over his chest and said nothing. Daralanteriel sighted in defeat.

'Someone help my scribe up,' Dar said, 'and take him to Ranadario. I don't think it would be wise to have Dallandra treat him.'

Calonderiel growled his agreement.

'Cal, go inside.' Daralanteriel pointed to the tent. 'Men, you keep him there. Wise one, come with me, would you please?'

Daralanteriel led her a little ways off to a reasonably quiet spot on the edge of the encampment. The prince hooked his thumbs over his belt and stared off to the north, where the forest hung like dark clouds in the last of the sunlight.

'I may be the prince,' Dar said abruptly. 'But Cal has as much authority as I do. More, maybe.'

'Not more, but as much, certainly.'

'Which means you're the only person who can do something about his fits of jealousy,' Dar went on, 'and I don't envy you the job. Meranaldar, on the other hand — I owe him my protection.'

'That's very true.'

'At the last council, I realized something. If we're going to keep from being swallowed up by the Roundears, we need more people. Oh, Prince Voran means well, and as far as I know, no one along the western border of Deverry wishes us the least bit of harm, but in the end, numbers will tell.' Daralanteriel turned to her with a tight smile. 'I'm sending Meranaldar back south to gather more Islanders. There's just time this summer for a trip across, if we get back to Mandra soon, anyway.'

'I can tell Valandario to make sure a ship waits.'

'Good.' Dar sighed and shook his head. 'This is what it comes down to, isn't it? Swelling our ranks. As many people as want to settle here with us, I'll welcome. We're going to have to assign them land, just like the Roundears do, and set up town councils like they do in the Rhiddaer. The swallowing's already begun, Dalla. All we can do is slow it down.'

'You're right, aren't you? Only time will tell if it's a disaster or a triumph.'

'Is that one of your omens?'

'No. Just common sense.'

They shared a grim smile.

'These new people will need a Wise One of their one,' Dallandra went on. 'Gavantar should return to the grasslands with them. I'll send a letter with Meranaldar.'

'Who? I've forgotten —'

'Aderyn's last apprentice. He went to the Isles years ago, to study or so he said, but really it was out of deference to me. It's time he came home.' A thought occurred to her. 'Does Meranaldar want to go back?'

'Probably not, but after what just happened, he'll agree. He's only tormenting himself, anyway, hanging around you without a hope.'

'What?' Dallandra felt herself gape like a village lackwit. 'Are you saying he's in love with me?'

'You hadn't noticed?'

'No, I honestly hadn't noticed.' Her face burned with a blush. 'Oh ye gods, the poor man! No wonder Cal – not that it excuses what he did – but – oh ye gods! I'll do my best to avoid Meranaldar till we get back to Mandra.'

'Good. I recommend it.'

'I'd better go calm Cal down.' Dallandra started to turn away, but the prince called her back.

'One more thing,' Daralanteriel said. 'Tonight, after everyone's eaten, I want to talk with Pir – do I have his name right?'

'The horse mage?' Dallandra said. 'Yes, that's it.'

'Good. I want to see if it's possible for him to work with our warhorses. If they learn to trust dragons, and the Horsekin mounts don't, we'll have another advantage over them.' He paused for emphasis. 'One that doesn't depend on dwarven devices.'

'That's a huge favour to ask him.'

'I know. We'll have to offer him something huge in return. Will you talk with him when I do?'

'Of course. But now I'd better go talk with Cal.'

When Dallandra returned to her tent, the three men on guard were more than glad to leave her alone with the banadar. She ducked inside, then created a gold dweomer light and tossed it to the roof, where it stuck near the smoke-hole. Calonderiel was lying on his back on their blankets, his arms still militantly crossed over his chest. With a sigh she sat down next to him.

'Did you seriously think I'd be interested in that tedious milksop?' she said. 'I'm insulted!'

Calonderiel smiled, uncrossed his arms, and sat up. 'I've made a fool of myself again, haven't I?' he said.

'No. You merely terrified me and everyone around us.'

'That's what I wanted to do, now that I think of it. Dalla, do you really love me? Sometimes I don't see how you could.'

'Sometimes I wonder myself, but I do.'

When he held out his hand, she took it in both of hers. 'There's something I've been meaning to tell you,' she said. 'I'm pregnant.'

He smiled, a slow, deep grin of utter satisfaction. 'Are you happy about it?' he said.

'Very, now that the war's over.'

He let the smile fade and looked away.

'It is over, isn't it?' Dallandra said. 'Cal –'

'It's over for now. That's the best I can offer you.'

'For now. How long –'

'I don't know. You're the dweomermaster, not me.'

'Well, that's true.' Dallandra let go of his hand. 'For now. That will have to do, won't it?'

'Unfortunately, yes.' He leaned forward and kissed her on the mouth. 'Forgive me for being jealous? Don't forget, I loved you in vain for five hundred years. Sometimes I just can't believe that the wait's over.'

'The wait?'

'Oh, I knew you'd give in eventually. I just didn't think it would take so long.'

'You really are an arrogant bastard.'

'Have I ever denied it?'

She started to laugh, laughed until he kissed her into silence. Yet even in his arms she felt a cold wind blowing, coming from a future that lay too clouded for her to see.

Sidro and Pir had taken to eating with the men of the Westfolk, as she'd learned to call them. She'd feared Lijik men for too many years to find it easy to be around them, despite the way that Gerran had saved her from the silver wyrm. She'd observed, as well, that Lijik men had woven a vast web of courtesies around themselves, customs that neither she nor Pir understood, while the Westfolk treated such things lightly and with laughter. *Vandar's spawn*, she would think. *They called them evil Vandar's spawn, and we believed them*. At moments she would shake with rage, remembering the lies.

Pir had even found himself interested in Westfolk music. Both of them loved to listen to the singing in the evenings, but the Westfolk harp especially fascinated him. 'It's got such a clear pure sound,' he said. 'It's a pity I can't sing.'

'Here!' Sidro grinned at him. 'I never knew you wanted to be a bard.'

'I didn't when it meant losing my eyes to the point of a knife. Besides, the gods marked me for something else.' He frowned, thinking. 'Or something marked me, anyway.'

One of the harpers, Adariel, was showing Pir how to hold the harp when Prince Daralanteriel strode up to their campfire. No one leapt to their feet; no one knelt. Adariel, however, did fall silent and set the harp aside.

'Pir, the Wise One and I would like to speak with you,' Daralanteriel said. 'Sidro, by all means come along too, if you'd like.'

The prince led them to the tent that Dallandra shared with the banadar. Calonderiel terrified Sidro. He always seemed to be standing, or sitting in this case, at the edge of things, arms crossed, glaring at someone in barely controlled rage. He did offer Pir mead like a host, but his purple eyes were as cold and bleak as always. Fortunately, during the discussion that followed he merely listened as Prince Dar talked, using the Lijik language.

'Pir,' Dar said, 'you and your woman are welcome to stay here among us as long as you'd like. I was wondering if that pleased you.'

'It does, your highness,' Pir said. 'We do have no other place to go except among the Red Reivers, and truly, there we'd rather not go. Exalted Mother Grallezar be an exile here, too, as be my men. If you will shelter us all, you will have Gel da' Thae to consult about your enemies' ways.'

'True spoken, and all of you are welcome. I have a task to offer you alone, however. You're a horse mage. We've heard of such, here in the Westlands. We know that your gifts are rare and immensely valuable –' He paused, noticing Pir's puzzled frown. '– of great worth, that means.'

Pir nodded with a brief twitch of smile.

'Do you think you could teach our horses to accept the presence, the nearness that is, of dragons? If so, we'd reward you highly.'

'And with those horses, you then do wish to slaughter more of my people?' Pir said.

Daralanteriel looked away, but not quickly enough to hide his grimace of guilt.

'So I thought,' Pir went on. 'An exile I be, but not yet a traitor to my kind.' He paused, visibly thinking something through. 'Though truly, I be Gel da' Thae, not a savage tribesman of the north, and it be the northerners who did ravage our cities and put their false goddess above all others. To them I be an enemy.'

'We also are their enemies,' Daralanteriel said.

'So we did see.' Pir glanced at Sidro. 'What say you to this?'

'Do what you want,' Sidro said in their own language. 'It's your gifts they need, not mine, so I don't see that I have any right to meddle in your decision either way.'

'Very well, then.' Pir continued in the Lijik tongue. 'So, your highness, if I agree, what be this reward you speak of?'

'Your own herd of Western Hunters, I was thinking,' Dar said. 'A golden stud, two golden brood mares, four other mares, ten geldings of whatever colour coat you'd like.'

'You do know how to tempt a man.' Pir thought for a long while before he spoke again. 'The northerners, they would put both me and Sidro to death, did they catch us. They do hate witchery.'

'We honour it here,' Dallandra put in.

'So we do see.' Pir nodded at her, then looked away, staring across the tent as if he were seeing a vision among the tent bags hanging upon its wall. 'Tell me, Wise One. Do you ken the story of the black stone and Laz Moj?'

'How your raven mazrak disappeared, you mean?' Dalla said.

'Just that.' He waited until she nodded a yes, then went on. 'Have you a thought on where he might have gone?'

'I haven't. It would gladden my heart to talk with you, Sidro, in fact, about just that, since you were there when it happened.'

'So I was.' Sidro felt cold grief clutch her heart. 'It were a terrible thing to see.'

Pir was watching her, his face carefully expressionless, his scent utterly noncommittal. Everyone else watched him. He fell silent again, thinking things through in his patient way. Finally he sighed and nodded to no one in particular.

'Here then be my price,' Pir said. 'If you do help us find Laz, then will I help you with the horses.'

Sidro gasped aloud, then clasped a hand over her mouth to hide her sudden flare of hope. The prince and the banadar both turned to the Wise One.

'At the moment I'm with child,' Dallandra said. 'Once the child is born, then I'll be able to help. In the meantime, others of our people have dweomer, Ebañy – Evan, that is – among them. There's also a dweomerwoman named Valandario who very much wants the black pyramid found and destroyed. She knows gem dweomer like no other has ever known it. If anyone can track the pyramid down, it will be Val. And we can hope that finding the pyramid means finding Laz. I can't promise, but I can hope.'

'And I'll still give you the horses,' the prince put in. 'They'll give you standing among us. You have the men in your band,

and we can give them sheep. Sheep and horses – they're our gold, out here in the grass.'

Pir considered, looking away, looking down, nodding now and then. At last he got up and bowed to the prince.

'Done, then,' Pir said. 'I do take your bargain. For truly, I do think I be able to teach your warhorses what you wish them to learn. There be a need, though, to have a dragon give me his aid.'

Solemn-eyed, Daralanteriel rose and held up his right hand, palm out. Pir laid his palm against it. 'You have my word upon it,' the prince said. 'The gods of my people have witnessed it.'

'So have mine.' Pir seemed unsure of what to say, but the prince nodded in satisfaction. 'So be it.'

'In the morning come with me,' Dar continued, 'and you shall pick out the geldings for your new herd. Once we rejoin the rest of my people and my herds, I give you my word of honour that I'll provide the stud and the brood mares.'

'Well, truly, your highness, never did I think you'd bring breeding stock along to a war.'

Pir smiled, everyone else smiled, but only Sidro could smell the bitter tang of sorrow in his scent. She supposed that he felt like a traitor, even as she did, despite their knowing that their own people had turned against them long before they chose exile. *And what of me?* she wondered. *He must know that in my heart I'm Laz's slave.* She found herself remembering the night of Vek's coming of age ritual. Most Gel da' Thae women would have taken Pir to their bed right then and there, but she had stayed chaste – like a good slave.

The men celebrated the bargain with a fair amount of mead, but once they were alone again in their tent, Sidro asked Pir outright why he'd chosen that reward.

'Do you want Laz to come back?' she said.

'I feel torn in half,' Pir said. 'I want him to be safe and well. He's my friend, after all. He hid me when the mob came after me. He took me with him when he went into exile.'

'I'd forgotten about that.'

'But then there's you,' Pir said. 'I'd rather have you all to myself. Once he comes back, well then, I'll be settling for the oats at the bottom of his manger.'

'Then why –'

'If you never see him again, you'll be unhappy, won't you? And then, sooner or later, you'll leave me anyway. You'll want something I can't give you, and you'll never find it without finding Laz, but you'll try.'

It took Sidro a moment to muster words. She could see herself, suddenly, going from man to man, whether Gel da' Thae or Westfolk, in a desperation that would grow worse as she aged.

'You know women as well as you know horses,' she said.

'No, but I do know you. I'd rather be your Second Man than not have you at all. It's a beggar's bargain, but that's what I am. A beggar, I mean, living on Prince Dar's charity.'

Once again she smelled the bitter tang in his scent.

'You should have been a great man among our people,' she said. 'You would have been, too, if it weren't for Alshandra's savages.'

He made a sound that might have been either agreement or scepticism. 'Doesn't matter now, does it?' he said.

'No. I'm afraid it doesn't matter at all.'

The army had crawled towards home at its usual pace for an eightnight before the Mountain Folk announced that they could no longer endure travelling with snails. On a last wave of promises and handshakes, they assembled in the dawn light, ready to march off north at their own quick pace. Dallandra made a last farewell to Kov.

'I'm sorry we couldn't unravel all the runes on your staff,' she said.

'Oh, please don't apologize!' Kov said. 'I know a fair bit more about them than I did before, and I'm grateful. Garin will be, too, I'm sure.'

'Do give him my regards when you see him. I remember him from the siege of Cengarn, and I think highly of him.'

'And he's spoken very well of you to me, Wise One. Perhaps we'll meet again someday? I'll hope so.'

'We may well do just that. I'd very much like to talk with Enj about Haen Marn.' Dallandra laid her hands on her stomach. 'But it will have to wait for a while, till the child's born and old enough to travel.'

A scowling Brel Avro strode over to them.

'I know what you're going to say,' Kov said. 'Everyone's ready to leave but me.'

Dallandra watched the dwarven ranks march off, hauling their carts with them, then walked through the encampment until she found Salamander, who was rolling up his bedroll. The servants had already packed away his tent. She knelt down next to him.

'Ebañy, what are we going to do about Neb and Branna?' Dallandra said. 'As decent a soul as Tieryn Cadryc is, his dun is not the right place for learning dweomer.'

'That's true, oh mistress of mighty magicks. Now, in a few more days, the army will split again. You'll be heading south to Mandra. I can ride east with the Red Wolf and fetch our two apprentices.'

'That's assuming they'll be allowed to go.'

'Fear not!' Salamander smiled at her. 'I have a ruse, ploy, or stratagem all planned. Since Meranaldar's taking ship for the Southern Isles, Prince Dar is going to need a scribe. What better scribe than a Roundear, to celebrate the alliance between our two peoples and to cement our enduring friendship and so on and so forth?'

Dallandra laughed. 'There are times,' she said, 'when your talent for blather comes in decidedly handy. I suppose Branna will simply have to go where her husband goes.'

'Under Deverry law she has no choice. Do you think our prince will speak to Tieryn Cadryc for me? The invitation will look much more official that way.'

'Oh, I think I can persuade him. As they say in Deverry, done then!'

When the messengers arrived at the Red Wolf dun, they brought with them the news of Tieryn Gwivyr's death, along with the deaths of so many other good men. Branna was shocked at her own reaction. While Galla wept, mourning her brother, Branna felt very little beyond sympathy for her aunt. *It doesn't seem real*, she thought. *Da buried in a foreign land, beside a foreign river.* As the days passed, and she found herself still unable to weep, she realized at last that death had taken on an entirely new meaning for her. She happened to be sitting on the window ledge in her chamber and remembering how it felt to fly when she thought of her father one last time. *I'll see him again if I need to*, she thought, *or if he needs to see me. In some When or another.*

The returning army arrived a full fortnight after the messengers. When they heard the tieryn's horn announcing their return, Branna and Solla rushed out of the women's hall and raced down the stairs to the ward. Lady Galla followed more slowly, yelling after them the entire way to mind their courtesies.

Men and horses filled the ward. The servant lasses whose men had come home rushed to greet them, while those who had lost their men busied themselves with their work, their eyes brimming with tears. Branna and Solla found a place to stand near the entrance to the great hall where they'd be out of the way of the confusion.

'I feel like running to Gerran's side,' Solla said, 'but what if he's changed his mind about marrying me? He never came right out and asked, you know.'

'Oh hush!' Branna said, smiling. 'Look! Here he comes!'

Gerran strode over to them. He'd made a heroic effort to look presentable, Branna decided, considering he'd been riding a long campaign. He was reasonably clean, freshly shaved, his hair trimmed up, and his shirt looked as if it had been dipped in a stream somewhere along the way home to get the worst of the dirt off. Tied around his left arm he wore Solla's blue scarf. Branna stepped back out of the way and stood watching.

'It gladdens my heart to see you, Lord Gerran.' Solla dropped him a curtsey.

'It gladdens mine to see you, Lady Solla.' Gerran bowed to her in turn. 'I have some interesting news. The Falcon clan's going to have a new dun, down in the Melyn River valley. I'd be honoured thrice beyond my worth if you'd be its lady.'

'My lord Gerran.' Her voice softened to a whisper. 'I'm a warrior's daughter, and the sister of a gwerbret, but I'll be the one honoured to be your wife.'

Gerran caught her hands in his. 'Done, then,' he said. 'My lady.'

For a moment their rigid courtesy held; then all of a sudden she laughed, a joyous ring of laughter, and threw her arms around his neck. He caught her by the waist, kissed her, then kissed her again, while all around them the ward rang out with cheers. Branna wiped a few sentimental tears away on her sleeve, then went into the great hall.

At the table of honour Cadryc and Galla had taken their places, and Mirryn, still sulky, sat with them. Branna glanced around for Neb and saw him standing at the honour hearth, talking with Salamander. She hurried over, paused to greet her uncle with a kiss on his bald spot, and joined them.

'I've received a very flattering offer,' Neb said with a wink in her direction. 'Prince Daralanteriel wants me to come be his scribe.'

'We'd live among the Westfolk?' Branna said. 'That sounds most interesting.'

Galla caught her breath with a gasp and turned in her chair to glare at Neb and Salamander impartially.

'Now, my love,' Cadryc said. 'I've already agreed that if Neb wants to take the offer, he can go. I'll be the prince's vassal in a few short months, you know, and so we've got to weigh his wishes carefully.'

'I suppose we must,' Galla said, 'but Branni, I'll worry about you, out there so far from home.'

'It's not like I'll be lonely, Aunt Galla. The prince travels with a huge retinue,' Branna said. 'I shall miss you, though.'

'And I shall miss you, dear. I do hope that you'll be leaving us that lovely wool-spinner of yours.' She glanced at Salamander. 'You must get her to show it to you. The Westfolk women will probably want one, too.'

Salamander smiled and bowed. Doubtless he had no idea of what she meant.

'Of course I will,' Branna went on. 'And you've got Adranna and the children here now, and Solla will be staying till Gerran gets his new dun. So you won't be alone any more.'

'Well, true spoken.' Galla sighed heavily. 'And no doubt the prince will visit us from time to time, and you with him. Neb, have you decided?'

'I have, my lady. I'm so truly grateful to you for everything you've done for me, taking me and Clae in, letting me marry Branna, but to take a prince's service – what an honour to come my way! Didn't you tell Branna that one day I might be attached to a great man's court?'

'Oh!' Galla made a sour face at him. 'Snared with my own wire!' She paused, thinking. 'You know, though, I must admit that it'll be a useful thing, having kinsfolk in our new over-lord's court.'

'Scheming already, eh?' Cadryc grinned at her. 'Now, what am I going to do for a scribe? Curse it all, I just got used to having one.'

'Solla can read and write,' Branna put in. 'It's going to be a while before the Falcon clan gets its new dun, isn't it?'

'A woman for a scribe?' Cadryc stared at her for a moment, then shrugged. 'Well, why not, eh? A pen doesn't weigh all that much. There's no reason a woman can't lift one.'

By the time the Westfolk army returned to the pastures around Mandra, the night winds hinted at the coming of autumn's chill, and Dallandra was feeling most assuredly pregnant. Calonderiel hovered around her, making sure she had the best food to eat and the softest blankets he could find for her to sleep upon, until she was ready to scream at him to stop fussing. It was Sidro, oddly enough, who told her that she should be grateful that her man cared so much.

'I did bear a child once,' Sidro said, 'to a man who cared not in the least. He did turn me out of his mother's house in his jealousy.'

'You mean he thought it wasn't his child?' Dallandra said.

'Nah, nah, nah, but that he were jealous of the child. He knew I would love it as much as I loved him, and he brooked no rival in his house.'

'That was Laz?'

'It was.' Sidro looked away, and for a moment Dallandra thought she might weep. 'But the child, he were born sickly, and he died. Laz did want me back, then, but I went instead to Alshandra's service.'

'I can see why! The selfish little beast!'

Sidro considered her for a moment, then smiled, but sadness welled behind that smile. 'He were that, then. Over the years, he did change for the better.' She paused briefly. 'In some ways.'

'It seems to me that you've got the better man in Pir.'

'Oh, he be that most certainly, Dalla. There be a need upon me to remember it if we do find Laz. Always has he held my heart in his fist.'

'He hasn't ensorceled you, has he?'

Sidro shook her head no. 'Only if love be sorcery, and truly, at times I think it be as dangerous as any spell.'

'I think you be right,' Grallezar put in. 'I do feel blessed that never did I succumb to such.'

'But Exalted Mother,' Sidro said. 'You did bear children of your own.'

'The children I loved. Their father –' Grallezar shrugged. 'I did pick him for his mach-fala and the lands they owned.

He did have a good scent, too.' She glanced at Dallandra. 'They all be safe upon those lands now, far from Braemel, so I think me I did pick well.'

Sidro smiled her agreement, then paused to sniff the air. They were all sitting in Dallandra's tent, while outside the rain drummed down, another omen of autumn. For want of much else to do, Sidro had attached herself to Grallezar as something of a serving woman and maidservant. Dallandra still found it unsettling to see the Gel da' Thae women constantly raising their heads to sample the smells around them, but she had to admit that at times it did come in handy.

'Exalted Mother,' Sidro said. 'Do you think Dallandra's child be female?'

Grallezar paused for a deep breath. 'I think you be right,' Grallezar said. 'I smell not the male taint.'

'Well, wonderful!' Dallandra said, simply because she knew they expected her to be pleased. 'I'm so happy to hear it!'

She would have felt as happy – and as burdened – with a boy as well, and in fact, she'd been expecting that the child would be male. Later, when she and Grallezar were alone and able to discuss dweomer and its secrets in their private language, Dallandra brought the matter up and mentioned how surprised she was to be carrying a girl.

'I'd been thinking that this soul would be Loddlaen's,' Dallandra said. 'I was sure of it, actually, the more I meditated upon it.'

'And why shouldn't it be?' Grallezar said. 'Male or female, the dweomer doesn't care.'

'You know, you're right. All this talk of Gel da' Thae and Mountain Folk, the People and the Roundears – I've fallen into tribe-bound ways of thinking again, I'm afraid.' She patted her stomach. 'I'm sure it is the same soul. I truly am.'

'You would know. Well, poor Loddlaen! At least you have the chance now to make things up to him. Or her, I should say.'

'What? I don't feel that I owe him anything. I did what I

had to do. Far more souls than one needed me desperately. The times now are dangerous enough that I'll have to do what I find the need to do again. But this time, I'll make sure that she's well provided for if I should have to leave her. And this time she'll be one of the People on both sides of her line, which will make her life much easier.'

'So it will. I just realized something. I've been trying to think what I might do for you, something to repay you for your generosity in taking me in –'

'You don't owe me anything.'

'Oh, I know, but we Gel da' Thae, we dislike feeling like useless guests. Look at Sidro, bustling around, washing my clothes and blankets, and her with dweomer gifts of her own! When the child's born, I'll be your nursemaid and help raise her.'

'Wonderful! She'll have a splendid start in life.' Dallandra suddenly laughed. 'Especially if she wants to be a commander of armies.'

Late on the following day, Salamander rode into the camp with Neb and Branna in tow. Since everyone knew that the two Roundears had come to study with Dallandra as well as write the occasional letter for Prince Dar, a tent stood ready for them on the edge of the encampment near Dallandra and Calonderiel's. The members of the royal alar crowded round them in friendly curiosity, and that first evening, Dallandra barely saw them. It would take them some days to grow used to the Westfolk way of life, Dallandra knew. In the long tent-bound winter they would have plenty of time to begin the methodical study of the dweomer that they both needed, as she informed them the next morning.

'It can get tedious, down in the winter camps,' Dallandra told them. 'But you'll have lots to keep you occupied.'

'No doubt,' Branna said. 'Dalla, will the silver dragon be there?'

'Not in the camps, but he should turn up here soon, once it stops raining. I've got to treat his wound.'

'Ah, I see.' Branna hesitated, thinking. 'I keep feeling like there's somewhat I should say to him, or discuss with him, more like, but I can't think of what it may be.'

'Well, you know, other than helping me lift the dweomer upon him, there may be naught for you to say. I've learned that at times, saying naught means more than words. It's a message in itself.'

Branna looked utterly puzzled, but Dallandra merely smiled. Evandar had taught her that some truths needed to be left as riddles so that the persons who needed the answers could find them for themselves. *It's the finding that matters*, she thought, *not the answer*. Dallandra did, however, have a straightforward question for Neb. She'd not forgotten Penna and Tarro.

'I remember Penna from the village, truly,' Neb told her. 'Tarro I only met once, when the gwerbret's captain let him come home for a visit. Penna was an odd child, but it gladdens my heart that she's been rescued from the Horsekin.'

'Odd how?' Dallandra said.

'First off, they were stepchildren. Their father was a river fisherman who drowned, and her mother married a farmer – his name was Gutyn – who took her children in and raised them as his own. He was a decent man, truly. The mother died before Clae and I got to Uncle Brwn's farm, so I never met her.' Neb suddenly paused. 'Gutyn must have been killed by the raiders, now that I think of it. Gods, it's horrible still, remembering all that.'

'Of course it is. Penna's still half in shock herself, I think. You could see her grief written on her face.'

'No doubt!' He frowned, thinking. 'She was terrified of the river, too.'

'Well, that's understandable, since her father drowned in it.'

'True spoken, but it had to be somewhat more than that. I found her weeping once because she was supposed to lead the cows down to drink. The river will take me one day, she told me. I thought she meant she'd drown, but she insisted it wasn't that.' Neb shrugged and spread his hands. 'She couldn't quite say what she meant. So I led the cows down for her, and after that, her half-brother took over the task.'

The half-brother had died in the raid, too, Dallandra supposed. The sudden look of slack-mouthed grief that crossed Neb's face confirmed it.

The dragon lounged in the lair he'd made in tall grass. The sun gleamed on his silver scales, tipped here and there with blue, as if he were wearing the finest mail in the world, made from some dweomer metal – except for the pink gash of his old wound, spoiling it. Branna could see where Dallandra had cleaned the dead flesh away, but the gash remained, stubbornly unhealed. Still, he sprawled comfortably enough. His eyelids drooped, and he yawned, revealing fangs longer than her arm.

'Rori?' Branna said. 'Are you awake?'

'I am now,' he said and raised his massive head.

His voice stirred memories, so deep in her mind that they brought no images or words with them, merely a piercing sense that she'd heard his voice before. Salamander had warned her about his eyes. Like Salamander, she nearly wept, seeing that human gaze, trapped behind the face of another order of being. He studied her with longing, a minute examination.

'You're no longer Jill,' he said. 'Dalla made that clear to me. I don't want it to be true, but I know it is.'

'Good. I don't want to be Jill. She's dead.'

'So she is.' He sighed and laid his head to rest upon his enormous front paws. His claws dug into the earth, then relaxed. 'It gladdens my heart that you've come out to speak with me. I hoped you would, in your own time.'

'You've not been here more than half a day.'

He rumbled with laughter. 'I've always been the impatient sort.'

'You could have sent a message back with Dalla when she tended your wound.'

'That would have spoilt it.' He raised his head to look straight at her. 'I wanted to – I needed to see if you'd come on your own.'

'Well, here I am.'

Branna waited, let him continue studying her with his all too human dark blue eyes. The moment had come that she'd been anticipating, when she would meet the silver wyrm at last and speak with him. The moment grew longer as she realized that she still had no idea of what to say. *There should be somewhat*, she thought. *Or is Dalla right?* Finally he sighed so deeply that the sound came close to a roar.

'Ever since that night in Cengarn,' Rori said, 'when you called out to me that you'd come back, I've been thinking of things to say to you. I might as well have been a bard, going through every fine word and phrase I knew. But now we're face to face, and none of the words are right, because you're not Jill. Now I can see it for myself. It's not just a tale that Dalla told me.'

'You know, I've been doing the same thing, but I don't remember who you were to Jill, so I'd not thought of much to say at all.'

'You don't remember anything?'

'Well, I know she was your friend. If there was somewhat more, my apologies, but I truly don't remember.'

'My friend? Well, she was that, too.' He sighed in a long hiss. 'You don't remember.'

'Does it truly matter? Dalla told me you want the dweomer lifted. One day I'll know what Jill knew, whether I'm her or not. And I swear it, Rori, I'll do whatever I can to lift that spell.'

'Will you? Then my thanks.'

His eyes, those striking dark blue eyes, filled with tears. *Dragons can't weep, can they?* Branna thought. *It's the man inside the form who's so sad.*

Rori raised his head with a shake to knock the tears away. For a moment he busied himself in rearranging his front paws on the grass. 'I'll be leaving for the winter in a little while. I can't take the cold in this body. Even cool days like this, they make me sluggish.'

'Well and good, then. I'll see you in the spring.'

He nodded, then lowered his head onto his paws and closed his eyes. She lingered, unsure if he were truly sleeping or if he were telling her farewell. Finally she walked away, heading back to the camp and Neb.

She'd killed some fine thing, she realized, some grand love, most likely, that she'd once shared with the man Rori had been. What precisely it was, she couldn't remember, and no more did she mourn the thing itself, but she wept, anyway, just a scatter of tears for all the honour and love that the river of Time sweeps away in its scouring flow.

AUTHOR'S NOTE

If any readers want to know more about the dwarven fire bolts, which are based on real weapons, they can find the source information in Aeneas the Tactician's *How to Survive a Siege*. Various reference books, such as Peter Connolly's *Greece and Rome at War*, have more detailed reconstructions. The falcata was also a real weapon, carried by the native Hispanic troops in Spain against the Roman army when Rome was mopping up after the Carthaginian Wars. Human beings have been wasting man-hours and resources on finding better ways to kill each other for a very long time.

GLOSSARY

Alar (Elvish) A group of elves, who may or may not be bloodkin, who choose to travel together for some indefinite period of time.

Alardan (Elv.) The meeting of several alarli, usually the occasion for a drunken party.

Astral The plane of existence directly 'above' or 'within' the etheric (q.v.). In other systems of magic, often referred to as the Akashic Record or the Treasure House of Images.

Banadar (Elv.) A warleader, equivalent to the Deverrian cadvridoc, (q.v.)

Blue Light Another name for the etheric plane (q.v.).

Body of Light An artificial thought-form (q.v.) constructed by a dweomermaster to allow him or her to travel through the inner planes.

Cadvridoc (Dev.) A warleader. Not a general in the modern sense, the cadvridoc is supposed to take the advice and counsel of the noble-born lords under him, but his is the right of final decision.

Captain (Dev. *pendaely.*) The second in command, after the lord himself, of a noble's warband. An interesting point is that the word *taely* (the root or unmutated form of *–daely,*) can mean either a warband or a family depending on context.

Deosil The direction in which the sun moves through the sky, clockwise. Most dweomer operations that involve a circular movement move deosil. The opposite, widdershins, is considered a sign of the dark dweomer and of the debased varieties of witchcraft.

Dweomer (trans. of Dev. *dwunddaevad*.) In its strict sense, a system of magic aimed at personal enlightenment through harmony with the natural universe in all its planes and manifestations; in the popular sense, magic, sorcery.

Ensorcel To produce an effect similar to hypnosis by direct manipulation of a person's aura. (True hypnosis manipulates the victim's consciousness only and thus is more easily resisted.)

Etheric The plane of existence directly 'above' the physical. With its magnetic substance and currents, it holds physical matter in an invisible matrix and is the true source of what we call 'life.'

Etheric Double The true being of a person, the electromagnetic structure that holds the body together and that is the actual seat of consciousness.

Falcata (Latin) A curved and weighted sabre derived from the earlier falx – an ancient weapon, carried in our world by Hispanic tribes of the second and third centuries BC, independently discovered by Gel da' Thae swordsmiths.

Gerthddyn (Dev.) Literally, a 'music man', a wandering minstrel and entertainer of much lower status than a true bard.

Gwerbret (Dev.) The name derives from the Gaulish (*vergobretes*.) The highest rank of nobility below the royal family itself. Gwerbrets (Dev. *gwerbretion*) function as the chief magistrates of their regions, and even kings hesitate to override their decisions because of their many ancient prerogatives.

Lwdd (Dev.) A blood-price; differs from wergild in that the amount of lwdd is negotiable in some circumstances, rather than being irrevocably set by law.

Malover (Dev.) A full, formal court of law with both a priest of Bel and either a gwerbret or a tieryn in attendance.

Mach-fala (Gel da' Thae) A mother-clan, the basic extended family of Gel da' Thae culture.

Rhan (Dev.) A political unit of land; thus, gwerbretrhyn,

tierynrhyn, the area under the control of a given gwerbret or tieryn. The size of the various rhans (Dev. rhannau) varies widely, depending on the vagaries of inheritance and the fortunes of war rather than some legal definition.

Scrying The art of seeing distant people and places by magic.

Sigil An abstract magical figure, usually representing either a particular spirit or a particular kind of energy or power. These figures, which look a lot like geometrical scribbles, are derived by various rules from secret magical diagrams.

Tieryn (Dev.) An intermediate rank of the noble-born, below a gwerbret but above an ordinary lord (Dev. *arcloedd*.)

Wyrd (trans. of Dev. *tingedd*.) Fate, destiny; the inescapable problems carried over from a sentient being's last incarnation.

APPENDICES

A NOTE ON DEVERRY DATING

Deverry dating begins at the founding of the Holy City, approximately year 76 C.E. The reader should remember that the old Celtic New Year falls on the day we call November 1, so that winter is the first season of a new year.

A NOTE ON THE PRONUNCIATION OF DEVERRY WORDS

The language spoken in Deverry is a member of the P-Celtic family. Although closely related to Welsh, Cornish, and Breton, it is by no means identical to any of these actual languages and should never be taken as such.

Vowels are divided by Deverry scribes into two classes: noble and common. Nobles have two pronunciations; commons, one.

A as in *father* when long; a shorter version of the same sound, as in *far*, when short.

O as in *bone* when long; as in *pot* when short.

W as the *oo* in *spook* when long; as in *roof* when short.

Y as the *i* in *machine* when long; as the *e* in *butter* when short.

E as in *pen*.

I as in *pin*.

U as in *pun*.

Vowels are generally long in stressed syllables; short in unstressed. Y is the primary exception to this rule. When it appears as the last letter of a word, it is always long whether that syllable is stressed or not.

Diphthongs generally have one consistent pronunciation.

AE as the *a* in *mane*.

AI as in *aisle*.

AU as the *ow* in *how*.

EO as a combination of *eh* and *oh*.

EW as in Welsh, a combination of *eh* and *oo*.

IE as in *pier*.

OE as the *oy* in *boy*.

UI as the North Welsh *wy*, a combination of *oo* and *ee*.

Note that OI is never a diphthong, but is two distinct sounds, as in *carnoic*, (Kar-noh-ik).

Consonants are mostly the same as in English, with these exceptions:

C is always hard as in *cat*.

G is always hard as in *get*.

DD is the voiced *th* as in *the*, but the voicing is more pronounced than in English. It is opposed to TH, the unvoiced sound as in *thin* or *breath*. (This is the sound that the Greeks called the Celtic tau.)

R is heavily rolled.

RH is a voiceless R, approximately pronounced as if it were spelled *hr* in Deverry proper. In Eldidd, the sound is fast becoming indistinguishable from R.

DW, GW, and TW are single sounds, as in *Gwendolen* or *twit*.

Y is never a consonant.

I before a vowel at the beginning of a word is consonantal, as it is in the plural ending *-ion*, pronounced *yawn*.

Doubled consonants are both sounded clearly, unlike in

English. Note, however, that DD is a *single letter*, not a doubled consonant.

Accent is generally on the penultimate syllable, but compound words and place names are often an exception to this rule.

Table of Incarnations

643	696	718	773	835-843	918
Brangwen	Lyssa		Gweniver	Branoic	
Madoc		Addryc	Glyn	Cardoc	
Blaen	Gweran		Ricyn	Maddyn	Maer
Garraent	Tanyc	Cinvan	Dannyn	Owaen	Danry
Rodda	Cabrylla		Dolyan		
Ysolla	Cadda		Macla	Clwna	Braedda
Galrion	Nevyn	Nevyn	Nevyn	Nevyn	Nevyn
Rhegor					
Ylaena				Bellyra	Glaenara
Adoryc				Burcan	
			Dagwyn	Aethan	Leomyr
			Saddar	Oggyn	
				Anasyn	
				Lillorigga	
				Bevyan	
				Merodda	
			Mael		Pertyc Maelwaed
				Olaen	
				Maryn	
				Elyssa	
				Brour	

980	1060s	EARLY 1100s	1150s
Morwen	Jill		Branna
	Blaen of Cwm Pecyl	Drwmyc	Voran
Meddry	Rhodry	Rhodry	Rori
Gwairyc	Cullyn		Gerran
	Lovyan		
	Seryan		Solla
Nevyn	Nevyn		Neb
	Caer		
		Carramaena	Carramaena
	Sarcyn	Verrarc	Aethel
	Gwin		Warryc
	Ogwern		Oth
		Kiel	
Lanmara		Niffa	Niffa
		Dera	Galla
Mella	Mallona	Raena	Sidro
	Rhodda	Lady Rhodda	
		Jahdo	Jahdo
		Yraen	Clae
	Alaena	Marka	
	Rhys		Ridvar
	Sligyn	Erddyr	Cadryc
Tirro	Alastyr	Tren	Laz Moj
	Perryn		Pir

Snare

Katharine Kerr

The Snare of Secrets

In despair at the corruption of his ruler, the despotic Great Khan, Captain Idres Warkannon sets out on a perilous journey in search of a saviour: the Khan's long-lost younger brother. Despite the strictures of his religion, he depends on the guidance of a mysterious sorcerer to cross the vast plains of purple grass in safety.

But the sorcerer, Soutan, is shadowed by a loyal member of the Great Khan's deadly secret service: Zayn Hassan has infiltrated a tribe of peace-loving nomads in order to carry out his spying mission. He certainly hasn't bargained for the simple pleasure of life on the plains, or the attractions of Ammadin, the tribe's fiercely independent spirit rider.

Journeying across the grass, centuries-old falsehoods are gradually revealed and all of the factions discover more about their histories and identities than they could ever have envisaged.

'A fantastic plot which turns a simple story into something far more original … a cracking read'   *SFX*

'Kerr traces complex emotional and intellectual relationships as they evolve amid the dangers and vivid wonders of a world you won't soon forget'   *Locus*

'A compelling standalone fantasy'   *Dreamwatch*

ISBN 0 00 648039 X